Parson Harding's Daughter
City of Gems

Parson Harding's Daughter
City of Gems

LONDON   NEW YORK   SYDNEY   TORONTO

This edition published 1999 by BCA.
By arrangement with Transworld Publishers Limited.
CN 8905

Printed and bound in the United Kingdom by
Mackays of Chatham plc, Chatham, Kent

Parson Harding's Daughter

For my mother and father

Author's Note

In the 1770s, the East India Company's Council in Calcutta was headed by Warren Hastings, and consisted of four men selected by Parliament under the premiership of Lord North. Thus the addition of Sir Edward Ashton, bringing that number to five, is purely fictitious.

I

The Reverend Henry Harding surveyed his congregation from the pulpit with a mixture of affection and exasperation. The affection flowed from his handsome and upright person, becomingly clad in Valenciennes-trimmed lawn over decent black, in a benign flood which spread over the whole gathering – save one pew. For that pew, the front pew across the aisle from his pulpit, he reserved his exasperation. He allowed something approaching a smile to lighten his face as his gaze swept over the well-filled silk and serge, the muslin and occasional smock frock of his village flock. It was early June 1775, and the silvery oak door of the church had been left open to allow the light and scent of a summer morning to remind the congregation of all that they had to thank their Maker for. With sunshine and butterflies at the western end of the church and that look of gracious kindliness from their pastor at the eastern end, the people of Stoke Abbas might be forgiven for thinking themselves in paradise already.

All the people, that is, except the luckless five in the front pew across the aisle. The Harding children were profoundly conscious of the exasperation they caused their parent, and of the affront he seemed to suffer anew every Sunday to see them sitting there, as alike as peas in a pod, beneath his well-chiselled nose. The eldest, Eleanor, did not suffer too keenly from her father's scrutiny since she was all too conscious of her own value in the world, and thus impervious, more or less, to the opinion of anyone else.

'There is no need', she would say to her brother

Robert, the only one she regarded as having any practicality or sensitivity, both of which qualities she reckoned on possessing herself to the full, 'for such a quality of port, such a needless extravagance of claret. Nor does Papa appreciate what sacrifices I must make to allow for the keep of his horses.'

Robert, for whom life at the Parsonage was only made tolerable by wine and horses, would nod and mumble that his father still needed compensation for the death of his wife. Eleanor would snort.

The late Mrs Harding had been very pretty. She had possessed that kind of soft vivacious prettiness that Josephine Buonaparte was to make so fashionable: on the occasion of her marriage to the undeniably handsome Henry Harding with the excellent living of Stoke Abbas, in the gracious gift of Lady Lennox, already in his pocket, the pair were pronounced a triumph. In a sense, the marriage had indeed been a triumph. They were both kindly, vain and self-indulgent. They were disposed to laugh and make others laugh and they liked life to be pleasant. It was pleasant, too, in the grey-stone Parsonage at the top of a street of model cottages, with the church and the river at the bottom and the green Dorset hills beyond. The only part of this life that was not pleasant for Mrs Harding was the bearing of children which tired her, spoilt her figure and made her, despite several servants, less able to please herself. But what truly distressed both her and her husband, and what really accounted for the irritation in his eyes as he frowned down on them that June Sunday, was that every one of the surviving five was as undeniably plain as their parents were handsome. They were like a row of changelings, a witch's prank played on an innocent pair to punish them for their good looks. It was a malevolent, envious trick of fate, Mrs Harding decided, and not one she cared to endure. She took a chill when the youngest, Harry, was six and made no effort to resist it. She lay in her half-tester bed while a small fire tried to combat the draughts and chills of February, and watched the grey countryside with disinterest until the infection spread to her lungs and killed her. That was ten years ago and the children endured an uneasy illusion that her fading was in some way their fault.

'Your mother's death,' Parson Harding said once to the elder three, 'has left me without a companion in the world. A companion, that is, who is to me as I am to myself.'

A sensation of guilty inadequacy planted itself in the breasts of the two younger listeners which was to blight their confidence for years to come. Eleanor, at nineteen, had felt that her father was being melodramatic and that he took no account of her, Eleanor's, feelings at the loss of her mother. Eleanor might not seem to care what her father thought, but she longed for him to acknowledge her superiority to her brothers and sister.

In the sense that Parson Harding appreciated how well she ran the family, he did acknowledge it. As his lips moved comfortably and sonorously through the familiar sermon on hellfire – '. . . therefore every tree that bringeth not forth good fruit shall be hewn down and cast into the fire . . .' – he glanced every so often at his family. Eleanor sat closest to him, her narrow bony face set in an expression of severe sanctity under her straw hat. She wore a gown of dark green silk a little too long to be fashionable, and her fichu had been draped too tightly to be at all softening or becoming to her narrow neck. Next to her sat Parson Harding's three sons: Robert, his eldest, and Charles and Harry, the two youngest members of the family. They too had narrow, long-featured faces, and reddish indeterminate-textured hair, but in them Eleanor's look of uncompromising certainty in herself and life was replaced by an air of doubtfulness. Robert was his father's curate until such a time as a living might be procured for him. At twenty-seven he had not married, since he seemed doomed to become enamoured of women who never noticed him, and as his father ceaselessly reminded him, he could not afford to marry for love alone. Charles and Harry, at eighteen and sixteen respectively, were in the Navy in the tradition of their uncles, and were enjoying a brief respite at home before embarking again on the high seas. Lady Lennox often remarked that she could not imagine whose notion of a sailor they were, for they certainly were not hers. Indeed there was no hearty openness about Charles and Harry Harding, no gallantry, no evident patriotism or sea fever; however, sailors they were and Harry was to distinguish himself under Nelson bearing just the self-mistrusting expression that he wore this present Sunday.

Finally, at the end of the pew, compressing herself into as small a space as possible under her father's scrutiny, sat Caroline. Lady Lennox had once said of Caroline that she was the least offensively plain of the Harding children but Caroline knew, as all plain people keenly know, that that was saying nothing at all. Her face was as narrow as her sister's, her nose as long, but her mouth was wider and softer and her grey eyes had a capacity for absorbing or reflecting light that made them gleam like moonlight. She did not raise them very often to give anyone the chance to observe this silver phenomenon. Conscious of her nose, and her straight colourless pale hair, and her unfashionably tawny skin, she was not prepared to give her eyes, or her sweet and diffident expression, any chance in winning her friends and admirers. By the old-maidish age of twenty-six, Caroline had only ever had one admirer, when she was eighteen, and he had gone to India and forgotten her. She did not blame him. She considered herself forgettable.

She looked down at her blue silk lap – a most frivolous shade of blue Eleanor had deemed it – and sighed, and wished she could be outside and not on this narrow over-carved Jacobean pew whose ornamentation dug into her spine. She always seemed to be shut in somewhere, shut in the house under Eleanor's tyranny, shut in church for most of every Sunday, shut in the monotony of her position as Parson Harding's second unmarried and unmarriageable daughter. She had plenty of inner resources, but she never seemed to be allowed to pursue them. She sighed again, audibly this time, and her father's frown deepened.

She was instantly sorry. She loved her father, and was the only one to understand his widowed loneliness. She loved her brothers, too, although she sometimes wished they had more enterprise, that the Parsonage might sometimes have that air of vigour and energy that impressed her so about the atmosphere at Stoke Park when she went on occasional and terrifying visits. As for Eleanor, Caroline supposed that in a dutiful sense she loved her, but Eleanor seemed to do everything in her power to make herself unlovable. She was didactic, undemonstrative and quick to take offence – and she had initiated the family habit of calling Caroline 'Carrie'.

The congregation rose in a flurry of creaks and rustles for the Old Hundredth. Caroline could hear Sam Wells, the tenant farmer from across the river, bellowing behind her with the joyousness of one who knows release is near. She smiled to herself and sympathized with him privately. He was such an amiable, clumsy man and his children were like a basketful of tumbling puppies. He would make a great success of the rich land beyond the river, for he worked it with an enthusiasm and dedication Caroline thought wholly admirable. She would go to buy bantam eggs from Mrs Wells occasionally, and would seize any pretext to linger in the dough-and-onion-scented kitchen, or out in the yard among the hens and pigs, and let Mrs Wells tell her of their achievements. Eleanor would scold her for unladylike behaviour and a taste for low associations, but Caroline took no notice. She liked the villagers and was interested in their lives, and was unaware that the age of Lady Bountiful had not yet officially come. She wanted to help where she could, and the cottage people, reassured by her appearance and shy manner, welcomed her help.

The last 'Amen' rang out with fervour. Two hours of a June Sunday morning with the sky as blue as cornflowers can easily appear as two and twenty hours if confined to the dimness of a Norman nave, however beautiful. Caroline rose, and shook out her skirts and gave a smile of appreciation at the Wells children behind her, suffocating in their Sunday cloth and unaccustomed shoes. Eleanor saw the smile, caught her sister's eye and gave the smallest and most unmistakable of frowns. When her upright dark green back was turned for a stately exit of precedence among her father's people – a privilege she could enjoy only if the Lennox family were absent from church – Caroline smiled again at the children. All but the youngest stared stolidly back at her. The youngest beamed widely, displaying two missing teeth.

'Fine children, Sam.'

'We'm blessed wi' healthy 'uns, Miss Car'line.'

She nodded and moved out of the pew behind Harry, still half a head shorter than she was. He and Charles walked closely down the aisle together as if seeking comfort from each other's company. Caroline noticed with affectionate despair how their stockings gave the effect of being made for much larger calves than theirs, drooping sadly as they did from the knee-bands of their breeches. Still, she thought ruefully, apart from Papa we are a shabby and shambling lot; we have no notion how to look. Perhaps St Peter will not refuse a man to paradise simply because his hose are wrinkled. She contemplated, briefly, a heaven full of bent haloes and crooked wings and smiled unconsciously to herself. The Stoke Abbas apothecary, poised in his pew for his proper moment to leave church, saw the smile and was fooled for a moment into thinking Miss Caroline Harding quite handsome.

14

Outside church, Parson Harding stood gravely and benignly among his flock, his silver locks gleaming in the sunshine, his elegant patrician hands folded in the lawn sleeves of his surplice. Eleanor stood at a little distance, her brothers in dejected attendance, and listened graciously to the garrulity of Miss Spears who captured her ear for no other reason than that she was an impoverished second cousin of Lady Lennox.

'My dear Miss Eleanor, you would never guess, never suppose – or would you? Yes, being a person of such amazing discernment and one who is the trusted repository of so many confidences, I feel sure, quite sure, that Lady Lennox . . . But, no – I must say no more, indeed I must not. It must be for Lady Lennox to – but I feel sure that already she has . . .'

'Caroline,' Eleanor interrupted imperiously, 'when did we last hear from Stoke Park?'

Caroline, far more absorbed in old Mother Crittall's ferocious complaints about arthritis, which seemed an unjust suffering for June, looked about her vaguely.

'Stoke Park?'

'Yes, yes,' Eleanor said impatiently. 'What news from Stoke Park?'

'I feel sure', Miss Spears began again, edging her absurdly frilled and flounced person nearer, 'that nothing of consequence that Lady Lennox has to impart could she possibly have imparted to my humble self before passing it first to a person of such consequence and absolute trustworthiness as . . .'

Caroline came out of her reverie.

'Is your cat quite well, Miss Spears?'

Miss Spears's social smile of false eagerness was replaced by one of genuine pleasure.

'Tabby? Oh, Miss Caroline, dear Tabby! So good of you to ask! Dear Tabby. After the little accident with the rat trap! Quite recovered, quite. So considerate of you to ask after her . . .'

'I am very glad,' Caroline said.

'When did we last hear from Stoke Park?' Eleanor said with alarming directness.

Caroline raised her eyes from Miss Spears and the inward vision of Miss Spears's Tabby.

'I have no idea, Eleanor.'

Eleanor's frown was awful.

'My sister, Miss Spears, is never aware of summer or winter, Christmas or Michaelmas. Time is of no consequence to Caroline. If a message from Stoke Park had reached her but two minutes ago, it would be to her as of two months since. There is no doubt a message from Lady Lennox awaiting our return. We will bid you good day, Miss Spears.'

Miss Spears smirked and opened her mouth for another flood of verbiage but something in Eleanor's severity and Caroline's kind but abstracted air gave her pause.

'Good day, Miss Harding, Miss Caroline.'

Eleanor nodded and swept on. Caroline paused and looked back at Miss Spears.

'I do not know what this business about Stoke Park signifies. There is very little communication between the Park and the Parsonage, Miss Spears. There is no need for it, you know. I hope Tabby continues well.'

She smiled, and turned to follow her sister, then stopped again.

'We have a cat at the Parsonage, you know, but she is not sociable like Tabby.'

Miss Spears, melted entirely, watched her walk away with affection. She saw her stopped half a dozen times before the lych-gate, stopped by village people, and saw her smile as she paused, and watched her down-bent head as she listened. Poor Miss Caroline, doomed by lack of looks and money, just as she, Jane Spears, had been doomed thirty years before. Miss Caroline had had a chance once but she had not known what to do with it and she would certainly never have a chance again.

16

One chance was, after all, more than many people ever got. Miss Spears looked up the slope of Stoke Abbas's village street and saw Caroline Harding moving slowly up it and wished for a moment with all the sincerity her trivial nature was capable of that something might glitter a little, just once more, for Caroline.

For her part, Caroline was not thinking of glitter at that moment, nor of Stoke Park, nor its inmates, nor even of Miss Spears's remarkable Tabby. She was walking, with her slightly stooping gait, up the cobbles of the steep street between these pairs of 'model' cottages: cottages no more than fifteen years old and still much admired for the aesthetic and liberal views that designed and built them. They were built of local stone, thatched and gabled, charming to the delighted eye of visitors bowling down the street to the comfortable elegance of Stoke Park in its great green dish of land below.

Caroline knew better. June might well be an unseasonable month for old Mother Crittall to feel her arthritis so acutely, but complaints of the circulation and joints do not stand much chance against walls of literally running damp and floors of beaten earth. Caroline knew too that the thick thatch, so satisfactory to the eye of an eighteenth-century gentleman at the height of fashion for elegant landscape and civilized nature, held the long winter rains with the eagerness of a sponge. The upper chambers of the cottages, where the thatch was unplastered and formed a rustling ceiling to the bedroom itself, always had a moist and marshy air about them and the makeshift beds beneath this dank canopy must always have been as clammy themselves. Caroline knew that interior walls seldom felt dry as she often had need to touch them clambering up rickety stairs to some sickbed above. She thought of Lord Lennox, so kindly, so affable, generally regarded as a most benevolent employer and landlord, and wondered it never occurred to him why a huge number of his tenants were so swollen and crippled and old before their time. Perhaps cushioned before a fire in the library at Stoke Park, such things as damp beds and dripping thatch and coughing children were as irrelevant as the thought of naked savages in the East dancing round in some awful revelry. Such things happened indeed, but not at Stoke Park.

'Carrie, Eleanor says you are to hasten, if you please.'

Caroline jumped. She had fallen into her reverie over the cottages, and had unconsciously ceased walking as she mused. Robert was standing before her with a smile of affectionate amusement.

'Day-dreaming again, Carrie.'

'Yes – no, no, not day-dreaming. I was worrying about these cottages, Robert, they are so damp inside, even in June. The walls are so thick and the windows so small that sunlight never seems to have a chance inside them. Did you see old Mrs Crittall outside church? So bent, Robert, in such pain . . .'

A spasm crossed Robert's face. He had all Caroline's sympathy of heart, and no strength of mind to put it into practice. He agreed, always, with all her altruism, but always wished she had not mentioned it. It embarrassed him because he knew it would be upon his conscience and he would be unable to act to shift it.

'They do not complain of Lord Lennox, Carrie, you know.'

'Of course not. He gives them a goose at Christmas, and buries their children handsomely when they die of diseased lungs.'

The indignation in her tone made Robert uncomfortable. He looked about nervously lest anyone should have overheard this slight upon the patron of Stoke Abbas.

'I was sent to bring you on quickly, Carrie. Eleanor . . .'

'Of course,' Caroline said hastily, 'I did not mean to delay you, dear Robert. I always seem to come out of church feeling not only reflective, which I should welcome, but melancholy, which I deplore. Why do I?'

Robert swallowed nervously. His own calling, which should have filled him with profound joy, often made him deeply melancholy too.

'Spirituality is a very solemn thing,' he began hesitantly.

Caroline made a small impatient noise, and flung out her hands.

'I am not aiming at spirituality, dear Robert, I would not be so presumptuous. It was merely an idle speculation as to why Papa's services, for I know no others, tend to depress rather than elevate me.'

Robert looked unhappy.

'I – I do not know,' he said.

Caroline smiled at him fondly.

'No, nor do I.'

They reached the Parsonage gate, and turned instinctively for one last look down that perfection of grey-gold thatch falling away symmetrically to the emerald sweep of the Park slashed across by the Stoke River. Beyond the green rose the hills, which in their turn matured into the great cliffs and bluffs of the Dorset coast. The air was as clear as crystal, every flower in the cottage gardens, every branch of the newly planted beeches in the Park was clearly, minutely visible.

'We are most fortunate,' Robert said, thinking how much of a solace the view was to him.

Caroline, her thoughts upon the comparison between her sparsely furnished but dry and comfortable bedroom and those in the cottages below, nodded and said fervently, 'Indeed we are.'

They opened the gate, and passed between the shrubs, planted by Mrs Harding as a bride, that bordered the apron of land on the south side of the house. Stoke Abbas Parsonage was low and grey, but Mrs Harding had used her charm to persuade Lord Lennox to replace the small Jacobean windows with large and fashionable ones. The new spaces of glass gave the Parsonage a slightly surprised air, but the rooms inside benefited greatly. Caroline and Robert walked silently over the smoothly mown turf and entered a small side parlour papered in a tiny flower-pattern and littered, though tidily littered, with the paraphernalia of family living. Through the doorway into the hall, they could hear their sister.

'My absence from the house for two hours must and shall not be taken as an excuse for unforgivable slovenliness. It is essential that Sundays are run to a strict timetable to enable Mr Harding to fulfil all his most exacting duties. One more lapse and you may seek another position.'

There was a pause, then the sound of footsteps hurrying in the direction of the kitchen. Caroline and Robert stayed where they were, despite a strong urge in the former to run after the footsteps. Eleanor appeared in the doorway, removing her hat as she did so.

'It is impossible to run this house as Papa would wish with such servants. I am quite exhausted. They seem to feel no loyalty to me after all I do for them, and to take a malicious delight in testing my patience. Patsy is well aware that we must dine early on a Sunday in order to allow Papa sufficient repose before the evening service. It is too bad, indeed it is, too bad!'

She sat down heavily and put her hands over her face. Caroline sought frantically in her mind for some distraction from this aggravation.

'Was Miss Spears right, Eleanor? Did a message from Stoke Park await you?'

Eleanor raised an entirely recovered face from her hands.

'Stoke Park? Indeed I do not know, Carrie. How am I to do everything in this house if you dawdle in the sunshine instead of assisting me in even the smallest way to bear my burden? Robert, pray go into the hall and see if any message has come from Lady Lennox this morning.'

Caroline, knowing that as usual there would be no message, stood silently by her sister while Robert left the room. Eleanor said nothing more, but sat upright and alert, her gaze fixed upon the door until her brother reappeared. He held a letter in his hand.

'To me,' Eleanor said imperiously and took the letter. It bore the Lennox crest upon the back. Eleanor tore it open and read it with maddening thoroughness, while Caroline and Robert exchanged glances of thankfulness above her head.

'We are bidden to dine at Stoke Park on Tuesday,' Eleanor said at length. 'Georgiana is engaged to be married, and we are to meet her future husband. The invitation does not specify Charles and Harry.'

'Might they not like to go?' Caroline suggested.

'Certainly not. Papa will be delighted. Georgiana has always been a great favourite of his.'

'I should not mind if Charles or Harry were to go in my place,' Caroline said, recalling the terrible shyness and awkwardness that afflicted her at Stoke Park.

Eleanor rose and tucked the letter into her fichu, patting it with satisfaction.

'Charles and Harry are not invited. You are, therefore you will go.'

2

On the Tuesday morning following Parson Harding's sermon on hellfire, Lady Lennox was in her boudoir, on the first floor of Stoke Park, contemplating in the intervals of her correspondence what would be, in sixty years' time, a most splendid prospect of oaks and beeches. As the trees had only been planted a maximum of twenty-five years, they only gave some idea of the splendour that was to come. Lady Lennox did not regard them from that point of view, however, but only scrutinized them keenly for any sign of blight or damage by sheep or deer. On the walls beside her bureau hung miniatures of her six children: Sophia—naughty, wilful Sophia, now being just as naughty and wilful a married woman as she had been a girl; then Henry, John, George; Jane – who would clearly remain always and invaluably at her side – and finally little Georgiana. It was Georgiana who was the subject of all the correspondence upon cream paper embossed with the Lennox arms. Georgiana was now officially to become Lady Lovell, and the world in general must be informed of the matter. Lady Lennox was a great believer in the dissemination of information. It led to far fewer mishaps if everyone knew everything and had no excuse for pleading ignorance as a reason for incompetence of any kind. Lady Lennox despised incompetence. She had by now told the entire neighbourhood of Georgiana's betrothal so that everyone might be prepared to perform any function required of them at the ensuing marriage. She had, of course, told Parson Harding first, as an old and valued confidant, and as a mark of special favour, subjected her lively family to the uninviting prospect of the three elder

Hardings and their father at dinner that day. There had been an uproar at breakfast over the matter.

'As the centre of attention,' Georgiana claimed, 'I refuse to be afflicted by any Harding at all if I cannot have Parson Harding himself by me. I will not endure Robert another meal, I declare I will not.'

Lady Lennox regarded Georgiana levelly.

'There is no question of Parson Harding sitting anywhere but by me.'

'I will not have Robert . . .'

'It is unlikely that you will ever have to sit by Robert again. You will behave to him tonight.'

'Mamma!' Georgiana wailed.

Her father patted her shoulder as he moved towards the sideboard.

'Think of me, my dear. I am doomed to Miss Eleanor Harding. I doubt I shall survive the ordeal.'

Lady Lennox said severely, 'Eleanor Harding is an eminently capable and practical woman.'

'Those are not qualities I seek in a dinner companion, my dear.'

The two Lennox sons at home applauded loudly.

'You should not encourage them, Harry.'

'Why did you ask them to dine at all, Mamma? Why could not you and Georgie simply have called upon them?'

'Because, my dear John, Parson Harding took up the incumbency of Stoke Abbas two years after your father and I were married, and thus is a person to be considered in all Lennox family matters.'

'You should have asked him to dine alone.'

'Unthinkable,' his mother said briskly.

'To whose lot falls the unlovely Caroline?' George wondered to the moulded ceiling.

'To Frank's,' Lady Lennox said, turning with a smile to her future son-in-law, until then fully occupied with his breakfast.

'Oh – oh, I say – I beg you, ma'am – I do not know the lady, may I not be excused?'

The Lennox brothers exploded again.

'It is a real chance for you, Frank,' Georgiana said with mock solemnity.

Frank Lovell looked pleadingly at his betrothed.

'Shall I be very wretched by her, Georgie?'

'Indeed no,' Georgiana cried. 'You will be quite fascinated, will he not, George? For beauty, wit and conversation, there is no-one to surpass—'

'Georgiana!' her mother said.

'Oh, Mamma, even you, with your heart of gold, must admit that Caroline Harding is surely the most insignificant person in the county of Dorset . . .' She stopped.

Lady Lennox had signalled to her husband, and he, rousing himself reluctantly from his lazy and good-humoured abstraction, said with unusual firmness, 'No more, Georgiana, not another word. If you cannot speak charitably, it is better you do not speak at all.'

Georgiana looked a little shamefaced, but brightened immediately at the sight of Frank Lovell's face full of the admiration he always felt at her daring.

'Come riding with me, Frank, and I will instruct you in the art of conversation to a Harding.'

'It is very simple,' George Lennox said. 'In the case of father and elder daughter one listens and never has the chance to speak, and in the case of the son and younger daughter one speaks and longs for a chance to listen which never comes.'

'I should prefer the former,' Frank Lovell said anxiously.

'We know that!' cried John delightedly. 'Why else are you marrying Georgie? You will not have to speak again for the rest of your life!'

Above the uproar, Lady Lennox said clearly that she did not wish to see any of them again until the dinner hour. When they had trooped noisily out, she turned

24

to her husband, idly reading last week's newspaper and humming beneath his breath.

'I am anxious, Harry, that Frank Lovell will not be firm enough with Georgiana.'

Lord Lennox yawned.

'Nobody is firm enough with Georgiana, my love, not even yourself.'

'She makes the boys behave so wildly.'

'Boys?'

'George and John.'

'Ah yes. George and John.' Lord Lennox's thoughts had run briefly upon his elder daughter Sophia and her effect upon young men. He rose slowly from his chair. 'They will be better when the hunting begins again, my love. The summer is a deuced idle time for a young man.'

'Endeavour not to yawn too frequently before Miss Harding, Harry.'

'We shall all, save yourself, my love, be yawning. It is infernal luck that Henry Harding should have produced such a family as his.'

'They have done quite well, Harry, indeed they have. The only one with no prospects of any kind is poor Caroline, but I do not think she ever hoped for any. Humility must be a great comfort.'

Lord Lennox laughed, and kissed his wife and strolled out into the sunlight to his horses. Lady Lennox, after a moment's regret over the excessive high spirits of her children, an indulgence she dismissed quickly as unconstructive, went in search of the excellent Jane, who always breakfasted early and would be about her household duties. Jane, Lady Lennox reflected, took after herself, and there was solace to be had from that thought.

At the Parsonage, Caroline spent the morning en-couraging a small throbbing in her temples to materialize into a headache sufficient to prevent her dining at Stoke

Park. She went out, at Eleanor's request, to pick strawberries, and did so in full sunlight deliberately without
her hat. The throbbing obstinately refused to intensify.
Having brought the strawberries into the kitchen, she
avoided Eleanor and escaped to her own room where
she proceeded to paint on ivory, without her spectacles.
Caroline was a talented miniaturist. She often felt it was
attributable to her short sight for only at close quarters
was she able to see anything in all its detail. She was
engaged upon an oval painting of field flowers com-
missioned by old Mrs Whitecross of Sturminster Newton,
and delicate attention to an ear of corn took all her concentration for a full hour. When she looked up, dazzled at
the largeness of objects in the room after the tiny intricacy
she had been absorbed in, she was dismayed to find the
throbbing quite gone, and her head lamentably clear.

Eleanor swept in, as usual without knocking. Caroline
wondered if all families were as insensitive to each other's
need or wish for privacy.

'Carrie – there you are! I have been searching for you
this good half-hour! I have had a thousand things to do
and instead I have been compelled to look for you.'

Her tone was accusing and offended. For a fleeting
second, Caroline thought of pointing out that anyone
with a pressing list of things needing to be done is better
occupied doing them than in hunting for a helpmeet.

'I am sorry, Eleanor.'

'So you should be. Sitting up here idly while I slave
for the family. How you would all get on without me, I
cannot conceive.'

'What can I do now to assist you?'

'Oh!' Eleanor gave a contemptuous glance at the ceiling and flung wide her hands. 'It is all done. I have done
it all.'

Caroline, on the edge of her patience, said, 'Then
why must you interrupt me?'

Unable to say truthfully that she had come to complain

and be self-righteous, Eleanor said firmly, 'It is time you were thinking of dressing.'

Caroline took out the watch that had been her mother's, and which she wore on a green ribbon at her waist.

'It does not take me two hours to dress, Eleanor.'

'I wish you to look well. It is most gracious and good of Lady Lennox to ask us, and I wish you to be a credit to Papa.'

'We are none of us ever a credit to Papa to look at. You know that as well as I. It is he who is a credit to us.'

'When you are in this frame of mind, Caroline,' Eleanor said furiously, 'conversation with you is quite impossible.'

'I am sorry,' Caroline said again.

'You are always sorry, eternally sorry, but I see no signs in you of any real desire to be other than you are. What is your life to become if you do not try to be more positive about it?'

Caroline shrugged helplessly. The question went far too deep for a quick answer. Eleanor was right, what was to become of her? Nothing, she supposed, as nothing always had. She expected nothing and there was after all nothing for a parson's daughter of limited means and no looks to expect in 1775. She would end up as companion to old Mrs Whitecross or Miss Lumleigh or Lady Fyfield and people would only remember her because she painted miniatures. She looked up at Eleanor with a face full of misery, and saw the severity in Eleanor's face and let her own gaze drop again.

'Please do not scold me,' she said in a low voice.

'If I do not scold you, Carrie, who shall? What use are you dreaming and idling your way through the days like this?'

The cottagers of Stoke Abbas might have had stout answers to this, but humble Caroline had none. Eleanor had abruptly opened such a black abyss before her through this sunny morning that she was horrified at the prospect.

When she considered in her mind, she could not think in what direction her usefulness, if any, lay. Eleanor ran the house, controlled the accounts, and shaped their lives to suit their father. Caroline was not at all sure that she could do any of those things even if she were given the chance. She taught some of the cottage children to read, but it never occurred to her that that was useful since her affection for the children made the lessons a pleasure to be looked forward to. She sat with bent head and despised herself.

Eleanor sighed and rustled to the window.

'I beg you will not wear the blue.'

Caroline looked up bemusedly, her mind still drowning in the prospect of her empty life.

'Blue?'

'Your blue silk. It is a most – most unsuitable colour.'

'Unsuitable? Unsuitable for what? I wore it to church last Sunday. Surely what is suitable for church is also suitable for Stoke Park?'

'It was not suitable for church,' Eleanor said firmly. 'I am sure Papa thinks so.'

'Indeed he does not!' Caroline said indignantly. 'He said it reminded him of Mamma, who loved blue above all colours!'

Eleanor's own colour rose.

'Papa has too good a heart to hurt your feelings.'

She moved back to the door, and stood with her hand upon the knob.

'I beg you will wear your grey. Or the muslin.'

Caroline raised her chin.

'I will be ready in one hour and a half, Eleanor.'

'In the grey if you please, Carrie,' Eleanor said, and closed the door behind her with decision.

When she had gone, Caroline went quickly to the door and bolted it. Then she crossed the small room and cast herself upon her bed, where she lay, staring dry-eyed at the ceiling, her hands clenched tightly at her sides.

Parson Harding still kept his own carriage. Eleanor complained that it was a needless extravagance, but it reminded her father of those happy days of early marriage when it had seemed possible to be both spiritual and extremely comfortable and he would not let it go. He climbed into it that afternoon, distinguished in his black, and glanced briefly at his children with the usual slight sinking of the heart that their appearance caused him. Why Robert seemed to feel that a clergyman had no sartorial obligation to both his Maker and his fellow man, Parson Harding could not conceive. He glanced from his own lean and elegant calves trimly clad in black silk, to Robert's which were approximately covered in black worsted. His coat wrinkled at the shoulders, and the sleeves were too short, and his wristbands had nothing of the dazzling whiteness of his father's. Eleanor looked neat and unremarkable in black, above which she wore an expression like a thundercloud. Opposite her Caroline sat wearing a dress of exceptionally pretty delphinium blue. It did not become her skin or her hair, both of which seemed deadened by the blue, but it was a pretty colour in itself.

'A charming dress, Carrie.'

Caroline looked up to give her father a delighted and delightful smile.

The journey to Stoke Park proceeded in silence. Eleanor was clearly in high dudgeon over something, and neither Caroline nor Robert were ever great volunteers of conversation. If it were not for the social burden they represented, Parson Harding would have thoroughly enjoyed the prospect of dining at Stoke Park. He probably knew Lady Lennox more thoroughly than any man alive, even her husband, and this knowledge gave an irresistible edge to their relationship.

Lady Lennox and her family were all in the drawing room grouped artistically about the great light white and blue room with its shining floor of parquet. Caroline's pleasure in her father's compliment and temporary small confidence in her appearance faded instantly the moment she saw Georgiana Lennox.

Both Caroline and Eleanor wore dresses of simple cut, the fabric of bodice and skirt falling unbroken by any seam but the waist seam, to the floor. Their necklines were modest and square cut, their sleeves only slightly caught at the elbow. As both dresses had been made by the village seamstress, there was a certain irregularity and puckering here and there, and Caroline was painfully conscious that the neckline of her dress was far from true. Their hair was unpowdered and caught up behind their heads, severely in Eleanor's case, and with an unsuccessful attempt at ringlets in Caroline's. But Georgiana was gorgeous in striped silk, a dress whose over-skirt was looped with ribbons over a matching petticoat ruffled and trimmed with narrow velvet. There were snowy ruffles at her throat and elbows ornamented with black velvet bows and roses, and her lightly powdered hair was piled into a ravishing cascade of curls and ringlets. Her plainly visible buckled shoes had scarlet heels, and the sticks of her fan were lacquered scarlet too. To Caroline, she was a wondrous and discouraging spectacle.

Eleanor was clearly unconscious of any sartorial discrepancy, but Caroline immediately felt the old sensation of utter dowdiness fall about her like a mantle. Her dress was too short behind, too low-waisted, too narrow in the sleeves and a crude colour. She bent her eyes upon the floor and was very miserable.

'Miss Harding! Miss Caroline! What a pleasure to see you on this beautiful day. Is it not a beautiful day?'

Lord Lennox stood affable and large before them. Eleanor made some suitable reply and Caroline managed to lift her eyes as far as her host's impeccably folded stock. Past him, she could see Jane and Robert in halting conversation, and her father and Georgiana laughing delightedly together. There seemed also to be an assembly of young men about, as usual, but Caroline dared not look. Lady Lennox did not allow her her solitude for long.

'Caroline! I have not seen you in a month. I suppose you have been much occupied with your charming painting and your little pupils. I wish to present Lord Lovell to you, Caroline.'

Caroline looked up briefly, and Frank Lovell caught a flash from those gleaming grey eyes that made him feel a little less apprehensive at the prospect of this dull and awkward creature in his charge for the next hour. Caroline managed a smile, but was inwardly much daunted by this fashionable young man in his exquisitely cut breeches and lavish linen.

'Delighted, Miss Harding.' He had a slight drawl, and when nervous, it became worse.

'You must tell her about India, Frank. I am sure you know nothing of India, do you, Caroline? Frank knows a good deal about India.'

Caroline, whose knowledge of India was confined to hazy notions of goats' milk in brass pots and thin brown men in huge jewels, said gratefully, 'I shall be glad to listen.'

'I hope you will help me a little more than that,' Frank Lovell said.

'I will try, Lord Lovell. I – I am not much use at conversation. But I should dearly like to hear of India.'

He offered her his arm, and they followed the older people into dinner. Behind them Georgiana was teasing Robert who sounded utterly bewildered and entirely bewitched in his stammering replies. Caroline smiled involuntarily, partly out of sympathy for Robert, and partly because she could see he was fair game for Georgiana. Frank Lovell saw her smile.

'Is she not fascinating?'

'Entirely,' Caroline said.

31

Frank Lovell beamed upon her with approval.

At the table, Caroline found that several feet of gleaming rosewood separated her from Lord Lovell on her left and John Lennox on her right. This isolation gave her some comfort. Across the table, Georgiana was showing Robert no mercy. His eyes were fixed upon her face and his expression was stunned. For a while it seemed possible for Caroline to eat in silence, since both her neighbours were engrossed in Georgiana and left her mercifully alone. She had not much appetite through shyness, but noticed that Georgiana ate almost nothing and thus felt it possible to leave her own plate half-finished.

As the lamb was borne in, Lady Lennox called down the table, 'Are you now much better informed about India, Caroline?'

To Caroline's horror, the table fell silent to listen.

'I – I am sure I soon shall be, ma'am.'

'Where have you been in India?' Parson Harding enquired.

'In Bengal, sir. My cousin is on the council of the East India Company at Calcutta.'

'Your cousin, Frank?'

'Yes, ma'am, my father's elder sister's only son, Sir Edward Ashton.'

'I knew an Ashton at Cambridge,' Parson Harding said irrelevantly, and the conversation flowed back again.

Caroline would have liked to ask whom Sir Edward Ashton counselled and on whose behalf, but she was afraid to venture a remark across four feet of space.

Lord Lovell helped her by saying, 'We had a wild time, Miss Harding, a wild time indeed. I think my cousin was thankful to see me leave.'

'Did – did you go with a companion, Lord Lovell?'

'No, no, I did not. But India is a most sociable place, you know. Calcutta is full of the best fellows imaginable and—' He was about to say some of the best women as well, but remembered in time that most of the women he had met in Calcutta were neither of a colour nor a status to be suitable for conversation.

'I was never in bed before four in the morning, Miss Harding—'

'And neither shall you be when we are married,' declared Georgiana from across the table. 'I intend to amuse myself all of every night and sleep during the day. Will that not shock you, Mamma?'

'Immeasurably, my love.'

'Can you be so dissipated in such heat as we hear of in India?' Parson Harding asked.

'Indeed yes, sir. I believe almost more than in London. I met one man who said he did not need above four hours' sleep in India.'

'Who was this phenomenon?' enquired Lord Lennox, ready to prolong any topic that gave him respite from Eleanor.

'John Gates, sir.'

The effect was electrifying. Every face around the table registered amazement and there was a sudden, concerted indrawing of breath.

'Johnnie Gates!' Lady Lennox exclaimed.

'Our bad Johnnie?' Georgiana said hopefully.

'I thought he was in Madras,' Lord Lennox said.

'He was, sir. But the Company moved him to Calcutta. I did not make his acquaintance intimately—'

'Just as well,' Lord Lennox said.

'Johnnie Gates!'

'We have not heard of him in seven years!'

Eight, Caroline said to herself. Eight years since Johnnie had been sent to India, eight years of knowing she must die an old maid.

'Was he prospering?' Parson Harding asked. 'He was indeed a bad boy, but something in him makes me hope he prospers.'

He was not bad, Caroline cried silently, he was just young and wild and – forgetful.

'I think he does, sir,' Frank Lovell said doubtfully. He had only seen Gates in the evening when he was more or less drunk. He was said to have several native mistresses, but to have made just enough money to be comfortable – well, to be comfortable in India at least.

'He is some connection of ours,' Lady Lennox explained. 'His mother was my husband's sister, and upon her early death and her husband's he became our ward. He grew up as one of our children.'

She did not add that she considered he had but poorly repaid that upbringing, nor did she mention, because she did not like to think of it, that a considerable part of the Lennox fortune left in trust for him by his parents would pass to John Gates on his uncle's death. He would get none of the property, and this she was most thankful for. However, a large sum of money that his mother had brought upon her marriage to his father, and that she would dearly like to see spread among her own six, was to be indisputably his.

'He was the best playmate in the world,' Georgiana said, 'and easily the most wicked. Do you remember, John—'

'Georgiana!' her mother said.

'Very well, Mamma, but if you will not let me tell tales of Johnnie's naughtiness in boyhood, will you please permit Frank to tell us of Johnnie's naughtiness in manhood, for I am sure he is no better behaved.'

'Is he, Frank?'

Frank Lovell looked doubtfully at his future mother-in-law, and seemed uncertain of speech.

'I see,' Lady Lennox said. 'We will discuss the matter no further. Now, Mr Harding, I hope you will confess that the strawberries at the Park are far superior to the strawberries at the Parsonage?'

Once more conversation spread gently along the table. Caroline longed to go home, to the seclusion of her bedroom and the privacy of her thoughts. When Johnnie

34

Gates had been mentioned so suddenly she had abruptly felt, only for a fleeting moment, that she was eighteen again and that all those emotions which had slept so quietly for eight years were free and dancing once more. She stared down at her plate and hoped nothing showed in her face. There was no doubt everyone had forgotten her part in Johnnie Gates's last months in England, and for the greater part of the last eight years, so had she. But she had remembered now, and she longed for the luxury of going on remembering, alone in her own room at the Parsonage.

Lady Lennox rose at last, and led her own and Parson Harding's daughters to the drawing room. To Caroline's dismay, card tables were set up.

'You were once very skilled at bezique,' Lady Lennox said to her.

'I am sadly out of practice now, ma'am.'

'Then you shall play with Lord Lennox who loves to win. Georgiana, do not yawn. Come and assist me with the cards.'

It seemed an age before the men came in, and another age before all the tables were seated to Lady Lennox's satisfaction.

After an hour of cards, tea was brought. None of the young Lennoxes made any attempt now to repress their yawns except Georgiana, who was seated by Parson Harding and thus kept very busy being fascinating. Parson Harding was delighted to be fascinated, and only with true reluctance, remembered the hour and rose to his feet. His children followed him obediently. He smiled and bowed and kissed Lady Lennox's hand and she thought for the thousandth time how unlucky it was that none of his poise and charm had descended to his children.

As soon as the Harding carriage had rolled away up towards the village, Lady Lennox went to her boudoir, and asked that Lord Lovell be sent to her. He entered looking extremely troubled.

'My dear Frank, pray do not look so anxious. I only wish to continue the conversation that it was clearly impossible to continue at dinner.'

'Johnnie Gates?'

'Precisely so. You say you saw him in Calcutta?'

'Yes, ma'am. Not above three or four times.'

'In his own house?'

'No, ma'am, always in the houses of others.'

Lady Lennox did not believe in beating about the bush.

'Was he drunk?'

Frank Lovell swallowed. 'Slightly, Lady Lennox. We all – it is customary – it seems in India that . . .'

'I understand you very well. Has he married, do you gather?'

'No – no, he is not married. There are not many married men in Calcutta. The Company tries to send possible wives out to Bengal, I believe, because the shortage of – of suitable women makes for – for men—'

'Taking native mistresses? Does Johnnie Gates have an Indian mistress?'

Although he would have delighted in imparting this information to his Georgie or her brothers, Frank Lovell was most uncomfortable at doing so to Lady Lennox. He avoided her eye and said indistinctly that he believed so.

'And has he children?'

'I have no idea about children, Lady Lennox.'

'Did you gain the impression, Frank, that he is extravagant?'

Being extravagant himself, Frank Lovell had no idea what extravagance was.

'I believe he has horses, ma'am, and an excellent cellar.'

Lady Lennox sat thoughtful for a while. Then she rose and walked to her bureau, and contemplated her children's portraits.

'Is it your opinion, Frank, that although we must take

36

for granted that men live a somewhat more unconventional life in Calcutta than they do here, John Gates's way of life is debauched even by the standards of Bengal?'

Frank thought of his cousin's orderly, almost scholarly life, and compared it with the other lives he had seen, those of Company men, attorneys, soldiers. They all lived self-indulgently by comparison to Sir Edward Ashton, but perhaps he had never seen anyone sprawled unconscious among the debris of dinner quite so often as Johnnie Gates.

'Your answer is important to me, Frank.'

'Yes, ma'am. I believe his life is perhaps a little more – more—'

'Exactly so. More than most of his peers?'

'Yes, ma'am.'

'Thank you, Frank. Now go and find Georgiana.'

After the door had closed behind him, Lady Lennox sat thoughtfully by her desk. Johnnie Gates had been sent to India because it was thought that the rigours of the climate and the discipline of the East India Company would reform him, and it was both irritating and disturbing to find that this plan had failed. After Johnnie had been gone a year and a half, Lady Lennox had ceased to write, and had thankfully assumed that her difficult and wayward charge of nearly twenty years was now in other and sterner hands. Indeed, if Johnnie's soul was all she had to worry about, she would not be worrying now, but it was not simply a matter of his soul. It was a matter of Lennox money. Lady Lennox had no intention of letting Lennox money pass into hands which would drink and gamble and squander it when it might be used far more efficiently. She was powerless to stop Johnnie receiving the money, but she was determined to use all the influence in her power to dictate how he should spend it.

There was, after all, only one way that she could ensure the money would not be wasted. Johnnie must marry. What is more, he must marry a sensible, thrifty, plain-living woman who would not abet him in his extravagances. It would also be an advantage if she was either of an age or physical type unlikely to prove fertile; since then the money would revert to what she considered its rightful inheritors. Only such a marriage, as far as Lady Lennox could see, would avoid shame and scandal being breathed about the name of Lennox, and the senseless waste of a good deal of money that her six darlings would have been able to make such excellent use of. It was a matter for true thankfulness that Johnnie would get no property, but the money was bad enough. And if Johnnie was behaving as badly as Frank Lovell described, Lady Lennox must take action soon before he was too dissipated for any sensible woman to look at him twice.

Caroline Harding had supposed inaccurately at dinner that no-one remembered her association with Johnnie Gates. Lady Lennox had glanced sharply at Caroline, and had recalled most accurately, when she saw Caroline's self-conscious downcast face, all that had taken place in the spring and summer of 1767. There, of course, thought Lady Lennox now in triumph, there is the perfect wife for Johnnie! She has a wretched position at the Parsonage, she has no occupations of importance, she was once deeply attached to him, and she is used to a most simple and inexpensive way of life. She is also, thought Lady Lennox, lucky to be offered a husband with those looks and manners, and the consideration of looks reminded Lady Lennox that Caroline's thin form looked splendidly unpromising for motherhood. Jubilant, Lady Lennox rose from her chair, and began slowly to pace the room. Letters must be written, to Johnnie himself, and perhaps to Frank Lovell's cousin to make it all seem as if every care for Caroline's happiness were being taken. Yes, she should enquire of Sir Edward Ashton if he thought the plan suitable, and as the Company had numerous employees in Calcutta it was to be hoped that he should not know enough of Johnnie Gates to disapprove.

The door opened and Lord Lennox came in.

'Well, my dear. And are you on your way to bed?'

'Not yet, Harry. Come and seat yourself.'

'I was rather thinking of bed, my love.'

'Not yet, Harry. I have a great deal to explain to you.'

3

Caroline Harding entered her bedroom at the Parsonage that evening in a very different frame of mind from that in which she had left it. She was agitated and slightly exalted, and very grateful that the day was done and that she had now time for her own thoughts. She undressed quickly in the darkness for the bright summer moonlight made nonsense of her candle, and in nightgown and cap, with her straight pale hair falling down her back, climbed into bed. She deliberately left both bed and window curtains open so that she might gaze at the pale square of June night sky as she gave herself up to the luxury of recollection.

She had known Johnnie Gates all her life, if you could call a furtive and frightened admiration from afar, knowing. When she was born he had already been at Stoke Park for two years, and was a vigorous and destructive child, adored by nursemaids for his looks and deplored by Lady Lennox for his mischief. Contact between the nurseries at the Parsonage and the Park was slight, but the Parsonage children knew via the servants every breath and deed of those gilded little children in their palatial quarters down the hill. The Parsonage children knew what the Park children ate and played with, heard every lisping cleverness repeated, knew all likes and dislikes. They saw them in church ruffled and beribboned, the boys in taffeta-tied shoes and pointed lace collars. They heard much about Johnnie Gates for there was much to hear. He upset churns in the dairies, tied the cats' tails together, hobbled the dogs, threw apples accurately at stooping gardeners, left toads in the maids' bedrooms and was entirely irrepressible when corrected. Robert, Charles and Harry sat open-mouthed as the nursery maid regaled them with fresh outrages as they ate their suppers by the fire. Eleanor would shake her head and click her tongue disapprovingly, and Caroline would long to hear more.

The children met seldom, on walks perhaps, or rides when the Parsonage children, taking turn and turn about on the old pony, would meet a fully mounted and beautifully equipped cavalcade of little Lennoxes, with the groom in attendance. Sometimes there were parties, sometimes there were agonizing visits when pretty Mrs Harding took her awkward brood to the Park and left them to be miserable in the great nursery while she chattered to the Lennoxes in the drawing room below. When adolescence came and all the boys of both houses went away to school, contact became even more broken but the snippets of gossip and news went on, so that Caroline still knew, with awe and fascination, that growing up was not having a sobering effect on Johnnie Gates.

When Caroline was sixteen, the gossip flared up into something more solid and dramatic. Sophia Lennox, at eighteen ravishing to look at and entirely heedless and reckless in her behaviour, had always been Johnnie's chief goad to wilder and wilder exploits. As children they had never been left alone together for long because the havoc they could wreak and the mischief they could concoct between them was terrifying. Gradually as their adolescence wore on, this partnership in misbehaviour deepened, as it was bound to do between two young, healthy and handsome creatures, into something more compelling for both of them. The groom noticed that on rides they managed to get themselves separated from the main party and Lady Lennox observed endless glances of complicity across rooms, or tables at meals. While she was gathering her information in order to confront them both with her displeasure – for Sophia was intended for someone much more considerable than the family orphan – matters came to a head of their own accord.

Caroline heard – or rather overheard – a conversation between her parents. Parson Harding had been summoned to Stoke Park in a hurry, and had gone immediately despite a wild wet October evening and no moon. The Harding children waited about the stairs and landings, burning with curiosity but not daring to risk a snub from their mother or a later chastening from their father for asking impertinent questions. At length Parson Harding returned and went straight in to his wife in the drawing room. Caroline, in the study across the hall ostensibly hunting for her mislaid Shakespeare, heard their muffled voices through the closed door.

'What will Lady Lennox do, Henry?'

'He must go away, dearest, and immediately. The carriage will take him to Salisbury tomorrow.'

'But what then? What will become of him?'

'Lord Lennox is to make arrangements for him to go abroad, probably to the East.'

'It is very dreadful for them all.'

'It was almost the ruin of Sophia, dearest. If the stable boy had not—'

At this point Parson Harding, who was apparently pacing the room as he spoke, came dangerously near the door and Caroline, with a beating heart, slipped quickly across the hall and up the stairs to impart whatever she knew to her brothers and sister.

By next morning, they knew it all. The house, despite Parson Harding's edict that the subject should never be mentioned again, was buzzing. The previous day, bored by the confinement indoors dictated by the weather, Sophia had gone down to the stables, followed after a decent interval by Johnnie Gates. They had been seen by the head groom patting the new grey hunter, and had then vanished. Some time later, a stable boy, climbing into the loft to hurl down hay bales for the afternoon feed, found Johnnie and Sophia tumbling in a flurry of

42

shirt tails and petticoats. As far as Sophia's marriage-ability was concerned, they were disturbed in the nick of time. Lady Lennox sent for Parson Harding at once with the sensation that the situation needed official moral authority as well as parental discipline and decisions.

So Johnnie was gone, not to the East as it turned out, but to a distant relation in Scotland which was felt to be remote enough to offer him no chance for wrongdoing. Before a year was up Sophia, who had shown nothing but resentment at being interrupted in the hayloft, had become a countess, and had been taken off to London. As the months wore on reports of her goings-on in London made the hayloft incident recede into insignificance. Gradually the whole affair dwindled, and with the two participants gone, there was nothing to prevent its vanishing into oblivion. General opinion blamed both Sophia and Johnnie equally for a few months, then they slowly ceased to be a topic of interest, and were talked of no more.

At the Parsonage it was quickly forgotten because other shadows were falling there. Eighteen months after Johnnie's dismissal, Mrs Harding was dead, and the lives at the Parsonage had to take a new and drearier shape. Of all the children, Harry and Caroline were the most desolated. Harry because he was only six, and Caroline because she had adored her mother and seen in her all the feminine charm that she knew she lacked herself. In that bleak spring of 1767, eighteen-year-old Caroline had been quite broken with grief and had felt that life would never have a light in it again.

One wet morning in April, Parson Harding was summoned to the Park. He returned for dinner punctually. His children waited silently for him to divulge any news he had, for he had unconsciously developed a habit, since his wife's death, of including his elder children in matters that before he would have reserved for Mrs Harding's confidence.

'Lady Lennox has received a letter from John Gates. He has written to beg her forgiveness, to assure her that he is a reformed character, and to ask permission to visit Stoke Park.'

Eleanor, in her new role as chatelaine, said, 'I trust you advised her to refuse him, Papa.'

Parson Harding looked up with a distinct amusement gleaming in his eye.

'Indeed I did not, Eleanor. John Gates did wrong, no doubt of it, but Sophia was no less blameworthy than he. He is not evil, Eleanor, merely self-indulgent and young.' He paused and looked out of the window at the wet garden. 'No, I advised her to forgive him and let him come.'

'For good?' Caroline asked, trying to suppress the eagerness in her tone.

'No. Only for a few months. The relation he has lived with in Scotland has obtained a post for him in Madras, with the East India Company. He sails for the East in the autumn.'

Caroline wondered if this move on the part of the Scottish relation meant that Johnnie was no better behaved than he had been. She said nothing because she was astonished at the flutterings of pleasure the news gave her. She looked up and smiled at her father, and he smiled in return, saying, 'I am glad you agree with me, Carrie.'

Three weeks later, it was known Johnnie Gates had come. Parson Harding and Eleanor went to dine at the Park, and the latter reported Johnnie wholly unchanged, adding that she felt Lady Lennox had made a grave error in accepting him back. Secretly, Caroline chafed to see him, though she knew she would have been tongue-tied if she had. She had not seen him since that episode in the hayloft and she burned with curiosity – and with something more.

One Friday a message came from Stoke Park begging that the Hardings might take advantage of the early peas, since there was such an abundance at the Park it was feared some might be wasted. Lady Lennox hated to see waste, but never thought of the cottagers when she had a superfluity of any delicacy. As Eleanor knew her father loved the first peas of the year, she found Caroline, absorbed in a book as usual, and despatched her, despite many protestations, down the hill with a basket and the old pony.

The only consolation of this alarming errand as far as Caroline could see was that she need only go to the kitchen door, and thus avoid the awesome terror of an official reception. She rode into the Park by the back gates, and trotted across the level grass in the direction of the orchard and kitchen quarters beyond. As she neared the orchard walls, she could hear voices, and the nearer she came the more obvious it was that the voices belonged to the young men of the house. Caroline thought of turning back, but then thought of Eleanor's displeasure, and decided that if she rode close under the orchard wall which was a good eight feet in height, she might get by unobserved.

The voices were shouting now, and there was a good deal of stamping and thudding. They must have a pony with them, she thought, pressing her own pony close to the wall, and bending low so that her hat was not visible.

'Johnnie, take care!' someone shouted. 'He will have you off under a tree . . .'

There was a crack, a shout and a heavy thud, followed by the pounding of hooves. Then Caroline could hear cries of:

'Catch him! Catch him!'

'Are you hurt?'

'Not in the least. Catch him, I say!'

'Not again, Johnnie, it is not safe . . .'

'Catch him, Henry, you fool, catch him!'

At this moment, to Caroline's horror, the wall stopped, and she found herself separated from the orchard only by a wooden gate and entirely exposed to the young men beyond. Henry Lennox and Johnnie Gates, dressed only in breeches and shirtsleeves, were standing panting and tousled by the nearest tree, Johnnie holding a plunging pony by its reins. They looked at Caroline in amazement, as astonished to see her materialize in the gateway as if she had dropped from heaven.

'It – it is Miss Harding, is it not?' Henry Lennox said at last.

Caroline nodded dumbly. Johnnie Gates's presence made it impossible to speak or to look up. His dark hair was rumpled, his colour was heightened by exercise and his ruffled shirt had come open at the neck. All this she took in at one swift and fascinated glance before fixing her eyes upon her pony's ears.

'May we assist you in any way?' Henry Lennox said. He had come up to the gate and was very near her. She could smell leather and sweat. She swallowed uncomfortably.

'I – I did not mean to disturb you . . .'

'You did not disturb us in the least, Miss Harding. I am only sorry you were too late to see Johnnie tumble off. Is there something I can do for you?'

'I – I was going to the kitchen for – for some peas. Lady Lennox kindly said we – we might have some.'

'I am delighted to hear it. We are weary of peas for every meal here and I should be glad to give you a cart-load. Hand me your basket, Miss Harding, and I will fetch you peas from the kitchen.'

Caroline was horrified. And leave her here alone with Johnnie Gates?

'Oh, no – no, you are too kind – no, it is no trouble – I had rather . . .'

'Nonsense, Miss Harding. Get off your pony and seat yourself on my coat beneath the trees over there, and I will not be ten minutes.'

Johnnie Gates materialized at her side. He seemed much larger and brighter than she remembered.

46

'Allow me.'

She felt his hands on her waist, and she was standing before him on the grass. He tied her pony to the gatepost and opened the gate for her.

'Entertain Miss Harding well, Johnnie.'

'Indeed I will, trust me.'

He turned and smiled at Caroline, and she felt a sort of breathlessness seize her.

'Do you ride much, Miss Harding?'

'Oh no – not much at all. Papa has horses, but Eleanor and I do not ride them.'

Johnnie Gates crossed to the apple tree where the pony was tethered, its flanks flecked with foam, tossing its head impatiently. With one hand on its neck, Johnnie turned and said slowly and casually to Caroline, 'Will you try this pony?'

Caroline's head flew up.

'That pony! No indeed! I should not dare!'

He did not take his eyes from her face.

'I think you would.'

'No! No. Indeed I should not! I should fall immediately . . .'

'I do not think so.'

Caroline was by now shaking with fright. All she could see before her was the pony straining on its tether, and Johnnie's half-shut eyes and small smile.

'Please, Mr Gates, I cannot, indeed I cannot! Do not ask me, I cannot, I cannot!'

Johnnie left the pony and came up to Caroline, standing so close that the open ruffles of his shirt nearly touched the sprigged muslin of her dress. His hand moved to brush her arm as lightly as a leaf.

'I think you can,' he said.

Something broke inside Caroline. The mounting panic and fright exploded in a crescendo and some strange unfamiliar strength, a sort of unnatural calmness, surged through her in its place. She waited a moment while this great wave of unaccustomed power spread itself through her body, then she walked towards the pony and put her hand on its neck.

'Will you help me up, Mr Gates?'

He said something she could not hear in an excited tone, and then she felt his hands on her knee and ankle, and she was astride the pony and the world was plunging and wheeling about her. She had no thought for what Eleanor would say to her, her skirts rucked up, her hat come off, her hair tumbled, being whirled about the orchard on a half-broken pony as the result of a dare. She had no thought of anything in fact, but that she must not fall, and with this consciousness lending steel to her muscles she clung like a limpet while the pony beneath her surged and spun in an attempt to be rid of its burden. She was dimly aware of Johnnie's white shirt here and there, of his shouts that seemed to come from far away, and of trees spinning about like grotesque creatures with a life of their own. Sky, grass, walls, trees all dipped and rocked in a crazy kaleidoscope, but still she clung. Johnnie's shouts came nearer, and suddenly the pony seemed to shudder to a halt and the world righted itself about her. Caroline looked down into blue eyes blazing with triumph below her. She crouched where she was while he led the pony to a tree, tied it, and then turned and lifted her down as effortlessly as if she had been a baby. He stood her on the grass before him, and he did not take his hands from her waist.

'You were afraid,' he said, and his tone was pure admiration.

'Yes,' she said, and raised her head and he caught his breath at the queer silvery gleam of her eyes in that thin tawny face.

'Why did you do it? Were you afraid I should laugh at you?'

'No. I was afraid of my own remorse later.'

He looked down at his hands and noticed how they

almost met about the slenderness of her waist.

'I will never laugh at you again,' he said fervently.

'There is plenty to laugh at.' She looked up at him and smiled with this beautiful new confidence borne of her success.

He thought of Sophia, of Jane and Georgiana with their luxuriant hair and shapely limbs and air of healthy vigour, and looked at Caroline and her frailty and light straight hair.

'I know no-one like you,' he said.

The intimacy of this remark made her realize that his hands were still holding her. She moved backwards to disengage herself and the moment she was free of his warm grasp began involuntarily to tremble.

'Come, you are shaken. Come here. Let me put my coat about you. I would not have frightened you for worlds.'

'I am not frightened,' she said truthfully, 'I am simply very surprised at myself.'

'I am surprised at you also. Surprised and delighted. Miss Harding, may I—'

At this moment, Henry Lennox called from the gateway.

'Your peas, Miss Harding! I hope you have been well amused. I see you have purloined Johnnie's coat which is very sensible of you as you will take much greater care of it than he.'

'Miss Harding was cold, Henry. You were such an age about those peas that she took cold.'

His arm was about her as they moved forward to the gate. Henry took that in, also the fact that Caroline's hair was loose on her shoulders, that she was hatless and looked much better than usual.

'May I fetch your hat, Miss Harding?'

Caroline was immediately confused and began to stammer. Johnnie said smoothly, 'Certainly you may, Henry, while I help Miss Harding to mount.'

49

Henry Lennox came back with the hat in his hand and his lips twitching. He bowed and handed it to Caroline who placed it on her head, and attempted with shaking hands to tie the ribbons. As she fumbled, two warm capable hands took over and tied the ribbons competently beneath her chin, lingering for a fraction of a second on her cheek.

'Now give me the basket, Henry, and tell Aunt I may be late for dinner. I am going to take Miss Harding home.'

Caroline spent the next three days in a trance of incredulous happiness. Luckily her return to the Parsonage was unobserved by her family so she was not molested by reprimands from Eleanor or teasing from her brothers. She felt the whole incident had been like some fairy tale, and found it difficult to recall any precise word or look, but simply dwelt in delighted astonishment upon the seductive atmosphere of dangerous excitement that had imbued it all. She remembered the sensation of feeling that she could do anything and, equally, that anything might happen, but she could not recall in any detail exactly what did happen. She felt intoxicated by the memory but, being Caroline, never expected any kind of sequel. It had been a small but thrilling adventure and she saw it as complete in itself.

But on the third day afterwards, crossing the Stoke River homewards after a visit to the Wells's first baby, she saw a lounging figure on a stile the far side of the bridge. Her heart beat a little quicker as it always did at the alarming prospect of a stranger, but she was too short-sighted to recognize Johnnie Gates. He watched her with amusement as she came, an amusement that now had no derision in it, realizing that she could hardly see him. She wore an old lilac print gown made over from one of her mother's and heavily frilled at the hem and elbows. Her wide straw hat was unadorned with any decoration but a wilting bunch of ladysmocks stuffed into the hat-band,

50

and she carried a small covered basket of fresh butter as a present for her father from Mrs Wells. To Johnnie, used to the rustle of silks and white hands unencumbered by anything heavier than embroidery wools, she was an astonishing and enchanting sight. He rose slowly from the stile and came towards her.

Caroline stood stock still on the grassy cobbles of the bridge, clasping the butter basket, and gazed at him with a smile of sheer delight.

'I am glad you do not frown to see me, Miss Harding.'

'Oh, indeed no, why should I?'

'I have thought I behaved hardly gallantly the other day. I should not blame you if you reproached me for it.'

'Reproach you? Oh no, indeed not.'

He shook his head in wonderment.

'I can scarcely believe it. I have never met a woman before who could resist the chance of reproaching me. What kind of miracle are you?'

Caroline reddened slightly.

'You promised you would not laugh at me.'

He took the butter basket from her hands, placed it upon the parapet of the bridge and came back to stand close before her as he had done in the orchard.

'I am not laughing at you,' he said in a low voice.

Not raising her eyes from the double row of buttons on his waistcoat she said, 'Now I do reproach you. I reproach you for laughing at me. You are quite aware of what the – the Lennoxes think of me, indeed I expect you join in the teasing. And they are right, quite right in what they say. So you can see that to be called a miracle when I know all too well what I am, only humiliates me.'

Three days ago she would never have believed herself capable of making such a speech. Johnnie, entirely unused to perception or introspection in women, bent to take her hands.

'I am not laughing,' he said again, stooping to see

beneath the brim of her hat, 'and every word you say induces me to believe more and more that indeed you are a miracle.'

Caroline tried to free her hands. The bridge not only led to the track that was a parallel and much-used alternative to the village street, but was also a most exposed and public place. Indeed, if Mrs Wells happened to glance from her parlour window at this moment, she would see them both quite clearly.

'I will let you go,' Johnnie said, 'if you will let me see you home again.'

The cart track led past the back of the Parsonage garden and was therefore as unobtrusive a way to go home as any. Caroline consented with a quick nod, and set off towards the comparative seclusion of the track, only to remember that she had forgotten the basket. She spun round quickly and was immediately caught in a firm embrace. Her hat, only balanced upon her head since she had long since lost the ribbons, slipped to the ground and her arms, wide flung in surprise, came to rest gingerly upon Johnnie's shoulders. Slowly her gaze travelled up the buttoned waistcoat inches from her nose, up the casually tied stock, and came to rest at Johnnie's chin. He took one hand from behind her back and tilted her chin further so that the sunlight struck full into her curious eyes and made them glimmer like moonlit water.

'I have thought of nothing else for three days,' he said, 'nothing. I am quite bewitched. You live up there like a princess in a tower and I could not think how to rescue you until I conceived a plan of discovering from your servants where you went and when. The Parsonage kitchen proved most fruitful.'

She did not dare to reply lest the wonderful dream should be broken. His hand moved from under her chin across her cheek to her hair and neck and came to rest across her shoulders, pulling her securely to him.

'When shall I see you again?'

She thought wildly. None of her little errands about the village seemed appropriate places for trysting.

'I – I do not know . . .'

'Do you not want to see me again?'

She nodded, her eyes now fixed on his.

'You have so much to teach me, gentle Caroline. We shall meet often. I must see you every day. Somehow we must meet every day.'

'Yes,' she breathed.

He released her then, and took her hands and kissed her palms and folded her fingers over the kisses.

'I – I must go home.'

'If I may come with you.'

'I have said you might.'

He smiled at her.

'Caroline,' he said.

For three weeks they met daily with a secrecy that astounded Caroline to look back upon. She devised lengthy routes home from all her missions about the parish – Eleanor luckily detested visiting cottagers – and always found upon the return journey that beloved lounging figure in some hedgerow gap or gateway. Some days they would wander on while he taught her popular songs and she returned speeches from Shakespeare and pieces of favourite poetry. Johnnie Gates's knowledge of literature was minimal and he had never before encountered a human being who read entirely for pleasure. Some days, as May blossomed into June, and the summer grasses were lush and inviting, he would take off his coat and make a couch for her.

'There, my Caroline, a sofa fit for a queen. Lie there and chant to me.'

She would lie down, pillowing her head on an upflung arm, and gaze at the blue sky behind his head, and recite to him until he silenced her with kisses. She had never been kissed before, and the first time quite literally took her breath away. She had been coming home from some outlying cottage when she had seen him racing and leaping towards her through the buttercup meadow that tilted away from her feet. She stood laughing as he came bounding and shouting on towards her, and then all of a sudden he was before her, his arms were about her and the summer day was quite blotted out. She pulled her mouth from his at last, quite gasping for excitement and lack of air.

'I am the first!' he shouted jubilantly, spinning her round him. 'The first! The first!'

Caroline cast herself into his arms to be kissed again.

It is impossible to keep any secret successfully in a small community like Stoke Abbas. At length the servants at the Parsonage, who were all too aware of Johnnie's reputation and Caroline's naïvety, deputed Patsy, who had served her master since his marriage, to inform Parson Harding of what was going on. The parson, with a secret leap of relief that Carrie was perhaps not wholly unattractive after all, received the news with due solemnity, and sent for his daughter.

'Well, my dear, and why have you not seen fit to inform me of this new acquaintance you have made?'

'I – I did not think to, Papa.'

'And why not? Is it of so little consequence to you that I need not know?'

'Oh no!' Caroline cried. 'It is of – of a great deal of consequence! To me,' she added in a lower tone.

'In that case, I must inform Lady Lennox. Unless, of course, Mr Gates has already done so.'

Caroline was sure he had not. She was, for the first time in a month, deeply apprehensive. What had seemed so free, so lovely, so possible, was about to be channelled by convention and authority into something dull and probably impossible.

'May I not see John – Mr Gates once more, before you speak to Lady Lennox?'

'My dear Carrie, I am aware that you are both young

and inexperienced, but surely you see that your behaviour has been quite improper enough already without compounding it with a further indiscretion?'

Caroline looked unhappily out of the window. Johnnie would be waiting for her in that part of Stoke Wood which came right down to the river and was thus an excellent and romantic spot for lovers. Perhaps he would guess from her absence that there had been some mishap. She looked miserably at her father.

'He has promised me nothing, Papa, and I have offered nothing. There is nothing to tell Lady Lennox.'

'I must acquaint her with what has happened, Carrie. I am not chastising you, my dear. I am sure you have been no more than foolish. Now go and assist Eleanor and think of something else for the present.'

Caroline spent an anxious afternoon and night, made worse by the fact that Patsy had seen fit to inform Eleanor while the latter was in the dairy that morning.

'Indeed, Carrie, I am quite astonished at you. Such a little mouse of a thing as you to throw yourself at a man whom we all know – except Papa whose heart is truly of gold – to have the worst of reputations. Who has seen you, I wonder, Carrie, and what must the village think of you? No wonder your dresses are always in such a state and your hair so disordered. I hope you are deeply ashamed of yourself for your own weak folly, that has brought such shame upon the Parsonage.'

At last Caroline fled to her room and bolted the door. She tossed herself on her bed and lay, without weeping, staring rigidly at the ceiling. She wished she could weep for tears must be such a release, but she was not a person to whom they came at all readily. So she lay, with clenched fists, and wide dry eyes, and listened to her hammering heart, and despaired.

The next day, to her terror, Parson Harding announced that she and he were to go down to Stoke Park.

'Oh, need I go, Papa? Can you not say to Lady Lennox

how much I regret any distress I have caused her? Can you not beg her pardon for me? Oh, please, Papa, do not make me, do not compel me to go!'

'There is no question of staying behind, Carrie. You are central to this whole matter.'

She was too agitated to notice the smile that sat upon her father's lips. In the turmoil of her own thoughts, she did not even notice that he was humming as the carriage jolted its way downwards. She descended clumsily at the Park and entered the house behind her father with downcast eyes. She was conscious that there were three people in the drawing room and she waited wretchedly for Lady Lennox to speak in a tone of icy displeasure.

'My dear Harding,' Lord Lennox said with great heartiness, 'and Miss Caroline! Charming to see you both.'

'It is indeed,' Lady Lennox said warmly. 'Now come here, Caroline, and give me a kiss.' Utterly dumbfounded, Caroline laid her cheek against that of Lady Lennox. As she did so, she saw that the third person in the room was Johnnie Gates, and that he was smiling broadly. She drew away, quite mystified.

'Seat yourselves, my dear Parson, Miss Harding. Well now, this is all very pleasant. Ring for wine, Johnnie my boy, would you?'

When he had complied, Johnnie came back across the room and seated himself close to Caroline. She felt she should not look at him but she could not help herself; and saw when she did so, that he was gazing at her quite openly with a mixture of understanding and encouragement.

'Will you speak to Caroline?'

'Certainly, Aunt. But I beg the privilege of doing it alone. As she was the only one not present yesterday, it seems hardly fair to astonish her in public.'

'Astonish her!' Lord Lennox said, with hearty derision, 'I hardly think she will be astonished!'

56

Johnnie rose and held out his hand to Caroline.

'May I take Miss Harding to the rose garden, Aunt?'

'Indeed you may, but do not be long about it. Rose garden, forsooth! Would not the library be more comfortable?'

'Comfortable, yes, but hardly romantic. And after all,' he added, greatly daring, 'we are used to the open air.'

Outside, among the pink and creamy profusion of flowers, Caroline woke a little from her trance. The flowers were real enough, so was Johnnie's arm under her own, but she could scarcely credit what he was saying.

'I fear I have done this in a somewhat backhanded manner, Caroline, but I did it to make certain you would not refuse. I am to go to India in September as you know, and I had intended that my life there should be a bachelor one—'

He stopped, and took his arm from hers in order to place it round her waist.

'I do not want to be a bachelor any longer, Caroline. I never expected to feel what I have felt this summer, I never thought to meet a being who would bewitch me as you have done. I do not think I could live without you now, and I have some little hope that you would be unhappy without me.'

'I should, I should!' she cried fervently. 'I could not bear it!'

'We must bear it just a little while. I shall sail in early September, and find a house in Madras, and engage servants for – for us. And then, perhaps you will come to me and we may be married.' He paused and said in a low voice, 'If you will have me.'

She flung herself into his arms.

'Oh, yes, yes, Johnnie! Yes!'

He relaxed his serious air, and whooped exultantly, whirling her round him on the smooth green grass.

'Then I have nothing left to wish for!'

'Nor I,' she cried passionately.

He pulled her to him and kissed her roughly.

'Shall you not mind India? The heat? The snakes? The strangeness? Will you dare it all for me?'

'Yes, I will!'

'My Caroline.'

'I love you,' she said fervently, 'I love you.'

He walked her slowly back to the house and to a benign reception. The whole matter had been settled when Parson Harding called the previous day to inform Lady Lennox of the affair between his daughter and her nephew. Johnnie had been summoned and had professed with such open sincerity that his intentions were entirely honourable, that both Lady Lennox and Parson Harding had felt their indignation mellowing into approval. The only person who was not there to consult was Caroline, but Johnnie was accurately confident of her response. She drove back to the Parsonage that night the promised wife of Johnnie Gates.

He sailed at the beginning of September, with promises they should be together by the Christmas of the following year. Caroline saw him go with anguish, partly at the thought of at least sixteen months' separation, and partly out of fear at what might happen to him on that dreadful and dangerous voyage. It would be six slow months of tedium, discomfort, and frequent alarm. The prospect did not alarm Caroline for herself, as she expected to sail the following summer but she suffered vicariously for Johnnie.

He promised he would write from every port, and at first they came, letters from Lisbon, letters from Cape Town, gradually moving further east. As the ship sailed further away, the letters grew further apart, and their tone became less loving and more informative.

In March of 1768 Johnnie wrote to say he had reached Madras, but added nothing of his search for a house or entreaties for her to join him. This unsatisfactory epistle reached Caroline in September, and it was the last she was ever to receive. Lady Lennox immediately began to besiege the Directors of the East India Company in India House in Leadenhall Street and was, to her indignation, brushed aside. They knew nothing of such trivia concerning a mere clerk in the Company, and they cared less. Letters to Johnnie, from everyone except Caroline, throughout 1769 and 1770 brought no response at all, and eventually even the indefatigable Lady Lennox told Caroline what she already knew full well, that she must resign herself to remaining at Stoke Abbas, a spinster.

What Caroline endured alone in her small bedroom, no-one knew, for she was stony in response to sympathy from anyone, even her father. The general assumption was, eventually, that she regarded the incident as over and done with, as everyone else was all too ready to do. And indeed it was true that after five years or so, although Caroline had not forgotten, the agonizing pain of heartbreak was over in its first raw savagery. She resigned herself to life as it must be for her, and never blamed Johnnie Gates for having shown her a brighter horizon for a while. He had been like a meteor across her heavens, had blazed a wonderful trail and had gone, leaving darkness. But the darkness was no blacker than before his coming, and Caroline was used to it. There was no doubt, however, that this evening, almost eight years after that parting, had brought a small glimmer back into the darkness. He was still alive, still in India, still, it seemed, a bachelor. She thought of the wild pony and the buttercup meadow, and with a little smile of remembered pleasure, she turned upon her side, and slept.

4

The month of December 1775 saw the arrival in Calcutta of two letters from Stoke Park, both addressed in the same firm hand and both asking for immediate response. The *Duchess of Grafton* was to sail again as speedily as she could be made ready and the writer begged she might not return without replies.

The letter addressed to Sir Edward Ashton found him soon after he had been respectfully awakened by a group of servants in his house near the Court House in Calcutta. It was not a fashionable house, being built of mud, not masonry as the new modern houses were, but the mud kept it cool, and its rooms were large with extensive views down to the Hooghly River. That December morning the Ashton servants were in a state of disarray and distress. Their equable, benevolent and ascetic master was in a mood so thunderous that they had leapt back from his bedside as quickly as if their politely folded brown hands had been scorched by touching him. In ten years of service, they had never known him to be so, and if he had chosen to confide in them, he would have informed them that in ten years he had never known himself so, and that was reason enough for bad temper. Sir Edward Ashton, scholar and statesman, one of the most respected members of the East India Company's Council in Calcutta, and a staunch supporter of the Governor General, had his first major hangover in a decade.

It was common enough for all his fellow Englishmen to get through seven different wines at dinner, followed by two or three bottles of claret apiece, quite apart from huge quantities of port, but Edward Ashton was the exception to the rule. He would drink but a glass or two throughout the length of those interminable and gargantuan meals, and was regarded with public amusement and private admiration by most of his contemporaries. He had no idea, searching his pounding brain, why he had indulged himself so insanely the night before, unless drink had seemed the only escape from the monumental boredom of the two pretty and witless girls either side of him at dinner. He was always given pretty girls at dinner, because his magnificent physique and air of distinction made mothers enormously optimistic about their daughters' chances of happiness with him. It was reasoned among the drawing rooms of Calcutta that a man of forty, prosperous, esteemed and solitary, must be sorely in want of a wife. Last night's hostess had exceeded herself in being able to produce two charming nieces who were under her protection for the winter and had watched in dismay while the decanter stopped constantly before Edward Ashton and he had regarded it alone with never a glance for poor Fanny or poor Sophia.

The truth was, in fact, that poor Fanny and poor Sophia were no more than the final straw in Sir Edward's burden of mounting contempt for Calcutta society in general. Indeed, if it had not been for his warm regard for, and much-needed support of, Warren Hastings, and his almost passionate fondness for India, he would have cut short his term of office years since and gone home to Herefordshire, however bleak an alternative that offered. As it was, he was only kept at a bare level of endurance in Calcutta because of an annual habit of setting forth to escape the European community in Bengal, and to find the alternative India. In this way there was hardly a Moghul palace or Hindu temple in Upper India, past or present, which had not had Sir Edward Ashton as guest or visitor. He had catalogued these edifices minutely, from the deserted red sandstone city of Fatehpur Sikri to the voluptuous carvings of the caves at Ajanta; the great forts of Agra and Delhi and Jaipur had all sheltered him at some point in the last decade. He had been one of the first European visitors invited to admire the new pink city of Jaipur, carved and fretted and painted the colour of peach sherbert. He had ridden elephants up the ancient rivers of the Jumna and the Ganges, camels across the desert wastes of Rajputana, and sailed at dawn across to the Lake Palace at Udaipur. After all these voyages, he had returned to Calcutta in elation with some measure of tolerance for the riotous and vulgar immorality of the city; but for two years now, pressure of work had kept him chained to a society which he could only endure with equanimity if allowed regular escape.

It was not that he was a priggish man, but rather that he felt that sin, like the classic definition of tragedy, only achieved greatness, and therefore any kind of distinction and interest, when committed by the great. Those people around him in Calcutta, those tawdry, scrambling little people, obsessed by their lust for gold and pleasure, seemed to him to fall as far short of greatness as was humanly possible. The stature of Warren Hastings as an administrator did, in some measure in Sir Edward's eyes, elevate his irregular cohabiting with a lady who was the estranged wife of Baron Imhoff, into sin of some consequence, but he was the sole example. For the rest, they aroused in Sir Edward nothing but scorn, and he retreated from them into the consolation of his studies in Persian and Arabic and his catalogues of Moghul architecture.

Persian and Arabic, however, could not shield him impregnably from the most determined of hostesses, nor from official obligation. Once or twice a week he must sally forth to witness just what he would have fled from and his ability to bear the onslaught of Calcutta society had been declining rapidly in the last year. He had sought refuge, first in silence, preferring his own thoughts to any conversation, but then, finding his muteness made him awkwardly conspicuous and a target for just the heavy rough-house he abhorred, he had discovered that to take a glass or two more than his customary small ration of wine gave him enough brief, false gaiety to participate sufficiently to escape notice. What had happened to that slenderly increased ration last night he could not recall, but clearly it had been no ration at all. The triviality and coarseness of the dinner party must have been in precise proportion to the quantity of wine he had recklessly swallowed.

Well, he thought savagely, surveying his bloodshot eyes and stubbled chin in the glass, he was paying dearly for his indulgence now. The headache and nausea and sense of utter dehydration were bad enough, but worse was his shame and humiliation. He could remember nothing after dinner, nothing at all. He was still in last night's shirt, a fact which repelled so fastidious a man, and which made him bellow furiously for the reason from the shaking clutch of servants in the corner.

They exchanged anxious glances, rolling their eyes, spreading their hands.

'Answer me!' Edward Ashton shouted. 'Why am I not in my nightshirt? Answer me, you dolts!'

Could this be the man on whom they relied so heavily for his steadiness and amiability, the man they had not thought of leaving for more glittering posts in the ten years they had served him? Could Sir sahib be sick? In the head, perhaps? Gocul, a little braver than the others, stepped out of the shivering band, shrugging his narrow shoulders apologetically.

'Sir sahib was so wild, we feared—'

'Wild?' Ashton said with incredulous emphasis.

Gocul waved his thin, muslin-clad arms and rolled his eyes.

'Wild, Sir sahib, that we were fearing injury.'

Edward Ashton regarded him sombrely. Had he been brought home, then, shouting and singing and flailing his limbs like any green clerk or cadet? Had he been so violent that the servants had been unable to undress him? They had clearly tried, he noticed, since he was without breeches or stockings. He surveyed his bare feet gloomily.

'Sir sahib is sick?' Gocul ventured bravely.

The other servants crept nearer. They had known full well that Ashton had been drunk the night before, but they had expected, so great was their faith in him, to see him rise refreshed at seven according to his custom, like a phoenix from the ashes of his excess. He raised his head despite the lead weights that slithered about inside it and managed, painfully, the smallest and tightest of smiles.

'Only sick for a little while,' he said.

'We are rejoicing,' Gocul said fervently amid a breath of relief from the men around him.

Ashton ran a hand over his chin.

'Where is the barber?'

'He is waiting, Sir sahib. He is waiting since seven o'clock.'

'What time is it?'

'It is being ten, Sir sahib.'

'Ten!' Ashton bellowed, instantly wincing with the pain his own voice gave him. It was unthinkable. He was, despite the Calcutta custom of not being at one's desk until nine in the hot season or ten in the cool one, always at work by eight. And now it was ten, and he had, unthinkably, missed a breakfast to be given by the Governor General for two most distinguished French attorneys passing through Calcutta. His absence would be a source of astonishment since he was commonly so reliably punctilious. Well, there was nothing for it but to shave and dress and rescue as much of the day as it was in his power to do.

Shaving was soothing. Warned by Gocul, the barber attempted no conversation and wisely desisted from his

64

usual morning practice of cleaning Ashton's ears. Ears, Gocul had pointed out, were not only sensitive but very close to what was, at the moment, an area of acute pain. Unable to refrain from all customary practices, however, the barber knelt reverently to clean and cut Ashton's nails and received a blow which sent him flying across the room.

'You did them but yesterday, you fool!'

'But they are growing,' the barber quavered from the corner where he had fallen, 'always, Sir sahib, they are growing!'

'Today, let them grow,' Ashton growled. A sweat of feverishness was beginning to mingle unpleasantly with the dampness of the skin that was customary in the wet heat of Calcutta. Noticing his master's beaded forehead, a servant with a fan came gingerly forward attempting to create a cool draught above that scowling brow.

'Go away!' Ashton shouted.

The man sprang back, caught the barber's table with his foot and overturned a silver bowl of soapy water and a clatter of razors upon the floor. Ashton put his head in his hands and groaned pitifully.

The door opened to admit Gocul bearing his master's dressing gown. Ashton was assisted into it and helped solicitously to a breakfast table in the adjoining room where tea and toast were laid out for him. He sat down weakly and surveyed the silver and china and white linen, but at the sight of the butter floating yellow and oily in a silver dish of water, he went greenish white and closed his eyes.

'Take it away.'

'All, Sir sahib?'

'All, everything, at once, far, far away.'

When he opened his eyes the table had gone, quite silently, and the hairdresser was standing anxiously across a space of carpet in the shadows. Sir Edward Ashton was a great disappointment to him always, because he refused to have his thick, strong hair powdered. The hairdresser had been trained by the most fashionable French coiffeur in Calcutta, and he felt it to be an insult to his professional skills that a man whom he could have coiffed so admirably would have no truck with powder, pomade or wigs. In vain he assured Sir Edward that in Versailles pomade was worn as thick as butter, and that if only he would wear three rows of side curls he would be able to sport one of those new and stylish French hats. On an ordinary morning, Sir Edward would merely laugh at these notions, and would then read absorbedly instead of indulging in the delightful gossip the hairdresser enjoyed so much. It was but the work of minutes to smooth that heavy chestnut hair back into its broad black bow, and it always left the hairdresser dissatisfied and unfulfilled. But this morning, he did not know if he even dared venture across the carpet. Sir Edward had no breakfast to distract him, no book even, and his expression made a typhoon seem a gentle thing by comparison. He looked about him desperately, licking his lips, and fidgeting his brushes. To his unspeakable relief, the double doors beside him opened and Ralph Buxby, Ashton's secretary, entered with a lacquer tray of the morning's papers.

Ralph Buxby had enormous respect and affection for his superior and was genuinely distressed to see him in such discomfort of mind and body. He motioned to the hairdresser to proceed, as he knew that an immaculate appearance would be soothing at such a frayed moment. The hairdresser scuttled like a crab round the outer edges of the room and reached the haven of the back of Ashton's head with visible relief. Buxby crossed the stretch of carpet slowly, his face registering both sympathy and concern. In his self-disgust, Sir Edward Ashton wanted neither.

'I require no pity, Buxby. I deserve every twinge. What have we this morning?'

'Not a great deal, sir, apart from more trouble at the silk mills up at Kasimbazar, and a packet of letters from England.'

To many Englishmen in Calcutta, the second item of news would have been cause for great excitement. Every East Indiaman coming up the Hooghly brought with it the chance of news from England. But Sir Edward Ashton had few contacts left in England now beside his sister who was keeping Ashton Court ready for his retirement, and she was a dull correspondent. She wrote dutifully and regularly, but her letters were no more than long household accounts and details of ailments among the servants and the dairy herd that grazed the fat Herefordshire pastures. Her letters never made her brother homesick but rather made him forget the particular and enchanting atmosphere that was so much a part of Ashton Court. He looked dully at the lacquer tray.

'What trouble at Kasimbazar?'

'More inland trading, sir.'

It was well known that clerks of the Company supplemented their meagre salaries of a few hundred pounds a year by steady and profitable private trading on their own accounts. It was possible to make five-figure fortunes in five or ten years, and to go home a wealthy man. But occasionally the private trading inland got entirely out of hand, and began to conflict with the Company's own profits and then, of course, it had to be curbed. Ashton looked up painfully.

'What has gone missing, Buxby?'

'The *Sea Horse* put in a month ago with broadcloth and fire-arms enough to exchange for two shipments of silks. Both guns and woollens have unaccountably vanished, and the silks sent down to be loaded at Calcutta were diverted on the way and have been sold to the French. They are now two weeks on the way to Marseilles.'

'Why did I not hear of this before?'

Buxby hesitated.

'I told you of it yesterday, sir.'

There was an uncomfortable silence. During it, the hairdresser finished a perfect job, and tiptoed away into the shadows. The hookah-burdar, waiting behind a screen, gestured to him to ask if he should go forward and slide the mouthpiece of the hookah's snake into Sir sahib's hand, as was the custom when his hair was dressed. The hairdresser, remembering the look on Sir sahib's face at the sight of breakfast, shook his head. The hookah-burdar nodded. He had spent the previous evening standing behind Sir Edward's chair, and understood better than any what ailed him this morning. He squatted down in the dimness behind the screen and resumed his endless, patient polishing of the hookah's silver chains and rosettes.

Ashton said, 'What letters from England?'

'Three, sir. Shall you read them?'

Ashton squinted at the covers and observed miserably that the writing on all three appeared to squirm nauseatingly across the paper.

'Read them to me, Buxby.'

With an ivory knife, Ralph carefully opened the first of the letters. It was from Ashton's London lawyer who, writing on behalf of the agent at Ashton Court, begged leave to restock the lake with carp and trout purchased with the profits from the sale of some veal calves. Ashton sighed irritably. It was precisely these minor decisions that he had hoped his sister and the agent would make between them without this tedious waste of time and money. It would mean a delay of a year in re-stocking the lake, and thus in fishing it again. His irritation mounted when the second letter proved to be from his sister with precisely the same question in it, in addition to the information that ten out of the thirty young oaks he had ordered planted had died and that her rheumatism was giving her no peace.

'Shall I open the third, sir?'

Ashton closed his eyes.

'Read it to yourself, Buxby, and repeat to me anything I might wish to hear.'

His head seemed almost worse with his eyes shut. He opened them again and noticed gratefully that the servants had placed the screens of dampened grass that usually stood across the doorways, across the windows, too. The glaring sunlight outside was reduced considerably by this means, and filtered faint and greenish into the cavernous room. He was sorry already to have shouted and bellowed at them this morning. He knew they were fond of him, and he knew too that they did not exploit him indecently. The servants' quarters contained far more human beings than the forty he employed – and forty was then a modest number – and he knew he provided for them all, but he was not prepared to complain without great provocation and that point had never been reached. He could see the hookah-burdar's foot protruding from behind the screen and guessed he had remained there out of diplomacy. Sir Edward smiled very faintly to himself, a smile that vanished abruptly, when Ralph Buxby cleared his throat loudly and sent an arrow of pain through Ashton's temple.

'I do not seem to understand this letter thoroughly, sir. It would appear it has some connection with Lord Lovell.'

'He is not coming back?' Ashton said in horror. He had never endured anything so stoically as those eternal months with Frank Lovell and his brainless, pleasure-loving energy.

'No, sir.' Buxby looked up and smiled at the relief on Ashton's face. 'No, far from it. It seems he is about to marry Miss Georgiana Lennox, daughter of Lord Lennox of Stoke Park in Dorset. This letter comes from her mother.'

'Her mother?'

'Yes, sir. Will you read the letter for yourself?'

'No – no, Buxby. Tell me what she says.'

'It appears that she has the incumbency of Stoke Abbas in her gift and it is presently held by a Parson Harding. He has a daughter, a Miss—' Ralph paused and searched the letter, while astonishment spread over Ashton's face, 'a Miss Caroline Harding, who was once promised to a certain John Gates—'

'What is this nonsense?' Ashton exploded. 'Who are these people? I have never heard of one of them in my life!'

'I am not quite done, sir.'

'Well, finish then, but quickly.'

'Sir, it seems that John Gates is in the Company's employ, and is yet unmarried, and Lady Lennox wishes you to inform her if you think he would make a suitable husband for Miss Harding.'

His eyes blazing with incredulity, Sir Edward Ashton rose to his considerable height.

'Are you telling me, Buxby, that a perfectly strange woman in – in Dorset, is asking me as to the suitability of some trifling clerk for the hand of a – a parson's daughter of whom I have never heard?'

'It seems so, sir.'

'It is perfectly preposterous. She must be a madwoman. What is the world coming to if I must be subjected to lunatic requests about possible nuptials from complete strangers half a world away? I am speechless, quite, quite speechless.'

Ralph waited a moment and then said, 'What would you wish me to reply, sir?'

'Reply?' Ashton said, as if his secretary had suggested flying to the moon. 'You will reply nothing. You will put that paper to the only use fit for it, that of a taper.'

Ralph looked at the coat of arms at the head of the letter, and the strong purposeful handwriting, and felt that he must make one more effort.

'May I not merely acknowledge it, sir, and say you have no opinion on the subject?'

Ashton cast himself back into his chair. The lead weights were now quite untethered and were crashing about his skull most agonizingly. It was useless to contemplate constructive thought of any kind that day.

'Oh, do what you will, Buxby, do what you will. I do not care. Today, I do not care for anything.'

Ralph rose, and picked up the tray. Kasimbazar would obviously have to wait. He stood looking down at his superior, and saw that a thread or two of grey hair was appearing on that handsome head.

'Shall you rest until dinner, sir?'

'I want no dinner, Buxby. I want no supper. You will cancel whatever engagements I have, and no-one is to come near me until seven tomorrow morning. If I am not recovered then, I shall throw myself into the river.'

Buxby thought of avowing that he would prevent that event at all costs, but decided this was no moment for protestations of loyalty.

'I shall see you are not disturbed, sir.'

He crossed the carpet again and turned in the doorway to look back. Sir Edward Ashton, in dressing gown and bare feet, looked for all the world like any other hungover Englishman in Calcutta, slumped in his chair, eyes closed, brows contracted. It was perhaps comforting, Ralph thought, to know such a paragon had some human failings, for there was normally precious little sign of any. He was charming to women, but appeared indifferent to almost all of them, he drank little, ate moderately, read interminably, and worked harder than almost any man in Calcutta. It was unprecedented that he should forget such a matter as Kasimbazar. Sighing, Ralph settled himself at his desk, and took out the letter from Lady Lennox. Unaccountable it might be, but it certainly provided light relief from the crushing load of official papers that littered

71

his desk. He pulled out a sheet of paper, took up his quill, and sat for a moment gazing at the quiveringly hot prospect beyond his window.

Dear Lady Lennox,
  Sir Edward Ashton begs me to thank you for your letter of June 16th, 1775. He instructs me to inform you that he knows of no objection to the proposed marriage between Miss Caroline Harding and Mr John Gates.
    I remain your humble servant,
        Ralph Buxby

He re-read it with satisfaction. It was a constructive letter, yet contained no absolute commitment. He folded it, addressed it, sealed it and then dropped it upon the brass tray whose contents were to be taken down to the *Duchess of Grafton* before she sailed.

Johnnie Gates was in high spirits. The profits from his share of the French deal were enough to cover all the gambling debts of the last six months which had amounted to the frightening total of twenty thousand pounds. It was a good thing the French appetite for silk was so insatiable. He had, for him, only a small headache that morning, he was to be permitted to stay in Calcutta for the remainder of the winter, and he had the prospect of an excellent dinner party ahead of him. Humming, he leant back in his chair while the dark curls that Caroline had admired so much were subdued beneath a wig that a friend had purchased for him at Boulogne when the *Sea Horse* had called there on her way east. Although he admired the effect of this splendid creation with its rows of side curls and high crest once it was on his head, there was no doubt it was confoundedly hot and his scalp frequently prickled maddeningly under its burden.

Tapping his teeth with the ivory mouthpiece of his

hookah, Johnnie surveyed the room. It was a shocking mess, shocking, he must get the servants moving, indeed he must. He shouted arrogantly. The sircar appeared, wiping his hands on the greasy tatters of his gown. It was a mystery to Johnnie that a man who absorbed so much money could manage to be so down at heel and disreputable. They had endless sessions, the sircar and Johnnie, the one whining, the other shouting, and the sircar invariably winning. He was responsible for hiring all Johnnie's servants, claiming a necessity for fifty-one, and arranged all the daily household expenses of which Johnnie had no notion at all. Visits to the money-lender, who always seemed to be a cousin of the sircar's, were frequent and expensive. Things had been better when George Campbell had shared the house but George had gone home and Johnnie found it unaccountably difficult to find another bachelor willing to live with him.

He regarded the sircar with imperiousness. 'I want this room entirely cleaned and put in order by nightfall. Indeed, I want the whole house attended to and there will be no more slovenliness. There are enough of you to keep a palace in order, let alone one man and a house.'

The sircar, servile and ragged, shuffled his feet. Being merely a broker, he had no direct responsibility for running Sahib Gates's household, but on the other hand, as he had installed himself in Sahib Gates's servants' quarters without permission, he did not like to point out that he was no housekeeper. It might bring his parasite's position to Sahib Gates's notice, and his profitable and comfortable way of life would be at an end.

'It is not being possible, sahib.'

'Not possible, damn you?' Johnnie roared. 'I do not care if it is impossible. It will be done, do you hear me, it will be done!'

The sircar shook his head.

'I cannot be doing it, sahib. You are not paying the

servants, they are going away and there is nobody to be cleaning.'

Johnnie clutched the arms of his chair while his face reddened with fury.

'I have paid them, you odious, cringing toad! I gave you money for wages not a week ago! What have you done with it, what, tell me what or I'll wring your worthless neck!'

The sircar backed away a little.

'There were many, many needing the paying, sahib, that I could not be paying for the servants. I am paying for the dhobi, and I am paying for the money-lender and I am paying for—' he stopped and gave a little yelp as a huge volume, its leather covers mouldy with damp, missed his head by inches.

'I would throttle you!' Johnnie yelled, 'but that it would foul my hands. Get out, get out or I will kick you out!'

The sircar, remembering a time when he had been quite literally booted from the verandah to fall ten feet to the shrubs below, hastily retired. The mornings were always the worst. By two, the sahib had gone to dine and thereafter the mellowing influence of wine caused him to forget household affairs. Most mornings, too, racking headaches and nausea prevented the sahib from thinking of anything but his own misery and it was only the occasional morning, like this one, that he was in a fit state to be a trouble to the sircar. He went to his rattan bed in the servants' quarters and drew out a small metal trunk from beneath it. It was satisfyingly heavy. From around his neck, the sircar took a key and unlocked the box. The sight within was very gratifying, very gratifying indeed. That was a lot of gold for a man who had been born on a mud flat in the Ganges delta. In gratitude to the good Sahib Gates who had done this kind thing, he, the sircar, would see that his bedroom was put in order. Not cleaned, of course, as that would be most wasteful for such a generous but unobservant sahib, but things would be picked up from the floor, and perhaps, as a special gesture, the bed linen might be changed. That was indeed a special gesture, as a drunken man does not notice his bed linen, but this month had been an especially profitable month for the sircar, and Johnnie should have a clean pillowcase for his generosity. The sircar went to the door of his hut and shouted for his sons and nephews.

In the house, Johnnie sat and fumed. The man was no more than a robber, a daylight robber. He looked angrily about at the dust and the dirty linen and his disordered bed. Every chair was heaped with clothing, none of it clean, and a heavy, unsavoury smell filled the hot, damp air. It was monstrous, Johnnie declared to himself in a wave of self-pity, monstrous that a man brought up as he had been should be condemned to live like this, deceived at every turn, uncared for and miserable. His mood of optimism had quite gone, ruined by that cringing toad.

With a final tweak and pull, the wig-barber stepped back, and Johnnie could not help a wave of gratification at the sight of himself in the glass. It was a pity he had put on weight so, but then, he had the height to carry it and he saw no diminishing of the handsomeness of those features he had gazed on so fondly for thirty years. He slipped into the heavy brocade coat held out for him, woven with a brilliant and complicated pattern of flowers, and consoled himself that so dazzling was his coat that the imperfect whiteness of his breeches would not signify. He was handed his snuff box, handkerchief and cane. A heavy signet ring was offered to him on a tray. It never struck him that the same ring was offered every day because all the others he had brought with him in a heavy morocco box had mysteriously vanished. Thus arrayed, he left the squalor of his bedroom, and proceeded on horseback across Calcutta to his desk.

He arrived, behind the customary procession of

servants, at eleven. His office had been busy for a good hour by then, and he took care not to swagger to his desk too ostentatiously. The twenty-minute ride in the blazing sun had done his head no good at all and he would have given a good deal for a bumper of claret. Breakfast had been inedible that morning as the bread was mouldy and the butter rancid, but at that hour he had been cheerful enough to overlook both. Now his stomach growled, and his head throbbed and his eyes felt gritty at the edges.

Nodding cheerfully to fellow clerks, for his main aim in life was the maintenance of appearances, he arrived at his desk and the disorder it bore. Other clerks around him discarded their gaudy coats for quill pushing, and worked in plain shirts and sleeved waistcoats, and starched white caps in place of their cumbrous wigs, but Johnnie disdained such practicality. When he had arrived in Madras almost eight years before, he had come with a magnificent wardrobe purchased at all the French ports his ship had put into. He had stepped from the masulah boat on to Indian soil resplendent in velvet and lace, strikingly handsome and debonair, and had been immediately christened 'Beau Gates'. It was the high spot of his popularity, and he was never aware that admiration for his wardrobe had dwindled as his taste and self-indulgences became more excessive. So he sat down at his desk in his stiffened and heavily cuffed coat, and prepared to attempt the task of writing, severely impeded by his ruffles and ring.

In the midst of all the thumbed and tattered papers that had lain gathering dust this last month, lay an unfamiliar item. It was a letter with an English stamp, addressed in a hand that was uncomfortably familiar. Johnnie stared down at the cream-coloured square, and from that bold black hand rose images of England, green pictures of horses and rain and hedged fields. He touched the letter nervously. He had thought and hoped she had

76

given him up, but he should have known Lady Lennox better. What could she find to say to him now? Was Lord Lennox dying? Johnnie, already sweating profusely beneath his wig and brocade, broke out into a fresh cold sweat of anxiety. He looked about him. Everyone seemed deeply absorbed, the only sound the swish of fans held by servant boys, and the buzzing of flies. Johnnie ripped the letter open.

His eye ran quickly and nervously down the page. She had crossed the letter, a sure sign she did not think him worthy of a second sheet of precious paper. He read it several times with slowly dawning comprehension and then replaced it with a shaking hand on his muddled desk. He felt sick, very sick indeed. The letter was a threat and a most unpleasant one. It amounted to the fact that if Johnnie did not marry, the money that he was entirely relying upon for his return to England, since he was too wasteful to make enough for his retirement in India, would go to his cousins. He was not at all sure that Lady Lennox could prevent his receiving the money, but presumably she had discovered some legal loophole and that was what had prompted her to write to him in this blackmailing manner after a silence of six years. After all, if she could not stop him receiving the money, why should she bother to write at all? He sat and shook, and concluded exactly what Lady Lennox had intended him to conclude.

After a long and sickening time, Johnnie picked the letter up again by the extreme edges as if it might bite him. One fact had now sunk in, the fact that he must either marry, or lose the money upon which his whole future depended. But there had been something else which his panicking brain had skimmed over at first reading. He looked at the letter again, and saw with renewed shock that Lady Lennox was not only dictating his marriage, she was dictating whom he should marry.

'I am sure you have not forgotten Caroline Harding,'

77

wrote Lady Lennox, 'and as she still lives at the Parsonage it is evident that she has not forgotten you.'

Johnnie put the letter down again, and closed his eyes. How Lady Lennox could manage to affect him so powerfully and distressingly from thousands of miles away he did not know, but there was no doubt that she was successful. If she could have seen him as he sat at his desk, shaken and entirely unmanned, she would have been highly gratified at the strength of her own influence. Luckily, Johnnie thought grimly, she could not see him and thus he could give way to all the upset and resentment that he so strongly felt. The more he thought about it, the more injured he felt. He was trapped and he felt it deeply unjust that he should be trapped. He had to comply if he was to have any comfort to look forward to, and he could not conceive of a life without comfort. The whole situation was intolerable, quite intolerable, and yet he had no choice, given his tastes, but to tolerate it.

He stared unseeingly at the confusion of papers in front of him. He, Johnnie Gates, Beau Gates, renowned in Madras and Calcutta for his dash and courage and gallantry, was to be condemned to marry Caroline Harding. He felt no particular fury against Caroline herself, indeed she had provided the substance of a very delicate and pastoral interlude in his life all those years ago, and he thought of her, on the rare occasions he thought of his English past, with a sort of pleasant sentimentality. He had been mildly sorry to let her down, but then he had been so cornered by his aunt and uncle and old man Harding that he really had had no choice but to profess honourable intentions of marriage. And she had been so sweet, and so very besotted that the notion of marrying her had briefly seemed a pretty thing. But of course he had never meant it, and he was sure that she would never blame him. She was not that sort of girl. Those mild, gentle, shy girls never blamed a fellow, they always supposed the fault their own and that was an aspect that made them such endearing companions. Endearing for a little while, that is, for no full-blooded man could want such milk and water stuff for his permanent diet.

Unfortunately, milk and water seemed about to form a major part of his future nourishment. Lady Lennox was a scheming old witch and would have no trouble in bending Caroline to her will. Caroline would arrive in Calcutta and be too frightened to speak and Johnnie's social life would dwindle to nothing, and he would die, within months, of boredom. A lump of profound self-pity rose in Johnnie's throat for the second time that morning and tears of sheer compassion at the intense pathos of his own situation began to prickle at the edges of his eyes. He looked miserably about him, and surveyed his fellow factors with an envy so violent they must almost have felt it burning through the brocade of their waistcoats. They were free, free as birds to live their lives as they chose, and he, Johnnie, was to be shackled as a convict upon a prison ship. There was no justice in the world, indeed there was not.

Across the room George Carew, a man who shared Johnnie's idea of pleasures to a large extent, had watched his companion with amused fascination for a good hour. He always enjoyed Johnnie's entrance in any case, with its peculiar mixture of swashbuckle and furtive anxiety about constant unpunctuality. But this morning had been a rare treat, beginning with the spectacle of that astounding wig (of which George Carew was a little envious) and then watching such a performance of writhing and blanching that the theatre at its most dramatic would seem tame by comparison. After an hour, however, the entertainment seemed to become more static and George perceived that Johnnie had now sat slumped and glum without stirring for at least ten minutes. Adjusting his cap on his glossy dark head, George was about to stroll casually in Johnnie's direction well armed with witticisms, when

Johnnie started up and cast such a glance of anguish round the room, that George was halted in the very act of rising from his chair. The poor old boy was clearly in a bad way. Subduing his facetiousness, George straightened, squared his shoulders, and began to pick his way among the servants crouched reverently about their masters' desks.

'Run out of luck, Johnnie boy?'

Johnnie raised a ravaged face.

'Clean out.'

George cast himself into the chair that had been instantly and silently provided.

'What's up?'

Self-pity had quite obliterated any discretion Johnnie might have had.

'I'm done for, George, quite done for.'

'No, you ain't. You won enough last night at whist to keep a king going for a week, not to mention the French fiddle.'

'It – it is something quite other.'

George Carew never beat about the bush.

'Poxed again, Johnnie boy?'

Johnnie shook his head miserably.

'No, no – I believe I'd almost welcome that. No, it is very much worse.'

George gave a yelp of laughter. If a man was clean and had a full pocket he could not imagine that anything else could ail him.

'There ain't nothing bad left!'

'Oh, you are wrong, George, so wrong. I am done for quite finished.'

'Spit it out, then!'

Johnnie leant forward, his eyes fixed intently upon George Carew. In tones of the deepest melancholy he said, 'I am to be married.'

The grin left George's face abruptly. In quite an altered tone he said, 'Married?'

'Married. I'm not to come into my family money if I don't marry whom I'm told.'

'To hell with family money!' George shouted. 'You don't need it! You're making your fortune out here!'

Johnnie looked at him without speaking, and in the silence that followed they both reviewed Johnnie's way of life, and saw what a struggle a fortune would have, to emerge from that extravagant circus.

In a much quieter tone, George said, 'Who is the bride?'

'Oh, a dear little quiet, shy creature,' Johnnie said scornfully. 'Wouldn't say boo to a goose.'

'Well looking?'

'N-no,' Johnnie said reluctantly, 'but quite a – a something – some sort of—'

'Pity. Docile?'

'Oh, very.'

George stretched his legs out, using a conveniently kneeling Indian as a footstool.

'Then you'll have no trouble.'

'Trouble?'

'About Rani.'

Rani! In all the turmoil of the morning, Johnnie had quite forgotten her. Rani! Reputed to be the most accomplished and sophisticated courtesan in all Calcutta and for the past two enthralling months his faithful mistress. How could he have forgotten her? Indeed, she had started last night in his bed, and where the deuce she had got to, he did not know. She was always doing that, vanishing and then reappearing at just the precise moment he wanted her. The possibility he might have to give her up was a fresh blow to his battered mind.

'God, George, will I have to give her up?'

'No, Johnnie boy, no, no, don't be absurd. You'd be mad to give her up. What I meant was that if your wife is a biddable, meek sort of creature, you can still do what you like, just as you always have, Rani included.'

It was the first ray of hope that had pierced the dreadful gloom of the morning. Johnnie seized upon it with desperate fervour.

'Do you think so, George? Do you know any fellows who have wives and can still please themselves? Do you really think it possible, George?'

'Certainly I do! She'll be as scared as a rabbit to be in India anyway, and you must see that you are master from the moment she steps on shore. You must begin as you mean to go on.'

Johnnie sat back in his chair and pondered a little. Small memories of Caroline were filtering back, the chief among them being those examples of her enormous desire to please him, to do just what he wanted. In his mind's eye he saw her standing before him when he had lifted her off the pony and saw again the strange light of glory in her curious eyes because she had done as he told her and was overjoyed to have pleased him. Perhaps, if he had to have a wife at all, Caroline Harding might not make such a bad one. She would never squeal, she would just endure. He looked at George gratefully.

'I think I might set her up right.'

George rose and clapped Johnnie on the shoulder.

'That's my Johnnie boy. You'll be as free as a panther and you'll get that pigsty of a house put in order for you to boot.'

It was yet another ray of sunshine. No more squalid and exhausting bellowings at the servants, no more inedible food and unwashed clothes, but instead someone to care for him and hold his head and shield him from the sordid everyday matters of living. The whole project seemed to be taking on quite another aspect and it appeared that he, Johnnie Gates, *bon viveur* and seducer of other people's wives, was going to be able, as usual, to have his cake and eat it.

He stood up and stretched, feeling his unpleasantly damp clothes peeling away from his skin as he did so.

'Where are you dining, George?'

'General Russell.'

'Shall we go together? I'm in no mood to work, and in any case it's too late to start now. Come home with me and help me to write my death sentence to England and we'll go on together.'

'I've a shocking thirst, Johnnie boy,' George said, linking his arm through the other's.

'We'll celebrate!' Johnnie cried. 'Come home and drink a toast to Johnnie Gates, husband and bachelor!'

5

The autumn and winter of 1775 passed with customary quietness at Stoke Abbas. All the issues raised so enticingly at the dinner party at Stoke Park appeared to have died a quiet and natural death as anything of interest always seemed to do in that remote and uneventful society. Caroline spent several weeks reliving her past in moments of solitude, then saw there was as usual to be no sequel to that brief glimpse of adventure, and banished Johnnie Gates from her reveries. Lady Lennox naturally said nothing to her of any schemes, and very soon the arrangements for Georgiana's wedding took precedence over any other consideration in all the minds at Stoke Park.

Unable to bear Eleanor's scoldings and goadings, and ever more conscious of her own futility, Caroline took to spending as much time as she possibly could away from the Parsonage. She made herself a regular circuit among the cottages and the inhabitants of Stoke Abbas became used to seeing her steady appearance, and in many cases began actually to look forward to it. Out of her slender means she bought expensive oranges which she would take to the malnourished cottagers, as well as chickens and broths begged from the Parsonage kitchens where she was a favourite and had staunch supporters. As the winter wore on, and the villagers saw that no weather seemed to daunt her faithful visiting, she began to gain a reputation equal to that of the local doctor.

Then, in March of 1776, she had a triumph. The cottage children she visited suffered very commonly from rickets and grew up with a deformity of limb that distressed Caroline acutely although the sufferers seemed quite cheerful about it. Caroline, who read voraciously upon any topic she could find, came across a pamphlet containing the novel suggestion from a London surgeon that a diet rich in calcium, most easily found in milk, might prove beneficial in counteracting the effects of rickets. It was a theory that appealed to Caroline for it caused no pain to the patient as many medical treatments did in the eighteenth century, and the milk was cheap and plentiful and readily available to the poor.

Among Caroline's regular dependants was a family whose steady courage in the face of poverty had always gained them a special place in her heart. Samuel Hedges had lost a leg in a man trap while pursuing poachers on the Stoke Park estate, and thus could now only do a limited range of work for Lord Lennox. Lord Lennox paid him the small wage he earned, but failed to take account of his disability, the circumstances in which he had been disabled, or his growing family. The family increased and the small wage did not. The youngest child, now two, had rickets acutely. The local apothecary had visited the family out of pure charity because he liked Sam Hedges, and had prescribed the customary treatment for rickets, that the child should be daily anointed with a scalding hot ointment, then have his limbs strapped to splints and that he should never leave his crib until the treatment was done.

One wild morning in March soon after the apothecary's visit, Caroline came battling across the windswept park with a basket of soup and fruit for the Hedges. Even before she reached the cottage she could hear the most bloodcurdling and terrible screams, the screams of some small thing in appalling pain. Alarmed that some evil had befallen the family, she picked up her skirts and ran as fast as she could against the buffets of wind to the cottage door. When she flung the door open, the sight that met her eyes horrified her more than the spectacle of any brutal attack might have done.

The littlest boy, dressed only in filthy rags, was being held forcibly by his brothers and sisters across his mother's knee. She appeared, with tears streaming down her face, to be smearing some greenish paste from a smoking pot onto his little crooked legs, already raw with the most terrible ragged blisters. The child was screaming with panic and pain, his face distorted with suffering, and all the children round him were almost in the same state. On the floor lay four splints of wood and coils of filthy greenish-stained bandages.

Caroline sprang forward to the group.

'Mary, Mary, stop it at once, what are you doing? Stop it, Mary, you are crucifying him!'

Mary Hedges could scarcely speak for tears.

'I know it, miss, I know it. But Mr Pears says I mun do it. I mun do it to save 'is legs. It do kill me to do it, miss, but he says I mun.'

'Nonsense!' Caroline said briskly. 'Absolute nonsense. And why is he so filthy dirty? You should be ashamed, Mary, you are always so particular. Why is he so dirty?'

'Mr Pears says I'm not to change 'im till 'tis done. 'E's only allowed from 'is crib for the treatment. 'E mun lie in 'is filth, miss, Mr Pears said so.'

Caroline glanced at the crib, and looked hastily away.

'Will you trust me, Mary? I have a notion that will get him better quicker than Mr Pears's remedy and will give him no pain at all.'

'Oh yes, miss,' poor Mary said, thankfully. 'I'll do anythin', miss, anythin' so's not to 'urt 'im more.'

'Very well.' Caroline looked round the poor, bare room and knew that there was not a morsel there to spare of anything. Commanding the boys to turn their backs, she lifted her skirt and slipped off her white cotton petticoat.

'Take off those disgusting rags, Mary,' she said, 'and we'll wash him, and wrap him in this.'

The baby's howls had subsided now to a whimper. He lay clinging to his mother, great eyes full of fear beneath his dirty, tousled hair. Caroline could hardly bear to look at the devastation of his legs or to see the shudderings of his little body under the remains of his shirt. She beckoned to the biggest boy.

'Take all that bedding and his nightshirt and those splints and that evil green mess, and make a bonfire of everything.'

'Yes'm.'

'Oh, no, Miss Car'line!' Mary cried, 'I've no more linen for 'im! I'll wash it best I can, but don't burn it, miss, please don't burn it!'

Caroline knelt down by her side and took one of the baby's filthy little hands in hers.

'I shall get you new linen,' she said gently. 'I shall send your Jane up to the Parsonage, and she shall ask in the kitchen for some old sheets we do not use, and for two little shirts I made for Tom Thwaites's boy, but he is not ill and so must do without. And I shall give your Meg money and she must go to the Park Farm and bring a quart of fresh milk.'

'Milk, Miss Car'line?'

Caroline smiled at the little boy.

'He must drink as much milk as he can. That will be his only medicine. And you must keep him clean and let him have plenty of air on those poor little legs.'

'I can wash 'im, miss, I'll wash 'im every minute if 'twill 'elp 'im, but we can't buy 'im milk, miss, you know we can't.'

'Don't worry about the milk, Mary. Just send one of the children to the farm and you will be given two quarts a day. Try and get him to drink all he can, and the others may finish what he cannot.'

Mere weeks later, the smallest Hedges was unrecognizably better. His legs were fast healing and though they would never be straight, their crookedness would never be worse. He had pink cheeks and clear eyes and Sam and Mary Hedges knew not how to thank Caroline.

She shook her head at them. 'I want no thanks. It is enough to see him so recovered.'

She wished she were brave enough to ask Lord Lennox to recompense Sam Hedges better for his long and steady hours of labour, but the confidence and ease she felt among the cottagers deserted her entirely among people of her own or a higher class. She knew she was cowardly, and she tried to still the voice of self-scorn within her by purchasing nourishing foods and making warm clothes for the needy. In some measure she succeeded and the recovery of little Abraham Hedges gave a distinct glow of achievement to her normally unconfident thoughts. She told nobody of her success, and meant no-one to know, but she had not accounted for the Hedges's admiration and gratitude.

Six weeks after that first visit to their cottage, she met Pears the apothecary on the field path behind the Parsonage. He had been attending a sick maid, and Caroline was returning for dinner. She saw him approach with some apprehension, fearing he would feel professionally insulted by her interference over little Abraham, and was astonished and relieved to notice the warmth of his expression as he came nearer.

'I am glad to see you, Miss Harding, very glad. I began to think you were eluding me deliberately.'

'Oh, no,' Caroline said untruthfully.

George Pears had not the social standing of Dr Thornton in the district, but he was an educated and perceptive man, and very little about Caroline Harding had escaped his notice.

'No, Miss Harding? Do you mean to tell me also that the rise in milk consumption among the cottagers in Stoke Abbas and the marked improvement in the ricketty children have no relation either to each other or to yourself?'

Caroline coloured slightly.

'I was afraid to offend you, Mr Pears.'

'Do you think I am so mean-spirited as to be offended by such sensible and effective help as you have offered? No, indeed, Miss Harding. You have been of more unobtrusive benefit to this village than it will ever realize. I have merely wished to see you to praise and thank you.'

Caroline's colour deepened.

'It – it was nothing – simply, only – only something I read—'

'And that I should have read and that I have indicated to Dr Thornton that he should read. He has been profoundly impressed by your actions, Miss Harding.'

Immense gratification and panic at the thought of such public notice battled visibly across Caroline's countenance.

'You are most kind – but Dr Thornton! He will think me unpardonably interfering!'

'He thinks nothing of the sort, my dear Miss Harding. You forget we are professional philanthropists, we medical men, and the improvement of human health is to be wished for at all costs and must override all petty personal considerations.'

Despite the splendour of this assertion, Caroline still looked doubtful.

'You have been more than kind, Mr Pears, more than generous. I meant no-one to know because—' she stopped, realizing that the chief enemy of her visits about the village was Eleanor, and that as a sister, even Eleanor deserved some loyalty.

'It is too late,' the apothecary said, triumphantly. 'Dr Thornton was appraised two nights ago and is full of eagerness to congratulate your father on his admirable daughter. I must bid you good day, Miss Harding, with the wish that your good endeavours may prosper.'

'Good day, Mr Pears.'

As she walked on homewards, even the fear of public attention subsided under the glowing realization of how sweet the apothecary's praise had been. He had not criticized her or patronized her but had spoken with frank admiration and gratitude to her, and had told her, actually told her in so many words, that there were people in the world who were the better for her existence. It was a dizzying thought. It meant not only that she had achieved something of her own, something attributable to nobody but herself, but also that she, as a person, mattered to some others. To the villagers, to George Pears, perhaps, oh shaking thought, even to Dr Thornton, she was a person of a little consequence. She was no longer simply Parson Harding's second plain unmarried daughter, but Caroline Harding who had helped a village's children most materially.

She leant on the garden gate and surveyed the vegetable plot, and observed that each little springing row of green seemed to have a new brightness, a new significance. The April sky seemed to be blue with a new delicacy, the air fresher than before, the day, the world, more full of promise. Caroline looked down at the grey stuff of her gown and felt its ugliness, for Eleanor had given it to her as a birthday present, to be immaterial. Her hands were shaking a little and she felt a sort of exhilaration that knows not hunger nor thirst nor weariness nor any bodily claim.

'I shall never forget this moment, never, never.'

'Miss Car'line?'

She spun round. Patsy was standing by her, twisting her apron in her hands.

'Beg pardon, Miss Car'line, but Miss El'nor says will you come in to dinner?'

Eleanor was sitting looking especially majestic and injured on her father's right. Parson Harding looked up and remarked inwardly how different Carrie looked, quite elated, almost approaching being a little handsome. Her eyes were gleaming like beacons and there was faint colour along her cheekbones.

'A good walk, Carrie?'

'Oh, wonderful!' Caroline said with more emphasis than any familiar walk could deserve. 'Quite wonderful.'

Eleanor sniffed.

'Which way did you go, my dear?'

It was always possible to be truthful about her routes, even if the omission of the visits to cottages almost constituted a lie.

'Down by the river, Papa. The air is like wine and everything is bursting out so new and bright and clean, it is quite a miracle to see.'

Eleanor sniffed again.

'Perhaps I should ride down there,' their father answered. 'I have not been near the river in months. Rivers are somehow most melancholy in winter.'

'Oh, Papa, today it was not melancholy! It was joyful, running over the stones in the sun, so clear and brilliant. It would do you such good to be away from the house!'

Eleanor spoke with awful emphasis. 'There are those whose duty and lot it is to stay within the house.'

'But that does not apply to Papa!' Caroline cried, thinking how appetizing the mutton looked and how unused she was to feeling so delightfully hungry.

'It is not Papa to whom I refer.'

A chill silence fell on the table. Caroline was astonished to find she felt none of the usual dread at the onset of one of Eleanor's outbursts. She said, as casually as she could, 'I imagine you refer to me.'

'I do.'

'Now, now, my dear Eleanor, let us have no unpleasantness. It is such a delightful day, and surely it is a harmless enough thing if Carrie has enjoyed her walk.'

'No, Papa, it is not harmless. It does a great deal of harm, and all to me: I must bear the whole burden of running the house and looking after you and Robert and the boys, because Carrie is too selfish and empty-headed to assist me in the smallest way.'

'That is wholly untrue,' said the new brave Caroline.

Eleanor's eyes flashed. 'It is absolute truth, Carrie. You use me as some manner of housekeeper, so that you may spend your days idling about the countryside and painting pictures. I work myself to exhaustion for you for not one word, or look even, of gratitude or—'

'Stop,' said Caroline. She put down her knife and fork, and stood up.

'I am very sorry to spoil dinner, but I am not sorry for what I am about to say. I am of no use in the house, Eleanor, because you absolutely will not allow me to be. I am permitted no duties, no responsibilities, I am not even allowed to arrange the flowers any longer. I am accused of being incompetent at everything, fit for nothing and best out of the way. So I have kept out of the way because I cannot bear the scolding and I cannot bear to be inactive. If you are short of assistance, Eleanor, you have no-one to blame on earth but yourself.'

She came quickly round to the head of the table, kissed her bewildered father, gave a brief but encouraging smile to Robert and left the room. When the door had closed, Eleanor began to cry. Parson Harding and Robert looked down at their half-eaten plates, decided the final half had lost its savour, and followed Caroline stealthily from the room. Under cover of Eleanor's outraged sobs, Parson Harding said quietly to his son, 'If anyone should want me, I shall be in my study until supper.'

From his study window, he witnessed the astonishing spectacle of seeing his daughter, Caroline, almost dancing down the steep road to the village. Her step was so light, so elastic that it could hardly be called walking, and her grey dress, whose solid fabric and outline her father deplored, swayed about her as if it were made of gossamer. What had come over Carrie? Was it possible that a pretty, though ordinary, April day could have this joyful effect on anyone, particularly one of Carrie's grave temperament? Parson Harding shook his head in puzzlement and sat down before the fire. It had rejoiced his heart to see her come in for dinner looking so illuminated, and it had discouraged him very much to have Eleanor's inevitable outburst act like a snuffer upon a candle flame. He was too tired to battle with Eleanor, whose energy in matters of her own emotions was inexhaustible. It was a pity the girls could not love each other, a pity they could not live in harmony. He regretted that Caroline no longer did the flowers for she had arranged them so beautifully, always putting sweet scented ones in the study, and Eleanor arranged them as if dragooning soldiers. All the bowls of pot-pourri had gone too, he reflected sadly, and the lavender bags he liked among his linen. Caroline had seen to those little touches. It was a pity, indeed it was. His head fell, with gentle regretfulness, onto his chest, and he slept.

Caroline spent the afternoon tiring herself out. She walked as far and as high as she could in the spring wind, and felt always driven on by a strange and wonderful sense of ease and power. She felt keenly observant of everything she saw, and deeply appreciative of it, and when she approached the Parsonage in the beginnings of dusk, she found her feet were indeed weary, but her heart and mind felt as buoyant as ever.

There was a strange cloak in the hall. Evidently her father had a caller. She went into the parlour, still cloaked herself, to make her peace with Eleanor who always spent the early evening there doing her accounts or mending church vestments. She was sitting, as usual, some distance from the fire, as if she would not allow herself the pleasure of being really warm.

'Eleanor?'

There was no reply. By the light of a tallow candle which she insisted on using for reasons of economy despite an ample supply of wax, Eleanor was writing minutely in her account book. Caroline had read it secretly once and could not believe such details were worth recording.

'Eleanor. I am come to apologize for distressing you.'

There was a sniff, but no word. Caroline laid her cloak on a chair and went to kneel before the fire.

'It is never my intention to distress you, Eleanor. I am all too aware that my cast of character is a great irritation to you, and that is why I try not to be before you too often.'

A page was turned behind her. After another pause, Eleanor said, 'Will you retract those evil things you said at dinner?'

'No,' said Caroline calmly. 'But I will modify them. I said them in the heat of the moment, and I meant them, but I can rephrase them to sound less fierce, if you like.'

Eleanor began to weep again.

'No-one understands the burden I bear. You least of all people, Carrie. You have no heart, no heart at all.'

Caroline rose from the hearth and came to kneel by her sister.

'Why will you not let me help you a little? Why should you suppose I like to see you so tired? May I not assist you in some things?'

Eleanor surveyed her over her handkerchief doubtfully.

'You are woefully undomesticated, Carrie.'

'No, I am not. Try me, why not try me—'

The door opened at the same moment as it was briefly knocked upon. Eleanor frowned at the servant.

'Th' parson wants Miss Car'line.'

'Are you sure?'

'Quite sure, Miss El'nor. Miss Car'line's wanted in the study.'

'I am coming directly, Patsy.'

The door closed and Caroline rose to her feet. Self-pity was beginning to suffuse Eleanor's features again.

'What can he want with you, Carrie?'

'I will go and see.'

Caroline put her hand on her sister's bony shoulder and pressed it, and wished she felt the smallest inclination to kiss her. Outside the door, Patsy was waiting with a candle, and escorted Caroline across the dusky hall. Caroline tapped on the study door. At her father's 'Come!' she opened it, and saw that on the hearth, his face illumined by six flames in a great candelabra, was the imposing figure of Dr Thornton.

'Come in, my dear, come in, don't hesitate so.'

'We only came in here for punishment as children,' Caroline said, 'and obviously that thought still lingers with me.'

Dr Thornton laughed genially.

'I am delighted to see you, Miss Harding. Your father and I have had a most delightful half-hour in contemplation of your success, but I would not leave until I had been able to congratulate you in person.'

Caroline came forward and seated herself by her father.

'Papa, I am having a most astonishing day. I met Mr Pears on my way home this morning, who said wonderfully kind and pleasant things to me, and now . . .' She stopped and looked down.

Her father took her hand.

'I am both very proud and very delighted, my dear. It does relieve my mind a little to know that all your long absences from home were not spent merely strolling the countryside, but I am delighted that your time has been put to such constructive purpose.'

'Admirable,' Dr Thornton said. 'Wholly admirable.'

Caroline found she could not raise her head. This morning's praise had quite sufficed and Dr Thornton's large impressive presence was superfluous.

'I did not want – I did not mean it to be known,' she said in a low voice.

'But, my dear lady, it is known,' Thornton cried. 'I called at Stoke Park this afternoon to ensure that Lord

Lennox's gout had not reappeared, and had the pleasure of informing both Lord and Lady Lennox what a remarkable daughter our Parson has.'

Caroline felt quite confused. Dr Thornton meant only kindness, but his excellent linen and air of health and great watch and seals only made her feel all her usual awkwardness. She had felt none of that in front of George Pears in his shabby coat that morning.

'Will you thank Dr Thornton for his great kindness?' Parson Harding said gently to her as if chiding a child.

'I do,' said Caroline to her lap, 'I do thank him – very much, but I – I did not do it – do anything for – for . . .' She stopped and rose quickly from the sofa. 'Will you excuse me,' she said, and was gone.

Both men surveyed the door fondly when she had closed it, the parson because he was genuinely proud of her, Dr Thornton because he felt a large man's protective fondness for feminine modesty.

'She does not mean to be ungracious, my dear Thornton. She is a very humble girl, very humble. She has never found it easy to be praised.'

'She seemed quite composed when she entered.'

'Ah yes, but that was before you praised her.'

'Admirable,' Dr Thornton said again with emphasis.

An uneasy truce reigned for some weeks between Caroline and Eleanor. Eleanor was mortified at Caroline's public acclaim, but forced, if not to submit to a position of utter ignominy herself, to show at least a small pleasure in her sister's success. She suggested on several occasions that the milk remedy had been pure accident, thus implying Caroline's achievement was no more than a mere stroke of fortune, but met only with rebuffs on all sides. It transpired also that rickets was not only confined to the poor cottagers round about, but prevailed occasionally in the more prosperous houses, and Caroline's name was thus often in mouths whose owners would not have countenanced her at all under any other circumstances. Both George Pears and Dr Thornton gave her, most handsomely, all the credit she deserved, and she became well known by name at least in the small locality that was her world.

Eleanor, with admirable restraint, said no more to her of their quarrel, but contented herself with a single quite different admonishment.

'I hope you will be very careful, Carrie. I can have, obviously, no objection to your visiting the cottagers since everyone seems to want you to continue, but it makes me very anxious that you may bring back some infection and we shall all be done for.'

Caroline laughed.

'Of course I am careful, Eleanor. What good is help if you endanger others by giving it? You are a goose to worry so.'

'I am not a goose, Carrie. I am simply thinking of Papa. In all I do I think of Papa.'

Caroline ignored the implications of that remark.

'I am glad you will not try to stop me, Eleanor, as it means more to me than you can know. I promise I will not endanger any of us.'

Eleanor sniffed self-righteously.

'Think of Papa,' she said.

6

By the summer Caroline had become something of a small celebrity around Stoke Abbas. She was even able to accept praise without blushing, although it never delighted her as her own sense of usefulness did. She attempted no more cures, but continued to visit, to feed, to bandage and soothe with an effectiveness borne entirely of her new-found confidence. To her secret joy, her relationship with her father blossomed out of this new security of hers, and they would spend long evenings together talking and reading, evenings of mutual satisfaction to both of them. Eleanor disliked this new bond, but could do nothing; instead she waited in injured silence for the time when she was sure her father would realize, and repay, her years of unstinting devotion.

In late June, Caroline had been very busy. There had been an outbreak of fever in the village, and, though mindful of Eleanor's fears for their own safety, Caroline was most attentive to the convalescent. In the midst of an extremely occupied week, a note came from Stoke Park summoning Caroline to see Lady Lennox.

'It is most strange,' Caroline said, holding the letter out to a resentful Eleanor. 'I have not seen her but once this whole year and that once at Georgiana's wedding. What can she want with me?'

Eleanor disdained to look at the proffered letter.

'Medical matters, I presume.'

'Most unlikely, I fear. Oh dear, I do not care for going to Stoke Park at the best of times, but going without any of you for support makes it very terrible.'

'How you do fuss, Carrie.'

'Should you like to go alone?'

'I should not make this undignified commotion about it.'

'Why do you not go instead of me and see what it is she wants?'

'It is not me she has asked for,' Eleanor said enviously.

Caroline sighed. She was dressed, as usual, for walking, and a visit to Stoke Park meant a change into the blue silk left from last year, about whose colour she now had her own doubts. She sighed again.

'Papa says you may take the carriage,' Eleanor said crossly.

Thus arrayed in the blue silk which looked even more antiquated this year than last, and full of trepidation, Caroline jogged down the hill behind her father's greys.

Lady Lennox was waiting for her in the south parlour, compiling an impressive list of the planting she was intending to do in the Park that autumn.

'Lord Lennox has such a fondness for beeches, Caroline, that I think we will make an avenue of them down towards the lake. Do you not think that would make a pleasant walk?'

'Very pleasant, Lady Lennox.'

'And then you may walk there whenever you have time from your duties about the village. Lord Lennox and I were most gratified to hear of your success.'

Caroline detected a coldness in her praise, and rightly deduced that she did not care to have her own lack of liberality thrown into contrast by Caroline's care. Perhaps that accounted also for the fact that no word of praise had reached the Parsonage from the Park except second or third hand. Caroline looked dutifully out of the window at the gentle sweep of valley soon to be cluttered with beech trees.

'Thank you, Lady Lennox.'

'However, Caroline, that was not the matter I wish to discuss with you. Will you be seated?'

Carefully, Caroline chose a small chair with its back to the light. Lady Lennox leaned forward a little, clasping her large ringed hands in a gesture of uncharacteristic eagerness.

'I have the most wonderful news for you, my dear Caroline.'

Caroline felt at once both astonished and suspicious.

'For me, Lady Lennox?'

'Certainly for you. For no-one else but you. You will recall, I am sure, dining here a year ago before Georgiana was married, and meeting Lord Lovell?'

'Indeed I do.'

'Then I wonder,' Lady Lennox continued with a hint of roguishness dreadful in so commanding a woman, 'I wonder if you recall a certain name that came into our conversation?'

Caroline recalled very clearly, for that was the only reason the dinner party was of any significance to her, but she was not prepared to be helpful.

'No name in particular, Lady Lennox.'

'Come, come, Caroline. Do you mean to tell me you did not colour up and start at the name of Johnnie Gates?'

To Caroline's enormous relief, her cheeks remained cool and pale.

'Perhaps I did, Lady Lennox.'

'Pooh, pooh, perhaps you did. Indeed you did, Caroline, I saw you do it. You are not going to deny that the name meant something to you?'

'It did . . . it might have done, Lady Lennox. Last summer, it might have meant something.'

'And now?'

'Now?' said Caroline with slightly less indifference, 'I do not understand you, Lady Lennox. What has now to do with it?'

With the triumphant air of a conjurer, Lady Lennox produced a letter from beneath a cushion, and brandished it at Caroline.

'Now for the wonderful news, my dear Caroline! I have here a letter from Johnnie, who remains a bachelor, a lonely bachelor, in Calcutta. He has written to me confessing his loneliness and the fact that he has never been quite heart-whole since he left Stoke Park – that summer. This letter contains no less, my dear Caroline, than a renewed offer of marriage. You are to set sail for Calcutta as soon as can be arranged as the future Mrs Gates!'

Caroline sat quite stupefied. The whole interview had become some monstrous charade, some scheme of tricks, some game where she knew not the rules.

'What do you say then, Caroline?'

'I – I do not know what to say. It is all so – so very astounding that—'

'Of course, of course, I knew you would be knocked quite breathless by it. Is it not quite wonderful? Shall I help you with a letter of acceptance?'

At the last question, Caroline's diffused gaze suddenly seemed to clear and concentrate.

'No,' she said.

'No? You will do it yourself? Of course, I was merely trying to—'

'Forgive me, Lady Lennox, but no, there will be no acceptance. I do not know by what machinations Mr Gates has offered for me, but I shall decline him.'

'Machinations? Decline him? How dare you, Miss Harding, behave in so insolent a manner? How can you refuse so magnificent an offer? You, insignificant, poor—'

Caroline rose from her chair and went to the window. She stood looking out at the sunshine with her back to Lady Lennox.

'Lady Lennox, did you persuade Mr Gates to renew his offer? '

'Indeed I did not, I merely suggested to him that his lot would be much happier—'

'If he married. And it would suit you well if he married someone who could be no rival to your own daughters. I do not, however, suppose he has any inclination himself to marry at all.'

Lady Lennox was hunting frenziedly again among the cushions. Eventually she produced the folded paper which she held out to Caroline.

'There is his letter to you. You will see for yourself how genuine is his desire to marry you. Read it, read it!'

Caroline looked at the strange desperation in Lady Lennox's face and made no attempt to take the paper.

'Thank you, no, Lady Lennox. As I am to refuse him, there is no point in reading his letter.'

Lady Lennox rose unsteadily and advanced upon Caroline.

'Do you mean to tell me that you will refuse him out of sheer obstinacy and pride simply because the marriage, though entirely at his will, was not completely at his suggestion?'

'Oh no, Lady Lennox, not at all. I am not at all too proud to accept a man who asks for me as he is bidden to do. Oh no, the reason is quite different. I have no wish to marry now. I am not as lonely and purposeless as I was and I have no desire to leave Stoke Abbas or my father.'

'Can you mean it?'

'I can.'

'That a handful of ragged cottagers and a few words of praise from a mere country doctor are sufficient to induce you to lead a life of obscurity for ever?'

'Quite sufficient.'

'I do not understand you.'

'Nor I you, Lady Lennox. I do not understand why you wish me to marry Mr Gates, and I do not understand why he is so anxious to do your bidding. But I will not do your bidding because I do not care to jeopardize the small happiness I have.'

Lady Lennox sat down abruptly in the chair Caroline had vacated. She appeared to be struggling forcibly with her temper, and eventually to be gaining control.

'I think I may have surprised you, Miss Harding.'

'You did, Lady Lennox, very considerably.'

'Knowing the secluded life that you lead, it was perhaps misguided of me not to prepare you more gently for the future. I see that I have alarmed you.'

'I am not alarmed,' Caroline said calmly.

Lady Lennox ignored her.

'I shall give you two months. I think that would be fair. I shall not raise the subject or allude to it again until the end of the summer. Then I shall ask you for your considered opinion. Caroline, I shall give you the summer to think it over most carefully.'

'I do not need to think it over, Lady Lennox.'

'Two months,' Lady Lennox said with finality. 'I shall not mention the matter to your father, but shall trust you to reflect upon your situation with all the good sense you can muster. I shall send for you in late August.'

She rose and rang for a servant.

'Miss Harding is ready for her carriage.'

'Good day, Lady Lennox.'

Lady Lennox nodded and looked at Caroline intently.

'I shall see you in August, Caroline.'

'There is no use, Lady Lennox, I shall not, cannot, change my mind. I have everything now to keep me here and nothing but memories to induce me to accept. Please do not expect anything from me but another refusal.'

'Two months,' Lady Lennox said relentlessly, and the doors closed upon her.

At the Parsonage, Eleanor was waiting with ill-concealed impatience.

'You are back very quick, Carrie. I did not look for you yet. I hope Lady Lennox was quite well and that you said nothing to displease her. You look quite queer, Carrie, indeed you do. Most strange and – excited. What did Lady Lennox want with you, Carrie? Why did she send for you so suddenly?'

Caroline, whose first sense of outrage had subsided in the carriage into feeling the matter was merely laughable, shook her head under this barrage of statements and questions.

'It was nothing of significance, Eleanor, nothing at all. She merely said a kind word upon my doings in the village.'

Eleanor eyed her narrowly.

'In that case, I cannot see why you are so flushed. You always assert, Carrie, that the notice of great people is of no consequence to you, and yet one word of praise from Lady Lennox appears to be sufficient to leave you quite breathless. I do not believe it is all that passed between you.'

'You may believe what you choose and you may suffer on the thorns of your own curiosity if you please. Lady Lennox clearly feels as you do about my visiting, and—'

'Ah!' said Eleanor with satisfaction, 'so Lady Lennox quite rightly tried to make you see sense about going into those vile hovels, and you had the effrontery to differ from her! You have no gratitude, Carrie, no sense of what is proper. Can you not see that a rebuke from such a quarter must and should be listened to? Indeed, Carrie—'

Caroline turned to leave the room, but paused long enough in the doorway to say furiously, 'Nobody shall preach to me any longer, not you, Eleanor, not Lady Lennox. I will do what Papa wishes because it delights me to please him, but I will not do the will of those who are merely attempting to exercise their petty power!'

After tea that night, Parson Harding drew Caroline into his study, declaring he had some work that must be copied before the morning, and that it pained his own eyes to do it himself.

With his eye sternly upon Eleanor, he said to Caroline, 'I will dictate to you, and you shall write, and in solitude thus we shall get along famously.'

In dudgeon Eleanor shut the parlour door with more emphasis than was necessary.

'Now we shall make ourselves comfortable,' Parson Harding said with some relief. 'If you will but put another candle by me and seat yourself where I may see your face.'

Caroline smiled.

'So the business of the evening is not to be copying, but Stoke Park instead?'

'Indeed it is. I have often thought curiosity to be sinful but then, were I not curious, how else should I know where to advise and where to console?'

'Which do you think I look in need of, Papa?'

Parson Harding studied her thoughtfully.

'I have been trying to decide throughout dinner, and have only concluded that you need neither, but that I, on the other hand, need the consolation of curiosity satisfied.'

Caroline laughed affectionately.

'I will satisfy it, Papa, but you must prepare yourself for a surprise – no, almost for a shock. And also to hear what may seem disloyalty to your patroness.'

'I must bear that, I think, Carrie.'

'Do you mock Lady Lennox, Papa? I am surprised at you.'

'I am ever surprised at myself, my dear, and I am very eager to be surprised at you.'

Seating herself on a stool at her father's feet, Caroline leaned her arms on his chair so that she might study every expression on his handsome face as she spoke.

'Lady Lennox summoned me, Papa, because she had wonderful news for me. She had written, for some reason I am not aware of, to Johnnie Gates in Calcutta and informed, or rather commanded, him to renew his offer of marriage to me. She was in receipt of his reply and had sent for me to inform me I was to be despatched immediately to Calcutta like any bale of broadcloth as Mr Gates's bride. There you have it, Papa, and I am gratified to see you look as dumbfounded as I felt this morning.'

Parson Harding put his hand over Caroline's. The news may have struck her forcibly at Stoke Park, but it dealt a much greater blow to her father who knew so much more of the people concerned and the world in general.

'Did – did she give you any reason for the plan, Carrie?'

'None, Papa, beyond saying that I had no life here and might as well accept—'

'No – no, my dear. I meant, did she tell you why she had written to Gates in the first place?'

'No, except for saying he was lonely.'

Parson Harding winced slightly. He had listened intently to all revelations of Johnnie Gates's Indian life, and had picked up all the implications of Frank Lovell's reluctance to be explicit. Furthermore, in his role as Lady Lennox's confidant, he was well aware of how the family money was to be disposed, and of her powerful opposition to any but her own children receiving any of it. It came upon him as he sat with Caroline's hand in his that Lady Lennox had been prepared to export Caroline to a life of heaven knew what suffering in order to ensure that Lennox money might be kept from being entirely dissipated. He could not quite visualize how she had put the matter to Johnnie so that he had come to heel so swiftly and compliantly, but he reflected that she was the only person Johnnie had ever feared or obeyed. He drew his breath a little and patted Caroline's hand.

'So what answer did you give to this dazzling prospect, my dear?'

'I said I must refuse.'

'Did you give any reason?' Parson Harding said quickly, to hide the spasm of relief that seized him.

'Certainly I did. I said I wished to stay with you, and

in Stoke Abbas. I feel I belong here, I am beginning to have a life here, and I do not wish to leave it.'

'I am deeply thankful to hear it.'

'Then I am glad.'

'Was – was there any part of you that wished to become Mrs Gates, Caroline?'

Caroline looked away from her father's face and into the dazzling glow of the candle flame.

'Once, Papa, once, all of me wished to become Mrs Gates, and I suppose some part will always remember that wish. But it is all so long ago, and I am changed and he must be changed so that it could never be as it once would have been.'

Parson Harding reflected gently that it could in fact never have been as she romantically imagined, for Johnnie had had too much of a fatal weakness about him to make a woman happy. It was by the greatest good fortune that Caroline had escaped marrying him, and Parson Harding felt a little mild guilt that he had once connived at such a marriage himself. But then, he consoled himself, safe in events as they had happened, how could he have known that Caroline would turn out to be too good a thing, for such a one as Johnnie Gates?

'So, my dear, you have handled Lady Lennox with great firmness and I see the victor in combat before me?'

'I believe you do, Papa.' She sounded surprised at herself still.

'And it shall be our secret, Carrie?'

'Oh, please, Papa. Except – except that Lady Lennox would not take no for an answer and insisted on allowing me two months to reconsider my decision.'

'As there is nothing to reconsider, my dear, we shall think no more of the two months. We shall instead plan a winter of reading the poets of the last century, and until that winter comes, you may occupy a little time with your favourite pursuit.'

'Painting, Papa?'

'No, indeed, you goose. Visiting the sick and needy. I saw Sam Wells today and he says the children have all had the fever, but are recovered, praise God, and are very low and dispirited and would like to play a few games with Miss Caroline.'

'I should love to go, Papa. They are such dear energetic children, usually so packed with health. I shall go tomorrow, and take some currants. We have never had such currants as this year before, black, white and red all together. They are like jewels.'

'You may take all the currants you wish, my dear. Now go and amuse your sister for a while.'

Caroline rose and kissed him.

'It does me good to know that you are happy, Carrie.'

'I am, Papa.'

The following day dawned grey and still with a heavy warmth. True to her word Caroline filled a basket with small bright fruit and set off down the field path to the river and the Wells's farm beyond. She was sorry she had not been before, but the Wells, isolated as they were from the huddled cottages of the village, were usually healthy and to be visited for pleasure rather than succour. The great kitchen of the farmhouse, almost untouched since its medieval building, had an uncharacteristic air of desolation about it. Commonly it was full of bustle and activity, a confusion of dogs and children, stray hens and baking. Today a few children hung dismally about the great table, and a little maid from one of the poorer cottages was anxiously stirring a pot over the fire. As she entered, several of the children came slowly forward to greet her.

'Sam, Charlie, Elizabeth, how are you? And little Robert. Are you better? I was so sorry to hear you were not well.'

The smallest Wells endeavoured to inform her that

he had been hot, so hot that he had thought he was burning all up. Caroline smiled.

'And now you are well again, and I have brought you some currants to help you get strong more quickly.'

She looked about the quiet room again.

'Where is your mother, children?'

'She hot now,' Robert said helpfully.

Caroline looked across at the little maid.

'Is Mrs Wells ill?'

The girl nodded fearfully. She was so terrified of Farmer Wells, and the fever and of her new and dreadful responsibilities that she did not know what she feared most.

'Where is she?' Caroline demanded.

'In – in her bed, ma'am.'

Caroline set her basket on the table.

'We shall make pastry, children, and then you shall cut pictures out for me from it while I go to see if your mother is comfortable.'

Ten minutes later, leaving all seven heads bent in concentration over the white slabs on the table, Caroline took water and a piece of clean linen, and climbed the uneven stairs to Mary Wells's bedroom. She lay in the bed in which her husband had been born, sweating and wretched, her face and hands scarlet with the fever's rash. She looked at Caroline wildly.

'Go away, Miss Car'line! Tidn't fit for you t'come near me!'

'I don't mind it, Mary. I have been by sick beds all year and caught nothing. Come, I will sponge and cool you and perhaps that will help to bring down the fever.'

'No, Miss Car'line! Tidn't right! Think if you was to catch the fever!'

'You will only make yourself feel worse, Mary, and you will not drive me away.'

Reluctantly Mary submitted to the cool water and gentle hands.

''Tis the nights as is terrible, Miss Car'line. Sam says

I do rave like a mad thing and 'e can 'ear me from t'next chamber. I sent 'im there to try and keep 'im from it. 'Tis the children I fear for, if both of us was to die.'

'You won't die, Mary. I've seen far worse rashes than this and felt far hotter foreheads. You won't die.'

Mary looked at her with fierce hope.

'You mean that, Miss Car'line?'

'Of course I do,' Caroline said comfortingly, smoothing the coarse linen sheet, 'and I shall come back often to make sure you don't.'

''Tis right what they do say of you,' Mary said with desperate gratitude. 'You'm an angel, Miss Car'line, there's no two ways about it.'

'Sh – sh, you are to sleep now. I shall make sure the children are fed and you are not to worry yourself about them.'

Mary closed her eyes.

'While you'm 'ere, I'll not worry.'

Caroline descended to the kitchen again to find the pastry sculpture had degenerated into a battle, helplessly watched by the little maid. She made them clear up the flung pieces, find their bowls and horn spoons, and did her best to make the mess in the pot appetizing. With the aid of chants and rhymes she induced them to finish each last spoonful, and then despatched them all to play peaceably in the orchard until their father's return from the first haymaking in distant meadows. She left instructions for the maid, made sure that Mary still slept, and then set off for home.

Her father met her in the Parsonage garden.

'Ah, the angel of mercy, I see!'

Caroline kissed him.

'Do not tease, Papa. I have been to see the Wells, and all the children are fed and, I hope, occupied. Poor Mary has the fever now but not badly. She will recover, but I must find her some more help from the village for she will be very weak for a while.'

'A good morning's work, my dear. You shall have your reward in the shape of some excellent pullets Lady Lennox has sent up. Perhaps you might care to regard them as some sort of feathered peace offering.'

Caroline laughed.

'I must wash, Papa, and then I shall be ready to do the peace offering more than justice.'

7

A week later, Mary Wells was able to leave her bed for a few hours at a time and sit by the kitchen fire, thin and weak, but mending, while the children leaned against her in relief. They all regarded Caroline as some being with superhuman powers, and Sam Wells vowed that the Parsonage should be provided with the best at pig-killing, all the cream and butter they could wish for as long as he had breath.

'It makes me uncomfortable,' Caroline said to her father. 'I have come to dread being thanked. It sounds complacent to complain of gratitude, but I simply do not know what to do with it!'

'If it comes in the form of bacon and butter, my dear, we shall all know what to do with it!'

'But if I keep going back to make sure Mary can manage, does it not seem as if I should like even more provender?'

'Certainly not. You must inform your conscience that oversensitivity is as bad as insensitivity. Would you be so good as to draw that curtain across a little?'

'Does the sun bother you, Papa?'

'I seem to have a slight headache, nothing more.'

She crossed swiftly to his chair.

'Papa, you never have headaches, never. What is the matter?'

'Nothing, my dear. I rode in the sun too long this morning, I fear. Now do not fuss or I shall send you away. Find some soothing verse and read to me. George Herbert perhaps, I have a strong notion to hear a little George Herbert.'

With half an eye upon her father, Caroline began. As she read she saw that he had closed his eyes, but his brows were still faintly contracted as if pain were drawing them together.

She put the book down.

'Should you like some water, Papa?'

He opened one eye.

'Do you fuss over your patients in the village like this?'

'No, Papa, I command them but I do not think I should have much success in commanding you.'

'Certainly not. Now get me some water and then leave me to muse upon eternity.'

Caroline found Eleanor in the kitchen sorting raspberries.

'Papa has a headache, Eleanor.'

'Papa never has a headache,' Eleanor said finally.

'He has one now. I am to take him water.'

Eleanor took her hands out of the great basket and wiped them vigorously on a cloth.

'I shall take it.'

'As you please. But I do not think he – I think he wishes to be left in peace.'

'You are not the only person capable of nursing the sick, Carrie. Indeed there are many more fitted for the task than you, I am sure. Of course I shall not disturb Papa, I shall merely take him water and reassure myself that he is quite comfortable. Perhaps you might continue with these raspberries – but no, I think not, on the whole. You would not sort them as carefully as I do and I should only have the task to do all over again.'

'If you were to tell me how—'

'No, Carrie, no. It is best that I do it. Heaven knows there is enough to be done, but it is best that I do it.'

Caroline went out of the room with tightened lips, and up to her bedroom to soothe her feelings by painting until dinner. Robert had managed to catch a swallowtail down by the river and had mounted it, its lovely wings outspread, upon a piece of wood for her to paint. She touched the fragile velvety thing gently, more sorry to see it thus than to be pleased to have it as a model. She had drawn the outline upon an oval of ivory, and now there was the pleasure of adding colour. She sat down at her table and took up her brush, looking carefully at the butterfly, and then a small nag of worry about her father came between and she laid her brush down again. He never had a headache. In fact he never seemed to suffer physically at all; Caroline could not remember a single occasion when he had complained of discomfort, let alone pain. And he was so precious to her now, their new companionableness was so wonderful to her, so unexpected. She looked at the butterfly again and forced herself to concentrate upon the tiny, tidy patterns upon its pointed wings.

At dinner, Parson Harding was cheerful, but his cheerfulness seemed to need an effort. Caroline did not like to pester him with anxious queries, but she doubted from the look on his face that his head was better. Eleanor, assiduous in the role of chief nurse and administrator, took over the task of carving, but when she placed a plate of chicken before her father, he pushed it away.

'Thank you, my dear, expertly carved, but I do not seem to have much appetite.'

'Papa!'

'Do not look so anxious, Carrie. I have simply exposed myself to the sun too long this morning.'

'The sun was not fierce today,' Robert pointed out unhelpfully.

'I expect at my age the sun does not need to be fierce to have a fierce effect upon my head. Would you forgive me, my dears, if I returned to the study? The sight and smell of food—'

He stopped and blanched suddenly. Caroline and

Robert were on their feet in an instant, but were motioned to sit down.

'No – no, sit down and eat. I shall be perfectly well if left to rest, perfectly well. Thank you, Eleanor, but I think I can manage the distance to the study un-accompanied. Forgive me—'

He closed the door behind him. The three left looked at each other doubtfully. A small and awful foreboding was beginning in Caroline's brain which robbed her immediately of appetite, but she would not speak of it. She might in any case be wrong and the consequences of raising a false alarm would be terrible.

'You are quite wrong to suppose the sun not fierce today, Robert,' Eleanor announced, 'and it was most thoughtless of you to allow Papa to ride so far this morning.'

'I could hardly prevent him,' Robert protested. 'He wished to go as far as Monk Hill for the view, and he was in such good spirits that it never occurred to me the sun might affect him thus.'

'Nothing ever occurs to either you or Carrie it seems. It is as well that one of us takes thought for the morrow. I hope you realize – where are you going, Carrie?'

From the doorway, Caroline said, 'To my room. I do not seem to feel hungry either.' She closed the door upon a tirade on wastefulness.

There was no-one in the study. Caroline ran to the window hoping to see her father under his accustomed tree in the garden, but he was not there. Filled with a sudden fresh anxiety, she went back through the room, across the hall, and up the shallow staircase. Patsy was coming along the landing with a bowl of water.

'Oh, Miss Car'line, I were comin' for you. The Parson ain't well, Miss Car'line, not well at all.'

'Why, Patsy, what has happened, quickly—'

'He'm sick, Miss Car'line. He just vomited, miss, and he do look like a sheet, so white—'

Caroline slipped past her to her father's room. He was lying, still dressed, on his bedstead, the half tester brought from France for his bride in which all his five children had been born, and in which his wife had died. He was ashen and his face looked alarmingly sunken. Caroline tiptoed to his side.

'Papa?'

He opened his eyes a little and gave her a glazed, unseeing look. He raised a hand from the bedspread and let it fall again.

'I – I fear I am not well, Carrie.'

'Oh – oh, Papa, I am so sorry, so sorry . . .'

She stopped quickly and bent to put a hand upon his brow. He was too hot to console her.

'Will you let Patsy and I make you more comfortable? May we put you in your shirt so that you may lie between the sheets?'

Parson Harding smiled faintly.

'I should be grateful, my dear. Perhaps you will be able to command me, after all.'

A lump rose in Caroline's throat, and she said with difficulty, 'I am so sorry there is occasion for it,' and could not trust herself to say more. Her father pressed her hand lightly and his touch was hot and dry. She went to the door and found Patsy waiting anxiously outside.

'Come and help me make the Parson comfortable.'

Patsy nodded. Gently they undressed the old man and slipped the folds of his nightshirt over his head. He lay unprotestingly at their mercy like a doll, his eyes closed, his limbs limp. As they pulled the fine linen down his body, Patsy suddenly gasped.

'Oh, Miss Car'line, see this!'

Caroline went quickly round to the other side of the bed and stooped to see what Patsy indicated. On the white skin of the rib-cage, spreading from armpit to hip bone, was the unmistakable flushed stain of scarlet fever. Caroline dropped, shaking, to her knees, staring wide-eyed at the rash as if her gaze could burn it out. It was her fault, that was the fact of it. She had gone to the Wells deliberately knowing there was fever there, because she could not resist the self-satisfying chance of doing good, and she had come home bearing the fatal contagion and given it to the person she loved most in all the world! She had been like Judas, kissing and betraying. She had come up the garden, with the fever all about her like a shroud, fresh from Mary's bedside, and had kissed her father and dealt him this blow.

'Forgive me,' she whispered fiercely. 'Oh, Papa, forgive me, forgive me!'

His hand strayed across the sheet in search of her.

'There is nothing to forgive, my dear. What did I say to you about oversensitivity but a few hours ago? There is nothing in the world to forgive.'

'But there is! There is! It is I who brought you—'

Parson Harding's hand came to rest with surprising firmness across Caroline's mouth.

'And I sent you to the Wells in the first place, Carrie, so you will not speak of such nonsense again. You nursed Mary Wells back to health, and now you shall nurse me.'

Caroline kissed his hand and rose unsteadily to her feet.

'Bring water and a sponge, Patsy. We must at all costs keep the fever down. Hurry.'

She went to the window and looked out at the rising, falling landscape, green and flowery under the June sun with the church steeple like a grey arrow against the soft hills. Slowly she drew the curtains across the brightness, and then went to sit by her father's side in the sun-speckled gloom. She must think collectedly, as calmly as she could always think when among the cottagers. But although she liked the village people, they were clearly not one hundredth part as dear to her as her father, and it was the very love she bore him that made it so difficult to be calm. The fever itself, she knew, was the danger. The rash would spread, but it was no more than an irritation and was itself no threat. But the fever must be kept down at all costs, and day and night someone must be by to sponge with cool water, endlessly sponge, to try to reduce the fever. She would do it all of every night as a punishment for her crime. She would sit alone through those long, silent, alarming hours and she would watch as vigilantly as if the lives of the whole human race depended upon her watchfulness. She stooped over her father and saw that he had fallen abruptly into the sudden, troubled sleep of illness, breathing fast and lightly. Eleanor and Robert must be told quickly, she must not be possessive. As Patsy came back into the room, Caroline rose.

'I am going to inform Miss Eleanor. I will only be gone a few minutes, and while I am gone you are to sponge his face and hands lightly and constantly. Do you understand?'

'Yes'm,' Patsy said tremblingly.

Caroline touched her shoulder.

'Do not be afraid, Patsy. I will only be a few minutes.'

Eleanor and Robert were leaving the dining room as Caroline descended the stairs.

'May I speak to you both one moment?'

Eleanor was instantly suspicious.

'What has happened?'

Caroline led the way into the parlour.

'It is Papa, Eleanor. When I went upstairs he was in his room, lying down, and he had vomited. Patsy and I have undressed him and I very much fear – no, I know, that he has scarlet fever.'

Eleanor's eyes blazed.

'Scarlet fever?'

Caroline's chin went up.

'Yes, Eleanor, scarlet fever. And you are right to be angry, becau   was I who brought it to the house just as you s   should. And now I mean to nurse Papa as I have ursed many others.'

Eleanor's face was terrifying in its anger.

'You shall not touch him, Carrie! I knew I should be vindicated, I knew it! Because you could not resist the praise of others, a little renown, you have deliberately brought this sorrow upon us. You . . .'

'Eleanor, Eleanor,' Robert remonstrated. 'Papa has seen sick villagers, too, as well as Carrie. There has been fever all over the village. Do not be so violent.'

'I deserve it, Robert,' Caroline said wretchedly, 'though nothing Eleanor could say could hurt me more than my own feelings. You shall nurse him by day, Eleanor, and I shall sit by him at night.'

'Indeed, you shall do no such—'

'Silence!' Robert cried with uncharacteristic firmness. 'Of course she must take a turn, Eleanor! You cannot sit by him twenty-four hours a day. Go to him now and Carrie shall relieve you at eight.'

Astonished, Eleanor did as she was ordered. When she had gone, Caroline looked gratefully at her brother.

'Thank you, Robert, but I do deserve her anger.'

Robert shrugged.

'That is debatable. It is surprising that no-one in the household has succumbed to the fever before. Do you think he has it severely?'

'I cannot tell yet. His age is against him, his health for him. It is the fever we must keep at bay.'

'He is in good hands,' Robert said, and smiled at his sister.

The fever rose and rose. By night Parson Harding was delirious, shouting and crying out, twisting and tossing in his bed so that Caroline needed help to prevent him injuring himself. By wavering candlelight she watched his desperate unconscious face as he wrestled with nightmarish images, soothing and sponging his burning skin and talking to him in a gentle monotone. By day he was a little calmer, and sometimes knew Eleanor. Once he made the mistake of asking for Caroline, and reduced his elder daughter to helpless angry tears.

A ceaseless procession of anxious well-wishers began to come to the Parsonage door. Although she desperately needed sleep by day, Caroline saw them all, and accepted their little offerings of flowers and fruit and eggs and gave them what crumbs of comfort she could. Lady Lennox sent daily to enquire, her notes accompanied by baskets of exotic fruits from the Stoke Park orangery. Daily Caroline wrote to thank her. She did the household tasks Eleanor had used to do, and the everyday business of life went on, Robert riding round the parish and taking services, but without his heart in it. The movements were made, but there seemed no point to them.

The scarlet rash spread its red stain all over Parson Harding's body, covering all his hands and face except for a small pale patch about his mouth. It became impossible to cool him, and he slipped even further into the grotesque inferno of delirium. For several days he knew nobody, and the house rang with his wild shouts, shouts that were terrifying from a man whom none had ever heard raise his voice. The servants huddled in the kitchen, and Caroline dozed fitfully between her duties. She became as pale and gaunt as a wooden peg doll, her eyes even larger and more extraordinary in her ravaged face. She took to pacing the landing during the day when not sleeping or working, straining her ears for any sound that might give hope.

On the tenth day, as she paced, the door of Parson Harding's room was opened, and Eleanor's weeping face appeared.

'Come, Carrie,' she said hoarsely.

But it was too late to come. As Caroline approached the bed, her father was slipping swiftly away from her. Her shaking hand found no heartbeat, nothing. The fever had won.

*   *   *

The time that followed was a kind of dreadful limbo, a no-time in which nothing seemed real or relevant. Sunk in her own agonizing dry-eyed grief, washed up alone again, Caroline moved through the business of laying out and burying her father as though her inner self had nothing to do with her body. Eleanor wept ceaselessly, sobbing and accusing, red-eyed with anger and grief, but her storm of abuse fell upon Caroline as if she were encased in armour. She had no feelings for anything because all her emotional energy was absorbed in her unbearable sense of loss. The village thought it strange that she did not weep at the funeral, as Miss Eleanor did so copiously, but concluded kindly that she must do her weeping in private. They were wrong. She lay awake night after night consumed with torturing sadness and could not cry.

A week after the funeral, Lady Lennox sent for Robert and informed him that he should be incumbent of Stoke Abbas in his father's place. She had confessed to Lord Lennox that she was deeply reluctant to do this since Robert was a mere travesty of his father, but she could see nothing but destitution ahead for the Hardings if she did not perform this magnanimous act. Lord Lennox pointed out that there were certain advantages in having a tame clergyman dancing as a puppet on the string of their pulling and that to set out to find a wholly new incumbent who did not know the place would be most fatiguing. So Lady Lennox was gracious, Robert was humbly and profoundly grateful, and his patroness sat back and waited for his younger sister to capitulate.

She had some months to wait. Caroline crawled back to life so slowly that she began to wonder if she would ever be able to feel again. It was a painful reawakening, seeing her father's possessions, recalling looks and words, and becoming gradually less deaf and more sensitive to Eleanor's accusations. The armour of numbness that had shielded her developed chinks, then great gaps, and gradually fell away altogether leaving Caroline as raw and twitching and vulnerable as she had ever been.

'You realize that you have ruined our lives, Carrie. You are aware, I am sure, that if you had listened to even a single word I said you would not have brought this tragedy upon us. I am sure you are well repaid for your selfishness, your greed for praise and your stupidity. I only hope you know the extent to which you have damaged us all.'

It went on and on. Caroline only had to make the smallest domestic error, to open a window a fraction too wide, to throw away a pea shuck in which a single pea remained, to set the process in motion. She had not the heart to escape any longer since the cottages only served to remind her of the tragic effects of her work among them, and she could not bear it. She felt guilty about her neglect of the villagers and began to take pains to avoid the very people whose company she had so eagerly sought before, because their reproachful faces caused her such added misery. Round and round the Parsonage and garden she went, fleeing before Eleanor's persistent recriminations, hopelessly trying to find some occupation that would fill her mind and give her some ease. She would spend hours standing at her bedroom window or pacing hidden corners of the garden, fruitlessly regretting and accusing herself until her mind was quite worn down.

There came a particularly bad day. Robert, out of sheer clumsiness, had preached a sermon the previous Sunday whose liberalism, meant only to be humane, had been taken as a direct affront to herself by Lady Lennox. Robert had not expected to see her in church – indeed she had not attended for weeks – and was far too inept to switch his planned sermon for some more diplomatic improvisation simply because his patroness had appeared unexpectedly. Lady Lennox had endured twenty minutes of diffident suggestion that all men were equal in God's eyes and only integrity and virtue made a true hierarchy, and then had risen outraged, in a flurry of rustling silks, and swept from the church. Robert was summoned the following morning and crept back to dinner at the Parsonage with an air of wishing himself totally invisible.

'What did she have to say to you, Robert?' Eleanor demanded at dinner.

'Everything you might imagine, Eleanor.'

Eleanor laid down the carving knife.

'Please answer me directly, Robert.'

'No, Eleanor!' Caroline said indignantly. 'No, he shall not! You may very well imagine what passed at Stoke Park this morning, and it is merely cruel to make poor Robert relive it.'

Robert gave his younger sister a covert but grateful glance. Eleanor swelled with anger.

'How dare you speak to me thus, Carrie! You of all people have the least right to call any fellow human being cruel! You have acted with more selfish cruelty than any being upon earth and yet you dare to accuse me!'

There was a choking cry from Caroline's end of the table as she sprang up and fled from the room. Robert, emboldened by her courage, said to Eleanor:

'You must cease to chastise her, Eleanor. Papa's death was no more her fault than any of ours, and you make her grief intolerable to bear with your accusations.'

Eleanor glared at him.

'So! I am to have no defenders! I may not speak the truth and I must comfort the sinners for the wrong they have done me! If that is your doctrine, Robert, you may feed upon it alone for dinner!'

With relief, Robert heard the door slam behind her. When the parlour door was banged shut in the same manner, he rose quietly and began to carve himself some ham. He gave himself a much larger helping than Eleanor would have allowed him, and began to eat it in a solitude that was far from unpleasant to him.

Caroline's solitude upstairs was a far wilder thing. She was pacing her small room with clenched fists, muttering and trembling, her face full of an anger that no-one would have believed she possessed. It was beyond tolerance, Eleanor's attitude, beyond anything that the most enduring of people could be expected to bear. It was bad enough that her own faults, however small and irrelevant, should be the triggers for Eleanor's tirades, but it was insupportable that any crisis in the house, even one that had no bearing upon Caroline herself, should be used as an excuse for a fresh flood of bitter reproach. I cannot bear it, she thought, I cannot bear it. I cannot live here for all my life and never be allowed to forget, never be forgiven. Robert is kind and fond of me, but he is too weak for Eleanor, and Eleanor makes no bones of her feelings for me—

She stopped abruptly as a thought cut suddenly across her mind. There was an escape, there was! She had meant never to take it and it would mean some humiliation, but it was a chance for freedom. Lady Lennox had given her two months to change her mind about India, and twelve weeks, twelve long and dreadful weeks, had gone by. It was to be hoped that Lady Lennox had not written to Calcutta saying the match was not to be; indeed Caroline must make all haste. She did not relish the prospect of submitting to Lady Lennox after all her fine proud words, but that was a small act of humility by comparison with the utter shame she endured hourly here. She went quickly to her writing desk. Patsy should take a note to Stoke Park immediately, begging that Lady Lennox might spare the time to see Miss Caroline Harding briefly the following morning. She wrote swiftly, and folded the paper. She must not think too hard about the consequences of that note, there would be plenty of time for thought later. The note must go before she had time to realize her future to the full. With it in her hand, she opened the door and ran quickly down to the kitchen.

8

In early October 1776, Robert Harding took leave of
his parish for a few days to escort his sister Caroline
to Gravesend. It was a wild and windy October, and
Caroline's last view of Stoke Abbas was through a whirling
cloud of golden leaves, flung about by impetuous gusts
of wind. The carriage came slowly out of the Parsonage
gates, for the horses were prancing and shying at the rough
weather, and thus the little group of villagers gathered to
wave goodbye had a long last look as Caroline moved
past them. Lady Lennox had sent a note to wish her
bon voyage so full of unconcealed self-satisfaction that
Caroline had tossed it straight into the fire, but this
small cluster of poorly dressed cottagers affected her very
deeply. She pulled down the carriage window, and leaned
out and called her thanks and good wishes into the gale
until she could no longer be heard.

Gravesend was to Caroline a most romantic sight.
They arrived in the damp dusk, and through the darkening air could see the East Indiaman that was to be her
home for six months. Straining her eyes in the dimness,
she could make out its great masts and the guns along
its bulwarks, and felt her heart leap with a mixture of
excitement and apprehension. Robert only seemed to feel
the latter emotion.

'Shall you really go, Carrie?' he said over supper at an
inn. 'I know all your belongings are aboard by now, but
I am sure we could get them taken off again.'

Caroline smiled and patted his hand.

'Indeed I am going, Robert!' she declared. 'Even if
my passage were not booked and all I have in the world

already on the ship, you must remember that my fate is already sealed in a letter halfway to India.'

She did not add that the prospect of returning to Eleanor's scorn and Lady Lennox's anger was far more terrifying to her than six months at sea and an almost blind marriage.

She looked at her brother's doubtful face above his clerical bands.

'Do not worry about me, Robert. I am sure there will be delightful company on board, and I will send letters home by every ship we pass.'

'I shall miss you sorely, Carrie,' he said painfully, suddenly envisaging what meals at the Parsonage would be like without an ally.

'Perhaps my absence will force you to find yourself a wife.'

Robert nodded without hope.

'I am going to bed now,' she said, 'for my last night on land until the spring.'

The momentousness of this fact struck them both into sudden silence, Caroline elated, Robert appalled.

'I shall never sleep for anxiety,' he said miserably.

'You must. I do not want to be waved goodbye by a long face, Robert. If it were not for leaving you, I should be entirely pleased to be going.'

If Gravesend had seemed a romantic sight at dusk, the dawn was almost better. Along the quay stood merchants muffled in cloaks, and sailors with gold rings in their ears were loading great quantities of cargo aboard the ship. Caroline stood on the wet cobbles, wrapped in her new boat cloak, and found it difficult to believe she was herself, or that before nightfall, she and that great ship would be slipping away from England together. She could see nobody who might be a fellow passenger, in fact nobody at all apart from the sailors, except for a most impressive person in a braided coat and buckled shoes whom Robert whispered he was sure must be the captain. Caroline regarded him with awe.

'I do not believe it is still too late to come home with me,' Robert pleaded.

Caroline shook her head.

'I do not want to go home, Robert. I could wish you were coming with me, but I do not want to go home.'

She remembered the brief dry brush of Eleanor's cheek which was all the farewell she had had and felt a sudden strong resolve to put all of such memories behind her. She turned to Robert.

'I think I shall go aboard now, and see to my cabin.'

'No, no, Carrie, there is no need before midday. I have express instructions that passengers are under no obligation to embark before noon.'

'Perhaps not, but I have an express need. I am not enjoying saying goodbye, and I should like to see you safely on your way.'

Robert looked deeply troubled. He hated hanging about in Gravesend, and he hated to see her go, but he was most relieved to be told what to do.

'Do not look so anxious, Robert. I promise you to board the right ship for the right destination, but I should do so with much more peace of mind if I knew you were homeward bound.'

Without further protestation, Robert allowed himself to be stowed comfortably in the carriage. He had meant to sell it on his father's death, but was, on this murky day, profoundly thankful his indecision had prevented it. He let Caroline tuck rugs about him and kiss him swiftly on the cheek.

'I shall say goodbye quickly, Robert, just as if we were to see each other in a few days. You must write, and so shall I, and give my dear love to Patsy.'

She watched the carriage rumble away, and then turned eagerly back towards the quayside. Burdened by no more than her small box of personal possessions, she went quickly among the bales and boxes that littered the greasy cobbles, nodding to any sailor who looked her way, and conscious of an exhilarating sense of freedom. As Robert jolted out of Gravesend westward, his sister Caroline mounted the gangplank of the East Indiaman, quite alone, on her way to Calcutta.

Lady Lennox, in a flush of gratification over Caroline's capitulation, had been generous. She had regretted the generosity almost instantly, but it was too late to recall it. She had booked Caroline one of the sought-after poop cabins, and had realized with annoyance too late that Caroline would have been quite content with something humbler. The poop cabins, after all, were usually occupied by persons of consequence, and Lady Lennox was perfectly confident that all the passengers would soon discover that Caroline was of no consequence whatsoever and thus the extravagance of a poop cabin would be entirely wasted. It was very vexing, and it was extremely doubtful that the vexation would have been lessened if Lady Lennox could have seen Caroline's huge gratification as she surveyed her little domain. She would have considered that gratitude was no more than her due for such reckless generosity.

A sailor equipped with a wooden leg limped before Caroline below deck to show her to her quarters. They passed a row of small cabins, divided only by canvas partitions, and in each one Caroline readily expected to see the narrow bedstead, washstand and small chair which Eleanor had graciously allowed her to take from the Parsonage. Each cabin was already furnished, mostly over-furnished, and great trunks stood on every floor, as well as piles of writing cases, fishing equipment, parcels of books and cases of wine. There seemed to be a flurry of servants everywhere, deep in trunks or gossiping between the cabins, and Caroline was suddenly bitterly conscious that she had no-one with her, no-one at all. It had crossed her mind to take a village girl as maid, but upon reflection, she had decided that it was too alarming a proposition to put to any girl who regarded Dorchester as the other side of the world, and had decided to manage on her own. Lady Lennox had pointed out, in her eagerness to encourage Caroline for her future, that Johnnie would provide her with a wealth of servants in Calcutta, where a raw Dorset girl would be quite superfluous. For a brief moment, however, Caroline would have given everything for the companionship of such a girl.

The sailor stopped before a pair of narrow wooden doors. He flung open the left-hand one and indicated that Caroline should enter. She took one brief amazed look and withdrew to the deck again.

'That cannot be mine.'

'You Miz 'Arding?'

'Yes, I am, but—'

'Port poop cabin, then, Miz 'Arding.'

He held his hand out hopefully. Caroline fumbled in her reticule and found a coin with no notion of how relevant it was to his services. He spat upon it, polished it, grinned and ambled crookedly away, leaving her small box upon the floor. After the crowded cabins behind her, Caroline's few bits of furniture seemed rather lost in the splendid space she had been allotted. The walls and floor were bare certainly, but the walls were panelled, and the end one was entirely occupied by a large window. A swinging lamp and tray were suspended from the ceiling, and Caroline's bed and washstand had been tidily arranged against one wall. Her writing case lay across the chair, familiar from the Parsonage nursery with its stretchers kicked bare by the boots of Robert, Charles and Harry. And there was something else, too, a small and pretty bureau, clearly the possession of some other passenger since it was quite unfamiliar to Caroline. She ran a finger over its satiny surface and admired the shell inlaid on the sloping front. She turned the small key to open it in case there was some hint of ownership inside, and found there a card from Lord Lennox, wishing her bon voyage and hoping she would accept this small gift on the occasion of her marriage. It was all quite delightful, quite unbelievably delightful. She threw her cloak across her bed and hugged herself and smiled out of pure pleasure.

A knock came at the door, which was then pushed open as unceremoniously as Eleanor would have done. But instead of her sister's uncompromising black figure, Caroline saw to her consternation that a ravishingly pretty girl, with dark curls and a high colour, was standing in the doorway.

'Now, do not look so startled. I know exactly who you are because I have just asked a matelot, and I also know from the same source that you have no maid, and so I am come with the express purpose of offering you mine for she is an idle madam and needs to be occupied.'

Caroline was stammering with amazement.

'You – you are too k-kind, b-but really, I—'

'Do not be a goose, Miss Harding, and refuse me. No-one wants to unpack their own trunks when someone could perfectly well do it for them. Why! Do you mean you only have one? It will take Fatima but a few moments, I assure you it will, and in the meantime you and I shall get to know each other.'

'You are m-most kind,' Caroline said faintly.

'Nonsense, I am not kind at all. I am extremely selfish because I want a friend exceedingly for this tedious voyage, and I am sure you will be she. Now, where are your rugs and pictures?'

'I have none—'

'None!'

'I have left them all behind. I was trying to – to leave as much as possible behind.'

The pretty girl surveyed her keenly for a moment.

'I understand you perfectly. Well, there is nothing for it but to lend you some of mine. I have brought an absurd amount as I always do, and shall be thankful to dispense with half of it. Stay here one moment, and I shall summon Fatima.'

She paused in the doorway, and added, 'My name is Isobel Grant, Miss Harding, and I know that yours is Caroline.'

Caroline stood quite stunned in the middle of her cabin and gazed at the doorway through which Isobel Grant and her green gown had vanished. It was clear that she occupied the adjacent cabin, and equally clear that she was of the class by whom Caroline was most alarmed. Poor Miss Grant would be doomed to find Caroline as dull and unrewarding as Sophia and Jane and Georgiana Lennox had all done, and it seemed wicked to accept her loan of rugs and ornaments when theirs was a friendship which had, because of Caroline's inadequacies, no chance of blossoming. But as Caroline stepped forward to try to prevent the transference of articles from one side of the poop to the other, Isobel Grant was already returning, her arms full of objects, with a plump, dusky-skinned maid in her wake.

'Now, Miss Harding, come with me and we shall sit in my cabin while Fatima makes yours presentable. What an enviable little bureau that is, to be sure, quite twice as pretty as mine. Fatima, to work, please, and we wish to be very much surprised and impressed.'

Isobel Grant's cabin could have been any small and fashionably pretty drawing room in London. Caroline sat nervously upon the blue silk padded seat of a small gilded chair, and looked about her in awe at the water colours and miniatures, rugs and embroideries.

'Are we not lucky, Miss Harding, to be in a ship so thoroughly modern? This is only her second voyage, you know, and these are supposed to be the most comfortable cabins in all the East Indiamen. I, of course, refused to go unless I was comfortable, and I am very glad that Lady Lennox felt you needed cherishing too.'

Caroline started.

'Lady Lennox? You – you know of Lady Lennox, Miss Grant?'

'Call me Isobel, Miss Harding, and then I shall be able to call you Caroline which I should much prefer to do. Yes, I know Lady Lennox, and now I shall tease you by making you guess how.'

Caroline could not help smiling.

'That is too difficult. I know nobody but Lady Lennox, you see, so have no knowledge to make guesses with.'

'How pretty your eyes are when you smile. Very well, I shall not torture you. I know Lady Lennox because my cousin Frank married Georgiana, last spring.'

'Lord Lovell!'

'The same. His father and my mother are brother and sister. I knew from Frank that you would be upon this ship, and I very much hoped we should be neighbours. Now, shall you tell me about yourself, or shall I tell you about yourself, instead, and then you can tell me where I am wrong?'

Caroline was laughing openly.

'You tell me.'

'Very well. You are the daughter of the Stoke Abbas parson who is recently dead, which is very sad, and you are bound for India to marry a childhood beau, which is more than I can say for myself, and you are wonderfully kind to the poor. Now, Caroline, I can see I am quite right because you are as pink as a rose.'

'You are almost right. Now tell me about yourself.'

'Oh, delightedly, there is no subject I am fonder of. I am very spoiled and very bored, and I am being sent off to stay with another cousin in Calcutta before I am clapped into irons and marriage for the rest of my life. My cousin is very important in Calcutta and much older than I am, and I am told I used to dote upon him when I was a baby. I very much trust he is preparing to dote in return upon me now.'

Caroline regarded her with warmth.

'I doubt he can resist you. How long shall you stay?'

'Until he throws me out. His mother was a most severe woman, very cross and disagreeable, and so is his surviving sister, and I am very much afraid that he will be entirely like them. So you see how I need a friend, Caroline, for I am so easily bored and cannot bear to be chided.'

'I should dearly like to be that friend, but I am afraid you will find me very dull.'

Isobel Grant looked at her in silence very carefully for a moment or two. Then she said decisively, 'I do not think so.'

The first few days of the voyage were terrible, and Caroline discovered that she was an appalling sailor. The moment the ship was beyond the safety of the Channel, storms fell upon her with fury, and waves as high as houses tossed her about as if she were no more than a toy. Sick and shivering on her bed, Caroline could hear the goats and poultry tethered in the round house above her bleating and squawking their dismay. She longed for air, but when her window was opened, the sea poured in in great grey gulps and swamped her cabin. If it had not been for Isobel, she did not know that she could have borne her wretchedness, but Isobel proved an excellent sailor and indefatigable nurse.

'You cannot imagine how much good it does me to be of use. I have never been of so much use before in my life. And I am so grateful to be safely here with you because you cannot conceive of how disagreeable the rest of the ship is. Everyone but me is ill, and all the furniture is rolling about through the canvas curtains like bulls got loose from their chains.

Fatima had wished to be ill too, but Isobel would not permit it.

'If I am to look after you, is it not entirely reasonable that she should look after me? When you are better, and this horrid sea is flat again, then she may dally with the sailors if she pleases, but not until then.'

As suddenly as they had pounced, the winds withdrew, and Caroline emerged from her cabin in the calm evening to find the air balmy and the rigging hung with coloured lanterns. Isobel was delighted with her progress.

'Caroline, I shall take all the credit for it, every scrap. I do believe if it were not for me you would have died.'

'You believe quite rightly. I cannot thank you enough, indeed I cannot.'

'You do not need to, for I shall exact my pound of flesh, I promise you. I shall start exacting it this moment too, for here comes General North, the heaviest gallant in the world, who has been plaguing me these last three days, and you shall take him off my hands.'

With an exclamation of distress, Caroline was about to protest, but the general was immediately upon them, smiling and genial.

'My dear Miss Grant, indeed my – may I say so? – very dear Miss Grant, I had hoped to find you here.'

'Good evening, General, and what pretty medals you are sporting, to be sure. Caroline, may I present General North to you? General, Miss Harding.'

The general bowed stiffly from his vanished waistline.

'*Enchanté*, Miss Harding. Any friend of Miss Grant's—'

'She is not any friend, General, she is my most particular friend whom I have snatched from the jaws of death.'

'Indeed?'

With a rush of courage Caroline said, 'It is true, General, quite true. I – I never thought it possible to feel so ill.'

'Aha! This must be your first sea voyage?'

'It is.'

'Then you must expect to feel the effects, my dear Miss Harding. When you have gone back and forth to India with the regularity that I have done, you will feel nothing, nothing at all.'

In the same breath, Caroline said, 'Then you know Calcutta well?' as Isobel declared, 'She is not going back and forth, General, she is going to be married there.'

'Married, eh? Married! Yes, I know Calcutta, Miss Harding, and I often wish I were spared its acquaintance. Madras is the place, you know, nowhere like Madras.'

'Is Calcutta so very disagreeable?' Caroline ventured.

'Pretty much so, pretty much. But I daresay you will not notice too much in your newly wedded bliss, eh?'

A small chill was creeping into Caroline's spirits.

'In what way is Calcutta disagreeable, General?'

The general looked about for Isobel to rescue him from the earnest direction in which conversation was tending, but found that she had slipped away in the shadows. He sighed a little, but endeavoured to do his best.

''Tis pretty hot, you know, and humid. And society there is very raffish. No standards, no propriety. Not, you understand, Miss Harding, that I do not know how to enjoy myself—'

He broke off, and said abruptly, 'Are you acquainted with Sir Edward Ashton?'

Caroline, whose thoughts were far away on the now slightly troubling prospect of Calcutta, looked at him perplexedly.

'Sir Edward Ashton?'

The name was very dimly familiar, but why she could not at present recall.

'Yes. Are you acquainted with him?'

'No – no, not in the least.'

The general looked disappointed.

'Pity. Fine fellow. He is the cousin to whom Miss Grant is going. He is one of the half-dozen most distinguished men in Calcutta, a member of the Council and a close friend of the Governor General.'

'The Council, General?'

By the faint light of the lanterns above their heads, General North regarded her with some surprise. This odd, stiff, plain girl whom that pretty creature seemed so fond of, appeared to have no notion at all of the place she was bound for for the greater portion of the remainder of her life. She appeared not to be aware of climate or conditions, nor of the administration that governed Bengal.

'Do you know anything of India, Miss Harding? Have you any connections there at all?'

'None – no, none, and I know nothing of India. General—' she said suddenly, 'will you instruct me a little? Will you tell me something of the place, and of the East India Company?'

The general looked at her again, and noticed her curious gleaming eyes for the first time, and the softening effect that eagerness had upon her features. He thought a moment upon the prospect of weeks of uninterrupted instruction, weeks with a humble and grateful pupil, and concluded that the prospect was entirely gratifying. He bowed again.

'It will be my pleasure, Miss Harding. A most delightful task. Now, may I escort you below where I gather we are to have some music before supper?'

Caroline was astonished at the spectacle of the second deck. Isobel had told her of the splendid dinners served there each day under the autocratic eye of the captain (of whom it was said that he had ordered a passenger to be clapped in irons for being so disrespectful as to whistle in his presence), but Caroline was not at all prepared for the gathering that confronted her. Several ladies, all dressed with considerable care, were grouped gracefully about one of their number who was playing upon an enormous harp. A respectful audience of men, mostly in uniform, but with one or two civilians, sat about at their ease, a bottle at every elbow. Except for the gentle motion of the ship, and the faint and not altogether pleasant odour that was to become an increasingly obtrusive feature of the voyage, it might have been a scene in any English drawing room.

General North escorted Caroline to a seat, then bowed and left her to join the serious drinkers in the round house. The ladies about the harpist looked her way briefly and slightly inclined their heads. The gentlemen, who had looked up hopefully as she entered, sought their liquid comfort once more. Caroline sat back thankfully in the shadows, and thought how strange it was to feel so solidly supported, so secure, in a little wooden vessel on the deep. She would never have believed whilst still on land that a ship could seem so stable and safe. She looked furtively round at the dozen or so faces in the lamplight, and thought how much she should know about them when they reached Calcutta, and how familiar they would become. The lamps swung gently from the low ceiling, the harp twanged in the silence broken only by the plash of the sea, and Caroline felt that Stoke Abbas was now a spot upon another planet.

9

A week later, the coastline of Africa was sighted amid exclamations from the ladies and the event was recorded at once in most of the industriously kept feminine journals. General North, by now delighted by his pupil's appetite and aptitude for learning, suggested to Caroline that as the equator approached, she might like to keep a map of the southern sky. Caroline agreed with enthusiasm, for she had already charted the ship's progress and course with an accuracy the captain had loudly admired, and liked to have some tasks to give shape to the by now sometimes tedious days. As the equator approached, the soft warm wind dropped and dropped until, after a week of no more than creeping through the water, it died away altogether, and they found themselves becalmed.

It was an eerie sensation, lying quietly there on the flat and glittering sea beneath the hard blue African sky. The ship, which had seemed so redoubtable a haven while slipping on resolutely through the sea, became a vulnerable little object, and a watch was set to keep lookout for pirates said to lie in wait for stranded vessels. Alarming tales were told of the savagery of these pirates, and the ladies' spirits dwindled a little in the hot silence of their predicament.

'Are you not afraid of this horrid situation?' Isobel demanded of Caroline.

'I do not like it, but I am not much afraid of it. It is not that I am brave, Isobel, but simply that the last weeks have been so novel that I do not seem able to feel that anything has much reality.'

'Oh, Caroline, you are exasperatingly patient, indeed you are! Does it not madden you to be so hot and so bored and fidgeted by so small a space?'

Three long days later, a little wind rose, and the passengers crowded excitedly on deck to watch the great sails begin to belly and fill. Slowly the ship moved forward and a cheer rose as the blessed breeze soothed their burned faces and tired eyes. Even while becalmed, most passengers had spent their days on deck because the smells below were becoming formidable, and their skins had inevitably become dried and scorched by the relentless sun. General North had told Caroline with pride that the East India Company insisted that its ships should be washed down twice a week – an unheard of standard of hygiene – but these salt-water swillings were no match for the cramped living conditions, the livestock tethered about the ship, and the unventilated areas of the lower decks. Caroline often had cause to thank Lady Lennox for her unwilling kindness, when she opened the window in her comfortable cabin and filled it with air and sunlight. Her little bureau was now strewn with maps and charts, meticulously kept, to the astonishment of Isobel.

'What can this mean, Caroline? What are all these little arrows and hieroglyphics? What are these strange names? Oh, Caroline, why will you not embroider with me like any civilized girl?'

Caroline had fallen in love with the southern night sky. Every evening, escorted by the captain, the ship's doctor and General North, she would repair to the poop deck, and watch the constellations rise in their astonishing and exquisite brilliancy. She had never imagined that a cloudless climate could make such a difference to the stars, and was amazed anew every night as these incredible diamonds wheeled across the velvety heavens. The ladies, however, were piqued at the attention shown her, for they considered her clothes and lack of grace and accomplishments still an insuperable stumbling block. If it had not been for the fact that the exquisite Miss Grant seemed to dote upon her, they would have ignored her altogether.

'Take no notice of them, Caroline!' Isobel declared. 'They are all disappointed spinsters save Mrs Mayhew, and she is a disappointed wife if you consider the insignificance of Mr Mayhew, and that must be worse. What is more, Caroline, they are jealous of you.'

Caroline looked up from her careful etching of the Southern Cross. 'Jealous! Jealous of me! Do not be absurd, Isobel. Nobody is ever jealous of me.'

'Indeed they are. Every night you are escorted to the poop deck by no less than three distinguished gentlemen, all of whom admire you profoundly. Shall I tell you something? Today the doctor caught a flying fish, and we begged him to dissect it for us, but he would not do so because you were occupied and he did not consider the rest of us a worthy audience.'

Caroline laid down her pen.

'You are teasing me, Isobel.'

'I would not dream of it. I never tease those I love best, never. I will tell you something else that makes these faded flowers green again with envy. They are all part of the fishing fleet, and you, the promised bride of Mr Gates, are not.'

'The fishing fleet?'

Isobel smiled delightedly.

'Guess what they are fishing for.'

Caroline considered a moment, gazing out at the shore of Africa that sometimes seemed to her as if it would never end.

'Come on, come on! You are so slow, Caroline, I do believe you are the slowest—'

'Husbands?' Caroline suggested doubtfully.

'Of course, you goose! What else! Husbands! The whole of Calcutta is full of eligible husbands!'

Caroline rose and went over to the window, standing for a long while looking out over the blue interminable sea.

'I wonder then,' she said at last, 'if they have even more to fear than I.'

Isobel came swiftly to stand beside her.

'Caroline! Caroline, are you afraid? Are you afraid of marrying Mr Gates?'

There was a pause, and then Caroline nodded.

'Yes, Isobel, I am.'

'But you have known him since childhood. He is the only man you have ever loved! Is it not the most romantic situation you can conceive of?'

'I – I think I hardly knew him. I can recall so little about him, although I can remember what I felt. But Isobel' – with a sudden rush of feeling – 'I have not seen him for nine years, nor he me. Suppose when I get there I – he—'

'Then you shall not marry him!' Isobel declared roundly. 'I shall see that you do not!'

Caroline took her hand and pressed it.

'I have never had a friend like you, Isobel, and I cannot express what your affection means. But I must marry, I must. I know myself well enough to know that I have to have a purpose, an occupation. I am only content that way.'

'Nonsense, Caroline! An unhappy marriage is not an occupation, it is a terrible affliction. I will not allow the martyr in you to have its way. Come now, there will be no more talk of Mr Gates until we get to Calcutta and decide whether he deserves you in the very least. The captain says we shall be at the Cape within a week unless the wind dies again and at the Cape there are the best grapes in the world and we may actually leave this floating prison for a while.'

Two days before the Cape was reached, with its promise of dry land and succulent fruit, the first sailors died of scurvy. Sewn into their hammocks, they were pitched into the sea during rough and ready funerals which afflicted the passengers deeply, but had very little effect upon the crew. In fact Caroline was much startled to notice that in the midst of reading a prayer, one of the ship's officers broke off to bawl an order to the helmsman, and then resumed his pious reading as if the interruption had never been. Isobel could not watch as the canvas bundles plummeted into the water.

'It seems so heartless, Caroline, they are vanished as if they had never been. Do you suppose anyone knows if they died, or cares?'

The Cape seemed like Paradise. It was decided by the captain to remain at anchor for some time since many timbers of his new ship had shrunk while becalmed in the blazing sun, and needed to be waterproofed. General North took firm charge of Caroline and Isobel and found them delightful lodgings with a stout Dutch widow in a house surrounded by blossom-hung terraces. In the midst of the flowers and ferns and trees, the sun no longer seemed oppressive but rather the greatest benefit upon earth. Caroline's room opened directly upon a terrace, its balustrade entwined with bougainvillaea, and beyond the roofs and gardens below it rose the square-topped splendour of Table Mountain.

She had initially been worried over money. Her fare had been paid, but it had not included a pause at the Cape since favourable winds often induced captains to · press on past that delightful place. But Isobel had discerned her difficulty and acted with her usual impulsive generosity.

'Do not think more about it, Caroline. You shall be my guest. I have the most dreadful tendency to waste money and should love to put it to good purpose. I could not bear to have you far from me after living but a wooden wall away these three months, so I will brook no argument.'

Caroline accepted gratefully, but as she unpacked her belongings in her sunlight-dappled room she reflected with a certain resentment how wonderful it would be not always to be the receiver, rather than the giver of charity. Briefly, before her father died, she had known how blessed it was to give, but now she was back in her old humble position of taker. She loved Isobel warmly, and was truly and deeply grateful for all her kindness, but some part of her felt herself diminished by this constant acceptance of others' generosity. She had nothing to give Isobel but love, and had she been surer of herself, she would have known that that was all Isobel wanted.

For three weeks, Caroline was entirely happy. The small circle in which she now felt quite comfortable, composed of herself, Isobel, General North and an increasing troupe of Isobel's admirers, met daily for the most delightful excursions. They rode out into the countryside, the admirers taking enormous trouble to instruct Caroline in the hope of ingratiating themselves further with Isobel, and stayed at little inns, where they breakfasted on vine-covered verandahs. The bacon, eggs and cheese were of the highest quality, but the fresh bread was a universal delight after the months of ship's biscuit. The gentlemen complained bitterly of the local wine, which they claimed was execrable to taste and appallingly expensive, but as Caroline observed, it did not seem to daunt them in drinking it.

One day they climbed Table Mountain itself, an arduous but satisfactory expedition, urging Isobel onwards with promises of the view to be had from the summit. Watching the general toiling upward in his full coat and heavy wig, it struck Caroline how inappropriately they were all dressed.

'Would it not be possible for you to walk in your shirt sleeves, General?'

General North stopped to mop at his streaming brow.

'Possible, my dear Miss Harding, but entirely improper. This heat is nothing in any case. Wait until you feel the steam bath that is Calcutta.'

Just below the summit, when Isobel was declaring that if she was to reach the top she should have to be carried, a surprise awaited them. General North, who knew the Cape well, had arranged refreshments and there, in a cool cave, stood a table spread with chickens and hams and great baskets of fruit. Sitting there in the shade with the exquisite bay spread out below her and a plate of peaches and grapes before her, Caroline felt a physical contentment she had never known before. The warmth, the colours, the comfortable companionship of people whom she would never have dared to feel easy with before, combined to make her feel both languorous and elated in a way she had not known she could feel. Great butterflies were drifting about a flowering shrub below her and a small bright bird chattered on a rock by her shoulder.

'I do not think I ever want to leave this place.'

'Nor I,' Isobel declared. 'Shall I send a message to my cousin Ashton and say I have changed my mind?'

The admirers looked horrified.

'You cannot be serious! You cannot mean it!'

'Of course I do not but I wish I did. I am anxious I shall not enjoy Calcutta.'

General North refilled his glass.

'My dear Miss Grant, you will move in the highest circles in Calcutta.'

'Perhaps she does not think that a recommendation,' Caroline said.

The general turned to her.

'Miss Harding, you disappoint me. After all these weeks of instruction, you should know better than to suggest that the highest circles in Calcutta are to be sniffed at. I beg you will inform Miss Grant of the circles I mean, and then I shall know if you have listened to a word I have said.'

Isobel clasped her hands.

'Recite it to me nicely, Caroline.'

'Then you must listen nicely.'

Isobel unclasped her hands and looked demure.

'Pray commence.'

'Calcutta is the chief port of the province of Bengal,' Caroline began, her eye upon General North, 'which is the most important of the Indian states to the East India Company—'

Here there were cries of 'To the John Company!' from a few young men lounging in the grass as close to Isobel's feet as they dared.

'Persevere, Miss Harding.'

'The Governor General of Bengal is Mr Warren Hastings—'

'I thought there was a man called Clive,' Isobel said. 'What happened to the man called Clive?'

'Warren Hastings is his successor,' General North said. 'Shall I continue for you, Miss Harding, since I shall be able to suppress interruptions by sheer volume?'

'I should be grateful,' Caroline said, sinking back into her chair.

'He is assisted in his administrative duties by the Council, a small group of men, selected in the main by my namesake, our Prime Minister, and of whom your cousin, Miss Grant, is one.'

'All I know of Warren Hastings', Isobel said, wholly unimpressed by her cousin's position, 'is that he stole someone else's wife which was most fascinating of him.'

'Warren Hastings is a man of the utmost rectitude,' the general said portentously. 'A man of excellent principle, abstemious habits and infinite industry.'

Isobel sighed.

'He sounds quite impossible, General. Will you please reassure me that my cousin Ashton does not resemble him in any way?'

'Your cousin Ashton, my dear Miss Grant, is a most

remarkable man. I believe', he added, turning to Caroline dreaming in her chair, 'that you, Miss Harding, and Sir Edward Ashton will find you have much of mutual interest.'

Caroline coloured and looked down at her lap. She did not observe the sudden and keen expression that fluttered for a moment across Isobel's lively countenance.

It was sad to leave the Cape, and discouraging to find themselves once more in the narrow confines of their cabins. Everyone seemed refreshed by the spell ashore, however, and one or two of the fishing fleet, as Isobel openly called them, were sufficiently revived to be almost gracious to Caroline. Caroline was grateful for these attentions, not simply because of her new-found delight in finding herself accepted by people whom she had formerly found terrifying, but also because they diverted her from her thoughts. As the ship moved away from the Cape and began to creep across the Indian Ocean, Caroline's thoughts were not of a kind to afford her much ease. Before she had started out, she had been so desperate to leave, so frantic to put thousands of miles between herself and the reproaches and bullyings of Stoke Abbas, that she had not given much thought to her future, except for the occasional grateful reflection that she had a future to go to at all. Even as they sailed away from Gravesend, she had been too preoccupied with seasickness and adventure and the dazzling novelty of Isobel to look ahead. All those long weeks it took to sail down the African coast had been so happily filled with little occupations and her daily instructions from General North about India that her mind was kept from being too reflective. The one pang of fear she had had, Isobel had diverted away, and then she had been so beguiled by the Cape and her pleasant little society, that she had felt herself secure in a magic world where the word future had no significance.

But the spell of the Cape was broken now, and Caroline felt the beginnings of a most alarming foreboding. She had little to divert her now, for General North, though he paid her steady and affectionate attention when they met, was now preoccupied with defence classes for the young men upon the ship, in order to be prepared for any sudden attack from French privateers. Isobel was with her a good deal of course, but she was herself chafing now at the tedium of the voyage and needed Caroline to amuse her, an occupation Caroline doubted she had much talent for. All her waking moments now had a dark shadow at the back of them, and while other passengers scanned the horizon anxiously for signs of pirate ships, Caroline watched, too, but with eagerness, for she now knew that she would have welcomed any event that prevented her arrival in Calcutta.

It was not the prospect of Calcutta itself that alarmed her. She felt well equipped with knowledge as to the habits, lifestyle, food, climate, pleasures and dangers of India and would under other circumstances have looked forward eagerly to the adventure of another continent. But her marriage filled her with mounting apprehension, and the more she thought of it, the more she became quite convinced that the whole enterprise was madness. If only, she thought fiercely, she were a person of independent means, she would not always have to be handed from one household to another like a piece of furniture. Isobel, for instance, with her private fortune and the connections that went with it, was going out to India under just those free and dignified circumstances that Caroline could never aspire to, while she, Caroline, must be handed, dowerless, from the support of her brother to that of a man she increasingly felt she hardly knew. She had read his letter to Lady Lennox, but it was not written in a style that she ever remembered his using before, and she had wondered fleetingly if it was all his own work.

What, in fact, could she really remember of Johnnie Gates, except a sort of buttercup-filled summer idyll that seemed more like a story that she had read than part of her own life? She remembered the pleasure the recollection of his courtship had given her, only eighteen months before, but that pleasure now shamed her by contrast with the emotions she had known since. She remembered Johnnie as tall, square-shouldered, with a handsome challenging face and disordered curls. She remembered his magnificent clothes, outstanding in the comfortable dowdiness of Stoke Abbas, she remembered his dare-devilry and teasing, she remembered being kissed by him but not how it had thrilled her. To the older Caroline, now seeking something far steadier and deeper, it seemed she could recall nothing of importance, nothing but the dashing trappings of romance any eighteen-year-old might harbour.

The night their ship made the mouth of the Hooghly River, Caroline was at her lowest ebb. She lay in her narrow bed, steady for the first time in months since the pilot had advised mooring away from the banks to avoid the very probable danger of tigers leaping silently aboard, and resolved to lie low in the ship and set sail again for England even if she had to work her passage. As if by some sixth sense, Isobel crept in to her before dawn and knelt in the blessedly cool air by her bedside.

'Have you closed your eyes at all, Caroline?'

'Not once.'

'I knew it! I have been on the point of tiptoeing in all night and now I wish I had. You have been wearing foreboding writ large all over your dear face these past weeks and I am very afraid you will do something foolish.'

Caroline said nothing but put out a hand in the misty light and felt it grasped.

'Confess, Caroline!'

'I – I was thinking of running home.'

Her hand was lightly slapped in the darkness.

148

'Shame on you! Back to demon Lady Lennox and dragon Eleanor? I know very well how apprehensive you are about the charms of Mr Gates, but do you really mean to run away again?'

'Again?'

'Again. Think, Caroline.'

Caroline thought. Pictures of Stoke Abbas, of her father's empty study, of Eleanor frowning in the pantries, of Lady Lennox in her drawing room, pictures she had not summoned for weeks on account of her acute apprehension about marriage, processed steadily across her imagination. Isobel was right in her inference that home was no longer there to go to, she had run away from it, renounced it, chosen an alternative.

'Why are you so pessimistic, Caroline? Why should Mr Gates not prove everything you wish him to be? And if he isn't why should you not refuse to marry him?'

Caroline sat up in bed.

'Because I do not really have a choice. That is what frightens me. You are young and lovely and independent and those things make your security. I am the reverse of all those assets, and am, in the eyes of the world, astonishingly lucky to be handed such a chance as I have. If I do not take it, if I do not marry, I might as well not exist. There is nothing else on earth for me to do.'

'Nonsense!' Isobel cried. 'You shall live with me! I have enough for ten extravagant companions, and a dear mouse like you would not so much as nibble at my money—'

'No – no! Isobel, please—'

'Should you not like to live with me?'

'I should love it above all things, but not – not as an object of charity. If I had my own fortune there is no other companion I should choose—'

'And if you are an object of charity to me, you goose, why are you not precisely the same to Mr Gates?'

'It is different as a wife! I have a conventional role to play, I can make his life comfortable, run his home, see to his wants, I can feel that in some way I am repaying being kept by him.'

Isobel got to her feet and shook out her bedgown.

'I fail to see the difference between doing all that for him and doing it for me, when he might not want you and I most certainly do. But at least I have made you talk yourself into marriage, and that I must conclude to be a good night's work.'

She bent and kissed Caroline's cheek.

'Bother your stiff-necked pride, you dear and tiresome thing.'

'Do you not – understand it a little, Isobel?'

'I might, but I do not want to – I want you to be happy and I long to be instrumental in your happiness.'

'You already are! More than you know. My courage is up again, thanks to you.'

Isobel opened the narrow door and moved on to the deck outside.

'You still shan't marry him if I don't think him good enough.'

When the door had closed, Caroline slipped from her bed and went to the window. The greyness of dawn was growing rosy now, and across the still pale water of the river she could see a low bank and the outlines of groups of alien-looking trees. Smoke was curling blue from some clumps, the smoke perhaps of early breakfasts, Indian breakfasts. Despite her wretched night, a leap of excitement warmed her as she stood there and looked at this foreign waking world. She, Caroline Harding, of the parish of Stoke Abbas in the county of Dorset, England, was about to set foot in India.

10

Johnnie Gates was ill-prepared for any bride that March morning. He had allowed George Carew to assist him in lamenting the end of freedom so lavishly the night before, that death would have seemed preferable as he opened stiff and sore eyelids upon the squalor of his bedroom the next day. No servants were hovering since they were disinclined to face Sahib Gates in such a condition one second before they were compelled to, and, in any case, Johnnie had quite omitted to mention that the pressing matter of welcoming the future Mrs Gates to Calcutta meant that he must be woken promptly and made as presentable as the limited resources of his house would permit.

'Ahmed! Ranjit! You insolent dogs, where are you? Here, I say, here!'

He raised himself from his greasy sheets and stared into the hot gloom.

'Ahmed! Ahmed!'

A shuffle of bare feet and two or three dim figures slipped into the room. They stood patiently by the door while Johnnie went into his customary morning pantomime of bellows and curses, interspersed with shrieks of pain at the suffering caused to his head by the volume of his own voice. When he was hoarse, they padded silently to his bedside and stood with folded hands, watching his frowsy, panting, bent figure as he sat on the edge of his bed quite spent with his own temper. After a considerable pause, he slowly raised his head and gazed at them with small red eyes.

'Clean linen. All clean linen. White breeches and my

blue flowered coat. My new wig. And cane. And a bottle of champagne.'

'But, sahib—'

'Now!' Johnnie roared.

They scattered. There was, as usual, no clean linen, but some was most certainly cleaner than others, and, if resourcefully folded and pressed with the flat of the hand, might pass. Sahib Gates's vision was none too good this morning. The blue flowered coat had suffered a muddy tumble in a brawl several nights before, and no-one had troubled to clean it, but if it were carefully presented to Sahib Gates with the back prudently concealed, what would be the harm in it? As for the wig and wine – ah, there mercifully there was no trouble, since no mice had yet taken up residence in the former, and the latter was the only commodity Sahib Gates made sure he never lacked.

An hour later, momentarily fortified by the champagne, Johnnie set forth in his somewhat grubby splendour. Shaved, scented, adorned with his single remaining ring – the sircar had plans for substituting an infinitely inferior copy but his cousin the jeweller had been so busy lately – and swinging his cane, Johnnie mounted his horse and set off in his personal cavalcade of ramshackle servants to the house of Mrs Rathbone. She occupied a house just on the edge of the desirable area of Garden Reach, and thus Fort William lay between her and Johnnie's less distinguished abode.

Johnnie had reason to be grateful to Mrs Rathbone. Though her husband might be the most unobservant upon earth, and though she might rejoice in the nickname of 'the Officers' Comforter', she was a generous and affectionate woman and boasted many true and loyal friends among those she had comforted. Some weeks before, she had come upon Johnnie sprawled unconscious on a staircase after dinner, his ludicrous wig tumbled off, revealing a tousle of dark curls, and a temporary air of attractive boyishness. She had summoned her servants, had them load Johnnie into her carriage, and had driven him home with her. She had left her fond husband a note to say she had retired with a migraine, knowing full well that port would have rendered him incapable of reading in any case, and took Johnnie to bed. He awoke in a surprising and unfamiliar multiplicity of frills and pink pillows, warmly – too warmly – cushioned by the affectionate amplitude of Mrs Rathbone. Falling upon her hopeful bosom he burst into tears and told her the whole story of his boyhood flirtation and how it had led to the jaws of matrimony that were about to close inexorably upon him.

'Silly boy,' Mrs Rathbone said cosily. 'Silly boy. Marriage will make you ever so much more comfortable, for sure it will. And if she's a nice girl, a sweet girl, as I am sure she is, she will not mind your visiting old friends just once in a while, now will she?'

Johnnie tried looking gratefully at Mrs Rathbone, but found her too close for comfort at this hour of the day. He edged away across the bed, took Mrs Rathbone's plump hand in his and kissed it.

'That is what George Carew told me.'

'Then George Carew is a sensible boy. Now then, when does your sweetheart come?'

Johnnie winced and fell back among the little pillows.

'In three weeks. She arrives on the *Sea Horse*. What am I to do with her?'

Mrs Rathbone gave Johnnie a playful nudge.

'As if you needed telling, you naughty boy! If I were to tell Mr Rathbone what you did—'

Johnnie put his hand over her mouth.

'Please!'

'Of course, I won't, silly boy: I'm no simpleton, I promise you and I believe in offering help where I can. So help you I will, and Miss Harding shall stop with me until your wedding day, and I shall befriend her and show her round the city.'

Johnnie looked about at the mirrors and gilding and plump pink furniture of Mrs Rathbone's room and contrasted it with the austerity of Parson Harding's study which was the only room he had ever been into in the Parsonage. Caroline would be like a cob nut in a dish of Turkish delight here, but it was a brave offer, indeed it was, and it got him out of a devilish hole. What else was he to do with her? Old Rathbone was a reasonable sort after all, said to be of quite good family, and the Officers' Comforter had a heart of gold even if her antecedents were unmentionable. He turned his head towards her.

'I thank you for that, indeed I do. And I accept your offer with the deepest gratitude.'

Mrs Rathbone wriggled coyly and pouted.

'Aren't you going to thank me, Johnnie? Thank me properly?'

Johnnie raised himself on one elbow, and swallowed.

'You know how I like men to say thank you, Johnnie boy, don't you?'

With a sigh and closed eyes, Johnnie flung himself across her.

Now, a month later, he was riding to escort her down to the quay. The tide was just right this morning, and all the tenders on to which passengers from the *Sea Horse* had been unloaded in the Ganges delta were due in at noon. By the dinner hour he would have seen Caroline again, and know the worst. This ride down the Hooghly to Garden Reach was the last entirely free ride he would ever have, the last time when he was able to do as he chose, and he alone. He looked at the dishevelled servants about him in the rags and tags of livery they wore as a sort of token to him, and envied them bitterly for their freedom. He looked about at Calcutta, blue and green and white in the spring sunshine, and thought of the free happy men everywhere in it, free to enjoy this gayest and wickedest of cities and not have to account for their every move to a wife. Engulfed in self-pity, he rode gloomily on.

Mrs Rathbone was not ready for him. There was a flurry of little shrieks from upstairs, followed by the startling appearance of Mrs Rathbone with her hair girlishly about her shoulders, clad in a peignoir the dhobi had not seen for some while. She kissed Johnnie warmly, emanating little stale puffs of last night's powders and pomades, rang for wine for him, and promised she would be but a moment. Johnnie drank his madeira in solitude, gazing miserably at his overstuffed, overdecorated surroundings, musing on his lot until he reached the conclusion that he even envied Mr Rathbone for the luxury of having such an accommodating wife. Caroline would never be like that, never. She would be shocked and resentful and priggish, and she was going to make his life a straitjacket.

Mrs Rathbone tripped in after an hour in a heavily embroidered gown of baby blue, looped up to show ruffled scarlet petticoats. There seemed to be a good deal of gold lace and fringing about her person, and she held yellow gloves and a parasol encrusted with embroidery in seed pearls and silver thread. She kissed Johnnie on the cheek.

'Do you like me, Johnnie dear? On the quiet side, I know, but I do not wish to alarm Miss Harding that we are too dressy here in India.'

'Admirable,' Johnnie said faintly.

The drive to the waterfront was not comfortable. Mrs Rathbone, delighted to be escorted by Johnnie, and equally delighted to be of service, waved and blew kisses to the smallest acquaintances they passed. The road was busy, for the *Sea Horse* was the first East Indiaman to put in for some weeks, and Calcutta was eager for news and letters and new faces.

'Is it not delightful, Johnnie? Are you not elated? I do not know when I have been so well amused! Look – look, I am sure that is Mrs Russell waving from her carriage – but no, I fear it – oh, but Colonel Bridgeman is bowing to me so nicely, Johnnie, and dear Mr Hicks, and that naughty Miss Glazer, what a wicked girl she is!'

By the time they reached the waterfront Johnnie wished to plunge into the river and drown. Sick with apprehension and misery, his head pounding and his face scarlet from his embarrassing journey, he felt his life had reached its lowest ebb. Because of Mrs Rathbone's delay, the tenders had all been in some time, and the quayside was a teeming confusion of Indians, passengers, soldiers, baggage and cargo. She was here then. Somewhere in this mêlée his fate awaited him. He glanced at Mrs Rathbone's rainbow finery and made a small but firm decision.

'I pray you will wait here in the safety of the carriage. I should hate to risk you being injured after all your kindness to me. I will go and find Miss Harding and bring her to the carriage.'

Bridling with pleasure at what she took to be the intended inference of 'all your kindness to me', Mrs Rathbone agreed. She watched Johnnie climb awkwardly from the carriage, then settled herself back to wave and smile at the crowd jostling by her.

Caroline and General North had been waiting on the quayside a full half-hour. Isobel had pleaded to be allowed to remain, too, but a magnificent person by the name of Sir Edward Ashton, with a posse of immaculate servants and a chaperoning widow of impeccable appearance, had swept her off. Caroline was desolate to see her go, but somewhat comforted by feeling that she did not want Isobel's perspicacious eye upon Johnnie at the same moment as her own. General North, staunch to the end, had offered to escort her until her betrothed arrived, and if he failed to show up, to take her to his old friends, Colonel and Mrs Clifton, who would welcome her as a daughter. As she stood on the hot busy waterfront, Caroline would gladly have exchanged being Mrs Gates for being Miss Clifton. She was disappointed with herself for being too full of misgivings to appreciate fully that her feet were now firmly on Indian soil for the first time, and these hordes of dark-skinned people were her first sight of real Indians. Suffocating in her boat cloak and unsuitable bonnet, she stood by General North, and waited.

They waited for an hour, while Johnnie plunged up and down through the crowds, uncertain of what he was looking for, and terrified of finding it. At last he found the *Sea Horse*'s captain and enlisted his help. He was directed back the way he had now been a dozen times, and told to look for a tall woman in a grey cloak, accompanied by a stout distinguished-looking soldier of sixty or so years of age. Ten feet away, Johnnie saw the grey cloak and almost panicked. He could not see her face, only the heavily pleated side of her blue calash, but as he dithered behind the bales and boxes that separated them, she turned and saw him. In the long moment before those glimmering eyes registered recognition, Johnnie took in her thinnness and plainness and unfashionableness and felt his heart plummet with dismay. She looked twenty years older, not ten, and had a maiden-auntish air that dismayed him unutterably.

Caroline's own feelings were no better. She had turned her head in no particular enquiry a moment before, and had seen a stout, florid, overdressed man in a wig like a cauliflower, and a coat of a colour that became summer skies but not his particular girth or complexion. Something in his eyes, his small and anxious smile, made her look a second longer and in that second, she saw the smile melt from his face, and that face resolve itself into a gross caricature of Johnnie Gates. She put out a shaking hand and grasped General North by the sleeve.

'Well, my dear?'

Awkwardness and confusion followed. Neither Caroline nor Johnnie knew what to say, and General North could ill-suppress his surprise and disapproval. In a series of inarticulate questions and half-finished remarks, the three of them fumbled their way back to the carriage, and the multicoloured glory of Mrs Rathbone. General North shot one horrified look at her and pulled Caroline abruptly away from the carriage.

'My dear Miss Harding, you cannot go with such people, indeed you cannot. I cannot allow it.'

Mrs Rathbone, delighted to recognize General North, was calling from the carriage.

'Have no fear, General, Miss Harding will come to no harm. I shall personally see that she don't, indeed I shall. She shall stop with me until her wedding day, and I shall be like a mother to her.'

Caroline looked at the carriage and its occupant and at large, wretched Johnnie, and then back at General North's anxious face. Resisting the strong temptation to cast herself upon his gallantry she whispered quickly, 'I am quite determined to go, General. I thank you from the bottom of my heart for all your kindness, but I shall be quite safe, I do assure you, and I must go.'

She pressed his arm and moved quickly towards the carriage, smiling up at Mrs Rathbone.

'It is truly kind of you to shelter me, madam, and I am very much obliged to you.'

'Nonsense, my dear, I shall enjoy it, and so, I hope, will you. Now up you get – no, no, let the servants help you – and we can get busy being friends, eh?'

General North appeared in the carriage doorway.

'Madam, do you still live in the Garden Reach?'

Mrs Rathbone dimpled and tapped his knuckles with her fan.

'Indeed I do, General, and I shall be ever so pleased to have you call.'

'I enquired,' General North said firmly, 'since I wished to have your permission to call upon Miss Harding. There are friends who will be very anxious for news of her.'

'Call when you like, General dear, and if Miss Harding and I are not dressed, then it will be your lucky day, will it not?'

The door closed, and the carriage jolted forward. If Johnnie had wished Mrs Rathbone a million miles away on the journey to the waterfront, he was, on the return journey, profoundly thankful for her chattering presence. With a plump bejewelled hand on Caroline's knee, she prattled away steadily, and Caroline, though startled by her appearance, could not but be grateful for her generosity and desire to please. She hardly dared glance at Johnnie, but sat with her eyes fixed upon Mrs Rathbone, thankful there was so much about the lady to look at. She was not listening to the endless stream of revelations about dress, and people's private lives and the latest wickedness of Mr Francis, another member of the Company's Council in Calcutta, but instead felt herself to be in a state of stupefaction, induced by the sheer improbability of what was happening. The ship had in the end become a reality, a small intense reality, peopled with a tight little group of friends, the first friends she had ever made on her own. Then, just as the ship had become a world in itself, a world to be relied upon, the Ganges delta had been reached, the mouth of the Hooghly, and that safe small world had been broken up abruptly and dumped anyhow in tender boats, and the sense of improbability had begun. All her anchors had been wrenched away, first Isobel's young men to serve in the Company's army, greeted by alarming uniformed officers, then, worst of all, Isobel herself in a whirl of officialdom and grandeur that was both terrifying and yet enviable in its purposefulness, and then General North, helpless in his gallantry in the face of her determination. But that was something to hold on to, was it not? She sat in the hot carriage hardly daring to look from the windows, and knew she had scored a small victory for herself, for Caroline. General North had offered to snatch her like an opportune eagle from a most bizarre fate, and she had said no, the fate was what she had come for and face it she would. She would rather not look at it again, slumped on the opposite seat of the carriage, but she would take it.

Johnnie sat and despaired quietly opposite her. He never had the energy these days to do any more with any emotion, than perform it quietly. Without the stimulus of drink or danger or sexuality, he was a dull dog, he knew it. He shot covert glances at Caroline from beneath frowning brows, and thought what a fool she was to tolerate old Madam Rathbone's chatter, and then worried as to how he should ever introduce such a yellow stick of a creature to George Carew and other cronies. He fought about resentfully in his memory for pictures of young Caroline by the river, on the field path, in the ten-acre meadow, and could only dredge up hazy images of print gowns and eagerness that did his sour present mood no good at all. Her grey dress was hideous, her calash a public disgrace – did they really wear such monstrous bonnets in England? – and her nose – enough to make the world pity him. He thought of Rani for a moment, her supple, caramel-coloured limbs, her shining eyes and hair, and could have wept for himself.

If Mrs Rathbone thought Johnnie hardly played the part of an eager bridegroom, she showed no sign of it. Caroline's appearance had struck her immediately by its ungainliness, but those brilliant silver eyes and that sweet and anxiously smiling mouth had overcome immediately the effect of her drab and clumsy clothing. Mrs Rathbone had decided, with the same maternal warmth that made her collect unconscious young men after dinner parties, that Caroline needed to be looked after and that she, Bella Rathbone, would perform that role.

'Here we are, dear,' she said unnecessarily as the carriage jolted to a halt. 'Home sweet home, and I hope you will come to regard it as such.'

Caroline looked out upon a house like a small replica of Stoke Park, a perfect small English house, set in an incongruously green garden of wholly un-English planting. She stepped out of the carriage on to a street of red dust, and smelt, for the first time away from the powerful odours of the waterfront, the curious sour, sweet, spicy, dusty, human smell of India. There seemed to be trees all about her, exaggerated, brilliant, alien trees, and scarlet and purple and cream and pink blossoms spread and fell all about the garden walls. She would have liked to exclaim at it all, and have run to examine and touch, but the phalanx of liveried Indian servants that lined the beaten dust path to the perfect Palladian-copy door seemed to make that sort of eccentricity impossible.

'A most elegant house, my dear,' Mrs Rathbone was saying, 'so fortunate, you know, to acquire it from dear Colonel Gordon when he went back to England, but it needed to be made more cosy, dear, more like a home, you know.'

Caroline followed Mrs Rathbone within, uncomfortably conscious of the unhappy bulk of her future husband behind her. They moved into a drawing room made dim by the screens of damp grasses at all windows and doorways, and still breathlessly hot, and Caroline perceived in the gloom that it was unlike any room she had ever entered before. There seemed to be a wealth of colours, an extravagance of gold, a proliferation of looking glasses. Every surface was littered, painted, gilded, stuffed and padded. For one brief mad moment, Caroline would have given all she possessed to shriek with laughter, but she pressed a corner of her oppressive cloak to her mouth and stifled it narrowly.

'Johnnie loves this house, do you not, dear? He is always here, you know; I think he feels at home. I like my friends to feel at home. Now, Miss Harding, dear, I shall have you shown to your room, and then we shall all meet again for dinner, shall we not?'

In the dimness, Johnnie made a small inarticulate sound. Caroline, who had no more wish to see him again at dinner, until she had adjusted her thoughts, than he her, said quickly, 'I am sure Mr Gates has a prior arrangement. It seems from what you told me in the carriage that Calcutta is very sociable so I am sure—'

'Indeed, no! Johnnie boy, can you think of dining elsewhere on such a day as this? The day your sweetheart comes to you. Fie, sir—'

'I must beg you to excuse me, ma'am,' Johnnie said on a high note of desperation, 'but Miss – Miss Harding is in a sense right, and I – I have not been at the office all morning, and am sadly behind in my affairs.'

Mrs Rathbone was scarlet with true indignation.

'You are a monstrous, mannerless boy, Johnnie, and do not deserve this sweet creature, indeed you do not! Indeed I feel—'

'Mrs Rathbone,' Caroline pleaded softly, 'let him go. I – I think no ill of it myself, and am quite confused enough by my travels to be glad of dining in a very small company.'

Johnnie shot a grateful glance not quite in her direction since he was terrified of meeting her gaze.

'Tomorrow then!' Mrs Rathbone commanded.

'Tomorrow, ma'am.'

'You will have to be very sprightly to make up for your behaviour today. Now bid farewell nicely to Miss Harding.'

'Until – until tomorrow, Miss Harding.'

His lips did not touch her hand.

'Good day, Mr Gates.'

By the time they met again in the overstuffed splendour of Mrs Rathbone's drawing room, Caroline had tried to spend twenty-four solemn hours with her thoughts. It had not been easy to do. Mrs Rathbone had wished to drive out and show her every inch of the glittering city, in the hopes also that members of its glittering populace might

162

be in evidence, but Caroline had pleaded weariness, and had managed to secure an evening and morning to herself in her lavish blue silk bedroom. Mr and Mrs Rathbone had confined themselves to a very small dinner party the previous afternoon, a mere dozen or so of overdressed and voluble people, and Caroline had felt no compunction in slipping away to her room – the moment port began to circulate and the favourite Calcutta game of bread-pellet throwing was at its height. Her hosts she felt were warm-hearted and good-natured, but their guests left her bewildered and dumb.

The morning was little better. She succeeded in persuading Mrs Rathbone that she must be left alone, but nothing seemed to daunt a steady flow of servants – amazing to her – wishing to dress her, dress her hair, manicure her nails and generally give her the kind of service she had never had in her life. A few spoke some words of English, most spoke only their native tongue, all were unobtrusive, smiling and astonished at her reluctance to be decorated. After futile attempts to make them leave her alone, she submitted miserably, so that by the time the dinner hour came she felt quite unlike herself and in the most distracted of humours. To come downstairs to the drawing room and find it full of brocade coats and spangled gowns, elaborately powdered heads and towering wigs, was no consolation. She felt protective and slightly defiant of her old blue silk gown and unpowdered hair and quite dismayed at the prospect before her.

'Ah, Caroline, my dear,' Mrs Rathbone cried, 'come forward, dear, so they may all see my new little English friend. There now! And where is naughty Johnnie, who is to be the lucky man! – there you are, you bad boy, now come along that we may all see you together.'

Cowering and wretched they stood together in a ring of false applause. Most of the women could scarcely restrain their amusement at Caroline's appearance, nor the men their barely concealed relief that she was poor

Gates's lot, not theirs. In that particularly shallow and gossiping circle, Caroline felt a small gratitude for Johnnie's presence, and Johnnie wished he was on the edge of the circle rather than at the centre of it.

'I – I hope you are comfortable here,' he said.

'Oh, quite. It is most good of Mrs Rathbone to shelter me. I do not know what else I should have done.'

Johnnie refrained from saying, 'Nor I' in heartfelt tones.

'General North called at my office this morning.'

He was dismayed to see Caroline's face light up with eagerness. He knew it was a blunder to let her stay here, but what more suitable houses could she have gone to? He knew no others – at least, none to whom he could apply for favours.

'Oh – how kind of him!'

'He gave me this for you.'

It was a note in Isobel's writing. Johnnie knew quite well who it was from, from whose house it had come, and what it contained, since he had read it. It did not improve his temper. Caroline took it eagerly and thanked him with real warmth. It was their first exchange alone, and it was terminated then by the announcement of dinner.

From the menu card held in an elaborate gilt fleur-de-lis before her, Caroline saw that seven courses were between her and escape. The array of glasses before her was prodigious, and the baskets of fruit that marched down the centre of the table would have supplied Stoke Abbas with such luxuries for months. Johnnie was on her left, and an empty chair was, to her relief, on her right.

'Do not feel neglected, my dear,' Mrs Rathbone said, laying a gloved hand upon her shoulder. 'A very special guest is coming to fill up that place of honour. Your Johnnie's greatest friend, George Carew.'

Johnnie blanched. It was insupportable. He had had no chance to warn George of his fate. What would George think of him, saddled with this prissy scarecrow for life?

He took up his champagne glass and swallowed the contents at a single gulp. It was instantly refilled, and as instantly emptied. Red-headed Mrs Grundy on his left, who had often much enjoyed him as a dinner companion and whiler-away of midnight hours, regarded him with a slight and cynical smile. Johnnie observed it. Caroline sat silent and tongue-tied. She wanted to ask Johnnie if they might meet somehow quite alone, but found it an impossible subject to breach. She looked furtively at him now and then, and was distressed to see the anger and misery that chased each other over his reddening countenance, but mostly she merely looked down at her soup and decided that, given the temperature of the room, nothing had ever looked more inappropriate or unappetizing.

The chair on her right was pulled back.

'Miss Harding, I believe? No, no, pray do not rise. I am unforgivably late. M'name's George Carew.'

'I am delighted to meet you. I believe you are a great friend—'

'Of the abominable animal's? 'Deed I am. Confounded hot, ain't it?'

'Why do we eat hot soup in this heat?'

'Deuced if I know, Miss Harding. Johnnie! Johnnie! Good day to you, sir. You've picked yourself a sensible woman here.'

'I have?' Johnnie said in genuine surprise.

'Don't care to drink hot soup in hot weather. What else don't you care for, Miss Harding?'

'Being made mock of, Mr Carew,' Caroline said boldly.

George Carew laid down his spoon and raised his glass to her.

'Caught red-handed, Miss Harding. Humble apologies.'

'Are you a Company man, also, Mr Carew?'

'For my sins, ma'am. How d'you like Calcutta?'

'I've not seen it yet. I arrived but yesterday and have been asleep or surrounded by servants since.'

'Won't change, won't change. That's how Calcutta is. Servants, sleep and much of this.'

He raised his glass again.

'Drink with me, Miss Harding.'

She shook her head.

'Why won't you?'

Caroline said levelly, 'I'll keep a clear head until I know more about you all.'

'My turn to be mocked, Miss Harding?'

'You must please yourself about that,' Caroline said daringly.

By dessert, Caroline was grateful for George Carew. Johnnie had said nothing whatsoever throughout dinner, but had eaten and drunk with the relentlessness of a man seeking both occupation and oblivion. Through soup and fish, mutton chops and quails, syllabubs and pineapple and all their accompanying wines, Caroline had watched him steadily plough. If it had not been for George Carew, she would have had no alternative but to gaze at her plate.

'Do guzzle, eh?' George said at one point, indicating Johnnie and a mountain of mutton chops. Caroline, who felt about hot meat as she felt about hot soup, preferred not to look.

At the end of dinner, Mrs Rathbone, pink with cherry brandy and heavily supported by the gentlemen on either side of her, rose to her feet.

'I wish to propose a toast, my dear! I – I wish to propose a toast of long life and happiness to my young friends, Miss Caroline Harding, and naughty Johnnie Gates! Now charge your glasses and drink with me!'

There was a good deal of roaring and shouting and everyone round the table rose unsteadily to their feet. Caroline dared not look at Johnnie. After a while the roaring subsided and George Carew hissed in her ear.

'Stand and say thank'ee, Miss Harding! They expect it, 'deed they do!'

Caroline looked at him in horror.

'Must I?'

''Pon my word, you must. Stand up and raise your glass and thank 'em. You too, Johnnie. Up we go!'

With a sensation of being fifteen foot high, Caroline rose to resounding cheers, her glass shaking in her hand. She raised it and felt the contents splash on to her hand.

'I thank you all,' she said, and her voice sounded small and unfamiliar and far away.

More cheers and shouts of 'On your legs!' to Johnnie. George went to the back of his chair and put his hands under Johnnie's armpits.

'Up, boy!'

Slowly, very slowly, Johnnie wavered to his feet. He raised his glass to Mrs Rathbone, drank from it, then prompted by shouts from the crowd tried to raise it to Caroline, failed and crashed prone, like a falling tree across the table, scattering pineapples as if they were no more than billiard balls.

There was a dead and expectant silence, while all eyes slowly turned and came to rest enquiringly upon Caroline. They were used to drunkenness, but was she? They waited, hopefully.

Caroline looked up from Johnnie's unconscious back.

'Would two gentlemen be good enough to help Mr Gates to somewhere more comfortable?'

'Bravo!' George Carew said under his breath.

Mrs Rathbone was mopping her eyes. All the romping that usually seemed so acceptable and amusing appeared deeply, dreadfully wrong in front of Caroline.

'Oh, my dear Miss Harding, my poor Caroline. Oh, forgive me dear—'

'There is nothing to forgive, Mrs Rathbone. You are hardly to blame. Mr Carew, would you escort Mr Gates home, since he clearly cannot take himself?'

George Carew bowed, and followed Johnnie's dragging figure from the room. Caroline, feeling that she could no longer bear that ring of incredulous and scornful eyes, went quickly after him, Mrs Rathbone sniffing and apologizing in her wake.

'I should have seen it coming, Miss Harding dear, indeed I should. Lord knows I've seen a boy with a skinful often enough! But before you, Miss Caroline! Oh, I could die of shame!'

Caroline put her hand on Mrs Rathbone's arm.

'Please do not distress yourself, Mrs Rathbone, pray be calm! I may not be as experienced in these matters as you are, but I have seen a deal of illness, and in many ways there is not much to choose between them. Come now, dry your eyes! It is hardly your fault, now is it?'

'For you to see him in such a state, Miss Caroline! For him to behave in such a way the moment his sweetheart comes!'

Caroline looked up and met George Carew's amused gaze.

'I feel that that may have everything to do with it,' she said.

George bowed again.

'You've a clear head on your shoulders, Miss Harding.'

Caroline smiled a little nervously and said in a low voice, 'It seems that I shall need it.'

'Oh come, come, Miss Harding! A douche of cold water and a bit of rest and he will be right as a trivet!'

'Until the next time.'

George Carew cleared his throat and did not reply.

'Oh, Miss Harding, dear!' Mrs Rathbone cried suddenly. 'Mr Gates and yourself were bidden to sup with General Russell this evening! And now what shall we do?'

Caroline gazed at her incredulously, visions of mounds of mutton chops dancing before her eyes.

'Supper, Mrs Rathbone? Supper? After – all this?'

'Oh yes, Miss Harding dear, it is quite the custom. You will find Calcutta very gay, will she not, George? We always sup at a late hour and hardly a week goes by without some dance or even a ball. We are never dull here in India, I do assure you.'

'I think, Mrs Rathbone, that I shall have to be a little dull to begin with, at least until I feel a little less disorientated. I hope General Russell will forgive me if I do not attend but I—' she looked across at Johnnie's bulk sprawled upon a sofa, 'I had rather not appear alone.'

'You'll not be alone!' George Carew cried. 'We'll swill the old chum out and he'll escort you, I swear it!'

Caroline shrank back a little.

'No – no, I thank you but no. Will you oblige me greatly, Mr Carew, by taking Mr Gates home, and – and would you tell him,' she added, gathering courage, 'that I shall call upon him at noon tomorrow – that is, ma'am, if I may borrow your carriage?'

'Certainly, my dear, with the greatest pleasure in the world.'

George Carew motioned to several of Johnnie's servants who had materialized by some sort of instinct in the doorway, that they were to bear away their master. He turned back to Caroline and said in a voice of undisguised admiration, 'You are a woman of spirit, Miss Harding, and I hand it to you, 'deed I do. He'll await you at noon, ma'am, if I have to lash him to his chair.'

He bowed to Caroline, kissed Mrs Rathbone's hand and went out.

'Will you not think me unpardonably rude, Mrs Rathbone, if I go to my room? I am so sorry to be such a poor-spirited guest, but I feel that I must – must think a while.'

Mrs Rathbone patted her hand with no small relief. An uproarious party was going on now behind the closed dining-room doors, and it seemed a shame that she, the hostess, should miss it all.

'Not at all, dear, very wise, very wise indeed. I'll have tea sent up to you later, dear. You'd like that, would you not? Remind you of home.'

'You are most kind,' Caroline said faintly, and escaped. Mrs Rathbone watched her fleeing through doors that were silently opened as she came, and then with the pleasure before her of making something of an entrance, turned back to the riotous remains of her dinner party.

Alone in the hot silence of her room, Caroline eagerly pulled out her note from Isobel. It seemed much crumpled, but that was probably the effect of spending two or three hours in her pocket. She took it to a window, where the afternoon sun might fall upon it, and felt a lump rise in her throat at the sight of that familiar handwriting.

My dearest Caroline,

I am quite desolate without you and my desolation is made much worse by anxiety. I am staying in a most stiff and proper house, and should suffocate instantly except that the maids are an excellent source of gossip and most speak good English. But I do not like the gossip, I do not at all like it. They say your John Gates is a depraved and licentious man, and they make fun of him for his style of dress. If you allow for the exaggeration of gossip, that still makes him a man grossly unworthy of you. Oh Caroline, do be careful! I beg you not to let your stiff and silly pride lead you into something rash! Both the General and Sir Edward forbid me to visit you where you are, but I shall find your address from the servants and come. I am in a ferment to see you. Why do you not come to me? I beg you to – Sir Edward would welcome you.

Yours in frenzy,
Isobel

Dear Isobel! Caroline looked up from the letter and out on to that strange brilliant green garden with its high mud walls and still tanks of water. She must not let herself see Isobel yet, much as she longed to. If she did, the whole beautiful allure of that confident world Isobel inhabited would sweep her away, undermine her resolve. The first person she must see, must be Johnnie. There was something at the bottom of all this, some explanation for his apparent ardour while she was safely far away, and his evident panic now she was close at hand. Perhaps his easy charm of ten years ago was all he had ever had and now it had gone for ever, its absence to be compensated for now with wine. Depending on the outcome of her visit to Johnnie, she would then decide about seeing Isobel. In the meantime she would write to her, reassuringly, very reassuringly. She crossed the room and rang for paper and ink.

II

Caroline hardly slept that night. The dreamlike sense of unreality, that had possessed her since her arrival and prevented her from feeling things too keenly, was slipping gradually away and leaving her to face facts unaided. The first fact she had to face during those long black rustling hours was that it was amazingly, incredibly hot. Mrs Rathbone had said it was still the cold season, if only by a matter of weeks, but Caroline had never experienced such laughable coldness in her life. As she lay and tried not to toss, her whole skin seemed damp, steaming damp, and the heavy black air about her bed seemed to have the density of hot velvet. Her hair was damp, her sensible cotton nightgown was damp, her pillow and sheet were damp. How on earth, she wondered, could those men at dinner today endure those layers of stiffened, gold-laced brocade, those great white wigs, cravats like perfect explosions of lace? And the women had been no freer, beneath towering wigs adorned with entire harvests of fruit and flowers and jewels, and although bare-bosomed, they still trailed pro-digious quantities of heavy silk about with them. Caroline had been very grateful for her cotton gowns during the daytime, and felt that her one silk was too shabby to matter spoiling, as it was bound to become. She had not believed it possible to sweat so much. Suppose one simply dried right out, like a husk or leaf, and blew away over the Ganges delta, unnoticed and quickly forgotten?

The second fact, even worse in its way, was the noises. Every so often there came a terrible anguished squeal, as of a child in pain, and each time it came Caroline would leap from her pillow, her throat constricted in apprehension. She had never heard a jackal call before, for General North's education had not extended to the sounds these beasts made, and every scream filled her with new terror. She began to wait for each next one, stiff and wide-eyed, straining to hear through the comfortable whirr of the crickets that soul-tearing shriek of sorrow and pain. In the intervals between the jackals, she could hear too the thin high drone of mosquitoes, wheeling and whining about in the dead hot air, many of them finding a successful entry through the shrouds of white gauze that wrapped her bed, and leaving her crazed with itchings. Starting up, casting herself down, thrashing and scratching, she gazed at the blackness of the windows and longed for the first glimmer of day.

When at long last it came, the sunrise was marvellous. A rosy glow began to steal through the billowing muslin and blue silk with which Mrs Rathbone had draped the windows and Caroline rose thankfully from her crumpled and unrefreshing bed and went to see what was happening. The skyline was sharply etched to the east in indigo, a skyline of flat-roofed dwellings, of trees, tall coconut palms with waving fronds, and the occasional dome and tower against an exploding apricot sky. The dreadful screams and rustlings of the night were giving way to more distinct sounds as the Rathbones's servants began to stir in their quarters, and the day was started in the small mud huts and houses beyond the garden walls. Plumes of blue smoke began to rise here and there, and with them curious cooking smells, strongly redolent of charcoal. She had spoken to no Indian successfully yet, she thought, a lack that must be quickly remedied. The little maids that had been sent to attend her remained dumb and smiling as they deftly fastened her gowns and brushed her hair. She hoped her tone conveyed what her vocabulary could not when she thanked them.

She breakfasted alone in the stuffy dining room, still faintly and unattractively redolent of last afternoon's cigars and mutton. She was brought toast and tea and butter, and the incongruous Englishness of it, in this opulent English room, made her smile to herself. She wondered if the silent servants who brought it thought it a curious meal and what had they eaten for breakfast instead. Rice perhaps? Scraps left from yesterday's banquet?

'Thank you,' she said.

They bowed.

'Will there be anything else the memsahib is wanting?'

'Nothing at all, thank you, until the carriage just before noon.'

There were three hours to think about that carriage drive, but Caroline resolved to be firm with herself and not to dwell on it. She would begin by a thorough tour of the garden, unadventurous perhaps, but a beginning.

The maids already busy in her room were horrified to see her come upstairs herself for her hat. They fluttered about her with little exclamations of dismay, tying the ribbons under her chin with light little butterfly touches. One held up a creamy pink flower with curved spikes for petals that Caroline did not recognize for her to smell. It gave off a rich, exotic, powerful fragrance. Caroline felt it tucked into the ribbon of her hat, another into the sash of her gown. Then they held up a looking-glass for her to see, and she felt it was so wrong that these little girls, so brown and pretty and doe-eyed, should be concerned with the adornment of a stiff plain spinster like herself. But they were so pleased with her, and with their efforts, that she smiled at each, and thanked them warmly, and they ran to open the door for her.

She felt a little leap of pleasure as she went into the garden. It was not fresh and cool and full of promise as an English spring garden would be, but the luxuriant and brilliant greenness was a balm to the eye after the heavily decorated interior of Mrs Rathbone's house. The garden

174

had been laid out with the sort of formality Caroline recognized from engravings she had seen of French gardens, symmetrical shapes of grass and gravel bordered with low box hedges, and brilliant unfamiliar flowers blooming in regimented patterns in formal beds of sifted red earth. Gardeners in loin cloths were crouched all over the garden on their haunches, neatly weeding with thin brown fingers, but when Caroline spoke to them in what she hoped was a gentle and congratulatory tone, they fell on their knees before her and made her feel abashed and uncomfortable. There were little water boys everywhere, with great earthenware crocks of water, to be sprinkled with reverence. It was all perfectly fascinating. Beyond the stretch of formal garden, Caroline found a wilder part in which she felt much more comfortable, where there was no gravel, only a stretch of elephant grass unevenly bordered with wonderful blossoming shrubs and trees, the blossoms in brilliant colours of scarlet and pink, purple and orange. She found one great beautiful white camellia with a scent like wine, and sat herself down in its shade to look at the splendours about her.

Shortly before twelve, she retraced her steps to the house, and waited in the drawing room for the carriage. Her calm solitary morning had both revived and soothed her spirits, and she felt, if not exactly prepared for the coming interview, at least not panic-struck with fear at the thought of it. She would not go upstairs to look at herself in the glass since she knew full well there was little point in that, but sat and waited in the dimness and heat and thought how infinitely preferable the camellia tree had been.

The carriage was punctual and emblazoned with gorgeous and thoroughly spurious-looking arms. Four servants in matching livery waited while Caroline climbed in, and she observed with a private twinge of amusement that their clothing was infinitely more splendid than her plain cream muslin. There was a pair of magnificently matched chestnuts to draw her, and a perfect army of servants to escort her. For a brief moment, which she despised herself for, she wished Lady Lennox could see her. They trotted forward over the smooth red dust road, and Caroline, having no Mrs Rathbone to distract her, watched eagerly from the window, determined to miss nothing, no detail of her drive.

She had not realized, when Mrs Rathbone had said that she lived on the edge of Garden Reach, how literal her hostess was being; but almost the moment the carriage left the coconut-fronded avenue outside the house, it plunged into quite another world. The green and white impression was gone, and in its place came a yellow and red impression, dusty and raw and dry. Leaving the smooth road, they began to lurch down lanes that were no more than rutted tracks, hard dun ridges of baked mud, between dwellings that Caroline at first mistook for mere piles of building rubble, such disordered heaps of planks and mud and mouldy matting they were. They huddled and straggled along the edges of these jolting tracks, the only shade afforded to them being from grotesque bearded trees, whose matted brownish tassels hung down from the branches like sheaves of unkempt hair. In the shade of these banyans were groups of squatting people, thin dark people in ragged cotton, their heads bound in cloths against the sun.

Dogs sniffed at the rubbish strewn everywhere, thin, dreadful limping dogs, and bare-bottomed children in tattered shirts squatted in the dust among goats and flies and mooning white cows. The children waved and smiled to her, the crouching adults raised faces with no animosity in them to her elaborate equipage, and went on calmly peeling oranges, fastidiously tearing away shreds of pith, and leaving the earth scattered with bright peels. The smells of poverty that drifted in to Caroline were very different from the smells of those poor cottages at Stoke Abbas; those stank of earth and mould and damp human dirtiness, but this powerful smell in Calcutta reminded Caroline strongly of the ancient dog at the Parsonage, tolerated solely because of his age, but banished always to the kitchen regions because of his almost tangible smelliness.

Eventually, these alarming lanes dwindled away somewhat, and the carriage entered small streets, not identifiable as such by their roadways which were of dried yellow mud as before, but because the hovels had given place to box-like mud houses, almost windowless to defeat the sun. Some of the houses were evidently in European occupation, with bright patches of garden and curtains at the glassless windows and an air of gentle activity that the presence of several servants gives. Occasionally, a house had clearly been modelled upon European style also, with steps up to double-leaved doors, and windows arranged with careful symmetry above and either side of them.

With a sinking presentiment that they were almost at their destination, Caroline's gaze fixed itself with almost prophetic certainty upon one of these small mud copies of houses upon Richmond Hill. It was yellow, like all the others, with a shallow flight of steps to a door beneath a chipped and crumbling portico that owed nothing to Greek art but the inspiration. The twin-leaved door had once been painted a dull terracotta, but this had almost all flaked off, leaving the gasping grey wood cracking beneath. Rows of dusty windows confronted a space of dun rubble that might once have been designated a garden, and among the piles of stones it contained, crouched several children, mostly naked except for bracelets.

When the carriage actually stopped before this spectacle, she saw with some dismay that she was evidently expected. A double row of servants lined the shallow flight of steps to the front door which itself was instantly opened to the dark interior. The livery this respectful double file wore was, she noticed, hardly fit to be exposed to the merciless brilliance of the sun, being both tattered and filthy, each garment only vaguely approximating to the size and shape of its wearer. She stepped out of Mrs Rathbone's gaudy but well-maintained carriage, and mounted the steps between these lines of calm-faced scarecrows, observing further as she went upwards that all the rubbish that had clearly littered the steps before her arrival, had been shuffled away by twenty pairs of bare feet in haste, and now lay in squalid profusion behind the rows of dark servants' legs. It was an inauspicious start to a daunting interview.

If George Carew had not arrived promptly at ten o'clock that morning and pummelled Johnnie mercilessly into consciousness, Caroline would probably have found him still deep in the slumber of the unjust. The night before he had indeed gone out again, a bucket of water being, as George had pointed out, all he needed to restore his wits to some semblance of order, and had proceeded to repeat the performance which had taken place at Mrs Rathbone's dinner party. He had not intended to specifically, but as all he sought at this moment was oblivion, however temporary, drunkenness was, for Johnnie, inevitable. George Carew had worked very hard on him for two hours, since the former had conceived a surprised, but undoubted admiration for Caroline the night before, and he now sat and shook in the drawing room, clad in the cleanest clothes George could find from a wholly dubious wardrobe. He was pouring with sweat, the cold sweat of apprehension mingling with the customary steam in which the occupants of Calcutta lived, and his every coherent thought, few though they were, concerned the desperate impasse to which his affairs had come. If George had not been lounging at the window, apparently relaxed but in reality ready to tackle Johnnie bodily should he so much as stir, he would have fled.

'Mis' Memsahib Harding, sahib.'

The drawing room was very dim, for the windows were screened with great blinds of dampened grasses, but despite being scarcely able to see Caroline was conscious of a well-proportioned smallish room which exuded a smell of warm mouldiness and dust. There seemed to be little furniture in it, and only pale patches on the walls instead of the pictures that once hung there. The sircar had cousins who repaired furniture broken in brawls and reframed pictures smashed by flying bottles, but somehow the cousins never seemed to disgorge these repairs.

'Good – good day,' Johnnie said in a low voice, his face slightly averted.

George Carew uncoiled himself from his sofa.

'Miss Harding, good day to you! Here's the rogue, good as my word.'

'I am grateful to you,' Caroline said doubtfully.

'Hope you will be, 'deed I do. I shall leave you together, but I'll not be far off, should you want me.'

Caroline curtseyed briefly, George bowed, smiled at her, grinned at Johnnie and left the room, humming. When his footsteps had died away across the hall, a thick silence surged back again into the room and seemed to stifle them.

At last Caroline said with difficulty, 'I hope you will not think me very impertinent, but I do not think I can speak to you in this darkness. Might at least one of the screens be moved?'

'Deuced hot,' Johnnie muttered, for whom the dimness was a comfort.

'Please.'

He barked a command briefly, and a shadow in the corner uncurled itself, and pushed away the screen from a small window at the end of the room. Sunlight blazed in, abruptly illuminating the dust and disorder, the bottles under chairs, books in mouldy confusion here and there, and Johnnie's hungover countenance.

'I have one more request,' Caroline said, looking with distaste about her.

Johnnie inclined his head without speaking. Fixing her level grey gaze upon him, she said gravely, 'Would you do me the great favour of removing your wig? It changes your countenance so entirely that I feel as if I am speaking to a total stranger.'

'Indeed, ma'am—' Johnnie exclaimed, backing away from her.

'Just for this interview, sir. Would you not be cooler without it in any case?'

With an oath, Johnnie tore his wig from his head and flung it into the chaos of a corner. He came closer to Caroline, glaring slightly.

'Do I please you better now, ma'am?'

She looked up at his disordered dark head and saw instantly the vanished and glorious Johnnie captured in this overweight and intemperate caricature.

'Infinitely so. I thank you.'

Grunting, he fetched a chair for her, and placed himself opposite, in the edge of the shadows. Where had that sweet and adoring docility gone, which was about all he could remember of her? She was looking at him, steadily now with those brilliant silvery eyes, and he was not at all sure that some tiny spark of mockery did not lie in them.

'We are in a fix, are we not, Mr Gates?'

He shrugged. She pulled a letter from her pocket and held it out to him.

'If I had believed what is written in that letter, I should have been broken-hearted at your reception of me.'

Unwillingly, Johnnie reached out and took the letter by its very edge. He turned it over and saw Caroline's name written upon it in his own hand, and remembered what George had assisted him to write within.

He said, 'It was written some time ago.'

'It was written after a silence between us of eight years. If eight years had not changed your feelings, I do not see that the one or two since its writing should do so.'

He said nothing, but sat gazing at his nails and hated her. She was his gaoler, his warder, she had come to India to put him in irons, to ruin the remainder of his youth. She seemed to have no sensitivity at all, for she was speaking again, still in that level, calm voice as if she were discussing something of no more consequence than the menus for the day.

'I asked to see you today, because I must discover the truth. I might not have believed this letter, but I did not disbelieve that you still had some desire, however small, to – to marry me. But I arrive here and find that I arouse in you a complete revulsion. You shun me, you can hardly bear to look at or speak to me. So I must conclude that there was more to your offer of marriage than I thought – or perhaps less, since you seem to have none of the feelings I – I hoped for.'

Her voice faltered a little, but she went on.

'You must try to imagine my situation a little. I have no-one, apart from my brothers, all of whom are busy, to turn to. I came to India because I had nowhere else to go and be – because I hoped I was wanted here. I see,' she hurried on self-consciously, 'that I was quite mistaken in that hope, but I am now in something of a predicament, as you must see. You may not – want me, but as I have come here at your instruction, I think you must help me in what I am to do next.'

The sourness of Johnnie's expression had melted a little during this speech with its increasing diffidence of tone. A small understanding of her loneliness flitted briefly, very briefly, across his own vista of self-pity.

'Have you any money, ma'am?'

'None,' she said almost in a whisper.

'Money!' he shouted, suddenly. 'Money! 'Tis true that it is always the root of evil! The lack of it and the need for it drives us to wretchedness, to untold suffering!'

She was looking at him in some perplexity. He got up and went to the window, standing for a moment with his back to her. He said, without turning round, 'If you have no money, ma'am, you are in the same case as I.'

'I – I believed you were employed here by the East—'

'Oh, I am, I am! But I am paid such a trifling sum that a dog could not live upon it!'

She moistened her lips.

'Perhaps I might help you to live upon it?' she suggested anxiously.

Johnnie turned from the window and came to sit quite close to her. Leaning forward, he said heavily, 'You are almost upon the truth of it.'

'I am? I do not—'

'I have little enough now,' Johnnie said, 'but if I do not marry you, I have nothing, no expectations, no future. If I do not marry you, I live like a jackal upon two hundred pounds a year until I die.'

Caroline leaned forward and, with a quite involuntary movement, put her hand upon his. He did not take his away.

'I do not quite understand you, I do not see why this should be.'

'Consider,' he said with something of a sneer, 'consider whose relation I am, to whose tune I must dance.'

Caroline sat bolt upright and said with a sort of angry triumph, 'Lady Lennox!'

'The very same.'

He looked up and saw the bright glitter of fury in Caroline's eyes.

He shrugged.

'Explain to me,' Caroline said in a voice full of anger.

'If you wish. Lady Lennox has contrived it that the fortune that is to come to me from my parents' will shall not be mine unless I marry. It is Lennox money, you see, brought to my father by my mother.' His mouth twisted a little. 'She does not like the way I live, reported to her in all its detail by that lily-livered traitor Frank Lovell, and thus wishes me to be curbed by marriage and its responsibilities.'

'But why should I come into any of this?' Caroline burst out.

'Because – because we once had an understanding, and because you are sober-living and used to poverty—' he looked pointedly at her meagre frame and stopped. Not even Johnnie could say that the other reasons were that no-one else would want a wife so plain, and also because her thin figure seemed ill-suited to the production of children, and thus she would present little threat to the Lennoxes as a producer of heirs.

Caroline looked at his troubled face with her clear gaze, and read his thoughts with unhappy accuracy.

She rose and began to pace about the room, twisting her fingers that were slippery with sweat by now. The heat seemed to intensify the oppression of her thoughts, pressing down upon her brow with a weight as painful as her new knowledge. She was simply a pawn in a game, an ignorant pawn in a sordid little game played by Lady Lennox. No wonder she had been so angry when Caroline had first refused to come to India! No wonder she had been so elated when Caroline capitulated after Parson Harding's death, and had written that infinitely complacent letter of godspeed when Caroline left for Gravesend! All her plans had worked quite wonderfully, quite as she had wished. She had killed two birds, whom she disliked, with one stone, and had ensured thereby that precious Lennox money should revert to her family upon Johnnie's death. Caroline bit her lip and felt herself more angry than she had ever been in her life.

'She shall not win!' she cried. 'We will not marry and she shall not win!'

Johnnie sighed hugely.

'If we do not marry, I am destitute.'

Caroline stopped pacing.

'I had forgotten that.'

'I had not. I never do. It has oppressed me this last year, I am never free from it.'

Caroline had an impulse to cry out, 'And what about me?' but saw the appeal would fall on stony ground and kept her lips tight shut. Johnnie's head was bent, he was clearly, she could see it, immersed in the sad contemplation of his own lucklessness.

She went over to him and said softly, 'All those years ago, did you even mean to marry me then?'

Johnnie looked away from her.

'I cannot say. I do not remember. My aunt and your father were so—'

'Please say no more.'

'But you asked me!'

'And I regretted doing so instantly.'

He shrugged. She walked away again into the hot stale gloom of the room and tried to cudgel her thoughts into some sort of order.

'It would seem to me that there is one sense in which each of us needs the other. You need me to secure your fortune. I need you to keep me from utter destitution.'

'I thought you had great friends here,' he said, not entirely pleasantly. 'I thought you were bosom friends with Miss Grant, now staying with Sir Edward Ashton. Would they not help you?'

'I do not choose to ask them.'

'You are very stiff.'

'Maybe so. I am also very tired of being an object of charity. To be someone's wife would give me a kind of status and an occupation. If I was your wife I would cost you very little as I am sure you have calculated, and in return I would make sure that you were comfortable. I would tidy up those servants and clean up this – this pig-sty, and I would see that your linen and food were as you liked them.'

Johnnie was listening more intently than he seemed to be. George Carew had said this very thing to him once, he distinctly recalled it. Perhaps she was right, perhaps she did have something to offer him, perhaps he might not do so badly after all. He stood up and looked at her. She was as plain as a pikestaff, but her added years had given her some strength of mind, no doubt about that.

'Shall we strike a bargain then?'

Caroline looked at his complacent smile and felt a surge of loathing. The promise of clean linen and swept floors had been all he needed to bring him out of his mood of petty self-indulgence. He had not thought once to ask how she felt, or to reassure her in the smallest way. In a tight voice she said, 'It can only be a bargain. Not a true marriage, only a bargain.'

'Agreed,' he said, and held his hand out. She put hers into it reluctantly and felt it slightly squeezed. When he smiled like that, little stabs of romantic nostalgia went through her. Perhaps she might get to be a little fond of him after all, recover a tiny part of the feelings of ten years ago. She smiled back.

'Your part of the bargain is that you shall support me and give me your name. My part is that I shall run your domestic affairs for you and make your life comfortable.'

He bowed.

'What freedoms will you allow me?'

Caroline thought with revulsion of dinner the day before, but recollected that the bargain allowed for no controls by one party of the other. She at least would stick by that.

'Any you care for – but one.'

'And what is that one, may I ask?'

Caroline hesitated, then said with a burst of courage, 'My bed. I do not want you in my bed.'

Johnnie's brow darkened instantly. It was true that nothing tempted him less than the prospect of making love to Caroline, but no woman in all his philandering life had ever laid down such a ban before. It was an outrage to his virility.

Caroline observed his reaction, and said quickly, 'If you think about it, you will realize I am only denying you something you do not want anyway.'

She suspected Johnnie's sexual habits after two days' conversation with Mrs Rathbone, but she did not wish to dwell on them, nor to give Johnnie overt *carte blanche* to indulge himself freely elsewhere. Those bridges, she decided, she would cross as they came.

'Is it possible that we can be married purely by civil ceremony?'

'There is no church in Calcutta.'

'No church!'

'Morning prayer is, I believe, said in the Customs Office every Sunday.'

Caroline looked relieved.

'I have no fear of desecrating the Customs Office. When should we arrange for – for it?'

Johnnie felt a slight rush of panic.

'You see,' Caroline went on, 'every minute I am still Mrs Rathbone's guest and, as I have already told you, I am anxious not to be in that position any longer. Must banns be read or may we be married soon?'

'George will know,' Johnnie said nervously.

'Will you call him?'

George was summoned, and came in with a quick light step and a distinct gleam in his eye.

'Congratulations in order, you old renegade?'

Johnnie nodded.

'Then my heartiest commiserations to you, Miss Harding! When shall it be?'

'That is just why we wished for your advice, Mr Carew. It must be soon for I have nowhere to go and I wondered if it was necessary for banns to be read?'

'Banns? In Calcutta? Nonsense, Miss Harding, we dispensed with such fripperies long ago. Deuce take it, I'll have you married by Saturday, on my oath I will!'

Three days later, Caroline Harding and John Gates were married in the Customs Office of Calcutta by civil ceremony. The only witnesses were George Carew and Mrs Rathbone, who wore purple silk and gold lace and cried a good deal. Caroline was thankful no-one who knew her was present at the small and shabby ceremony, in which the bride and groom made their promises in tones quite devoid of any conviction and the drone of flies all but obscured their voices in any case. Caroline did not permit herself the indulgence of reflecting upon what she was doing, but went through the motions of the day in as mindless a state as she could manage. A subdued dinner and an even quieter supper followed the wedding, and Caroline went to bed alone on her wedding night, placing a chair back beneath the door handle before she slept since she had observed the lock was broken.

12

For Caroline, the first few weeks of marriage resembled nothing so much as the month of April at Stoke Parsonage, when Eleanor made everyone's life insupportable by relentless spring cleaning. She rose the first morning of finding herself Mrs Gates with the firm intention of making the house immediately habitable, and providing Johnnie with an alternative to his luxurious but dingy linen. They breakfasted together in some embarrassment, both slightly stunned at the speed at which they had become bound as man and wife, and parted for their separate days with ill-concealed relief.

Caroline had no qualms at dealing with her new army of dark-skinned, silent-footed servants; indeed, she rather looked forward to it. She ascertained from Johnnie, after a few days of finding how difficult it was to make any headway domestically, that household affairs had been in the sircar's hands for the last few years, and that if she wanted anything done she must apply to him. General North's instructions had included the information that a sircar was a broker, responsible for the hiring of servants and domestic finances. Looking about her, it seemed to Caroline that the latter responsibility appeared to weigh very lightly on the sircar indeed. When Johnnie had departed for the office with his retinue, resplendent in glittering white linen washed by Caroline herself at the cracked washstand in her bedroom, the sircar was summoned.

The feelings of warmth Caroline had so spontaneously for all working people cooled considerably at the sight of the sircar. He stood in the doorway, cringing slightly, dressed in a greasy robe of grey cotton over various unattractive and dirty rags. He smiled hopefully, clasping his hands before him in a humble manner; his smile displayed broken teeth, and never reached his small brown eyes which watched Caroline with a steady beadiness. Caroline, her hair tied up in a kerchief in preparation for an assault upon the drawing room, surveyed him without compassion.

'The memsahib is wanting me?'

'I have a good deal to ask you.'

The sircar winced a little at the relentlessness in her tone. He attempted a little fawning, a technique that had proved highly successful with Sahib Gates in the early days.

'It is not being seemly for the memsahib to be dirtying her hands so. If she permits, I will be sending servants to do the work that she may rest as is proper.'

'I would rest if I thought any work would be done, but I do not. Why is every corner of the house so filthy? Why have I had to turn away breakfast every morning because the milk has soured and the butter was rancid oil? Why is no laundry done? Why is the house cluttered with servants who do nothing but loll in the shade picking their teeth all day? Where is the rest of the furniture and the pictures? Why is the garden no more than a wilderness?'

The sircar tucked his hands into the sleeves of his gown, and began a long wailing, whining explanation. His heart was in it too, for he had detected in Caroline's quiet and steady voice a distinct note of purpose. After enduring the sing-song for two minutes or so, Caroline motioned him to be silent.

'That will do. It comes to nothing but the grossest negligence. You have been entrusted with the money to run the household, and the household receives no benefit from it. I wonder where the money has gone?'

The sircar fell to his knees.

'Always, always there is so much to be paying for, memsahib! Sahib Gates is not giving me what is necessary—'

'I do not believe you. I think you are a rogue and a liar.'

The sircar's forehead touched the floor at her feet. He lay there, glumly awaiting dismissal.

'Get up,' she said.

He shuffled to his knees, but deemed it politic to remain on them.

'You are angry with me, memsahib. But if you are sending me away, what am I and my children to be doing? In all Calcutta, there is nowhere for I and my children—'

'I never spoke of dismissal.'

The sircar ventured a brief glance upwards. She was not smiling, but her eyes looked very promising.

'I shall not dismiss you. I shall simply make you answerable to me in everything you do. You will hire no-one and dismiss no-one without reference to me. Food will be ordered by my consent, and the money you use must be checked before and after any purchase. Everyone will be given duties and will be expected to perform them scrupulously. An inventory of everything in the house will be made and missing items will be instantly reported. Do I make myself clear?'

'I am without speeches,' said the sircar, groaning inwardly at this appalling prospect of discipline and accounts.

'In return,' Caroline went on, now smiling broadly at his discomfiture, 'I will do what I can for you. If any servant is in trouble, and it is a trouble I know something of, I will help. If any servant is sick, I will try to make them comfortable.'

The sircar shrugged. The mere idea of a white lady being of any use whatsoever in that comfortable rat-run that constituted the servants' quarters was perfectly laughable.

However, if she chose to entertain such ludicrous notions, he could not stop her. He felt very gloomy about the future, and saw what a painful necessity for deviousness there would be. For the past few years he had not had to tax his wits at all; now he would have to cudgel them. He would also have to see Sahib Gates alone on little matters of money. He sighed deeply and shook his head.

'Get up,' Caroline said again.

He rose slowly, and stood dejectedly before her with his shoulders and head bowed.

Caroline looked at him levelly.

'Shall we begin?'

A few days later it became necessary to apply to Johnnie for money. Huge quantities of whitewash had appeared mysteriously at the sircar's reluctant command and the house resounded with the slapping of brushes. A dhobi, yet again a relation of the sircar's, had agreed to take away every remnant and rag of fabric in the household and return it pristine, on condition that he might be paid upon the spot. Caroline promised readily, entranced at the prospect of fresh curtains and sheets, and then found she had nothing to pay with. At dinner that day, she ventured to broach the matter. Johnnie seemed in quite a good humour, encouraged by the new order sweeping through his house, and by the excellent mutton he was eating. His benevolence was further increased by the comfortable self-satisfaction of being very good to his new bride by staying in with her during these first few weeks until she felt able to venture into society.

'I regret having to petition you,' Caroline began, 'but I fear it will not be possible to run the household without money.'

Johnnie waved a hand airily.

'Think nothing of it. 'Tis the sircar's affair. When we are in straits, he always has a cousin who is a money-lender, and at most reasonable rates. Leave it to him!'

'I'm afraid I cannot.'

'Cannot?'

'No. I cannot. I have every reason to believe he has been pocketing money entrusted to him.'

Johnnie's brow darkened. It would not only be deuced inconvenient if that were true, but also make him look a pretty fool before the world to be tricked that way these last few years.

'Rubbish!'

Caroline said nothing.

'How do you know?'

'Because no bills have been paid this last year, laundry has seldom been done, furniture sent to be repaired has not come back, and yet the sircar has had a steady supply of money from you or from the bazaar on your behalf.'

Johnnie put down his knife and fork.

'Damn you!' he shouted.

Caroline had an impulse to flee, and resisted it.

'I – I am trying to improve matters—'

'You are an interfering woman, that is all you are and no more! What ailed this house until you came into it, may I ask you?'

'Everything,' Caroline said stoutly.

'Rubbish! It ran like clockwork and it suited me, thank you, it suited me very well!'

'Did it?' Caroline said maddeningly. 'The dirt suited you? And the filthy clothing and rotten food suited you?'

Johnnie glared at her.

'Damn you,' he said again.

Caroline waited a moment and then said as gently as she could, 'If you would tell me how much I might spend in running the house and paying the servants, I will make quite sure that sum is never exceeded.'

'I don't know how much,' Johnnie said crossly. 'It is the sircar's damned business. Anyway, I have no money to give you. You know that.'

'What are we to live upon, then?'

Johnnie shrugged.

'It comes and goes. I make a little here and there, I never know when.'

'How much is the house?'

'Two hundred pounds a year. It's robbery. Who would live in this part of town unless you were condemned to as I am? And I have just spent forty pounds upon you, for that is the price of matrimony in Calcutta. Forty pounds!'

Caroline felt a slight chill come over her. She knew nothing of the inland trading with which the Company clerks heavily supplemented their meagre incomes, and it seemed to her that destitution was as near to her in matrimony as it had been when single. She knew that Johnnie's salary was only two hundred and fifty pounds a year, therefore fifty pounds only remained for domestic expenditure when the rent was paid. Servants' wages, if the sircar spoke anything like the truth, were exorbitantly high by comparison with England, and the number of servants wickedly extravagant.

'If I were to dismiss some of the servants—' she began.

'Dismiss them!' Johnnie shouted. 'Are you mad? The servants are wholly necessary for me to maintain my position. I cannot dispense with a single one.'

'I have nothing to sell, I fear. If I had, I would, to help us until matters are better, but I have nothing.'

A slight gleam came into Johnnie's eyes. George Carew had mentioned the whist club that morning, and Johnnie had made a laborious performance of refusing because he had been married only a matter of days. But he was good at whist and lucky, and it was a wonderful chance of escape. He'd not drunk above three bottles a day since their marriage and felt himself to be quite parched with abstinence. He leaned across the table and patted Caroline's thin hand.

'I'll have money for you by morning.'

'How? How can you?'

He laid his finger to the side of his nose.

'Ask no questions.'

Caroline looked profoundly troubled.

'Is it something wicked?'

'To a parson's daughter, very wicked. To a man of the world a mere nothing. I shall see you at breakfast.'

'Breakfast? Shall you not be in to supper?'

'I shall not. Back to your whitewashing, my girl, and see that I've clean linen for this evening. I'll see you at breakfast.'

Inadvertently she saw him some hours before that. A terrible commotion aroused her from the deep hot sleep she had fallen into, and she went out in her dressing-gown to the landing, sure the servants were fighting. Below her, on the now gleaming and polished marble floor of the hallway, her husband was struggling and bellowing in the hands of his servants. Nobody noticed her, and as she went forward to the banisters to call down to him, he suddenly pitched forward and was violently and copiously sick. She drew back in revulsion and shock, astonished at herself for her own squeamish-ness. She stood indecisively for a while, unable to look down again into the hallway, then retreated back to her bedroom and despised herself.

Johnnie was assisted to bed by well-practised hands, hands that had been astonished at how little of this sort of work they had had to do in the past week. In the midst of shovelling Johnnie unceremoniously onto his bed, fully clad and still shod, Caroline appeared in the doorway. Amazement struck every servant into rigidity. She approached the bed and lifted her candle to look at Johnnie's face, but gave it no more than a glance.

'Undress him,' she said quietly, in a voice that was not quite steady, 'and wash his face and hands, and put him into a clean nightshirt. I will return shortly and see that he is comfortable.'

She waited on the landing, telling herself that to satisfy her own standards she should have washed him herself, with her own hands, but she did not think she could bear to touch him, not any longer, now that his flesh had become so gross and his temper so petulant. She went quietly back into the room and saw him lying there, decently clad in clean white lawn with his dark hair rumpled and his mouth open.

'Thank you,' she said to the servants.

The sircar, who had come to watch this astonishing entertainment, made an elaborate ritual of hanging up the gorgeous coat in which Johnnie had graced the whist club. As he did so, he removed the pouch of money carelessly thrust into an outer pocket and slipped it neatly among his rags. He felt much soothed. It was a small but sweet revenge for the misery his life had become.

'I am wishing you peaceful sleep, memsahib.'

She nodded, and went back to her room and her thoughts.

It soon became abundantly clear that she must manage on her own, both for money, and for amusement. The whist club had whetted Johnnie's appetite for pleasure, and almost no subsequent evening saw him at home. He still dined with Caroline, for he had a profound reluctance to exhibit her as his chosen bride, and interfering gossips such as Mrs Rathbone were told not to call upon her until she felt more settled. Mrs Rathbone was secretly relieved for though warm-hearted, and very sorry for Caroline, she had found her slightly forbidding company. Caroline was indeed quite happy on her own for the moment, while she was so much occupied, and although the cheering thought of Isobel came into her mind quite frequently, she would not let it dwell there since she knew she had put herself upon another planet to that happy one Miss Grant inhabited.

As for money, she saw that she must borrow it. It seemed Calcutta did borrow money as a matter of course, and she must steel herself to do it. Unaware that she would cause a stir in the bazaar, she summoned the sircar and instructed him to assist her in this matter. The sircar was incredulous and horrified at the suggestion that she should visit a money-lender in person and flung himself prostrate again in an attempt to prevent her.

'Do not be absurd,' Caroline said calmly, poking him with the toe of her shoe. 'If I do not come myself, how am I to understand what I am doing?'

The sircar wished to explain that her lack of comprehension was what his own profit depended upon, but found it difficult to do. Wretched, and feeling himself to be a laughing stock among his fellow countrymen, he trailed after her into the bazaar, noticing she created the most sensational disturbance as she rode down the narrow and stinking alleys bordered with ramshackle little open shops and resounding with the din of little hammers upon brass and copper and the shouts and whines of pedlars. Tailors sat sewing cross-legged on the raised platforms of their shop fronts, and spice sellers, their garments splashed with ochre and vermilion, weighed their wares in brass pans, handing over the purchases in twists of rag. There were pyramids of oranges and watermelons, appalling butchers' shops where flayed hunks of meat hung on iron spikes in a fog of flies, and sandal makers stitching in a raw stench of poorly cured leather. The alleys themselves were jammed with people, some almost naked, some in brilliant silks, some turbanned, some moustached and sporting long black pigtails, and all of them with one amazed accord looked up at this astonishing white-skinned apparition, riding through them, and then down, with equal disbelief, at the figure of the sircar, shuffling miserably behind her. His cousin, the money-lender, squatting on his mat by a mud wall with his scales and neat piles of coins before him, was equally staggered and dismayed.

There was a rapid exchange Caroline could not follow between the two men, while the sircar explained how necessary it was that there should be two rates of interest to justify the rigours of his own life at the moment, the difference between the two rates amounting to his commission for such suffering. The cousin promised rapidly, his eyes darting in bewilderment from the sircar to the astonishing figure of Caroline in her lilac cotton gown and straw bonnet. Little naked children, their eyes swarming with flies, were gathering round her, also an interested white cow, who clearly felt its sacredness allowed it an extremely close inspection. The heat was intense down here in these swarming alleyways, crammed with people and thick with the smells of dung and cooking and dust.

'My cousin will be helping you,' the sircar said.

'I need to borrow a hundred pounds,' Caroline said directly, conscious she needed to borrow twice that amount but not daring to be so bold.

Using the sircar as an interpreter the cousin explained his terms and rates of interest. Caroline considered them for a moment, weighing what seemed an exorbitant rate of interest against her desperate need for the money.

'It is too much,' she said at last.

The cousin argued violently for some moments, then conveyed the information through the sircar that he would reduce the rate by one per cent. Caroline was adamant. The cousin struck his forehead and whined and adjusted his figures again. Still Caroline shook her head. The cousin waved his arms and shook his head in reply.

'He is going no lower, memsahib,' the sircar said, conscious that one more drop would eliminate all his own profit.

Caroline picked her skirts up and said calmly, 'Then you may tell him that I will do my business elsewhere.'

She turned to go, full of a sudden sweet elation. Both men leapt at her at once, kneeling by her in the dust among the press of children, and pulling at her skirts. If she did not deal here, the cousin would never oblige the sircar again so accommodatingly, the sircar knew that, and the cousin was conscious that the steady flow of demand from households like the Gates's provided the basis of his livelihood.

Ten minutes later, she had mounted again and was picking her way back to the thoroughfare with a hundred pounds in her pocket, and the sircar growling in her wake after making the smallest profit on a deal he had ever had to lower himself to. Half a per cent! It was monstrous, truly monstrous to be outwitted by someone who had nothing but ignorance and strength of mind to recommend her. As she emerged from the packed squalor of the bazaar and was blinking in the brightness of the sunlight, Caroline saw a familiar and gaudy carriage bowl past her in the dust. She had just time to see Mrs Rathbone's incredulous face, and smile and raise her hand to it, before it had whirled away. It never struck her that there was anything odd in being seen riding, with only one bedraggled servant in attendance, out of a native bazaar.

At home, she proceeded to exert the authority of her borrowed wealth. She summoned all the servants together, and found that over a hundred persons lived, somehow, in the servants' quarters of her house. She selected all those whom she recognized from household duties and found herself left with a motley assortment of women, children, old men and cripples all of whom claimed the closest of relationships to one or other of the servants. She hated to send any away, but she could not afford to support them. She explained that she was forced to cut their wages considerably and that any servant and his dependants who were dissatisfied by the new rate were quite free to go and she would give them references.

The room erupted at once in a perfect babble of dismay, which Caroline thought slightly illogical since no servant had received any money at all for some months, whatever his rate of pay was supposed to be. When the shrieking and scrambling had died down a little, Caroline perceived that the room was now only half full, and that the sircar was not to be seen. She counted those in livery of sorts, and discovered she now possessed eighteen servants and their families, which seemed grossly extravagant still, but a definite advance upon the fifty or so the sircar had claimed. She explained that they were to work for a fortnight more, and she would then pay them for the month they had served her since her arrival. There was a little shuffling and muttering at this, but no direct protest. She then delivered her bombshell.

'I am now coming to inspect your quarters. I wish to see how you live and see if there is any way in which it might be improved.'

Consternation broke out again. Caroline wondered uneasily if she sounded exactly like Eleanor preparing for her weekly inspection of the attics where the Parsonage servants slept in draughty discomfort. But she did want to see how they lived, and perhaps help them a little, especially those pathetic little children with their dull eyes and swollen bellies.

Accompanied by a nervous escort of servants, Caroline went out into her dusty and disordered garden and through a broken hedge of tired oleander to a strange and wholly Indian world. Curious huts of mud and dung were grouped about an irregular courtyard dotted with cooking fires, and bisected by a stinking ditch. There were a few goats, and a dusty hen or two, and the sound of someone singing a high monotonous song. The huts were windowless, and contained nothing but mats, except for one which had a low bed and the disturbed air of very recent occupancy. A tall and serious Sikh, whom Caroline had already noticed with approval for his gentleness and industry, came forward and explained that this hut had belonged to the sircar.

Caroline looked more closely. There was a clean square in the dust under the bed, and blurred marks before it as if a heavy object had been pulled hastily out. A tin or a box, Caroline thought, and wondered how much of their possessions and money were now being hurried away into the depths of Calcutta. She straightened up and looked at her dependants waiting patiently outside in the sun. She smiled at them, and called the Sikh to her, since he spoke some English.

'Will you explain to them that it will make them ill to have that ditch so near to where they live? Tell them it must be dug behind the compound, far from the huts, and that the animals must not live with them. It brings the flies.'

She stopped, suddenly overcome by an enormous weariness, the weariness of considerable exertion in intense heat. Ranjit said, 'You must rest, memsahib.'

She nodded blindly. Gentle hands took her arms and she was led back to the drawing room and seated by the open window with its scarcely moving grassy screens. Ranjit stood before her.

'I will help you, memsahib, now that the sircar is going.'

Caroline shook her head. General North had told her that the Sikhs were proud and warlike, and regarded the call to arms as the highest calling a man could aspire to.

'No, Ranjit, no, not you. Not a Sikh. It would demean you.'

'I am a servant already, memsahib. One day I will be a soldier again, but now I am helping you.'

Caroline looked up at his serious thin face.

'I thank you,' she said with fervour.

He left the room silently, and she lay back and gazed at the blank whiteness of the newly painted walls. The triumph of the day's achievements was receding with her tiredness, and she began to be apprehensive of Johnnie's reaction when he discovered what she had done. It was his household after all, and perhaps she had no right, however practical she thought herself, to diminish it for him without permission. She passed a damp hand over her damp face and abruptly wished very much for Isobel to lighten her spirits. She had told Isobel that she would see her in a few weeks, but now, looking at this shabby, empty little house, and knowing herself to be in debt for the first time in her life, she did not think she could. Every day seemed to cut her off further from any chance of maintaining her friendship with Isobel. In her present mood, it seemed a bleak and hard prospect, and it was made worse by knowing that the people she would have to force herself to know very soon would be just those loud and jeering people who had frequented Mrs Rathbone's house. She could not keep to the house for much longer on her pretext of becoming used to India, in fact only the day before Johnnie had mentioned a dinner party he had no intention of missing and at which he advised her to make her debut as it would be a large crowd which would easily absorb her. The thought was alarming, but some day it had to be done. Her mouth drooped unconsciously. Caroline let her head fall back against her chair and dropped into a hot and troubled slumber.

13

Isobel would have been fiercely indignant at the suggestion that Caroline had in any way slipped her mind. It was true that she was exceedingly, delightfully busy, that all Calcutta seemed to have taken a great fancy to her, and subsequently the days seemed full of charming, flattering people, but in any moment of quiet, such as the dawn or her prayers at the end of the day, she thought very fondly of Caroline. The periodic presence of General North reminded her of Caroline, though he seemed slightly reticent now on the subject, and Isobel concluded that his natural taste for pretty girls had reasserted itself over his brief absorption with a girl who had everything to recommend her but her looks. Isobel had received one letter from Caroline which had sounded both calm and happy and she had deduced that Caroline was disproving all the gossips who said such evil things of Johnnie Gates. Initially Isobel had fretted dreadfully over these snatches of malice the servants brought her, but Caroline's letter had dispelled her distress. How could anyone write a letter of such serene contentment if they did not mean it, and Isobel prided herself on knowing Caroline so well that she might see through any attempt at false courage.

She kept Caroline's letter in her jewel box and thus had reason to see it several times a day. Unfortunately, this habit had the effect of all familiarity, and the folded square of cream paper became as comfortably invisible as all the other objects in daily use upon her dressing table. Never in all her twenty years had her dressing table been so busily in use. She sat before it in the charming, light, white gauzy bedroom in Sir Edward Ashton's

202

comfortable house, at least three times a day for prolonged periods, dressing with enormous care for morning calls, for dinner and then finally for supper parties and dances. She wore through three pairs of satin slippers in the first weeks simply by dancing, for she never sat out a single dance. She was indeed the toast of Calcutta, for no-one a quarter so pretty had stepped ashore for a good five years, and even if any rival had been as pretty they could never have matched her spirit and wit.

These last two qualities had proved themselves extremely useful in outwitting the amiable chaperone Sir Edward had provided in the shape of old Lady Renton, widowed five years after a skirmish on the North West Frontier. Bewitched earlier and bemused, Lady Renton quickly succumbed to Isobel's powerful will, and at dances retired thankfully to the card room, leaving her charge to flirt with whom she wished on the dance floor. Sir Edward seldom accompanied them since he did not care for dancing, but on the rare occasions Isobel teased him into coming – 'so that I may exhibit my splendid cousin, dear Sir Edward!' – he was helplessly gratified by Isobel's undoubted success. He had dreaded her coming as a disruption of the quiet pattern of his life, but now she was here, he could not but appreciate the colour and light she spread about her. What was even better was that she bothered him for very little. He was accustomed to think that young women pestered one ceaselessly for frocks and ribbons, parties and parasols, carriage rides and lap dogs, but Isobel asked him for almost nothing. There was indeed one topic she referred to every few days, but he remained, upon General North's advice, adamant.

She seemed to have made a close friend upon the ship, a very quiet ladylike person upon General North's account, of whom she had grown very fond. The ladylike person was clearly, however, not what she seemed, for upon arrival in Calcutta, General North had seen with his own astonished eyes that she was greeted by a known renegade, and handed into a carriage belonging to, and occupied by, one of Calcutta's most promiscuous women. While uttering this sanctimonious speech, the general forebore to add how many times he had had reason to be grateful for Mrs Rathbone's easy generosity. The ladylike person was now residing in Mrs Rathbone's house in the Garden Reach, and Isobel longed to call upon her there.

'I fear, my dear, that it is quite out of the question.'

'But why, Sir Edward, why may I not?'

'Because I am reliably informed that Mrs Rathbone is not the sort of person with whom you should have any sort of association.'

'But I do not want to associate with Mrs Rathbone, I do not care a pin for Mrs Rathbone! I want to see Caroline, who is one of the dearest people imaginable—'

'So you informed me yesterday, and several days before that, and yet several more days before that. I am sure in your eyes, my dear Isobel, she is a perfect paragon, but in society's eyes she is living with a woman whose company renders her quite the reverse.'

Isobel began to protest, but he held up a hand to silence her.

'Society may be an ass, Isobel, indeed I frequently think it is, but as I am in the position of your guardian here, I cannot pursue either my or your inclinations and flout society.'

'Then poor Caroline must suffer because you are so pompous?'

He smiled at her.

'I take it you infer that the lady is poor because she must be deprived of your company?'

'Do not tease me. I wish to see her because I love her very much, quite as well as because I know I do her good.'

'I do not doubt it, but I am afraid that as long as she

204

remains where she is, you must remain where you are. And if you disobey me,' he added, 'I shall replace Lady Renton with a much keener-eyed companion. Now go and change. The hot season will take its toll of you and you will find you are too wearied by it to dance another step, so you must make the most of your energy.'

'It is limitless,' Isobel said airily.

She went lightly up the shallow staircase, and into her bedroom, to find her bed already strewn with pale clouds of silk and lawn for her to change into. She sat down at her dressing table and opened her jewel box to look for the lovely rose quartz earrings Mamma had given her that would look so well with that pink silk gauze. As she took out the top tray a square of paper slipped sideways and fell among her brushes.

With Caroline still fresh in her mind from her conversation, the paper had a new significance. She unfolded it and ran her eye down the fine, neat writing. Yes, it was certainly a happy and contented letter, there was no real need to worry. Idly Isobel glanced up at the date on the head of the letter and had a small and guilty shock. It was two months old, a whole two months and Caroline had lived all that time with that disreputable woman and never had a word from Isobel! Poor neglected Caroline, she would write this instant. But as she rose to find pen and paper, a new thought smote her, a thought that took away her complacency and left disquiet instead. It was one thing to say that Caroline had been neglected by herself, but was it not quite another, and more anxious, to realize that she had had no news from Caroline? What of that childhood sweetheart, of that planned marriage, surely some progress in that direction must have been made?

Isobel sat down again, frowning and uneasy, suddenly filled with new and unpleasant apprehensions. She glanced at herself in the mirror and said resolutely to the pretty reflection there, 'I shall have to break the rules, shall I not? While Sir Edward is working tomorrow morning, I shall have to give Lady Renton the slip and go down to Garden Reach myself. There is nothing else for it, is there?'

Then, because the prospect of action always pleased her, she rang the bell for assistance and went about the business of the pink silk gauze with a much lightened heart.

Mrs Rathbone was very alarmed to hear that Miss Grant awaited her below. She knew very well who she was, since the newspapers and the gossips were full of little else, and after all, had poor Mrs Gates not travelled with her and no doubt entertained high hopes of such an association? Mrs Rathbone could only suppose, scrambling out of her beribboned bedgown into a brilliant assortment of clothes, that it was on the subject of poor Mrs Gates that Miss Grant had come. But what was she to say? She was not at all sure that what she knew was all truth, although there was no doubt that she had with her own eyes seen Caroline coming brazenly out of the native bazaar with all the nonchalance of someone riding in Rotten Row. But whether the gossip that she had dismissed half the servants, and dosed the children of the remaining half for worms, and then been hit by her drunken husband for her pains, was true, Mrs Rathbone really did not like to say. She surveyed herself in the imitation French glass that a man in the bazaar had made so cleverly, and wondered unhappily if emerald green and brilliant yellow were really too striking a combination when set off with gold fringing and orange braid?

She entered her drawing room wearing an anxious and placatory smile above this dazzling combination. Isobel, faultless in white and pale blue, fought down an enormous desire to laugh, and simply held out her hand, saying gravely, 'How very good of you, Mrs Rathbone, to allow me to interrupt your morning.'

'Interrupt? Oh no, my dear, it is a pleasure, an – an honour, my dear, I am charmed, quite charmed.'

She stopped uneasily, and motioned Isobel towards a fat satin chair on gilded bow legs.

'Make yourself comfortable, my dear, please do. Will you take some lime juice, so cooling, I always say, in this dreadful climate?'

Isobel accepted both offers, and watched with pleasure while Mrs Rathbone clucked and bustled among her silent servants. When at last she seated herself, and had spread out her green and yellow skirts to their best advantage Isobel saw no reason to waste time.

'Forgive me for being a little abrupt, Mrs Rathbone, but there is someone of whom I long to have news, and I believe you are the only person who can give it to me. In fact I believe the person I seek still resides here.'

Mrs Rathbone fidgeted miserably, making her glittering fringes quiver. Oh dear, it was as bad as she thought, and clearly this elegant young person had no notion of the truth. She opened her mouth to reply, but could find no words, and gazed speechlessly at Isobel, her little round eyes full of distress.

'I seek Miss Harding,' Isobel said gently.

Mrs Rathbone nodded.

'Is she still with you? I know this is where she came. Is she still here?'

Mrs Rathbone shook her head and a small chill crept over Isobel.

'Where is she, Mrs Rathbone?' Isobel said in an altered tone.

'She – she is gone, Miss Grant. She left about two months ago. She – she—' she stopped, and then said in a sort of rush, 'She is married, Miss Grant.'

'Married?' Isobel sprang to her feet, knocking her glass of juice onto the carpet. 'Caroline is married?'

Mrs Rathbone was much alarmed at her manner and voice, and could only nod again, like a mechanical doll.

Exasperated, Isobel seized her shoulders and shook her.

'Tell me!' she insisted. 'Tell me!'

'She married John Gates, Miss Grant. They were married in the Customs Office, only myself and George Carew to see them wed, Miss Grant.'

Isobel let go of her and straightened up. Caroline had promised, she was sure she had promised, not to take any step without consulting Isobel. She had been most apprehensive of the marriage, indeed dreadfully so, and Isobel had sworn to save her from it if she wished, and now she had plunged into it without a word to a soul, and who could tell with what misgivings. Idiotic General North, who might have been such a source of information, was evidently too frightened to jeopardize his social standing with Sir Edward, by being seen too frequently at Mrs Rathbone's. Isobel clenched her fists.

'Is she happy?' she demanded.

Mrs Rathbone spread her plump hands hopelessly.

'Who can say, my dear, who can say? You don't look for happiness in marriage, Miss Grant, and maybe Mrs Gates has found what she was looking for—'

'She was looking for happiness,' Isobel said.

'Oh – oh, well, then—'

'Is he as bad as the gossips say?'

Mrs Rathbone smiled indulgently.

'Oh no, dear, not a bad boy, not a bad boy at all. A bit naughty now and then, but you know how boys are, Miss Grant. He's a heart of gold, my dear, would not hurt a fly.'

Doubtless the rumour of Johnnie striking Caroline had no more truth in it, than the one that she was teaching some of her servants to read. People hit each other endlessly in Calcutta, it was the heat, simply the heat, bad for your temper it was, but blows meant nothing, nothing at all.

'Where do they live?'

Mrs Rathbone gave the address with some doubt. It was

not a good part of the city and she was sure Miss Grant's distinguished guardian would not like to see her driving there. Tentatively, she offered herself as chaperone.

'No, thank you, Mrs Rathbone. You have been most helpful, but the rest I intend to see for myself, and by myself.'

In a flurry of fuss and anxiety, Mrs Rathbone watched Isobel mount the elegant carriage she had purloined from Sir Edward's stables, and be driven off towards what could only be the upsetting fact of Caroline's marriage. It was no consolation to her, in the turmoil of her thoughts, to be patted absently on the shoulder by her husband, who had seen Isobel depart, and now remarked that, as callers went, the last one was a cut above the average.

Isobel could hardly have chosen a worse morning to make her call upon Caroline. She had bargained on finding Caroline alone, on the understandable assumption that Johnnie would be at his desk until dinner, and she was not to know that a wild night the evening before on Johnnie's part, and a most disagreeable breakfast with his wife on the following morning, meant that he was still pacing furiously about his drawing room at noon.

Caroline watched him from her seat by the window. She had learnt so much in the last weeks she felt as if she were quite another person to the ignorant and unsuspecting creature who had landed on that brilliant waterfront in March. She had learned, with the gentle help of her servants, that she must not expect her huge Pathan bearer to have anything to do with the sweeper who dealt so humbly with the household refuse because of caste. For the same reason, she had learned that she must not touch utensils belonging to her servants, for she had seen the same sweeper dash his drinking bowl to the ground after she had picked it up out of curiosity and therefore defiled it for him. She had learned that to insist upon doing her own shopping only exposed her to the grossest exploitation, but that if she allowed Ranjit or the cook their small 'dastur' or commission on everything they bought for her, she was treated with faultless honesty and loyalty. She had learned that the Mohammedan cook must never be asked to cook bacon and that the gai-wallah who brought his cow to the door each day must be prevented from watering the milk. She had learned to stand all the legs of furniture in bowls of water to protect it from marauding armies of white ants and she had learned that the only way to deal with the agonizing menace of prickly heat was to resist the powerful temptation to scratch. She learned that her servants had their own highly developed sense of demarcation in the tasks they were prepared to do, but that they were equally prepared, given this condition, to serve her impeccably. They were proving themselves as easy to respect and love as the circle into which Johnnie had unwillingly introduced her had proved itself despicable and dislikeable. Caroline could find nothing sympathetic about them, but she had, in a hard lesson in self-schooling, learned to endure. She had also learned not to ask Johnnie for money.

This particular morning, however, she had been forced to ignore this lesson and petition as delicately as she could for money. Her hundred pounds, so dashingly captured, was dwindling fast now that the servants had all received their long overdue wages, and the drawing-room and dining-room furniture and pictures had been reclaimed, with difficulty, from the bazaar. All these expenses came on top of the normal running expenses of the household, and the cost of living in Calcutta seemed to Caroline exorbitantly high. Imported commodities from Europe such as ham and cheese, both of which Johnnie claimed he could not do without, cost twelve and thirteen shillings a pound, and Johnnie's twice-daily visits from the wig barber would have kept the whole household in ham and cheese for months. But if Johnnie was the prime incurrer of such expenses, he did not seem to see that he should pay for them. He appeared, Caroline thought, to regard her part of the bargain they had made as the ability to wave a magic wand over all domestic troubles and expenses, and make them vanish.

'What can you want money for?' he shouted ill-temperedly, his head thudding with pain.

'Merely to pay for what we eat, what we drink and for – for your expenses.'

'My expenses?' he said in outrage.

'Your tailor, your barbers, your wig, your horses—'

'Leave it to the sircar!' Johnnie bellowed. 'Don't meddle, woman! Leave it to the sircar!'

It was the Parthian shot he had intended it to be and Caroline fell silent. He knew as well as she that the sircar had gone a month since, and he only wished to remind her of the rage he had been in when he arrived home to find his household arbitrarily sliced in half. He had been incoherent with anger, and she had had a black eye for two weeks to bear witness to it. He had not meant to hit her or at least not to hit her so hard, but her prim parsonage ways, her mealy-mouthed competence and prudence, her exasperating predilection for being right had driven him to it. And now she was whining on about money again, having chosen precisely the morning when he was hard-pressed himself to meet debts incurred the night before. He glared at her, and thought that it would become a woman in her supplicating position to weep just a little; but she was looking back at him, evidently distressed but maddeningly dry-eyed.

'How are we to live?' she said faintly.

'I shall live as I have always done,' he said, 'and you will keep your side of the bargain and see that I am comfortable.'

She wanted to scream that his side of the bargain had been that he would save her from destitution, and how was she to make even a dog comfortable without a single penny, but pride forbade her. She would not beg or appeal any more, not to such a man – or monster – as this. Indeed she would not. She had made her spiritual independence before, and now, though God alone knew how, she must make her material independence too. There was a hundred pounds to be restored at interest at the end of three months, and somehow she would achieve it. If Johnnie would give her no money, she would sell some of his pictures to raise it. He had not noticed their absence for repair, so it was strongly probable that their final disappearance would be equally invisible to him. She lifted her chin and stared levelly at him.

'Bargain!' Johnnie said with furious despair. 'Bargain! A man-trap maybe, but a bargain!'

He moved heavily towards the door, which swung open silently at the hands of servants and revealed the immaculate white figure of Isobel without. Caroline sprang up with a cry of heartfelt delight and pushed unceremoniously past the bulky figure of her husband to fling her arms about her friend. Johnnie, whose instincts for gallantry were highly roused by this ravishing apparition, masked his fury and headache with just those smiles and impudent glances that had been so fatally attractive when he was twenty. Isobel, her arms tight about Caroline, despite the temperature, regarded him coolly over Caroline's shoulder.

'Mr Gates, I imagine?'

Johnnie bowed with a flourish.

'The same, Miss Grant.'

Her likeness had been in all the papers, there was no mistaking her. His eyes travelled lingeringly over her face. What a jewel!

Caroline released Isobel, and lifted a face quite transformed with delight. Isobel looked at her critically for some moments and then, without taking her eyes from Caroline, she said to Johnnie, 'What have you done, Mr Gates, to deserve this angel in the smallest degree?'

Johnnie floundered. The harsh words of the morning were still thick in the air about them, the effect of his temper still written on Caroline's countenance.

'Nothing,' he said weakly.

'I am glad you admit it,' Isobel said, and turned her blue gaze upon him, scrutinizing him as carefully as if she were assessing every particle of him, every stitch he wore, for its possible purchase value. Under her unfriendly eyes, his flirtatious poise began to diminish into just the nervous awkwardness only Lady Lennox could reduce him to. In his reddened eyes and extravagant clothes, Isobel saw everything she had feared to see. Caroline's old cotton gown, drearily familiar from those daily appearances at sea, and extreme thinness spoke equally eloquently. And what was that faint smudge along her cheekbone? Isobel's heart was twisted with pity at the spectacle of Caroline's evident suffering and equally evident gallantry in the face of it.

'May I speak to Mrs Gates alone?'

Johnnie bowed.

'I should not wish to intrude, Miss Grant.'

When he had gone, Isobel turned and took Caroline's hands in hers.

'I had hoped you would weep in relief at seeing me,' she said teasingly.

'I wish I could, dearest Isobel. I feel the relief, but I cannot weep, I never could. Even when Papa died I – but how blooming you look! Everywhere I hear of your charms and how the beaux fight to quaff from your slippers!'

'I have not come to speak of that.'

'I was afraid not,' Caroline said sadly.

Isobel seated herself on the newly restored sofa, and pulled Caroline down beside her.

'Now then. What is the meaning of all this?'

Caroline looked away. 'Please—'

'No, you shall not get away with it. I want to know

what you mean by throwing yourself away in this dismal manner.'

'Please do not let us speak of it, I beg you, please.'

Isobel dropped her bantering tone and spoke with unaccustomed earnestness.

'You promised me you would do nothing without telling me. You promised you would not throw yourself away. You promised.' She felt a sudden thrust of self-reproach and said in a low tone, 'I know I have neglected you dreadfully, and been giddy and silly and all the things Sir Edward says I am, but why did you not tell me?'

Caroline had a sudden mental picture of the shabby incongruous figure she would have cut in Sir Edward's splendid apartments, for splendid they must be, and could not restrain a small smile at the thought of it. 'Do not be absurd,' she said gently, her hand on Isobel's. 'What sort of reception would I have had, dusty and down at heel, asking you among all these glittering people whether you thought I should marry or not?'

Isobel looked at her solemnly.

'Are you very unhappy?'

'Not very.'

'Oh, Caroline, Caroline! Not very. You deserve, oh how you deserve to be intensely happy. And that brute—'

Firm fingers were laid across her mouth.

'No, Isobel. We will not speak of him. I married because I should have begged otherwise and he married because he does not know how to keep house. That is all.'

'I do not believe you. Why must you insist on your stiff-necked pride always? Why could you not let me help you? I should love to help you! There is no-one I'd rather help!'

Caroline kissed her cheek.

'And I love you for that. But if you will not think me ungrateful, I must tell you that I am tired of gratitude, tired of being obliged to people. I must have been born with the wrong spirit for my position, a spirit that only likes to receive when it feels perfectly sure that it is fully entitled to receive. I felt that briefly once just before Papa died, and I feel it now. As far as Mr Gates is concerned, I will truly fulfil my part of the bargain.'

She did not add that as far as being kept by him went, it very much looked as if she would have to keep herself from now on. Isobel still gazed at her with eyes full of troubled incomprehension.

'I know you think me mad. How could it be otherwise? You, with your gentle upbringing, how could you bear to live in this sad little house with no-one to amuse you? But it is different for me, indeed it is. I love my household! I do not care very much for the house itself to be sure, but at least it is my domain and I have it mostly to myself. The garden may look to you like a dreary little desert, but the malis and I have great plans for it next cool season and it will blossom like the Garden of Eden. I intend to learn all about Indian flowers. Come now, dearest Isobel, none of it is so very tragic and really there never was anything else to be done.'

'Given your character, there never was, and that is what I cannot bear.'

Caroline stood up.

'Then you must have a diversion, and think no more of it. Look, it is nearly one. Does Sir Edward know where you are?'

'No,' Isobel said absently, her mind still bowed down with anxiety over Caroline's lot, 'I stole his carriage and ran away. I was so desperate to see you.'

Caroline looked horrified.

'I could not bear him to be angry with you on my account.'

'He will not be. He is a kind of angel too, though not of the arch variety that you are. Promise I may see you again soon?'

'If – if Sir Edward thinks you may.'

'He must,' Isobel said decidedly. 'I shall insist you are invited.'

'No.'

'What can you mean, no? Do you not want to see me?'

Caroline's gaze dropped.

'Above everything. But we – we are not fit for the kind of society you move in now.'

'Nonsense!' Isobel said furiously. 'Unspeakable nonsense! Wait but a day or two and you shall see whether it is not the most ridiculous nonsense!'

'Please think no more of us,' Caroline cried apprehensively. 'It would only be awkward. Use your excellent sense and you will see how awkward it might be for all of us.'

'No,' said Isobel decidedly. 'The time has come to please myself, and as what pleases me in a feminine capacity is your company, I shall have it if I can. Every other woman in Calcutta is a dolt compared to you. Do you want to make me miserable?'

Caroline smiled affectionately and shook her head.

'Then leave everything to me. I must go now, but we shall be together again shortly.' She kissed Caroline warmly. 'I have plans for you,' she said.

14

If the invitation consequent upon Isobel's visit had come during the long hours of Caroline's solitude there is no doubt what its fate would have been. Caroline would simply have torn it up, and said nothing of the matter to Johnnie, while steeling herself for Isobel's indignation. But fate did not decree it thus. A packet was delivered by a bearer in unmistakably splendid uniform at just the moment that the Gates – on Caroline's part most reluctantly – were setting forth to dine with George Carew. The packet was addressed to Caroline, and Johnnie commandeered it on its way across the room to her. She said nothing with difficulty, feeling that if he came across some indiscreet opinions of Isobel's about himself, it was no more than he deserved for his mannerless interference. He ripped the paper open and gave an exclamation of delight.

'Ah, madam! I see you are to be some use to me after all! We may yet shoehorn ourselves into higher circles, indeed we may. I imagine we owe this honour to your imperious little friend – ah, a note from her, let me see—'

'You shall not,' Caroline declared, springing from her seat and whipping the paper from his hand.

Sneering faintly, but too satisfied with the splendid social prospect before him to be bothered to retaliate further, Johnnie withdrew, saying she had better be in the carriage in two minutes or he should leave without her.

Isobel's note was highly self-satisfied. She had secured an invitation for the Gates for an evening party to be given by the Nawab of Fultar, and all high Calcutta was to be there. 'I promised I would try to rescue you from your dismal little situation,' she wrote, 'and this is only the beginning. Sir Edward is persuaded and I am delighted.' She did not add how difficult Sir Edward had been to persuade, nor how he had only consented because he said that the Nawab always gave enormous parties, thus dubious guests such as Isobel suggested would, with luck, be lost in the crowd.

He was, in fact, irritated by Isobel's persistence in a matter that seemed to him tasteless and trivial, for his mind was much more occupied with professional matters at the moment. Not only did the Governor General need every ounce of support Sir Edward could give him against the opposition he faced in almost all matters from the other members of the Council, none of whom knew Bengal as Hastings did, but there was a new and thorny problem for the East India Company. The outbreak of war between England and her American colonies had diverted British eyes westwards, and the French seemed to be seizing the chance offered by this averted gaze to recover the losses made in the seven years of war. A French agent had arrived in western India, and was doing all he could, and successfully so far, to make French interests a formidable opponent to British interests. The best way to thwart these designs occupied most of Sir Edward's waking hours at present, and to be constantly diverted by a matter which seemed to him wholly worthless made him irritable and irrationally dictatorial. He had given way at last out of sheer exasperation and immediately thought no more about it.

Caroline would have been grateful to be able to think no more of it either, but she could not. Isobel followed up her initial assault by a series of flying visits, all made when she was officially on the way elsewhere, to bully Caroline into accepting the loan of her hairdresser, the gift of a dress.

'No,' said Caroline to the latter.

Isobel stamped.

'I despair of you and I begin to think you are growing horns where once I thought you had wings. I insist you have a dress, I absolutely insist. I have given you no wedding present since I am so disgusted with your wedding generally, but you will simply have to regard a dress as such if you will take it no other way. You are hardly gracious, Caroline, indeed you are not.'

Caroline was instantly contrite.

'I never meant to offend you, Isobel, and I cannot tell you what a welcome change a new gown would be. I am only – only sorry that I need to be assisted thus, if you understand me. I had hoped by marrying that – but no matter. You are good and generous and a new gown will be a joy to me, I promise you. The ones I have are worn threadbare by the vigorous attentions of the dhobi, I have nothing fit for a party.'

Isobel was delighted.

'It shall be cream-coloured, Caroline, to set off your skin, silk gauze, I rather think, over underskirts of satin—'

'Simple,' Caroline begged.

'Be quiet, Caroline, you have no taste whatsoever and must heed mine until you know better. In any case it is my present and I shall therefore dictate my terms.'

Like an eager Pygmalion, Isobel set to work on Caroline. The latter, who had no notion that Isobel had concocted a far more complicated plan than the mere attendance at a party, submitted with surprised pleasure, surprised because it had never struck her before that personal adornment could be pleasurable. To a pretty person certainly, such as her mother had been, or Isobel was, but not to her plain, awkward self. Her aim had always been to look inconspicuous at best, and inoffensive at worst. Isobel, it seemed, took quite another view.

On the day of the party, an elegant French coiffeur arrived, despatched by Isobel. Despite the disdain he clearly felt for this humble little household, and Caroline's panic at having him there at all, he managed to effect a complete transformation. She clung tenaciously to her refusal to be powdered at all, and watched in the mirror as he grimaced with despair at her lack of sophistication. After an interminable space of time, he stepped back, and declared he could do no more. Caroline surveyed herself and thought that the whole effect was very artless and milkmaidish for so many hours of effort, with its tumble of loose curls at the back of her head and the smooth rise above her forehead. But there was no doubt it was extraordinarily becoming and presumably it was fashionable; at least she trusted so. It looked like no head she ever saw in Calcutta, but perhaps that was no guide. He had managed to create an effect of having far more hair somehow, it really was most flattering, most – Caroline hardly dared admit it as she sat in unaffected delight before the glass – most encouraging.

The exquisite gauzy dress which had seemed such an incongruous garment for her but that very morning, did not seem quite so inappropriate now. She had never possessed a dress remotely like it, and it filled her with a kind of awe. She stepped into the underskirts of cream satin, lightly quilted in swirling patterns of shells and ferns, and felt the overdress of cream-silk gauze, satin-striped and edged with fragile embroidery in seed pearls and silk thread, lifted over her head and arms like a cloud of petals. It might be absurd, but she could not help smiling. Despite the desperate wet heat of the June night, despite the terrors of the party ahead and the known pitfalls of going anywhere with Johnnie in public, she could not at this moment feel anything but the most piercing, elating delight.

The servants were enchanted with her. Chinking with jewellery themselves, it seemed most strange that the memsahib should possess no adornment at all except the little watch she always wore at her waist. Nothing daunted, however, they darted into the rapidly darkening garden and came in with handfuls of creamy jasmine blooms, the last brave flowers to survive the onslaught of the summer heat. Choosing the freshest, they pinned them into the curls behind her head and crowed with delight at the effect.

Even Johnnie, Caroline was gratified to notice, looked considerably startled when she entered the drawing room. He was fortifying himself with a little champagne against the dangers of the journey ahead – dangers that only existed because the drunker he was, the more insistent he became about driving the carriage himself. He had twice upset them both, and the last party had ended with Mrs Rathbone bringing Caroline home since Johnnie, bellowing furiously from the box of the carriage, seemed in a mood to break their necks.

'You look very fine, ma'am.' A thought crossed his mind that he might be called upon to pay for the finery, a thought so painful to him that his face contracted abruptly.

'It was a gift,' Caroline said smoothly, reading his expression as if it had been a book. 'It was my wedding gift from Miss Grant.'

'Wedding gift? Wedding gift to us? What use is a dress to me, may I ask?'

'It was a gift to me.'

He snorted.

'May you get good use from it, for you'll not have another in a hurry.'

They drove in silence, the coachman for once being permitted to perform the duty for which he was hired. Night had fallen with the Indian suddenness Caroline still found surprising, and only the red glow of cooking fires and the dull yellow of oil lamps here and there along the way enlivened their rolling passage. The Nawab of Fultar, although he possessed an admirable palace in his dominions down in the Ganges delta, preferred to entertain in a magnificent new pleasure dome he had built himself among the parks and gardens of fashionable Calcutta. Caroline wished she could see more. She knew, from Isobel's chatter, that there was a part of Calcutta that in no way resembled the mud-built sprawl of her own area, indeed, she had had brief glimpses of green splendours when she sheltered with Mrs Rathbone. It was clearly this area of trees and luxuriant gardens and great houses that they were bound for now, and it was most frustrating to be able to see nothing in the velvety blackness but the occasional pinprick of light.

As they drove onward, they were joined by other carriages, and the streets began to boast, albeit ineffectually, some sort of lighting. The phaetons dashing past them were all full of groups of uproarious people, it seemed to Caroline, and the passing of their carriage lamps gave her brief but unmistakable glimpses of the envious dissatisfaction on her husband's face. If it were not for her, she thought, he might have been in one of those noisy carriages of bachelors, but then cheered herself by recollecting that if it were not for her, he would probably not be going at all.

The Nawab of Fultar did not wish his palace to be mistaken for any other. Enormous forethought went into these huge receptions he gave; forethought that began by illuminating his house with such myriads of lights and permanent explosions of fireworks that the glow surrounding it was visible a mile off. The sky all round the building was rippling with waves of brilliant light, green and rose and white, and as they drew nearer, in a now jostling throng of carriages, the thin high wail of an oriental band came floating down to them.

Johnnie groaned. 'God help us, not that, not their music. I've not come out simply to hear Indians caterwaul. It's nothing but the most horrid screeching.'

Caroline, leaning from the window, hardly heard him. They had swept through a gateway like a triumphal arch, and were now bowling up a great sweep of drive, bordered by the tallest palms, beyond which stretched lawns and huge tanks of water strewn with perfect floating blossoms. Every tree was hung with lights, every tank edged with them, and servants in gold and scarlet turbans stood at the edge of the drive, shoulder to shoulder, bearing flaming torches. The carriage suddenly swept round in a circle, and came to rest at the foot of a great flight of white marble steps, leading up to the most incredible and magnificent building Caroline had ever seen. Huge white domes seemed to float like giant pearls above her, supported on columns and fretted pillars with screens of pierced marble between. The whole seemed illuminated from within by a shimmering glow which made the entire building look as if it was as insubstantial as gossamer.

'Oh, do look!' she cried to Johnnie, but he was looking the other way, to see if he saw familiar faces among the carriages around them.

They climbed the steps several feet apart, seeming to onlookers that they had no wish to be regarded as arriving together. A ribbon of crimson carpet ran down the steps, and muffled their tread. At the top they passed between huge doors of latticed marble, set with panels of jade and coral, and before them lay a breathtaking vista of white space, and light and height and size. Caroline gasped, and heedless of the people pressing behind her, stood stock still on the threshold of this gleaming spectacle to stare and stare. The ceiling vanished away into the vaulted domes that roofed it, domes inlaid with a mosaic as intricate as embroidery, and seemingly as high above Caroline's head as the heavens. Delicate fluted pillars, like the slender trunks of young trees, soared upwards in support, their surfaces inlaid as the entrance doors had been, with semi-precious stones fashioned into flowers and birds and fruit. The floor was white, the walls were white, all made of marble and thus gleaming like the inside of an oyster shell. The window spaces were screened with marble, too, marble worked as if it had been as malleable and fragile as lace, carved into twisting patterns of amazing intricacy. Perhaps there were five hundred people there, perhaps more, but they seemed diminished to far fewer by this glowing white cave of a room.

Caroline looked round to express her feelings to Johnnie, and found him gone. She peered anxiously about her in that throng of brocade and powder but could see no sign of his cornflower blue coat or considerable stature. He had clearly spied some acquaintances, and used her absorption in her surroundings to make good his escape to their comfortable company. It was too bad of him, too bad indeed. She had no notion of how to proceed at an occasion such as this, she could only stand by a pillar, grateful for its smooth coolness, and hope that she did not look as miserably awkward as she felt. Should she slip down those steps again and see if their carriage still lingered, so that she might flee home unnoticed? Should she patrol the room to find an ungracious and unwelcoming Johnnie? Should she wait and hope for a glimpse of Isobel? She laid her cheek against the coldness of the marble and surveyed the crowd of Indians and Europeans surging brilliantly before her, and prayed that a familiar face might come.

'Are you admiring my house?'

Caroline took her cheek away abruptly from the pillar and looked round. A small, old Indian, in a turban encrusted with jewels and a tunic of purple brocade, was smiling at her with enormous kindness.

'Oh! I beg your pardon, indeed I was only—'

'There is no pardon to beg. I observed you in the doorway and I was much gratified by what I saw. Do you like my house?'

Caroline said with fervour, 'I do not believe I ever saw anything more astonishing. Or beautiful.'

He bowed.

'I am most pleased. Are you not amazed that my English is so excellent?'

Caroline smiled.

'It is indeed excellent.'

'My father was a most modern man, a most modern man. He did much business with English merchants and instructed all his sons in English. I am most pleased you like my house.'

Light suddenly dawned on Caroline.

'*Your* house?'

'Indeed so.'

'Then – then you are the Nawab of Fultar?'

'That is so.'

Stammering a little, with a faint colour along her cheeks, Caroline said, 'You must forgive me if I did not react properly when you addressed me. I fear I am but newly come to India and most ignorant. Should – should I have curtseyed to you?'

The Nawab laughed delightedly, clasping his little brown hands before him, and shaking his turbaned head.

'I do not wish it, no, no, I do not wish it! You smile for me and that is enough.'

'You are most kind.'

'No, no, I am not kind, I am pleasing myself. Always I am pleasing myself. It pleases me to give parties, it pleases me to hear music and drink wine, it pleases me to have in my house ladies like flowers who admire my house.'

Caroline's answering smile was radiantly grateful. Ladies like flowers indeed! Never, never could she remember anyone saying anything so delightfully poetic, so wonderfully romantic to her. Her eyes were as brilliant as moonlit water as she looked down at the gallant little Indian.

'Will you tell me about your house?'

'Most gladly. I have the inspiration from the Taj Mahal. You know, of course, of the Taj Mahal?'

Caroline shook her head.

'The Emperor Shah Jehan built it in the last century as a tomb for his wife whom he loved dearly. He built it in the plains of India, and he built it all of inlaid white marble, in domes with screens and pillars. It is most beautiful and I wished very much to have one too. But mine is not a tomb! Mine is a place for life!'

Across the room Isobel was flirting competently with two young officers steaming in the splendour of full dress uniform. Beside her, immaculate in dark blue with white linen, stood Sir Edward Ashton, fighting with boredom and a mounting desire to go home. He had not wanted to come in the first place, but Isobel had been most insistent and in the end he had agreed to stay for supper only, but to drag her home before the nautch began. He used to enjoy a nautch once, but Europeans were so sneering about them now, so supercilious, that the comments of his fellow guests ruined his pleasure and made him ashamed to be one of them.

He looked round for the Nawab, to congratulate him on his architectural skills. He was nowhere to be seen, which was hardly surprising since he was, like most native princes, an impeccable host, endlessly circulating at these huge receptions to make sure each guest had what he wanted. Shifting his shoulders uncomfortably, conscious of the linen peeling away from the damp skin of his back, Sir Edward put his eyeglass to his right eye and looked irritably about. The usual faces, of course, the usual unremarkable faces saying the usual unremarkable things to each other. Across the nodding sea of powdered and turbaned heads, Sir Edward found the unmistakable figure of the Nawab at last, solid with jewels, and talking animatedly to a most remarkable-looking young woman. Sir Edward took out his eyeglass, and polished it vigorously on his handkerchief, then replaced it for closer scrutiny. She was a most fascinating-looking creature, all the colour of honey, hair, skin, dress, and although no beauty in the accepted sense, she had a face of considerable distinction. Her hair was unpowdered, too, and woven with flowers. She was unlike anything Sir Edward had ever seen before, and she was conversing with the Nawab with an air of concentration that represented a challenge to the watcher across the room. He turned quickly and gestured to Lady Renton, seated peacefully gossiping by the wall.

'There is someone I must speak to, Lady Renton. Would you be so good as to look after Miss Grant for me?'

He threaded his way rapidly through the crowd, unaware of Isobel's satisfied gaze watching his passage. Caroline, deep in her first lesson of Moghul history, was unaware that anyone had joined herself and the Nawab, until a voice beside her said, 'Would it be unforgivable to interrupt, Nawab?'

She looked up and found herself immediately dismayed. This tall, impressive man, with his splendid presence and air of dignity, was none other than the alarming person who had whisked Isobel away on the waterfront three months ago. He was the man who had forbidden Isobel to see her and who openly disapproved of her and her husband. Muttering stammered excuses, she endeavoured to curtsey and move away, for it was evident that it was the Nawab Sir Edward sought.

'I beg you will not go,' he said in a low voice.

'No, indeed, you shall not go. You have listened to me so charmingly and now you shall listen to Sir Edward for a change. This delightful lady much admires my house, Sir Edward.'

'I am not surprised, Nawab.'

'I must present her to you, Sir Edward, but I have been so charmed by her conversation I have quite forgotten to ask her name.'

'It is of no consequence!' Caroline cried hastily. 'Please, it does not matter. I am sure I am intruding and that

you wish to speak without me. I will withdraw, indeed
I—'

A firm hand held her elbow.

'I hope you will do nothing of the sort, and I hope the
Nawab will forgive me if I tell him that I did not cross
the room to speak to him, but to speak to you.'

Startled out of her shyness, Caroline looked straight
up at him and saw that his eyes did not belie his words.
He did not take his hand from her elbow but went on
holding her with his firm grasp.

The Nawab, observing this, was chuckling delightedly
again, rocking back and forth on the toes of his golden
slippers.

'I see I have two guests who will be happy! It pleases
me to have guests who are happy! May I persuade you
to stay after supper for the nautch?'

Caroline removed her bemused gaze from Sir Edward
and said dazedly, 'The nautch?'

'Aha!' the Nawab cried delightedly. 'You have never
seen a nautch! You have not lived, you have not lived! I
have the most beautiful, the most witty, the most graceful
girls in all India. I have girls from Lucknow, girls from
Delhi. I have the best of all girls to perform for you!
Is not that true, Sir Edward?'

Sir Edward said to Caroline, 'Will you stay? If you will
stay, the Nawab may at least count upon an audience of
two.'

'I should like to if—' Caroline began doubtfully, still
anxious as to the effect of the revelation of her name.
But the Nawab waited for no more.

'Splendid! I am delighted! Now, Sir Edward, you will
look after this charming lady for me at supper?'

'If she will allow me.'

The Nawab bowed, smiled and vanished into the throng
to seek out any other lonely guest.

'Will you take my arm?'

Caroline hesitated.

'I – I feel I should tell you who I am. I know who you are, I am sure most of this room knows that, but I fear you – will be displeased when you hear my name.'

'I refute that entirely. Will you trust my equanimity and reveal this dreadful truth?'

'I am Caroline Gates. I came out on the *Sea Horse* with your cousin, Isobel Grant, to marry a man I have known since childhood.' She stopped, and then with a burst of honesty said, 'You do not countenance the man I have married and you have forbidden Isobel to visit me.'

'I must be mad,' Sir Edward said.

Caroline looked up at him earnestly.

'Please do not make light of it. You have been very angry with Isobel for visiting me, and I do not want to embarrass you by being seen with you!'

For answer Sir Edward picked up her hand and placed it within his arm.

Supper was laid in a room whose floor space almost equalled that of the great reception hall. The ceiling was painted with jungle beasts and men in turbans and girls in veils and jewels, and from it hung hundreds of lamps suspended on brass chains threaded with flowers. Sir Edward took Caroline to a table by a screened window and introduced her to the dozen or so men and women already seated there. She was greeted most kindly and sat down with the feeling that she was in a most happy dream which was certain to be broken by the coming of morning.

'Tell me again why you are in Calcutta,' Sir Edward said, pulling his chair close to hers.

'I came to marry.'

'And did you?'

'Yes – yes, I did.'

'I do not give a fig for that,' Sir Edward said.

'But it is – how things are.'

'Maybe. And how were things before that?'

'I come from a village in Dorset, a very small village called Stoke Abbas.' She stopped. It was so long since she had tried to recall it that the wheels of her memory seemed stiff. 'It is supposed to be a model village, of grey stone cottages running down a steep green hill to a river and a park. I think it is perhaps more a model to look at than to live in.'

Sir Edward looked at her keenly.

'Do you miss it?'

'I – I do not know. My feelings are so bound up with the people there. I did think today, however, that I would give a good deal for a wild autumn English day, with wet gusts and keen air. I was in the garden with the mali this morning trying to learn what I can expect to grow in the cool season, and I suddenly longed so passionately for a windy October day of driving clouds and yellow leaves!'

'You are as remarkable as you look,' Sir Edward said. 'I know no woman in India who bothers with her garden herself, who will take trouble to learn from, rather than instruct, the mali. I know no woman who sensibly attempts to grow Indian fruit and flowers instead of trying in vain to rear frail English ones. And I know nobody, man or woman, who has been able to induce in me the smallest pang of homesickness in ten years in India before now. But you have, and like you I would give anything at this moment for a stormy autumn morning in England.'

'I would not willingly induce homesickness in anyone.'

'Do you suffer yourself? I asked you before and you evaded me. Do you want to go home?'

Caroline looked down at her plate.

'Since my father died, I have not really got one to go to. The house is there still – but not what is necessary.'

'I understand you.'

She looked directly at him.

'Do you?'

'Certainly I do. I have a house in Herefordshire I have not missed in ten years for there is no-one there to return to, and I have no-one to take back to it. It is simply a house.'

Caroline felt her arm touched. The man on her left, a distinguished servant of the Company who had known Bengal for twenty years, wished to compliment her upon her hair.

'I hate this powdered fashion, hate it. Your curls are a pleasure to look at, my dear, a feast for the eye.'

Sir Edward could not hear her reply. He looked at those light twists and loops of hair, and their burden of flowers, and had to restrain in himself the desire to thread a finger through a loose curl lying on her shoulder. Her shoulder itself caught his attention, and the skin of her arm, so smooth and tawny, quite flawless, quite even. So strong was his inclination to touch this time, that he found his hand had involuntarily curved itself in the air above her arm that lay on the table, and he had to clench his fist to stop himself. He waited impatiently for her attention once more.

'You have no jewellery,' he said to her abruptly, forcing her to turn to him.

'I possess none.'

'Your flowers are perfect. Will you eat nothing?'

'I am not hungry. There seems to me too much food in India, too many meals.'

'You are too thin,' he said. 'You must not be too thin, you must look after your health.'

The nautch passed for Caroline in a dream. She was dimly aware of shrill oriental music, and of astonishingly supple girls in scarves and jewels dancing endlessly and tirelessly on a shining space of floor. They sang occasionally, answered repartee from the Indians left among the guests, and passed before Caroline's eyes in a blurred haze of gleaming skin and gems. She sat in the shadows at the edge of the room conscious of very little beyond the fact that Sir Edward Ashton was behind her chair and that she only had to tilt her head back a matter of inches for her hair to brush his waistcoat front. She did not do so. She sat and stared before her and never noticed that Johnnie had gone or that Isobel, from her circle of beaux across the room, was regarding her with an expression of delighted achievement. When the nautch ended finally in the dawn, and the lamps were re-lit to show only a small and yawning group of Europeans remaining, Caroline woke from her trance and asked for her carriage. Sir Edward endeavoured to prevent her, to escort her home himself, but she was adamant. Day had come and ordinary life must be resumed. She stepped into her carriage just as the first glorious glow of a Calcutta sunrise was spreading over the sky, and turned to say goodbye with no idea of how she should do so. But he was before her.

'*Au revoir,*' he said as he kissed her hand, and stepped back for the carriage to roll by.

Half an hour later, at six in the morning, Ralph Buxby was woken by a bearer. He was initially extremely angry, assuming the bearer had mistaken the hour and woken him early in error. However, a paper was thrust into his hand, and a lamp was brought so that he might read. The message came from his superior, Sir Edward Ashton, and contained express instructions that Buxby was to discover everything he could about a man named John Gates, and to have that information on Ashton's desk by noon.

15

Ashton was at his desk by ten. His servants had watched his homecoming with some trepidation, for only once before did they recall his returning at dawn and the consequences of that had been terrible for all of them. This time, however, though elated, he was clearly entirely sober and wore an expression of private joy that made them put him to bed with more than their usual reverence. They were summoned three hours later since he appeared to wish to rise, and found him still and most uncharacteristically remote and calm in his manner. He seemed not to notice as he was shaved and dressed, appeared unconscious that breakfast had been put before him and when the hookah-burdar slipped the mouthpiece of his pipe into his hand, he let it slip to the floor as if he could not feel it. Only when seated at his desk did he seem to recollect himself, and summoned Buxby with almost more than his usual vigour.

'Well, Ralph, and what news have you for me?'

'You indicated noon, sir,' Buxby said anxiously. 'It wants still two hours to noon.'

'It does?' Sir Edward said vaguely, looking about him as if evidence of the correct hour hung about him in the damp hot air.

'I am doing all I can, sir, I do assure you.'

Buxby licked his lips. He remembered very clearly the tiny episode eighteen months before in which John Gates had figured, and in which he, Ralph Buxby, had taken it upon himself to play an unauthorized part. He knew, for half Calcutta knew by now, exactly whom Sir Edward had spent the previous evening with, and now feared some consequence of his presumption.

'I am sure you are, Buxby. Do not look so perturbed.' He gazed into the spaces of the room in an abstracted way for a while before pulling himself together with a visible effort. 'Any news from the Governor General?'

There was plenty, Buxby was relieved to be able to say. The French were digging themselves comfortably into Poona, and were doing all they could to undermine the Company's presidency in Bombay, a presidency that had none of the strength or wealth of that in Calcutta. They were employing a divisive policy among the Marathas, the ruling people of that part of western India, and it seemed that assistance from Calcutta in the form of money and men was imminently necessary. Hastings had, as usual, his own decided ideas on the best course of action, and was, also as usual, opposed by all other members of the Council in what he wished to do, and therefore desired to hear Sir Edward's views as soon as possible.

When Buxby had gone, Sir Edward sat with pen and paper in a kind of benign abstraction. His views on dealing with any challenge to British dominion in India were usually as adamant as Hastings's own, but somehow this morning it was curiously difficult to bring his mind to bear on the probable necessity of raising several more regiments of sepoys, and the difficult task of selecting a man to lead them. He drew patterns idly on the margin of his paper, watching with interest the dimples of dampness his hand left upon it in the heat. After a while he gave up the task of even attempting to marshal his thoughts on paper, and flung his pen down, his hand then reaching out instinctively for the soothing influence of his hookah. The smooth coldness of the mouthpiece was briefly pleasant to the touch, and the comfortable bubbling sounds and draughts of spiced Persian tobacco contributed to his instinct for reverie.

Ten minutes before noon, Buxby was back, visibly damp with effort. He came into the room cautiously, not in the least sure of his reception, and found to his astonishment that, instead of the furiously scribbling figure Sir Edward usually presented, he was lounging back in his chair with an expression of indescribable pleasure.

'Sir Edward?'

'Ah! Buxby!' The lounging figure swung abruptly upright. 'What news have you now?'

'I have information, sir – and a confession.'

'Which will you give me first?' Sir Edward enquired serenely.

'The information, sir.'

Sir Edward nodded and fixed his eyes upon Buxby's sweating countenance.

'John Gates is the nephew of Lord Lennox, sir, Lord Lennox of Stoke Park in Dorsetshire. He was apparently something of a reprobate as a boy and, after a skirmish with Lord Lennox's eldest daughter, was sent out to Madras. I gather a relation in Scotland had some influence with the Company and obtained him a post as a clerk. It seems that his ways are unchanged from his boyhood.'

Ralph paused. He knew George Carew reasonably well, and therefore had a great deal more detail about Johnnie's life to hand than he had given. He decided that, in view of his superior's present mood, sordid revelations of Johnnie's habits were unnecessary.

'Lennox,' Sir Edward said thoughtfully. 'Lennox. Why do I have a small recollection of a Lennox?'

'We are coming more nearly to my confession, sir. May I say in advance that I deeply regret my presumption and never, since that time, have I exceeded my duty in such a manner.'

'I expect you to exceed your duty, you dolt,' Sir Edward said with a smile. 'What use to me is a secretary with no head on his shoulders?'

'Two years ago, a man came to Calcutta who forms a link between yourself and – John Gates. Your cousin, Lord Lovell—'

'I do not wish to recall him, Buxby.'

'I must, sir, in order to remind you that he married Lord Lennox's youngest daughter, and it was through his information that it came to be known to the Lennoxes that you were in Calcutta. They might not have needed this knowledge except that it seemed Lady Lennox wished for your opinion on a matter relating to John Gates over a year ago and I – I gave it to her.'

'What?'

For the first time that morning, Sir Edward's eyes seemed to be focusing clearly upon his secretary. Buxby quailed a little, but persevered.

'I gave her an answer, sir. She wrote to ask you if you knew any reason why the daughter of the incumbent of the living in her gift should not marry John Gates. The daughter was a Miss Caroline Harding. I replied by saying I knew of no impediment.'

He watched while his information was translated into understanding in Sir Edward's eyes.

'You said, Buxby,' Sir Edward said slowly, 'you said you knew no reason why this innocent girl should not marry a known blackguard! You said that?' His voice suddenly exploded into a bellow. 'How dare you presume to decide such matters? How dare you act in such a manner without consulting me?'

'I did consult you, sir,' Ralph said staunchly.

'You did?'

'Yes, sir, I did. But I do not think', he added bravely, 'that the matter concerned you as nearly as it does now.'

'When was this?' Sir Edward's tone was still dangerous.

'The winter before last, sir. During the troubles over excessive inland trading. Lady Lennox's letter came on an – unfortunate morning, sir.'

'Unfortunate? Why was it unfortunate?'

236

Buxby shifted uncomfortably. Most men had hangovers as their houses had mice, but if a man only has one monumental hangover in ten years it becomes both legendary and unmentionable.

'It – it is difficult to remind you, sir.'

There was a pause.

'I need no reminding,' Sir Edward said shortly. He sat bent over his clasped hands for a while and contemplated the consequences of the past. He could remember very little of that painful day except the suffering of his spirit as it wrestled with humiliation and self-disgust. He could recall that Ralph had presented him with a whole series of matters he could not begin to deal with in such a state, and he had no reason to doubt that in such condition, blind to everything but his wretchedness, he had allowed Caroline Harding to be sent as a lamb to the slaughter.

It was no good reasoning to himself that he could not possibly have known what she might mean to him, nor in arguing that if he had prevented the marriage she would never have come to Calcutta in the first place, and thus he would never have known her. The facts of the matter bore down all such reasonableness and left him full of remorseful anguish. Her look of happy gratitude last night, her thin and fascinating face dominated by those exquisite eyes and crowned with a halo of pale hair and flowers, flashed suddenly upon his inward eye and gave him resolution. She should not be squandered upon a reprobate, especially not when he was so entirely sure that he would want her for himself. If convention had to be flouted, well, so be it. He had trapped her in this marriage, and he would now open the cage and release her. It was as simple as that. He rose and smiled at Buxby.

'Find Miss Grant for me, would you, Buxby? I have a small task for her.'

*　　*　　*

237

Caroline's morning had given her no chance for happy reverie. She had been woken after a few hours only of deep unnatural slumber, because Ranjit's anxiety that Sahib Gates was still not home could be contained no longer. None of the servants who had accompanied them to the reception had seen him leave, all assuming that while the memsahib was still present, the carriage must stay and them with it. They stood before Caroline with clasped hands and bent heads and awaited reprimand. Her Hindustani was far from good, but she had enough now to speak simply to them.

'Did you see him go? Did any one of you see Sahib Gates go?'

They shook their heads. One had in fact noticed him climbing into a carriage with George Carew and a party of ladies, but he did not feel he wished to mention the matter. Johnnie had not summoned anyone to attend him and therefore wished to be left alone. He stared at his feet and said nothing.

'Then, Ranjit, you will take a letter to Sahib Carew for me.'

The note despatched, she sat down to a breakfast she did not want and tried to put her thoughts into some kind of order. She had scarcely even allowed herself a glimpse of the recollection of Sir Edward Ashton before there was a knock on the door and the great Pathan who had his eye upon Ranjit's position announced that a money-lender from the bazaar wished an audience with the memsahib.

Caroline felt a clutch of panic. In the last few days of fairy tale, when she had been so absorbed in sartorial delights and the joy of Isobel's enlivening company once more, she had quite forgotten that the repayment of her loan must begin. What was worse, was that the household was in want of money again, if she was to pay the servants as promptly as she had promised, and keep the kitchen stocked with the expensive European commodities Johnnie demanded. She rose with as much calm as she could muster and asked for the man to be shown in.

He entered with a smile that bore a disagreeable family resemblance to the sircar's.

'You are very prompt,' she said in a faintly accusing tone.

'And the memsahib is being most honourable, I am sure.'

She thought rapidly. Her one desire was to get him out of the house in case Johnnie should return and her secret be revealed. A few rupees still remained out of the hundred pounds, a few rupees destined for that week's food, but it would have to be sacrificed.

'I shall pay you a little today, and more next week when – when I can lay my hands on a larger sum.'

'The terms, oh gracious memsahib, were repayment in full after three months—'

'It cannot be,' Caroline said, surprised at the decisiveness of her tone. 'You shall have your money, and the interest, but I do not have it by me today.'

The money-lender shrugged. He was not unduly concerned, and knew very well how to make himself a nuisance, so much a nuisance in fact that no sum of money seemed too much to pay to get rid of him.

'I will return, memsahib.'

'I do not doubt it,' Caroline said faintly, and turned away as he left the room.

No use now to let her thoughts dwell luxuriously on forbidden pleasures. If she were to survive at all, she must put her thoughts to work and cudgel out of them some solution, however temporary. There were Johnnie's pictures still, of course, but the notion of taking those, however justified she might be, had grown distasteful to her. She must calm herself, she must. Nobody could think constructively while their minds were so distracted with anxiety. She cast about the room for some occupation with which to settle her wits and her eye lit upon the only painting of her own she had presumed to hang up, a miniature of the Parsonage painted from memory on that long and happy voyage. She would paint again! That was it. She would force herself to tackle some intricate and detailed subject, something so absorbing that it would allow her mind no escape until it was calmed and would once again work for her.

There was something heartachingly familiar about her materials, the ovals of ivory, the paints and brushes, the rags of torn-up petticoats still smeared with the paint and memories of the past. She looked out of the window on to the baked yellow earth of her garden with its struggling shrubs dusty in the merciless sunshine and saw no inspiration there. She glanced back at her miniature on the wall, and a sudden idea came to her. She would not paint India at all, India was all around her, she would paint something English, some cool, wet, green evocation of England. She closed her eyes for a moment and saw a tuft of young bracken, the brilliant green fronds uncurling soft and moist from damp dark earth, and snails among them, tiny snails with iridescent shells and questing horns. The idea was so captivating, so far removed from the oppression of her present situation, that she was suddenly in a ferment of eagerness to begin. She sat down at the table and sought her pencil and a suitable piece of ivory. There could be a spider's web, spangled with drops, and a ladybird for a single note of scarlet, and a mossy cushion at the base.

She was so deeply absorbed that the announcement that she had a caller startled her. She was dismayed to find her mood abruptly shattered, so dismayed that she could not move for a moment but sat bemused on her chair until Mrs Rathbone grew tired of examining the shabbiness of the drawing room and sought her out unheralded. She was bursting to see Caroline, to talk over the night before, and to see whether this odd self-contained girl was in the least affected by the great attentions paid to her.

'My dear Mrs Gates, Caroline, dearie! And how are we this morning? We are the talk of Calcutta, I do declare! Sir Edward Ashton has never been known to pay the smallest attention to any woman before, and it is said he did not take his eyes from you once! What a conquest, my dear, what a triumph!'

Caroline was silent. The mere thought of being the talk of Calcutta was repugnant to her, even though she knew the city thrived on gossip and grew quickly tired of any item of it.

'I am sorry to be the subject of any talk, Mrs Rathbone.'

'Sorry? Sorry? My dear, you are a foolish girl, my word you are. Sir Edward never stays anywhere beyond midnight, and there he was still dancing attendance at dawn. You should be pleased as Punch, my dear, I vow you should.'

Caroline shook her head helplessly. She knew Mrs Rathbone meant to congratulate her, and she knew that one of the motives, albeit a small one, of her visit was kindness, but she could not bear that the previous evening was the plaything of vulgar gossip. She had hardly had time to reflect upon it at all, but she sensed that it was probably one of the most precious occasions of her life and for that reason she bitterly resented that it should, even briefly, be public property. Mrs Rathbone watched her brightly and deduced that she had either been hopelessly overawed or entirely infatuated by her distinguished admirer.

'And what are you doing in here at this hour, my dear? I thought you were our early bird, always breakfasting with the dawn, putting us all to shame—'

'I was painting.'

Mrs Rathbone glanced at the table, and her casual air immediately became bright with interest. She peered intently down upon the little painting.

'My dear! I had no notion, no notion at all, that you had such a talent! It is charming, quite charming. It reminds me so of England, my dear, I could quite weep, I declare I could.'

She looked up at Caroline with the slightly challenging air of one who cannot resist acquisitions.

'Would you paint one for a friend, my dear, as a very great favour?'

'No,' said Caroline suddenly, seized by an inspiration. 'I wish I could afford to do that but I cannot. I only paint for purchase.'

'Hard-headed creature, Caroline!' Mrs Rathbone laughed and tapped her with a tasselled fan.

'Not by nature, Mrs Rathbone, but out of necessity.'

Mrs Rathbone looked about her at the run-down air of the room, the whitewash already streaking, the patched curtains and absence of silver and an inkling of the nature of Caroline's life came to her.

'Are you short of money, dear?'

'Yes,' Caroline said briefly.

'Does – does Johnnie keep you short, dear?'

Caroline said nothing, but fidgeted the pieces of ivory on the table. Mrs Rathbone clicked her tongue sympathetically.

'What shall you do, my dear?'

'I will sell miniatures, Mrs Rathbone, if you will help me. I wonder I never thought of it before, but Calcutta is so full of idleness and money that I feel I must have some small success.'

Mrs Rathbone's eyes lit up with pleasure at the thought of such a project.

'Caroline, what a wise head you have upon your shoulders! I think we may well start a new fashion for mementoes of England, indeed I do.'

'Will you help me? Will you be very kind and show my work to your friends?'

Mrs Rathbone thought of the happy diversion that the examination of miniatures would provide from the endless, though pleasurable, topics of dress and scandal. Quite apart from that she could see clearly that help was necessary, and help was something she liked to give. Within a quarter of an hour her carriage was bowling homewards, and she carried with her Caroline's promise that within two weeks some half-dozen of these tiny paintings would be at her house ready for sale. For every ten she managed to sell, Caroline would paint an eleventh of a subject of her own choice as a gift. Mrs Rathbone smiled contentedly to herself. Would people pay four guineas apiece, or dare she ask five? She thought of Caroline's neatly mended gown and the dining-room furniture placed discreetly so as almost to cover, but not quite, the worn patches in the carpet and decided she would stick out for five. Five guineas was, after all, no more than an average hairdresser's bill and Caroline was quite evidently in desperate need. Naughty Johnnie, Mrs Rathbone reflected with cosy disapproval; what a reckless, extravagant boy to keep his poor wife in such awkward penury, and what a providential thing that she, Bella Rathbone, had chanced to call. Suddenly Mrs Rathbone sat upright. It was too bad, indeed it was! In all the happy little arrangements about the pictures she had entirely forgotten to squeeze from Caroline every drop of fascinating information about Sir Edward Ashton!

Still in the dining room after Mrs Rathbone's departure, and elated at the prospect of some small release from her difficulties, Caroline went back to her painting with renewed vigour. If she rose each morning early, she calculated, and instructed the servants as to their tasks while she breakfasted in order to save time, she could see that five or six hours were at her disposal until the dinner hour, five or six hours for her meticulous work. Her father had once said it was hardly good for her weak eyesight to strain for long over the tiny details, but he had never contemplated that she would be in such straits as she now found herself. She had always worked fast, it was in her nature, and now she imagined that with practice she would become faster, indeed she had to. Over twenty miniatures had to be sold before she could regard herself as out of debt and beginning to make a profit. Twenty miniatures were well over two months' relentless work, given that she had no interruptions. She shook herself resolutely and settled sternly to the completion of the first.

She had not been working above a further hour when a letter was brought to her, a letter in Isobel's dear and familiar hand. It was an invitation to dine on the morrow for both herself and Johnnie, and Isobel indicated that Sir Edward was in no frame of mind to brook refusal or a prior arrangement.

'We dine at two, and will be eagerly looking out for you. You shall not refuse, dearest Caroline, without causing the wrath and dejection of your host, at whose command I gladly write. Tell Mr Gates I shall be sure to give him amusing companions at dinner, since I feel he may need some lure to be got up here at all to a house where his wife will be made so rapturously welcome.'

Caroline sat and gazed at the letter with a mixture of apprehension and joy. Within twenty-four hours or so, then, she was to see him again, he had remembered her, he had asked for her! Her face was illuminated by a quite involuntary smile, a smile of absolute happiness that was abruptly extinguished as she remembered guiltily for the first time in hours that not only could she not at this moment accept for Johnnie, but she also had not the smallest notion where he was. She rang immediately.

'Have you any news of Sahib Gates?'

'He will be returning after dinner, memsahib,' Ranjit said. 'He is detained but he is returning then.'

'Why have you not told me this before? Where is he? Is he hurt or ill?'

Ranjit could not look at her. He had not come to her immediately with the news of his master's whereabouts because he had been busy in the servants' quarters with a fierce dispute over whether he should tell her at all. The great Pathan had declared that the memsahib had the heart of a lion and could bear all truths, but Ranjit's own gallantry had made him wish to temper the truth and not put that lion's heart to the test. The truth was that Johnnie had indeed been at George Carew's house, and the servants there had informed Ranjit that Rani, Sahib Gates's old mistress, had come there in the dawn and that Sahib Gates had wept when he saw her, and pressed gold into her hands, and they were still together. Sahib Carew had told Ranjit that he would see Sahib Gates was home before nightfall, and that the memsahib was not to worry. This part, at least, of the message, Ranjit felt he could give.

'Then I will dine alone, Ranjit,' she said quietly. 'I will dine at four since I wish to continue painting. And I thank you, Ranjit,' she added, discerning from his manner that his news was edited, 'for what you have left unsaid.'

Johnnie came home in a lowering temper and last night's sweat-soaked linen. Only when he wrenched himself from Rani's entwining arms to seek the rival attraction of George's cellar at the dinner hour, did he hear of Caroline's triumph the night before. His reaction was initially to be furious, to feel himself cuckolded and diminished, and to declare roundly to the table of red-eyed, stale-mouthed gentlemen in George's dining room that Sir Edward Ashton must be an ass to waste his attention on a woman with no more charms than a broom handle. He muttered and complained his way through a prodigious quantity of claret, swore that some rogue had thieved what he had won at whist the night before, and was packed into George's carriage to go home, still demanding the company's pity for the fool he had been made to seem. He arrived back to find Caroline still wearing the traces of the previous night's elation, and in possession of an invitation to dine at a house where Johnnie had fruitlessly sought entry for six years or more. He cursed and swore at her for a little while to soothe his feelings and to disguise his eagerness to accept, and then, shouting for fresh linen, he declared his intention of passing the evening at the whist club. Out of an unspoken mutual desire not to know the truth, he did not ask her about the previous evening, and she made no enquiries as to where he had been.

16

At two the following day, Johnnie was nowhere to be seen. He had breakfasted with Caroline in silence, casting her resentful glances and heaving sighs of self-pity, and had only broken his silence to say he would return at noon and she was to order the carriage for a quarter to two. She had tried to paint that morning, but was in such a state of happy trepidation that she knew the results were not her best work. She was slightly ashamed of how frequently her thoughts ran on the vexing problem of how she should dress. Isobel's present was clearly out of the question, being a dress only for after dark, but the choices it left were in truth extremely dreary, and would inspire none of that sartorial excitement she had felt when dressing for the great reception. At long length she selected a dress of pale blue muslin, for although the fabric would be conspicuously humble amid the splendours of Sir Edward's dining room, it was the dress that fitted her best and contained the Stoke Abbas dressmaker's fewest errors. She only possessed one silk dress in any case, and she had come to detest it for it had been the last new dress before her father's death and was inextricably mixed up in her mind with her guilt and suffering over that event.

She sat in the sweating gloom of the drawing room and waited for Johnnie. Her servants had made an excellent imitation of her French hairstyle of two nights before, and one had, in a last moment of inspiration, wound a blue ribbon high about Caroline's throat for ornament. It chafed her when she swallowed, but the effect was almost elegant. It was difficult to sit still, difficult not to glance eternally at her watch, difficult to subdue her mounting excitement. At a quarter past two, she made a sudden resolve and rose to her feet. She would go, she could not bear not to, and Johnnie must follow as best he could.

Her consciousness of being late filled her mind with far more alarm than the decision whether or not to wait for Johnnie. As her carriage halted before the great square white house by Calcutta's Court House, with gardens about it and the river glittering below, she felt it would in fact be impossible to mount those steps alone and enter a room full of self-possessed strangers knowing that she was late and with the added embarrassment of being unaccompanied.

As she stepped reluctantly from the carriage, a young Englishman appeared at the top of the steps, called to a servant and then, before Caroline was even halfway up that daunting flight, Sir Edward Ashton himself was in the doorway and leaping down the steps towards her. He was beside her in a moment, seizing both her hands in his, all without giving a single glance towards the carriage which he must have presumed still held the unwanted Mr Gates.

'I thought you had failed me.'

She looked up at him with difficulty in the blinding sunlight.

'Oh, no, no, I would not – I am so sorry to be so late, I do apologize, but my husband is not home, he has sent no word, I—'

'Think nothing of it.'

Still holding the hand closest to him, he began to lead her up the steps.

In the stripes of sun and shadow of the doorway, he turned her to face him, and in the shadows behind them, Buxby waited in interested amusement, watching their black profiles against the sunlight turned earnestly to each other.

At last Sir Edward raised the hand he still held and kissed it.

'I fear I must share you with some dozen others. It is all arranged by Isobel for I have the social instincts of a hermit. Buxby, do not slink in the shadows like a servant. Come and be presented to Mrs Gates.'

Ralph bowed before her with a hint of self-consciousness. She smiled and he saw her eyes and the warmth and happiness in them, and a pang of shame made his own returning smile difficult to achieve.

Isobel was waiting in the drawing room in ill-concealed excitement.

'Oh, thank heaven you are come, Caroline! I thought you had played the coward at last, I truly did, and Sir Edward has been pacing like a caged tiger since noon—'

'Hush, Isobel!' Caroline said in a shocked whisper, keenly aware of the sudden attention of everyone else in the room and of her left hand still firmly and conspicuously imprisoned.

'Caroline, you are a goose,' Isobel declared. 'I do assure you', she went on to a man beside her, 'that Mrs Gates has more to congratulate herself upon than the rest of us women put together, but she has not the first notion how to do it.'

The man came forward, took Caroline's free hand and kissed it.

'We can only admire such modesty, Mrs Gates, and school ourselves to the impossible task of ignoring your enchanting friend. Your servant, John Eyre, ma'am.'

They all seemed about her then, smiling and presenting themselves, eager to see, in all her detail, this phenomenon who had so obviously captivated Calcutta's most eligible and obstinate bachelor. There was to be much discussion later, of course, discussion on the provincial drabness of her dress, the remarkable fact of her unpowdered head, her astonishing quicksilver eyes and her quietly independent behaviour. She was pronounced hopelessly plain, unfashionably thin and awkwardly shy, but there were also opinions that declared her face to be one of considerable distinction, her manners appealing in their gentle diffidence, and her figure elegant among some of the more solid flesh about her. Whatever the world, in the shape of twelve English people in Calcutta in the summer of 1777, thought of her appearance, their views were all coloured by respectful astonishment before dinner was over.

Caroline found herself on Sir Edward's right, her own right flanked by the comfortable stocky figure of John Eyre. The room bore many resemblances to the dining room at Stoke Park, except that the painted wood that panelled it was laid against mud, and the floor was of marble. She looked about her with pleasure, at the pictures on the walls that spoke so powerfully of England, at the pierced brass hanging lamps one saw everywhere in Calcutta, at the polished wood and silver, the Indian rugs and embroideries.

The talk ranged easily about her, talk of the French, talk of the decaying Moghul princes living out lives of voluptuous splendour, talk of England and Lord North's government that sought to direct the East India Company with a more official hand than it had ever felt before. Caroline listened with absorption, ate a little of everything that was put before her, and raised her glance every so often to reassure herself that everything was real, and to find Sir Edward gazing at her often with a kind of delighted triumph.

When the fruit was laid upon the table in great woven baskets, a man who sat several places down the table from Caroline, and who had introduced himself as Piers Lawrence, called to attract her attention.

'We have given you enough time, Mrs Gates, to establish your composure, and I now propose to test it.'

'You will do no such thing,' Sir Edward asserted.

Caroline had detected a gleam of challenge in Piers

Lawrence's eye, and felt herself serene enough to meet it. He was a handsome man, a black-haired handsome man with a sardonic air and mocking eyes.

'Oh, please, Sir Edward, let him speak.'

'Do you wish it?'

Caroline nodded.

'You are a fortunate man, Piers, but I will brook no insolence, not the smallest suggestion of it.'

'Insolence could not be further from my thoughts, Sir Edward. I merely wish to know from Mrs Gates if certain rumours are true.'

At the mention of rumours, Caroline froze, but it was too late to retract now.

'Rumours, Mr Lawrence?'

'I gather, Mrs Gates,' he said slowly, 'that you are perhaps the most intrepid in our number. I gather you have been seen in the native bazaar, attended by no more than one servant, I might add—' he paused, and a little ripple ran round the table.

'Pray go on,' Caroline said.

'Perhaps you are unaware that it is hardly customary for an Englishwoman to enter the bazaar? Perhaps you are equally unaware that it is not expected that an Englishwoman shall meddle with her servants' lives, dose their children, teach them English, interfere with their living habits, and be on terms with them that I can only describe as familiar?'

Sir Edward was on his feet.

'Get out! I said there was to be no insolence and you have exceeded yourself! Get out, I say!'

'No – no, please, Sir Edward!'

He looked down. Caroline had her hand upon his sleeve and was looking up at him with irresistible earnestness.

'No, you must not dismiss him, Sir Edward, you must not. Everything he says is true. It is only that the interpretation I put upon my actions is wholly different to his.'

The table, which had erupted into excitement, was instantly stilled. Unwillingly, Sir Edward lowered himself into his chair again.

'I have every faith in your interpretation,' he said.

Caroline looked down at her lap for a moment, aware that while she could defend her affection for her servants, she could not explain the emotional desert and threat of destitution that had driven her to them and to visit the bazaar. She raised her eyes at last and stared unwaveringly down the table at Piers Lawrence.

'This country is not ours, Mr Lawrence, we may plunder it and use it to our advantage, and many Indians may profit from our being here, but it is not ours. It seemed to me, arriving as a complete novice, that I would only understand India through the Indians. It seemed to me that the society which involves most of Calcutta could be better found in Bath or London. We English live a parasite's life here, and I did not wish to do that. How do I know if Indians resent my presence here, your presences, all our presence? It would seem that the humblest way to live here for me – I do not speak of men of affairs – is to let India teach me. How do I do that if I do not know my servants, the people who are closest to me? How do I learn not to offend them if I do not know how they live, how they market, how they pray? And if I come to the conclusion that I like them, that I admire them and that there are ways in which I can help their children to be less sickly, make their problems of speaking to their employers less difficult, why should I deliberately hold back that help because I am English and they are Indian? They help me immeasurably. May I not return some of that help? If you disapprove of such opinions, Mr Lawrence, I cannot help it, but I could wish, for India's sake, that your mind were not so narrow.'

She was trembling when she stopped. She realized that all these thoughts had been mere instincts before, that she had never rationalized them until now, and that in doing so she had sounded as dangerously priggish as Eleanor. She dropped her eyes.

'Forgive me,' she said in a low voice to the table at large. 'I fear I have presumed a superiority I do not feel. I have no right to judge Mr Lawrence, no right at all, forgive me—'

There was a burst of cheering. She could not look up, but sat and wished very much that she had held her tongue. In the babble, she was conscious of Isobel kneeling at her side, smiling, and talking rapidly, but she could make no reply. Someone broke through the circle and stood by Isobel, someone whose exquisitely cut breeches and silk stockings, which was all Caroline dared glance at, betokened a man of fashion.

'I surrender completely, Mrs Gates.'

'It is Piers!' Isobel whispered. 'Be gracious, Caroline!'

Caroline looked up and saw that his eyes were no longer mocking.

'It – it is very handsome of you, Mr Lawrence, I feel that I—'

'You were magnificent, Mrs Gates, and I have nothing but admiration for your spirit. Will you accept my humblest apologies?'

'Gladly.'

He drew back a little, and the press of people, still murmuring in undertones of excitement, drifted back to their places. Caroline ventured to steal a glance in her host's direction, terrified to find, because of his silence, the blackest disapproval written there. But he was regarding her with a look of admiration so unmistakable that she was held motionless by it, as a rabbit in a snare.

'You are matchless,' he said at last. 'Matchless!'

At home in the gathering dusk a most peevish Johnnie awaited her. He had deliberately delayed himself that morning out of a small resentment that Caroline should be the instrument by which he entered great houses, and also because he was perfectly certain her social timidity would force her to wait for him, however late he was. He arrived but minutes after her departure, and burst instantly into the flaming and violent temper the servants had known daily in his bachelorhood; now he vented it upon Caroline instead, and they were out of training for such an onslaught. By the time he had been changed and had consumed a bottle of champagne to console himself for his wife's callousness and shameless social climbing, Ranjit was forced to point out gently that it was almost three o'clock.

'What of it, you dolt?' Johnnie shouted.

He strode out on to the landing and bellowed for the carriage.

'Memsahib is taking it, sahib.'

It dawned slowly upon Johnnie that if he wished to get there at all he must ride and furthermore the distance would take him twenty minutes or more, at which point he would be an hour and a half late, not to mention dusty, exhausted and drenched in sweat. Swearing and cursing, Johnnie kicked his way downstairs, banged into the dining room and bellowed for mutton and wine. All Calcutta would be dining by now, all his friends deep in happy conversation and quaffing wine they had not had to pay for, and all because of Caroline's inordinate selfishness he was forced to sit here alone with a solitary chop and only a bottle for company. She had promised always to look after him, she had sworn to make him comfortable, but clearly her idea of comfort only concerned herself. Oblivious of the days and nights Caroline had spent alone in their gloomy rooms while he was out pleasuring, forgetful of the fact that she had made his life more comfortable than it had been in ten years in India, Johnnie sat in the dim room and chewed and muttered and vowed he would be even with her.

When she did return at last, and he marched out into the hallway to vent his furious resentment on her, he found that he might as well have addressed a brick wall. She gazed at him with a kind of calm remoteness, her eyes fixed upon some inward picture, not absorbing the spectacle of his temper at all, and then, without so much as a word, she shook her head slightly as if to get rid of some disagreeable sensation about her ears, and climbed the staircase to her room. He shouted still as she went, but his words and insults bounced off her like hailstones, and then, as he paused for breath, he heard the door of her room shut softly. He started up the stairs after her still bellowing, then halted abruptly halfway up.

'Damnation take you, you bitch!'

The key would be turned by now. She had had the lock of her door mended.

17

By the time the monsoons came, Calcutta was weary of the subject of Mrs Gates and Sir Edward Ashton. Affairs, after all, only retained their fascination if one or both of the participants was prepared to be flamboyant and thus sustain public appetite for sensation. By September, Calcutta was used to them and bored by them, and now had a new target in any case. Warren Hastings, having lived with the Baroness Imhoff openly in Calcutta awaiting her divorce, at last received that eagerly awaited news in the summer of 1777, and instantly married his lady. With a new Mrs Hastings to flatter and toady to, who could be bothered any longer with plain Mrs Gates, however impressive her admirer?

For her part, Caroline was thankful when the glare of public interest was diverted. July and early August had passed for her in an enchantment so powerful she had quite forgotten to observe the reactions of those around her. If she had looked, she would have seen that the gossips were still astounded that Johnnie could not quite bring himself to behave heavy-handedly, because he was very doubtful he was a match for Sir Edward, and that Isobel, Mrs Rathbone and George Carew saw in Caroline what could only be called a flowering. There was a distinct bloom about her, an aura of freshness and vitality despite the appalling heat. Her hair seemed thicker, her cheeks to have more colour and her body seemed less the awkward collection of angles it usually presented.

'My dear, it is no more nor less than a fairy tale,' Mrs Rathbone said to a friend. 'She'll never be a beauty, poor dear, but you never saw such a change in anyone, I swear it.'

Isobel, free now to see Caroline as often as she chose, observed the same to her friend's face.

'Dearest Caroline, you are hardly the same person. Indeed, if it were not for these dreadful old muslins you will wear of a morning, I doubt I should recognize you.'

Caroline knew she was indeed not the same person. The combination of the difficulties of her everyday life in Calcutta and the splendour of being loved by such a man as Sir Edward Ashton, had caused her to emerge at last from the chrysalis of her diffidence. Mrs Rathbone had proved, for all her garrulity, a faithful ally in the matter of the miniatures, and the little paintings, diplomatically unsigned, were now springing up in drawing rooms all over Calcutta. It was in truth becoming quite the fashion to have a whole collection of these nostalgically English miniatures hung tastefully to one side of the chimney-piece; so much the fashion, Mrs Rathbone reported, that she had even seen two dormice and a bunch of primroses hanging incongruously among the jewelled splendours of an Indian harem. Prices in Calcutta were so outrageous that Caroline found she could ask ten guineas quite brazenly, almost all of that sum being pure profit since Ranjit brought her all the ivory she could want from the bazaar at a price she could hardly credit was so small. She was, as a result of this secret and successful traffic, out of debt and well on the road to running the household without having to apply to Johnnie for anything, a fact he never seemed to notice, but rather took for granted.

It was, indeed, all deeply satisfactory, except for the fact that to comply with what seemed an insatiable demand she was having to force herself to paint eight or ten hours a day, and her eyes were sore and strained as a result. She rose at dawn, painted until the dinner hour, and then, if she were not dining out, painted again until the light failed. The results were not as meticulous as those first few she had done in the weeks of oppressive need to pay her debt, but they seemed to suffice. Calcutta's taste, she concluded, was for show and, fortunately for her, not for exquisite workmanship.

But all this paled into insignificance beside her other achievement. Supporting herself and, in some measure, her household was indeed a matter for congratulation, but it was a small thing, a trivial, material thing, beside the fact that she was in love for the first time in her lonely adult life, and that that love was returned an hundredfold.

Sir Edward did not seem to find her dull or gauche or plain, he did not appear to think her existence pointless or her ideas trivial. No opinion seemed too small to excite his notice, no gesture or comment too slight to excite a reaction from him. She saw a good deal of him all that summer for between them, he and Isobel saw that she was invited to anything they might attend themselves. At every meeting he would bear down upon her like a knight who has at last found the Holy Grail, and carry her off to some secluded corner and the miracle of his undivided attention. He never, in all those glittering weeks, said in so many words that he loved her, but Caroline, timid, pessimistic Caroline, who had doubted almost every pleasant occurrence in her life, never doubted for one moment that he did. She only had to look up to him and find his steady gaze bent upon her to reassure herself that it was true, it was real, it was her he wanted.

In any other city, the consequences of such an entanglement would have pressed upon Caroline and Sir Edward Ashton quite quickly; but not in eighteenth-century Calcutta, a city so rife with reckless immorality that high-principled behaviour was conspicuous rather than the opposite. It was also assumed that any affair that did take place was doomed to a short life, since the climate, the short terms of office of most Europeans, and the presence of plenty of other and more tempting fish to fry, conspired against emotional steadfastness.

Caroline had horrified herself initially, but then even she saw how calmly her own behaviour was taken, and abandoned herself to the happiest weeks she had known. She tried not to think ahead, discouraged Isobel from speculating, and presumed Sir Edward was in the same thoughtless limbo of bliss as herself.

She was wrong. Sir Edward had never been a soldier, but his mind had the same aptitude for successful forethought and planning as an able commander's. Wrenched, albeit willingly, from the Persian and Arabic studies with which he used to beguile his solitary hours, to dote upon Caroline, he did not allow his wits idleness. The very morning after he had met her, he had resolved what he would do for her, and he was simply, with a fierce and possessive tenderness, waiting for such a time as she might feel she could trust him without reservation. It was not a plan he could have proposed in London, perhaps not anywhere save Calcutta, but luckily society here, much as he might disapprove of it, made it possible.

'I beg you,' he said to her once in his own drawing room, while the monsoon rain fell from the sky in solid masses, 'that you will gradually, as you feel comfortable, tell me everything of your history. You must know by now that I am greedy for every crumb that you can give me as soon as you feel it is possible.'

Caroline had never believed it would be possible to speak of such matters as her father's death, or to recall her relationship with Eleanor impartially. They were all so bound up with her own sense of inadequacy that she had believed they would be too painful to voice, but not, it proved, to Sir Edward.

'My dear Caroline, I would give a good deal to love my own sister, and the fact that I do not is quite as much her responsibility as it is mine. Eleanor must come to meet you halfway.'

It was a novel idea. When she eventually told him of her father's death and the lurking fear of responsibility that shadowed her memory of him, Sir Edward reacted just as her father himself had done.

'Why your fault? Why any more your fault than any servant's?'

Caroline remembered the Judas kiss.

'Did your sister never kiss him? Did the servants not handle the food he ate? Come, look at me and do not turn away. Don't indulge yourself with these morbid fancies. I could wish selfishly that he were not dead so that I might indulge myself in talking to him of you, but if he were not dead you would not be here and—'

He stopped abruptly, and reached out to take her hands.

'There is one more avenue we must explore if you will not think me an intruder. Not today,' he added, observing the effects of recalling Parson Harding's death still evident on her face, 'but when you are ready. Will you tell me how you came to agree to be Mrs Gates?'

Caroline nodded.

'Another day.'

He raised her hands and kissed the fingers bent over his own.

'When you wish it.'

In all these weeks of happy confidence, Caroline saw little of Johnnie. He had, at the beginning, intended to demand honourable satisfaction for being cuckolded, and to challenge Sir Edward to a duel. George Carew, lazing beside him at his desk, pointed out the absurdity of the notion.

'You'll look a damned fool, my boy, indeed you will. You're no cuckold for a start, for I'll wager all Calcutta will tell you he's done no more than kiss her hand. Deuced if I know what they're up to, but it ain't what you're up to seven nights a week.'

'I look a fool,' Johnnie complained. 'She's never with me, and all the world knows where she is.'

'You don't want her with you,' George pointed out

reasonably. 'You do nothing but shout at her when she is. Added to which, you're a damned poor shot these days and I'm told Ashton has the eye of a hawk. Pity to die for a woman you don't want.'

'I do—' Johnnie began petulantly.

'Do you, my boy?'

Johnnie shifted in his chair and muttered inaudibly.

'I will say', George said idly, 'that you are a prettier sight since she came, and you wouldn't know the house from the hovel it was. But you don't lust for her, boy, do you?'

'Certainly not!' Johnnie said indignantly.

George got up slowly.

'Then leave her be. Why shouldn't she have her bit of fun, then? Deuced sight more harmless than yours. It'll all be over by Christmas in any case, and then you'll thank me for not getting yourself winged for nothing.'

The monsoon vanished as abruptly as it had come, and the blanket of wet heat that had accounted for the large number of funerals in the past weeks lifted, and air with a delightfully crisp edge to it came as a reward for endurance. Caroline, temporarily secure in her financial affairs, spent hours with the mali in the garden, kneeling beside him to press seedlings into the damp red earth. Things grew with gratifying speed, she observed, as she watched this veil of brilliant green, the result of the recent rains, bringing the dry yellow bones of her garden to life.

Not only winter was stirring in Calcutta. With quite a new source of information in Sir Edward Ashton, Caroline was beginning to be conscious of an India far and away beyond her small house and even the furthest reaches of Calcutta. The French, working on in western India, were now posing themselves as a considerable threat in reality, and it was Warren Hastings's opinion, an opinion shared by Sir Edward, that war between the English and French in India was a strong probability.

261

'War!'

'Do not look so alarmed,' Sir Edward said. 'Calcutta is quite secure. In any case, we have a lot to do in western India before the French spread here. But it does have some unhappy consequences, one of which is that I must send Isobel home.'

Caroline was aghast.

'You cannot, truly you cannot! She was to stay for a year, till the end of the cold season! She will miss all the things she loves most! You said yourself the French are no immediate threat, so why send her so soon?'

He came to sit close by her.

'It must be soon. If war breaks out between us, the seas home will not be safe and in half a year Calcutta may not be safe either, and I shall have failed in my guardianship lamentably. If I send her now, she will reach England in the spring, and it is unlikely that there will have been much direct conflict here by that time which means that English ships will not be molested on the high seas.'

Caroline thought of life without Isobel, without that delightful companionship, that spirit-lifting gaiety. As if he read her thoughts, Sir Edward touched her hand lightly and said, 'I shall see that you are not too desolate.'

'Oh – oh, forgive me, I did not wish to seem – it is just that she has opened up such a life for me, she has meant so much to me—'

He nodded. They looked at each other gravely for a moment, aware of what each owed to Isobel.

'Send her,' Caroline said at last. 'I could not bear harm to come to her. Send her at once.'

In the slightly reflective and vulnerable mood that fell upon Caroline after Isobel's departure, Sir Edward saw his chance. He was aware he must take it quickly, for his opportunities to meet Caroline were fewer now that Isobel no longer offered a ready and eager excuse. In any case, he had subdued his natural impatience long enough, and although he knew, from a boldly outright question, that she did not leave his company at night to share her husband's bed, his desire to have her for himself was increasing daily.

They were invited to supper one clear November night by John Eyre and his pretty, indolent wife. Johnnie was, as usual, about business of his own, and Caroline, since it was perhaps the twentieth occasion she had done so, felt no compunction in setting off to sup in this new and happy circle of friends, without informing him. It was an occasion late enough, she felt, to warrant Isobel's dress, but slipping into it this time, she had a sensation of melancholy rather than excitement, for the donor was no longer there.

She arrived alone at the Eyres's house, quite accustomed now to doing so, and was ushered into their most elegant drawing room, ablaze with candelabra. In an alcove, she noticed with pleasure that there was a familiar miniature of cowslips.

'Is it not charming?' Mrs Eyre was saying of it in her comfortable drawl. 'I cannot discover where they come from, but I dare say that does not much matter.'

'Finely done,' a gentleman said, screwing in his eyeglass. 'Must be English in execution. Exquisitely observed. Wonder who does them?'

'Do you buy them in Calcutta, Mrs Eyre?' Caroline asked innocently.

'Yes, yes, I do. Should you like me to obtain one for you? It is no trouble. I do it through friends.'

'Thank you,' Caroline said with an irrepressible smile. 'I do thank you, but I must not indulge myself just now.'

Sir Edward Ashton was at her elbow.

'Then let me indulge you. You will not allow me to indulge you in anything, and I long to shower you with treasures. Even the books I would gladly give you, you only borrow. Let me buy you one of these enchanting pictures. Please me this once.'

Caroline, her face alight with laughter, shook her head.

'You cannot,' she said with difficulty. 'I fear you cannot.'

He eyed her suspiciously.

'There is more to this than it would seem. What is the reason for all this mirth, Caroline?'

'I cannot tell you just now,' she said looking up at him with eyes still shining with laughter. 'One day I will tell you, I promise it, but not now. And when I tell you, you will understand my laughter.'

'I don't care for riddles.'

She shrugged delightedly and walked with him to supper. Whatever her secret was, it had illumined her face like a lamp within and given her a gladness and a confidence that encouraged him to feel that tonight was the time he should speak. Even the sight of George Carew, an unexpected guest at such a gathering, did not diminish her gaiety, and the moment supper was over, and card tables were being set up, Sir Edward drew Caroline away to a secluded corner by open windows where the sweet cool air could blow in upon them.

Whatever Sir Edward had decided for that evening, Caroline seemed to have made resolutions of her own. It was in just such a mood, it occurred to her at supper, that she could tell Sir Edward of how she had agreed to be Mrs Gates without becoming oppressed at the memory of Lady Lennox's successful trap. She felt buoyant enough to treat the matter quite lightly, and thus, when Sir Edward seated himself opposite to her, as he loved to do, she gave him no chance with the matter on his mind.

It sounded a curious story as she told it. She hoped her portrait of Lady Lennox was a reasonably fair one, but felt very much as she drew to a close that the person who emerged most feebly from the whole pattern was herself.

'You will think me very weak, I fear, to comply so obediently with what were strange commands but I was

264

so – so desolated by Papa's death, and the future looked so empty, that I made the only decision I felt I could.'

'It is an outrageous story.'

'Do not be angry, Sir Edward! Please do not. I know it seems to you that my behaviour was feeble-witted—'

'It is not that in the least,' Sir Edward said, leaning forward to take her hands. His eyes were blazing. 'It is nothing to do with you. You, as usual, made precisely the choice I find understandable. But that – that woman! Lady Lennox. What proof have you – no, look at me, do not turn away for an instant – that Lady Lennox had any legal right to withhold an inheritance from John Gates?'

'Proof?' Caroline said stupidly.

'Yes, proof. By what information did you learn that she had such power over the inheritance?'

Colour was beginning to rise in Caroline's face.

'Johnnie – told me. He had a letter. A letter from Lady Lennox. He said that she told him if he did not marry me he—'

Her voice tailed away. Sir Edward continued to look steadily at her.

'Do – do you mean we – we have been duped?'

'I have no proof of that any more than you have proof Lady Lennox had a right to direct you both as she has done. Have you seen no legal document, no lawyer's letter, even?'

'Nothing,' Caroline whispered.

They sat in silence for a minute or two, Sir Edward contemplating with inward fury, some of it directed at himself, what an innocent pawn Caroline had been in the lives of people to whom she was only useful for a brief interruption; Caroline was only appalled at her own naïvety, at the raw gullibility which had led both her and Johnnie to accept Lady Lennox's word as law. After a while she raised a confused countenance to Sir Edward and said in a low voice, 'You must think me – unforgivably incompetent and unworldly.'

He was on his knees by her chair in a moment.

'If I did think so, I can promise you I would think it no fault. If being unworldly results in a nature so deeply sympathetic and gentle as yours, then it is something we should all strive for.'

She bent her head, struggling with her own humiliation after these months of independence that were so sweet to her.

'Listen to me – Caroline, dearest Caroline, for so you are.'

He put a hand beneath her chin and turned her face forcibly to his.

'There is nothing about you that I would change, nothing, except your married state. I see in you all I have unconsciously sought all my life, unconsciously because I did not know such a creature existed, a woman of strength and sympathy, a woman of pride and compassion, the only woman I have ever met who had every cause on earth to be self-satisfied, and who is humble through it all.'

'Please—'

'Does it displease you to be spoken to thus? I have waited all these months because I feared to alarm you, but I cannot wait any longer. Is what I say unwelcome?'

'Nothing – nothing, no speech was ever more welcome.'

His hand still firmly beneath her chin, he leaned forward and kissed her.

'If you knew how I longed to do that! Every night I have seen you I have hardly known how to restrain myself. What are you thinking, my Caroline?'

'You – you are sure?'

He smiled at her incredulously.

'Sure? I was never more sure of anything in my entire life!'

'But—' she hesitated, it seemed so foolish a thing to say, but then, it was something that had haunted her all her life, 'but – I am considered – I mean, I – am so very plain.'

'Plain!' he shouted. 'Plain? How can you possibly be plain when I love so to look at you?'

At the sheer arrogance of this remark, Caroline burst out laughing.

'You are anything but plain. You are fragile and delicate and lovely, and I shall never tire of gazing at you. Indeed,' he said ruefully, 'I find it very difficult indeed to keep my hands from you.'

'I wish – I wish—'

'And I shall grant it.'

'You can't,' she said.

'Can't?'

She did not speak, but simply held out her left hand which was adorned with nothing but a narrow wedding ring.

'So?' he said dismissively.

'It – it is all too late. You know it is. I am not free to – to—'

'Nonsense,' he said.

He stood up and pulled her to her feet. His face was alive with excitement.

'There need be no obstacle. You shall come to live with me as my cherished wife, mine in everything but the eyes of the law and somehow we shall obtain a divorce for you and then the world will be satisfied. I do not give one anna for the world's opinion personally; but I want the world to treat you as you deserve. You see, dearest love, how simple it is and how happy we shall be. Your past life is over, over for ever, and no woman on earth shall be prized as you shall be.'

There was a fractional pause, and then Caroline raised her eyes to meet his elated gaze.

'No,' she said.

'No?' He was shouting again.

She freed herself from his embrace and stood a little apart, her eyes glittering with quite a new expression.

'No, Sir Edward. No, it must be no.'

He came a step nearer.

'Is it convention that troubles you? Do you think anyone in Calcutta cares for it? If it disturbs you, I will build you a palace outside the city and you may live there in perfect seclusion. May I remind you that Mr and Mrs Hastings are but lately wed themselves? I do not think you need fret yourself over convention.'

'I do not. I do not care for it any more than you do. It is not that.'

He was close to her again, his hands on her shoulders, and through them she could feel that he was shaking.

It was so difficult to articulate, so painful to explain. Her brain surged with powerful feelings of obligation and duty, and among these emotions shot bolts of panic, at the thought of losing the independence she had struggled so hard to gain.

'I – cannot leave him, he is so weak and – and helpless. And I cannot be – your possession, your object, I cannot—'

'You would be my treasure, can you not see that? If only you will live with me I will allow you any freedom you require. I no more want to cage you than a songbird. You owe that blackguard nothing, nothing at all. I will not hear such pointless loyalty. Come to me, Caroline, I beg you—'

'No,' she said.

He took his hands from her shoulders.

'You do not care for me, then. Were you flattered, was that it? It is unlike you to take and not give. I must assume you do not care!'

'I care—' she said desperately, almost in a whisper.

'You do not,' he declared furiously. 'Look at you! You are stony-hearted and dry-eyed, the sight of my despair squeezes not one tear from you, not one! You are in love with your own achievements, Caroline, that is what it is, nothing but that! You want no human love for you have nothing to repay it with now, nothing! If that is the price of freedom, madam, you are welcome to your liberty!'

Hardly conscious of what she did, Caroline turned and stumbled from the room. His voice followed her, still accusing, as she hurried through the drawing room while people and surroundings passed in a blur around her. In the hall, George Carew, bored by the sheer respectability of the evening, was pulling on his gloves while waiting for his carriage. He saw Caroline come flying through the double doors of the drawing room as if pursued by some spectre, and purely instinctively held out his arms and caught her in flight. She was not weeping, but looked as if she longed to.

'Mrs Gates, ma'am!'

'George – Mr Carew – George, I beg you, take – take me home.'

She was shuddering violently. George took off his cloak and wrapped it round her.

'Directly, ma'am,' he said.

18

The atmosphere in Calcutta throughout that winter was a disturbed one for the Council of the East India Company. Sir Edward Ashton had not exaggerated the threat of French invasion. Although it was unlikely that they would attack Calcutta and Bengal by sea, it seemed increasingly probable, given their growing success in western India, that they might attempt an attack by land, their own army reinforced by native troops as they crossed and subdued the princedoms on their journey across India. Sir Edward was of the opinion that the French needed less than a thousand men, trained in European military discipline, to educate huge numbers of sepoys into fighting most effectively. As this French army crossed the vast states of upper India the numbers of natives whom they could quell and enlist as allies was truly terrifying, and, should this happen, all the areas of India upon which British dominion depended would, as Warren Hastings said, 'lie at their mercy'.

This threat to the entire stability of the Company was something Sir Edward might deplore, and resist to the last breath in his body, but this winter he was grateful for such an absorbing problem to divert his mind. Although he was a man of energetically held principles, he was not someone subject to cravings in life – until he had met Caroline. He had wanted her above all else, with a single-minded passion, and when she had so obstinately withheld herself, he was desolated.

He tried to throw all the energy of his anguish into the thorny problem of subduing the French where they were, in western India, before they began to seep eastwards, and in some measure he succeeded. His household found him so changed that a kind of anxious reverence hung about the rooms, the sort of respect for grief so evident at funerals. Buxby found that his working hours, delightfully diminished during Sir Edward's absorption in Caroline, were infinitely extendable these days, but the sight of his superior's countenance caught occasionally off his guard was a deterrent to even the gentlest of complaints. He naturally dared not utter on this most delicate of subjects and, as for Sir Edward, the matter lay sealed in silence within him, and only from the abruptness of his manner and the tirelessness of his industry could it be deduced how much he suffered.

If he had some release, Caroline found she had none. She painted, of course – she had to paint – and she gardened, and she shunned company with all the panic she used to feel long ago in Dorset. Day in, week out, all those long months of winter, the months that should be the most pleasurable in northern India, she hardly left her little compound. As George Carew had said so casually to Johnnie, it was all over by Christmas.

All over. It was indeed. She would stand in her garden, now a cascading and brilliant tangle of bougainvillaea and jasmine, orchids and oleander spilling onto a green carpet of some close-leaved herb the mali had persuaded to grow like an English lawn, and consider that she was everything her garden was not. It was burgeoning and rioting, full of promise, and she was now no more than the dried-up yellow shell of dust and thirst it had been all summer.

During those long days, and longer nights, Caroline had come to realize, with a bitterness she could hardly bear, that she had made a mistake which would cost her her happiness for the rest of her life. For two days after the quarrel, she had been upheld by a kind of righteous elation, a feeling that she had stood up for what she felt to be true and vital, and that she had done a noble thing in paying such an agonizing price for it.

Was it not the greatest thing in life to be able to hold up your head with the self-respect you had built yourself, painful brick upon painful brick, all yourself, from no beginnings? Indeed it was, and she had been right, very right, not to throw it away simply because she had found the companion of a lifetime.

Was it not also equally laudable to cling to your obligations, all the tighter simply because those obligations were so burdensome and unpleasant? Did she not owe Johnnie the fulfilment of her promise to him? Merely because he seemed not to feel any reciprocal debt to her was no reason, she felt in this high-minded vein, for shirking her side of the bargain. No, indeed, she, Caroline Gates, would be an example to all of endurance and courage, a pattern of honourableness.

After forty-eight hours of this exalted condition, reality and Caroline's true nature began to tarnish the splendour of her attitudes. To realize that what she took for a noble gesture was in reality a hideous and self-gratifying mistake was a dreadful experience, and one that stripped her, in a few short days, of all the confidence and contentment she had taken more than a year to acquire. There was plenty of time and solitude – indeed too much of both – to see the damage she had done.

Slowly but surely her own honesty asserted itself and she began to see that her freedom was nothing in itself. She had sought it because it gave her courage and because it was the only way she could endure to be married to a man for whom she had no feelings at all save disgust and contempt. She had thought, in her folly, flushed with her own success, that this independence was a prize in itself, but now, too late, she knew better. Her independence should have made her free to choose what she pleased, released her from her bondage to be unconventional and happy and oblivious to the world's finger pointing at her. She had made herself able to be Sir Edward's mistress, free enough to make that choice, and she had out of obstinate pride refused him and lost him, and lost herself in the process.

Mrs Rathbone was a steady visitor. She not only called to collect new batches of pictures, but also because her cosy and maternal heart could not resist Caroline's wretchedness.

'Come now, dearie, we mustn't give way like this. There are plenty of fish in the sea, and whatever we have done once we can do again.'

'It is myself I despair over,' Caroline said, 'I am so ashamed of myself, so weary of my lack of judgement—'

Mrs Rathbone patted her hand.

'There, there, my dear, we all make mistakes, do we not. To be sure, I've made many, my dear, so many—' she paused and reflected with pleasure on a number of them, 'but you must not brood, indeed you must not. Tomorrow is another day and you must put it all behind you.'

Caroline managed a small and rueful smile.

'You are most kind to me.'

'Nonsense, my dear, it is no more than common charity. Besides, now that Miss Grant is gone, who are you to confide in, if not in me?'

'I feel that – that I deserve to bear the pain alone.'

Mrs Rathbone clucked disapprovingly.

'What a silly notion, my dear. Anyone would think you enjoyed being unhappy, I vow they would. Now then, what are we going to do to cheer you up?'

'I should dearly love to stop painting. It must seem ungrateful to you after all the months of help you have given me, but I am becoming unoriginal and the pictures are no longer fresh, I do too many.'

Mrs Rathbone eyed her for a moment, and saw the smudges of weariness under her eyes, and the tired droop of her shoulders.

'You need more company, my dear.'

Caroline looked startled.

'Oh – oh no, indeed no. I mean, I thank you for your concern, but I am grown so awkward in company, just as I used to be.'

'Not dinner parties, my dear!' Mrs Rathbone said recalling what a difficult guest Caroline had been, sitting remote and shy among the flying bread pellets. 'Some companion. Some friend other than myself.'

Caroline was seized with contrition.

'Oh, Mrs Rathbone, I should hate to be a burden to you! Please do not feel you must come here if you have other calls—'

'I like to come, my dear. And you need a friend, but it's my belief you need more than just myself. I have an idea.'

She leaned forward confidentially, and spoke in the whisper she had perfected for passing on gossip in crowded rooms.

'Listen, my dear, I've a friend, a nice boy, a soldier, and he's being sent across to Poona under Colonel Leslie to fight the French. Six battalions are going, I'm told, to show the French they can't do as they please in India, for it's not theirs to have. Now, my friend, a Lieutenant Wheeler, has a little wife here in Calcutta, a pretty little thing she is, and a baby, and they have nowhere to go while he's away. Now, of course, I offered to have them just as I offered Johnnie—' she hesitated for a moment then hurried on. 'But why do you not have them here? Frank Wheeler will pay their board, I am sure, and would it not amuse you a little? Think of a baby to play with, Caroline!'

'Would – would not Mrs Wheeler find it very dull?'

'Why should she? She's quite a timid soul herself, for all her looks, and has only been here a few months. The baby was born at sea, would you believe it, and Frank is as proud of him as if he'd borne him himself. Now, what do you say?'

Caroline still looked doubtful.

'I do not feel I am fit company for a pretty girl, Mrs Rathbone. I should dearly love to have a baby here, and I should be more than glad to help, but—'

'No more buts. I shall bring her to meet you. Now, then, what pictures can I take away with me this week?'

Ann Wheeler turned out to be a slight dark girl, quietly pretty but with an expression of gravity that did not lighten her features. She seemed quite undismayed at the prospect of living in the Gates's silent house, and her serious appearance stilled all Caroline's fears about her vulnerability to Johnnie should he feel moved to exercise his gallantry once more.

She had engineered that Mrs Rathbone should tell Johnnie of the arrangement, so that he might feel he was the first to know.

'Johnnie boy, I want you to do me a great favour. I think you'll feel I deserve one every so often, do you not?'

Johnnie, amply supplied with Mr Rathbone's port, grunted his permission for her to continue.

'There's a girl needs caring for, Johnnie boy.'

'A pretty girl, Bella?'

'You don't change, do you, you naughty boy? Pretty she is, but not for you. It's Frank Wheeler's wife. She'll be left all alone when the army moves west, and I wondered if you would offer her lodging.'

'Will she pay?'

'Naturally, she will! Though I hardly think that is the question of a gentleman.'

'I'm pressed for money, Bella.'

Mrs Rathbone thought of Caroline's lonely struggle with money and eyed Johnnie with less than her usual fondness.

'Don't tell me such stories, Johnnie. All you boys line your pockets with gold here in Calcutta, you know you do. There's not a man among you not amassing a private fortune enough to buy half Mayfair when he goes home—'

'Not me, Bella,' Johnnie said glumly. 'I'm beset with ill-luck.'

He gazed glumly down into his glass. He didn't even seem able to win much at whist these days and his facility for private deals which had paid for his lifestyle so comfortably a few years back seemed to have crumbled to dust.

George Carew had simple reasons for it. 'If you soak and whore as you do, my boy, you can't expect miracles. Damned if I know how you're still alive.'

Mrs Rathbone, once a faithful ally, seemed no more sympathetic.

'If Lady Fortune frowns on you, Johnnie, it's because she's tired of your selfish ways. You've a wife you don't deserve, indeed you don't, and if you knew what she did for you without a word—'

'Don't speak to me of her,' Johnnie interrupted savagely. 'No man was ever cursed with such a wife, never. When her great friends noticed her she was never there to do her duty by me, and now that they have tired of her, as I knew they would, she mopes about the house all day. Mark what I say, Bella, mark it well. The moment that woman stepped on shore, here in Calcutta, my life went from bad to worse. There was never a man as beset in his marriage as I am.'

Mrs Rathbone had risen.

'I'll hear no more, Johnnie, in truth I'll not. You'll not have a soul left who will speak to you if you go on in that way. Now pull yourself together and do not always be so sorry for yourself. I shall send Frank Wheeler to you and you may make what arrangements you will.'

The arrangements that resulted were not wholly to Caroline's advantage. After an unseemly wrangle, which Mrs Rathbone insisted on watching to see fair play, it was grudgingly decided that half the money Frank Wheeler would contribute should go to the housekeeping costs of maintaining Ann and little Francis. The rest, Johnnie insisted he needed.

'I must have it, I must. It will go towards the cost of the additional servants we shall have to have with two extra people in the house.'

Tight-lipped, Caroline said, 'We have more servants than we need already, and in any case it is I who pay them, not you. I know full well the extra will go to the whist table and your other – pleasures, but I would rather not touch a penny than that we should squabble for it.'

Mrs Rathbone came to her rescue. A lump sum should be paid to Johnnie on Lieutenant Wheeler's departure and his wife would then give a weekly amount to Caroline.

Caroline was deeply distressed at the squalor of the arrangement.

'Forgive me, Mrs Wheeler, for this shameful penny-pinching. I would give anything to be able to offer you our house as our guests, however long your husband is away, and perhaps in time that will come to be.'

Ann Wheeler, in full knowledge of all of Caroline's history regaled in every detail in a whisper by Mrs Rathbone, merely inclined her head, and said gravely, 'It would embarrass me, Mrs Gates, to be dependent upon your charity for what might be months. I am easier in my mind that things are as they are.'

Within weeks, Caroline actually ventured to return one of Mrs Rathbone's endless calls. She found her friend in a flurry of excitement over a box of hats from Rheims come by the last ship, and sitting in her bedroom in a perfect ocean of plumes and ribbons.

'My dear, did ever you see such pretty things? I feel I shall go mad with delight, indeed I shall. Come now, try the blue. Do, my dear, try the blue!'

Caroline resisted, laughing.

'No, no, thank you. They are charming, much too

charming for me. I am come anyway to thank you, not to accept more favours.'

'Thank me, my dear?'

'Yes, indeed, most warmly. I am come to thank you for the introduction to Ann Wheeler. I am in your debt, once again, and most grateful.'

Mrs Rathbone turned from the mirror under a palm tree effect of nodding pink plumes.

'Do you suit one another, my dear?'

'Oh, so well! She is such a sweet, serious person, we have much in common, and she is so unobtrusive that I often do not know whether or not she is in the house. And the baby is a delight. I do not know what I should do without the baby.'

Mrs Rathbone removed the pink palm tree and came across to Caroline.

'Are you quieter in your mind now, my dear?'

Caroline nodded speechlessly. It seemed ungrateful to tell a lie and say her heart was quite healed when in fact it was as sore as ever, but on the other hand what kind of reward for Mrs Rathbone's kindness was the truth?

Mrs Rathbone considered her for a moment, accurately interpreting her silence. Mrs Rathbone had had a most strange encounter two nights before, and the memory of it tempted her to ignore her small reserve of discretion. She had been asked to dine with Mrs Eyre, as a favour, she supposed with her no-nonsense awareness of social differences, after supplying the latter with four or five of Caroline's paintings. At the table had been, to her consternation, several of the great persons of Calcutta, including Sir Edward Ashton. He looked as impressive as ever, but the new hard lines about his eyes and mouth suggested to Mrs Rathbone that he had schooled himself rigorously in the last months. The idea of this made his presence less awe-inspiring to her and emboldened her considerably after dinner when the miniatures were again being admired.

She edged her plump person through the group of people in the drawing room until she was at Sir Edward's elbow, and could share with him a view of the picture of wild strawberries he held in his hand.

'Forgive my being so bold as to address you in this way, Sir Edward, but I can tell you something you might like to hear about these paintings.'

From his considerable height, Sir Edward looked down in some surprise at this highly coloured little person below him. She appeared to wish to emulate a rainbow in her style of dress, and was gazing up at him with a sort of roguishness women never dared employ with him usually. Mrs Eyre came to his rescue.

'Mrs Rathbone, Sir Edward. It is through Mrs Rathbone that I have acquired these charming miniatures.'

The light dawned.

'And so, madam, I presume you wish to inveigle me into a purchase too?'

'Will you step a little apart, sir? I feel we can talk more comfortably then, do not you, sir?'

Sir Edward gave Mrs Eyre a resigned smile and followed Mrs Rathbone to a sofa.

'Now, sir, you quite misunderstand me. I do not wish to sell you a picture, no indeed, for I have more orders than I can deal with as it is. No, it is not about the paintings I wish to talk, but the painter.'

Sir Edward looked at her with mild interest.

'The painter? I thought one of the charms of these miniatures, one of the elements that gave them such cachet, was that the painter was anonymous.'

Mrs Rathbone leant very close to him, and in the cloud of violet-scented powder she exuded, said, 'Anonymous to all Calcutta, but not to me!'

Sir Edward endeavoured to sound interested.

'Indeed, madam.'

Mrs Rathbone edged her brilliant skirts closer to him.

'And not to you, either, Sir Edward.'

'Really, madam?' The interest was less feigned this time.

'No, indeed. In fact, I believe the painter was at one time most – most—' here Mrs Rathbone temporarily lost courage, but rallied to deliver her triumphal shot. 'It is Caroline Gates, Sir Edward, none other than Caroline Gates!'

If she had hoped for a reaction, she was not disappointed. He blanched completely, and the gaze directed at her grew so intense that she was suddenly frightened. Moving away a little, she began to apologize hurriedly for her intrusion, she would leave him in peace, he must forgive her, she only meant for the best, indeed she did. His hand shot out and held her like a vice.

'You – you know Mrs Gates?'

'I do, sir,' Mrs Rathbone said apprehensively. 'She – she is a dear friend of mine,' she added staunchly.

At that his hand relaxed a little on her arm.

'You see her then?'

'Oh, yes, often, often, several times a week.'

'How is she?'

Not entirely sure yet of Sir Edward's reaction, Mrs Rathbone determined to be loyal to Caroline.

'Doing very well, sir, to be sure. She has a sweet friend living there, with a baby, and they suit each other excellently.'

'She is quite content, then?'

Mrs Rathbone did not understand his tone. It was an alarming sort of tone, and she did not want to be alarmed again.

'Dear me, yes, I believe she is.'

There was a silence. Mrs Rathbone would have moved away, but she was still held captive by Sir Edward's hand. He sat gazing at the floor, and she could see from his hardened profile that every muscle in his face was tensed.

'What about these paintings, then, Mrs Rathbone?' he

said at last, in an altered voice. 'Why does she not sign them?'

'She cannot, sir! No-one must know! Can – can I trust you with a confidence, sir?'

Sir Edward looked at her pityingly.

'You may, madam.'

'The truth is, Sir Edward, that she is so shamefully used by her husband – a good boy at heart, I do believe, but weak with it – that if she did not paint she would starve.'

The hand on her arm tightened uncomfortably again.

'What?'

'It's as I say, sir. He never gives her money, and he never pays the servants, and she's that fond of her servants I believe she'd sell the clothes off her back to give them what she owed them. They'd die for her, Sir Edward, I truly believe they would. But we're getting good money for the miniatures now, you know – why, Mrs Eyre said she'd give me fifteen guineas for another if I could have it ready by the end of February! Think of that, Sir Edward!'

He said thickly, 'How long has this been going on?'

'Oh, all summer, sir, all autumn, seven months or more. Mind you, she is tiring a bit now, she's worked so hard.'

'All summer, all the time I—'

'Oh yes, sir.'

Sir Edward muttered something savagely to himself.

'Sir – Sir Edward? Would – would you like me to obtain one for you?'

Thoughts of a reconciliation were fluttering hopefully round Mrs Rathbone's head, but really he was a most difficult and daunting man to deal with, not at all like her boys. He looked at her now suddenly, and then almost as if he had forgotten it was there, removed his hand from her arm.

'Yes, I – no, thank you, but no, I could not bear—'

He rose and stood looming over her.

'Why did you tell me all this?'

Mrs Rathbone summoned all her courage with difficulty.

'I thought you should know, sir. I thought you should know what she has had to bear.'

'You are right. Quite right. But you do not think she has so much to bear now?'

Mrs Rathbone did not know what the reply was that he wanted, or indeed what the truth was. Caroline seemed content enough now but then, she never was one for opening her heart. She would consider Mrs Rathbone a gossip for meddling with Sir Edward, and suddenly Mrs Rathbone felt that indeed that was what she was. She gave Sir Edward the smallest shake of her head, and watched him stride away in silence. She left soon after, and at supper that night, drank too much cherry brandy to distract herself, and could not sleep a wink as a result.

Now, regarding Caroline rather gravely, she was considering whether to report this conversation. It struck her that she had not given the right answers to Sir Edward, for it was patently obvious now that Caroline was as far from contentment as she had ever been. She picked up a straw bonnet woven with lattices of ribbons, and played with it a little.

'I've something to tell you, dear.'

'Oh?' Caroline looked startled.

'Oh, never fear, my dear, nothing nasty. Quite the reverse. Guess who I met but two nights ago?'

Caroline looked at her steadily.

'None other than – Sir Edward Ashton!'

Caroline went pale.

'No – no, please, dear friend, do not, do not speak of him, I beg you, do not—'

Mrs Rathbone dropped the bonnet and seized Caroline by the elbows.

'You must listen to me, dear, you must! It is pleasant things I have to tell you!'

Caroline freed herself.

'No,' she insisted, 'please say no more, please. I have cut myself off quite from any – any possibilities – I have angered him beyond any redemption, it is no use. Nothing is any use,' she put her hand up to silence Mrs Rathbone. 'If you are truly kind as I know you are, you will not – not mention him again. I beg you will not. I will never – never heal again if you do. His – his name opens up everything, all the wounds. Forgive me, but I must go, truly I must. Ann is dining out, and I have promised to look after little Francis. Thank you for everything, thank you again and again.'

Mrs Rathbone felt a light kiss on her cheek, then the door flew open and instantly closed behind Caroline. For a few minutes the wind of her going still eddied among the finery on the floor.

19

Caroline had not exaggerated when she said she did not know what she would have done without the baby. He was a charming baby in any case, an open-faced laughing blond baby, with his father's merry blue eyes and a wealth of endearing dimples and creases, and his happy innocence, coupled with the inevitable demandingness of all babies, rescued Caroline in the nick of time from the blackest despair. The ayah whom Frank Wheeler had engaged found that she had to watch like a hawk for the scant hours when Mrs Gates was painting in order to get any share in her charge at all, and often was reduced to sitting dumbly by the baby's cradle watching his hot, damp, rosy daytime naps. Ann Wheeler was a mother whose children would grow in value to her as they grew in years, and she was entirely happy to surrender the repetitive amusement of a year-old baby to another, especially when that other seemed so passionate to be involved.

In the relative cool of the mornings or glowing early evenings, Caroline would take little Francis out into the garden and play with him on a blanket under the old banyan tree that grew close to the house and spread its hideous shaggy branches beneath her bedroom window. He would crawl and crow and examine minute objects in the dust about him with solemn absorption, before cramming them into his mouth. Caroline would sing to him and read poetry to him, out of volumes which she had failed to return to Sir Edward Ashton prior to their quarrel, and which she now could not bring herself to give back. Both the baby and Caroline were watched by a circle of malis affecting to garden, and by the under-occupied ayah. Ann Wheeler, free to play in the music groups she loved and to dine and sup out as much as she pleased, came to regard Caroline as one of the most benevolent accidents of her life.

'I fear that I exploit you, and I would wish you to know that I feel the deepest gratitude for the freedom your love and care for Francis gives me. I have missed my music sadly since coming here, indeed I did not know how sadly until I took it up again. Frank said I was silly not to trust the ayah with little Francis, but I think he is wrong. If he could see you with his precious son, he would acknowledge that he was wrong.'

Caroline looked up at her from the rug where she knelt by the rolling baby.

'You must not thank me, indeed you must not. It is I must thank you. I was in a very sorry plight before you came, and you cannot fail to have observed how solitary I am, thus your two presences here have meant more to me than I can express.'

She might have expressed much more, but she did not care to. The truth was that the baby, with his golden blitheness, and his promise of future life and his demands for attention, was providing her with just the oblivion she sought. Not only did occupying herself ceaselessly with him prevent her dwelling on her own deep, private misery: it also partially obliterated the fact that her painting was becoming an intolerable burden to her; but the necessity of doing it, with the added strain of the Wheelers on the household, was no less pressing. If she painted five or six hours a day now, she could just run the household, provided that Mrs Rathbone could obtain a minimum of ten guineas for each one, but it was becoming uncomfortably evident to both Mrs Rathbone and Caroline, that as the early summer drew on Calcutta was beginning, with its usual fickleness, to tire of the enigma of these nostalgic and anonymous miniatures. Caroline painted on, doggedly and increasingly mechanically, and pushed her realization of the dwindling numbers Mrs Rathbone took each month to the back of her mind by absorbing herself, in all free moments, with the baby.

What she would do when she could no longer earn a living, she could not imagine and dared not even try to contemplate. The spectre of destitution, of being forced to beg for some kind of help again, drove her to bury her face and her thoughts in the baby's neck and seek forgetfulness in the seductiveness of that contact. She had contemplated either telling Ann Wheeler or admitting to Mrs Rathbone that she knew her market was declining, but she had shrunk from both, preferring to go blindly on, too tired by the strains of the last year in an exhausting climate to confront the awful possibilities with her usual courage. The baby was her buffer against the future, her talisman, her touchstone. She carried him about with her and talked to him and gave him flowers, and reassured herself constantly that while he was with her, fate could strike no blow.

The Wheelers' coming had estranged Johnnie even further from the house. Within a few days he had recognized in Ann Wheeler's steady dark glance a girl who would be flinty in response to his decayed charms, and had come to see also that her allegiance lay increasingly with Caroline. With this new grievance of being driven out of his own house by a pack of malicious women and a squalling baby, he was only at home to sleep the last few hours of each night, and seldom even that. His sense of intense injustice was heightened by realizing that Caroline, either bent myopically over her damned daubing, or cooing over the brat, simply did not care whether he was there or not. His linen was immaculate still, he supposed his food was still provided though he never troubled now to come home to eat it, and it never crossed his mind as he departed in the third clean shirt of the day, to wonder how she managed to do it on no money whatsoever. She seldom even looked up now when he passed her, and if shouted at, replied with a vague remoteness that seemed to indicate she had no recollection at all of who he was.

George Carew could not understand why he was not satisfied. 'It's what you wanted, eh? Ain't it? All the comfort and none of the commitments?'

'It's my house, George, my house, and I'm a stranger in it! Those she-cats don't care if I live or die, all they care for is that drivelling brat.'

'Jealous of a baby now, Johnnie?'

'Confound it, I'm not!' Johnnie yelled. 'I'm not jealous of a soul on earth except the man who isn't cursed with a wife!'

In the hot dreadful weeks before the monsoons in the summer of 1778, Ann Wheeler became increasingly involved in a quartet who were to play a selection of Italian composers at a much-publicized musical soirée to be given by Mrs Hastings.

'I fear I shall be from home a good deal, Caroline, and I am anxious that Francis, as he becomes more active, is distracting you from painting. Would you allow the ayah, or any person you think fit to engage, to take the burden of his care from you?'

Caroline held the baby tightly to her and shook her head vehemently.

'Indeed no. I do assure you that the care of him is only a pleasure to me, never anything else. I beg you will go and practise your music with the freest conscience possible, knowing that you leave me doing what I love to do.'

Her tone was so eager that Ann Wheeler thankfully acquiesced, and took to spending the occasional night away at the house of the friend who had organized the quartet in the first instance. In these absences, Caroline, on the pretext that the baby was teething and restless, took little Francis into her own room at night and beguiled the black and awful hours in watching him and defending his small sleeping form from mosquitoes. During these vigils she would sometimes hear, in the dawn, the crashes and oaths of Johnnie's unsteady return, but more often than not, only crickets and jackals broke the hot and heavy silence and she would see the dawn come up brilliantly over a city in which her husband lay oblivious of her and her lover lost to her.

Three days before the soirée, Caroline had an unintentional caller in the person of George Carew, unintentional since he had not meant a formal call, but merely to offer Johnnie a seat in his carriage on the way out to dine. George had not seen Caroline since that fateful evening when he had escorted her home, and was struck by her dispirited and withered appearance, after the temporary bloom that Sir Edward's attentions had given her. She stood before George in a dress of faded lilac print, the rosy cheek of a plump baby pressed in painful contrast to her own thin one.

'You ain't unwell I hope, ma'am?'

'No, indeed, Mr Carew, I am not unwell at all. Like everyone I shall find the rains a great relief. Is there anything I can do for you?'

'You might produce your husband, in a trice if you would. We're deuced late as it is.'

Caroline's gaze dropped hastily.

'I would if I could, Mr Carew,' she said in a low voice, 'but I have no notion where he might be. He has not been home these two nights.'

'Not home? Have you not sent the servants for news of him?'

Her head still bent, she said in an even lower voice:

'No, no, I have not. It is hardly the first time. He comes home merely to change his linen.'

George Carew's drawl did not alter in speed as he said, 'And you think that no reason for concern, ma'am? Is a wife to show no more care than the orders she gives to a dhobi? Might he not be home more if he had more to come home to?'

Caroline's head jerked up abruptly and she glared savagely at George Carew over the round blond head of the baby. Tiredness and a sense of hopelessness were winning over her natural reticence and humility. To think that George Carew, rogue as he might be, saw any cause at all to pity Johnnie for a fate which was entirely of his own making, was more than her wearied mind and heart could bear.

'If this house is empty for him, Mr Carew, it is because he has made it so! Everything about it, even the fact that I am here at all, has been arranged to suit his monstrous selfishness. He pays for nothing and takes everything. I have, in every mechanical sense, kept the promise I made him and, if I have withheld my heart, it is because I would not squander it on a creature so worthless!'

The baby, sensing the upheaval in the bosom to which he was pressed, began to whimper. George Carew took a step backwards, grasping his hat more firmly in his hand.

'Beg – beg pardon, ma'am, I'd no notion—'

'Oh no, you have not, but you will have.' She was horrified at herself but unable to stop. 'I have a small talent which is luckily sufficient to pay for all household expenses. I have not received one penny from Johnnie since I married him, not one penny, not to mention a single flower or ribbon. The only money he has ever expended upon me was the forty pounds for the marriage licence, and I am sure that, indiscreet and greedy for pity as he always is, he has confided in you the reason for the marriage in the first place. He scorns me and insults me, so why should I care what sordid ends he comes to. If you care what has happened to him, you may find him.' She stopped for a moment and then said in a lowered voice, 'I will not lift a finger.'

George Carew was not a man who cared for apologies.

He stood, turning his hat slowly for a while, wishing very much he had not been so foolhardy as to involve himself, and reluctantly coming to the conclusion that he had put himself into a position where he was committed to seeking Johnnie. It was damned awkward, for in truth he would not give any more to know where Johnnie was than his wronged wife did, but he saw no alternative.

'I'll fetch him home for you, ma'am.'

Caroline inclined her head, seeing no reason for gratitude, and hid her face in the baby's neck. George moved to the door and stood there for a moment, wrestling with vague feelings he did not recognize as familiar. After a long pause, he looked back at the still figure in the lilac print holding the baby, and said, 'Damned bad business.'

Watching him cross the hall, Caroline realized that she had just received both apology and commiseration.

It was after dark when George brought his prize home. Ann had gone, and would not be back until after the soirée; she had managed to obtain an invitation for Caroline, to the hopeful delight of Mrs Rathbone who knew Sir Edward Ashton was bound to attend, but Caroline had been adamant in her refusal. Ann had been quite open in revealing that a fellow musician in the quartet was a young man named Ralph Buxby, although she did not add that he was also a most open and ardent admirer of hers, and the combination of this link and the house in which the soirée was to be held made Caroline quite convinced that the presence she most wished to elude would have to be unavoidably confronted. So Ann had hired a carriage alone and gone off with her maid, genuinely grieved that Caroline would not come but profoundly relieved to abandon her child to such tender care. Thus, when George's carriage halted outside the small mud house where the only candle visible was burning in one of the upper rooms, Caroline was alone with Francis, and singing to him as he lay and tossed wakefully in the steaming heat of his cradle. Reluctantly she summoned the ayah, crouched hopefully as always outside the door, and went downstairs full of apprehension.

Johnnie was being carried across the hallway as she descended, on a sort of makeshift stretcher to which he had been tightly bound with a number of shawls. The reason for this became quickly evident; he was delirious and would have twisted himself to the floor in seconds if not strongly confined. His face was scarlet and running with sweat, and the shirt he wore – his coat being respectfully carried by a servant – was as wet as if he had swum in it. George Carew had found him in a bawdy house down on the waterfront just as he was, delirious, with a high fever, abandoned on a heap of sacks in a welter of empty bottles. It seemed he had succumbed to unconsciousness and fever twenty-four hours before after a night and day of relentless drinking, at which point the bawdy house lost interest in him as a potential customer and had tossed him into a corner to recover.

Caroline pressed herself to the wall as this grotesque little procession of servants, lit by flickering torches held by those below, bore its muttering and rebellious burden past her to Johnnie's bedroom. George Carew waited below in the hall, his face illuminated by the leaping flames about him, and looked upward to the jumping shadows where Caroline stood.

'What ails him, Mr Carew?'

George cleared his throat.

'The usual, ma'am, and a touch of fever. Will you have me fetch a physician?'

Caroline hesitated. She knew what she expected of herself, and she could not do it. She willed herself to want to nurse him back to health and sense, and could make nothing of it. A doctor would give instructions the servants might carry out.

'If you would be so good, Mr Carew.'

He bowed and left. With mounting repugnance, Caroline moved slowly towards her husband's bedroom. Johnnie had been rolled upon the bed, and the servants were now standing back in some disarray, unsure what next to do with his flailing and slippery bulk. Two candles burned at the bedside, and the heavy bed hangings had been tossed up on the canopy to allow air and easier access. Caroline advanced to the bedhead and stooped to look closely at Johnnie's face, bloated and distorted with excesses and fever, and recoiled sharply at the stale stench he emitted.

'He must be sponged with warm water. Warm water, not cold. And he must be put in fresh linen, and left covered lightly.'

A wave of nausea rose in her throat and she stepped back quickly. A chair was instantly brought, and she sank into it thankfully, accepting the offered cup of water, and leaning her forehead against the smooth wood of the bedpost. She seemed to feel quite shaken, giddy and helpless and sick, so she did not move away from the sordid spectacle on the bed, but regarded what was going on there with the remoteness of an uninvolved spectator. When the physician came, to pronounce Johnnie thoroughly over-indulged and to prohibit all alcohol for a month at least, he found a touching picture of a devoted wife sitting at her sick husband's bedside to ensure the servants treated him as they should.

'You must be very firm with your husband, Mrs Gates. He is endangering his liver mightily with the work he gives it to do. Continue warm sponging as you have been doing, and administer this medicine four-hourly. It will clear the system and thus help to reduce the fever. He is to be on light foods, plenty of oranges, and no wine whatsoever until I pronounce him fit to take it.'

Caroline stood up, swaying a little, unintentionally

giving every impression of a wife worn with loving anxiety.

'I fear that will be very difficult to achieve, Dr Campbell.'

He laid a hand upon her arm and said confidentially, 'But you women know how to gain your ends, do you not? He'll not refuse you if you plead your case prettily enough. I'll call again in a few days or so and expect to find him supping broth. I'll bid you good night.'

When he had gone, Caroline turned back to the bed, aware that she should now sit by and watch the unattractive processes of Johnnie's system endeavouring to rid itself of all he abused it with.

As if he read her thoughts, Ranjit stepped from the shadows and said softly, 'There is no need for memsahib to be watching. We are watching and will call if we fear anything.'

With a look and smile at him of the purest gratitude, Caroline thankfully escaped to the sanctuary of her bedroom. Though still stiflingly hot, the air smelt only of flowers and dust, and above the gentle sounds of the baby's breathing and the old banyan tapping against her wall, she could hear nothing but the comforting crickets in the garden below.

Twenty-four hours later, Johnnie's fever had abated remarkably, and he was peevishly conscious enough to complain bitterly that he was denied any wine. Caroline could hear him ranting as she moved about the house, and knew full well that the curses he was hurling were all directed at her. She had told him that she was only repeating the physician's orders, but he chose to ignore her.

'You'll kill me, won't you! You'll murder me slowly and painfully, by depriving me of anything I need! No man has ever had wine withheld for medical reasons, not ever! It's a witchlike scheme of yours, you shrew, to make me suffer so that you may gloat over my pain!

Well, I'll tell you something, you milksop daughter of sanctimony, you may starve me to death, you may dry me to death, but when I'm in my coffin, I'll have my revenge on you! I will, I will! When I'm gone, you mealy-mouthed prig, you'll not see a penny of Gates money nor Lennox money, not one penny. It will all go back to those who know how to spend it, and you'll beg for your bread and live to regret the shameless manner in which you treated me!'

To prevent his getting anywhere near the tempting bottles in the dining room, Caroline instructed the servants to keep his room locked. The insult of the imprisonment, added to the injury of being denied the wine he craved, caused his bellowings to rise to a crescendo, and the second night was rent with moans and cries and yells of rage as the craving and fever took their toll of him. Caroline spent the night apart, shuddering and sickened, kneeling by the baby's cradle with her fingers pressed to her terrified ears. What she would have done without that stoical and loyal band of servants, she could not imagine, for they pursued their duties about their master as if the sole aim of each one was to save the memsahib any knowledge, let alone hardship.

The second day was no calmer than the first. Ranjit intimated reluctantly to Caroline that his master was very violent when she pressed him for information, and when she went out into the hall after pushing away her untasted dinner, she could hear above the thuds and crashes of some unseemly struggle. Alarmed anew, she summoned Dr Campbell back.

'There's nothing I can do beyond give you an opiate for the nights, Mrs Gates. He's suffering badly from needing his wine and that's souring his temper in addition to the fever. But he'll have to sweat it out if he's to regain his health. You've no call to worry, with that fine bearer of yours, and in a week or so he'll be calmer.'

294

He did not stay above fifteen minutes, brisk, professional and entirely unaware of the engulfing undercurrents of the situation, of this man and woman bound by nothing but law, and existing in a state of siege between each other in the stifling little yellow house. As the evening wore on, Caroline's sleepless two nights began to tell on her with blessedly welcome heaviness of head and eyelids, and before ten o'clock struck she had closed her door firmly upon the ravings down the landing and climbed thankfully into bed.

Almost as she did so, Johnnie was dashing his sleeping draught to the floor. The bed linen was already splashed with the juices and medicines he had roughly spurned during the day, and the servants, without Caroline to make them fastidious, saw no reason to change the dirty sheeting. Tousled, sweating and foul-mouthed, Johnnie swore and ranted at them, falling back on his pillow in weakness every so often and groaning with pain.

Patiently, Ranjit prepared another draught and approached the bed again, only to see the glass swept from his hand a second time to splinter against the wall. He said nothing, but his mouth tightened beneath his carefully plumed black moustache, and he resolved that if the sahib was bent upon suffering, suffer he might. With a few swift, decisive gestures, he moved about the room extinguishing candles and drawing down the blinds, so that within a few moments, Johnnie found himself alone in the absolute blackness, not a servant within call, a prisoner of his own wretchedness. He bellowed and shouted until he was hoarse, and tears of self-pity were coursing down his streaming face. No-one came. No-one cared. Along the landing Caroline and little Francis slept in oblivion; outside his door, the servant left squatting as sentry stuffed rags into his ears and buried his head in his folded arms. Johnnie sobbed and swore and punched his pillows.

At long last, as Ranjit had surmised, he wore himself out and slept a hot, troubled, unnatural slumber among the squalid tangle of his bedding. The sentry servant unlocked the door, and tiptoed with a candle to the bedside to make sure that sleep held his master mercifully silent, and then, reassured, crept out and closed the door behind him. He then lay down himself across the doorway and pulled up his dhoti to wind about his head preparatory to the luxury of his own rest. Silence at last, silence after two days and nights of maniacal roarings, fell upon the house.

A few hours later, Johnnie woke in the thick blackness of his solitude with only one desperate thought in his mind – wine. He fumbled about for a moment or two in a vain search for either tinder or candlestick, and was about to shout for assistance when the extreme silence of the house struck him forcibly. He sat up in bed to listen more intently, and could hear nothing, no sound, no indication of humanity anywhere near. He tried to stand but found that his head whirled wretchedly, so dropped to his knees and began to crawl, ignominiously impeded by his nightshirt, towards the door. In the eagerness of the dawning of a new idea, he quite forgot that the door would be locked and thus felt no surprise when he reached up to the handle and felt it turn smoothly in his grasp as the door swung inward. By inches he missed stumbling over a prostrate figure across the threshhold, dimly outlined in the greyish light on the landing, and, with a supreme effort, he managed to pass the obstacle and continue his lumbering progress along the landing.

All around him, silence reigned. Caroline, Francis and the ayah slept on, the servants, far away in their quarters, secure in the knowledge their master was a prisoner, enjoyed the sleep of the just. Step by step, Johnnie lowered himself shakily down the staircase, his head spinning and his limbs weak and unreliable, but driven on by a blinding desire for his goal. His eyes became gradually used to the dimness, and as he dragged himself, trembling violently, across the hall, he could make out the three-branched candelabra that stood on the chest by the dining-room door, a tinder box beside it.

Painfully, he lifted it to the floor, and pushed it and the tinder box before him into the haven of the dining-room. Once inside, with the door securely closed, he gave himself up to a moment of triumph and relief, stretched sweating and shaking upon the carpet. It took him an age to light even one candle, but at last, by dint of holding one jerking hand in the other, he managed a blaze of two lights and the room – and his goal – were clearly illuminated.

The wine, several bottles of claret, stood on the sideboard by the window, the curtains drawn as they had been since the dinner hour to keep off the afternoon sun. His heart bursting within his chest, Johnnie heaved himself to his feet with the help of the table and hauled himself around to the wine, pushing the candelabra across the table as he did so. He was sobbing with relief as he reached the first bottle, tearing the cork out with his teeth, and pouring· the wine down his open throat while it splashed his face and hair and nightshirt with dark stains. It was gone almost in a moment, leaving him gasping and almost insensible, but possessed solely with the desire for more. He reached unsteadily for a second bottle, swayed as he lifted it to his mouth, and then, as the impact of more than a pint of alcohol hit his weakened system, a blackness blotted out his wits and he fell backwards against the lit candles, rolling with them into the folds of the curtains.

Caroline came down a long tunnel of nightmare to consciousness, a tunnel lit by a red glare and echoing with a faint but sonorous roaring. She fought her eyes open at last upon the spectacle of her bedroom door edged with a quivering line of scarlet and the sensation that the air about her had dried to a stifling cindery dust. She took a gasping and appalled breath, and her lungs filled immediately with acrid smoke, causing her to double up violently, choking out the fumes into the sheets of her bed. At last, holding her breath painfully, she stumbled to her washstand and the jug of tepid water that waited for her morning toilette; the movement seemed to bring her to full consciousness, to the sharp and frightful knowledge that a blaze roared beyond her door and would soon burst in upon her – and that little Francis was coughing desperately in his crib across the room.

Within moments she had dashed to the baby's bedside, and snatched him to her, pressing a soaked linen towel to his small, choking mouth. Then, with her free hand, she wrenched open a drawer in her chest and pulled out as large a handful of stockings as she could seize, and ran with both them and the baby to her bed. Perched upon its side, half her attention upon the strengthening flicker of flame around her door, and half upon what she was doing, she knotted the stockings hastily into a long bandage, and then, manoeuvring the baby so that his body lay against her bosom, lashed him as firmly as she could manage, twisting frenziedly to pass her makeshift rope across her shoulders and round her back for safety. The ends were firmly tied across the baby's back, and then, gasping and with streaming eyes, Caroline stumbled to the window and her only chance of escape – the banyan tree.

For a moment she sat upon the sill to breathe the blessed air outside, but for no longer. Behind her, tiny, evil tongues of fire were flickering into the very room, and, in addition, the naked branch that stretched itself perilously below her was at least thirty feet from the ground, and did not invite contemplation of its possible dangers. It *was* dangerous, especially imbalanced by a now protesting and writhing baby, but it was not a danger to compare with the one behind her. As she lowered herself on to the scaly bark, and observed that she must inch her way astride for at least eight feet with no support whatsoever except that of desperation, she felt a sudden blast of heat and a dull roar as the fire sprang like a dragon into the room she had left but seconds before.

Below her now, the garden was full of little scurrying figures, the servants presumably, running hither and thither distracted by their own helplessness. Swaying and sick with dizzy fear above them, Caroline could hear their cries of alarm faintly above the fire, and although nothing on earth would have induced her to look down, she was aware of a leaping light below her as the fire fought at the windows of the drawing room, shuttered at night against thieves.

For several desperate moments, Caroline thought she must fall. She crouched over the branch, the baby kicking and screaming perilously in his frail harness and threatening to tip them both on to the baked earth far below. She could hold with nothing but her hands before her, and her thighs were clamped tight to the branch on which she sat. Then the baby struggled suddenly and violently, and in a frantic effort to save them both, Caroline dug her feet inwards and found them held in the comforting growth that bearded the branch below. Very gradually, using these wiry tassels for purchase, Caroline inched her way forward, her feet and hands gripping and pushing, her hair tangled and damp about her face and her breath coming in little gasps of strain. About halfway to her goal, there was a sudden explosion below her, and a yellow sheet of flame sprang out of one of the drawing-room windows, illuminating Caroline's struggling figure high in the shaggy tree, and blinding her with abrupt light.

She stopped, and cried out in shock and bewilderment. There were shouts from the servants and then a surge forward as, headed by Ranjit, they plunged towards the tree. Trembling violently, Caroline could move no further, but crouched, bowed and clinging, while her teeth chattered and her toes and fingers clenched themselves on the tree and its growth for support.

'Memsahib! Memsahib! This way! Look this way! The baba!'

In the jumping light, Caroline peered through her tangled hair. Ranjit was braced against the main trunk of the tree, his arms out towards her, his hands but eighteen inches from the baby. She must go on, she must. Staunchly refusing to look down but keeping her smarting eyes fixed upon that narrow dark face under its white turban, she began to creep on again along the branch, inch by inch, her skin grazed and sore beneath her nightgown, the baby loosening all the time against her heaving chest.

Then Ranjit was there, deftly cutting the baby free and handing him downwards, and his thin strong hands were on her shoulders, her waist, balancing her respectfully against the trunk so that she might recover breath a moment. Then she felt more hands on her ankles, guiding her downwards, and always Ranjit's on her hands and shoulders, downwards, shakily but blessedly downwards, until her feet felt the miracle of the dusty earth beneath her.

She turned dazedly.

'Francis? The baby? Where is—?'

'Baba is safe, memsahib. Quite safe. All is being safe.'

She stretched out her hands blindly for him, and said something but her voice was faint and strange and far away and the baby did not come. She tried to step forward, but her knees were now shaking so convulsively that she could not seem to order them to obey her in the smallest way. Everything seemed to be throbbing and receding, black and yellow and jumping red. She saw Ranjit's face wheel past her, as big as the sun, before she crumpled soundlessly to the earth.

20

Mrs Rathbone was in her element. Her spare bedrooms were both occupied, there was a baby in the house, and the stream of callers to enquire after the consequences of the fire gave her a feeling of limitless popularity. She had been woken at dawn almost a week before, by Caroline's bearer, in a state of the greatest agitation and bringing news which, Mrs Rathbone uncomfortably suspected, would have caused a person of more gentle birth to faint outright.

But being merely Bella Rathbone, she did not faint. Instead she summoned her carriage and drove at once to the smouldering ruins of the Gates's house. Even she, with all her good sense, could not look at it, nor contemplate whose tomb it had become, but as an antidote to such ghoulishness, she had become extremely brisk and had collected Caroline and the baby from the corner of the garden where they had lain, and brought them home with her. Caroline had not spoken a word, but had lain back in the corner of the carriage with her eyes huge and vacant, seemingly unconscious of anything about her. Mrs Rathbone had thought it most improper to see Ranjit lift his mistress's body into the carriage with the most proprietary tenderness, but Caroline had seemed as oblivious of him as she was of Mrs Rathbone, her own safety or her grimed and half-naked condition. Mrs Rathbone watched her all the way home, examining her bare and dirty feet, her broken fingernails, her snarled hair and her great smudged empty eyes and could hardly see anything in her that was recognizable as Caroline. Only once that whole morning, when she went up to see

Caroline, now washed and dressed in one of her own extravagantly ruffled nightgowns and lying in bed, was there the smallest sign of any kind of life.

'There, dearie, that's better, is it not? Bella will care for you, that she will, so you are to sleep till you are better.'

Caroline lay with no sign of seeing her, her eyes still open and as dark as thunderclouds. Mrs Rathbone took her limp hand and bent to kiss her forehead.

'I should have a good cry, my dear, I should indeed. Many's the time I've calmed my feelings with a hearty cry. It does you no good at all to keep it pent up inside, my dear, no good at all.'

She pressed Caroline's hand and smiled kindly, and saw her head on the pillow give a tiny, but unmistakably negative shake.

Ann Wheeler got no better response. She had been brought news of the events of the night while she breakfasted, basking in the success of the evening before and contemplating, not without pleasure, the basket of orchids which had awaited her wakening. They were from Ralph Buxby, and expressed a far more profound admiration than that felt by one musician for another. Into this mood of happy languor Ranjit had broken, bringing with him a tale that drove all thoughts of fiddles and orchids and compliments from her head. The house which had sheltered her for three months was a smoking ruin, Johnnie Gates and all her possessions were ashes, but her baby was safe, and it was Caroline who had saved him. She fled to the Garden Reach at once, delirious with terror and gratitude, and pausing only to give her surprised son an uncharacteristically passionate embrace, rushed to Caroline's bedside to pour out her blessings and thanks.

Caroline lay as if she could not hear her, her thin hands lost in the elaborate ruffles of her cuffs, as limp upon the sheet as if she could not feel them.

'I owe you everything, everything! I am desperately ashamed of my frivolity and cannot in any way express to you the gratitude I feel! I shall never be able to repay you, never, never! My life would have been a ruin if – if—'

One of the thin hands came up and brushed against Ann's mouth as if to silence her. Then it dropped and Caroline turned her head away, seeming to indicate that it tired her to hear more. Ann was weeping, hot thankful tears dropping on to the bed, Caroline, her own hands, but Caroline lay as if she were deaf and blind. At last, choking with emotion, Ann bent to kiss the hand nearest to her, and then crept reverently from the room.

Caroline lay entombed in silence for four days, accepting only the merest nourishment, and giving no sign to anyone what she thought or felt, if indeed she thought or felt anything at all. Mrs Rathbone sent for the physician, to whose examination she submitted as limply as if she were a rag doll.

'There is nothing to warrant anxiety, Mrs Rathbone. I would say that Mrs Gates is suffering no more than the effects of shock and strain upon a highly sensitive and over-wrought system. Give her light nourishment and let her rise when she will. Rest will be the best medicine.'

Clothes – the most subdued gown Mrs Rathbone could find in her extensive wardrobe, a dress of burgundy silk trimmed with cream lace – were laid ready in Caroline's room in case she should wish to rise from her bed for any other purpose than necessity. Trays of broths and custards were brought to her constantly, but mostly they were carried away again quite untouched. Her thinness began to acquire a fragile transparency and when the fifth day dawned, Mrs Rathbone confided to Ann that she was deeply concerned.

'If only she'd speak, my dear, I'd be so much easier in my mind. But nothing seems to rouse her, nothing at all. I sometimes wonder if she even knows I am in the room at all. If her eyes weren't open, I wouldn't believe her alive, I swear I wouldn't. I even offered her Baby to play with yesterday, but she didn't flicker an eyelash.'

Ann Wheeler reflected a moment.

'It can hardly be grief for – for – can it?'

'For Johnnie, dear? I hardly think so. I spoke to her of the funeral arrangements only yesterday, just to tell her how good George Carew is being to take it all off our shoulders, and there wasn't a sign she'd heard me.'

'He – he was not a man one would be likely to miss. He was a brute,' Ann added with some vehemence.

'He was a foolish and self-indulgent boy,' Mrs Rathbone said firmly, 'but I'll admit she was too good for him by many a mile. Now, my dear, do you go up and have one more peep at her before I summon the physician again.'

Ann went up the staircase with some trepidation. There was something alarming in the consistency of Caroline's immobility, especially as Ann could not believe that those wide dark grey eyes hid a sleeping brain. She tapped at the door, but as usual heard nothing and slipped quietly in, to find Caroline fully dressed and seated in the speckled shadows by the screened window.

'Caroline! My dearest – should you be up? Why did you not call for help?'

Caroline turned a little, her neck startlingly narrow in its collar of extravagant ruffles. The dress hung hopelessly from her shoulders, designed for a body with many more amplitudes than hers, its swags and ruffles drooping dispiritedly towards the floor. Her face looked calmer, less empty of expression than it had, but her eyes were still as dark as if she had been contemplating nightmares.

'Caroline?' Ann said again, more softly.

Caroline nodded.

'Can you hear me?'

'I have heard – everything.'

'Then why—'

Caroline made an abrupt gesture, and Ann stopped. She came across the room and knelt by Caroline's side. Caroline put out a hand and touched Ann's dress, a green figured silk also from Mrs Rathbone's wardrobe while Ann's own surviving dress was hastily copied. She smiled faintly.

'We hardly look our best, do we?'

Tears were rising fast in Ann's eyes.

'It matters not a whit, dearest Caroline. All that matters is that you have spoken at last.'

'How is little Francis?'

Ann could not reply. The tears spilled over and she seized Caroline's hand and pressed it fervently.

'He is well?'

Ann nodded vigorously.

'Then all is well.'

There was a silence for a moment, while Ann fumbled for a handkerchief with her free hand, and Caroline sat quite still, gazing into the shadows of the room. Then she began to speak, in a low, quiet tone, never looking at Ann, never moving.

'I have come full circle, you see. For years, it seems, I have struggled to make something of my life, of myself, I have built up my courage, tried to make myself free of my inadequacies. Once or twice I thought to be happy, but I see that was not a very possible hope. But I've had moments of contentment, moments of feeling I have done what I could. I am so limited by my own self, but I have tried. I fled from the things that bound me, and tried to do what was best in what was new. I made many mistakes, many, oh yes, one that cost me – but that is history. And now everything is history, too. All my life up to now has become history. I have travelled all this weary way in my life and I am only back where I began. No, it is worse, for I am less than I was. I am older, tireder, sadder, and quite destitute. I have nowhere to go but back to what I left – and which rejected me. You

305

must forgive me for being so melancholy and self-pitying, I dislike myself so much for being so.'

She stopped quite suddenly and gave Ann's hand a little shake.

'Were you – did – did you ponder all this all this time? All these days, is that what your poor brain was about?'

'Yes.'

'But why do you think so sadly? Are there not countless people who would value your companionship in their households? Myself, Mrs Rathbone, Miss Grant—'

'No – no, please. Forgive me for sounding so ungrateful, but you see – you see, the unkindest cut of all is that I have always wanted to work out my own salvation. I have a tiresome nature that wishes to earn what it gets. Isobel said I had a stiff-necked pride, and she was right. I have. It is not so stiff as it was, and it has a great deal of fear in it also, but I suppose it is still a kind of pride. It – it is really all that is left, you know. All – all I have. I shall find myself a position as some old lady's companion, never fear. I thought when I was eighteen that that was what I must come to, so I am not quite unprepared.'

Ann said gently, 'You are very difficult to help.'

Caroline smiled and leaned forward to kiss her.

'I know it. It is a dreadful fault but I don't think I can root it out without destroying my will to live completely.'

'Is there nothing, nothing I can do?'

'You do it already. You do the only thing I have really ever wanted from anyone, I suppose. You show me affection. No – no, Ann, you must not weep again. There is nothing now to weep for. Your baby is safe, thank God and I – I am free.'

Ann wished to question her, but could think of no way to frame the words. After a while, Caroline added in a whisper, 'I cannot speak of that. I cannot. All I can tell you is that I shudder to think that the merest living creature should die that way.'

Later that morning the stream of callers included Ralph Buxby. He had been every day since the fire, finding it all too easy to obtain permission from Sir Edward Ashton to leave his desk earlier than was customary, and had brought profusions of flowers with him each time until Mrs Rathbone's drawing room was richly scented and quite obscured beneath blooms. Ann, sensible and sincerely attached to her husband, received him with frank pleasure but never permitted him to speak to her alone. This morning, however, he found her by herself, lost in subdued reverie in the drawing room with none of the open gladness in her face that he was accustomed to see.

'Mrs Wheeler – Ann – I do trust that nothing ails you, troubles you?'

She looked absently at the crimson roses he held, but not at his face.

'I am preoccupied with Mrs Gates.'

'Is she still not well? I am sorry to hear that she still has not rallied.'

'Oh, she has rallied. This morning I found her up and dressed, but so sadly depressed in spirits, so brave still, so—' She stopped hurriedly and bit her lip.

Ralph Buxby put his roses on the nearest chair, and assisted Ann to seat herself.

'If it would not be indiscreet, could you not tell me more?'

'How much do you know?'

'You forget whose secretary I am. I know a good deal.'

'And of Johnnie Gates? And her family in England?'

Ralph shrugged.

'Of the late Mr Gates I know what all Calcutta knows. Of her family, I know nothing. I believe she scarcely has one.'

'That is part of the trouble.'

'You mean that she has nowhere to go?'

'I mean that she will not go there. She has one sister whom – whom she does not care for. She came to India in part to escape her. Oh, Mr Buxby, it broke my heart to hear her talk so today! She will let no-one help her, she is resigned to throwing herself away as companion to some old lady, she – she said she never wanted anything from anyone but love—' here a sob broke from her, enabling Ralph Buxby to take her hands in sympathy. 'She has worked so hard, and been so good and she has nothing now, nothing at all. She deserves such love, oh, how she deserves it! Do you know that her bearer will not go? Mr Rathbone has been most good about arranging for other employment for her servants, and most of them wailed bitterly at leaving her, but we cannot make Ranjit go! He says he wants no wages, only to serve her. He has waited for her to see him ever since the fire, and he will not move from the house. That, you see, Mr Buxby, is the kind of creature she is, and that is why the awful emptiness of her fate is so hard to bear!'

Ralph was silent for a moment, part of his brain concerned with how enchanting Ann looked in her grave eagerness, and the other part involved with a dawning notion that he might in some way repay Caroline for the injury he had unwittingly done her three years before. He had told Sir Edward Ashton the outline of the story of the fire, in order to gain as much of his superior's sympathy and thus time away from his desk as possible, but as all mention of Caroline was painfully impossible between them he had not elaborated on her resourcefulness and courage.

'You say she will not be helped?'

'Oh, no. She admits it is a fault but says it is all she has to stiffen her.'

'Suppose we were to help her without her knowledge?' Ann's dark eyes glowed.

'You have some plan?'

'Only a vague one. And given the chief participants, it may be doomed from the outset. You say that she wants nothing but love, and that her future is quite barren. I am in no doubt whatsoever that Sir Edward cares for her as deeply as he ever did, but that he, like her, is afraid to expose himself to hurt again. As they both so evidently need each other, may we not contrive to throw them together again?'

'She would never agree!'

Ralph Buxby smiled conspiratorially.

'Then she had better not be told.'

The following day, Caroline was persuaded to come down to the drawing room when she was sure that no more callers would come.

'Such a shy thing you are!' Mrs Rathbone exclaimed, 'when all that anyone wishes to do is to admire you for your courage, and praise you and make much of you!'

Caroline blushed and said nothing, but Ann spoke for her.

'That is precisely what she does not want.'

Caroline looked up at Mrs Rathbone from her seat on a low chair, the baby on the rug at her feet.

'I do not know what I should have done without you. You have been the most staunch of friends and your kindness has been unbounded. I do hope I will not have to trouble you much longer—'

'Trouble? Trouble, my dear Caroline? It has been the greatest delight to me to have you here and I will not hear any nonsense about leaving, I most certainly will not. Your head is full of the most absurd notions of independence, and until you are fully well, I will not even permit you to speak on the subject. Now come, my dear, and tickle Baby, for see how he longs for it!'

Before dinner was announced, Caroline insisted on returning to her room, despite the fact that Mrs Rathbone said that there was to be almost no company that day, a mere handful, not above three or four extra people. On the following day, Caroline again came downstairs, this time for a little longer, but again retreated to her own room before the house began to resound with Mrs Rathbone's hospitality. That evening, however, she came downstairs for supper, during the course of which she mentioned that she would like to see George Carew.

'Ann tells me he has been so good to me. He has – dealt with everything. I would like to thank him.'

'I shall tell him to call tomorrow, my dear. I shall send a note directly, and he may call on his way home from his office.'

Caroline nodded gratefully and bent her head over some fruit, while Ann and Mrs Rathbone exchanged a glance of some significance. When supper was over, and Caroline had gone slowly up the staircase, Mrs Rathbone drew Ann aside.

'Well, my dear, and is not her asking for George Carew an excellent sign? She is waking to the world at last! I think in a day or so, for we must capture her before she is strong enough to think of leaving, she may be ready to see quite another caller, do you not think?'

'I will write to Mr Buxby.'

'Do, my dear, this very evening. Now I must go, for I am bound for the tables again. I confess I am having such a run of luck at present that I can scarcely bear to be away from them!'

George Carew came as bidden, as languid and elegant in appearance as ever, but with an uneasy air as if he had recently been floundering in waters of sincerity hitherto quite unknown to him. Caroline received him still clad in the capacious and unbecoming wine-coloured gown, and with an unaffected warmth she had never felt for him before.

' 'Twas nothing, ma'am, nothing.'

'It was a great deal, Mr Carew, and no-one else was about to do it. I – I do not quite know how to express my gratitude—'

'I'd rather you don't try, ma'am.'

An awkward silence fell between them which George occupied by rubbing his thumb round and round on the silver top of his stick, and Caroline in wondering how she could ask what she felt she owed it to Johnnie to know.

'Mr Carew?'

'Ma'am.'

'Was – did, did anyone attend the funeral? I did not know myself that it was to take place, you see, so that I— '

'I never meant you to know, Mrs Gates. Had to shove the old rogue off quickly in this climate. No point in you knowing.'

Caroline was startled at his perception.

'But – but was there no-one there? Besides yourself?'

'No, ma'am.'

'No-one from the Company? No-one at all?'

'Just myself, ma'am.'

She could not ask the next question, but as if he read her thoughts, George said simply, 'There was nothing left, you know. Nothing.' He stood up, and looked down at her for a moment as she sat contemplating the desolation of Johnnie's going. She roused herself abruptly and rose to bid him farewell.

'You have spared me so much, Mr Carew, and I do thank you for it from the bottom of my heart.'

George Carew bent briefly over her hand.

'Better I than you, ma'am,' he said.

'Yes, Mr Carew. Yes, you are right. Better in every way.'

Two days after this visit, Caroline was just preparing for her daily descent to an empty drawing room when Mrs Rathbone intercepted her.

'Caroline, my dear! Just in time! Look what I have brought you! Now, is that not pretty? I said to myself that you must be sick to death of that old red of mine, and I had the tailor take in this blue which is a prettier colour for you by far. Now come, dear, and we shall try it.'

Caroline demurred.

'You are so kind, but may I try it later? I would so much rather not change now. It does not signify to me how I look, I do assure you, and I am dressed for the day now. It is very pretty but I am quite used to this, and who is there to see me?'

Mrs Rathbone seemed strangely anxious, barring Caroline's way with her arms full of blue silk, but Caroline was adamant. She would not change, she saw no reason for it, and eventually escaped downstairs in the despised burgundy gown to the empty drawing-room. She looked about her – in some surprise. Usually, at this hour between callers and dinner, Ann would be seated there waiting for her, with little Francis on his rug, allowed as a special privilege to roll about in the drawing room for the delight of Mrs Gates. But today there was no-one there. Presumably, Ann was on her way, perhaps she was still practising her music. Caroline listened, but could hear nothing. Well, she would wait. She would choose a chair near the roses that Ann's admirers, unspecified to Caroline, seemed to bring so abundantly, and sit quietly and inhale the scent and wait.

After some moments, she heard footsteps in the hall, male footsteps. Clearly Mr Rathbone was home, for there had been no sounds of a stranger being let into the house. The footsteps approached the drawing-room door and Caroline sprang up, ready to greet her host with the gratitude she felt he richly deserved for his hospitality, and found herself confronting Sir Edward Ashton.

She groped blindly about her for a chairback for support. He closed the door behind him, without taking his eyes from her face, and then began to move steadily across the room towards her. His face, oh his face! As remarkable as ever, as powerful, but so sad, so weary!

Had she done that? Had she carved those long lines beside his mouth and across the forehead? And her dress! Her dreadful hideous dress, no wonder Mrs Rathbone had wanted her to change! It was all a plot, that was what it was, a plot to get her here alone—

'I fear you are the victim of a scheme,' Sir Edward said. His voice shook.

'Yes.'

'I hope you are not angry.'

'I – I am very much surprised.'

'But not angry?'

She shook her head slightly.

'I hear – heroic things of you.'

'Please, do not speak of it. It was – what anyone might have done—'

'That', Sir Edward said with more of his characteristic firmness, 'is nonsense.'

Caroline felt giddy. There was no time to collect her spinning thoughts, and precious little reassurance in Sir Edward's manner. He had addressed her by no name as yet, and it was impossible to tell what he intended from what he had uttered so far. He was speaking with the concern shown to a recovering invalid, and his hesitancy could be accounted for by the fact that their last exchange had been acrimonious.

She raised her head and said formally, 'I am most obliged to you for calling.'

He looked startled, began an incoherent sentence which he soon abandoned, and said, 'I wished to offer my – my sympathy and my admiration.'

She inclined her head but did not speak.

'You have suffered a great deal, I wished you to have my sympathy.'

'I thank you.'

Silence again.

'I wonder, Mrs Gates, what your plans are? May I assist you in any way? Do you need a sea passage to England?'

'I am most obliged, but I have all the assistance I need. I – I shall be returning to England certainly.'

'I should be delighted to help you get a passage should there be any difficulty.'

'There will be none.'

There was a pause. Caroline felt unfamiliar sensations of tension in her breast and throat, and her eyes were burning so that she could not raise them from the carpet.

'Would you think me impertinent, Mrs Gates, if I were to ask what you intend to do upon reaching England? If you will not let me help you here, perhaps my influence might be of some help to you there?'

'You are very good but – but I shall manage quite well. I can return to my sister in Dorset for some – for a short time, and then I shall – I shall—'

She stopped in unutterable confusion, aware only that some extraordinary exploding loosening was taking place within her, some strange wave of relief, set free it seemed by the desperate contemplation of her future. Clinging to the chairback with both hands she felt her face helplessly flooded with a wash of tears, hot, painful tears which coursed down her cheeks, while her throat tightened uncontrollably on sob after sob. It was terrible, appalling, unutterably humiliating to shed these violent tears, the first tears since childhood, in front of Sir Edward Ashton, of all people. Struggling blindly with the physical difficulty of weeping in itself, and the seeming impossibility of checking it, Caroline stretched out a hand in her helplessness, as if to make a gesture to indicate that she would recover herself in a moment, and felt it warmly clasped. She tried to pull away, but not only was one hand firmly imprisoned, but the other was then captured from the chairback and both were pressed to Sir Edward's shirt front while he spoke to her through her sobbing confusion. She strove to hear him but could make out no words; it seemed she hardly needed to, for his voice was full of all the old urgent tenderness, whatever he was saying. Then he separated her hands from his own, so that he might put his arms about her and hold her strongly to him.

'Caroline, my Caroline.'

She could only cry.

'You shall never leave me again, never. Do you hear me? If I have to chain you to me to keep you, chained you shall be.'

She said something brokenly.

'Forgive you? Of course I forgive you! I have nothing to forgive, nothing, all is past, finished, forgotten, everything is but beginning. Look up at me, look up.'

She sniffed. She could not.

'I – I am ashamed of how I must seem—'

'You are absurd,' he said with the utmost indulgence. 'Also uniquely courageous, sympathetic, remarkable – and mine.'

The tears would not stop; it seemed as if twenty years of weeping must be accomplished in a few minutes.

'Yours,' she said with difficulty.

'Ah! Always?'

His voice rang with triumph. She nodded, wishing to heaven she might speak her promises, not be confined merely to indicating them. Sir Edward ran a finger gently along her cheek and contemplated the tears he had collected.

'I should preserve these, should I not, my dearest? Like you they are unique, for I shall see to it that they are the first and last of your time—'

The door opened; there, framed in the opening, stood Mrs Rathbone, Ann with her baby in her arms, and Ralph Buxby. The faces of all four wore the expressions of unconfined delight that follows a plan of perfect accomplishment.

21

It was a fresh November morning in 1778, one of those clear, bright days of the upper Indian winter that is a just reward for the heats and rains of summer. Mrs Rathbone, clad in a new boudoir gown of yellow Chinese silk, embroidered heavily with oriental hieroglyphics in emerald and scarlet, was seated at her new escritoire. It was new for she had never had occasion for one before, writing letters being an anathema to her and her family in England being without sufficient education to read any epistles in the first place. But she now had a new correspondent, and her life had blossomed so strangely and wonderfully in the last few months that she found herself eager to relate all that was happening to a sympathetic ear.

Ann Wheeler was now with her husband, having most properly decided that Calcutta was no place to be left without official protection. She had set off across India intrepidly in the rains of late summer, to be greeted with rapture by Frank Wheeler, whose regiment had been encamped some distance short of Bombay for many weary months while its commander endeavoured to coerce his natural dilatoriness into some sort of decision. Before she left Calcutta, she had extracted from Mrs Rathbone a promise that she would write with faithful regularity. Hence the new escritoire – beautifully copied from a French one by a clever man in the bazaar at one quarter the European price – and hence also an impressive quantity of thick new writing paper, emblazoned with arms which owed most of their flourishes to Mrs Rathbone's imagination. Mr Rathbone had pointed out that the most he was entitled to was a mailed fist, but Mrs Rathbone had added a laurel wreath, a rose of England and a portcullis, quartered on a gilded shield. She sat down before a sheet so glorified now, and selected a quill; it seemed that there was some pleasure to be gained in writing after all, when the results of one's labours were so eagerly awaited.

My dear Ann,

I hardly know how to begin, I have so much to report. It is quite difficult to think how changed everything is and in so short a time. I was looking at my green silk – the green with silver lace that you wore after that dreadful fire – only the other day and reflecting how long ago that seems already. I hope Baby is well and bouncing and that you are nicely settled.

My dear, you cannot imagine the circles I move in these days! Mr Rathbone says he hardly knows me, I am grown so grand. Only yesterday, Lady Ashton invited me to dine – that will be six times, my dear, in as many weeks – and I was put upon Sir Edward's right hand at table, would you believe! The place of honour! I said to myself, Bella Rathbone, you have little left to wish for, indeed you have not. I shook in my shoes for fear at the thought, you know, but he was quite delightful and not at all fierce, and only wished to dote upon Lady Ashton in conversation, which I was glad to assist him in. And during dessert, Lady Ashton said she wished the party to drink a toast to me as one of her most valued friends! My dear, I did not know where to look. I was quite ravished with delight and fear, but I managed to stand and thank them all, though my face was fiery, and then Sir Edward said he did not know how to thank me for the support I had been to his wife. And then, my dear, the Governor General came up to me himself and spoke so civilly that I could not utter a word, but stood like a dumb thing. I was much pleased I wore my new cerise, it is really very pretty and a perfect background

317

to my peacock feathers. They are said to be unlucky, but what could be more lucky than such compliments? I declare, my head is quite turned.

You will want to hear more of Lady Ashton – she is so changed, except, of course, in her manner which is as sweet as ever, that I find it hard to think of her as our dear Caroline – and indeed she is the rage of Calcutta, would you believe it? I declare that wigs and powder are quite going out of fashion, and we all strive for curls like hers and hair on our shoulders. She has filled out a little, and her looks are so much improved, she has that bloom about her as she did when Sir Edward first loved her. She wore a gown of cream figured silk over an underskirt embroidered in pink and green and gold thread, and though it was all a little quiet to my taste, I must say she looked very well in it, and I expect to see copies all over Calcutta before the week is out. Sir Edward has given her a collar of pearls so lustrous that I could not keep my eyes from them, but she only wore flowers in her hair which seemed strangely countryfied.

My dear, I never saw a man dote as does Sir Edward! I do declare he is not happy if she is not by him, and his eyes follow her as if he could not see enough of her. It warms my heart, my dear, it does indeed. There's not a woman more deserving than she in all the world, nor is there one who knows her luck better. I am to sup with them tomorrow before a ball, and Lady Ashton insists I join them for a great picnic to celebrate her husband's birthday. I am in quite a flurry of choosing dresses, as you may imagine, and await the next ship with impatience as I have had to order a quantity of new things to befit the company I now move in. You would stare to see how grand I am become!

I must make the most of it, my dear, for Lady Ashton has whispered to me – in the strictest confidence, you understand – that they will go home at the end of the cold season. Sir Edward has done enough in India, and now is impatient to take his bride home to Ashton Court, which I hear is very fine and set in extensive grounds. It will be very dreadful without them, but I hope I can persuade Mr Rathbone to follow shortly.

Lady Ashton says she is about to write to you, but it's my belief Sir Edward scarcely allows her a moment to herself. She says she prizes the letter your husband sent her about little Francis above all others she has ever received, but says that all the thanks she ever wants are letters with news of Baby. Is not that like her?

I also hear news that Miss Grant is to be married next spring, an excellent match it is said to be, but Miss Grant has declared she will not allow any man to put a ring upon her finger until Lady Ashton has approved him. So you see, my dear, there are many reasons for her going back to England, and in any case, she has not the constitution for this climate. She thinks she may have to allow Ranjit to come with her as he will not leave her, but she is anxious he will find England unpleasantly cold and damp.

My dear Ann, how I have run on! I must close now as it is time to dress and the hairdresser has been clearing his throat this half hour. Send me news of how you do, and a kiss to Baby.

Ever yours Affectionately,
Bella Rathbone

THE END

City of Gems

For David

Mandalay, November 1979

Acknowledgements

I should like to thank Peter Pointon most warmly both for the truly encouraging interest he has shown in this project and for all his invaluable guidelines for my research. I have benefited enormously from his expertise on Burma and also from material most kindly lent to me by David Brown. I am also very grateful to my father whose painstaking research for me has been used to the full in this book.

Glossary

Kalā foreigner

Thakin sir, equivalent of 'sahib' in India

Thakin-ma memsahib

Salun-daw low backless couch

Kinwoon Mingyi Prime Minister

Ashin-nammadaw-paya formal title of the Queen

Poon-dawgi-paya formal title of the King

Hlutdaw parliament

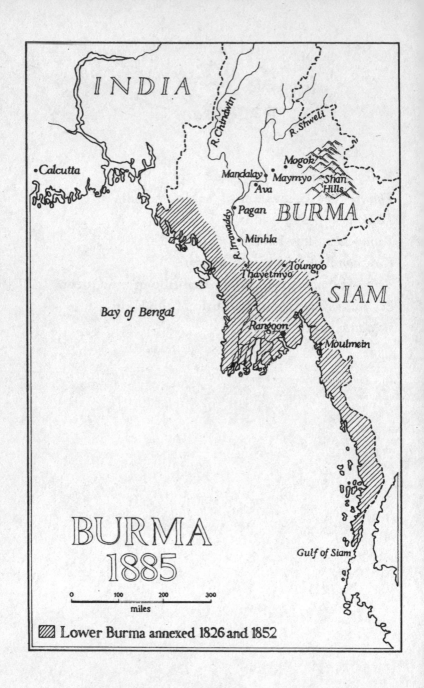

INDIA

• Calcutta

R. Chindwin

R. Shweli

Mogok

Mandalay •   • Maymyo
        • Ava   Shan
                     Hills

R. Irrawaddy

• Pagan   BURMA

• Minhla

        • Toungoo
Thayetmyo   SIAM

Bay of Bengal

Rangoon

        Moulmein

BURMA
1885

Gulf of Siam

0   100   200   300
        miles

▨ Lower Burma annexed 1826 and 1852

PART ONE

1

On 15 February 1879, the day on which Queen Supayalat, wife of King Thibaw of the Kingdom of Ava in Upper Burma, ordered eighty members of the royal family to be clubbed to death, Maria Beresford celebrated her twenty-first birthday in Bombay.

In the furious February sunshine grim processions left the rose-brick walls of the royal Gem City in Mandalay by the ill-omened western gate and made for the great yellow breadth of the Irrawaddy, bearing with them red velvet sacks which were hurled into the slow-moving waters of the river. In sunshine almost as fierce, tables had been spread in the shade of trees in the garden of Hubert Beresford's bungalow in Bombay, for Maria had been seized by the whim of a picnic for her birthday and in this, as in almost everything, her father delighted to indulge her.

The near-naked men carrying the red velvet sacks – red velvet because the luckless contents were of royal blood and also because that same blood would be less visible on its plushy surface – were criminals let out of gaol for their grisly duty, armed with sandalwood clubs and primed with a raw local spirit. The people on Hubert Beresford's lawn, retired – or failed – tea-planters like himself, soldiers, civil servants, their wives and daughters, despite the heat, dressed in tight-bodied gowns of enormous complication, the skirts either elaborately swathed or sporting ruffled trains, ate salmon mayonnaise and cold curried chicken and told each other exhaustedly what a novel idea an al fresco party in a temperature around the hundreds was.

Within six months, Maria Beresford, who had never given Burma a moment's thought in her secluded life, would be congratulating herself on being one of the few European women welcomed at the court in Mandalay.

But this, on the day of Maria's party, was yet to come. Burma had as much significance for Maria that day as Iceland might have done, or the remote islands of the Pacific. She had evolved her plan for a picnic with great care, determined her birthday should be memorable, unlike anyone else's, widely talked of. When she suggested it to her father, she had used her little-girl voice, implying that she needed to be indulged, that he was the protective all-provider who could make her happy.

'Such a little thing, dearest Papa, but such a big thing in terms of its effect! Only think. A mere luncheon party so not a quarter as dreadfully expensive as an evening party might be – and your Maria knows full well how careful we must be and how no-one must know about our carefulness. It is our secret, isn't it Papa? – and outside under the trees so that everyone may walk about and not be stuck with anyone tiresome. And then we shall set up the butts and the croquet and we shall have an archery competition and I shall present the prizes, shan't I, Papa, because it is my day.'

Her day it was, whatever the inconvenience and discomfort for anyone else. She was woken with her customary breakfast tray upon which her father had laid a bunch of flat white Indian roses. She dressed then, in a morning gown of relative simplicity in order to be unimpeded as she swept about the house and garden being commanding to the servants. They had only to put a table down to be told to move it. Tablecloths were declared to be creased, even when freshly ironed, flower arrangements went in and out of the house endlessly as Maria first wished to see their effect in certain places and then insisted that their transient freshness would be gone if they were not kept cool and dark.

Flies descended in thick clusters on servants and furniture. Fruit was ordered out, shrouded first in white muslin, then in flies, and ordered back again. She called for the ice boxes, saw their contents running into the red earth, and commanded them taken away. Glasses were finger-marked, silver improperly arranged, the boys set to fan the whole proceeding with palm leaves were idle and inefficient.

At noon, Maria abandoned the chaos she had created and went in to dress. Hubert, ponderous with significance, waylaid her in the hall.

'One moment only, my dearest.'

His study was dim and hot, the punkah only succeeding in moving clouds of dust about.

She sat down, prettily expectant.

'And did my dearest think I should forget her on such a day?'

She played up to him, eyes wide. 'Oh no, Papa! I know you did not! Those lovely roses on my breakfast tray!'

He said with smiling dismissiveness, 'Oh, roses!' and then he took a red morocco case from his desk and put it in her hands.

She looked up into his face for some moments rather than at the case and then he said, 'Open it! Open it!' delighted at the sweetness of her response, and watched her as she lifted the lid and revealed two pearl earrings, large lustrous teardrops, each swinging from a fleur de lys of diamonds.

She said, 'Oh Papa!' and remained gazing downwards.

'You like them, my own one?'

'More – more than anything I ever saw. But you should not spoil your Maria so, I know you should not. What with my party—'

'Hush,' Hubert said. He lifted an earring from its nest of velvet and deftly screwed it to Maria's ear. She turned her face.

'Now the other one, Papa!'

16

He surveyed her with pleasure.

'I – don't know how to thank you.'

She rose and put her arms about his neck, so that their handsome profiles were nose to aquiline nose.

'You are the dearest, best Papa in all the world.'

'And you are the dearest and best of daughters.'

Automatically their eyes slid sideways to a dim portrait on the wall, a painting of a sad, faded woman with large pale eyes full of bewildered injury.

'Poor Mamma,' Maria said and sighed.

They smiled at each other.

'Poor Mamma,' Hubert said.

Poor Mamma was scarcely even a memory. She had died when Maria was eleven, protesting faintly as she had done for the previous four years, that Maria should go home, home to England. She had protested, in the same exhausted manner, all her married life, about India, the servants, Hubert's neglect of her and indulgence of Maria, about her health, her loneliness, her boredom. She saw herself as a victim, and it suited her husband and daughter very well to agree with her that she was, indeed, one of nature's victims about whom nothing could be done and of whom little notice need be taken.

She had been very pretty when Hubert married her and had brought with her, apart from her looks and malleable character, twenty thousand pounds. Hubert might have wished that the money had not been made among the potteries of Staffordshire, especially as the pottery concerned made the coarser articles of domestic use, but he needed the money quite enough to blink easily at its origins. He himself brought to the marriage, as he told his admiring bride, such intangible and invaluable qualities as his name, his education, his culture and a family who had lived in the same house in Shropshire for five generations. That his own generation was hopelessly improvident and therefore impoverished he did not choose to tell her, nor that he was, as the third son, destitute and badly in debt. He put the situation to her quite another way.

'And now we shall realize my lifelong dream, together! I have always, all my life, been stirred by tales of India. Indian stories were the chief passion of my boyhood. And what have we to keep us here?'

Fanny Beresford wished to point out that an old mother in Burslem very much wished to keep her there, but did not like to say so.

'Nothing, you see! Nothing at all! We are as free as birds. We shall go to India, we shall buy ourselves a part of India, we shall have our children there. Fanny, it will be our kingdom.'

The Anaimalai Hills had certainly looked like paradise, a fair setting for Hubert's kingdom. The brilliant green slopes around Tirimbatore in southern India had rich, bright earth and rioted with flowers and birds. Hubert bought eight hundred acres and, leaving Fanny miserable as the guest of a formidable colonel's wife at Pondicherry, chose the highest point of his estate where he proceeded to supervise, for almost a year, the building of a magnificent bungalow, luxurious and splendid enough for a viceroy. When the first tea bushes were planted on the surrounding hills and the last rug laid and picture hung, Hubert came to Pondicherry and carried Fanny off to his kingdom. He deposited her in the gleaming bungalow on the hilltop in which absolutely nothing, not even her boudoir, had been of her own choosing, and demanded that she be as elated as he was. She drooped. Alone all day but for the servants, three days' journey from the next Englishman, she began her steady, faint complaining. Hubert, beyond allowing her three months in Madras for Maria's birth, took no notice. He was lord of his domain, always well, vibrant with energy.

Maria was like him. By the time she was four, the missy-baba in her vast sunbonnet was as familiar a figure on the plantation as her father. Her amah came to Hubert for orders; he chose her dresses, taught her French and mathematics, drawing and music, and insisted, after her seventh birthday, that she should sit up to dinner.

When Fanny had said she should go home, she had clung to her father and shrieked.

'Would you break my heart?' Hubert cried.

'And hers? Would you tear away our chief of pleasures?'

Fanny had sulked. 'No-one else does. No other children stay. They are all gone by Maria's age. It will look so odd. You have lived up here too long, you have forgotten what people do.'

'Bah!' Hubert cried. 'Convention!'

Maria had stayed, the blue gaze she turned upon her mother ever more scornful and triumphant. She was given duties in the house, instructed in the affairs of the plantation, given a small fiddle as well as her piano and a showy little mare to complement her considerable skill on horseback. Fanny requested a governess and was ignored; suggestions of boarding school, of a companion even, went quite unheard.

'I am Papa's only companion,' Maria informed her mother. 'We do not need anyone else.'

What else was there for Fanny to do but die? She took some mild infection, gave way to it greedily and was buried in Tirimbatore in a ceremony whose elegance owed much to Hubert's reading of elegiac verses. Her going left no mark, indeed it lent an exuberance to meals that her husband and daughter had not felt before; there was an air of holiday about. At eleven, Maria had her own boudoir – it had been her mother's but Hubert let her now have it, redecorated, for herself. He was like a bridegroom. The house must be quite made over. All the old furniture went, all the rugs, all the curtains, most of the pictures, and beautiful things came from Europe to replace them, things that scarcely anyone but Hubert or Maria saw.

Three and four years later, the crops failed. A blight struck the tea bushes withering their brilliant little leaves into rusty uselessness. Hubert had never been a good manager, never prudent with money. For three years more they struggled gallantly on, selling acres to neighbouring plantations, praising each other for small economies. When Maria was eighteen the end came. If they were to have anything to live upon, they must retrench at once. Tirimbatore was sold to a hefty young Scot whose small appraising eyes roused Maria to furious indignation and they took themselves and their possessions to Bombay.

'I shall find employment,' Hubert said. 'I have connections in Bombay.'

If he had, they appeared fairly tenuous. They bought a bungalow on the northern slopes of the city – 'Where else, for my dearest one!' – despite the fact that prices there were the highest, and settled back confidently for offers to pour in for Hubert. None came.

'I don't believe anyone knows you have come,' Maria declared.

She began to call on people; they were asked out to dine. Maria, out of her father's earshot, pleaded prettily with directors of the small trading companies with which Bombay abounded. At last a position was found, much too humble of course, nothing more really than

21

chief clerk in a tea-exporting house, but the money would pay for everyday life and appearances might be kept up.

'You see, my dove, what connections will do for a man.'

Maria said, 'And daughters' silently to herself and put her arms about his neck.

She saw him off to Parsee Bazaar Street every morning and welcomed him home to luncheon. She spoke of his work in the light in which he saw it, not as it actually was, and when an Indian director of the company, one stout and strutting Pranjeevan Jeena, came to complain of the shortness of Hubert's office hours, he found himself confronted by such a terrifying example of English superiority in Miss Beresford that he went away again, mission unaccomplished and his tail between his legs.

'It is of the utmost importance, my darling,' Hubert would say, 'that one puts the highest value upon oneself. The rest of the world, after all, only takes one at one's own valuation.'

With that principle in mind, Maria's birthday guests might have been forgiven for thinking they had really been asked to a viceregal durbar. Maria, always handsome, always much admired by the gentlemen and reluctantly by the ladies, who found her proud and egotistical, was dressed to kill. A new dress had been made for her of blue silk precisely the colour of her fine eyes, its skirt swathed in front, caught up at the sides in wreaths of white gauze roses and flowing gracefully behind into a train edged with lavish pleating. The bodice was also edged with gauze roses, the elbows ornamented with them, and around her long neck of which she was so proud was a blue velvet ribbon on which was threaded the lovely old cameo her father had given her at Christmas. Her new pearls swung in her ears, her dark blonde hair curled becomingly on her forehead and then was swept up into curves around a hat made of yet more gauze roses and blue ribbons. The ladies of the party, dressed merely for luncheon and conscious of the damp armpits and sweat-beaded brows that were inevitably part of life in India, felt themselves deliberately outstripped.

Grace Prior, shyly clinging to her father's arm, was particularly conscious of the discrepancy between her own appearance and Maria's. If their circumstances had not been so similar – single daughters of widowed fathers bravely making do on insufficient money – she would not have felt so keenly the endless unhappy comparisons which blighted her every meeting with Maria. She looked down at her own dress, a shapeless green thing she had sewed herself, inspired by the paintings of Sir Edward Burne-Jones, and felt she might as well have come dressed in bedclothes for all it did for her figure. Maria swept up to them, cool and immaculate, received her father's hearty congratulations smilingly, glanced briefly and killingly at Grace's clothes, and swept on, indicating the laden tables with a graceful gesture of her fan.

'Will you do battle with the flies for a little pilau, my dear?'

Grace smiled lovingly at her father. His great brown beard almost hid his clerical bands, flowing down to meet the waistcoat he was sure to bespatter with food.

'It – it's very grand, Papa. I – I am not at all properly dressed. I had not imagined it would be like this at all. I wonder why we were asked?'

'*De rigueur*, my dear. I am the regulation holy man. Over there is the regulation doctor, and beyond him is, I think, Colonel Browne, who must count as the regulation senior officer, as well as the prize guest. We balance the thing.'

A plate of rice and chicken, liberally sprinkled with flies, was pushed into Grace's hands, speedily followed by a napkin, a fork, a glass of warm champagne. Colonel Browne, coming up to the tables for his own luncheon and seeing her difficulties and her father's equal preoccupation with a similar burden, relieved her of all but her glass and found her a seat in the shade.

'Miss Prior, isn't it? Thought so. Horace Browne at your service, ma'am. We met before you know, at the mission house. I brought along some of my more troublesome boys. Rum do, this, eh?'

'I shan't miss this sort of thing,' Grace said with vehemence.

'Miss it? Miss it? Why, where are you off to? I

24

thought you were pretty much a fixture here, Prior, Anglican mission humming along nicely and all that. Excellent congregations you get here, I'm told.'

Tom Prior smiled again in the depths of his beard. 'Ah, Colonel, and that's the trouble. Much too excellent. I've no challenge left at all. It might suit a parish priest but not a missionary. It was another matter when we came, you know, my wife and I – we had to leave Grace in England, you know, she only joined me two years ago – empty church, total indifference, nothing doing at all, wonderful, simply wonderful.' He paused, and gazed away, his fork in mid-air, his eyes clouded with memories. He recollected himself with a jerk and dropped a forkful of curry onto his trousers. 'It's too easy now, Colonel. A curate could do it. It's time for me to be off, me and my helpmeet here.'

Grace leaned over and dabbed at her father with a napkin.

'Where are you going?'

Tom Prior's mouth was full but Grace, still scrubbing vigorously, said, 'Mandalay.'

'Good God,' Colonel Browne said, and then added, 'I do beg your pardon, Miss Prior. We soldiers, you know. Mandalay!'

'We have a great man there,' Tom Prior said earnestly, brandishing his fork, 'a true soldier of Christ. Doctor Marks. He has had the most immense influence with the kings, the late king especially. He was permitted to instruct some of the princes even. But he is not so young, he needs another pair of arms, a comrade in God.'

'Buddhists,' Colonel Browne said musingly.

'Yes,' Grace said, giving up the unequal struggle with the flies, and putting her plate down. 'At least they will make a change from Hindus.'

Colonel Browne said, 'Of course, I know Mandalay. First went there in fifty-nine, you know, on one of Phayre's missions, and then led the survey expeditions in sixty-seven. Fascinating business. Took them up into the mountains north-east of Mandalay. First European up there, complete terra incognita. The whole thing would have been a great success except for poor Margary being murdered. He was consul in Shanghai and had come to meet me but insisted on going ahead of the armed escort back to China. Fatal mistake. I've been in and out of Burma for the last twenty years. Extraordinary place. In my view we should annex the whole country, not just content ourselves with Lower Burma. All very useful, of course, a port like Rangoon on the way to Singapore, but I doubt we'll ever really use it. What we need to keep an eye on is the teak. There's going to be trouble over the teak. The French want it. You mark my words, we shall have trouble with Upper Burma before a few years are out. But will the government here or in London listen? Not a bit of it. All eyes on South Africa and Afghanistan. The Resident up in Mandalay is an excellent chap, former tea-planter like Beresford here. He shares my views, says you can't get the government to budge on anything to do with Burma unless it's a question of British dignity, like all that shoe nonsense.'

Grace, who had been suppressing small yawns, she hoped invisibly, into her champagne, looked up. 'Shoes?'

'Yes, my dear, shoes. The court in Mandalay insists all visitors remove their shoes in the presence of the king. Of course that is out of the question for an Englishman.'

'Difficult to,' Tom Prior said, 'to remove, I mean. Eastern sandals are much easier.'

'Just what the Resident said to the Burmese. Do we ask you to take your hats off to us, he said, just because it is a gesture of politeness among us and our hats come off easily? Of course he won. He and the Italian consul were the only foreigners allowed to wear shoes at the late king's funeral. You'll have to watch out for that sort of thing.'

Tom Prior smiled. 'I'm after their souls, not their shoes.'

A cool breath seemed to refresh the air around them. Maria had come over and was standing smiling down on them, particularly at Colonel Browne.

The men got to their feet.

'Are you enjoying my picnic, Colonel?'

'I'm enjoying the company, my dear, but I can't say I'm managing my fodder very well. I'm better off with a table indoors, truth to tell.'

Maria laughed with great good nature and turned to Grace. 'Miss Prior. Do you have everything you want? I am so glad you could come, especially when you are leaving so soon. It is so stupid of me, but I quite forget where you are going.'

'Burma,' Grace said.

'Oh,' Maria said faintly, 'Burma. But I have come to take you away, Miss Prior. I have a lonely young subaltern who needs diverting.'

Captain Murray Shaw of the Queen's Own Bengal Infantry saw Maria coming across the lawn to him with a leap of pleasure. He had three weeks' leave in Bombay, had met Maria at a dinner party on the third night and here he was, two days later, at her birthday party. She was the best-looking girl in Bombay, he thought, perhaps the best-looking in India, but then, hc had been stationed in such out-of-the-way spots recently that he fancied he might have found a Hottentot desirable.

Behind Miss Beresford, half hidden by her parasol, trailed a slender discouraged-looking girl in green. Her stalk-like neck seemed to be wilting in the heat as if her small head and fine silky-brown hair were too much of a burden for it to bear. Her dress had no shape to it, nor did her depressed-looking hat from which a tired feather hung. With a sudden sinking sensation, Captain Shaw deduced from Miss Beresford's purposeful walk and bright smile that she was not bringing him the charm of her own company, but rather the doubtful society of the gloomy girl in green.

Maria introduced them with animation. Murray Shaw gave her a glance of deepest reproach, was rewarded by a conspiratorial smile and turned to do his duty by Grace. She was much alarmed by his impeccable appearance in uniform.

'Why do you go to Burma, Miss Prior?'

'I shall accompany my father. He is to run the Anglican mission in Mandalay.'

'Are you not afraid to go? I believe there are very few European women in Burma. Shall you not be lonely?'

'I am used to it,' Grace said, simply. 'We are not going for society you see. We can do our work better if there are difficulties, we can be better Christians.'

Captain Shaw looked at once respectful and mildly embarrassed. A change of subject was imperative.

'Have you known Miss Beresford long?'

Grace followed his longing gaze across the sun-soaked lawn to the tall blue figure deep in conversation with Colonel Browne.

'About two years, I think, but – but we do not see much of each other. She – she is very accomplished.'

'By jove she is,' he said fervently. 'I admire her awfully. I suppose all the fellows do.'

'There are not so many young ones here,' Grace said to encourage him. 'Most are away with their regiments.'

He smiled down at her gratefully and thought that if she had been taller and fairer and better built, she really would not have been a bad-looking girl at all.

Across the lawn, Maria had pinned Colonel Browne between the knotted trunk of a peepul tree and her own slender form. She had presumed upon the slight acquaintance between the colonel and her father, founded in the Malabar Club, to issue an invitation, and had been immensely grateful when it had been accepted. Colonel Browne was highly regarded in both military and civilian circles, with a sound reputation as an explorer and administrator. He was a bigger fish than Maria had hoped to catch for her party and, having caught him, she now wished to make full use of her success.

'Can't think why your father retired,' Colonel Browne said. 'Always imagined those planters led wonderful lives, splendid country, your own man entirely.'

Maria said in a low voice, her eyelids downcast, 'It was circumstances, Colonel, not choice. Leaf blight—'

It was perfectly possible to say leaf blight, but it would have been out of the question, even had she admitted such weaknesses as existing, to add extravagance, careless investment, general improvidence.

'My dear. Forgive me.'

She put her hand on his arm and smiled directly into his eyes. 'There is nothing to forgive.

We are hardly destitute but we must be a little careful. It is not that I mind at all, money means nothing to me, but – but—'

Colonel Browne patted the white glove that rested on his sleeve. 'Can I help you, my dear? Are you in difficulties? You ladies—'

'Oh no!' she said and shook her head. 'It is not that at all. It is not money, Colonel, it – it is more self-esteem. It is for Papa that I care so much, not for myself at all.'

'Suppose you tell me right out, my dear, suppose you tell me just what it is that troubles you.'

She hesitated for a moment and gave her parasol a twirl or two as if she needed to gather courage. 'It – it is his dignity, you see, Colonel. He was, as you say so rightly, his own master. He ruled our little world down there oh so well, Colonel. You cannot imagine how much they all loved him. And then – my mother died and then came the blight and he was forced to sell before the estate was worth nothing at all because we had to keep selling land, you know, to manage. And he came up here – for me really, because I had known no society and nothing, I think – though he is too good to speak of it to me – has quite gone as he had hoped. He was educated at Harrow, Colonel, and then at Cambridge and his family is very old and has produced many distinguished men and here he is, Colonel, scratching away in an office all day like – like any *Indian*. He is so good, he never complains, but he must feel the indignity of it. I know I do. And I wondered, Colonel, since you are a man of such influence, if you would at least remember him when administrative posts need filling. I don't ask for favours outright, I just beg you to keep him in mind.'

Colonel Browne considered her for a moment, shrewdly aware that if she had adopted an artificial pose to plead her father's cause, her desire to help him was genuine enough.

He said, 'As he, your father, my dear, knows nothing of the Civil Service here, I couldn't ever suggest him for anything considerable. I hope I don't offend you.'

She smiled. 'Not in the least. I am perfectly realistic, Colonel. I just don't want to see him perched on a stool with a quill and a ledger for the rest of his working life.'

Hubert's elegant figure was clearly visible to both of them now, stooping to hear something Grace Prior was saying and plainly alarming her by his handsome condescension.

'I understand you, my dear. I do indeed. And if there's a man who might help you I have to say, without undue modesty, that man is myself. Very wise of you to speak to me. And I shan't forget. Never do. Don't expect miracles, Miss Beresford, but I will see what I can do.'

She put out a hand and said, 'Thank you,' in a firm and decided tone, and he thought how splendid it was to meet a young woman who didn't gush. Having made polite speeches about her party, he said, 'Trust me, Miss Beresford,' and pressed her hand and she watched him stride across the lawn with the greatest satisfaction.

Captain Shaw, desperate not to have to leave without the smallest conversation with Maria, found that he had abandoned Grace despite the precepts of his upbringing, and had almost run across the garden to waylay his hostess without having been aware of doing any more than harbouring the desire to be beside her. She shook her fan at him.

'Oh, Captain Shaw, I am going to be very severe with you. How could you leave poor Miss Prior standing all alone like that? I have a good mind to send you straight back again.'

'Then I should disobey,' he said daringly.

She laughed. 'Insubordination in my own garden? That will never do. Tell me what brought you racing over in such a headlong manner.'

He coloured and said something indistinctly, cleared his throat and stammered out a wish to see her, if she would permit it, during the two weeks that remained to him in Bombay.

She raised her eyebrows. 'Permit it? Of course I do. Unless you know some secret reason why I should not? I hope you will dine here on Tuesday. My father will be so much pleased if you would.'

She nodded and smiled again and moved gracefully away, leaving him gazing after her, at once rapturous at the thought of dining with her and cast down that she had only declared how pleased her father would be to see him.

Hubert met his daughter before she descended upon the next group of guests.

'A delightful young man, my dear.'

'Oh, Papa? Is he? What makes him so delightful?'

Hubert leaned a little closer. 'Eldest son of Sir Murray Shaw, baronet, of Battrick, Northumberland, and a present income of three thousand a year which rises considerably on his twenty-fifth birthday, which, I am reliably informed, falls this autumn.'

'Oh Papa, you have been busy!'

'And you, my dearest one? Have you been busy and happy?'

Maria, her mind upon Colonel Browne, glanced over her shoulder to reassure herself that Captain Shaw's admiring gaze followed her still. He did not appear to have moved a muscle since she left him.

'Oh yes, Papa. Very busy – and very happy.'

2

15 February 1879, in the City of London was one
of those days that make an Englishman feel that
the winter will never end. A raw yellow fog had
settled thickly in the courts and passages, blotting
out the sky entirely and giving an eerie sensation,
on account of the gloom, of its being no particular time of day at all. It was bitterly cold and a
thin layer of evil, half-frozen mud made the
cobbles alarmingly slippery.

Archie Tennant, the collar of his greatcoat
turned up around his ears and his hat jammed
down as far as it would go to meet it, had walked
from Liverpool Street Station to Austin Friars in
order to get his circulation going. The train had
been miserably cold and he had had to get up at
intervals, all the way from Ipswich, and stamp
about and beat his chest until a dyspeptic-looking
man in the innermost seat said he thought
Archie's fidgets were worse than the cold. Archie,
at nineteen easily disconcerted and by nature
eager to please, sat down at once and felt the last
traces of warmth ebbing for ever from his large
and loosely jointed frame.

His mother had said he must go to London.

She had seemed rather tearful at breakfast and refused to tell him why he had been summoned from Oxford in the middle of term. He was used to her being tearful and had always supposed resignedly that widows, without exception, were. So he had eaten his way through an immense breakfast and she had sat behind the coffee pots and sniffed, only remarking now and then that he must not miss the train and cause inconvenience to poor darling Frederick on such a day as this.

'As what?' Archie said through his smoked haddock.

His mother merely sniffed again and said, 'Your brother is so dreadfully busy. I really do not know anyone who works harder and it will be wicked of you, deliberately wicked, to be late and cause him inconvenience.'

Archie did not reply. Nineteen years of being the unsatisfactory son had taught him how useless it was to contradict his mother and nineteen years of close proximity to his elder brother Frederick had taught him equally clearly that he could not bring himself to agree with her about him. He put a good deal of marmalade on a muffin.

'Why does Frederick want to see me at the office?'

His mother looked at him quellingly from behind her battery of silver. 'Where else should he wish to see you? Where else does he ever spend his time, poor hardworking darling?'

The theatre, Archie thought of saying, Epsom,

Newmarket, actresses' bedrooms. Aloud he said, 'I hope he isn't going to go on at me about joining the firm. I have no inclination at all to have anything to do with Far Eastern trade. I want to be a lawyer.'

Mrs Tennant's eyes filled with tears. 'It is as well, Archie, that your beloved father cannot hear you talk with such disgraceful ingratitude, such wicked lack of duty.'

'He was a lawyer,' Archie pointed out reasonably, picking up a second muffin and realizing sadly that even his capacity had its limits. He replaced it reluctantly on its silver dish.

'Only so that he might serve the company better.'

Archie shrugged and stood up. 'I shall go straight back to Oxford tonight, Mother. Straight from London. The drag hounds meet tomorrow.'

'Pleasure!' his mother cried resentfully. 'Pleasure! It's all you ever think of. Not a day passes but I thank God on my knees that He has given me one son at least who is a support to his poor mother, who showers on her the love that your beloved father's passing took from me so cruelly.'

Archie said, his voice a little hardened, 'Hunting is the only pleasure, as you call it, that I do indulge in. I don't gamble, I don't drink much, I only eat because I am always so hungry. I say, Mother, could you lend me twenty pounds?'

'You must ask Frederick. He deals with all the money matters. What I should do without him, I cannot imagine—'

'If I must ask Frederick, I shall have to do without my twenty pounds.'

'Then you must do without,' Mrs Tennant said, and when Archie had left the room in silence, reflected that he had never kissed her goodbye and that Frederick would hardly ever leave the room for a five-minute absence without an affectionate farewell.

Now, on the steps of number 4 Austin Friars, the offices of Tennant Phillipson, Far Eastern traders, Archie remembered he had not said goodbye, and was instantly contrite. He resolved to write a note to his mother and post it at Paddington before catching the train to Oxford. The double doors ahead of him swung open and old Tremlett, who remembered his grandfather, the company's co-founder, said, 'Bad day, Mr Archie,' and held out a trembling hand for Archie's hat.

The reception hall at Tennant Phillipson was panelled in wine-red mahogany, floored in black and white marble and decorated with nothing except two sombre portraits of the founders. There was no fire in the fireplace and Archie didn't wonder that old Tremlett, in his glazed dog kennel by the door, should shake so much.

'How are you, Tremlett? Pretty fit?'

'Not so much as I was, sir. *Anno domini*, sir. Seem to feel the cold so.'

'You should retire, Tremlett, and dig that garden of yours. I'll never forget the raspberries you brought up for me last summer. They deserved an award.'

Tremlett beamed upon him.

'You shall have more this summer, Mr Archie. Mrs Tremlett will be honoured. I'll retire, sir, when I've seen you settled into the company, sir, but not before. I gave my word to your father. And I don't want to lose touch, sir, you see, seeing as how I am a shareholder, sir.'

Archie's father had hit upon the enlightened notion of paying his clerks as little as he could get away with and encouraging them to put their small savings into shares in the company. 'In that way, Tremlett,' he had said thirty years before, 'Tennant Phillipson will pay for your working life and your retirement as well.' It had become a company obligation.

'Is my brother expecting me?'

'Yes, Mr Archie. Mr Frederick said to me this morning, "Now, Tremlett, that young scamp of a brother of mine will be in this morning. Be sure you leave him to cool his heels a while." But I wouldn't do that, sir. I'll get Norris to take you up, sir.'

Archie protested that he could find his way up quite well alone, but Tremlett considered this idea quite unsuitable and so Archie found himself escorted by a spindly boy of fourteen or so whom the company employed as a messenger. When he was announced, Archie heard his brother say, 'Tell him to wait a moment,' and was strongly tempted to cuff the weedy Norris aside and march in to Frederick's office. He calmed himself however, and picked up the bound volume of the company report that lay on the table in the anteroom outside his brother's office. Such extraordinary things Tennant Phillipson dealt in, indigo, fish oil and yak hair, salt and ngape – what on earth was ngape? Ngape – dried fish, explained a helpful footnote. The door opened.

'Come in,' Frederick said abruptly.

Archie followed him into the large square office furnished with his grandfather's monumental desk and chair.

'What on earth do you deal in yak hair for?'

'Fly whisks,' Frederick said briefly.

He looked tired and older than his twenty-eight years. His suit was as beautifully cut as ever, his linen as immaculate, his meticulously trimmed whiskers still gave off a faint odour of bay rum, but his face had an exhausted, dishevelled look. Archie, whose entire appearance was dishevelled more often than not, cast himself into a great wing chair opposite his brother's desk.

'Well, what's up? I'm in the middle of a particularly thorny patch of Roman law, you know, and it really wasn't easy to get away. Mother was crying at breakfast.'

Frederick made a small sound of irritation. 'I hope she did more than that.'

'Not beyond saying I mustn't be late.'

Frederick said with sudden vehemence, 'Confound it! I expressly asked for you to go home first so that she could – could prepare the way a little. Before you came here.'

Archie was grinning. 'You are the man of the house, you know. All burdens are for you to bear—'

'Take that stupid grin off. What I have to tell you, thanks to Mother, will wipe it off soon enough anyhow. We are washed up, Archie, absolutely done for. The firm is finished.'

Archie, lounging in his chair, froze rigid. 'What do you mean?'

'You wouldn't understand,' Frederick said impatiently. 'You'll simply have to take my word for it. There's not a penny left, all gone. In fact, we are unpleasantly in debt—'

Archie stood up. 'But why?'

Frederick waved his hand. 'Oh, some pretty wild speculation on someone's part. Could happen to anyone. A lot of forward buying of some rather expensive rice and now a bumper harvest in south-east Asia and a bit of a dabble in rhinoceros horn which the Chinese swear by as an – an—'

'Aphrodisiac. I know that perfectly well. But *whose* speculation? *Whose* dabbling? Yours?'

Frederick shrugged. 'Never made a mistake before.'

'Not such a big one, anyhow,' Archie said.

Frederick shouted, 'Don't you preach to me! You're only a boy. You know nothing about trading!'

41

'No,' Archie said, 'I don't.' He walked to the window and stood looking down at the fog-filled zigzag of Austin Friars, his broad shoulders blocking almost all the light that struggled into the room.

'What happens now?' he said.

'We fold it all up. End of Tennant Phillipson. I've tried to get someone to buy us, but there are no takers. We're too specialized, we don't deal in the big commodities like timber or rubber, nor in the really expert, difficult things like precious stones. The offices will be closed by the end of the month, and I shall sell the building—'

Archie spun round. 'You can't! Have you told the staff? You can't just fold everything up and throw them out on their ears in a fortnight!'

'I'm not asking for your advice, Archie. I'm telling you what is going to happen. No, they don't know. I shall tell them in good time. I'll probably put the proceeds from the building into setting myself up in something in Ipswich. It'll be precious little but it's all I'll have.'

Archie loomed over his brother. 'But your creditors! And the shareholders! What happens to them?'

'Luck of the draw,' Frederick said.

Archie's fist came crashing down on the desk. 'You can't behave like that! You will have to put any monies you receive for the building towards paying debts and shareholders. The law will make you!'

'I'll fight,' Frederick said, 'Why should I be left with nothing? The building is mine in any case, not the company's. I bought it from them some time ago. It's mine to sell. I've sat in this dismal place for nine years now and I'm not going away empty-handed.'

Archie said, 'You are not only unprincipled, but extremely stupid.'

Frederick yawned and looked at his nails. 'I should go if I were you, Archie. There was no reason I had to tell you any of this except that, as you were coming into the company, I thought you should know.'

Archie said furiously, 'I can't wait to be back in Oxford,' and then he realized with a leap of dismay that his Oxford life would presumably crumble with the company.

'Damned annoying,' Frederick said, 'the whole business. I should think number eight out there are laughing themselves sick.'

'Number eight?'

'Wallace Brothers. Number eight Austin Friars. Six of them, four with beards, and trading out of Bombay like nobody's business. Teak, mostly. They are a bunch of canny Scots and they have been waiting to see me fall.'

'What about old Phillipson?' Archie said suddenly.

'I haven't told him yet. He comes up once a year for the board meeting this month, and I can't say I look forward to seeing him.'

Archie remembered an old man in a summerhouse wrapped in a plaid shawl. He had given him a ginger biscuit and told him horrendous stories of the Indian Mutiny.

'Will he have lost a lot?'

Frederick shrugged again. 'Not much. We never saw eye to eye. He managed to palm a lot of his shares off on me seven or eight years ago and then he made a fuss when I bought the building. Rumour has it that he reinvested in Wallace Brothers. He's kept some money with us, "for my father's sake" he always said, the old hypocrite.' He paused and added with bitterness, 'He'll be all right.'

'You must go out to Henley and tell him. You can't just wait for him to struggle up here, believing everything is all right. It would be intolerably cruel.'

Frederick stood up and glared at his brother. 'The whole thing is intolerably cruel! I have to give up the house in Wilton Crescent, my horses, probably my tailor, my wine merchant, everything. I think that's pretty cruel. I don't have, quite frankly, much pity left for a crafty old bachelor with enough money to do just what he wants! If you mind so much, Archie, you can damn well go and see him yourself!'

Two minutes later Tremlett reverently and shakingly assisted Archie into his coat.

'When shall we see you here on a daily basis, sir? When your university time is done, sir?'

Archie took his hat and gazed earnestly into its depths since he could not bear to look at Tremlett's face. 'I don't know about that, Tremlett. I really haven't made up my mind. But I'll be back to see you all very soon, I promise that.'

At Didcot Junction, Archie left the train and ordered a cab to take him to Henley. The fog had trickled up the Thames from London, but hung white and limp here in the river valley having lost the yellow filth of the city. It was even colder however, and the cab was draughty, icy blasts whipping up the fragments of straw that littered the floor and making Archie's boots feel as insubstantial as if they were constructed of paper. He slumped in a corner, plunged in his collars, and continued to fume.

He had been boiling with anger all the way from Austin Friars. At Paddington he remembered his intention to write to his mother, recalled the next moment the knowledge she had withheld from him at breakfast, and her hopelessly partisan feelings for that scoundrel, Frederick, and decided she deserved no letter. He hoped, glaring out of the train window as the red and blue tenements of outer London slid by, that she had spent all day in tears. He could not, even inspired by his fury, think of a fate worthy of Frederick's monstrous incompetence and dishonour. A woman climbed into his compartment at Reading and motioned the child with her to take the seat next to Archie, but the boy, with one alarmed glance at Archie's knotted brows, prudently decided that to disobey his mother was the lesser of two evils, and chose the farthest seat he could.

Even on such a day, Riverdene was a pleasant house. Old Phillipson had built it for himself in the early twenties, intending it to house the ineffably sensible girl with a comfortable fortune whom he had selected as his bride. The sensible girl had spoiled these level-headed plans by running off with an attractive and unprincipled army officer, later to be cashiered, and George Phillipson, adjusting himself to the situation with very little trouble, had shut the house up for thirty years and gone to have a look at business prospects in south-east Asia. He was drawn, like so many young men at that time, to Singapore, established by Sir Stamford Raffles as a free port, free that is of the royal monopolies that so dogged trade with such places as Siam or Cochin China. In Singapore, on the steps of the Malay Institute, George Phillipson met a large, ill-coordinated young man called Frederick Tennant, six months out from England and in search of something more to occupy himself with than a squire's life in Suffolk.

They were chalk and cheese, the two young men, yet wonderfully compatible. George Phillipson, with his unimaginative careful ways, was much attracted to Frederick's inventive brain and impulsive flashes of brilliance. Frederick in his turn found himself steadied and calmed. For three years they travelled together, the large untidy young man with his mass of baggage and

46

boxes full of 'collections' and the tidy and well-organized one, accompanied by the minimum of luggage and the maximum of order.

Nine months of those three years were spent in Hong Kong and nine in Singapore and the experience of both taught Tennant and Phillipson that most of the trading companies mushrooming in the new free economic climate would deal in the most obvious commodities, tea and timber, silk, rubber and rice. It seemed to them that a good many more specialized goods might find an equally hungry market in the West and that in addition, many of these commodities could be traded around the Far East itself, satisfying such curious oriental tastes as dried fish.

They considered setting up an office in Bombay; Riverdene had waited now beside the Thames for five years and could wait longer, and Hasham Hall, Frederick supposed, was quite as competently run by his mother as he could ever manage himself. No, George Phillipson said, there was no point in them both being away from England, no point in their both being in India. He should take a small office in Nesbit Road, Bombay, and Frederick should return home and find somewhere suitable in London. In 1830, Tennant Phillipson was born, operating from number 4 Austin Friars, London, and number 4 Nesbit Road, Bombay, a coincidence which both partners felt to be a good omen.

It was not only a good omen but a good partnership. There were times when Frederick wanted to move faster, take larger risks, buy land, and wrote thunderous letters to Nesbit Road. George moved ahead with sure steadiness, ignoring explosions from London, profiting always from the flashes of imagination that interspersed the expletives in Frederick's letters. The American Civil War eventually proved the great turning point for Tennant Phillipson. The cotton mills of Lancashire, cut off from the supplies in the Southern States of America, turned to Bombay instead, and this time George listened to the urgent recommendations that poured from Austin Friars to buy land for development. He listened and acted and by 1860 the nominal capital of the company had risen to twenty lakhs of rupees, divided into a thousand shares at two thousand rupees each.

By 1860 also, Frederick Tennant had married and was father to one son and seven daughters. George Phillipson possessed a godson of almost thirty he had never met and, motivated by that and a desire to see Riverdene once more before he was too malarial to enjoy it, he sailed for England. The Bombay office was left in the capable hands of its major shareholder besides the two partners, a Parsee merchant who had been responsible for excellent advice to George Phillipson during the cotton boom.

George had come home and stayed at home. Riverdene, with its pleasant rosy bricks and long windows, its lawns and trees and access to excellent fishing, proved the love affair he had been thwarted of thirty years before. His godson had entered the firm eight years previously after reading law at Oxford and had shown himself a worthy successor to the founders. George travelled to London for the three middle days of each working week, slept the nights at his club, and travelled back to Riverdene thankfully on Thursday evenings. Frederick, racked now with gout, had much the same routine, varied only by staying with his son and daughter-in-law in St John's Wood for the nights he had to be in London. Young Frederick worked six days a week, frequently seven, travelled eight times to Bombay in fifteen years, hardly saw the two sons born to him at an interval of nine years and in 1870 followed his gout-ridden father to the grave, felled by a massive heart attack.

Old Phillipson continued to come to the city for a year or so, 'to see the grandson settled' as he put it to himself. The third Frederick resembled his father and grandfather in nothing but name and, within two years, old Phillipson had not only withdrawn the major portion of his money but also himself to Henley, except for an annual excursion to Austin Friars. Riverdene became his life. He kept an indoor staff of ten and an outdoor staff of six. Archie, climbing out of the cab, stiff with cold, thought that despite the gloom cast by the fog, he had never seen a house so utterly, unmistakably cherished, the white window frames gleaming, the creepers up the walls thick and immaculately trimmed, the lawns green and smooth and empty, even in February, of so much as a single dead leaf.

He stamped numbly on the gravel for a while, blowing on his fingers and looking admiringly about him, and then the glossy white front door opened above him and he was asked his business.

'To see Mr Phillipson,' he said.

The old butler, who had looked after River-dene for the thirty years of his master's absence, inclined his head and looked sceptical. Archie hunted about in his pockets, failed to find a card and was reduced to saying, in more supplicating a tone than he intended, 'I – I'm Archie Tennant. Would you tell Mr Phillipson that I should like to see him?'

At the name of Tennant, the butler's brow darkened. He held the door barely wide enough for Archie to squeeze his bulk into the hall and left him waiting, without taking his hat and coat, to contemplate a handsome pair of elephant tusks that embraced the chimneypiece. There was a fire burning beneath the chimneypiece and a thick Turkey rug on the polished floor, and the panelled walls were painted white and hung with sporting prints of the last century. The air was warm and welcoming and above the scent of firewood and wax polish Archie caught a faint but heady drift of hot buttered toast.

The butler came back and handed Archie a note on a silver tray.

'Which Tennant? What do you want?' old Phillipson had written.

Archie attempted to write a reply but was too much impeded by his greatcoat. Not daring to ask for help, he struggled out of it alone, dropped it clumsily onto a nearby chair, watched implacably by the butler, and with fingers stiffened with cold wrote awkwardly in reply. 'Archie, sir. The company. I am very worried and angry.'

He then thought family loyalty should have precluded the last remark but he could hardly cross it out. He dropped the pen on the tray and remained standing while the butler vanished again. The fire was beginning to thaw him slightly and with returning warmth came courage and a determination not to touch his hat and coat again for himself.

The second note took longer to come but was, for various reasons, much more welcome. 'Come in. Hope you like muffins.'

Old Phillipson, in a velvet dressing-gown, his thin silver hair brushed smooth as metal and his knees covered in a fur rug like a brown bear, was sitting in a room lined entirely with books and looking down to the river. There were several large tables bearing portfolios of prints, a globe, a telescope, objects in ivory and jade, and in the window embrasure a grand piano, open, with music on the rack. Everything, the books, the furniture, the white-painted shelves, gleamed with care.

'You are as large as your grandfather,' old Phillipson said.

'Yes, sir,' Archie said. 'I feel every inch of it. I expect he managed it much better than I do.'

Old Phillipson motioned Archie to a chair. 'No, he didn't. Always knocking things over, chairs, tables, coolies, everything. I'm as old as the century and in all that time I've never met a clumsier man. Tea for Mr Tennant, Ford. You mustn't mind Ford. He thinks all Tennants are like your brother. I expect you had to take off your own coat, eh? He did that to Frederick. Upset him so much he wouldn't even drink his tea. Are you too upset to drink your tea?'

Archie gazed worshipfully at the muffin dish, the fat-bellied tea pot, the rich dark fruit cake. 'I could eat a horse, sir.'

'Then eat one. Talk afterwards. I never did have much appetite, less after India. Your grandfather always ate as if each meal was his last. Remember him?'

Butter running down his chin, Archie nodded vigorously. 'He was pretty lame, sir. But I was ten when he died so I remember him quite well.'

'Worst funeral of my life, that,' old Phillipson said, 'and your father six months later. Terrible year. Fill Mr Tennant's cup, Ford, and then leave us. I'm sure my guest will have the strength then to cut his own cake. Like my house?'

'Enormously, sir,' Archie said with enthusiasm.

'Perfection, ain't it,' old Phillipson said with contentment, 'Perfection. Worth waiting for. Ever been East?'

'No, sir. I'm at Oxford, sir.'

Old Phillipson regarded him with his bright birdlike glance. 'I remember. I gave you ginger-nuts when you were only a little chap. In the summerhouse here. Oriel, isn't it? Undistinguished college but I suppose that can't be helped. Never seemed to do your father any harm, or your grandfather either for that matter. Another muffin?'

Archie shook his head. Old Phillipson nodded at him. 'Mustn't let your appetite run away with you. All very well when you're young but you don't want a load of extra flesh to haul about when you get older. Your grandfather got heavy, far too heavy, but then, he was too gouty to move about much. You've got his frame. Now then, what are you here for?'

Archie went scarlet. 'I – I thought I ought to come, sir. I went – I went to Austin Friars this morning sir, and – and – I saw Frederick and, well, the fact of the matter is, sir, that something awful has happened and – and I thought – I thought one of us should tell you, sir, and Frederick is so awfully tied up, you see, sir, so I thought that on my way back to Oxford, sir, I would come and, well, and tell you, sir—'

Old Phillipson leaned forward, his pale, well-manicured little paws resting calmly in the brown fur of his rug. 'You may stop now. Have some cake. No? Oh, I should you know, because I am going to tell you my side of the story and you would be much better with something to occupy yourself with.'

Archie gazed at him, the cake knife suspended in his hand. 'Then – then you know, sir?'

'Of course I know. I have my contacts, I haven't lost my touch. Your brother Frederick has got, in common parlance, his comeuppance. That's the fact of it. Always saw Tennant Phillipson as another Jardines, always wanted to be in the first eleven. That was one of the things we fell out about. One of many, mind you. I suppose our worst battle was when he wanted to buy the building in Austin Friars. I should have stopped him, I should have held out, but I'm not as young as I was and he would have his way without my consent. He persuaded all the shareholders. Bombay did their best to keep him in line. Mr Jivanji's a shrewd customer, but what can you do from India, and your brother would never leave London. Miss all his dancing girls? That would never do. So speculate he must and he's been riding for a fall these last five years. Hunt, do you? Good, good. Best thing in the world for the liver. I tell you, young man, the amount your brother knows about rice you could write on a sixpence. He had no business to go experimenting with a commodity where the sums involved are huge and the field is full of experts. It was lunacy. And, of course, he had classic beginner's luck a year ago so he doubled his stake. Bought twice as much at almost twice the price and, as any halfwit in the East could have told him, if he'd only listened, they were heading for the best harvest in years. To cap it all, he'd neglected all the things we'd made our name in, Burmese earth oil, musk, salt, things like that, so of course the producers turned to other traders and there are no markets for him to go back to. What was Frederick's version of all this?'

'He wouldn't explain, sir. Quite rightly, I suppose, since I don't know the first thing about it.'

'Don't defend him to *me*,' old Phillipson said with the first flash of anger he had shown. 'To the world if you must, but not to me. He's an incompetent blackguard, your brother. My money might be safe, young man, but my pride isn't.'

Archie, scarlet again, nodded vigorously in sympathy.

'Nearly half a century,' old Phillipson went on more calmly, 'founded 1830, died 1879. My life work I might say, if I were an emotional man like your grandfather. You're like him. I might also say it if I didn't have this house to console me, if I didn't have something to put my heart into. In fact, young man, I've said it for the last two months to myself but I've scolded myself for doing it. So Frederick refused to be a gentleman and tell me face to face? And you, because you are your grandfather's grandson, felt you should do it? And being an impetuous, headstrong fellow like your grandfather you came straight here from number four without even letting your temper cool?'

Archie hesitated a moment, playing with the cake knife. 'Yes, sir.'

'Thought as much. How d'you like Oxford?'

'Enormously, sir. Law has its dusty side, but everything else is splendid, sir.'

'And who's going to pay for it now?'

'I – I expect it will come to an end.'

'And you will be sorry?'

'Yes, sir.'

'How long have you to go?'

'The rest of this term and four more.'

'And have you been a credit to your brains?'

Archie looked up, caught his host's humorous eye and smiled in relief. 'Two shots at moderations, sir, which wasn't very popular. But I've worked harder since then.'

'And played too? What do you amuse yourself with besides hunting? Share your brother's taste for actresses too, no doubt.'

Archie shifted a little. He had become quite used to paying for the satisfying of his more urgent physical needs, although he came away after every visit to the Jericho slums of Oxford considerably disquieted in mind however much his body had been appeased. He had observed too, without liking to draw conclusions from the fact, that his visits to Jericho were more frequent than a year ago and that he looked forward to each one more eagerly.

'Your grandfather married before he was thirty,' old Phillipson said comfortably. 'I meant to but she wouldn't have me. You Tennants can't do without a woman. Not keeping one, eh?'

Archie shook his head vehemently. 'No, sir. Just – well, you know, sir. There's something else that's worrying me awfully, something apart from your not being told properly about the company. And that's the small shareholders. I don't know much about business, Frederick's quite right, but I do know that most of the clerks in the office have at least part of a share, it was father's policy. Old Tremlett, sir. I mean, what happens to them when the company's bankrupted?'

Old Phillipson looked levelly at Archie. 'When everything has been sold up in Bombay and London, all the buildings, whatever is left in our godowns, the creditors and the shareholders are the first to be paid. But the creditors are in the first place many, owing to your brother's way of doing business, and in the second place, the company debts exceed at this moment its nominal capital. So I shouldn't imagine there will be a brass farthing left.'

'But old Tremlett!'

Old Phillipson shrugged. 'A sad story, young man.'

Archie got up and began to walk about the room rapidly and clumsily, catching his coat tails on piles of books as he strode past.

'Sit down,' old Phillipson said.

'It enrages me,' Archie said from across the room, taking no notice. 'I can't bear to think that that old man who has given so many years' service to the company, who is only waiting for

57

me to join – although I've told him I never shall – because he promised Father, I can't bear to think – it's intolerable—'

'What shall you do?' old Phillipson said composedly.

Archie strode back to the fire. 'How much does he have in the company, sir? What is he expecting to see?'

'Five hundred pounds, perhaps. Not more.'

Archie's face broke into a delighted smile.

'Capital, sir! It's just what I have. I was trying not to touch it because I knew I should need something to tide me over until I am called to the Bar. Father left it for me until I am twenty-one, then I think I shall have – I mean I should have had – some more. But Tremlett shall have it.'

'And the others?' old Phillipson said. 'Philpotts has been at number four just as long, Rigby and Newton forty years to my certain knowledge.'

Archie slumped into his chair in despair. 'I don't know, sir.'

'I'll strike a bargain with you. You rescue Tremlett. I will rescue the others.'

Archie leaped to his feet with a shout.

'Sit down!' old Phillipson said commandingly. 'You are quite as noisy as your grandfather. So that's settled.'

'I think you are – are *splendid*, sir!'

Old Phillipson sighed. 'No,' he said, 'I can afford it. I took all my money bar a few thousands out of the company. I just left enough to give myself a seat on the board still. It was a sentimental thing to do but I could afford it. I can afford to recompense those poor old pen-pushers too. *You* can't though. That five hundred is all you have.'

'I'll manage, sir.'

'Oh yes,' old Phillipson said. 'You will.'

Archie stood up for the third time. 'I must go, sir. You've been awfully good to give me so much time and to have been so generous. Perhaps you would let me call again sometime.'

'I'm not letting you go now, young man. There's one of my own ducks for dinner and it's an abominable night. Comfortable room you'll have here.'

Archie said, stammering, 'But – but I've – I mean, you can't want me, a Tennant—'

'I do. And I want my pound of flesh.'

'I don't understand you, sir.'

'I don't expect you to. I haven't explained myself yet. I'll tell you now and then you can go and fiddle about on my billiard table and think about it. It's a splendid table. I brought the mahogany home from the East with me and I went to Wales myself to choose the slate. Now listen to me, young man, and don't say a word. We'll discuss it at dinner. Don't fuss you've no evening clothes, I didn't ask you to stay for your clothes. I've struck one bargain with you. I'll strike another. I'll keep you at Oxford until you are finished and I'll be liberal with you. A couple of hunters, good rooms, a good cellar. And you in return will do what a son, if I'd had one, would

59

have pleased me by doing. You'll go to Wallace Brothers at number eight Austin Friars and offer yourself as a recruit. They are just about to take young men on to work up country in Burma and Borneo for their sister firm in Bombay, the Bombay-Burmah Trading Corporation, and they are a first-rate company. They've looked after my money in a way I couldn't have bettered myself. Your brother knows that's where I put my money; it's another reason for his hating me so. So that's the long and the short of it, Archie. I'll see you handsomely through the next eighteen months and you'll give up the law, just as your father did, and be one of the first young Englishmen Wallace Brothers ever sends to the East. Now off you go. Don't touch the cue with the ebony handle. It's mine and it doesn't play the same if anyone else uses it. I dine at seven.'

3

Four months later, in the decrepit and squalid British Residency in Mandalay, Queen Victoria's official representative in Upper Burma died of rheumatic fever. He was mourned by the Burmese people as a true friend, although his relations with the new young king, Thibaw, had never been as cordial as with Thibaw's father, Mindoon. He had been a diplomatic and scholarly man, had put up patiently with the tyrannical inconsistency of palace dealings, with alternating insult and warm patronage, with knowing how much the Upper Burmese wished to remain on good terms with the British occupiers of Lower Burma and with seeing the Residency of those same British crumble, through lack of funds or interest, into a collection of decaying wooden huts in a compound walled in matting.

His immediate replacement as British Resident in Mandalay was Colonel Horace Browne, fluent Burmese speaker and experienced explorer in up-country Burma. Colonel Browne was in Rangoon when the news of his appointment came, and before setting off up the Irrawaddy in one of the steamers of the Irrawaddy Flotilla Company – a journey of some eight or nine days – he remembered a conversation he had had the previous February with Miss Maria Beresford at her peculiarly uncomfortable birthday party in Bombay.

A telegraph was sent at once to Bombay, followed by a more explanatory letter. Although the appointment of his staff in Mandalay was not altogether a matter for his personal choice, he wrote to Hubert Beresford, it was of course within his power to make warm recommendations. His own appointment was only temporary but he supposed it would occupy a year at the least and as all the assistants at the Residency in Mandalay were young men, he himself would feel the benefit of an older aide. The salary would not be great – rather under a half of his own annual four thousand, though he did not specify this – but the opportunity might in some way compensate for the lack of ample payment. Colonel Browne, having inquired meticulously about Hubert Beresford, had no intention of allowing him much responsibility, but was aware that, first, his slightly rash promise to Maria must be honoured and, secondly, Upper Burma was precisely the place where a man of Hubert's good but idle wits might best profit himself. Colonel Browne intended to introduce him into Burma, and then, tactfully, to withdraw the support of the government of India and leave him to his own devices.

*　　*　　*

Thus it was on a stifling hot July morning, a morning drenched with the steam heat of the monsoons, that Maria looked out from the steamer as it drifted, hooting, in towards the riverbank at Mandalay and saw with irritation Grace Prior, in a hideous cape of green rubber, waving to her from the top of the bund. In addition to the cape, Grace wore a monstrous matching hat-cover of her own devising which did away with the encumbrance of an umbrella, and she was attended by a crowd of chattering Burmese with whom she seemed much at ease, and this, as well as her clothes, made Maria stare disagreeably back at her.

Maria's temper had been sorely tried of late, in any case. She had felt triumph and a thrill of secret power when Colonel Browne's letter had arrived in Bombay, and had derived enormous pleasure from the ostentatious packing up of the bungalow on account, as she put it to anyone foolish enough to ask, of her father's 'diplomatic appointment'. The few good possessions that remained to them from palatial days in Tirimbatore would accompany them to Mandalay where Maria envisaged them standing about graciously on the gleaming floors of the British Residency. Colonel Browne was a bachelor; he would, without the smallest doubt, be thankful for her talents as hostess. She saw herself at the head of a long table glittering with silver and glass, having managed the servants with serene confidence and receiving, as awed and grateful guests climbed reluctantly into their carriages after magnificent parties, the warmest tributes of gratitude from the Colonel, a gratitude not untinged with respect . . .

Buoyed up by these visions of their new life together and the public role she would play in it, Maria invested in as many new clothes as she dared, and sailed for Rangoon with Hubert in the best of spirits. Not only had there been a flattering number of farewell parties at which she found herself the undisputed centre of attention, but the day they departed she had received from Bengal a letter from Captain Murray Shaw, now back with his regiment. He heard of her going, he wrote, with the deepest regret, and was consoled only by the rumour that her father's appointment was likely to be temporary. Maria felt quite sure that if Murray Shaw's twenty-fifth birthday had already come, bringing with it his accession to a comfortable income, the letter would have been an open offer of marriage. As it was, it would do very well for the present, and she put it among her numerous personal possessions to be carried onto the ship. Once on board she found herself the only lady. Her new muslins were delightful for the bright breezy days on deck and the captain came as near to flirting with her as he dared. She stepped down onto Burmese soil with every expectation of finding red carpets and a brass band.

There was nothing. Rangoon was pleasant

enough in an unutterably provincial way and would presumably, in view of the amount of European Gothic building going on, be a place of some presence in ten years or so. But now it was a low-built, unfashionable town, boilingly, steamingly hot, the river fringed with godowns, the streets pitted with holes. There was nowhere like Marine Drive in Bombay, to show oneself off, nowhere to see or be seen. The only object that could possibly arouse interest was the Shway Dagon pagoda and that, with its smooth, soaring pinnacle of brilliant gold tinkling and winking with bells, Maria considered hopelessly vulgar. She was taken to visit it by no less a person than the Chief Commissioner of Lower Burma and when she discovered that to step onto the pagoda platform she must remove her shoes, she turned to her guide with a laugh that was not entirely without irritation.

'Mr Aitchison! You cannot suppose I should really take off my shoes! Look at the pavement. It is indescribably filthy and in any case the Burmese walk all over it – in bare feet!'

The Chief Commissioner shrugged and said that in that case he had brought her on a long climb to no purpose. They descended the steps from the platform to his carriage in silence and Maria was left with the feeling that if a mistake had been made that afternoon, it most certainly was not hers. When she drove past the Shway Dagon three days later to board the steamer for Mandalay, she gave it a quelling and reproving glance and resolved to put all memories of Rangoon behind her.

There was precious little to remember in any case, no garden parties, no receptions, no dinners, not even anyone to tea. She had been subjected to an awful performance – again by Mr Aitchison who, for all people said he was a sahib, had clearly lived too long among native peoples – called a *pwe*, where girls with barbarously painted faces and hideous tawdry costumes stiffened into ludicrous points on shoulders and hips, danced in a fashion that was scarcely even decent and sang screechingly to the accompaniment of tuneless gongs. Maria had had an agonizing headache throughout and there had been no European woman in the audience who came even halfway to being a lady. In fact there were very few women at all beyond a garrulous contingent of American female missionaries whose sartorial neglect affronted Maria quite as much as the winged costumes of the dancers.

It will all be all right she promised herself, when I am on the steamer. That is when it will become our new life, that is when everything will be elegant and suitable and deferential. The steamer, one belonging to the Irrawaddy Flotilla Company, was a huge three-decked affair, the top deck screened with awnings as much against the thick black smoke from the funnel as against the furious rains or the blazing sun. Behind the steamer were towed two vast flats piled with dried fish with a smell so violent that

Maria declared at first that she could not stand it.

'Make them take them off,' she cried to her father, angry-eyed across a scented handkerchief. 'Explain who you are! Insist they are removed!'

The flats and their stinking fish remained. Maria, exhausted by the disappointment of Rangoon and the heat and the wet, retired to her tiny none-too-clean cabin and burst into tears. She refused to come out to look at the little villages they stopped at, refused to admire the charming children playing in the river shallows or the pretty little Burmese women in their bright cottons who brought fruit on board in baskets whenever they moored, refused, in fact, to do anything but sit in her cabin and complain. She complained at the mould growing daily on her shoes, at the coarse food provided on board, at the jovial, beery manners of the captain, at the ceaseless melancholy chant of the leadsmen up in the bows, testing the depths of the river with long poles as they steamed onwards.

Hubert made promises about Mandalay.

'You will see, my dearest, you will see. A place of wonderful primitive beauty, the kind of beauty you knew in your childhood! The presence of royalty always gives a place an air. What could you expect of Rangoon? It's a place for petty provincial administrators, the dullest sort of civil servant. But Mandalay will be another world!'

And here now was that other world. All she could see from the taffrail was the huge, ugly, ochre breadth of the Irrawaddy dimpled with rain and stretching away to her left to some undistinguished dun-coloured hills. To her right was the high river bund, crowned with dripping trees, its steep flanks crowded with brown Burmese, some of whom were washing clothes in water the colour and substance of liquid mud. She could see no roof, no tower, no pinnacle. Certainly no palace.

She turned to exclaim her disappointment to her father and caught for a fleeting moment on Hubert's face a look of intense apprehension directed at her and that look, so vulnerable, so beseeching, so quickly gone, transformed her dismay at once to resolve.

'So, Papa! Here we are! And there is Grace Prior looking exactly like a toad in that dreadful arrangement of green rubber and, if I am not mistaken, there is Colonel Browne to welcome us. Just as I thought he would. Well, Papa, is this not exciting? A royal city!'

Hubert straightened his back and smiled at her with undisguised gratitude. Despite the wet heat, the pale grey cloth stretched smoothly across his shoulders, his collars rose to his distinguished jaw line unwrinkled and stiff. Maria, conscious that this horrible climate had caused a dampness that appalled her at her waist and beneath her arms, straightened too, unfurled the handsome green parrot-handled umbrella she had bought in Bombay and brought it up smartly over her new hat, a hat of grey velvet roses tied on with a huge and becoming bow of green moire ribbon beneath her chin. As the umbrella went up, so did her chin and then she put a grey-gloved hand on her father's arm and stepped ashore.

Grace Prior, so properly subdued in Bombay, seemed full of a new and wholly unattractive confidence.

'I do hope you will like Mandalay, Miss Beresford. It really is such an interesting place and so beautiful and Papa has done wonderful things at the mission school. The numbers have gone up to forty! It is such a pity it is raining so, people say the climate in the winter is quite perfect and when we came it was quite dry and the sun shone brilliantly, oh, for weeks and weeks! And I am learning Burmese, Miss Beresford, and the children are so charming and tease me so—'

'Indeed,' Maria said and moved smoothly forward to be greeted by Colonel Browne.

'My dear Miss Beresford! How very fine you are! Quite an ornament to Mandalay. Good journey, eh? Only eight days, you know, not bad at all. It sometimes takes nine or ten and if the steamer gets badly stuck, longer still. No trouble from the banks?'

'Trouble?'

'Dacoits. That's why they always moor the steamer in mid-stream at night. Ah, Beresford. Good to see you, welcome to Mandalay. Your fame is before you, Miss Beresford. The Queen has expressed a desire to meet the European lady who plays the pianoforte so well.' He lowered his

69

voice. 'The ladies from the missions only play hymns you know. Evangelical music don't seem to suit the Burmese ear. Now then, I'll show you to your quarters. I haven't put you up in the Residency, it's hardly fit for pi-dogs let alone a lady. But there's a pleasant bungalow and I've given you half of the Residency guard. Ten Madras sepoys, Beresford, not much use but better than nothing.'

Dismay was beginning to creep lumpily up Maria's throat once more. Not stay at the Residency? Her vision of green lawns, flights of white steps, wide cool rooms – was that not to be? And Colonel Browne himself was wearing some dreadful tartan tam-o'shanter, not at all as she had remembered. But there was at least the invitation to the palace. The Queen with the outlandish name had asked to hear her play. If Maria did not think the bungalow Colonel Browne had found them suitable, she would of course ask the Queen to use her influence. Cheered at the thought, Maria did not even object when she discovered Colonel Browne had offered Grace Prior a lift back to the mission in the same carriage.

Carriage? On the other side of the bund, down its equally steep eastern bank, waited a row of bullock carts.

'Does the luggage go first?' Maria inquired of Grace.

'Oh no! We do.' Grace turned to smile at Maria, caught her look and said encouragingly,

'They really are not so bad, you know. You get used to them quite quickly. And the roads in Mandalay are so rutted that anything else would be broken to pieces.'

'Even in Rangoon,' Maria said with tightened lips, 'there were rickshaws.'

Grace shook her head.

'Not here. There aren't any rickshaws here. I expect we have to use bullock carts because we are *kalās*, foreigners, you know. The Burmese despise *kalās*, they really despise any foreigner except the Chinese. Sometimes I rather see why. We look so huge and clumsy beside them, we must seem like big children.'

Stiff with outrage, Maria descended the slope to the waiting carts. It was difficult to do, for mud clung stickily to her shoes and hem and her hands were quite preoccupied with her umbrella and her reticule. Little Burmese watched her impassively, their dark eyes taking in her height, her blondness, her strange and fantastic dress. They themselves wore pasos of checked cotton and tight fitting cotton jackets and only a few held umbrellas over their sleek black heads. A handful of children smiled shyly, filthy naked children with navels protruding like acorns from their swollen stomachs, inhabitants of the huts that clung to this slope of the bund, made of matting and broken lattices, indistinguishable in colour from the mud that surrounded them.

Poor Miss Beresford, Grace thought pityingly, poor Maria, in her lovely clothes, so used to

71

everything being comfortable and elegant. So awkward, climbing into a bullock cart for the first time, before one gets used to the way Burmans stare so, before one realizes that ankles really don't matter a fig in Mandalay. And of course there is never anything to sit on in bullock carts, just the planks and that green silk will get horribly dirty. It must be awfully expensive silk, it is so thick and rustling. At least carts can't harm my mackintosh, though I can see Miss Beresford thinks I look a perfect fright. I always will beside her, though I look better in Burma, being small is more suitable somehow and they have thin wrists too—

'My dear,' Hubert murmured in Maria's ear. He had put his arm across her shoulders to protect her from the rough planking side of the cart.

She smiled at him bravely. 'The royal coach, Papa!'

Grace Prior leaned forward. 'This is such a beautiful place, Mr Beresford, even the *kalā* town is beautiful but, of course, today it is a bit difficult to see . . .' Her voice trailed away doubtfully.

Hubert Beresford looked about him. 'Quite,' he said.

The rain had almost ceased, but the air was thick with steaming dampness making it almost impossible to see anything at all. The *kalā* town, the city for foreigners, had been built inside a wide, western-swinging curve of the Irrawaddy, so that the river embraced it on almost three sides, and all the rutted lanes that passed for roads led down to the water. The lanes near the river were lined with the hovels of the poorer Burmese which, although squalid in themselves, were greatly improved in appearance by an enormous number of trees, mangoes, peepuls and feathery tamarinds, that grew everywhere in profusion.

As the carts jolted bone-shakingly away from the river to the east, the huts gave way to large compounds, low houses with verandahs and courtyards thick with mango trees, and every so often among these low bungalows an unmistakably oriental building appeared through the foliage, roofed in a double or triple layer of corrugated iron supported upon eaves of vermilion-painted timber.

Colonel Browne followed Hubert's gaze. 'We sold them tons of the stuff. Corrugated iron. There's an ancient custom in the orient that royalty must be roofed in silver or lead, but of course the Burmese are too practical to follow that to the letter. It was Mindoon, the last king, who hit upon the notion of corrugated iron. He could buy it very cheaply in Europe. He roofed the whole of the Gem City in it. It looks fine in the sunlight, too. Here we are, Miss Prior. Tell your father I'll be in to see him later today.'

The springless cart had crashed to a halt outside one of the oriental buildings, one with a triple roof. It was built high on pillars of teak, and a flight of worn steps led up to a wide covered verandah which surrounded it. Like the houses all around it, it was sunk in rampant foliage.

Grace climbed down neatly, turning when she was on the roadway to say to Maria, 'If you are not too tired to come at teatime, Miss Beresford, my father and I should be so pleased to see you.'

Maria nodded and smiled tightly. Presumably at some point she should have to call on Grace in that peculiar crooked, carved dwelling, but not until she had made of their own infinitely superior house a place to be envied.

Colonel Browne leaned out of the cart and patted Grace's wet hand. 'Course she'll come. I'll bring her myself.'

Under Hubert's arm, Maria's back stiffened with irritation.

'Triple roof you see,' Colonel Browne said as the cart jolted on. 'Mindoon built it for Doctor Marks, Prior's predecessor. They got on very well. Marks was even allowed to teach some of the princes. I remember seeing them when I first came up to Mandalay in fifty-nine, all processing off to the mission school on an elephant apiece under a pair of royal golden umbrellas. It was a great mark of favour to have a triple roof; Mindoon meant it as a compliment. Wait till you see the royal city, Miss Beresford. The King's own apartment has seven roofs. I've only had two audiences and I must say kicking my heels doesn't suit my temperament. I shall send you in,

74

Beresford, and you can sit about for a few days instead of me, and wait for Thibaw not to appear. Well, here we are, my dear, home sweet home.'

Hubert's hand tightened on Maria's shoulder. Together they looked across the backs of the bullocks towards a small, shabby compound with great unkempt mangoes flopping over the walls of matting. Between their pointed leaves was visible a modest timber bungalow with a narrow verandah – and a single roof. No lawns, no prospect, not even the dull gilded carving that had covered eaves and doors at the mission, just a squat, weathered, wooden building crouching warily under the thunderous drip of overhanging leaves.

'Has it been uninhabited long?' Maria said, her voice quite steady for Hubert's sake.

'Not more than a few months, my dear. There's more room than there looks. I expect, being an Englishwoman, you could make something of the compound.'

'I have never had anything to do with a garden,' Maria said and then, with as much dignity as possible, she clambered from the bullock cart into the mud of the lane.

4

Grace Prior, behind the teapot at the mission, looked at the room with less satisfaction than she had felt with it before. When she first came, she had liked the simplicity of it, the way the windows and doors were the same thing – long shutters of carved wood, faintly gilded – and the great soaring roof had seemed to her noble, almost spiritual, like a cathedral, arching over all the little rooms that were clustered below it. Of course, as these rooms were divided from each other only by partitions, there was little privacy, but she and her father lived at either end of the building so she need fear no indelicacy . . . In any case, the screaming of ungreased axles from the lane and the ceaseless knocking of the coppersmith birds from the trees outside were enough to drown any other sound. Since school, and the agonizing sharing of a dormitory, Grace had always been afraid of snoring, utterly humiliated at the prospect of unconsciously causing other people to regard her with disgust. She was quite sure Maria Beresford never snored.

But then, Maria Beresford had this steely quality of success. She had been a month in that most undistinguished bungalow and already it was, Grace was sure, the most elegant house in the *kalā* town. Grace had gone down to it in a spirit of intense curiosity thinly veiled as helpfulness to assist in the unpacking of innumerable boxes and had watched the dull little wooden rooms brought to life and character with rugs and embroideries, little tables, pictures and ornaments. The simplicity of the mission that had seemed to her so beautiful, almost holy, now only looked raw and bare.

Colonel Browne had laughed about the Beresford's bungalow, but then you couldn't expect a middle-aged bachelor to admire that charming sitting room littered with pretty things.

'I said to him,' the Colonel had said to Tom Prior, 'I said to Beresford, bring as little as you can, we shall only be here a matter of months – and they turn up with enough knick-knacks to fill a mansion! Game girl, Miss Beresford, though, I'll hand her that at least. I imagine she's had to get used to making silk purses out of sows' ears.'

Tom Prior was a great liability in Maria's house. Smiling and kindly, frequently abstracted, he blundered into frail objects like an amiable bullock while Grace fluttered round him, all at once terrified at what he might break and mortified, yet again, by her own clothes when seen against Maria's.

Clothes don't matter, she told herself regularly and resolutely before the little freckled glass that hung on the wooden wall of her bedroom. Not

77

outward clothes, just the clothes of one's personality, one's soul. Even if I had some silk as delicious as that yellow afternoon dress of Maria's, I should only spoil it in the making up and anyway I am too pale for yellow. I really am very pleased with my new pink, very pleased, even if it is a little harsher in colour than I meant, in any case, it doesn't matter at all, it isn't what God minds about—

Now presiding over her tea table, she began again, dismissing and despairing over the simple furniture at the mission, the absence of ornaments, the fact that the only pictures were badly drawn prints of martyred saints. Her father liked them. He teased her and said she liked them too really, only she would not admit to a taste for the melodramatic.

'Do you have more tea in that pot of yours, Mademoiselle?'

Grace blushed at once. This was the third time the young French engineer Bonvilain had come to tea, and she blushed every time he spoke to her. He was handsome too, which meant she could not look at him because of being afraid of looking too much. She poured tea silently into his cup and with relief and disappointment watched him go back to the group of men around Colonel Browne.

They met like this three or four times a week, her father, the colonel, Mr Beresford, sometimes the intriguing Italian consul, Signor Andreino, sometimes the French engineer, very occasionally a peculiar and disconcerting man called Denzil Blount. Grace had noticed, pouring tea and slicing the cakes she had taught the Burmese cook to make, that if Monsieur Bonvilain or Mr Blount were there, the conversation was always more stilted, no-one seemed so relaxed, the talk was always more general. She wondered if Monsieur Bonvilain's being a Roman Catholic or Mr Blount's being, shockingly, an unashamed atheist had anything to do with the constraint, but her father had laughed at her. He never, Grace reflected, took any of her opinions quite seriously.

'If I don't get any satisfaction from the palace soon,' Colonel Browne said, 'I shall call it a day. I shall have to anyway, because the Residency is about to fall down, quite literally, and Thibaw won't produce a farthing for repairs. I am not received at court, we are not properly housed or guarded—'

Bonvilain said smiling, 'You should be prepared to remove your shoes.'

A disapproving silence followed this remark. After savouring it for a while, Bonvilain drained his cup, stood up in a leisured manner and then came to bow alarmingly over Grace's hand and take his leave.

'Mademoiselle,' he said and looked at her directly and for a second she looked back and was quite overwhelmed. Then he turned and bowed easily to the men, and Grace saw Hubert Beresford give him a more than cordial nod of farewell. Then his footsteps rang out on the verandah and down the steps to the road.

The Italian consul, his fingertips lightly together, surveyed Colonel Browne with amusement. 'Too much said, my dear Colonel. It was you who first told me that the French were to be watched up here, oh, nearly twenty years ago, and now you slip up yourself. That young man is only supposed to be building bridges but he looks too clever for that. And he has taken off his shoes several times and been granted audiences. Thibaw seems to be as much taken by his moustaches as Signorina Prior—'

Grace, mortified, bent her head.

'Of course,' her father said, gazing upward into the dark peak of the roof, 'we are all on a knife-edge here, all we foreigners. Only money or God keeps us here, and for the money to flow we need the favour of the King. And the Queen.'

Grace came out from behind the table, drawn by the mention of Supayalat. 'I saw the sisters from the convent today. They were summoned to see the Queen yesterday and had to sit in an apartment while some women were beaten in the room next door. They said Supayalat and her ladies laughed at the cries, and afterwards she made them translate a very vulgar French novel and ordered them to send to Paris for heaps of things, watches and photograph albums and French silks, expensive things. The sisters are worried about payment because the Queen keeps ordering things and never pays for them.'

'I imagine,' Andreino said, smiling at Grace, 'that the handsome Frenchman will find himself soon in much the same case. Supayalat is assuming more power each day and although she likes to spend, she does not like to pay. Her own troops are short of money, and foreigners in the royal service will be next. I am grateful for the agency of the Bombay-Burmah Trading Corporation for without their interests to guard in the teak forests, I should be penniless too. I am afraid my country does not think a consul in Mandalay necessary to pay for.'

'And mine,' Colonel Browne said abruptly, standing up, 'will not have such a necessity to pay for much longer. My position is absurd. I have been here two months and done nothing and every time I complain to Rangoon, Aitchison says he quite understands but the governments in London and Calcutta are far too preoccupied with trouble in South Africa and Afghanistan to be bothered with Mandalay at all. I fail to see the point of going on. Beresford, I'm going back to the Residency. Will you walk with me?'

Hubert Beresford declined with perfect courtesy. He wanted to walk towards the royal city, he said, it had almost become a habit with him in the early evening.

'My regards to Miss Beresford,' the colonel said.

When he too had gone loudly down the wooden steps to the lane, the Italian looked across at Hubert Beresford. 'And if the colonel withdraws from Mandalay, what shall you do, signore?'

Hubert, who seemed to have been dreaming, turned his fine head and said calmly, 'I think there will be plenty to keep us here, Signor Andreino. Plenty. We are a resourceful pair, my daughter and I, and although there would of course be absolutely no difficulty in my going back to Bombay, my old position being always open to me naturally, we are disinclined to re-trace our steps so soon.'

'I must warn you,' Andreino said smiling, 'Mandalay is full of strange people, people who cannot live anywhere else, people who are not welcome any longer in Lower Burma, British Burma. Tom says we are on a knife-edge here. We are indeed. We must be very careful not to fall nor to get sliced in two.'

Hubert, regarding him, made no reply.

Andreino went on, 'There is much to be gained here, especially with royal patronage. But royal patronage is as fickle as it is heady. There is also much to be lost.'

'Not,' Tom Prior said smiling, 'if you come for God. Only if you come for money. Forgive me, gentlemen, I am going down to the chapel for a while. Grace will look after you—'

'I will come,' Andreino said, 'I will come with you.'

Grace, afraid of being left alone with Hubert, was relieved to see him rise too, look at his watch

82

and declare that it was now time for his stroll towards the palace.

'Of course,' Grace said, too eagerly, 'it is very beautiful, isn't it? I don't wonder you go every evening, it is so lovely.'

Hubert, looking at her abstractedly, thought what a pity it was that the only girl of Maria's age in the *kalā* town should be this unremarkable little thing with her anxious eyes and terrible homemade clothes. He said goodbye to her with the gracious kindliness he reserved for the very young and the very old, took up his beautiful silver topped cane, and went down the verandah steps.

As he reached the lane, Grace saw to her consternation that Mr Blount appeared to be approaching the mission. She keenly did not wish to have to entertain him alone, but observed with relief that Mr Beresford seemed to have diverted him from his purpose for the two men, having exchanged a word or two, set off together in the direction of the palace. Grace stood and watched them for a while, tall formally clad Europeans among the scattering of little brown Burmese in the lane wrapped only in their lengths of bright checked cotton, and then her gaze wandered up among the damp green trees to where the sun, exhausted by the effort of trying to penetrate the monsoon steams all day, was about to slide thankfully to rest in the Irrawaddy.

★　　★　　★

Denzil Blount, negotiating the puddles that made the roadway more lake than lane, observed how very much better polished Hubert's boots were than his own. It was also extremely obvious to anyone interested in such discrepancies that Hubert's suit was better pressed, his linen better laundered, his hat better brushed. Denzil's clothes had begun their lives superbly in St James's entirely on credit, and were now, after years of neglect in punishing climates, both travel-weary and still unpaid for. If Denzil were ever unwise enough to go back to London, he doubted St James's would provide him with so much as a new necktie.

Of course, Hubert had a helpmeet in his splendid daughter. Miss Beresford had been seated in her pretty drawing room, immaculate in yellow silk, when he had met her the day before and she had made him, for all the confidence he felt in his charm, feel crumpled and not in charge of the situation at all. She had given him tea with distaste and had then proceeded to manage her father with such affectionate adroitness that any resentment Denzil felt at being treated high-handedly vanished quickly into a mounting admiration. Hubert's connections with the British establishment, his vanity, his need for money, the credentials of his manners and appearance, coupled with his daughter's shrewdness, strength of mind and devotion to her father – all these things, Denzil felt, accepting a second cup of tea humbly, boded very well for the future.

After tea he had boldly expressed his admiration for the bungalow and all Maria had done to make it so charming. Maria had bowed stiffly but her eyes had gleamed for a second.

'Shall I have the pleasure of seeing you at the mission tomorrow?' Hubert had inquired in his incurious drawl.

'No. No, you won't. I seldom go there. I believe I shock good little Miss Prior.'

Maria had looked up then with a real smile, made brilliant with a touch of malice. 'Then we have something in common, Mr Blount. I seldom go to the mission either. I am always asked but am always deeply depressed by going. I prefer boredom here with pretty things to look at than boredom there in the company of St Stephen being stoned without proper perspective.'

Denzil smiled back at her with the lazy, intimate smile that had proved so invaluable with women all his life. 'Since we are in such perfect agreement, Miss Beresford, perhaps you will allow me to waylay your father after his visit to the mission tomorrow. We could stroll by the palace walls and I might amuse him with tales of Mandalay.'

She nodded assent but withdrew her smile, deepening his admiration. Now glancing at Hubert as they made their way towards the palace, Denzil envied him not only for his clothes, but also for his daughter. She would prove, Denzil had no doubt of it, an admirable asset in all the plans he was revolving in his mind.

They did not speak much, being too occupied with keeping their feet dry and when the palace walls and the moat came in view, they fell instinctively into complete silence, standing and gazing as all Europeans were wont to do, however familiar they were with the spectacle of the City of Gems, the golden city of Mandalay. Before them rose walls of coral-red brick, the top crenellated into shapes like spear heads, running away to the east and north for more than a mile towards the blue Shan hills. They marched for more than a square mile, those coral-red walls, broken only once in each flank, to the north and south, to the east and west, by the blinding white structures of the massive gateways each crowned with a spire of five-tiered roofs, winged delicate roofs, edged with carved wooden eaves painted in scarlet and gold.

Between the walls and the muddy roadway where Denzil and Hubert now stood stretched the moat, more than two hundred feet of still and shining water, its gleaming surface broken only by the brilliant green pads of the water lilies and the pink lotus. Some distance away, by the southern gate, just visible from the south-western corner where they were, floated two golden royal barges, delicate winged boats like gondolas, with prow and stern upswept into pennants of wood which looked as if they might lift the barge right out of the water and bear it away to Mandalay Hill which rose, blue and misty, to the north-east of the palace walls.

Despite the thick damp air, the prospect was very brilliant, the red walls, the white gateway, the blue shining water, the green lily leaves, the glittering golden boats basking in their reflections in the moat beside the white bridges. And if one raised one's eyes, and looked beyond, inside the walls, it was almost dazzling to contemplate the strange loveliness of the Gem City. The square mile inside the walls was packed with roofs, glittering tiered roofs of pagoda and palace, all edged with winged eaves in red and gold, all soaring into spires between the feathery fronds of the tamarind trees. The whole palace complex, temple, bedrooms, audience hall, kitchen, every single building was of wood, teak wood from the forests to the south-east of the city, carved and fretted and painted vermilion. Here and there a watchtower rose, a red column up which a gilded staircase wound in a spiral, up, up to the lookout at the top. It was magical but somehow, to a European eye, unnerving, so much red and gold, so many shining tiered roofs, so many spires, everything so brilliant, so winged that only the trees seemed natural, the frothy pale green of the tamarinds and the dark drooping branches of the mangoes.

Hubert said, a faint note of regret in his voice, 'My daughter does not much care for it. She thinks it showy.'

Denzil laughed. 'It is. Decidedly. I should not expect a lady to enjoy it.'

Hubert had been disappointed at Maria's

disgust. They had come on a relatively fine evening, soon after their arrival, and he had felt himself frankly overwhelmed, responding to the sinister splendour with a wholeheartedness that surprised him. Maria had not descended from the bullock cart, but merely surveyed the view from beneath her parrot-handled umbrella, pronounced it vulgar, flashy and ostentatious, and had then suggested returning home. He sighed faintly now, remembering.

'Have you had audience?' Denzil said casually, moving to lean against one of the mangoes that fringed the moat.

Hubert looked shocked. 'Naturally not. The shoe question—'

'Ah,' Denzil said, 'the shoe question. Representatives of Her Imperial Majesty Queen Victoria, etcetera. Well, Beresford, nothing venture, nothing gain. And there is much to be gained, much, so much. But,' he said with careful nonchalance, 'I doubt Horace Browne will gain it. It needs a man of – a different mettle altogether. A man of the world, of assurance, of polish, a man understanding in the ways of men.'

Hubert drew his gaze reluctantly from the pinnacles of the palace. 'I believe,' he said, 'that Colonel Browne was glad to have me here. I can only suppose he felt I should have a better chance of an audience than he. Being, you understand, rather less martial in my approach.'

'Precisely.'

Encouraged, Hubert said, 'It seems to me a

little strange that we have made no progress in seeing the King. I have no vaulting ambition myself, but I cannot help feeling that if the matter were in my hands, we should be farther forward than we are.'

'If Colonel Browne,' Denzil said, his eyes fixed on the moat, 'were to withdraw to Rangoon, wash his hands of the whole affair, what should you do?'

'My position in Bombay is always open to me—'

'But should you like to resume it?'

Hubert studied his gloves and considered a reply.

Denzil ceased to look at the moat and regarded his companion instead. 'You see, Beresford, if the British withdraw, the field will be open to the French. You cannot imagine that young Bonvilain is only here to make roads and bridges. The French will move into the teak forests and drive out the Bombay-Burmah and our consular friend Signor Andreino. And they will work upon Thibaw. They will not hesitate to take *their* shoes off. He is a weak young man; he was a monk before he was King. He isn't much more than twenty and the French have already wooed him with wine and champagne for which he has developed a violent fondness. He may be weak but he has much power, and that power could be of real use to you and me, Beresford, could we tap it. Thibaw holds the great royal monopolies in his drunken hands, the monopolies of timber and earth oil and precious stones. Would you wish, Beresford, to see the concessions to those monopolies fall into French hands?'

'But the British government, the government of India, they would never allow—'

Denzil laughed and snapped his fingers in Hubert's face. 'My dear fellow! They don't care *that* much for Burma! Their hands are quite full with trouble from the Afghans and trouble from the Zulus; they have not a moment to spare for Mandalay.'

Hubert drew himself up. 'Colonel Browne assured me that a post in Mandalay was of very real significance to the government of India.'

Denzil said nothing in immediate reply but anger flared for a second in his eyes. When he spoke, his voice was tightly controlled. 'Try not to be an ass, my dear Beresford. A diplomatic post up here is not worth an anna. Burma is a backwater to England, a disagreeable steaming place which usefully provides us with timber. It is not a place of consequence, not to governments. But it could be to *us*. It could be to you and me, Beresford, if we play our cards right, if you listen to me, if you stick by me when Browne goes down to Rangoon as he surely will do before the monsoon ends. Don't look mortified, dear fellow. Don't sulk on me. You *know* this is a hole. You *know* assistant to the Resident carries as much weight as his bootblack. I am offering you more than Browne ever did. I am offering you a position with the King, wealth, status, *real* wealth and status. You can help me. I can help you.'

Hubert seemed to consider for a moment. Then he said slowly, 'Monsieur Bonvilain and I – have spoken, only very generally you understand, on the matter of the royal monopolies. He is as you say, a clever young man, but not an experienced one. He cannot, of course, offer me anything except the fruits of his observations and it is perhaps fortunate that he is sharp-eyed. I should, of course, be only too pleased to help you, Blount, should my influence be required—'

'It is,' Denzil said shortly.

'In that case—'

'Listen to me, Beresford. Those concessions to the royal monopolies are ours for the taking if we go the right way about it. We, Beresford, you and I, Bonvilain even, on the right terms, though I am reluctant to put a farthing in a French pocket – we could win the right to work the ruby mines, to cut down the forests. You, with your manners, can work upon Thibaw for me. I will do the sums, I will arrange the business but *you* will smooth the way with the King. And the beautiful Miss Beresford—'

Hubert looked up sharply. 'My daughter?'

'Your daughter. Your lovely and admirable daughter will be covered with rubies from head to foot if I have my way. She will be of inestimable value to us, because she will be our path to Supayalat.'

Hubert said, 'When we arrived, we were told

that the Queen wished to see Maria, to hear her play on the pianoforte. But the invitation has never come. I find it most surprising.'

'I can make sure it is renewed.'

Hubert regarded him. 'You can?'

Denzil smiled. 'I have a *petite amie*. Among the maids-in-waiting. She will remind the Queen. You must never underestimate the Queen, Beresford. She is young, but she is worth a dozen of Thibaw. She has allowed him only one other wife, her plain and pious elder sister, and she rules him completely. He is enslaved by her. She will soon be the power in this country, the only power that counts. It was she who ordered the massacre of the royal rivals. She will stop at nothing to achieve her ends, nothing at all. And your daughter will become her companion. She will like Miss Beresford, she likes all things that are striking, dramatic. Miss Beresford will tell her in carefully chosen words of our plans and she, in turn, will tell the King.'

Hubert was visibly gratified. 'There could be no more fit setting for my daughter than a palace.'

'Even if she does regard it as hopelessly vulgar.'

'The chosen companion of the Queen – that puts quite another complexion upon it.'

'And does it,' Denzil said, leaving his mango tree at last and coming close to his companion, 'does it also put any kind of complexion upon my offer to you?'

Hubert said superbly, 'I shall be happy to help you.'

Denzil's hand came up involuntarily, as if it wished to strike Hubert of its own accord, but it was restrained and returned to a pocket.

'We must work fast, Beresford. We must get ourselves locked tight in with the palace before the Residency is closed and all the British have a bad name. The Burmese will not take Browne's departure kindly; we will all be tarred with the same brush. But if Miss Beresford has made herself indispensable to the Queen, and you have made yourself wholly agreeable to the King and not, repeat not, initially asked for any favours, we will prove the exceptions to the rule. I will obtain an invitation for Miss Beresford at once and you – you will present yourself at the Hall of Audiences tomorrow. Without your shoes.'

'No,' Hubert said. 'That cannot be done.'

'Then neither can our fortunes be made.'

Hubert regarded his boots for a moment almost regretfully. 'Very well.'

'And Miss Beresford? Will you permit me to see Miss Beresford?'

'Tomorrow,' Hubert said, 'you may come for tea tomorrow.'

'And you will also ask Bonvilain?'

'No,' Hubert said. 'I will speak to Bonvilain. In due course. It will be more satisfactory that way.'

When he had bowed and moved away along the western road that led back into the *kalā* town, Denzil realized that there was perhaps a compensation for dealing with a man so inordinately vain. There had been moments in their interview when vanity had quite obscured Hubert's wits, but that same vanity had happily rendered him totally incurious about Denzil's past, his reputation or his soundness as a partner in such an adventurous scheme as this.

5

Grace Prior was in Maria's drawing room when the royal summons came. She had arrived half an hour before accompanied by Hosannah Manook, an Armenian whose father was the *Kalawun*, or minister for foreigners. Hosannah was plump and dark and lively, with brilliant black eyes and startlingly colourful clothes and Maria had, from the moment they met, and despite Hosannah's father's position at court, regarded her in much the same light as she did Burmese architecture.

Grace, no longer even fractionally confident of her new pink, had come with another purpose than simply introducing Maria to the cheerful Hosannah.

'Miss Beresford, you must come with us! We are going to the Denigrés, the French weavers, you know. They weave velvet for the court, all those apricot velvet robes the ministers wear on feast days. They are father and daughter, Miss Beresford, just as you and Mr Beresford are, and father and me. Do come!'

Maria laughed a little. 'My dear Miss Prior! I have no need of any velvet. One hardly would in this climate. And I am sure that if I did need any,

Mademoiselle Denigré would come to me.'

'Oh, *no*, Miss Beresford, not like that at all. Not a business visit. A social call! They are so charming, both of them, and the daughter is so dignified and amusing and she is very well received at court. The house is delightful, just like a house in southern France, not Burmese in the least and Julie bakes the most delicious cakes you ever ate. Oh do come, Miss Beresford. I have promised I will bring you and told them so much about your lovely dresses!'

'No doubt you have,' Maria said without a hint of gratitude at this compliment, 'but you should not presume on my time in this manner. Living here may be quite extraordinary in all sorts of ways and compel one to do all kinds of things one would not ordinarily do, but there is a limit to one's eccentricities all the same. And calling socially upon a weaver's daughter is definitely beyond that limit.'

Grace, goaded by this supercilious ungraciousness and inspired by the knowledge that Maria had never left India before coming to Mandalay, retorted bravely, 'Oh, of course, one would not do it in *England*, I am sure, unless it was a pastoral call, but Mandalay is so very different from England.' She paused and then said, 'Is it not, Miss Beresford?'

Maria, outraged, looked past her into the compound where the mango trees dripped drops the size of marbles onto the soaked earth. Hosannah Manook, quite unperturbed by the barbed exchange, burst into a flood of enthusiastic praise for Mademoiselle Denigré and the taste she displayed both in her work and in her house.

'It could not interest me less,' Maria said, her voice taut with fury.

'Of course not!' Hosannah cried gaily. 'How could it until you have seen it, and observed how charming it all is! And when we have taken you there, we shall take you to the little cigar house by the western gate and you shall see the Burmese women rolling cigars with their little brown fingers and then you shall choose cigars for your revered father! And probably Julie will send one of her special *gâteaux au chocolat* home with you for Mr Beresford too and when he eats it he will be happy! And you will be happy too, for the Denigré house is always full of sunshine and pleasant people, all the charming French people in Mandalay, such as that delightful Monsieur Bonvilain!'

Grace coloured so quickly that Hosannah never noticed the brief gleam in Maria's eye.

'Oh, my dear Grace! Pink as your English rose! I don't blame you, my dear, he is so very amusing. Now, Miss Beresford, why do you not run and fetch one of the pretty hats I have heard so much about and let us take you there with no more objections?'

The door opened and a black Madrassee bearer – taken from the guard by Maria, who was used to Madrassees in the house and preferred them to the little Bengali Colonel Browne had brought from Calcutta and spared, at great cost to his own comfort, for her use – came in with a folded paper on the silver tray that used to wait in the hall at Tirimbatore for the calling cards that never came.

Maria, still flushed a little with temper, took the paper in her most haughty manner and, without begging pardon of her companions, proceeded to read it. She read it very thoroughly, several times, and as she did so her proud and disagreeable expression changed to one of open exaltation.

'I fear I cannot come with you this afternoon, Grace – Miss Manook. I have been summoned to court. Queen Supayalat has requested me to attend her.'

Hosannah laughed heartily. 'But not now, my dear Miss Beresford! Not in the afternoon! The King and Queen sleep now and then they will lie all afternoon in the gardens and watch the king-fishers! And then the Queen will change again for she changes three times a day, fresh tamein, fresh jacket, fresh pawa, different jewels. Never never does the Queen hold audience in the afternoons!'

It was too much that this dreadful vulgarly dressed person with her loud, jolly laugh should know more about palace life than she did. She rose, signifying that the visit was at an end.

'I am well aware, Miss Manook, that I am not required until the morning. But I wish to make sure that everything is in perfect order for tomorrow and also I do not wish to be tired out and shaken to pieces by bouncing about in a bullock cart. I will bid you both good day.'

When they had gone, Maria read the note over and over again, as greedily as if it had been a longed-for love letter. She had entertained Mr Blount to tea two days before – at Papa's request – and had been pleasurably surprised to see how much improved he was in appearance. His suit now looked worthy of its origins and his hair and moustaches had been neatly trimmed. Maria took all these significant changes in him as a compliment to herself and allowed herself to own that he was an extremely pleasing-looking man and one who clearly admired her more than any man had done since Murray Shaw had so nearly declared himself in Bombay. Murray Shaw had been an attractive proposition, it was true, but a callow and unformed one beside the practised ease of Denzil Blount. Of course, Mr Blount was hopelessly disadvantaged by having no money, but then, as he revealed his schemes to her in an irresistibly humble and self-deprecating manner, it appeared that his embarrassment in this matter was likely to be only temporary.

'So you see, Miss Beresford,' he said to her in conclusion, 'I am about to discover what your fortunate father has known for years. Namely, that we cannot do without you. It is only by your intercession with the Queen that we have any chance at all.'

Later that night as they dined together, Maria, using her little-girl voice to disguise a question she felt might be naive, said to her father, 'But Papa, there is nothing wicked in these schemes for the royal monopolies, is there? There is nothing naughty in our trying to gain the concessions?'

Hubert put down his soup spoon to stretch his hand across the table – it was a pitifully small table, they had only used it as a tea table at Tirimbatore – and clasp hers warmly.

'My darling girl! As if Papa would ever stoop to such a thing whatever the gain! It is as open a scheme as I ever saw! The King has a monopoly of these mines and forests but he does not always have the engineers to work them, so he will allow someone else to work them for him and to benefit from the results. That is all! All, my dearest. Mr Blount is simply anxious to secure the concession to at least one of these monopolies before, for example, the French do. And he needs my advice, my influence and your brilliant way with people to achieve his ends.'

Maria smiled and lowered her eyes, releasing Hubert's hand after giving it a grateful squeeze. The blue silk she wore, a strong soft blue, would be wonderfully set off by some sapphires . . .

Now, having slipped the note into her pocket, and abandoned the drawing room for her bedroom and a little sartorial deliberation, she acknowledged that it was not only the prospect of sapphires that excited her, but equally that of action. The idea of having something to dress for, somewhere to go, someone to meet – all these things aroused her as nothing had done since she left Bombay. And the fact that the somewhere was a palace and the someone a queen brought an animation to her whole being quite spontaneously, an animation she had had to force for the last few months whenever her father crossed the threshold.

They had been, for Maria, months of the acutest disappointment and almost intolerable boredom. There was no-one in Mandalay to see her clothes, to dine with, to play music to, to be admired by, no-one at all. Apart from Colonel Browne – and Maria had long since ceased to be grateful to him for bringing them to Burma, indeed she now regarded him with powerful resentment – there was no-one in Mandalay whom she could begin to countenance. The visions of the Residency and its life that had sustained her as she journeyed up the Irrawaddy had been dashed by the reality of the people who lived here, the rogues and ruffians of a dozen nationalities all hoping for the fruits to be gained from royal patronage, all unacceptable either in British Burma or in their own countries. They were ill spoken, badly dressed and worse behaved. Many of them even kept native women in their houses, a notion almost too disgusting to contemplate. Maria really felt that most of the *kalās* in Mandalay were worse even than the Burmese themselves, and she was not capable of a more insulting thought than that.

She chose a dress of rose pink, its skirt looped

up to show underskirts of cream embroidered in pink, and laid it on her bed to contemplate. It was the best of the new dresses from Bombay, dresses she knew with a pang of guilt had cost far more than they should have and which she had had no chance to wear at all for anyone of any consequence except her father. Hubert had intimated, very gently and with a regret that broke her heart, that the Bombay dresses must be the last for the moment and Maria knew that they had not been paid for before they came away, that money must be sent from Mandalay. Of course it would be sent, Papa was so honourable, but she regretted her extravagance bitterly. Perhaps when Mr Blount's schemes bore fruit, there never need be any worries of that kind again; money would be as unthinkingly plentiful as it had been in her childhood. Such a happy prospect was worth every effort, indeed it was, and Supayalat must be impressed at first glance. Even if she had nothing finer to wear than the rose pink, it would remain in the Queen's mind that Maria always dressed as magnificently, because she had first seen her thus. As Papa said, people only took one at one's own valuation and therefore one must put a high price on oneself.

With her dress decided, there was little else to worry about. It was the custom to take Supayalat presents, European presents for which she had an insatiable appetite. Mr Blount had said anything would do, any frippery she had no use for and that mirrors were particularly popular. That was easy. Maria would take her mother's hideous old-fashioned silver-gilt looking glass, its handle shaped like a fish, a dreadful object that had come from that happy childhood in the big, new, vulgar red brick house in Burslem. The fish on the handle had red glass eyes and the rim of the mirror was studded with imitation stones. Maria, not disclosing its origins of course, had shown the looking glass to Mr Blount with a deprecating laugh, saying she could not think how such a thing came into her possession and Denzil Blount had laughed too and said it was the very thing for the Burmese Queen. Supayalat might be a queen but she was, after all, only Burmese.

The present was chosen, the dress, the hat, the parasol. Maria surveyed herself piece by piece in her glass and decided that the elements that the Almighty had chosen would do very well also. It was a pity she had grown thinner in the last weeks but her blondness and elegance were un-diminished, even though she had been so starved recently of the admiration that was life blood to her. Even if they had shown it, she would have despised admiration from the extraordinary handful of nonentities gathered in Mandalay. Tom Prior was amiable enough but, being a missionary, hardly counted, of course, as a human being socially speaking. Grace ditto, and she was not even so amiable; the Frenchman was handsome but quite evidently bourgeois; the Italian was as good as bourgeois and horribly casual over clean linen and fingernails; Colonel

Browne had proved a bitter disappointment; and Denzil Blount – not quite to be relied upon somehow . . . That was her audience, she reflected bitterly, that was what she had had to substitute for her visions of Residency elegance and a full social life of which she was to be queen.

She looked down at her mother's looking-glass. Tomorrow it would be in other hands, royal hands. Perhaps tomorrow would bring something else also, a life more like the one she had hoped for. She picked up the silver bell on her dressing table and rang sharply for her maid.

The following morning, she was kept waiting two hours. She rose very early, poured tea for her father at breakfast, saw him off through the rain to the Residency and then was dressed with the utmost care and slowness on account of the heat and the wet which seemed to fill the little house with a sticky steam. Once attired in the rose-pink silk, she sat down to wait for a carriage from the palace, arms carefully akimbo in that awful temperature to avoid the horrid possibility of staining her dress.

She sat and sat. In the lane outside wheels screamed past and the Burmese shouted to their bullocks and two coppersmith birds in the nearest mango knocked maddeningly, not quite together. Tuneless singing and an intermittent clatter came from the servants' quarters across the compound, but no royal messenger, no sound of trumpets. Maria sighed impatiently and stayed motionless, watching with distaste a pair of geckos flickering across the walls behind the pictures and a stout blood-red cockroach which, supposing the room to be empty, had come trundling out of the damp woodwork in search of crumbs.

She consulted her pocket watch as seldom as she could bear to and told herself that if no word had come by eleven she should ring for her maid to help her change. At twenty past eleven, when her impatience had flared into fury, a dark-skinned little person in white muslin with an absurd straw hat bobbing with cherries came tripping into the compound accompanied by a Burman holding an umbrella over her head. Maria remained where she was, only taking up a book from a side table and opening it at random.

'Miss Beresford?'

Maria started admirably and made a pretty show of almost dropping the book.

'Oh, did I disturb you? Forgive me, do. Miss Beresford, I am Mattie Calogreedy, I am European maid of honour to Queen Supayalat. I am come to take you to the palace.'

Maria rose and surveyed Miss Calogreedy. She had Eastern blood there was no doubt of it, with that dusky skin and slightly slanting dark eyes. She would also in a few years be extremely stout, although pretty and soft enough at the moment. She was smiling up at Maria from beneath her ribbons and cherries, showing teeth as small and even as a child's.

'You will wonder at my name, Miss Beresford! My father is Greek and much in favour at court. That is one reason why I am maid of honour. Come, Miss Beresford. We must not keep the Queen waiting. She is so anxious to see you and asked most particularly that you should wear your jewels.'

Maria's chin went up and her pearl earrings swung against her cheeks.

'Miss Calogreedy, I am wearing such jewellery as is appropriate to my dress.'

The royal carriage was yet another bullock cart, although the floor had been covered with a particularly hideous carpet of pink and yellow roses on a ground of emerald green.

'French!' Mattie said, patting it proudly.

Maria seated herself with as much dignity as she could and was disconcerted to find that two Burmese bearers sprang in after her and held umbrellas above her and Miss Calogreedy. The cart squealed atrociously and what with the axle and the rain and the wheels hitting ruts in the lane, conversation was hardly possible. Mattie Calogreedy sat and smiled at her or looked about her with an enjoyment that seemed to Maria both incomprehensible and distasteful. For her own part, she stared straight before her and let the wet trees and low buildings slide past her gaze, looked at but unseen.

It was only when the cart halted on the bridge to the royal city that Maria allowed her eyes to take in what was before her. Even her outrage at being kept waiting half a morning must give way to curiosity when actually about to enter the royal Gem City of Mandalay, and she leaned forward and observed that a guard of soldiers was coming forward to meet them, soldiers dressed in long red cloth coats over baggy white breeches, and wearing on their heads little winged red velvet caps embroidered in gold and surmounted by tin hats. At the head of the group was one who was evidently an officer, to judge from the coil of gold tinsel that adorned his hat and the embroidered velvet coat, bordered in gold, that almost obscured his balloon-like breeches. He spoke to Mattie Calogreedy in Burmese and, to Maria's disgust, Mattie dimpled and giggled in reply. When the bullock cart lurched forward, she actually waved her plump little hand to him coquettishly.

'Of course, we have permission to go in!' she cried to Maria. 'I can come and go as I please! I run in and out of the city all day, to see my mother and father and my friends, in the *kalā* town! Did you meet my friend Julie Denigré, Miss Beresford? Or Hosannah Manook? Or that dear, sweet thing at the mission who wouldn't say boo to a goose? There now, Miss Beresford, look about you, do!'

The rain had almost ceased and a milky sun was beginning to burn fiercely through the pearly vapours of steam. In the strange misty light, Maria saw the City of Gems for the first time, rising like a fairy city from the clouds, a

107

dim magical spectacle of spires and wings and pinnacles, red and gold and glittering silver set in spaces of brilliant green grass and cushioned among trees.

'It is a square mile!' Mattie Calogreedy said. 'And almost a quarter of it was given over, in the late King's day, to housing the lesser queens. Look. There, over there in the middle, the seven-roofed building, that's the Glass Palace, that's where we are going. And the little one next to it is the royal kitchen and then there is the theatre. They are all on platforms, Miss Beresford, that is why they are so high. Perhaps I may show you the Lily Throne Room, it is quite lined with mirrors!'

The street along which they rumbled was packed with people, all Burmese, all prosperous looking and dressed in the slender tameins that they wound so deftly about themselves from waist to ankle. The tameins in the royal city seemed all to be of silk too, a rough gleaming silk in brilliant clear colours, jade and pink and sky blue, apricot, yellow, purple and grass green. Above the tameins were neat white muslin jackets, long-sleeved, close-fitting and at the neck little scarves of yet more brilliant silk. The oily black hair of this busy crowd was for the most part done up in a sleek cone on top of their heads and ornamented with flowers.

'We must walk now, Miss Beresford.'

They had halted at another gateway, almost as massive and quite as blindingly white as the one they had passed through at the bridge.

108

'You see,' Mattie said, sliding a confidential and unwanted hand beneath Maria's elbow, 'the outer part of the city, where we have just been, is for shopkeepers and merchants and lesser courtiers, but now we are going into the inner enclosure reserved only for the great ministers, the Prime Minister and such like, and in the heart of that, we shall find the palace itself!'

More soldiers in their strange uniform of scarlet and white escorted them through, and into another area of straight streets and wooden buildings and green grass mown as close and smooth as velvet. Before them rose a massive building supported on red and gold pillars and roofed in iron decorated with a wealth of curious carved animals and plants.

'The palace?' Maria said, startled out of her disagreeable silence by curiosity.

Mattie Calogreedy squinted up at the huge building. The gold on its pillars was beginning to dazzle in the strengthening sun.

'No. No, that is the *Hlutdaw*, the parliament. There, over there is the palace.'

There was another gate to be negotiated first, a little postern in a wall, and Maria was reminded of a Russian doll she had been given as a child – and despised – which had come apart at the waist to reveal a second doll and the second doll held a third and on and on until she was left with a tiny solid doll no bigger than half her thumb. But the sight through the last door was infinitely more rewarding than the last doll. The streets ended, the bustle of people vanished and instead Maria found herself in a vast, park-like place, a space of gardens, of lawns, fountains and trees and, here and there, the palace buildings on their great platforms. They were of teak too, like everything else in that extraordinary place, oiled dark teak, but the pillars that supported the entrances were lacquered in red and gold and set with mirrors, and the roofs, the glittering winged tin roofs, balanced on wooden eaves carved and painted to resemble scarlet flames, soared up into the sky.

There were some people about, after all, Maria realized, staring round her, unable to help herself, but only women – women and children. The grass was brilliant in itself after the rains, but the little bright figures that ran about on it were more brilliant still in their silks, like butterflies, like flowers, like scraps of coloured paper.

'Who are they?' she said, gazing. 'What are they doing?'

At the sound of her voice, many of the little creatures turned to stare at her so tall, so fair, so stately in her strange and elaborate clothes. Mattie laughed and called out to them in Burmese.

'They are the maids in waiting, Miss Beresford! The maids of honour. And the children of the court. We play all day, Miss Beresford. You cannot imagine what a delightful time we have! The King and Queen love the gardens as much as we do, they use the summerhouse over there, you see? The little one with the five roofs. Come, Miss Beresford, come.'

Outside the central hall, Mattie Calogreedy kicked off her slippers and indicated Maria should do the same. There was a moment of rebellion, a memory of the Shway Dagon pagoda in Rangoon, and then Maria recalled that her father had taken his shoes off, that Mr Blount had said success depended upon her friendship with the Queen. Slowly and stiffly she stooped and eased off her shoes, not best pleased to observe how large they were beside Mattie's little velvet slippers.

After the steam and the glare outside, the dim splendour of the central hall was a cooling relief. The doors were all thrown open, but they were low and narrow and only admitted enough light to see where one was going.

'Sit,' Mattie whispered, 'like me.'

The room was quite silent, carpeted in layers of rugs, some old and oriental, some new and European. There were maids of honour here and there, but no-one spoke. Mattie had dropped flexibly into the required sitting position with her feet tucked under her and Maria, attempting to imitate her, thought crossly that if Mattie's father was a Greek, her mother must certainly be Burmese, which would account for her catlike suppleness as well as the darkness of her skin.

It was agonizing, sitting like that. The bones of her corset dug viciously into her sides and it was impossible to breathe comfortably. The impression of coolness one received coming in from the outside proved only an impression and the heavy wet heat began to oppress Maria dizzily in her discomfort. She could feel a sliding finger of sweat running down her backbone and her upper lip was wet. Desperately she began to count objects in the room as a distraction, pillars, girls, mirrors—

At the far end of the hall, a golden door was opened. Instinctively, Maria attempted to rise.

'Sit,' Mattie hissed, seizing her. 'It is polite. It is the most humble.'

The girl who came into the room seemed to dart rather than walk. She stepped in quickly and lightly, her head turning this way and that, the diamonds in the tall cone of the hair catching the faint light, like cold fire.

'Down,' Mattie whispered and bringing her joined hands up to her forehead, bowed to the ground. Maria, uncomfortably impeded by her corset, followed suit as best she might.

In the silence, the girl spoke. Her voice was harsh and clear. Maria waited, head bent still, the blood thudding in her cheeks, and heard Mattie reply.

'We are to follow her,' Mattie said urgently. 'She wishes to see you in her own apartments. Come quickly, Miss Beresford.'

Stumbling over her flounces, clutching her hat and skirts, Maria followed Mattie up the hall and through the gilded door onto the scorching palace platform once more. Then Mattie went running down the platform and Maria hurried to follow her, through a doorway, across a small chamber, through a further doorway and into an empty room full of light where the small, imperious figure of Queen Supayalat waited in the centre of a rug that was almost a twin to the one that had lined the bullock cart.

Maria knelt.

'She wants you to rise,' Mattie said. 'The Queen wishes to look at your clothes.'

The Queen was very small and very supple and, Maria noticed with a shock, heavily pregnant. She prowled round Maria like a little brown snake that has swallowed a coconut, reaching out with her flickering fingers to touch the silk and velvet, talking all the time in her clear, harsh voice. She was not beautiful, not pretty even, but she had an allure, a power that Maria could feel as an almost physical influence, and when she raised her magnificent dark eyes to Maria's face and smiled, Maria felt herself for a second ready to faint.

'The Queen admires your earrings,' Mattie said. 'She asks if you have rubies for that gown.'

Maria smiled with difficulty down at the little glowing creature. 'I have no rubies, Your Majesty.'

Supayalat clapped her hands and called something sharply. She wore a tamein of the most lustrous silk, pink and green, embroidered in gold, and the muslin of her jacket was stretched tight over her silk bodice and the smooth high mound of her belly. Her small brown feet were thrust into red velvet sandals whose soles were edged with rubies, and the diamonds Maria had seen in her hair were echoed in her ears and hung in glittering strands around her neck.

Two maids of honour came running in with lacquer boxes which they placed on the carpet before the Queen. Supayalat took Maria's wrist in her thin tight grasp and drew her down to her knees, flinging open the lids of the boxes and revealing a heap of jewellery in each, a dazzling tangle of red and green and white and blue necklaces, bracelets, earrings, all thrust pell-mell in together. Supayalat laughed and pushed Maria's hand into the jewels; it was intoxicating, her fingers deep in such a pile, deep among the cold smooth smallness of the gems.

Supayalat pulled out a bracelet of pale pinkish rubies set in gold and held it against Maria's dress. Then she nodded and said something to Mattie and pushed the bracelet onto Maria's wrist.

'The Queen asks what you have brought her.'

Maria took the looking glass from her reticule and offered it to the Queen. Supayalat took it in silence, sitting on her heels, studying her fascinating, vivid little face in the glass and then she looked up at Maria and laughed again and began scattering jewellery all over the carpet, diamonds and emeralds and rubies rolling like marbles into the corners.

'The Queen is very pleased with your present,

114

Miss Beresford. She wishes you to keep the bangle.'

Supayalat stopped throwing jewellery and began to speak quickly and without smiling, her eyes fixed upon Maria's face.

'The Queen wishes to know why you are in Mandalay. There are few European women in the Kingdom of Ava.'

Maria looked steadily back at Supayalat. 'I am here because of my father. The Queen will know he is assistant to the British Resident. I go wherever my father goes. I am his chief companion.'

Supayalat smiled at her.

'Do you have a husband, the Queen wishes to know?'

'No,' Maria said, 'my father is all I need.'

A young man appeared in the doorway, a plump young man with deep sunk eyes in a faintly puffy yellow face, dressed in a green silk paso with a spray of diamonds in his top knot. Supayalat and Mattie instantly bowed upon their clasped hands and Maria, startled but entranced to find that she was almost alone in a room that held both King and Queen of Upper Burma, followed them.

Thibaw's voice was soft, almost hesitant. He glanced at Maria nervously once or twice, then crossed the room to sit cross-legged on the low gilded couch, a *salun-daw*, that was the only furniture. Supayalat, answering him in her rapid way, moved to sit beside him. Maria remained where she was upon the floor.

'The King says he has given audience to your father,' Mattie said. 'He says he wishes you to play music for the Queen. He has a German pianoforte that he would like you to play on. The Queen wishes you to rise in order that the King may see how tall you are.'

In silence the royal couple surveyed her and, despite the fact that her silk was now crumpled with so much getting up and down Maria looked back at them serenely.

'The Queen wishes you to learn Burmese so that you may speak together. She asks if you draw.'

'I do.'

'Could you draw Their Majesties?'

'Most certainly.'

Supayalat and Thibaw turned to each other in delight. Then Thibaw spoke once more, not to Maria, but to the carpet and her feet.

'His Majesty wishes to impress some things upon you. He wishes you to repeat them to your father. There are very few royal monopolies left. His father, the late King Mindoon, abolished almost all of them, leaving only those in teak and earth oil and precious stones. The teak is leased to the Bombay-Burmah Trading Corporation but, that lease aside, His Majesty wishes to establish a relatively free market. He wishes you to tell your father this.'

Maria bowed a little and looked at Thibaw. His face was quite expressionless but Supayalat was regarding Maria with a look at once determined and encouraging. She smiled quickly and spoke to Mattie.

'We should go, Miss Beresford. The Queen is tired. You will return in the morning.'

Maria subsided to the floor once more, her forehead bent upon her hands. When she looked up again, Thibaw was walking from the room, Supayalat behind him. Almost at the door the Queen spun round and darted to Maria's side, seizing her hand and saying something to her with rapid eagerness before running back to Thibaw who waited for her like a dog under orders.

Mattie Calogreedy put her plump little hand on Maria's arm and smiled knowingly up at her. 'Oh, Miss Beresford, you have been a success! The Queen tells you that your father must not be disappointed, that he must persevere, that the notion of free trade is only an idea so far. And when you come tomorrow, Miss Beresford, the Queen wishes you to bring your sketchbook.'

6

The colonel, waiting for Hubert in the Residency, was occupying his time in pondering. Before him on his desk lay a letter from the Chief Commissioner in Rangoon which had arrived on that morning's steamer, and which indicated that London and Calcutta had roused themselves sufficiently from their anxious contemplation of Afghanistan and South Africa to decide to close the Residency at Mandalay.

'It seems nothing can be gained by your remaining,' Aitchison had written, 'and you have endured enough indifference and humiliation. I have begged the Viceroy to reflect upon the indignity of your situation and at last he has listened. All British subjects in Mandalay should be informed of our withdrawal, naturally, although I suppose those who insist upon remaining might trust themselves in times of trouble to the ingenious Signor Andreino.'

Outside his study windows creamy frangipani and the blood-red blooms of a gold mohur tree were shuddering under thunderous raindrops. Two Indian servants, crossing the compound, had adopted the Burmese custom of wearing palm leaf hats a yard wide and they moved into the colonel's view like a couple of mobile umbrellas. Within a fortnight perhaps he would be gazing out, not at the unkempt and exasperating splendours of Mandalay, but at the ordered grounds – equally wet to be sure but ordered – of the British High Commission in Rangoon. Oh the wet! The ceaseless, exhausting monsoon season of Burma, rain and heat and rampant mildew from June to October, day in, day out. Turning back to his letters, Horace Browne promised himself a month in Simla.

His reply to Aitchison was written and sealed. The Residency would be left in the care of one of his junior assistants for a few weeks more, but he assured the Chief Commissioner that he and his staff should board a steamer for Rangoon within days. He agreed there was nothing for him to stay for. Thibaw seemed inclined to see anyone, everyone, and appeared unimpressed by a history of cordial Anglo-Burmese relations in the last twenty years. He had as yet ceded the royal monopolies to no-one, but Andreino had ferreted out the fact that he was in correspondence with the Czar of Russia and in any case the matter was not so much in his hands as in those of his Queen. If Supayalat went on in the way she seemed to be going, Colonel Browne doubted that even the Italian consul would be a match for her. That was what worried him. If Supayalat became obsessed with the notion that Burma was for the Burmese, that Ava could do without the

119

kalās, or at least, those *kalās* with whom her father-in-law had had such steady and mutually profitable relations . . .

Hubert was announced, as impeccable and unruffled as if he had never heard of either bullock carts or monsoons. Colonel Browne rose to greet him in profound embarrassment, sore with the knowledge he should never have encouraged him to come to Burma in the first place and also uncomfortable under the sharp consciousness that his future was now something of a liability as well as a responsibility. Hubert seated himself, folded his hands upon the top of his cane and waited with composure.

The colonel picked up the Chief Commissioner's letter as a talisman to give himself courage. 'Bad news, Beresford. At least, bad for you and not so good for me, though it's all that can be done in the circumstances. The Residency is to close down. I'm to go down to Rangoon with my staff and the sepoys as soon as possible, perhaps even tomorrow. I'm sure you'll understand why. Thibaw won't see us without our shoes off and of course the alternative is not to be thought of. I've always been grateful that you are a staunch supporter of me in this. So he doesn't see us and therefore we can't achieve anything. It's inevitable. I'm – I'm damned sorry Beresford, I feel badly about it all, bringing you up here and then dragging you back almost at once, but affairs of state, you know—'

Hubert, whose face had not moved throughout

120

this speech, merely said, 'And is the closure of the Residency permanent?'

The colonel brandished his letter. 'Good heavens, no! At least, I should hope not. But it's the only way to teach these people that they are not the centre of the universe, that they cannot treat us like this. They'll miss us, mark my words, they'll come to see what an influence for the good we were.'

'And you, Colonel? Shall you go to India?'

The colonel's discomfort increased visibly. 'I – I had thought so. A spell in the hills, you know – But you, Beresford. Shall you go back to – to Bombay?'

Hubert smiled. 'Indeed no. I shall remain here.'

'You can't,' the colonel said flatly.

'Oh?'

'It would be madness. It is extremely unsafe. You cannot remain here. The Residency will be almost under siege, I am instructed to leave no sepoys. The mood at the court is extremely dangerous.'

Carefully Hubert said, 'I do not think so.'

'You know nothing about it!' the colonel shouted. 'Don't be a dolt, Beresford. Your daughter playing the piano at court every morning means nothing, nothing at all. If the Queen decides to take any revenge for our going, you will be the first victims. Do you understand me? It is imperative, absolutely imperative that you and Miss Beresford accompany me to Rangoon.'

Hubert rose and came to stand close to the colonel.

'You underestimate my daughter's relationship with the Queen. We shall not be harmed—'

Horace Browne threw the Chief Commissioner's letter to the floor in exasperation.

'Listen, Beresford. Listen to me. I know you haven't much to go back to in Bombay – no don't flannel me, I know – but I got you into this hole and I – I'll find some way—'

'I am not returning to Bombay, Colonel. I am not prepared to discuss the matter beyond telling you that my daughter and I are in no danger, we are not afraid and we have plenty to keep us here. You need have no regrets about bringing us to Mandalay and no doubts about leaving us—'

An accented voice from the doorway said pleasantly, 'And who is leaving?'

Colonel Browne said angrily, 'I am, Andreino, and so should Beresford here be.'

Signor Andreino came forward into the room, bringing with him his usual aroma of hair oil and garlic. 'Calcutta says withdraw, Colonel?'

'Yes. Lord Lytton has taken his telescope off Kabul long enough to order us down to Rangoon.'

'All of you?'

The colonel shrugged. 'I shall leave one of the juniors to close things up. There's nothing to stay for. This absurd shoe question. Beresford and I have sat for hours waiting for an audience.'

'And Thibaw won't see you,' Andreino said

softly, his eyes on Hubert, 'because you will not remove your shoes. Will you, Signor Beresford?'

'Naturally not,' Hubert said blandly.

Andreino smiled. 'Precisely, signore. Naturally not. So now you must go down to Rangoon.'

The colonel groaned faintly and Hubert said, 'We shall stay. My daughter and I.'

'Look,' Andreino said, 'look, Beresford. You make the poor Colonel ill at such a suggestion. You should not torment him so.'

'I wish you would assist me in reassuring Colonel Browne that my daughter and I are not his responsibility. He is under no obligation to ensure our safe conduct out of Mandalay. It is our choice to stay.'

'It's lunacy!' the colonel shouted. 'All the British here will be in the gravest danger. You might as well put your head in a noose—'

'Nonsense,' Hubert said sharply. 'I want no more of this. I appreciate your concern, Colonel, but I do not need it. We are well established, Maria and I.'

Horace Browne passed his hands over his face. 'Very well. You must do as you wish. Of course, you realize that your salary from the government must cease if you remain—' Here Hubert gave a small dismissive wave of his hand. '—and that you will no longer be regarded as having any kind of official capacity. If you are in any kind of difficulty, I am sure Signor Andreino will do his best to assist you. In fact that is the Chief Commissioner's wish.'

Andreino said smiling, 'I shall be happy to oblige him. I will, of course—' He glanced quickly round the room and said in a lowered voice, 'I will, of course, be happy to be, shall we say, news collector for the government of India? Lord Lytton's ear in Mandalay?'

'You would be of inestimable value.'

Andreino spread his hands, displaying the grimy fingernails that offended Maria so. 'I think it would be mutually valuable. It will be only one more little duty to add to my other little duties. So, Colonel, you are to leave us. There was a rumour on the wind this morning, that is why I came with such dispatch. Shall you take the steamer on Thursday?'

'May I,' Colonel Browne said in one last desperate attempt, 'may I not even take Miss Beresford down to the safety of British Burma?'

Hubert shook his head. 'You may not, Colonel. Thank you for your solicitude. But she would not wish to go. Her life is much occupied here in the last few weeks.'

Andreino smiled to himself. 'So it is, Signor Beresford. So it is. Now, we must leave the good Colonel to sort out his papers and pack his trunks. You will accompany me?'

Only Hubert's bullock cart waited in the dripping lane. Andreino had clearly, from the state of his boots, adopted his usual habit, and walked.

'May I give you a lift?'

Andreino shook his head. 'Thank you, no. I have business down on the bund. I wish only to say one word to you, signore, one word of warning. I know you have been most – most assiduous in your attempts to see the King, properly shod as a representative of Her Majesty should always be. I also know that you have made some of those attempts in, shall we say, another guise, a guise that does not require such formality of dress. Do not walk away, Signor Beresford, do not ignore me. All I say to you is that you must be careful. I can guess why you remain here; I know what the prize is as well as you. I know also Bonvilain and Blount. There is little in this steaming spot I do not know. And I tell you, you must be careful.'

Hubert, seated now in his bullock cart, merely touched his stick to the brim of his hat. 'I will bid you good day, Signor Andreino.'

Smiling under his moustaches, Andreino bowed elaborately and then, when the cart had jolted round a curve in the lane, turned his steps towards the bund and the river.

Maria did not go down to the bund to bid the colonel farewell. The steamer's departure time would have conflicted with her preparations for her daily visit to the palace and in any case, she wished the colonel to feel himself snubbed. So Grace Prior, enveloped in her green rubber costume, found herself the only English person by the river.

Tom had wished to come, but the colonel, striding, booming into the mission the afternoon before, had said he wanted no ceremony. 'Life must go on, Prior, just as usual. I know you are occupied with the school in the mornings and I don't want lessons broken up for me. No, no, my dear fellow. I shall see you in Rangoon one of these days, who knows—'

Grace too was occupied with lessons in the morning, but they were sewing lessons – *only* sewing, she told herself – and therefore it was perfectly possible to put strips of white cotton into all those deft little dark hands and promise a great reward upon her return for the smallest hemstitching. She had then, guiltily, gone back to the mission to change out of the grey cotton she always wore at the school, into her pink, telling herself that it was not on Maria Beresford's account that she was changing – for Maria would surely wish to bid the colonel goodbye – but on Colonel Browne's.

She gazed dismally at her small blanched face in the spotted glass on her bedroom wall. Colonel Browne once said he liked me in pink, that it became me and I look terrible in grey, quite washed out, but it is practical and Maria doesn't have to do anything so practical so she can wear yellow silk and not worry all day if she wants to. Imagine rustling round the palace, talking to the Queen, a real royal queen covered in diamonds, even if she is a wicked murderess. And I'm sure Maria isn't frightened of her, not one bit, not like I should be. I should shake and tremble and not know what to say. There now. I've gone to all this trouble and put on my pink and I look awful in it because I am particularly pale today for some reason and I have mosquito bites on my nose and anyway I am going to cover it all up with my mackintosh which I know she despises—

Half an hour later, standing ankle deep in the pale yellow mud beside the Irrawaddy, Grace reflected that she had, in the event, put on her pink dress to no effect at all. Maria was not there, nor was Mr Beresford, nor Mr Blount, nor, to her mingled relief and disappointment, Monsieur Bonvilain. The only European besides herself was Signor Andreino, whose eyes were horribly bloodshot today and who had kissed her hand with a flourish that made her feel unaccountably silly. She stood for a long, long time it seemed, steaming inside her green rubber and watching while near-naked Burmese coolies carried all the bundles and boxes from the British Residency on board the steamer. Every so often, Colonel Browne's tam-o' shanter could be seen here or there on one of the steamer's three decks and his sepoys, white smiles of relief at leaving breaking their black Madrassee faces, stood lining the gangplank until the last piece of luggage had been carried aboard.

It wasn't only the colonel's going that made Grace miserable, though, goodness knows, it was a dreary enough spectacle in that never-ending rain, with the Irrawaddy the colour of milky coffee, streaked with long, evil-looking smears of scum. She knew perfectly well that both her father and the colonel had supposed her out of earshot the day before when Colonel Browne had confided his anxiety about the safety of the remaining British in Mandalay. She had said she was going down into the garden, but something had made her linger on the verandah and she had been well repaid for her dishonesty by what she heard.

It wasn't simply that what the colonel had said had frightened her. It had, of course. Who, she asked herself wretchedly in bed later, who really relishes the thought of dying at the hands of furious natives? And then it came to her that her father almost – yes, he almost did. He certainly didn't shrink from it, he'd said – and she could tell he was smiling from the warmth of his voice – he'd said, 'Colonel, you must remember that I am a *soldier* for Christ. A soldier.' That was what really dismayed her. Not that her father felt like that, but that she, Grace, *couldn't*. And neither could she tell him she couldn't. She was sure he believed she had his heart and stomach for Christ. Well, she did have the heart, she did, she *did*, but the courage, the physical courage, that was something else altogether.

And funnily enough, she thought Colonel Browne understood it. He had suggested, with a touching and awkward diffidence, that he should take her down to Rangoon and confide her to the care of Doctor Marks at the Anglican mission there until Tom could join her, and her heart had leaped at the thought and been outraged all at once. And her father had laughed gently and said, 'God bless you, Colonel, but there is no need of that. She is at one with me, my Gracie. You'd break her heart to take her.' Then the colonel had asked if he might ask her directly, and Tom had refused, smilingly, and Grace had suddenly felt that the colonel saw more than she thought, that he wasn't so bluff and straightforward as he seemed . . .

Now he was going away, taking with him this newly appreciated sympathy, and she was to stay in Mandalay, with her father, whom she loved with all her being, and the Beresfords, whom she feared, and all these odds and ends of people and they *all* had something in common, something she didn't have; they were all brave, properly, truly, physically brave. She was the only one who feared for her skin and the only one to bear the bitter shame of such cowardice, bitter because anyone who had grown up hand in hand with God as she had done was the last person to be so utterly, despicably weak.

Colonel Browne, standing in front of her and holding out his hands, 'My dear child! If you look so woebegone at my going, I shall be discouraged all the way to Rangoon. I can't express my delight at your coming, my dear. The only one! The only one to take the trouble.' He leaned forward, showering Grace with heavy drops from his tam-o' shanter, and said confidentially, 'It won't be too long before I see you in Rangoon, I think. The Queen may decide it all for us, you know. I can't see that a continuing mission school is quite in her line.'

'I – I couldn't leave Papa—'

'I know, my dear. No more you should. I only meant that he will probably come down to Rangoon soon himself.'

Grace's eyes were filling with tears. 'Will you write, Colonel Browne?'

He looked visibly startled. 'Will – I – why – yes, yes, of course, my dear. If you'd like me to. Not much of a hand at letter-writing—'

The steamer trumpeted in a melancholy way from the river. Colonel Browne took Grace's wet hands and squeezed them painfully.

'Goodbye then, my dear. God bless—'

She nodded, her throat swollen with tears. He stumped down the last few feet of the bund, turned to wave once more and then disappeared across the gangplank into the steamer. A small detachment of Burmese soldiers in their absurd tin hats were ordered nearer the water's edge, but made no further move and simply waited there, in slightly ragged formation, while the steamer churned its way into the deeper channel in the centre of the river.

'Miss Prior, you pleased our old friend,' Andreino said at Grace's elbow. He peered to see her face, observed that it was pinkily blotched with crying and insect bites, and put a firm hand on her arm.

'I need two favours from you, Signorina. First I should be very grateful for a ride in your horrible cart. And second I want your help, with a girl. A Burmese girl.'

Grace, mindful of what rumour said about Signor Andreino's domestic arrangements, shrank visibly. Her own little maid, recruited from the mission school as being too intellectually idle to benefit from instruction and therefore better practically employed, had told her in a delighted whisper, that Signor Andreino had at least two *bo-kadaw*, possibly three. Grace's Burmese was now sufficient for her to realize, with a sensation she took for shock, that *bo-kadaw* meant white man's wife . . .

Andreino laughed and gripped her elbow more firmly. 'Ah, you English misses! I will do nothing to offend you, Signorina, nothing at all. I wish only that you should see a girl who deserves a better fate than the one she has been reduced to in a cigar factory. She is a girl unlike the other native girls. All Burmese are intelligent, but she is particularly so, sympathetic. I wondered, Miss Prior, if perhaps there is a place for her in your household?'

Grace struggled to explain that the mission was in the first place always straitened for want of money and, in the second place, heavily exploited already by Burmese in whom Tom Prior genuinely thought he saw Christian possibilities.

'Come all the same,' Andreino said.

'I have been,' Grace said, a little desperately, longing now to get back to the safe familiarity of her sewing class. 'I am sure you mean the cigar

131

factory by the western gate. I have been. Hosannah Manook took me. She goes often to buy cigars for her father.'

'Then it will be no surprise to you,' Andreino said, steering her firmly through the Burmese gathered on the bund. 'You will know what to expect.'

Grace, with a flash of temper, pulled her arm free. 'No, Signor Andreino! I don't wish to go and I can't help you. Nor can I see why you should – should—'

'Take an interest in this particular girl? I am trying not to offend you, Signorina, but perhaps the truth is more important. She has – shall we say been misused by an acquaintance of mine?'

Grace blushed hotly beneath her hat-cover and bending her head muttered that she did not know Signor Andreino saw himself in the role of knight in shining armour. He laughed at this and then gave her a great deal of alarm and a fair amount of pleasure by picking her up in his arms and lifting her easily into the bullock cart.

'You are as light as a child!'

Grace, confused and excited, said nothing. Andreino climbed in after her and seated himself so close that the smell of garlic and coconut oil was almost overwhelming.

'Miss Prior, I see you are astute as well as feather-light. You want to know what advantage there would be to you in taking such a girl in. Is that not it? I will tell you, Signorina, I will explain. Colonel Browne is not wrong to think these dangerous times. It is well for us Europeans to take all the precautions we can, and one of the best precautions, Miss Prior, is to have Burmese who are in some way indebted and thus more likely to be loyal in our households. It would be wise for you to have in the mission an intelligent girl who would, as you say in English, keep her ear to the ground. I have found you just such a girl. I do you a favour and also one to the man I spoke of, the man of my acquaintance. He has given me some information I needed and it is now my turn to do him a little service. The girl has behaved with great dignity since – since she left his house, but her mother and sisters give him no peace. They say they are disgraced by his being a *kalā*, a foreigner. They will not take the girl back, she is an outcast. She has been put to the lowest work in the factory, she is almost a beggar. The man in question – Miss Prior, you do not ask me who he is?'

Grace turned her face away. 'No,' she said stonily.

'I will give you a clue,' Andreino said, enjoying himself hugely. 'I will tell you that mine are not the only moustaches you admire. I have undertaken to help the girl because my friend is not experienced enough in Burma to know what to do. And he is trying, Miss Prior, to behave like a gentleman but, of course, as you English know, we Europeans are not so skilled at it.' He paused. 'Will you try to help me?'

'I – I don't know.'

133

Andreino waited a moment and then he said softly. 'The girl is fifteen. Fifteen only.'

The cigar factory was a low brown wooden house in the usual matting-walled compound some hundred yards short of the moat and the western gate to the royal city. The house was used mainly as a shop, the biggest room being furnished with a few crude European armchairs upholstered in red velvet and the walls were lined with shelves stacked with cigars in neat bundles. Each bundle was wrapped in newspaper – Grace could make out the familiar columns of the *Rangoon Gazette* here and there – and bore a band of coloured paper to denote the quality of the cigars. There was a smell of dust and mould and the sweet pervasive vegetable smell of tobacco.

The proprietress, an implacable-faced Burmese woman in her fifties, dressed in a tamein of wine-coloured silk and smoking a green cheroot, came forward to fawn upon Andreino. He smiled, pointing out various packets he wished taken down and sent to his house, while Grace stood by him and felt both bewildered and discomfited.

'And now, Hnin Si,' Andreino said. 'We wish to see Hnin Si.'

The proprietress shrugged, her usual impenetrable expression blotting out the brief eagerness of the saleswoman. Stumbling in Andreino's wake, Grace followed him out of the dusty room and down into a muddy courtyard in which a few bedraggled hens pecked moodily. The courtyard was lined with open sheds upon whose tin roofs the overhanging trees dripped in a dull tattoo. Women crouched in the damp dimness all along the earth floor of the sheds, thin, bent women in filthy ragged cotton tameins. Grace, who had never penetrated beyond the shop before, was horrified to see how old some of them were, old and crooked and almost toothless.

At one end of the sheds great piles of yellow-brown tobacco leaves hung in hammocks suspended from the ceiling. What the women squatting below them were doing Grace could not imagine but the women close to her, the ones she could see, were spreading a smooth leaf on a little board before them, laying upon it a handful of leaves and then, using a metal spike for shaping which was withdrawn at the last moment, were rolling the leaf up into a smooth and symmetrical cigar. None of them looked up.

'This way,' Andreino said.

Grace followed him dumbly, picking her way between the crouching figures on the floor and the piles of tobacco.

'Hnin Si,' she heard Andreino say, 'I have brought the English *thakin-ma*.'

Beneath the hammocks of dried tobacco, four or five women were sorting leaves, pressing out smooth the big unblemished ones that would serve to wrap a cigar, and heaping up the pieces that would stuff it. They were even, if it were possible, older and more ragged than the women who rolled cigars, for the job of sorting was less skilled and therefore more poorly paid. But among the grizzled and wispy heads was one sleek black one, decked with flowers.

'Hnin Si,' Andreino said again.

The girl raised a face that was not exactly pretty, though so delicate and fine-skinned that it almost passed for such. Her eyes were too slanting, her nose too snub for beauty, but her skin had a faint pinkness along the cheekbones uncommon among the Burmese and the bones of her face were beautifully moulded. She wore a checked tamein of poor cotton whose hem was splashed with mud, her feet were filthy and her torn cotton jacket revealed collar bones like wings and arms like brown sticks.

'You see,' Andreino said to Grace in English, 'she needs help.'

Hnin Si, after an anxious glance at the proprietress, raised her thin brown hands to her forehead and shikoed to Grace on the earthen floor of the shed. Grace knelt at once beside her.

'Oh don't!' she cried in distress, 'don't do that! Please don't do that!'

'We will speak in French,' Andreino said. 'The proprietress does not understand it but, as you may imagine, Hnin Si has learned a little in the last months. And you, Miss Prior?'

'Schoolgirl French,' Grace said, getting to her feet and feeling that what little grasp she had of the situation was slipping from her fingers. The girl was pathetic, and had such a sweet face, but how was one to cope with the responsibility of such a human being, recommended by Signor Andreino and cast off by . . . by . . . It did not bear thinking of.

Hnin Si was saying softly, 'I would work. I do not fear work. It is the shame I fear. I do not fear foreigners.'

Andreino stooped and said something in almost unrecognizable French, of which Grace caught only her own name and the words 'Christian' and the Burmese word for priest, *poongyi*.

Hnin Si turned her slanting gaze upon Grace and repeated, 'I will work,' and the sudden look of childlike pleading that came into her face made Grace burst out, 'But how could he, how could he be so cruel, so wickedly cruel—'

Andreino shrugged.

'These things pass, signorina. You cannot expect miracles. He has moved on, chosen elsewhere. You know his new companion, Miss Prior. She escorts the elegant Miss Beresford to the palace each morning.'

Grace exclaimed, truly shocked. 'Mattie! Mattie Calogreedy!' She took a step backwards, away from the Italian with his operatic moustaches and gusts of garlic, away from the silently pleading figure on the mud floor of the shed. 'I must go, I must go home! Don't make me stay, don't ask me any more. I must go—'

Andreino reached out and took her arm. 'If you insist—'

'I do, I do! I am so sorry, so sorry for – for that

poor girl, truly I am, but I can't – I can't bear – Where is the way out? Where is the cart? You should not have told me, why did you—'

Briskly, Andreino propelled her across the courtyard and up the steps into the musty, cigar-lined room. In the lane outside, the bullock waited between the shafts and the four mission servants, without whom Grace was not allowed now to stir outside the compound, lounged against the wheels, a reassuring reminder of home. Without speaking, Andreino swung Grace into his arms as he had done before and set her in the cart, and when she glanced agitatedly at him, she was astounded to see that he was smiling.

'How can you smile? How can you? If you are laughing at me, you should at least have the courtesy to do so behind my back, but I hope you are not laughing at the – the situation this morning. I think – I think,' she cried out, gathering courage, 'I think your conduct is despicable, Signor Andreino! Despicable! You pretend friendship with the English and yet from what you have said to me this morning, you are plainly on very cordial terms with the French also. I see it – it is not only the Burmese we have to be suspicious of in Mandalay!'

And then she burst into tears. Andreino continued to smile and offered her a disgusting handkerchief she was too confused to reject. After a while, when her sobs had subsided, he leaned into the cart and said gently, 'Miss Prior, you are perfectly right. I do ride, as you say, two horses. I should ride three if I could. But you forget two things. One, I will ensure that the best horse wins. And two, I am an excellent horseman.'

He shouted to the driver and the cart lurched forward among the ruts away from the western gate. Grace did not look back but sat and stared stiffly before her, trying to keep her mind as blank as possible. When they were almost in the *kalā* town, a bullock cart came splashing past at a great rate, heading for the royal city. As it lumbered by, the tall graceful figure in the back, an unmistakable figure in yellow silk with pearls in her ears, raised a single gloved hand in brief salute to Grace, but the person next to her, a plump laughing little person in pink muslin, waved and blew kisses in a way Grace found utterly repugnant.

It was almost two weeks before Grace saw Maria again. During those two weeks, since the lanes in the *kalā* town were considered dangerous and her going out was discouraged, she immersed herself in the school in the daylight hours and prayed long and desperately in the black clammy nights for peace of mind. At the end of the first week of September, she arrived back at the mission at teatime one day to find her father already there, in company with Signor Andreino. She attempted to smile and murmur some excuse and slip past them to her room, but her father caught her sleeve.

'My dear Gracie, you must not run away, you must listen. What Signor Andreino has to say most nearly concerns yourself.'

Grace could not look at Andreino. She simply stood silently by her father and heard the Italian say, 'The British Ambassador in Kabul, Sir Louis Cavagnari, has been assassinated. The Viceroy in Calcutta has decreed that no unnecessary risk shall be taken with British lives further and that the Residency and mission in Mandalay are to close forthwith. Miss Prior, you are to go, for your own protection, by the next mail steamer to Rangoon. All the British colony will go, even the Chinese and the Indians.'

Grace clutched her father.

'But Papa! You must come! I can't go al – I mean to say, you must not stay if the danger will be worse—'

Tom Prior's face wore the expression of crusading zeal she had come to dread.

'Dearest child, of course I will come. In time. But I cannot let all our precious souls slip back. God is not accountable to Lord Lytton and in His service no more am I. You shall go down to Rangoon and be the invaluable handmaiden to Doctor Marks that you have always been to me. The nuns at the Convent of the Good Shepherd will take you in. And when things are quieter again, back you shall come.'

Andreino said, smiling beneath his moustaches, 'You must not weep on me again, Signorina. Come, dry your eyes. I have a task for

140

you, Miss Prior, a task I think you will enjoy. The news of Afghanistan reached me but an hour since and Miss Beresford and her excellent father are still in ignorance. Will you go to her and tell her for me and then you may both make your preparations for the journey to Rangoon together? My own servants will escort you. You will have nothing to fear.'

So Grace, still in her regrettable grey cotton schoolroom gown, her feelings in a perfect turmoil, found herself being ushered into Maria's drawing room and confronting not only Maria, resplendent in rose pink, but the terrifying Mr Blount. He reminded Grace of nothing so much as the ferret that the school gardener in Brighton had kept to put down drains after the rats.

Grace sat down unhappily, accepted tea and cake she had no appetite for and waited an interminable ten minutes – during which time Maria and Mr Blount talked with perfect ease and a good deal of laughter across her before an opportunity arose for her to speak. At last Maria turned and observed that as Grace had very evidently run straight from her little pupils, she must have some quite urgent errand. Grace stammered a little, forgot the name of Afghanistan's capital, confused the name of the luckless ambassador and had, scarlet with shame, to begin her story twice over before she could tell it coherently.

When she had finished, Mr Blount and Maria exchanged glances.

'Signor Andreino,' Grace added diffidently, 'and – and my father, they say we must go down to Rangoon. At once. They think we should take the next steamer! There is a mail steamer waiting up river a little, ready to take all the British colony to safety. They think everything will become dreadfully dangerous here.'

Maria said to Mr Blount, 'They do?' and laughed. Then she turned to Grace and said, 'Miss Prior, I wish you godspeed upon your travels. However, I shall not be joining you. I am sure you will appreciate that my position now with the Queen means that I have nothing to fear here, nothing that is, one-hundredth part as unpleasant as the dreadful tedium of Rangoon. And in any case, my father and I – and Mr Blount – are much needed here now. Much needed. I am sure you have heard that the Queen gave birth to a son but a few days ago. I believe I am the only European to have seen the child. But that is not all.' She paused and then added in a voice of undisguised triumph, 'My father – and Mr Blount – cannot possibly leave Mandalay. Queen Supayalat has been gracious enough to award them the concession to work the ruby mines at Minhla. She gave me the news today.'

Grace rose unsteadily to her feet. 'Yes, yes, of course, I quite understand. I hope – I hope you will be very – very successful. I will say goodbye then, Miss Beresford, that is, until things are calmer, until I come back—'

When the door had closed behind her, even as

she hurried through the tiny hall, she could hear them laughing together in the drawing room and it seemed to her that she had never heard any sound so triumphant, so satisfied, so entirely self-congratulatory.

PART TWO

7

On a brilliant October morning in 1884, Archie Tennant, aboard the SS *Nimrod*, entered the mouths of the Irrawaddy. He had been at sea for a total of thirty-seven days since leaving Liverpool, not counting the week he had spent in Bombay at the offices of the Bombay-Burmah Trading Corporation at number 1 Nesbit Road, a mere three doors away from the now departed Indian headquarters of Tennant Phillipson.

He had been received cordially by a Mr Richardson, the senior representative of the corporation in India, and had been informed that his salary would be one hundred and fifty rupees to begin with and that he would be provided with a house, servants, transport and most importantly, water, while in Upper Burma. Mr Richardson had then shown him into a small panelled room, an identical copy of the room in which he had been interviewed in Austin Friars the previous summer, except for the stifling heat, and had left him with a high sloping desk, a clerk's stool and copies of the corporation's annual report to divert himself with.

He had started by taking off his jacket,

waistcoat and cravat. Five years had hardened the lines of his face to good advantage, but also deposited extra girth, which he detested but seemed unable to control, beneath that same waistcoat. Old Phillipson had warned him ceaselessly about the dangers of obesity until Archie grew to dread the powerful allure of the excellent food on his patron's table. He hoped that the East would simply, with its heat, melt him back to the size he had been when at Oxford and hunting four days a week.

The corporation's reports, satisfactory though they were to the directors, were not what Archie wanted of his week in Bombay. He learned painfully and with cavernous yawns that the present year had been a good one even though the rains in Upper Burma had not been sufficient to float down the Rangoon all the teak that had been cut in the Ningyan forests to the south-east of Mandalay. Despite this drawback, the directors could report an overall profit of more than five thousand rupees and reserves of above forty thousand. The corporation, Archie read with slightly more interest, possessed five thousand rupees worth of elephants and sixty-four thousand rupees worth of unsold timber. A twenty-five per cent dividend had been paid to all shareholders, the capital stood at – Archie yawned widely enough to crack his jaw and closed his eyes once or twice in an attempt to force his wits to cohere and concentrate, but they were disobliging. He put his forehead down upon the report balanced in front of him and felt his skin adhere damply to the paper. Figures in this temperature were intolerable; everything was a struggle, a battle against mental sloth. The only thing he really wanted to do was sleep and sleep or perhaps, he thought drowsily, feeling that there was something a little ignoble in wishing only for slumber, to try his hand at polo before the week was up—

The door opened and Archie peeled his face away from the annual report. An Indian clerk, beneath a pile of ledgers large enough to crush him, padded softly to Archie's side.

'Mr Richardson says you will be needing these now, Mr Tennant. These are the detailed accounts in which you will be seeing quite clearly the pattern of the annual finances, the debts and liabilities, the reserves, the needs for insurance, particularly against fire, the progress in ship building, the losses sustained by mortality among the elephants, the rise in dividends paid upon both shares in the original and in the second issue—'

'Go away.'

'Mr Tennant?'

'Go away. And take every scrap of paper in the room with you.'

A pause.

'But Mr Richardson is wishing—'

'And I am *not* wishing.'

Another pause.

'What shall I be saying to Mr Richardson?'

149

'That I am too hot, too weary and too stupid to take any of this in. And that I should like to play polo.'

'Hot, weary, stupid, polo—'

'Yes! Yes, all those! Now go away.'

Later that day, dining with Mr Richardson off mulligatawny soup and innumerable tough little roasted fowls, Archie found himself sitting next to a blandly good-looking young man in uniform.

'Digby Shaw,' the young man said, shaking red pepper into soup which had already filled Archie's eyes with scalding tears. 'Gather you're off to Burma. Hellish hot. Know my brother?'

Archie closed his eyes and swallowed one more spoonful of soup as if it were medicine. 'No. I'm afraid I don't. Should I?'

'No reason really, except that when the lid blows off in Mandalay, Murray will be in the thick of it. He's with the Hampshires and they are stationed in the Madras Residency so, when the call comes, they will be one of the closest regiments to Burma and the first to go and teach those—'

'I'm afraid I don't understand you at all.'

Digby Shaw looked up from his soup to give Archie's civilian clothes a pitying glance.

'No. Well, I suppose you wouldn't, fresh out from England . . .' He sighed, took a huge swallow of wine and said with the patience of someone speaking to the very simple, 'There is going to be trouble in Burma. Over the teak. Your outfit, you know. And the King is rotten through and through and drinks like a fish. He's quite willing to sell anything and everything to the highest bidder. If he tries any funny business with us, we'll send the redcoats in. And my brother Murray will be in the front line. White's his commanding officer. Know him?'

'Of course not,' Archie said irritably. 'How could I? I was a lawyer in London until two months ago, and on a ship until the day before yesterday.'

'I've an uncle who's a judge,' young Shaw said unperturbed. 'Sir Barnet Shaw. Know him?'

'Yes,' Archie said, 'I do.'

Young Shaw lost interest at once and fell upon the wizened little fowl that had been placed before him with an enthusiasm Archie found incomprehensible. The huge dusty fringe of the punkah swung relentlessly back and forth over the table, creating an unpleasant draught about his head and ears and not getting to the heart of the matter at all. A boiling yellow-brown sauce had been spooned over the poor little burnt bird on his plate and an array of chutneys, livid yellow, olive green, burnt sienna and shining brown was being held out for his choice. He waved them away. The only thing on that table laden with steaming dishes of terrifyingly coloured food that Archie could feel any affection for was a lonely pineapple in a silver dish shaped like a vine leaf.

Digby Shaw, having discovered that his other

neighbour ran a shipping business out of Bombay and knew nobody of interest either, swung back to Archie and said, 'Pig sticking?'

'Hardly,' Archie said, 'in England. But I'd love to have a try at polo. Do you play?'

'Rather! Most evenings except when it's too damned hot to do anything but die. Made up a team with Bruce Gardiner and his brother and Miles Lumsden. Know them?'

Archie ignored him. 'Could you help me, then? I know it's an awful lot to ask to borrow a pony but I can't tell you how grateful I'd be.'

'Absolutely,' young Shaw said, waving a hand airily. 'Be pleased to help,' and promptly forgot all about it.

The only advantage of that week in Bombay, Archie thought, boarding the *Nimrod* in relief, was that if he were not actually any thinner, he was certainly no fatter. He had spent every day at Nesbit Road and every evening in company with tea brokers, rice shippers and silk merchants. The notion of playing polo died as it was born and Archie steamed away into the Indian Ocean with not a single glance of affectionate regret behind him.

The mood of slight despair lasted him into the Bay of Bengal. There were a number of English and German merchants aboard the *Nimrod*, but no one of his own age or tastes, and in the intervals between meals he sat mostly alone on deck, trying to accustom himself by force to the sunshine and to think of old Phillipson with all the unstinted gratitude he knew was due him. Old Phillipson had, indeed, been better than his word. Archie had come down from Oxford in the summer of 1881 with a perfectly respectable second and, thanks to his patron's enormous generosity in the matter of horseflesh, with two splendid hunting seasons behind him.

He fully expected to be sent straight to Austin Friars, and thence, equally straight to the Far East, but old Phillipson, while beating him soundly at billiards, said that he had changed his mind.

'Or shall we say, postponed it a while. Don't want all this law to go to waste, no indeed. You eat your dinners my boy, and get called to the Bar and then we'll see about the East. And I've a cousin in Northamptonshire who'll let you have his lodge to use for hunting. How old are you? Twenty-one? Let us say in three years, three years from now.'

They had been wonderful years to Archie. He found the law a very different matter in practice and hunting in the Midlands a glorious improvement on the southern country. Old Phillipson gave him a gig and a splendidly matched pair of bays and he pursued a happy triangle around London, Northamptonshire and Riverdene. Once a year he went home to Suffolk for his mother's birthday and after a day or so of being ignored or gazed at in virulent reproach, left again hastily.

'You should go more,' old Phillipson said. 'Once a year and a jeweller's box ain't enough. Not that I like to spare you, mind you—'

Frederick had survived quite comfortably from the dissolution of the company. What he did precisely Archie could not tell and refused to find out, but it involved a good deal of time in Newmarket and the entire refurbishment of the stables at Hasham. He brought his dubious friends home with him, who made great inroads upon the excellent port his father had left for both his sons, and Mrs Tennant, who now had real cause for distress, wept almost all the time so that the atmosphere about her was always damp like the air above a marsh. Archie did not know what to do about her and could not bear the situation in general, so he stayed away.

When his three years were up he went obediently to Wallace Brothers. He had half expected to be greeted as rather a catch by them, but was treated in a brisk and businesslike manner, informed that he should be posted to up-country Burma and that he should board the SS *Nimrod* from Liverpool in the second week of September. He had only agreed to pause in Bombay to please old Phillipson, because he might very well have been briefed about his duties in Rangoon, but old Phillipson wanted to know at first hand how Bombay did without him. Archie had attempted, not at all successfully, to write a letter that was both truthful and which said Bombay was splendid and that he was sure he should find absolute satisfaction as a recruit for the Bombay-Burmah. He felt, steaming down the Indian coastline in the shimmering heat, that Bombay was as exciting as an English suburb peopled with clerks and that the only thing that had ever given him absolute satisfaction in his life was to come first of the field over a particularly difficult fence and gain an appreciative nod from the master of the Pytchley.

Subtly, as Burma drew nearer, his reluctance began to disperse. He could not tell why, except that he was approaching a country of which only half was regimented by British bureaucracy and that half not the one he was destined for. It was difficult to visualize precisely how life would go on in a teak forest, with himself the only white man for miles and miles and his companions Burmese foresters and elephants. He could not, come to think of it, visualize Burma at all. People in Bombay had said, slightly disparagingly, that it was where the Orient began, rather as if civilization as known to the British, and therefore the only kind worth having, stopped abruptly at India. And then all of a sudden, after days of glittering sea and the thudding of the engines and the remorseless boredom of confined life on board, Burma had come and was slipping past the *Nimrod*, and the blue waters of the Bay of Bengal were changed to the milky-greenish ones of a great river.

The mouths of the Irrawaddy were many, he discovered, and the low-lying fingers of land which divided them were emerald green with young rice. Here and there among the paddies rose the gold-tipped white spires of pagodas and along the raised paths of beaten earth that crossed the rice fields plodded bullocks in wooden yokes drawing flat carts, small Burmese wrapped in checked cotton and occasionally the saffron-draped form of a priest.

Archie's spirits rose as the steamer churned onwards through the increasingly coffee-coloured river waters. Beside him on the taffrail, the Englishmen and Germans began to grumble about the climate, the awful Burmese climate that soaked you and roasted you and wrung you out entirely. Archie, his eyes smarting from the glare of the green and white and gold and the sun bouncing blindingly off the water, felt abruptly that none of that mattered, that his discomfort was nothing beside the sudden buoyancy that filled him, lifted him up with elation and expectation, making him peer ahead for his first glimpse of Rangoon.

The first glimpse did not fail him either. Up the pale brown breadth of the river they steamed to a shore lined with trees and low white buildings. Far away to left and right, Archie could see the bulk of godowns and shipbuilding yards, but ahead it was only delightful, a green and white contrast to the choking urbanity of Bombay, crowned with something that made Archie clutch his neighbour's arm in amazement. Above the city, some way to the north, a glittering gold pinnacle sprang hundreds of feet into the hot blue sky like some divine finger.

'The Shway Dagon,' Archie's neighbour said. 'Over two thousand years old.'

'Yes,' Archie said, 'yes.'

The pinnacle had a smooth dome-shaped base out of which it rose with the grace of a swan's neck. Its goldenness was a miracle, all at once blazing and glowing, breaking out at the tip into a shower of little bells they were too far away to hear.

Archie's neighbour removed his sleeve from Archie's grasp. 'It's four miles away, but a clear day like this makes it seem closer. It's a perfect forest of pagodas up there, all round the base, there must be over fifty. If you ask me, it's better than anything they've got in Siam but then it's all they *have* got. First time?'

'Yes,' Archie said from far away, 'first time.'

'Rangoon?'

Archie shook his head, his eyes still fastened on the soaring golden spectacle to the north. 'No. To Mandalay. In a day or two.'

The man looked at him admiringly. 'That so? Well, well. You are in luck though. Best week of all the year to be in Rangoon. It's the autumn meeting. Rangoon races, you know.'

Archie's gaze left the Shway Dagon for a moment. 'Local races?'

'Some local riders, a few boys from Rangoon, always some Bengalis from Calcutta. But mostly Englishmen. You a horseman?'

'Yes.'

His neighbour surveyed his bulk. 'They're only ponies, you know.'

Archie sighed. 'I don't suppose a newcomer could ride in any case.'

'Why not? If he's good enough. Race secretary is a great friend of mine. Would you like me to have a word?'

Archie, full of the frustration of his dashed hopes over polo and his eagerness to seize life in Burma with both hands, said with fervour, 'I'd be so grateful, you cannot imagine—'

'Who are you joining?'

'The Bombay-Burmah.'

'Ah,' the man said, 'a teak boy. Look. Here's my card. Got anywhere to stay? Good. Now come round to that address the day after tomorrow, after dinner, and I'll take you to the assembly rooms. That's where they have the lottery the day before the big race, and we'll see what can be done.'

Archie indicated the card. 'I'm an Archibald, too. You are very kind, Mr MacGregor.'

'But you're no Scot?'

'By family, not by birth.'

The steamer slid competently into her berth by the dockside. Down below on the wooden quay was a solid mass of Burmese, their gleaming black hair coiled in top knots, almost all of them, even the children, Archie noticed with surprise, smoking green cheroots.

'Every man jack of them,' Archibald MacGregor

said, 'puffing like trains, day in, day out. There, look down there, the man in light grey, that's your man in Rangoon, the Bombay-Burmah fellow. Come to meet you. That's decent, isn't it, young man? Well, here we are, and although I can think of places I'd rather be, one of them certainly isn't Aberdeen. I'll be seeing you then. Day after tomorrow.' He paused and put out a freckled hand to shake Archie's. 'Welcome to Burma, young man.'

8

The atmosphere in the assembly rooms was like a steam bath. Archie, sweating freely in evening dress, joined a crowd of civilians dressed likewise, officers in mess dress and a vast number of Chinese, Burmese and Indians who were comfortably and intelligently wrapped in loose lengths of cotton. Among the civilians Archie, as he pushed behind Archibald MacGregor's back through the crowd, heard Greek spoken as well as German and English and he felt his face being minutely examined from all sides as a newcomer about whom nothing was known today, but everything doubtless would be tomorrow.

The race secretary, a small spare man with the wiry look of an ex-jockey, was standing below the stage at one end of the room beside a table which bore a thick coating of dust and the lottery box. He held a large yellow handkerchief in one hand and a wooden hammer in the other and the sweat was gleaming on his forehead just as Archie could feel it shining on his own. MacGregor made introductions and Archie shook hands damply.

The secretary eyed him critically. 'I've found

you a mount. Not up to much but MacGregor here said you'd need a weight carrier. We've three classes of horse here, Indian Arabs and country breds, pure Burmans and half-breeds. I've got you a half-breed. Sluggish fellow, but you might get something out of him. Give you a ride in any case.'

'I'm awfully grateful, sir—'

The secretary waved his hammer and handkerchief. 'Think nothing of it. Only too pleased to have boys from home riding. These local johnnies ride like the very devil. It'll amuse you. Point-to-point, do you?'

'Yes.'

'You'll stand a fair chance then. Look, I have to start, nearly nine thirty. Infernal hot tonight. I don't advise betting myself, but if you must, stick to your own kind. The Chinese are very devils, gambling is like mother's milk to them—'

MacGregor drew Archie to the side of the room where a group of young officers were eyeing him speculatively. 'Gentlemen, a rival,' MacGregor said.

One of them, his shoulders to the wall, said, 'What have you drawn?'

'Jack Tar.'

'Wish you luck. Ugly beast.'

'To look at or by temperament?'

'Both, I'm afraid.'

The hammer crashed for silence. When the voices fell, the mosquitoes could be heard plainly wheeling and droning in the thick, hot air. One landed on Archie's wrist and before he dashed it off, he observed that it was as large as a wasp and speckled in dun and black.

'Who'll bid for The Parson?' the secretary was saying, his hammer poised. 'Great pony. Winner of – I don't know how many—'

The Chinese and Burmans on the floor had stopped their indolent squatting and smoking and had crowded to the front. The secretary fixed his fierce blue eyes on a huge stout Burmese like a swollen brown fruit, wrapped in a paso of pink silk.

'Wake up, Maung Hpo! Ain't you listening? Now, a hundred rupees at a time. Bid up now. Who'll start me off? Fifty rupees for The Parson, sixty, seventy, eighty – one hundred. One hundred to Ah Sin. One hundred and fifty? And fifty, Maung Hpo. Come on, gentlemen, bid up, bid up. Fine pony. Don't keep me here all night—'

'Worth six hundred,' one of the officers near Archie said. 'Rode him in the Grand National here myself last year. Slow starter but stays like anything.'

'If you have the winning horse,' Archie said, 'what might you win from the lottery?'

The officer shrugged. 'Three thousand, perhaps.'

'Three *thousand*!'

'Ah, but if your horse loses, you must pay out the lottery and the man with the losing ticket on your horse. You see, they all buy lottery tickets to get a horse in the race. There'll be seventeen runners tomorrow, therefore seventeen lottery tickets out of perhaps, twenty thousand applicants for those seventeen tickets. They gamble like fury here, even the women. Jack Tar is owned by a woman.'

Archie took his eyes off the flailing yellow handkerchief.

'A woman?'

The officer grinned. 'A little Jill Burman. There's a number of women owners. There are women in everything in Burma. You'll see.'

The following day seemed, if it were possible, even hotter than the one before. Archie lay for hours in a large tin tub while a bearer poured can after can of cold water carefully over his shoulders and he waited with each canful to see steam rising as the water hit his burning skin. The tub stood in a small stone cell, almost windowless but for a square cut high in one wall, adjoining the bedroom in which he had battled with mosquitoes his first two nights in Rangoon. His host, the corporation's representative in Lower Burma, had been meticulous in describing the precise operation of the mosquito net, but Archie, covered in agonizingly itching bumps, was convinced that the mosquitoes crawled into his bed in the daylight and lay in wait there, licking their lips, until both they and their victim were safely tucked in together at night.

He was, despite sleeplessness, highly elated

both by Rangoon and by the prospect of steeplechasing. He had spent two happy days ambling among the corporation's godowns and admiring the seemingly endless stores of long, dark teak logs that lay there in the dusty, timber-scented gloom. He had seen the first consignment of logs lying in the river after being floated down from the northern forests after the rains and had watched the nimble Burmese skipping from log to log with their spiked implements, deftly keeping this vast and unwieldy flotilla in unified movement. He had also spent a sunset hour at the Shway Dagon and had felt himself ready to faint at the splendour of it. There had been moments in Oxford, summer moments when the setting sun lay golden on Christ Church meadows or lit up the spires and bell towers clustering round Radcliffe Square, when he had felt his soul filled with a sweet contentment. But that was gentle soothing stuff. This soaring stupa, at once barbaric in its magnificence of gold and size and civilized beyond anything in its grace, almost prostrated him with a mixture of awe and rapture. He had stood at the base and flung his head back to the heavens and gazed and gazed until his throat ached and his eyes were dazzled.

The bearer, Ah Chun, stepped back and said, 'Dressing, *thakin*.'

Archie shut his eyes and slid beneath the water, blowing bubbles like a hippopotamus. When he surfaced, Ah Chun was smiling, showing teeth blood-red from betel juice. He was from Mandalay, recruited there by some mysterious Italian who seemed to combine being both Italian consul and agent for the corporation, and he was anxious to get Archie, his *thakin*, back to territory he knew. He held out a vast rough towel and waited for Archie to heave his bulk out of the tub and spray the air and floor with flying drops of water.

'*Thakin* will be winning.'

'I doubt it,' Archie said, succumbing to the pleasure of being rubbed dry by other hands than his own. 'I'm overweight and out of practice.'

'In Mandalay, no racing.'

Fresh sweat was beginning to run down him with the water drops. Ah Chun knotted the towel deftly round Archie's waist and stood back for him to pass into the bedroom. The silks of his owner lay upon the bed, a thoroughly Burmese combination of pink and lime-green.

'I shall look like a sherbet.'

The breeches he had not worn since England felt pleasurably loose at the waist but the light-weight borrowed boots were, whatever the number stamped on the sole, too small.

'Must bear, *thakin*,' Ah Chun said from knee level, pulling and tugging. Even with such exertion his even brown skin remained smooth and dry. He was a Shan, he had told Archie, born in the blue mountains to the east of Mandalay and he had lifted his high cheekboned, slant-eyed Chinese face to Archie to prove it. Shan food was the best in Burma, he said, delicate and delicious, smoked duck in ginger, spiced chicken cooked with half-raw sprigs of cauliflower and watercress, pure white rice, slightly sticky, better than any rice, even the rice of the Rangoon delta.

'Winning,' he said now firmly to Archie, surveying his pink and green quartered master.

'Have you money on me?'

Ah Chun shrugged.

'Not much, I hope,' Archie said. 'You'll surely lose it.'

'My *thakin* win, I am much respected.'

Archie grinned at him. 'Your *thakin* win, I am much surprised.'

Down in the drawing room furnished with oak from England and brass from Benares, two people were waiting in the gloom caused by the drawn-down shades. Wates, the representative of the corporation, stood by the unnecessary fireplace and jingled coins in his pockets, and the nearest chair, a giant affair with wings upholstered in burgundy leather, completely dominated a small young woman in white who sat unhappily on its extreme edge.

'Ah,' Wates said, 'Ah. Archie. Dressed for the fray, I see. This is Miss Prior. Miss Grace Prior.'

Archie stooped and held out his hand, smiling. Grace forgot to be taken aback by his size or his clothes and smiled back at him rapturously. She was sure she had never seen so large a young man, nor one with so peculiarly sweet a smile.

'Are you coming to watch me make a fool of myself, Miss Prior?'

'She is, indeed, Archie. And then she needs a favour in return.'

Archie and Grace gazed at each other in embarrassment.

'Of – of course—' both said together.

'Fact is,' Wates said, taking his hands out of his pockets, 'fact is, Archie, Miss Prior needs an escort up the river to Mandalay. Her father is – is—'

'My father,' Grace said with difficulty, wishing suddenly and to her horror, that Tom were not what he was, 'my father is the Anglican missionary in Mandalay. He has been there four years. He sent me down here when the British Residency closed in Mandalay in seventy-nine. But I must go back to him. I must.'

'Is he ill?' Archie asked helpfully.

'Oh no! Not that kind of need, Mr Tennant. He needs me as – as a helpmeet you see. The nuns have been so kind to me here but I want to go back. I loved Mandalay and there doesn't seem to be any danger any more. It was just the journey, you see. I mean, the steamers are perfectly safe and the captains are such kind fatherly men, but Papa felt, I mean, I wasn't sure—'

Archie said, smiling, 'I think the escorting will be the other way about, Miss Prior. I'm a babe unborn in Burma. It will be wonderful for me to have a guide.'

In order to express her gratitude at this

gallantry better, Grace rose eagerly from her chair and Archie found that her head barely reached his shoulder. She was wearing some extraordinary garment, goodness knows, he had little opinion and no knowledge of women's clothes, but this strange draped affair reminded him strongly of the choristers in Christ Church Cathedral and gave no indication at all of the outlines underneath. Looking amiably down at her while she thanked him breathlessly for his kindness, he thought that perhaps missionary's daughters *had* no outlines out of sheer godliness, and even if they had, one certainly should not be thinking of them.

She was quite pretty really, in a pale and unspectacular way. Her wide, light eyes, turned with childish warmth up to him, were fringed with soft, brown lashes that matched her hair; her nose was small and straight; her teeth even. But she was a watercolour girl, a faint and delicately tinted thing, and Archie had the sensation that if he stretched out his lime-green right arm and laid his hand upon her head, he could crumple her up as easily as if she were made of paper.

'Walked the course, have you?' Wates said, tiring of Grace's effusiveness.

'Early this morning. It doesn't look too alarming except I don't much like the look of the stone wall at the fourth and of course the ground is like iron.'

'I think it's so awfully brave of you, Mr Tennant. I do hope—'

'You shouldn't have much trouble,' Wates said. 'At least you know what you are doing. You will find three or four professionals from Calcutta but the others are either local boys from Rangoon or chaps who've done no more than follow the Rangoon beagles. Of course, the soldiers think they can do it backwards—'

'They probably can.'

'Are you nervous, Mr Tennant? I am awfully nervous for you. I wasn't before we met, but you have been so kind that I, that I—'

Wates looked at his watch. 'We should be going.'

Grace picked up her parasol and moved ahead of them into the hallway which was furnished with stuffed heads and oak chests just as it might have been in Perthshire. Behind her, Wates said in a low voice, 'Nice little thing. Hope the chattering won't be a burden. It's a real kindness, Archie. Andreino asked me that the next recruit I sent up, you know—'

Archie nodded. 'No trouble at all.'

In the hall, Grace was counting. There was today, and the races, and then tomorrow and then the next day the steamer would leave and she would have at least eight days with him, eight or maybe nine or even ten if, by great good luck, the steamer got stuck on a mudbank, and she would be able to tell him so much, all she knew about Burma, maybe even the language. Including today, there would be ten days at least. Ten days of being very happy. She turned as

Archie and Wates came out to join her.

'Oh, Mr Tennant, I do hope you will be careful!'

Jack Tar had a short neck, small eyes and ears, and feet like soup plates. He glanced contemptuously at Archie and curled his lip, showing huge yellow teeth. Then he laid his ears back and braced his powerful shoulders as if prepared to resist any attempt to mount him.

Archie said to the grinning syce at his head, 'Hold his head up. *Up*. As high as you can.'

Jack Tar's sneer vanished as he felt Archie's weight and his expression became startled for a moment and then sullenly resigned.

Archie leaned down. 'The whip.'

The syce handed it up, still grinning.

'I'm going to ride longer,' Archie said, pulling up the saddle flap. 'I have to, there's too much of me to ride as short as they all are—'

Around him several dark little Indians and Burmans crouched on their ponies. The officers of last night were mounting in a leisurely manner amid a good deal of laughter and chaffing from fellow officers who had gathered round to make a crowd. The heat was terrific and the earth under Jack Tar's great hooves was baked as hard as a rock. Behind Archie rose the skeleton of what would be the grandstand, a distinctly oriental-looking structure in teak, with wide verandahs and up-winging roofs. The space of grass between this and the white-painted rails that edged the flat course was entirely jammed with people, thousands upon thousands of people, mostly Burmese in their bright silks and cottons, the air above them quivering and slightly blue from the smoke of innumerable green cigars.

Archie's owner had been pointed out to him. If he won, they would meet; if not, not. She was small and perfectly finished, like some little piece of enamel work, and there were diamonds blazing away around her throat and in the black tower of her hair. Her husband, gross with prosperity, trod softly behind her, his small eyes bright with intelligence in the smooth yellow moon of his face. Archie watched them for some time. She so small and contained and cylindrical, he so vast and sleek, like a great swollen yellow candle, how did they ever—

'Starter's orders, Mr Tennant.'

The starter was flustered. All the horses were milling and wheeling about him and he shook his flag at them as if it were an angry fist.

'In line, gentlemen, in line, if you please.'

Jack Tar felt wooden and reluctant in Archie's hands. He planted his hooves firmly as if setting himself against Archie's weight and then dropped his ugly head dispiritedly.

'In line, damn you, get in line!'

A local boy, frail and brown in blue and scarlet silks, jostled clumsily into Archie. Jack Tar affected not to notice and hung his head still farther. The starter's flag went up. Archie pulled at Jack Tar's head, but the horse appeared to ignore him, merely shifting the bit to a tougher and more comfortable place in his mouth.

The flag went down and Jack Tar leaped forward almost taking Archie's breath with him. The pace was tremendous immediately, accentuated by the hard ground which made each drumming stride shudder and jar. Around Archie, pressed close, several native boys clung to their ponies, not riding, he could see, but simply hanging on limpet-like, their slight bodies arched over their mounts' necks. The first fence, a hurdle, seemed to flash by with Jack Tar hardly altering his stride, then came a nasty double, flanked by ditches, and Jack Tar pecked on landing, forcing Archie to collect him and his own scattered wits at once.

The third fence came wheeling up, a low mud wall with a ditch on take off, then the three-foot stone wall which Jack Tar took with surprising ease, only grunting as he landed, and then the course swept round and it was the water jump by the grandstand and all those little butterfly ladies and a blur of brilliant colours. Ahead of Archie, The Parson, a bay, and a lean chestnut were going with comfortable competence. A quick glance over his shoulder told him that the water jump had checked a large part of the field, although a couple of good-looking little Arabs he had admired in the paddock were gaining ground on him. Jack Tar's ears were flat back and it felt to Archie as if he had the bit clamped between his teeth.

At the sixth, an in-and-out about ten paces

apart, he stumbled and the little Arabs sailed by. Archie's blood rushed up. The seventh, a teak post and rails of terrifying solidity, loomed ahead and Archie shortened the reins more savagely than he would have dared to do on an obliging and delicately brought-up English hunter.

'Get *on* with it, you clumsy—!'

Jack Tar took it like a bird but his ears didn't move. Five of the fences to take again, the last one being the water and a grand finale in front of the ladies . . . Archie took out his whip. If Jack Tar could have slotted his ears into his skull he would have done so, but his heavy shoulders, flecked now with foam, moved as steadily and powerfully as pistons. He gained on the Arabs steadily, took the double beautifully and left them behind. Archie let him have his head a little and he stretched his neck in pursuit of the bay and the chestnut, still stride for stride ahead of him. At the stone wall the chestnut swerved abruptly flinging his rider over the rails into the rough dry grass beyond and the bay, unnerved, jumped too late, lost the rhythm of his stride and allowed Jack Tar to thunder by. Only the water jump now and the crowd roaring at him like the sea coming in and The Parson's sweat-dark rump nearer and nearer, and then the collecting under him and the leap and The Parson's nose passing his knee, backwards and backwards and the roar of the crowd turning to thunder and the white disc of the winning post fifty yards ahead, forty, thirty . . .

Jack Tar slackened. Archie took the whip to him, shouting, but the great muscles which had served him so well were now entirely directed against him, not for him. The thudding gallop broke down to a canter, Jack Tar let his head go down, bunched his neck. Slowly, inevitably, The Parson drew level again, more than level, half a length ahead, a length . . . At a ragged and surly trot, Jack Tar passed the winning post in second place.

Grace, hoarse with screaming, was now in tears. Wates and MacGregor, who had failed to find alternative escorts to themselves for her, passed her their handkerchiefs in silence and turned their backs discreetly.

'He should have won, he should have, that horrible horse. Oh, what happened? It's all wrong. Poor Mr Tennant, he should have won. It isn't fair—'

'Told you he was a bastard,' The Parson's rider said cheerfully to Archie as they unsaddled.

'Does he always do that?'

'Not exactly that. New trick every year. But he's always in the frame. Madame May will smile upon you, never fear. She'll be at least four thousand to the good so she can afford to smile.'

'Madame—?'

'Daw Kyn May. Your owner. I say, watch out!'

One of Jack Tar's huge hooves lashed out and missed Archie by an inch.

'You *are* a bastard,' Archie said in amazement, 'a real, through and through *bastard*.'

Jack Tar swung his ugly head round and regarded Archie with his small malevolent eyes. Then for a fleeting moment his ears went up and he drew his lips back over his ochre teeth in the grotesque semblance of a smile.

'Five thousand rupees!' Grace said in genuine admiration.

Archie nodded. Madame Kyn May had not thought it necessary to see him, send him a message even, but just as he was boarding the steamer, not ten minutes before it churned out into midstream, a boy had come up, running, with a packet and a message.

'Look!' Archie said. 'Look at that! And will I ride him in the spring meeting! I *say*, oh I say, five hundred, over three years' salary, five *hundred*—'

Grace said, meaning it, 'Oh, Mr Tennant, I am so awfully pleased for you!'

There was everything, today, to be pleased about. She looked down at her blue muslin lap and was particularly pleased about that and full of gratitude for dear Hosannah Manook, who had been in Rangoon for a month or two and had said that if Grace were to charm a young man all the way to Mandalay, she must do it properly dressed. And then, because there was so little time, she had taken two of her own dresses – they were slightly over-flounced, Grace felt, and they made her go in and out in a way she didn't at all naturally and was perhaps not quite decent

175

– and reefed them in to fit Grace and here she was, blue muslin frills and parasol, and a tiny straw hat with daisies and blue ribbons, and then Mr Tennant all to herself and the journey ahead and now the money and him so excited . . . Everything looked so lovely, the blue sky and the green banks far away across the glittering stretches of water and the golden finger of the Shway Dagon dwindling in the distance, fiery in the sunlight.

'I wish she'd done it sooner,' Archie said. 'I could have bought a horse. Yesterday, I mean. Or a couple. And brought them with me.'

'Can't you do that in Mandalay?'

He turned to look at her. She looked quite changed today, even a different shape somehow. He wondered how it was done.

'I doubt it. There aren't enough Englishmen up there to ensure good horses. Never mind. I'll save it to buy myself a beauty on my first leave. Five hundred! I say, Miss Prior, what shall we do to celebrate?'

'Oh, we can't, there's nothing!' she cried, despairing at once. 'Oh, you should have, I don't know, champagne or something or make a speech, but there's nobody, just me. Oh poor Mr Tennant!'

Looking at her, smiling and thinking of the money, he said, 'I don't think I am poor at all,' and Grace, understanding him as she wished to, fell at once from admiration into love.

'It will be – eight days, you know,' she said,

'at least. Eight days of just this steamer and – and—'

'And then Mandalay.'

'Yes,' she said sadly, 'then Mandalay.'

'Don't you want to get there? And see your father?'

'Oh, yes, yes, of course, I do! But I love this kind of journey, so peaceful and safe and nothing mattering. I love Mandalay. You will too, it's so beautiful, so strange. Some of the people are, well disconcerting I suppose, not like they are when they are in England—'

'Men like me? Teak boys?'

Grace raised her eyes for the luxury of looking at him.

'Oh no. Not like you. Odd sorts of people. Papa said they were speculators. I am not sure whether that necessarily means that they are wicked or just that they are ready to take a great gamble to be rich, but they used to hang about the court and fawn upon that terrible Queen to try and get permission to work the forests and the mines. There was one—' she stopped. This golden day, this golden time ahead could all be spoiled entirely if she began to think about Maria Beresford.

'Go on,' Archie said. 'Please. I want to know all I can about Mandalay.'

'There was a girl,' Grace said carefully, wanting very much to put her hand in Archie's for reassurance, 'a girl I knew in India, before Mandalay, and her father was some sort of – of administrator, I think. At least he was a tea-planter first but he lost his money. And she was very – very handsome,' Grace said, forcing herself to be honest, 'and she became a great favourite with the Queen and the Queen gave her father and – and, oh, Mr Tennant, an awful man, a sinister sort of man called Mr Blount, well, the Queen gave them permission to work the ruby mines at Minhla. And there was a Frenchman involved too, a *Frenchman* and they are English. And Papa tells me they are so rich now and the Queen has built them a house with a triple roof, just like Papa's mission, and Maria can do anything she likes and she has lovely jewels and they call her the Queen of the *kalā* town—'

Archie passed her his handkerchief. 'Please don't look so distressed, Miss Prior. What is the matter? Did this person upset you, do you an injury?'

'Oh, no!' Grace said vehemently, clutching the handkerchief with fervour. 'She didn't upset me, well, not much, by what she *did*, but by what she *was*. She always dressed so wonderfully and knew what to say and didn't mind at all what people thought of her. I'm so sorry to talk to you like this, Mr Tennant. I really am. I never meant to. It is simply that you have been so kind and I feel you are a friend.'

'Oh, yes,' Archie said, 'I hope so.' Then he stood up and held out his arm. 'We are going to walk three times round each deck, otherwise we shan't deserve our luncheon, and you can begin teaching me Burmese. The only phrase Ah Chun has taught me is "Give me the money!" '

Grace stood up laughing. 'Oh yes! *Pike-san pay-like*, they all say that a great deal! Don't expect too much of luncheon, Mr Tennant, the food on these steamers isn't good at all. One can never look forward to it. I find the only thing I do look forward to very much is the evenings, when they moor near the villages and the people come out in their little boats. That is lovely.'

It was indeed. The steamer lay like a great whale in mid-stream while the boats of the villagers jostled round her in the fawn-coloured waters. Above them the sky was rose and apricot and thin, clear faded blue, and here and there from the banks a pagoda caught the last light, its whiteness flushing pink and amber. In the boats the villagers shrieked for custom, holding up chickens in wicker baskets, necklaces of persimmon seeds, chunks of sugar cane, trays of heart-shaped betel leaves, green coconuts, melons, fans of little bananas. Archie bought a bundle of green cheroots tied neatly with a plait of grasses and leaned on the rail, smoking and gazing, while item after item was held up for his inspection. And then the moon came up, white and brilliant, and the river waters became like polished jet and a velvety softness fell upon the banks out of the deep hot darkness of the Burmese night.

9

Afternoon sun fell golden on the heavy leaves of the mangoes and the blood-red blooms of the mohur trees. Between their leaves, Maria could see the creamy sweeps of frangipani and the delicate pink of Chinese roses and the brilliant purple – a colour she detested even in flowers – of the bougainvillea climbing like wildfire over anything to hand. That sunlit spectacle was framed by the blue-shadowed posts of the verandah and again by the wide-flung doors of her drawing room, doors lacquered vermilion inside and hung upon wonderful brass hinges fashioned like dragons. Between herself and the doors stretched a satisfying sweep of teak floorboards, gleaming with oil and scattered here and there with silk rugs from China in duck-egg blue and pink and cream, rugs that had been carried by coolies over the Shan hills to be sold in Mandalay.

The little table upon which they had been forced to dine five years ago now stood at Maria's elbow and bore a crystal bowl of water in which three perfect white hibiscus floated – and the tea things. Maria herself, almost as perfect, wore a dress European in cut but made of rough gleaming Burmese silk and in her ears and round her wrists shone rubies as dark as good claret. The chair she sat in was French, gilded and upholstered in rose brocade, and its companion stood opposite her, across the best of the Chinese rugs. On the teak walls hung French looking glasses and the watercolours that had dictated the colours of all Beresford drawing rooms since the days of Tirimbatore, interspersed here and there with groups of eighteenth-century French miniatures that Supayalat had demanded from adventurers seeking to win her favour, and then laughed at as soon as she had them and handed them directly to Maria. In corners stood exquisite old Chinese lacquer cabinets, pieces that had also found their way over the eastern hills to the bazaars of Mandalay and on them were delicate old blue and white bowls which Maria had filled with glimmering, quartz-like pieces of rock from the mines, valueless but highly decorative.

The room was her domain. When the house was built two years ago she had begged that one room might be much larger than most Burmese rooms, at least thirty feet in one direction, because, she explained laughingly to the Queen, when one was so tall, one needed space to move. Supayalat had been in high good humour that day. She was wearing a watch Maria had given her, a watch made like a tiny enamelled beetle whose jewelled wings flew open to reveal the face – it was a watch that Maria had no business to give to anyone, being Hubert's wedding present to his wife, but Hubert knew better than to remonstrate with Maria in any way these days – and it was always a good sign when the little beetle adorned the white starched muslin of the royal jacket. Yes, Maria should have her great room, as great as she wished, two perhaps . . .

Now she sat in it and waited. The teatray was level with her elbow, laid with English silver and bone china and a plate of almond biscuits made from Chinese almonds as sweet as honey. Her gaze wandered round the room in self-congratulation but her thoughts drowsed in the heavy warmth of late afternoon. The morning had been spent at the palace, as usual, a morning like almost every morning in the past five years, attending Supayalat's ritual bath and first dressing of the day, helping to oil that silky brown skin or stitching the lining of soft muslin that had to be put in, fresh at each wearing, as the tamein's only undergarment. The Queen was pregnant again, smoothly swollen, and she was sullen and dangerous for Thibaw had been caught with a mistress and the court was waiting in trepidation to see what would happen next. Maria knew what would happen, she now knew the Queen too well. The little mistress would be summoned to play a game with all the other little maids of honour and then gradually the game would become a scuffle and then the scuffle would become a battle and the little mistress would limp disgraced from court, her teeth broken, her face a livid mass of bruises, her hair pulled out in handfuls, her hands and feet stamped on, twisted. And the Queen would watch, laughing. But that had not happened yet, nothing had happened but that Supayalat had smouldered in her garden pavilion and would, as usual, only allow near her the tall *kalā*, the Englishwoman in her sweeping silks.

Unfortunately, there had been little to divert her with that morning. Maria had been meticulous in showing the Queen every drawing, every plan to do with the ruby mines and they had spent many hours poring over Bonvilain's diagrams and charts. The Queen was in many ways a frustrated businesswoman and her sharp little brain was easily diverted from domestic upsets by the prospect of new and improved schemes to work the mines. But today there had been nothing to give her, not even a selection of rubies from which she could choose the best as the terms of the concession dictated. She had shrieked for music to be played louder and louder and had sat upon her cushion, smoking furiously, exuding sparks of danger and temper.

Five years of that now. Five years of that red and gold palace, the gardens with their grottos and waterfalls and summerhouses, the little maids of honour in their butterfly silks, who came and went as if they were as disposable as paper kites. Five years too of Supayalat, of her fascination, her power, her passionate possessiveness of the King, her conviction that she was the centre of the universe, her beastliness and cruelty and charm. Five years of a tinsel world, where a king and queen above the earth played all day like children while royal prisoners starved beneath it in dungeons of unspeakable squalor; where one trod upon precious carpets and lay upon soft silks and threw the empty food tins of asparagus and artichoke hearts imported from Europe to stink beneath the palace platform in the rat-infested gloom. Five years of intrigue and spying and an uncertainty at once heady and terrifying. Five years which had given Maria position and admiration and jewels – and dulled her hair a little and drawn fine lines beside her eyes and mouth. Five years—

A fifth of her lifetime, no less – of a chance for queenliness, the chance that she had, since those arrogant childhood days in South India, felt she was not so much lucky to have, as entitled to. Her first great public moment in Burma, a year after her arrival, had satisfied her absolutely and had given her proof that this was the kind of position which should be hers by right. In the late autumn of 1880, that most lovely of the Burmese seasons when the stifling, drenching rains had given way to clear, strong sunlight, Maria, attended by her father and Denzil Blount, had gone down to Minhla to inspect the ruby mines. In addition to her father and Denzil she had full royal escort, particularly ordered by the Queen as a mark of most especial favour, and she rode out of Mandalay upon an elephant, preceded by yelling lictors in royal livery, followed by a detachment of the Queen's own bodyguard and surrounded, for every step of the way, by a surging and fascinated crowd of Burmese.

She did not observe, swaying down towards the river where a royal steamer had been put at her disposal for the journey down the Irrawaddy to Minhla, that in contrast to the magnificence of the elephant trappings and the scarlet and gold of the soldiers, the crowd that gaped at her magical progress were barefoot, filthy and ragged. She did not look down at them but gazed superbly before her, only conscious that she was the focus of all attention and that both Hubert and Denzil rode some way behind her, on inferior animals, attended only by a handful of soldiers attired in the uniform of the guard of the Gem City, not the Queen's own livery.

The journey had lived up to its beginning. She was allotted two staterooms aboard the steamer, even if they were furnished with a Burmese disregard for European lack of suppleness, and four of the little maids of honour from the court knelt reverently in corners awaiting her pleasure.

'One might say,' Denzil said, looking about him at her borrowed splendour, 'that you have, my dear, arrived—'

Maria regarded him without smiling. 'And not, I may say, before time.'

More elephants awaited them at Minhla and huge tents, carpeted and with gilded guy ropes, had been put up a little distance from the mines.

It was an unprepossessing area, a flat plainlike stretch of dun country, its surface scarred and pitted with the mine workings, baking beneath the relentless sun. Robed in a flowing white dustcoat over her silks, Maria arrived to inspect the site and found a delegation awaiting her with garlands of jasmine and a canopy of cheap English umbrellas obtained, no doubt with enormous difficulty, as a compliment. The manager of the mine, a scrawny and scarred individual with the keenly intelligent look of a practised exploiter, offered to show her the mines themselves.

'On no account!' Hubert cried, horrified.

Maria turned to him. 'Papa! Why not?'

Denzil said, 'You have no conception of how rubies are mined. It's an appalling business. The tunnels in which they work are improperly shored up, the heat is terrible, not to mention the smells. And the depth—' He paused and looked over her shoulder. 'Take a look for yourself. Those are the men that work here.'

At the mouth of the main entrance to the mine, a square hole cut in a shallow mound and lined with teak trunks, a small band of men was being marshalled into order for inspection. They were, for the most part, almost deformed in appearance, with grossly enlarged joints, humped shoulders and thrust-forward necks. They were also naked, apart from filthy loincloths and turbans.

Maria looked at them swiftly and turned back.

186

'But I should be escorted. I am under royal protection. There is nothing to be alarmed about.'

'There is no question of it,' Denzil said shortly. 'Pierre has been down, merely to satisfy us that the gem-bearing seams are as rich as we think. You are here merely as a figurehead. Choose some stones for the Queen and then we shall go.'

Maria said furiously, 'You treat this as if it were a charade—'

'It is.'

'Dearest,' Hubert said, 'do not upset yourself. Come—'

'We would not have this concession if it were not for me! If it were not for my intercession with the Queen, almost a year of paying court, of daily attendance, of presents and flattery—'

'Forgive me,' Denzil said, 'I apologize. You are too precious to risk in a Burmese mine, believe me. Out of kindness to myself and your father, don't think of it. Do as the Queen would do, choose jewels, let them gaze at you and come back to Mandalay.'

With four magnificent rubies, two cabuchon and two brilliant cut, in a gilded lacquer casket lined in velvet, Maria made her stately progress back to Mandalay. A detachment of soldiers waited on the bund to escort her back to the palace for Supayalat was impatient to see her, eager for trophies. She was entranced with the jewels, holding them up to the light, putting them between her small, strong teeth and then selecting one, a cabuchon, and holding it out to Maria, laughing, as a gift. It was memorable, that day, the Queen's narrow little hand in hers, the smooth small egg-shape of the jewel falling into her palm, the sense of triumph, of power. Four years ago now and, had she but known it, only a beginning—

A voice from the doorway said, 'I disturb you, Mademoiselle.'

'Pierre, you are late.'

'Five, it is only five—'

'I did not say five.'

Bonvilain came into the room, grinning and shaking his finger. 'Don't scold. You must not scold. I bring excellent news.'

She held out her hand. 'I know perfectly well you do. That is why I am impatient.'

'And Denzil? Him also? Is he coming?'

Maria rang for hot water. 'Later,' she said, 'Later. When you have told me.'

He settled himself in the empty chair opposite her. 'Ouf. This chair is terrible. Our French chairs are to look at but your English ones are to sit in. You would not give me whisky instead of tea?'

'I would not.'

'So beautiful and so severe—'

'Don't flirt with me, Pierre,' she said, not meaning it, turning her head a little.

'I can't help it. And you like it.'

Maria's Madrassee bearer, now in a sort of livery she had devised for her servants out of

188

yellow Burmese silk – the only thing she had ever done which Denzil Blount had dared to tell her was utterly ludicrous – came in with hot water and green Chinese tea and Maria busied herself with the pretty ritual of tea-making, delighted to have Bonvilain's eyes upon her.

'When I am married,' he said, putting his sunburned hands fingertip to fingertip under his chin, 'I shall still flirt with you.'

She looked up, the teapot poised.

'Marry! Are you to be married? But not, surely not, Pierre you could not—'

'Marry Mattie Calogreedy? Naturally not. She feels herself to be married in the Burmese sense, which is sufficient for her self-esteem, but she knows that as a Frenchman I cannot marry her in the European manner. I doubt she would expect it and in any case, she is growing stout and yellow—'

'She does expect it.'

'Then I shall not tell her.'

Maria shrugged. 'It is your affair.'

'I wish you could be *mon affaire*. I am going home to marry a sweet child my parents have chosen, blonde *comme une ange* and good as gold. I have only been waiting for her seventeenth birthday.'

Maria said nothing. Five years in Burma had not increased the liberality of her views in any way, notably those she held about the free-living behaviour of Europeans in Mandalay. Mattie had been undeniably useful to Maria, but being half

189

Burmese, could not expect to count as a full human being in her consideration and although Pierre's liaison with her was in the first place disgusting, his planned abuse of her was certainly not more so. It was rumoured too that Pierre had once had some little native thing from the cigar factory in his protection and Mattie had behaved just as you would expect someone like her to do and screamed and wailed. She had tried to tell Maria about it one day in the palace and Maria had turned her back.

'I will send Mattie a dress from Paris.'

'I expect that will seem to her as good as a marriage.'

'I have drunk my tea. Now will you give me some whisky?'

'When you have told me what I want to know.'

'Ah,' Bonvilain said and leaned back, stretching his legs. 'My information. My information is no less than that Thibaw has sent a mission to Paris. I have not been idle at court either, you see. A full-blown Burmese government mission has left Mandalay for France, ostensibly to assemble information about arts and sciences, industrial progress, that sort of thing. They all speak French and English and it is being put about that they will go first to Paris and then to London. But the *atwinwun*, the officer of the royal household, who leads them tells me that they mean to go no further than Paris. And while they are in Paris, they mean to offer to the French at the King's, and therefore the Queen's, instructions, concessions to work mines of coal, of lead, of sulphur, of silver, of rubies, the ruby mines at Mogok—'

'Pierre!' Maria said, her eyes shining, 'Oh Pierre!'

'It annoys me a little that my charm cannot make you smile at me as such information does. It piques me. I am not used to this. Now you see why I must go home. Just for a while. I shall follow the mission and make sure that nothing happens on the Quai d'Orsay that is not to our advantage and, of course, while I am there, I shall marry my little Marie-Thérèse and everyone will say Bonvilain has gone home to fetch a wife.'

'Mogok,' Maria said, 'Where is Mogok?'

'East of the Irrawaddy, high. The Shweli, the tributary of the Irrawaddy, goes almost all about it.'

Maria rose and paced slowly towards the open doors. A coppersmith bird beat in the trees outside and the late sunlight was as thick as syrup.

'When the present business has passed,' she said, 'the business between the King and Queen, I shall speak to her.'

Footsteps sounded on the verandah. Denzil Blount, not supposing for one moment that Maria was in the doorway because she had risen to greet him, took off his hat and remarked that she looked like a cat with cream.

'Not cream. Rubies.'

'More! But my dear Maria, you are stiff with rubies. There cannot be one single item of jewellery in which rubies can be used that you do not possess already—'

'Mogok,' she said, and laughed and went back to her chair to pour tea for him.

Denzil followed her, nodded briefly to Bonvilain and said, 'Ah, Mogok. Pierre, you are before me. I had promised myself the pleasure of telling Maria.'

He took his tea and went to stand against the shining wall between the chairs, the space that in European houses was given over to a fireplace. 'I don't think I'm altogether pleased, Pierre. And I hear you are going to Paris too.'

Bonvilain shrugged and smiled. 'My dear fellow, if it was not for me, for my being French and an engineer, we should never have got the concession to work the mines at Minhla—'

'Nonsense,' Denzil said crisply. 'Your nationality has nothing to do with it. I may not be much of a patriot but even I would rather you were not French. It is your engineering skills we prize you for, as well you know. Just as you could not do without our diplomacy and standing at court. Not to mention our ability to borrow money. And this delegation of Thibaw's is going to London after Paris, therefore English links with Mandalay will be just as much strengthened as those the court has with France.'

'No,' Maria said, 'it is not.'

Denzil glanced at them both, gestured defeat with his teacup and said, 'Then I suppose the die is truly cast. We must choose between Queen

Victoria and Mogok. How do you know the Burmese will not go to London?'

'The *atwinwun*, the officer who leads it, he told me. He says they will put about that they will go but they will not go.'

Denzil put down his teacup. 'Is this your doing?'

Bonvilain looked amused. 'Not entirely.'

'What is being offered to work the mines at Mogok?'

Maria leaned forward a little. Bonvilain, on the other hand, leaned back and put his hands, fingertip to fingertip, beneath his handsome chin.

'Three lakhs of rupees annually. No parties other than ourselves admitted. The King to have first choice of all rubies but to pay full value for any he chooses. The rest ours to sell as we will, where we will.'

Denzil let out a breath. 'Three lakhs! We don't pay half that for Minhla. But then on the other hand the King does not pay full value for the best stones either. And no hindrance to our taking all the rest out of the country!'

Maria said, 'The royal coffers are empty. Thibaw and Supayalat know that. They are monstrously extravagant, they always have been. Three lakhs will be a drop in the ocean. I lend the Queen a little here and there – at least I give it for there is little chance of seeing it back and it is a good investment. She is really pressed for money, ready money.'

Denzil smiled down at her. 'Does the Queen know of Mogok?'

'No,' Bonvilain said, 'not yet. But our charming ambassadress here—'

'You mean you have worked out these terms with the King alone?'

'And his adviser, Prince Yanaung. Yes.'

'Then we cannot rely upon them.'

Maria rose and swept rustling to the open doors. 'Oh, yes, we can. I shall speak to the Queen and Pierre will accompany the Burmese mission to make sure no higher bidders win Mogok.'

Denzil said, 'I don't underestimate your power in any way.'

'Don't flatter me.'

Bonvilain got up, smiling. 'I will leave you, Denzil, to see if you may soften her heart any better than I. She refused to let *me* flirt with her either.'

'Ah, but you are French and therefore not to be trusted. When do you leave?'

'At once.'

'I am a little envious of your going to Paris. I have not seen Paris in sixteen years. Paris—' he stopped. Maria's back, suddenly stiffening in the doorway, reminded him that she did not care to hear Europe spoken of so. She had never seen it. Piere, glancing at him and understanding, moved to Maria's side and took her hand to kiss it.

'Shall you come and wave me farewell with tears in your eyes?'

194

'I only ever have tears in my eyes on account of the dust.'

'The man who wins you will be a conqueror beside whom Alexander will pale. You will speak to the Queen? Tomorrow? And send me word before I go?'

'If I think fit. Naturally.'

When Bonvilain's footsteps had resounded down the verandah and he could be heard shouting for his servant in the lane, Denzil said, 'I do not really flatter you, you know.'

'Of course I know. That is why I won't allow you to pretend to.'

'Will you come and sit down?'

The room was growing dim as the sun sank lower. The Irrawaddy would be copper in the early evening now, its farther banks violet, the trees along the bund smudges of indigo and the dying sun, poised above it, would be veiled in dust. Denzil, seated opposite Maria with his back to the open doors, was almost invisible apart from the white of his shirt front and the sudden gleam of his teeth.

'You know why I do not flatter you. If I did, it would prove that I was hiding my disappointment in you. As it is, I admire you more than any woman I have ever encountered and I would not dare to flatter you. So I will do the opposite. I will warn you.'

Her chin went up. 'Oh?'

'Yes. Mogok is by no means a certainty. Whatever,' he said emphatically, gesturing her to

195

silence, 'you may say to the Queen. I tell you why. This is not simply a trade mission going to Paris nor is Pierre merely going to collect his child bride. It is a political mission as well. Pierre will see Jules Ferry, the French Foreign Minister. That means one thing only and that is that the French mean to cut out the British here, the Bombay-Burmah, all that teak—'

'Cut out the British? Why do you say it so lightly? Don't you care?'

Denzil smiled at her. 'Don't be queenly with *me*. You know I don't. I may have been born English but that I regard as a sort of accident. Don't misunderstand me. I don't mean that the remoteness of my feelings for England makes me in the least partisan towards the French. I care nothing for either. I care only, as you know, for myself. But you are not the same. Whatever the circumstances of your life, you are English. I only wish to make it clear to you that if Bonvilain brings back all the prizes you hope for from the Quai d'Orsay, you will be throwing your lot in with the French. It will not be the same as with Minhla. There the concession was to a group of us, two Englishmen, one Frenchman; patriotism, for want of a better word, was not involved. But Mogok – with Mogok, it will be. It does not bother *me*. *I* want you to speak to the Queen. But it is sufficient proof of my real admiration for you that I ask you to consider whether your own feelings will permit you to help the French so much.'

She stared at him with her cold blue stare. 'Why has this come about? Why has it all become a French affair? Why does it not stay as it was with Minhla?'

'Your friend, Pierre Bonvilain.'

'And you, presumably. You to encourage him.'

'A little. I am prepared to help the French because in so doing I help myself. I would help Germans, Greeks, Italians in just the same way if I saw in their dealings an advantage for myself. But would – could you?'

Maria wanted to ask, 'And Papa?' and would not let herself. Hubert spent a good deal of time at court, strolling through the audience halls, advising newcomers, being enigmatic with acquaintances, persuaded always of his own usefulness. Maria knew quite well where his usefulness lay. His clothes, his air, his manner, all these had been invaluable in persuading the Indian and Chinese merchants of Mandalay to lend them all sufficient money to pay the first enormous instalment to the Burmese government for the right to work the mines at Minhla. In two weeks only, Hubert, languid and self-confident, had borrowed the rupees that were necessary for the project even to begin. It was a talent the others could not do without. On the other hand, Maria knew but would not acknowledge, it was his only talent. Pierre and Denzil would not tell him of Mogok until they had a task for him. Maria's spirits soared and sank at once at the knowledge that she was told in full and that he would not be.

'I must, of course, tell Papa.'

'It is unlike you to be unable to make a decision on your own.'

'That would not be the reason!' she said angrily.

'Why must you build up his self-esteem so?' Denzil said, leaning forward in his chair. 'Why always present him to himself as greater than he is—'

'Stop it!' she said. She was almost shouting. 'Stop it! I – I *order* you not to speak so!'

She saw his smile glimmer maddeningly in the gloom.

'Let me tell you some news, then. Tomorrow's steamer brings an old friend of yours to Mandalay. Little Miss Prior.'

'Grace! But I thought she was in a convent. In Rangoon.'

'She was. I saw Tom today. She has decided to rejoin him. He is, of course, enraptured. She is landing tomorrow. Tom said she was in the care, would you believe it, of one of those over-educated schoolboys the Bombay-Burmah sends out to die in the jungle. What possesses a young man to take such a job? This one is to go down to the Ningyan forests it seems, not up the Chindwin like so many others. Of course, if Pierre does his job properly, there will be no jobs for these boys at all and the teak forests will be full of Frenchmen.'

'So Grace has not married.'

There was a pause.

'No more, my dear, have you.'

Maria said smoothly, 'My choice has been severely limited.'

'Certainly. A situation intensified by the fact that you would not have *me* if I asked you.'

'You would not ask me.'

He laughed easily. 'Quite right. I would not. And yet I come closer to it with you than with any woman before. No, Miss Prior is not married. Her father claims proudly she is quite unchanged.'

Maria looked about the room with its lovely objects and colours, at her dress, at the jewels on her wrists. She said with complacency, 'I wonder if she will find me much changed,' certain of his agreement.

He laughed again.

'Oh, no, my dear Maria, she won't. She will find you much the same only, if you understand me, very much more so.'

10

Archie, leaning on the taffrail, felt he had been in Burma for weeks. He also felt – guiltily because it was not an entirely satisfactory sensation – that he had known Grace Prior all his life. They had been together nine days, one day of which had been spent motionless and blisteringly hot upon a sandbank (the leadsman who had thus failed in his duty had been flogged by the captain and Grace had cried and cried and needed hours of comforting), and all that time Grace, in her blue and pink borrowed muslins, had been at his side, chattering and laughing and gazing earnestly up into his face. In many respects, he told himself sternly, he had been very glad to have such a companion, a pretty girl who had lived in Burma for four years and who had a tolerable command of the language, but their being such an obvious couple and the only white people on board had segregated them from many other passengers Archie would have liked to talk to. He leaned heavily forward on the taffrail now so that she could not possibly take his arm.

'Look!' she was saying. 'There's Papa! Oh, dear, *dear* Papa! I can see his clothes need mending from here, and his beard – Oh, and there is Signor Andreino! He isn't a bit changed! And little Ma Zan, Papa has brought her too. She used to be my maid, you know, because she wouldn't work in the school so we took her into the house. I wonder where you will live? I expect Signor Andreino will have found you a bungalow—'

The day was brilliant. The wide sluggish breadth of the Irrawaddy glittered with points of sunlight and the hard blue sky rose like a shell behind the heavy trees along the bund. The bund itself was hardly visible under a crowd of Burmese, some dressed in their bright cottons, some entirely naked or almost so but for a strip of dingy cloth around their hips.

'Mandalay,' Archie said to himself, 'Mandalay.'

Little houses had been built out into the river on stilts with crude boats moored to the posts and lines of washing from house to house like coloured flags. There were children in the water too and a good deal of rubbish and, along the river's edge, women slapped and banged their laundry against stones. Voices came floating to Archie above the chug of the steamer, shrill Burmese voices like the dawn chorus in England, echoing and dancing on the water. He straightened up, feeling his clothes peeling damply away from the skin of his back and smiled delightedly at it all.

'Papa has seen me!' Grace cried, forgetting her

parasol in her rapture so that it swung dangerously close to Archie's eyes. 'Oh, how wonderful!
I do so want you to meet him, he will be so
pleased you have come and so grateful to you for
looking after me!'

Beside the bearded missionary, who was now
waving in huge wide sweeps like a windmill,
stood another European with tremendous black
moustaches and extravagant linen. He was talking with a great deal of gesturing to Tom Prior
and some stone on his finger caught the light
with every movement and flashed like fire. At
Archie's elbow, Ah Chun said, '*Thakin* Andreino.
He was finding me.'

Archie nodded. The deck was becoming
crowded as all the passengers pushed towards the
rail, eager to land. Ah Chun started shouting and
waving, vigorously clearing a space around Grace
and Archie with his knees and elbows.

'I wish the journey wasn't ending! I cannot
thank you enough, you have been so kind, you
have amused me so well. I do hope we won't lose
touch – when do you go into the forests?'

Passengers, despite Ah Chun, were beginning
to push between them, barging through with
bundles and baskets and chickens in wicker
cages. Across the stream of people, Archie
shouted, 'I – I don't know! It's been a great
pleasure, I've enjoyed it too, can't really believe
I'm in Mandalay—'

They seemed almost to be washed over the
gangplank on a river of people. Grace was terri-

fied to see that the gangplank had no sides and that the Irrawaddy, ten feet below, was choked with children and refuse, so she clung to Archie like a limpet and said she must close her eyes, he would have to guide her. Archie saw Andreino watch them as they came unsteadily towards him and wished he did not look so wonderfully amused.

'A good journey, I am sure, Mr Tennant.'

'Excellent,' Archie said, attempting as gently as possible to disengage his arm.

'And the boy? Ah Chun? You are satisfied?'

'First class.'

A voice behind Archie said, 'How good you have been to my Grace! She could not have come without you. I cannot thank you enough.'

Archie turned with difficulty. Grace let go of his arm and sprang into her father's embrace. Over her head Tom said to Archie, on a note of amusement, 'Still a most affectionate child.'

Archie grinned in relief.

'Have you clung to Mr Tennant like a creeper all the way from Rangoon?'

'Almost,' Grace said happily.

'Then I give you your freedom, Mr Tennant. And when you have savoured it a little, come to us in the mission. Come and see us. The cooking has fallen off a little since my daughter went away – apart from a brief spell when a young American Baptist was here, a Miss Newman, an excellent cook – but I hope the welcome hasn't.'

'He should not be here,' Andreino said,

looking after him, 'nor should Miss Prior. I fear you have not come to a safe nor a comfortable place, Mr Tennant. We Europeans are a dwindling band. I expect you were warned of all this in London.'

'No. No, I wasn't. Warned of what?'

A crowd of children was gathering round them, drawn like magnets to gaze at Archie's fair skin.

'Ah!' Andreino said with annoyance, 'typical! Always, *always*, the British ostrich has its head in the sand when it comes to Burma. It drives me mad. Still, all the British government, all the Viceroy can think of, still it is only Africa, Afghanistan. The Transvaal is their great obsession at the moment. And much though I bless the Bombay-Burmah for the use they make of me, they are not much better. The teak is so important they will not heed the dangers. Mr Tennant, life will not be very comfortable here.' He took Archie's arm and began to steer him down the far side of the bund, the knot of children keeping pace with them, their circle unbroken.

'I didn't suppose it would be,' Archie said, his mind filled with schoolboy images of jungles, images he had been trying to replace with something more realistic ever since he left Liverpool.

'When you are in the forests,' Andreino said as if reading his thoughts, 'then you will be safer, I think. Even with dacoits. The boys who work on the elephants are peasants, far from court influence, quite reliable in their way. But

Mandalay is not good, now. Only a few *kalās* are safe. I suppose the Queen would hesitate actually to kill a British subject but, of course, accidents can be arranged here so easily. You will be sharing quite a comfortable bungalow. No small matter to have such a place, I can tell you.'

Archie stopped. Several children cannoned into him from behind and there was an explosion of giggling. Andreino spoke to them sharply.

'I don't mind them,' Archie said, 'it would take more than a few children to knock me over. But I thought I was to go out into the forests straight away. I didn't really imagine needing a bunga-low.'

Andreino stood aside with a flourish by the bullock cart for Archie to climb in ahead of him.

'You will go in a couple of weeks, when you have the feel of the place. Mostly they fell from November to March and float from March until October. It was a poor floating season this year, there's far too much timber still lying. Not enough rain, though on a daily basis it seemed hard to understand how that could be.'

Archie settled himself with discomfort in the cart. The trees and huts around him were obscured with dust which he could see rising in soft choking clouds and feel gritty on his lips and tongue.

'How old are you, Mr Tennant?'

'Twenty-four.'

'Then you have an excellent chance of

becoming a forest manager. How many other Bombay-Burmah recruits have you met?'

'None,' Archie said.

'There are plenty here, but mostly up the Chindwin. All sorts but very well educated. I sometimes wonder what use an intimate acquaintance with the ancient languages is in a remote Burmese forest. There – that is the Anglican mission.'

An ancient-looking, weathered building of carved wood could be glimpsed among the dense foliage.

'Did you say I should be sharing a bungalow?'

'Indeed yes. You will find Frederick Winser there. He knows a lot about your forests, he came from the Burma Police. And a couple of others. You won't be lonely. I don't think that in Burma you will be bored either. I just ask you to be careful.'

Archie lifted his face to the sky and felt the sun smite it like a scalding iron. He was full of a most peculiar contentment, peculiar because he had expected to feel the keenest apprehension at all that lay ahead of him, and he felt nothing of the sort. He felt instead a great and comfortable happiness, despite the tremendous heat, despite the springless cart with its gaping sides like wooden ribs, despite the dust and his sweat-soaked shirt and the utter unknown of the next few weeks. He closed his eyes and let the sun burn into his skin like a brand. The air smelt of heat and dust and dung and various fruit and vegetable smells, slightly sweet with an edge of decay. He breathed in deeply.

'Mr Tennant,' Andreino said, 'look.'

Reluctantly, Archie straightened his neck and opened his eyes. The world swam in a dazzle of sunlight.

'Look.'

Before him was a fairytale. A shining moat filled with lilies and dotted with golden boats and white bridges encircled a magical city apparently made of gold and silver and scarlet lacquer. Great walls of russet brick, edged in white, rose out of the waters of the moat and above them soared the towers and spires and pinnacles, the tiers of roofs like winged saucers, everything shining, glittering, glowing, a shimmering fantasy place—

'My God,' Archie said, 'my God. I never, I mean, nobody ever – nobody said – it must be the palace. Is it? The royal city? Is it? I can't believe it—'

'It is.'

'The City of Gems.'

'The same.'

'I – I saw the Shway Dagon. In Rangoon. But this – this—'

'It is extraordinary. Some Europeans hate it.'

'I can't believe that I see such a thing—'

'No. Sometimes nor can I. But I have known it so long now that those times are only when I am a little drunk.'

'It makes me feel drunk.'

A tiny breeze blew from somewhere and a ripple of sunlight ran down the moat like a tinsel ribbon.

'What is that hill?' Archie said, pointing to the north-east.

'Mandalay Hill. There is a gigantic gold Buddha at the top, pointing down upon the city King Mindoon built. And those, to the right, those are the Shan hills. And there,' he said, his pointing finger swinging to the south-east, 'over there are your forests. Ningyan and the Pyinmana forests. Trees and elephants, elephants and trees.' He looked at Archie. 'You must make the most of Mandalay.'

Archie nodded in silence, still gazing.

'You must call at the mission,' Andreino said after a while, smiling, 'just once, perhaps. But you must go. Tom Prior is a brave and interesting man, he will intrigue you. And the little signorina—'

'Yes,' Archie said, not listening really, 'yes,' and then he took his eyes from the blue line of the hills that hid China and feasted them again on the gold and scarlet glory of the royal city.

It was a week before he got to the mission and even then, it was only because Andreino prompted him. The delights of a bachelor chummery were too strong for Archie to remember much else, his days, after the weeks of inactivity on board ship, too headily filled with games and exploration, and the nights, blue with cigar smoke, too absorbing with tales of the forests, discussions on the habits of elephants, reflections on the mysterious and powerful allure of being alone in such places for weeks on end. Frederick Winser seemed to know an encyclopedic amount and preferred to instruct Archie while occupied, so that his first days in Mandalay were spent in happy pursuit of snipe accompanied by Frederick's running commentary on Burma.

'The Kingdom of Ava,' he said, waist high in the grasses of the foothills to the east of Mandalay, 'is about five hundred miles from north to south, three hundred east to west. The population,' he brought his gun up sharply to his shoulder and squinted along the barrels, 'is about three million. I suppose the most revolting aspect of Thibaw's reign—' a short pause while a snipe rose and began its darting, zigzagging flight away from them, followed by the sharp report of Frederick's gun, '—is that the sovereign has a right to whatever adult labour he chooses. A vile slavery, that's what it amounts to.' He then waited while the bird was brought back to him, examined his shot without comment and resumed. 'Quite a substantial army, though none of them but the Palace Guard are much use. Must be ten thousand, all told, but they lack horses and guns shockingly and the officers! *We* know more about things military than they do.' His gun swung up again. 'Good at river fighting though. Thibaw is utterly improvident. They say he is going to import plates from France to print his own money. Fondly imagines that's how you have enough. How are you doing? Fine, fine. Want to call it a day and wait for some geese this evening? Best geese and duck shooting I've ever had. Can't fish though. Coarse, bony fish, like all tropical rivers. I say, good shot. Nothing like snipe, eh?'

When they paused for a moment or two out of the blistering heat and Frederick had time to look at other things than snipe, the sight of distant hills and forests would remind him of Archie's future.

'Of course, it's a roughish life. You'll be superintending the felling and dragging of the timber. Mind you, the forests are far too full, some places we won't have to fell for years, the ground is simply solid with fallen timber. Want a cheroot? We pay the King a royalty on each log and about four and a half lakhs of rupees annually for the concession to fell in the area I'm taking you to. That's a pretty fine gun you have. Present, eh? We pay the foresters in silver, terrible stuff to carry about, weighs a ton. I suppose there are about three hundred foresters in all down in Ningyan, each with his own elephant. We have to give them an advance each season before they'll lift a finger, it's the custom here. And, of course, you'll be doing a bit of exploring. There are no maps, we make 'em. Right then. On your feet. Any good at languages? Won't get far without a bit of dialect here. I say, don't forget your topee. Shouldn't stir an inch without it in day-light.'

In the late afternoons, before the sun sank low enough for the heavy flights of ducks to come winging across the sky, Frederick and the two Chatsworth brothers, who shared the bungalow, would take Archie lime-cutting. Deprived of polo, he was in his element. Mounted on an amazingly game Burmese pony – 'Ought to take one home with you,' Frederick said. 'They'd be perfect for hunting' – and armed with a Burmese *dah*, he rode full gallop at a stick planted in the ground and crowned with a lime. The aim was to slice the lime as cleanly as possible from the stake as one thundered by. Archie's skill was such that even Ah Chun almost forgave him for his failure steeplechasing in Rangoon. After these bouts, he would return to the bungalow and stand naked in his brick cubicle of a bathroom while Ah Chun hurled bucket after bucket of water over him with as much force as he could muster.

It was during the exertions of one of these improvised showers that Ah Chun's impeccably folded garment parted a little to reveal the skin of his thighs darkly and horribly mottled in deep blue, like a matted tracery of veins. Archie pointed, gasping, his face and hair running with water and trails of soapy bubbles. Ah Chun put down the bucket and parted the cotton that wrapped him with pride. Archie, squatting before him, blowing soap and water out of his mouth and nose, saw that Ah Chun was tattooed, closely and evenly, all over his skin from his waist to his knees, every inch. Since Ah Chun wore an expression of extreme satisfaction, Archie did not quite know what to say and contented himself with, 'Did it hurt?'

'Much, *thakin*. But me, I take no opium. Many boys, they take opium for tattoo.'

'Good Lord,' Archie said and stood up. He surveyed his own thighs and found that, despite the heat, he was goose-pimpled at the mere notion.

'They all do it,' Frederick said later at dinner, his mouth full of mutton. 'It's a sign of manhood. Must be agony.'

The tablecloth that stretched between the four men was linen, made in Manchester, the laundry label told Archie. On it, apart from the heavy paraphernalia of knives, forks and glasses, stood a huge pot of yellow mustard and a blue glass bowl – doubtless also from Manchester – which held custard apples, greenish yellow and covered in spikes, mangoes and small sweet bananas like little yellow fingers. They had eaten a thick brown soup, an extremely dull fish full of peculiar wedge-shaped bones, and were now contemplating a dish of tough chops. Archie, replete with air and exercise, found himself enthusiastic about every mouthful.

'Of course,' Frederick went on with one of the abrupt changes of subject Archie was becoming used to, 'you should have had a squint at Moulmein. That's where most of our teak is

212

exported from. Rangoon is nothing much yet. It's Indian railways that will do it. Teak, teak and more teak. Thousands of tons, can't get enough. Don't be put off by the smell of those things,' waving his fork at the custard apples, 'they are pretty good. What do you think of Andreino?'

The Chatsworth brothers, due to go up river to the Chindwin forests, said they couldn't see why a company as prosperous as the Bombay-Burmah needed a greasy little foreigner to look after their affairs in Mandalay at all.

'What d'you think?' Frederick asked of Archie.

'I supposed,' Archie said carefully, much preoccupied with the prickles on his fruit, 'that it was because of his relations at court. With the King. But that was only what I supposed.'

'Quite right,' Frederick said, 'quite right. Don't like him much myself.'

Archie looked up. 'I do.'

'He is an Italian,' the elder Chatsworth said reprovingly. His nose had burned and peeled to a brilliant rose pink.

Archie grinned at him. 'Yes,' he said.

Frederick finished his last chop and threw the bone onto his plate. 'Hundred thousand people in Mandalay. Four of us. Next week in the forests, it will be one of us and fifty natives or so apiece. I'll keep you with me a while until you know what you are doing. Show you how to measure the logs, what to look for in terms of quality. You'll need a bit of help with negotiations over money too, I should

213

think. Throw me a mango, Archie, would you? Bridge?'

The next morning Andreino was there on the verandah when Archie got back from an early ride. The temperature was fierce already, but the light was clear and lovely and the cartwheels had not yet had time to fill the air with clouds of dust.

'You see,' he said to Archie, smiling beneath his moustaches, redolent of hair oil and garlic, 'I told you that you would need some time to settle. You enjoy yourself, I think. You Englishmen are never happy without a horse. I am come to widen your horizons a little, to interrupt your bachelor games. You should meet the other Europeans in Mandalay before you go. There is not so much time.'

Frederick had promised Archie guinea fowl that day. Andreino laughed and shrugged.

'As you wish. I will return this afternoon. English teatime still happens in Mandalay.'

Ah Chun came out and handed Archie a towel. He rubbed his face and neck vigorously, saying as he did so in tones occasionally muffled by terry cloth, 'It's no time to ask you and in a way none of my business, but I have been wondering a little why – I mean what made you – rather why you should choose the Bombay-Burmah—'

Andreino leaned smiling against the verandah rail. 'It chose me. Most fortunately. I am a creature of no place, born an Italian, adopted by nowhere. My early career does not matter except that it was quite respectable and somehow –

214

perhaps it was the respectableness – I came up here and found myself consul for Italy. I don't think Italy really wants or needs a consul here, we have so few interests to protect, but she has one and I am he. It was William Wallace of the Bombay-Burmah, the Wallace who gained the first big teak contracts here, he asked me if I would be agent. You can do nothing without the King up here and I was close to the King's father. He was remarkable, Mindoon, the best and wisest of these kings. I have not lost my touch, I know almost all that goes on. A young lady of your acquaintance once told me I had no principles. She felt I, as you English say, rode too many horses. I told her and I tell you, that I do, I ride as many as I can, it is my survival. But in the end, I will always ride the winner.'

'Even if it is Burmese?'

Andreino leaned forward and said softly, 'The Burmese winners? With this king? Young man, there will be changes. You will see them. If you keep your head and take no foolish risks, you will find you are here at a golden time.' He straightened up and took a long green cigar from his pocket. He turned the end up and with a none too clean thumbnail, neatly skewered out a small plug. 'Keep close to me, young man. Tell me anything you see. You will not regret it.' He put the cut end of the cigar into his mouth and Ah Chun, whom Archie had supposed inside, came forward with a match. 'Look at this!' Andreino said. 'Matches from Sweden in Upper Burma!

Absurd.' He spoke sharply to Ah Chun who retreated at once. 'The French must have an eye kept upon them. These teak forests are worth thousands of lakhs and the French are well into the Far East, Cochin China, Tonkin, why not Burma. There is a mission—' He stopped and smiled. 'But I can tell you all this later. I shall come for you at four. I wish you a good bag.'

He was late, which was just as well since Archie, tumbling dust and sweat covered off his pony that afternoon, was late also. He had shot better than ever before in his life and had, with the deepest reluctance, left Frederick and the Chatsworths waiting for the twilight and the geese. He thundered into the bungalow, shouting for Ah Chun, and saw formal clothes laid out upon his bed with a sinking heart. But the exhilaration of his success that day uplifted him to such an extent, despite the prospect of a tea party, that he became aware as Ah Chun doused him and he sang lustily, but flat, well-known opera choruses, that he had become thoroughly aroused. This confused him at once and, not sure whether Ah Chun had noticed, he turned his back and endeavoured to fill his mind with thoughts of the most unstimulating kind. His efforts were partially successful, sufficiently so at least for him to leave the bathroom only a little stooped and to climb hurriedly into his underclothes while in his wake Ah Chun protested at such independence. When at last he clambered into the bullock cart with Andreino, he felt that the Italian, with his amused black glance, knew exactly what had happened and understood precisely the disconcerted but elated state the incident had left behind.

Grace Prior, all in white with a sash of pale blue, was the only woman present at the mission house. Besides Archie and Andreino there was a man of perhaps sixty immaculately dressed in white, a garrulous Armenian called Manook with some position at court, and an Anglo-Indian with responsibility for the mails up from British Burma, a duty of which he was inordinately proud. Grace sat behind a tea table which reminded Archie very much of the ladies' bazaars his mother used to hold complainingly at Hasham in aid of converting little heathen souls in some outpost of the Empire – and then he realized, taking a cup of tea, that he was in just such an outpost and indeed in a mission, and he laughed outright so that Grace, who had ventured some mild remark about the enduring quality of English habits even abroad, felt that Archie was quite as pleased to see her as she was to see him, and gave him a smile of purest adoration.

Archie observed the smile but not its implication, and grinned amiably back before going to seek his host and apologize for not calling before as invited. Grace watched him walk across the room with a possessive delight that rendered her immune even to the daunting prospect of Maria's imminent arrival.

'But I agree with you,' Tom was saying earnestly to Manook. 'I don't disallow at all the liberality and generosity of Buddhism. But I cannot regret too bitterly the principle of annihilation which Buddhists covet so, it is so negative, so low spirited, it can only destroy the soul by weakening it – Mr Tennant. How enormously glad I am to see you. Mr Tennant escorted my Grace up river ten days ago. Without him I think the journey would have been unthinkable.'

'In Rangoon, were you?' Manook said, his plump sallow face creased with friendliness. 'And did you see my daughter Hosannah? And my wife? I sent them to Rangoon for safe keeping, you know. I thought it only wise—'

'I am afraid I did not,' Archie said, straining to be back with Buddhism. 'I was only there a few days. I saw all the corporation's godowns and offices and I failed to win the Grand National, but that was all. Do the priests believe in this annihilation principle too?'

Tom, not in the least disconcerted by the leap from race course to religion, put his hand on Archie's arm. 'More than anyone. The *poongyis* are men who have renounced their lives in order to work towards the principle more fully. Mendicants, ascetics—'

'*Professed* mendicants,' Manook said with smiling emphasis, '*Ostensible* ascetics.'

'And every man must pass through a monastery at some time?'

218

From outside in the lane a woman's clear voice rose above the creaking of passing carts. 'You may tell him to wait, Denzil. I shall only be a quarter of an hour. I mean simply to say what is necessary, remove Papa and come away.'

Archie looked inquiringly at his companions. Manook was laughing, Tom had glanced towards his daughter. Grace was pouring tea for Andreino and appeared to have heard nothing.

'Who was that?'

'Miss Beresford, Miss Maria Beresford. That is her father in white.'

Archie said, 'Grace told me about her. She is a favourite with the Queen and has some connection with ruby mines?'

'Yes,' Tom said sadly, 'yes. I fear that she and my Grace were not destined to be companions. The only Englishwomen here too—'

Sweeping along the verandah in her silks with Denzil reluctantly at her heels, Maria was at her most imperious. The morning had been a great success, during the course of which Supayalat had said, 'The mission to Paris can do nothing without my orders. I shall give no orders that do not please me. You know what pleases me. Bring me the plans for Mogok.'

Maria, kneeling before her in the garden pavilion, had bowed her head. Thibaw was present too, but cowed and silent after the dismissal of his mistress and slightly fuddled with the wine he had taken in consolation. Maria knew she need not do more for Thibaw than observe the formalities.

'The English and the French are great nations, Majesty. They have powerful armies. They want the riches of your kingdom.'

Supayalat drew on her cheroot. Her brilliant eyes flickered with amusement. 'Bah! Great! No nation can touch us, they must beg for what they want, *beg*, not take. They cannot take. Cannot. We will consider all these mines, coal, lead, silver, all of them, and our orders will go to Paris.'

She had given Maria, then, a box like a golden bird, its wings outlined with emeralds and rubies, a box that her father-in-law had used for his betel nuts. With this proof of supreme royal favour clasped to her bosom, Maria had first prostrated herself before the Queen and had then risen to withdraw, observing as she did so that Thibaw had fallen asleep, slumped upon his *salun-daw* like a stout and sulky boy.

Supayalat's manner had remained with Maria as it frequently did, and she bore with her into the mission house an impossible haughtiness. Her glance swept around the room, took in nothing new beyond a large, loosely made young man with rumpled brown hair and no distinction, and then, without so much as a nod of greeting to either Grace or Tom, she moved swiftly over to her father.

'Papa! I thought I should find you here. It is quite time you came home, do you not think?'

'Oh yes!' Grace said, too eagerly, 'Mr T – Tennant was so kind—'

'Mr Tennant. Of course.'

Behind her, Hubert said, 'Dearest, may I present Mr Tennant to you?'

She was, without doubt, the most wonderful and disagreeable creature Archie had ever seen. He stepped forward, forbidding himself to smile until she did, and bowed very slightly but did not offer his hand. She remained holding hers out, imperious.

'Mr Tennant,' she said, with more than a hint of command.

Archie's hands remained by his side. 'Miss Beresford.'

Behind her, Denzil Blount gave a snort of laughter. Archie inclined his head a little once more, retrieved his teacup from the table where he had left it and went purposefully across the room to Grace.

'Would I be allowed another cup? I was shooting all day and I feel I could drink a river.'

Grace, with a heart that was almost bursting, seized his cup. 'Oh, Mr Tennant, of course, of course, as many as you like!'

'Snipe?' Denzil asked, his eyes still upon Maria, 'You were shooting snipe?'

'Guinea fowl.'

'Not quite such sport but plenty of them.'

Hubert said, 'Better game here than I ever saw in India.'

222

'I think it's splendid, sir,' Archie said, 'the whole place.'

Grace said, 'Will you have some tea, Maria?'

'Thank you,' Maria said furiously, not moving. Grace poured out a cup and placed it carefully on the edge of the table, keeping her hand upon the saucer to prevent any of the men picking it up in helpless gallantry.

'There,' she said, 'your tea.'

In silence, Maria stalked to the table. Across her Denzil said to Archie, 'I wonder how splendid you will think Burma when you have been out in the forests for weeks.'

Archie grinned. 'I'll tell you. When I come back.'

Maria, her cup rattling in its saucer, said, 'Papa, we should not be long.'

'Up the Chindwin?' Hubert said to Archie.

'No, sir. The other direction. I shall be working with Frederick Winser under Eisenhauer. He is the manager of the Pyinmana forests, I believe.'

'I would not know,' Hubert said.

'Papa, when you have finished—'

'Have you any experience of dacoits?' Denzil said.

Grace gasped.

'No. But I imagine I soon will have.'

'Andreino has been telling me,' Tom said from the other side of the room, a spot he had not moved from since Maria's entrance, 'that now the Bombay-Burmah extract all their own timber,

223

now they no longer use contractors, that they plan to build a hill station for all you young men, somewhere for you to recuperate.'

'Papa! I am waiting!'

'Yes,' Archie said, 'a place called Maymyo, I believe. It has a lovely climate, you need a fire at night in the winter.'

Denzil put down his teacup. 'Forty degrees not uncommon. You should go and see it. It isn't more than forty miles or so though, of course, the road is hardly more than a track. Poinsettias grow there like rhododendrons in England.'

A small spasm crossed Maria's face.

Archie said, 'Do you know Maymyo, Miss Beresford?'

She did not look at him. 'No. No, I do not. I have been too much preoccupied with court affairs during my time in Mandalay to go on excursions. Papa, we must go.'

'Court affairs?'

Maria did not like the tone of Archie's voice. Her own was at its most haughty as she replied, 'I have daily audience with Her Majesty Queen Supayalat.' She turned to Grace. 'I hope you will find it – pleasant to be back in Mandalay.' Then she nodded to the men present, paused fractionally before Archie as if she might say something but changed her mind, and swept, head high, out onto the verandah.

Hubert paused long enough to say to Archie, 'Of course, having been here so long, we are reasonably experienced and you should not hesitate to ask us if there is anything you wish to know,' before following her.

'Not,' Tom said quietly to Grace, bending over her, 'a success, my dear.'

She looked up, smiling. 'I don't mind. Not any more.'

'Ah! The comforts of growing older.'

Grace dared not look at Archie.

'Well?' Andreino said, 'Mr Tennant. What do you think of our self-appointed first lady?'

'Very, very handsome.'

Denzil laughed. 'Oh yes. Undeniably that.'

'Come,' Manook said, 'come. We must talk of serious things. Are you not perturbed, you British. The French—'

'No,' Andreino said smoothly, his eyes flickering towards Denzil, 'we are not perturbed in the least. I speak as agent for the corporation, you understand, not in any way as a mock Englishman.'

'Signor Andreino, I wish I had your confidence.'

'You must keep it,' Denzil said. 'It might sustain you in time of trial.'

Andreino glanced at him again. 'It will also prove justified, Signor Blount.'

Grace had left her post to stand as close to Archie as she dared. 'Will you go soon? Will you go to the forests soon? And will you stay there all winter, will I – will Papa and I not see you until the rains begin?'

He looked down at her. She wore an

225

expression he had been used to see on the liver and white face of the springer spaniel he had reluctantly left at Riverdene with old Phillipson. His response to the dog had always been to put a brief but grateful hand upon her head. Grace's head was the perfect height for such a caress and her hair as fine and smooth as silk. Archie thought what a stir he would create if he touched her thus. He smiled down at her.

'Oh, you should pity me, Miss Prior! I go next week into the forests where I shall probably catch a fever from the night dews and if I don't die of that, die of the frustration of not being able to make myself understood by the fifty elephants and foresters in my charge. There are leeches and probably snakes and any books I take will go mouldy and goodness knows what I will eat—'

'I know you are teasing but there's too much truth in it for me to bear. Are you really to be so wretched?'

'I shall be as happy as a king.'

Grace looked down. 'I shall not, thinking of you there.'

Unaccountably, Archie's heart sank a little. Too heartily he said, 'Then don't think of me. Four months will go by very fast, you'll see. And you have the school here and your father—'

'Yes,' she said, 'yes.'

Andreino was bowing before her. 'I must take your escort away, Signorina. It is a great pleasure to have you back with us in Mandalay. We were sadly deprived of pretty faces.'

'Come again,' Grace said to Archie, 'before you go. I am always here in the afternoons. Please come.'

A minute later, clattering down the verandah steps to the lane, Archie had the sensation that Andreino, for the second time that afternoon, knew precisely his state of mind. He was even laughing softly.

'Well? What would you do?'

Andreino put a hand on his shoulder. 'Just what you are about to do, my friend. Go to the forests.'

11

Ah Chun was squatting, waiting, in a corner of Archie's bedroom.

'*Thakin* Winser. Has fever.'

'Good God!' Archie said. 'But he was fine! I left him this afternoon absolutely fine—'

'Fever here so sudden. *Thakin* Winser coming home on pony, lying so, on pony, arms hang.'

A mosquito net shrouded Frederick's bed so thickly that he was scarcely visible within its folds. The drill trousers and tunic he should have worn that evening lay neatly across the only chair, and his bearer, a fly whisk in one hand and a palm leaf fan in the other, crouched on the floor, swatting and waving, with an expression of the most intense gloom.

'Frederick!'

A muffled oath came from within the white folds, followed by a sharp command. The bearer leaped to his feet and pulling up the net, revealed Frederick, stark naked and pouring with sweat, his eyes closed. His fists were clenched and he was shaking uncontrollably. Archie put a hand on his shoulder and almost leaped back at contact with that scalding skin.

'Don't worry,' Frederick said without opening his eyes or unclenching his teeth. 'Over soon. Always is. Got some stuff to take but it needs time to work. Quinine mostly.'

'Can I get you anything? Or do anything for you?'

'No. Nothing thanks. Doesn't usually hit me until I'm in the jungle. Still work then. Takes my mind off it. Always pounces on me. Never know it's coming.'

'Shouldn't you have a doctor?'

Frederick gave a short yelp Archie took for laughter. 'Might as well ask for the moon here! Europeans don't know any more than I do and the Burmese a good deal less. Remind me to tell you what they do to women after childbirth if you want a taste of Burmese medicine. I say, Archie—'

'Yes.'

'It shouldn't take long. This, I mean. I usually sweat for a couple of days and then stagger about finding my legs for three to four. We won't have to postpone departure for more than a day or so. D'you want to go ahead of me?'

'Not particularly.'

A spasm shook Frederick so violently that his teeth chattered. When it was over, Archie said, 'Shouldn't Ba Sein be sponging you? To bring the fever down a bit?'

'Good idea. I'd rather you didn't go ahead. You are perfectly capable I know, but I'd like to show you the ropes. Especially as you don't speak the language much yet. Mind?'

229

'Of course not.'

'Tell that idle brute to get water and a sponge. Thanks, Archie. I say. Say good luck to the Chatsworths for me will you? Off tomorrow. Shan't make dinner.'

Dinner was dull without him. The Chatsworths were understandably preoccupied with the following day's journey and either ate with dedication or muttered remarks to each other in the telegrammatic manner of family familiarity. The younger one, tilting his chair back at the end of the meal, eyed Archie across the debris of crumbled bread and banana skins.

'What about your tea party, then? Pretty girls?'

'Two.'

'Ah!' young Chatsworth said knowledgeably. 'The two. Miss Prior and Miss Beresford.' He looked at his brother. 'The corporation don't mind, you know. There's no policy. About Burmese girls.'

Archie tried to subdue the eagerness in his voice. 'Really?'

'No. They are pretty open minded. One of the managers down in Rangoon said to me, "I have neither attitude nor rules." Of course, the Burmese regard it as an honour.'

Archie leaned forward. 'To – to be an Englishman's mistress?'

'Surely. *Bo-kadaw*. White man's wife, they say. Doesn't spoil their chances of marrying a Burman later either.' He looked at his brother again and grinned. 'You can take them into the forests with you. If you like. They regard themselves as married to you as long as you want them. Marriage here is purely civil. You can get rid of them the moment you are tired of them. No trouble.'

The other Chatsworth said with elder brotherly tolerance, 'Oh, of course, he knows all about it. One whole forest season behind him and I don't remember we saw a woman in months.'

'Does Frederick—?'

The elder brother shrugged. 'I don't know. I'm not interested really, not like young Robert here. To tell you the truth, I don't like the idea of native women much, never have. Now, Miss Beresford—'

'Yes,' Archie said, remembering.

'*She* wouldn't have any of us if we were the last men on earth,' young Chatsworth said. 'Give me a Burmese girl any time. Eh, Archie?'

Archie said, 'And they will come with you into the forests? They don't mind?'

'They are proud to.'

The elder Chatsworth stood up. 'Bed, Bob. We're to be off by sunrise. We go in one of the Irrawaddy Flotilla Company steamers with one of their managers from Rangoon. He wants to see how far up the river is navigable for him. We have got a pretty unchartered area this season, Bob and I. Should be amusing. These infernal insects!'

He gave a wild slap on the side of his neck and

a huge speckled mosquito went singing off into the shadows of the room.

'Worse in the forests,' he said. 'Well, goodbye, Tennant. And the best of luck. See you in March.'

'Frederick said to say good luck to you.'

'Poor devil. Never known him ill before. Come on Bob, chop, chop.'

When they had left the room, Archie became aware that he and the mosquito were not the only living things in it. He turned in his chair and observed Ah Chun squatting by the doorway.

'You devil! Were you listening?'

'No, *thakin*.'

Archie strode over to him and pulled him to his feet. 'Not only an eavesdropper but a liar! Either stand behind my chair so that I know you are there or keep away! Don't sneak in corners.' He gave him a rough shake. 'All right, then, Ah Chun. You heard what you heard. And this afternoon you saw what you saw. Do something about it then. Now go and let my net down. I'm going to bed.'

The bungalow was strangely empty the following day. The servants went on padding about their duties in house and garden, wheels screamed as usual outside and the coppersmith birds knocked as relentlessly as ever, but there was no-one to breakfast with, no-one to shoot with, no Frederick shouting at his bearer. He was no better. His skin was greyish in the morning light and Archie, putting a hand on his forehead, doubted that his temperature was any less. Archie decided he would order Ah Chun to take turns with Ba Sein in sponging him and that, if necessary, he would himself sit up with him the following night.

He wandered from room to room, aimlessly. There was a pile of old copies of the *Rangoon Gazette* – always at least ten days old on account of coming up river with the mails – but these were as unalluring as they had ever been, partly because events had overtaken all the news and partly because there was so little mention of anything to do with Mandalay in them. Archie did a clue here and there at random in the crosswords but soon gave up and allowed himself the pleasure of flinging the newspapers all over the floor in the comfortable knowledge that within minutes someone would have picked them up and reassembled them in their neat stack.

He thought of shooting and decided he was not in the mood to do it without a companion. He thought of riding and maybe practising his lime-cutting and then came to the conclusion that it was the one thing he seemed to be able to do without practice and, in any case, he liked an audience. He remembered what Andreino had said about the corporation's plans to build a hill station for its forest employees at this place called Maymyo, and he was half out of his chair at the thought that he might go up into the hills and see it, when he remembered that a forty-mile journey up a rough road and back could not be accomplished in a day and that he should not leave Frederick overnight. He slumped back in his chair and bit his nails and sighed.

Andreino's voice, calling for Ah Chun from the verandah, was unbelievably welcome. Archie leaped up and went out to meet him.

'Ah, my friend! I hear poor Winser has the fever. So you are all alone. I saw the brothers Chatsworth off on their travels three hours ago. What are you doing with yourself today?'

'I thought of riding up to Maymyo. But it would take too long.'

'Three days, to do it comfortably, there and back. But you should go, it is a most lovely place—'

'I don't want to leave Frederick.'

'No. No, of course not. But you may leave him for a few hours? Take off those clothes and dress properly. I shall take you to the palace.'

'The palace!'

Andreino shrugged. 'I fear it won't be very amusing. I have to do this at the beginning of each season. We will squat for hours on some floor in the palace while we negotiate the price of the leases, the price the King must pay for any timber he wants, the wages of the foresters. But I should be glad of your company.'

'Do we negotiate with the King himself?'

'Ah, no. Only with ministers. It is a very lengthy business. But you will like to see the

234

palace and the royal city. Wear shoes, not boots, they are easier to remove.'

Archie looked both astounded and indignant. 'Remove them!'

'Of course. We must all do so. The old British Resident here, he managed to keep his shoes on and, of course, Miss Beresford is permitted to appear shod in the palace. Even I was allowed to keep my shoes on for the late King's funeral. But that was an especial favour. In the ordinary course of events, we must humble ourselves and appear barefoot.'

Archie nodded. 'Actually,' he said, 'I'd humble myself much further in order to get inside the palace.'

Once there, however, nothing was quite as he had expected. There was more space everywhere, the streets of the city were wider, straighter, cleaner than he had imagined. There were plots of grass scattered among the wooden houses with their winged and glittering roofs, the harshness of the scarlet and gold was softened by the frothy boughs of the tamarind trees. A procession came out of the palace as Archie and Andreino approached, a procession headed by a general dressed in scarlet velvet and copper, who held his reins high and wide in an extraordinary formal fashion and rode with two huge brass shields suspended from the saddle between his legs and the horse's sides. Over him a bearer held an umbrella on a long curving pole and behind him walked a column of attendants, barefoot but wearing turbans of gold-embroidered velvet. Behind them was a detachment of much more poorly dressed men, each carrying a rifle with a roll of cloth bound to one end and a cooking pot swinging from the other.

'Ah,' Andreino said, 'the Burmese army. That wadding on their rifles, that is a sleeping mat. And there is rice in those pouches at their waists. Each soldier is self-sufficient. This way, through this postern.'

Archie followed him through the low doorway and past the parliament building and a gilded and mirrored structure outside which a sickly looking elephant with a strangely mottled trunk stood glumly, head hanging.

'The sacred white elephant?'

'The same.'

'He looks the same as any other elephant to me. Only not so healthy. What is the matter with his trunk?'

'That's the whiteness,' Andreino stopped and regarded the elephant. 'He takes milk directly from the breasts of nursing women. They clamour for the privilege. It does not seem to do him much good, does it? They line up here, a dozen, twenty sometimes, and he goes along the line from breast to breast, his trunk—'

'Stop it,' Archie said, revolted.

'I shock you?'

'He does.'

Andreino laughed. 'You will get used to it. The East does not have the same regard for the flesh

236

as the West. You will see. Now you must take off your shoes. We will climb onto the platform.'

The audience hall into which Andreino led him more than fulfilled his expectations of Eastern royalty. The huge teak pillars which marched down the length, on either side, had been lacquered in scarlet and studded with scraps of mirrors so that the room was filled with a winking, darting light as of a million fireflies. The floor was of teak, huge, wide, gleaming boards, down the centre of which ran a strip of vermilion carpet bordered with capering yellow dragons. The walls were panelled with mirrors edged in dull gold and the ceiling, high and dim above their heads, was intricately painted and carved. There was no furniture beyond a low *salun-daw* on a platform at one end, but the room was lined with people, some Burmese, some Europeans, all squatting in groups in such privacy as the spaces between the pillars afforded.

'We wait,' Andreino said. He chose a corner at some distance from everybody else and lowered himself onto the floor. 'Those two there are Greeks, engineers, and the big one, he is a German, a railway specialist, and the two Indians are British subjects – which reminds me. Some other Indians, British subjects also, whom Mindoon gave land to for building themselves houses, they have been turned out, no compensation, nothing, and their property given to Burmese. And what is worse, two traders from Madras, British subjects again, have been murdered in prison. No-one knows why they went to prison in the first place. I have managed to get their wives and children places on a steamer for Rangoon, but what they will do there, I don't know, poor creatures. I don't keep warning you for nothing.'

Archie, shifting uncomfortably in an attempt to find a bearable arrangement for his legs, said, 'But would we be touched? We white men?'

'Three, four years ago, I would have said no. Today I only say maybe not.'

'But there are white people in high favour at court, Miss Beresford, her father, the Frenchman everyone speaks of who has recently left—'

Andreino shrugged. 'This is such a fickle place. Like a firework. One match and it can all go up, very pretty, very spectacular, all gone in a moment.'

'I've seen nothing,' Archie said. 'I've been here a week and the nearest I have come to hostility is a sullen look or two in the roads, nothing more.'

'Even while we sit here, even beneath us, the violence is happening. The dungeons are full of royal prisoners, princesses, queens, anyone who might suggest that the present rule is in any way corrupt or ill-judged. Do you know how they live, those poor women? They are bricked up except for one small opening, their legs are ironed, the temperature must be always over a hundred. If the Burmese behave like that to their own people, what might they not – Bow, Archie, just a little. Our ministers are coming.'

Four men were advancing down the strip of red carpet. Despite the heat, which had reduced Archie's shirt to a clammy skin he was trying not to think about, they wore velvet robes to the floor with high tunic collars and surcoats of gold brocade. Huge winged over-collars stretched out to the edges of their shoulders and down to their breasts and on their heads they wore incredible hats, pinnacles of gold and scarlet rising from wide brims of beaten copper. Behind them attendants padded softly.

Andreino said something to them, in a tone of respectful formality. The smallest of the ministers replied in the same rhythms, and then all four seated themselves kneeling upon the floor, their hands folded in their brocaded laps, their slanting eyes fixed incuriously upon Archie.

He understood almost nothing. It seemed to him an interminable time while Andreino and the ministers talked in the strange yawning vowels of the Burmese court language. He dared not move, for no-one else had, and his limbs ached intolerably. The air, which had seemed so mysteriously dim when they first entered, he now perceived to be thick with dust and flies, and the humming of the latter and the muttering of the crouching groups among the glittering pillars filled him with a drowsiness so heavy that once or twice he caught himself swooning forwards onto the floor. He was rescued by a gecko which darted around the pillar nearest to him and began to move desperately back and forth on the mirrored surface, as if frantic to escape the jagged little fragments of its own reflection. Archie watched it with interest, as it quivered and flickered, its tiny hands clinging for a fraction of a second, now here, now there—

'We may go,' Andreino said softly.

Obediently and stiffly, Archie bowed. The four little brocaded figures in their absurd hats like temple roofs rose easily to their feet and retreated up the red carpet in precisely the formation they had come. Archie stood with difficulty, grimacing.

'Not what I had hoped,' Andreino said. 'The King is becoming more demanding each season and more intransigent. It is not what it was in the old days with Mindoon, with his father. There were difficulties then, but we adjusted them. This King is a spendthrift, the Queen is worse.' He spoke so softly, Archie had to crane to hear him and his eyes moved round the room ceaselessly, watchfully. 'It seems the King will soon require a loan from the corporation if he is to renew the leases. The figure mentioned is twenty-two lakhs of rupees. That is well over one hundred and thirty thousand pounds. His ministers say he is increasing the royal lotteries by the fantastic method of decreeing that each rupee shall be worth sixteen, not fourteen, annas so that every person shall have two more annas to put into the lottery and thus fill the royal coffers. If that fails—'

'It's mad!' Archie said. 'Can't he see?'

'No. You must understand the nature of royalty here. They are omnipotent. All powerful, quite literally. They do not see themselves as men among men, not in the smallest degree. Come, we should go. I have had to promise more to the foresters, I fear. It means that you will have even more rupees to carry, the coins are so bulky I am afraid. Ah, what a world, what a world.'

The sunlight and heat outside smote them like a blow in the face. They descended carefully from the palace platform, retrieved their shoes and retraced their steps past the despondent elephant and the parliament building to the gate that led into the city. As they stepped through, watched with disconcerting intentness by the guard in his velvet cap and tin hat, a bullock cart drew up outside containing a plump little woman, obviously part Burmese despite her European clothes, and Miss Beresford, cool and pale beneath a parasol of pale green silk.

The little woman leaned forward excitedly, grasping the ribs of the cart's sides. 'Why! Signor Andreino! Have you been having audience? We go each morning, you know, every day I come to fetch Miss Beresford. I don't suppose there are two Europeans who know the court so intimately—'

Maria, who had been gazing steadfastly ahead with no apparent consciousness that Archie and Andreino stood in the road below her, said coldly, 'We should not linger, Miss Calogreedy. The Queen does not like us to be late.'

Mattie gave a peal of laughter and put a smooth plump little brown hand out of the cart for Andreino to take and kiss. Her eyes, black like any Burmese, but lidded and fringed with thick lashes like those of the Mediterranean, flickered appraisingly over Archie. He bowed very slightly.

'Miss Calogreedy, may I present Mr Tennant to you. Miss Beresford, I believe you have already met Mr Tennant.'

Archie rested his elbows on the side of the cart. 'Good morning, Miss Beresford.'

The green parasol gave a small shake. 'Please do not attempt to delay us, Mr Tennant.'

'I do not suppose there is any frantic hurry, Miss Beresford. Signor Andreino and I have sat for two hours over a ten-minute bargaining point, having waited above an hour before that.'

'Audiences with the Queen are entirely another matter, Mr Tennant.'

'Am I to believe,' said Archie conversationally, aware that Andreino, though ostensibly flirting with Miss Calogreedy, was listening with amusement, 'that you have done nothing in all the last four years but go in and out of the palace at the whim of the Burmese Queen?'

The smooth line of Maria's throat bulged a little as she swallowed her temper. 'Can you imagine a greater or rarer distinction, Mr Tennant?'

'I wasn't thinking so much of distinction, more of amusement, of enlarging one's knowledge, one's sympathies. Have you not ventured outside Mandalay in five years?'

Maria, from the moment she had observed Archie climbing stooped through the palace postern, had resolved to remain as aloof as possible in order to impress upon him her superiority to and her disdain for people of his sort. But he seemed strangely impervious to the manner she used so successfully upon everyone else and, what was worse, he was even beginning to disconcert her with his comfortable persistence. The grey flannel that clothed his folded arms she observed to be only inches from her own skirts. In order to descend with proper dignity from the cart, she would have to ask him to move and, preferably, to move away altogether since, even after years of practice, it was not an operation that could be performed with reliable dexterity. The bullocks occasionally lurched forward or the cart tilted abruptly for no apparent reason, or one simply missed one's footing. She turned her head at last and looked down at him as chillingly as she could.

'The court has not thought it necessary to leave the royal palace and therefore any movement has been unnecessary for me also.'

'I thought of going up to Maymyo,' he said. 'A little mountain air, see the pineapples being harvested. My departure into the forest has been delayed a few days, Frederick Winser is unwell. If I were to make up a party, a sort of excursion, to go up into the hills, would you come? Would you forsake your duties at court, duties you must be heartily sick of, and come for just two or three days?'

Dignity or no dignity, Maria rose in the cart. 'It is an absurd idea. Most certainly not.'

Archie shrugged. He said to Andreino, 'Then it seems that in a few weeks I shall have the privilege of knowing more about Burma than Miss Beresford has known in five years.'

Mattie Calogreedy began to giggle and clapped her hand to her mouth. Andreino, bowing to hide his own smile, took a step away from the bullock cart.

'We must not detain you further, ladies. We must bid you farewell.'

Slowly, Archie took his arms off the cart and put his hands into his pockets. He walked a few deliberate steps from the cart and then turned to say his goodbyes. Maria had remained quite motionless, standing stiff and furious in the cart in the watery shadow of her parasol.

'Miss Calogreedy, Miss Beresford, good morning—'

'Mr Tennant!'

'Miss Beresford.'

There was a small pause. Archie waited, his eyes screwed up against the glare.

'Mr Tennant. Do you never smile?'

He shook his head. 'Very seldom, Miss Beresford. And then only – it is my strict rule – as a reflection of another's.'

Andreino took his arm as they walked away

244

and through it Archie could feel convulsions of laughter.

'You English! You English! Where do you find the courage? Ah, you have lightened my morning, more than you know. "Mr Tennant, do you never smile?" "Very seldom, Miss Beresford—" Magnificent! Wonderful! She is becoming absurd, our Miss Beresford. It is not before time she is mocked a little. She was always proud, now after these years at court, she is really intolerable, scarcely human. Her father dares say nothing. Signor Blount, who might, values her influence with Supayalat too much to chance a correction and, in any case, he does not care, she amuses him! I think you are like him, you too are amused.'

Archie looked over his shoulder. The palace postern was empty but for the guard, not so much as a flicker of green silk.

'Partly I am amused, partly—' he stopped.

'And the other partly? You find her handsome?'

'The other partly,' Archie said firmly, quickening his stride, 'the other partly does not matter in the least.'

He slept heavily that afternoon, a hot troubled sleep full of dreams that were lunatic but so powerful that their influence dogged him through an early evening ride and even his solitary dinner. He ate mechanically and without appetite, a mildewed copy of *Punch* from March 1880 laid out before him, and he chewed and gazed at the parliamentary report and saw and tasted nothing. Frederick was as hot as ever but had had sufficient strength to say between his clenched teeth that the last thing he wanted was Archie brooding over him like some damned old woman all night and, if Archie wanted to make himself useful, he could remove those two infernal blacks and their sponges before they soaked him, Frederick, into an early grave.

Huge blue flies crawled across the tablecloth towards the crumbled bread Archie had scattered. He watched their progress mindlessly, pushing crumbs in their path, making obstacles they maddeningly refused to acknowledge. One flew heavily into the water jug and floundered there, buzzing, knocking itself helplessly on the glass walls. Archie peeled a banana, took one bite and threw the rest across the table. He then occupied a full five minutes by making bread pellets and attempting to hit the banana target with them. When he had scored eleven out of sixteen attempts, Ah Chun padded into the room and put a port decanter at his elbow.

'No,' Archie said, 'not in this heat. Take it away.'

'*Thakin.*'

'Yes?'

'In two days we cannot be going. *Thakin* Winser more ill. Six, seven days maybe. Maybe eight.'

'Then we will go ahead.'

'Alone, *thakin*?'

'Alone. Even danger, Ah Chun, is preferable to sitting alone gazing at a whole lot of bluebottles.'

Ah Chun waited a moment. 'I have family in Maymyo. You are going to Maymyo, I tell them. They cook for you, make welcome.'

Archie shook his head. 'I don't know, Ah Chun. Ask me in the morning. I simply don't know. I feel too stupid tonight to think about anything.'

'*Thakin* need me, want—?'

Archie stood up. 'No. No, nothing. I shall sleep off my lethargy. I'll be better in the morning.'

His bedroom was ready for him as it was every evening, the folds of the mosquito net let down, the nightshirt he never used lay on a chair as a sort of ritual to please Ah Chun, and two oil lamps, giving off their sickly odour and dim yellow light either side of his bed. The floor was bare, the screened window curtainless, the walls empty but for a scattering of geckos. There had been a single picture when Archie arrived, a framed reproduction of Queen Victoria by Winterhalter, the infant Prince of Wales cradled in her arms, but Ah Chun, dismissing the significance of any queen but his own, had said that the picture would attract ghosts and had taken it away.

'He'll sell it of course,' Frederick said, 'in the bazaar.'

Archie did not mind much. The romantic and

sentimental image of motherhood, swathed in white frills and flowers, had only seemed to him extraordinary. He would have liked some hunting prints, the hand-coloured Jorrocks with their balloons of comic conversation that had decorated his bedroom at Hasham perhaps, but failing those, the geckos would do very well. He sat down in the cane-bottomed armchair, unbuttoned his collar and began to pull off his shoes. Ah Chun had initially been most put out at Archie's insistence on undressing alone but had been forced to give way. Archie did not understand it himself but only knew that whereas for the whole of the rest of the day he liked to have Ah Chun at his elbow in case he should need him in any way, last thing at night he needed his solitude. He would sit down to take off his shoes and socks, then wander about the room, dropping his clothes on the floor as he removed them before climbing naked into what always seemed to him the ridiculously bridal folds of his mosquito net.

He let one shoe fall onto the floor.

The laces of the second one twisted, knotted and when he jerked at them irritably, broke. He swore.

In French, a girl's voice said softly, 'May I help you? My fingers are smaller than yours.'

In the darkest shadows by the doorway leading to the bathroom, a small figure was kneeling, small enough to have been a child, but for the silhouetted cylinder of hair upon her head.

Tom's immensely kind face tautened with displeasure. Archie, quite bowled over by the splendour of Maria's appearance, was rooted to the spot and could take in nothing properly except that tall, long-necked figure in its wonderful clothes.

'Miss Beresford,' Tom said, his voice quite unnatural with self-control, 'how good of you to come.'

She turned slowly, with a small smile. 'I heard that your daughter was back in Mandalay, Mr Prior.'

Hubert's hand came out and lightly touched Maria's sleeve. She drew her arm away at once, but smiled at him as she did it.

'Grace, Miss Beresford, has been home a full ten days.'

Grace rose from behind the tea table. Beside Maria she seemed hardly to exist at all but became as insubstantial as a shadow, her pale face and smooth hair seeming as gauzy as her dress.

'Good afternoon, Maria.'

Her voice was almost steady. She had achieved this by gazing relentlessly at Archie since the moment Maria had entered and drawing courage from his solid and comforting presence.

In silence, Maria turned slowly towards her. Colour rose in Grace's cheeks like a pink tide, suffusing even her forehead.

'I trust,' Maria said, 'that you had a pleasant journey.'

'Who are you?' Archie said. 'What are you doing here, who let you in?'

The girl rose and came silently forward to kneel at his feet. She wore a cheap tamein of pink cotton, a jacket of coarse muslin over a band of patterned stuff bound tight across her breasts and tassels of jasmine flowers in her hair. She brought her hands up, palm to palm, the fingertips touching her forehead, and shikoed low before Archie who still sat, gazing at her, one foot bare, his shirt open, his fingers clutching the broken shoelace.

'Don't do that,' he said. 'Who are you?'

'I don't please you?'

He blushed. He said quickly, 'Yes, yes, of course, I do not – I do not know anything about you. Why are you here?'

She leaned forward and began to pick at the broken shoelace with slender brown fingers. 'My name is Hnin Si. Signor Andreino has been very kind to me. For years I must work in the cigar factory, now I am one of the best, the quickest. Ah Chun brought me here tonight. He put me in your room, to wait for you. He bought new clothes for me, these clothes. He says you will give me money for these clothes. There. There is your shoe. Tomorrow Ah Chun will find you new ribbons.'

'Laces. Why do you speak French?'

'During one year I am the lover of a Frenchman. Five years since. You will know him. He is named Pierre Bonvilain. He has just gone back to Paris with the King's mission.'

249

Barefoot, Archie stood up. She knelt still, staring up at him, her flat oriental face enlivened by the character in it and the rosy colour that spread along her high cheekbones.

'I don't please you, *thakin*?'

'Ah Chun brought you?'

'Yes. You are angry? You did not tell him to?'

Archie stooped and took hold of her elbows, fragile as bird bones in his grasp, and lifted her to her feet.

'I – I almost told him to. I am not angry, no, nor displeased. Just – just – Tell me. Bonvilain, Andreino, many others? Many other white men?'

She shook her head. He did not know if she were lying and discovered that he did not seem to care. He bent down to peer closely at her, at the tight smooth cone of her hair, her finely textured skin, and caught the mingled scent of jasmine and coconut oil and garlic that floated from her. Her body was tiny, as straight and featureless as a sapling, showing no curve of breast or hip and her wide brow, smooth as brown satin, was barely level with his chest.

She said, 'Ah Chun say you are a good man.'

'A good *master*, perhaps. I don't beat him.'

'You can beat me. If you like.'

He gripped her elbows more tightly. 'I do *not* like.'

She smiled then, her eyes vanishing into dark

slits of delight. She brought her hands up and laid them lightly, flat against his chest. He swallowed hard.

'Do you know any English?'

She said in English, with a heavy accent, 'I love you.'

'That is a silly thing to say. Is that all you know?'

She nodded.

'I will teach you some more.'

'Then I may stay?'

He did not seem able to let go of her elbows. He said, 'Yes. Please stay.'

She leaned forward and put her cheek on his chest between her two hands for a moment, then straightened up to smile at him again. 'Let go of my arms, *thakin*.'

Reluctantly his hands dropped to his sides. She reached up and began to unbutton his shirt, picking up first one arm and then the other to undo the cuffs. Archie watched her, mesmerized, entirely absorbed in her and the boiling turmoil that was going on within.

'Have – have you ever been in the forests?'

She shook her head. 'Not before.'

'Before?'

'Before this time. Come,' she said, taking his hand, '*thakin*, come,' and she put her hand on the buttons of his trousers.

'No,' Archie said, 'don't—'

'I don't please you?'

He shouted, 'Don't keep saying that! Of course

251

you do! You know you do! It's simply that I want
– I have wanted – it's so long—'

'*Thakin*,' she said, 'I have not come to talk.
Now take my hand.'

Huge and naked beside her, he said, 'But I am
so big, I will hurt you, you are small, so small—'

She shook her head. 'Not hurt. I am small but
not weak. You will see. Come. Come and I will
show you,' and gripping his hand in her small
calloused fingers, she towed him across the room
behind her towards the waiting bed.

12

In the dim greenish light of her bedroom, Grace
stooped before her little speckled looking glass.
Since the day before, when Tom, confessing
himself at last to be weary and sadly in need of a
change, had said that after all they should both
go up to Maymyo on Archie's expedition, she
had been in raptures of happiness. If Tom
wouldn't go, she couldn't and she had been in
the depths of misery at his obstinacy, his insistence that his task must keep him in Mandalay,
day in, day out, kings and queens and politics
notwithstanding, until the mission school was
thriving, packed to the doors with eager little
Burmese Christians. Grace had been afraid to
beg too hard, afraid that she might suddenly say
that she didn't care where they went as long as
she might have three days with Archie, so she had
sat and prayed, with her eyes tight shut as they
had been during childhood prayers, and chastised
herself for praying such a selfish prayer, and then
Tom had said suddenly, framed in the doorway
on his way down to the school, 'Gracie, we shall
go with Mr Tennant. It can't hurt to be away
only for a few days and I think I am tired, though

I don't like to think it. Perhaps I shall come back
a lion refreshed—'

That was yesterday. That was before she
had discovered that all her muslins were like
limp rags after two weeks in the steam heat of
Mandalay and before Mr Blount, coming by
at teatime for some undisclosed reason, had
said that he and Mr and Miss Beresford had
been invited too. Grace had handed him his tea
and, muttering hastily about having some dust in
her eye, had fled to her room and its scanty
privacy.

It is not fair, she said wretchedly to God, I
don't ask you for much. I try not to bother you
with little things, with details, but this is not a
little thing, this is desperately important to me. It
is the last chance I shall have of seeing him before
the rains because he will leave on Saturday. Mr
Winser will be well enough then to travel and
they will be in the forests all that time. I know
you think that human love shouldn't matter beside divine love, and I do try, I *do*, but we have to
live our life here, we have to get through the days
and it can't be wrong for me to long for the
days when he is part of them and find the ones I
don't see him so long. And I shan't see him for,
oh, more than a hundred and fifty days perhaps,
so why can't I have these three, only three, to
myself, why must she be there . . . ?

'My dear,' Tom said, outside her door, 'Grace.
Are you unwell?'

'Oh, no,' she said, forgetting the excuse she

had made to Denzil, 'just a slight headache, nothing much.'

'Come back, then,' Tom said, 'come back. We have guests.'

It was only Manook who was there, rubbing his hands and smiling, and Mr Blount still, his cup half full, his eyes appraisingly on Grace. He rose as she came in and drew a chair up close to her tea table.

'Tell me, Miss Prior, your friend Mr Tennant. He has been to the palace. You are great friends, are you not, after that long and intimate journey? You will know why Mr Tennant has been seeking an audience?'

She blushed a little and shook her head. 'No. I know nothing. I – I have not seen Mr Tennant since you have, not since you were both here—'

'But you will go up to Maymyo?'

'Yes,' Grace said carefully, pouring more hot water into the pot, 'I believe we will. If Papa can get away.'

'He intends to. He has just said so.' Denzil took his cup from her. 'I am not sure that I will go and you know Miss Beresford does not like to leave Mandalay. So I imagine you will be quite a small party. Perhaps you would do a little favour for me?'

Grace, aglow with sudden gratitude, beamed upon him. 'But of course, Mr Blount! I should be happy to. I am so sorry Miss Beresford has decided not to come. Maymyo is reputed to be so lovely and the air of course is so much superior to anything one breathes down here in Mandalay. What can I do for you?'

'It isn't much,' Denzil said, 'but I should be most interested to know what Archie Tennant thought of the palace, which ministers he saw and so forth. Don't mention my name, of course, because if I can help him – and I might well be able to if I know, through you, what it is he was seeking – I had rather not be burdened with gratitude. You understand me, Miss Prior?'

'Perfectly,' she said. 'And if he cannot be grateful to you, I can.'

He stood up. 'Please don't,' he said. 'I never know what to do with gratitude. When will you return? Friday? I look forward to it, Miss Prior. And a *bon voyage* in the meantime.'

Since that conversation, her every waking moment had been devoted to thoughts about or preparations for the journey. Most of those thoughts and preparations had been – to her despair and inability to do otherwise – concerned with her appearance. She had a new straw hat with a deep crown smothered in marguerites. It had come by steamer from Selah in Rangoon with a note to say that it was Parisian and a little present and that they missed her sorely at the convent and were very dull. Grace sat up half the night changing the pink ribbons on her muslin for yellow, too excited to sleep and terrified of having circles under her eyes the following day through not having slept enough. When she heard Archie on the verandah the next morning, talking to her father, she had dropped on her knees by her bed, for once careless of crushing all those flounces, and said a heartfelt prayer of thankfulness.

Archie was dressed as usual in the khaki drill trousers and tunic that were to be his uniform in Burma. He was swinging his topee by its strap in one hand and listening to her father with the intentness that made him such a flattering companion.

'You should not be surprised that the Beresfords will not come,' Tom was saying earnestly, forgetting the cup of tea he held so that his own clothes were becoming liberally sprinkled as he gestured, 'but I am disappointed for you. Indeed I am. Of course, Miss Beresford's head has been a little turned, but she has sterling qualities and it is a pity you should not have a chance to see them, a great pity she only appears to you at her worst. Her father is indeed a vain man, pitifully so, but the love and loyalty she gives him are unstinted, she would do anything to protect him, promote him. It is a great misfortune for her to be motherless. A mother would have a balancing influence—'

Grace tripped along the verandah and put her arm through her father's. 'Papa will forgive anyone for anything. He simply does not have the capacity to see ill for more than two seconds together. Mr Tennant this is such a lovely plan! It will be – I mean, it will do Papa so much good!'

'We will not be very many,' Archie said. 'Only

four in fact, yourselves, Signor Andreino and me
– but we have an army of servants, all armed to
the teeth.' He smiled down at Grace. 'Frederick
insisted, so did Andreino. Neither of them sup-
poses we shall have the smallest interference but
they want us to be prepared. Prepared! Two
elephants, four ponies, a bullock cart, enough
provisions to feed an army – it's astonishing. The
Burmese—' he checked himself. Hnin Si, pressed
close to him in the hot heavy blackness of the
previous night, had said that if he permitted her
to come into the forests with him, she would be
no trouble, get in no one's way, bring nothing
that she could not carry in a Shan bag slung over
one shoulder. He had been about to contrast this
economy of luggage with their own extravagance
and had suddenly realized the impossibility of his
remark and blushed hotly.

Grace gazed at him with earnest sympathy,
hoping that she might relieve whatever discomfiture he was suddenly afflicted with, but he did
not look at her, only regarded his boots for a
while, very intently, and then announced that if
the Priors were ready, they should be off.

The elephants had departed some hours before in darkness, shuffling on their huge dry feet
away towards the east and the first rosy streaks of
dawn. They carried a cooking stove, an immense
quantity of rations, bedding, mosquito nets,
folding tables and chairs, brass lamps and the oil
to fill them, canteens of water and a considerable number of green rubber groundsheets. The

258

bullock cart, canopied against the sun, was for Grace, and the gentlemen were to ride, a syce leading the fourth pony should Grace become weary of her springless conveyance and need a change. The entire caravan would set off, leaving the statutory quarter of a mile between each group to allow the dust to settle, the gentlemen going ahead, the cart and the bulk of the servants following.

The ponies and the cart and all the servants who could be spared from the corporation bungalow and Andreino's house had been assembled in a dusty space under some tamarind trees at the south-east corner of the palace walls.

'Rifle to each man,' Frederick had said the previous day, sitting on the bungalow verandah with an abacus and a series of much-altered account books. 'Any trouble, don't stand any nonsense, shoot for their feet. Tie 'em up, tie 'em to a tree and leave 'em to sweat until you come down the hills again.'

Archie, feeling that it all sounded as improbable as a story in a boy's adventure book, grinned and said wasn't he supposed to hold his fire until he could see the whites of their eyes?

'Don't be an ass,' Frederick said shortly, and returned to his checking and muttering.

Grace was settled in the bullock cart and cushioned with the ponies' haybags, the gentlemen were mounted, and had already begun to move off eastwards when rapid hooves were heard from the city and a voice was heard calling in commanding English, 'Don't move yet! Don't go! We are come to join you after all!'

Maria did not quite understand the powerful impulse that had woken her at dawn and driven her to persuade Hubert to accompany her up into the Shan hills. There were plenty of excellent outward reasons and she had advanced all these to her father; Supayalat was to be confined within a day or so and, of course, at such a time, could not let even so favoured a foreigner as Maria near her; also she, Maria, considered her father to be looking a little fatigued and in need of a change and – she put this argument most forcibly of all – the waiting for news from France was already irksome and likely to become more so and a diversion could only be beneficial. As for the expedition itself, Maria said scornfully, pouring tea for Hubert at an extremely early breakfast, that of course held very little charm for either of them, in the company of that mousy little Grace and the raw boy from the Bombay-Burmah who had fewer manners than any man she had ever come across. Signor Andreino had manners to be sure, but of an unpleasantly oily kind that made one wonder if Archie Tennant's boorishness were not in some ways preferable.

Hubert, deep now in an indolence of five years' standing, drank his tea and smiled at her fondly. He loved to see her animated, absorbed in some scheme; it reminded him of those far off days in Tirimbatore, days when he had seemed consumed by energy himself, driven on ceaselessly by it, days that seemed so distant and strange to him in his present, almost drugged condition, that he could hardly believe himself to be the same man. Perhaps, he reflected, Maria had taken over from him; perhaps Maria had drawn so greedily on the life force they shared as father and daughter that there was nothing left for him now. This notion, surging unbidden into his brain, was not particularly comfortable for a second or two, and when he looked up at Maria her face was to him, for a moment only, that of a hard and calculating stranger.

Breakfast had been followed by the usual whirl of activity that accompanied Maria's dedication to some purpose. Hubert's customary white linen suit was taken away and replaced by a grey one – 'More practical, dearest Papa, on account of the dust' – bags were packed, orders and counter-orders were given to servants and syces, Maria's jewels were packed in chamois leather and hung in a pouch at her waist, messages were sent to Denzil, to Mattie, to the corporation bungalow, to the mission—

'Good Lord!' Archie said, turning in his saddle, quite forgetting Tom's presence. 'Good Lord! Look!'

Maria felt it unnecessary to make any explanation at all. Never mind that she had first refused to come on any terms, then exercised her own unassailable privilege of changing her mind – she now sailed into the small company's midst without the slightest consciousness of doing anything other than granting the most immense favour. Everybody stared to be sure, Tom and Archie in amazement, Andreino smiling and Grace in horror, but she was used to stares, took them as her due. She bowed slightly to them all in turn and, riding to the head so that her pony's nose was clearly in front of Archie's, said over her shoulder, 'Should we not be off?'

Dumbly in their appointed order, they followed her. Early though it still was, the heat was terrific and the white dust of the road, laid briefly at night by the light dew, began to rise in soft puffs and clouds about their hooves. The road was built on a kind of embankment between paddies of young rice which stretched away bright, clear green to the blue hills ahead, the even greenness broken only by the occasional white stupa or clump of darker trees or peasant's hut built of grey weathered teak and tottering on unsteady stilts. It was all very quiet and still except for the shuffle of hooves and bare feet and the grinding squeal of the ungreased axle of Grace's cart in the distance behind, and the silence was made worse by the tension. Only Hubert seemed not to feel it, riding with a faint smile upon his handsome face and his eyes fixed upon the hills ahead or upon his daughter's upright back in her blue-grey habit.

After three or four miles, Archie could bear it no longer. He was about to expostulate to Tom but found he did not wish to be talked out of his anger and into a more Christian and forgiving frame of mind, so he merely muttered that he was going forward a moment and kicked his mount to a trot.

'Miss Beresford.'

She did not turn her head but continued to look ahead, presenting him with her elegant profile under a charming small bowler hat trimmed with grey feathers.

'I may not have had the distinction, the *doubtful* distinction, of knowing you long, but I think one hour's worth of acquaintance would justify me, in the present circumstances, in saying that I find your behaviour perfectly intolerable.'

A small lurch took place somewhere deep in Maria but she gave no outward sign of it. She continued to ride forward, looking fixedly ahead.

'It is one thing,' Archie continued furiously, riding so close to her that their knees almost touched, 'to refuse an invitation with the utmost lack of grace. It is quite another to change your mind with no reference whatsoever to the convenience or feelings of anyone else and to arrive, unannounced, with an air of the most intolerable queenliness and proceed, without a word of explanation or apology, to lead the expedition you spurned contemptuously a few days ago. What made you change your mind I neither know nor care about, but I do know that you have upset everyone here and I do care that their pleasure should be spoiled.'

Sweat had broken out unaccountably on Maria's upper lip and in her armpits and down her spine. It was indeed a blessing that she did not seem to know how to blush, but unfortunately she did not appear to have the same immunity to trembling. She clenched her hands upon the reins and stared rigidly before her, taking deep breaths and holding her smarting eyes forcibly wide open.

She said, 'I will not be spoken to so!'

'And I,' Archie said, in a more normal tone, 'will not be used so. You will oblige me by reining in and dropping back to ride with your father.'

She opened her mouth to overwhelm him with all the imperiousness that had rendered her untouchable in the last few years, all the biting haughtiness that had kept people at bay, and made them afraid to cross her in the smallest degree – and found that she could not trust herself to utter. There seemed to be an obstruction, partly caused by the most blinding fury and outrage, partly by something less manageable and familiar, which made her distrust her ability to be even halfway articulate. Almost choking in her angry confusion, she uttered an unintentional almost pitiful sound, a sort of low moan, and pulled fiercely at her horse's head.

'Dearest!' Hubert said anxiously as he drew level and observed her bent head. 'Dearest! What is the matter? Are you unwell? Come, look at me, you frighten me!'

There was a short pause and then Archie heard her say in a voice of almost steady cheerfulness,

'Dear Papa, how you do fret! Of course, it is nothing. I merely received a whole cloud of dust in my eyes and they are smarting terribly. May I ride with you, Papa? I should so much enjoy it, we never seem to have enough time together, do we, and if I ride with Mr Tennant, we shall only argue about the best route as we did just now and that would hardly be profitable, would it, since neither of us has been this way before!'

At the back of the procession, Grace's teeth were being almost shaken from her head. She had at one moment tried to cry out to her father, riding far ahead with Signor Andreino and deep in conversation, that she should like to get out and ride herself. But he was too far away, too absorbed in what he was saying – indeed it was a good thing Archie had found him a docile and sensible pony for he frequently dropped the reins altogether in order to gesture more eloquently towards his companion – to hear her and, in any case, she supposed miserably that as she did not possess a beautiful habit like Maria's she would only, in her crumpled muslins, look like a bag of laundry on horseback. In any case an unfamiliarly violent headache, brought on no doubt by this horrible cart, was beginning to grip her skull in iron pincers, and if she exposed herself to the sun, as she must do on horseback, she would only make it worse. She concentrated her energies on praying that Archie might drop back and ride beside her, but he appeared, after a few words to Maria, to have taken a decisive lead and was farther away from her than ever.

At last the flat white road between the paddies began to climb a little and the trees of the hills ahead came creeping down the slopes and sheltered them all a little from the now burning sun. Archie had promised that they should stop every eight or ten miles and rest, but Grace was sure he had forgotten this for he was now so far ahead that curves of the road sometimes entirely hid him from her view. Then Mr Beresford stopped for a moment and dismounted while a syce took a stone from his horse's shoe and Tom and Signor Andreino went arguing on past him and his daughter, so that now the only people Grace could call out to were the Beresfords and she would rather die from the heat and her headache and the jolting than address one syllable to them. She watched the trees jerk past, the dappled patterns of light and shade, and tried not to feel that the bumping and the squealing and the disappointment of her hopes might at any moment reduce her to hysterical crying.

So determined were her efforts at self-control that she hardly noticed the moment at which they fell upon her. It seemed that she was, at one second, sitting swaying and wretched and pricked maddeningly by little ends of hay which protruded from the nets, and the next that the hysteria she had supposed she was fighting from inside had fallen upon her from the outside. The bullock driver seemed to tumble abruptly from his perch, the bullocks themselves began to lurch about, bellowing awfully, and the cart, which had held only herself and the hay, was suddenly full of writhing, filthy brown bodies clad only in disgusting rags and screaming heathenishly. She heard her own screams coming high and shrill from far away and felt the crucifix that had been her mother's wrenched from her neck, the chain slicing cruelly into her flesh, and the canopy of the cart was ripped away to reveal a dizzying world of trees and savages and panic whirling round her in an incomprehensible nightmare.

When the shot rang out and the cart emptied as abruptly as it had filled, she was past noticing. Maria, handing her small revolver, still smoking, to her father, with a quelling and decided look to him as if to forestall any argument, swung herself down from her pony, stepped with distaste over the man whose knee she had wounded and climbed into the cart. When the gentlemen and the servants, clattering back down the road in an agony of alarm, arrived at the cart, they found Hubert standing beside it with a look of understandable confusion and Maria kneeling beside Grace, smelling salts in one hand, while she pushed Grace's head down between her knees with the other in a manner that was by no means ungentle.

'They must have thought the cart held our possessions,' she said, cutting short their breathless inquiries and indicating the slashed haynets and the hay scattered everywhere. 'I don't suppose they bargained for poor Miss Prior. There's one of them in the road.'

Archie stooped over the man. His hair was done up in the typical topknot, slipping now to one side of his head, and he wore nothing but a filthy loincloth around his tough little body.

'There,' Andreino said on a note of unnecessary triumph. 'One of the dacoits about which I have warned you all so often.' He stooped and slid a short knife out of the man's loincloth, holding it out as if it were some sort of proof.

Archie looked up. 'Who shot him?'

Maria said clearly, her back to him as she bent over Grace, 'My father.'

'Good shot, sir,' Archie said admiringly.

Hubert with a slight start bowed a little. In the cart, slumped against Maria's shoulder, Grace began to cry. Tom climbed in beside her and put his arms about her, taking her from Maria and cradling her against him, crooning and soothing.

It was clearly impossible for them all to go on. The dacoits, having attacked in error, would not do so again at once but might well spring upon the elephants some miles ahead. This possibility meant that some of the party must go on until the elephants were found and that some must escort Grace home at once to the relative safety of the mission. It was hardly mid-morning, they had not come twelve miles and the expedition was in ruins.

'I shall return,' Andreino said. 'And if you are

wise, you will all accompany me. I shall turn this rogue over to the authorities, of course.'

'Papa?' Maria said, but her tone made the query rhetorical.

Hubert appeared to be dreaming. He said, from far away, a little coldly, 'Whatever *you* choose, dearest. I am not afraid.'

'Mr Tennant?'

Archie looked a little guiltily at Tom. 'I – I do not wish to appear unfeeling but I should quite like to go on. That is, if no-one objects. I don't need anyone but Ah Chun. I should like all the rest to go with Miss Prior.' He leaned over the cart side and took Grace's hand. 'I would not have had this happen for the world.'

She said shakily, smiling at him, 'Not – not your fault, how could you know? Please go on and – and forgive me for wanting to go back.'

'But *I* want you to go back. I want to know you are safe.'

Behind him, Maria, who had descended from the cart when Tom took his daughter from her, said, 'May we accompany you, Mr Tennant?'

He looked round. She was not smiling but her voice was quite altered.

'Of course.'

Tom called from the cart. 'Miss Beresford!'

She went over to him, placing her hands on the wooden sides.

'I do thank you, Miss Beresford. I do thank you most sincerely.'

She said, 'But it is my father—'

'Yes,' Tom said, his eyes full of discerning kindness, 'Yes. But all the same I thank you,' and then he looked up briefly, caught Archie's glance and stooped over Grace again.

They did not find the elephants until mid-afternoon. Some time had been spent at the spot where the cart was attacked ferreting about in the undergrowth but nothing had been found. Grace had been sure there had been twenty dacoits, Andreino of the opinion, after questioning his prisoner, that there were only three or four. However many there were, they had vanished among the trees taking Grace's crucifix with them. The party separated, the bulk of the servants accompanying the Priors and Andreino back across the paddyfields to Mandalay.

Archie and his companions rode on in silence. They were preceded and followed by servants and they rode three abreast, Maria in the middle, up the rough track which deteriorated sharply at intervals or vanished altogether in a pile of boulders. The hillside was growing considerably steeper and once or twice they emerged out of the trees and could look down upon the plain below them and the winking, glittering roofs of the royal city, set within its square mile of walls. It was not a comfortable silence that enveloped them and it was made worse by their inability to break it and so there was nothing for them to do but ride steadily on while crickets chirped in the grasses beside them and, every so often, a clearing appeared beside the track planted with orderly rows of pineapple. They passed few people, only a labourer or two with broad calloused feet and faces of brown leather, and the only village they encountered was a dilapidated shuttered place, seemingly quite asleep in the midday heat.

Maria, her spine still straight beneath the now burning cloth of her habit, determined that she would not complain, nor ask to stop. She had ridden endlessly as a child but had had very little occasion to since coming to Mandalay and could feel her legs beginning to ache violently at this unaccustomed time in the sidesaddle. Hubert seemed still to be in a dream, only emerging from it now and then to glance at his daughter, and Archie, thrown into confusion by the collapse of what had seemed to him a pleasant, mildly exploratory excursion, was too preoccupied to think of anything very much but that they must find the elephants. Of all the peculiar things he had done in his few short weeks in Burma, this hot ride up a stony track to look at a place which hardly existed in the company of two people whom he scarcely knew and barely liked seemed to him by far the most fantastic.

With the elephants, luncheon also waited. A huge repast of curries, bowls of rice, dried prawns and sliced green mangoes lay spread out upon the folding tables in the shade of some trees. A field kitchen had been set up at some distance away, the whole spot having been chosen because of the view across the falling wooded hillsides to Mandalay, no more than a blur some twenty miles distant. They sat down in the chairs provided and were handed plates and bowls with as much formality as if they had been in a dining room while the elephants, tethered in the bushes below, tore off whole branches at once and crushed them noisily into their mouths.

Conversation even with food was only desultory. Hubert observed how extremely unlucky it was that the most timid member of the party should have been the victim and Maria said with unexpected charity that, whatever one's constitution, it must be terrifying to be fallen upon when trapped in a bullock cart and unable to escape, as one might on horseback.

'How far ahead were you?' Archie said, his fork poised.

'A hundred yards perhaps. Perhaps a little more.'

'My daughter has extraordinarily swift reactions.'

'You too, sir, if I may say so.'

'No,' Hubert said, looking down, 'Not so quick.'

Maria stretched out a hand and took her father's.

Archie said, 'Do you feel you are quite in another world up here? Do you feel everything is entirely different?'

Maria looked at him oddly. 'I do not know,' she said.

They reached Maymyo the following day, stiff and saddlesore. Ah Chun had been as good as his word and his relations had prepared what would in India have been a dak-bungalow in which they slept in tolerable comfort, apart from regiments of cockroaches which swarmed across the floors in a blood-red river. Conversation at dinner, eaten by the yellow light of the oil lamps, flowed no more easily than it had at luncheon, and Archie flung himself under his mosquito net profoundly thankful that in two days he would be back in Frederick's idiosyncratic but easy company. At the other end of the bungalow Maria was disgusted to discover the state of her clothes and berated her maid as sharply as if the climate and nearly six hours in the saddle had been her fault alone. Hubert, taking Maria's revolver out of his pocket, looked at it for a long time with a kind of resentment, and then placed it under his pillow. He imagined, staring up into the thick blackness above him as he lay in bed, that he was a young man again, the pioneer of Tirimbatore, riding about the neatly planted hills below that palatial bungalow with an imperious little thing in a sunbonnet demanding that he go faster, that he race her. He had used the revolver he kept in his belt only once, to prevent the flight of the only dishonest overseer he had ever had. He had shot him in the leg, below the knee, or was it in the knee itself . . . ?

They slept badly despite the sharp night air of the hills and the complete silence. All three were pervaded with a sense of oddness, of improbability, which made them restless and uneasy, despite the fatigue induced by long unaccustomed hours on horseback. They came to breakfast each with a profound desire to return to Mandalay and an absolute determination not to suggest it. It was the third meal over which silence had hung oppressively, a silence broken only by the self-conscious clatter of plates and knives. Maria ate almost nothing, but watched her father relentlessly, leaning forward when breakfast was almost over, to say in a voice which had more of command than cajolery in it, 'But you have not drunk your tea!'

And Hubert, looking up from his plate, said in a tone of irritation he had never used before to her in all her twenty-five years, a tone sharp with resentment, 'Do not treat me like a child.'

Archie, expecting this to be a common sort of exchange between a father and daughter thrown always together, was astonished to see all the colour drain at once from Maria's face and her eyes and mouth widen in an expression at once horrified and vulnerable. He said, 'I should be grateful for more tea myself' as a diversion, but she did not hear him and went on gazing at her father with that stricken look, her lips trembling very slightly. Then she rose abruptly and left the room and they could hear her outside on the bungalow verandah calling for her maid.

Hubert seemed not to observe her going and merely said calmly to Archie, 'I think we should be mounted soon. It would be preferable to ride before midday.'

'Yes,' Archie said, 'Yes, it would.'

'Then, if you will excuse me—'

'Of course, sir.'

Hubert rose slowly and left Archie alone with the teapot. His cup of tea, Archie noticed, had remained untouched.

In the tiny cabin of a room in which he had tossed all night, Hubert stood for a moment to compose himself, his eyes closed upon his clamouring thoughts. He was thirsty still, but nothing would have induced him to drink his tea after such an instruction, and so bear his thirst he must. It was, after all, a distraction from his state of mind.

He could not recall ever having suffered so from a state of mind in all his life as he had that previous night, pressing his cheek into the hard pillow of cotton wadding and feeling the revolver there, like a probe in a wound. He had believed – fondly, now he told himself, foolishly – that Maria had always wished to see him appear well in public for the best of reasons, merely that she admired him, was proud of him and wished others to love him and respect him as she did. Now it seemed otherwise, subtly, disturbingly otherwise, and a conviction was worming itself into Hubert's brain that she only saw his good public performance as a necessary appendage to her own reputation, an extension of her own success, window dressing for her image in other eyes.

So that, he told himself, if it seems to her that I might fail in any way, she quickly takes over the action to avoid the possibility of failure. I may still get the credit publicly but she and I know I do not deserve it. I might have shot the bandit – I might – but she would not risk being seen as a successful woman whose father might, even in the smallest measure, be a shame to her. She protects me, but only for her own ends, and because she protects me, she has come to think she has a right to control me.

He opened his eyes with an effort. A bright square of sunlight fell on the rough disordered sheets of the narrow bed. Hubert put his hand beneath the pillow and drew out the revolver. It was small and elegant, the barrel finely inlaid with brass. When he had given it to Maria it had seemed to him then such a dashing present, a gallant gesture with a flavour of intrigue to it, from a worldly father to a beautiful daughter. It was a symbol of their companionship, their unique association. Now – Hubert tossed it onto the bed for the bearer to find. He would not look at it again. Lying there gleaming blue-grey against the white bedclothes it seemed to tell him, as plainly as words might have done, that Maria, for a quarter of a century such an ineffable delight and satisfaction to him, had ceased to love him.

the trees edged with rocks that would make a natural grandstand.

Hubert said, 'I have never much cared for cricket.'

Maria said nothing.

It was, in view of the constraint now added to incompatibility, as endless a morning as the previous afternoon had been. For the look of the thing as much as to satisfy his own determination not to call the expedition a failure, Archie rode determinedly all around the village and all over the gentle hillsides immediately to the north and north-east which were the obvious sites for a European community. He was, to his incomprehension and mounting irritation, followed, and in silence. He tried humming to show of what little consequence the Beresfords' presence was to him but found he could not seem to hold any tune and relapsed into silence himself.

Luncheon was spread out with the same meticulous care and superabundance of food as the day before and eaten with as little animation. Maria watched her father with an expression of both bewilderment and alarm, but said nothing to him, and he ate placidly and did not return her glance once. Archie ate voraciously to give himself some occupation and wished both Beresfords at the bottom of the ocean.

When the fruit had been removed, Hubert announced his intention of sleeping before they returned to the bungalow. Archie most powerfully did not wish to be left alone with Maria but could see no way to avoid it without adding to the wretchedness she was already and most evidently suffering from. When Hubert and his servant had gone in search of a suitable spot among some neighbouring bushes, Archie remained slumped in his chair, enervated beyond all ability to make either conversation or decision.

Maria said abruptly, 'I am afraid we have been an intrusion, Mr Tennant.'

'Oh – oh, no – Miss Beresford, of course you haven't – only too pleased—'

She said, 'I must apologize.'

Archie ducked his head and groaned inwardly. He wanted no reference at all made to the day before, nor to his reprimand to her.

'You did not want us to come up to Maymyo with you, Mr Tennant. I forced our company upon you. It has been very awkward for all of us – ' She stopped, her voice shaking a little, took a breath and went on, 'I had rather you were not polite, Mr Tennant. I had rather you told me the truth. I find – I find I prefer it. From you, at least.'

He risked looking up. She sat in a camp chair, bolt upright, but looking at him with an expression of determined candour. He said bravely, 'Very well, Miss Beresford. I *have* found the last two days difficult. We have, none of us, anything to say to each other. It makes such an expedition, as you say, very awkward.'

She said unexpectedly, 'I am not used to conversation, you see. I do not have any here. There is no-one to talk to. I discuss things, of course, plans and schemes, but that is not the same as conversation.'

'Perhaps you are not much interested,' Archie ventured.

'I thought I was not. I thought it a waste of time. But I have had some hours to ponder on – on everything while we rode about this morning. I do not seem to feel sure about anything up here, I seem to feel – almost another person—'

She stopped and then she said, with extraordinary deliberateness, 'It was not my father who shot the dacoit yesterday. I did it. There is no particular merit in that since my father taught me to shoot when I was only a child and I showed great aptitude at once. I hit the bandit exactly where I intended to and then I handed the revolver to my father. I feel that I should apologize for not telling the precise truth, for misleading you—'

Archie said hurriedly, 'Please do not feel you have to confess anything to me, Miss Beresford. You hardly know me. I do assure you that what is done is done and forgotten. You will only embarrass me by apologizing.'

'I have already apologized,' she said calmly. 'I shouldn't do so again. I am merely making the truth clear – and perhaps thinking aloud. You see,' she said with a sudden rush and in quite an altered tone, a tone he found inexplicably touching, 'you see, I am English and I have never seen England. I know only India and now Burma. I have no roots, only my father—' She paused for a moment and a look of pain passed swiftly across her face, 'my father. We have been inseparable – all my life. All of it. First in India and now in Mandalay, and Mandalay, as you said to me, has been my world. My only world. Coming up here has made me think, Mr Tennant. It has made me remember that there is another world, the world of everything outside Mandalay. And I thought, riding about after you this morning among the trees, what will become of us after Mandalay, what will we do next? Or will we do nothing, will it be Mandalay for ever and ever? Papa and me and the Queen and the mines, on and on.' She stopped again and then she said, 'What do you think?'

He put his elbows on the table between them and leaned towards her. 'Why do you ask me?'

'Because you are the only person I have met here who is here for a conventional reason. Your coming makes me see what strange and improbable people I live amongst – or at least I have seen it this morning.'

He grinned at her. 'If I am the most conventional person in Mandalay, Miss Beresford, you must be one of the most unconventional.'

'It is not in the least remarkable to be unconventional here. As I said, we are two a penny. I begin to see that when everyone around has to some extent lost their heads, it seems perfectly commonplace to lose one's own. What is your background, Mr Tennant?'

Startled by her directness, he told her. She listened to him most intently, regarding him with great seriousness and, because of the compliment of having her attention so absolutely, he found himself telling her far more than she had asked for, even so far as to describe the birth and death of Tennant Phillipson.

When he had at last finished, she said, 'Thank you, Mr Tennant. Thank you very much.' And then she paused and looked away among the trees for a moment. 'So you see, I was perfectly right to ask you how you see the future of someone such as myself. We are both English, but our growing up has been as different as it possibly could be. Yours, I perceive, has been a proper education in the most solid and full sense. I really am – today – at a loss to describe mine at all—' She looked back at him and gave him a smile of startling brilliance. 'Do you see me as an adventuress?'

Overwhelmed by the smile, he stammered a little and said, 'Of – of a sort.'

'And I shall come to a disgraceful end?'

'I hope not.'

'You say that as if you really meant it, Mr Tennant.'

He stood up and stretched, looking down at her. She seemed to him extremely beautiful at that moment. 'I find I do.'

'You are my junior by two years, yet I do not seem to feel that you are younger. I think perhaps you are a great deal more worldly than I am—'

'Oh no,' he said hurriedly, 'not at all.'

She smiled again. 'We shall see,' she said and rose also.

'Miss Beresford—'

'Yes?' she said.

'Miss Beresford – why did you insist it was your father's shot that wounded the dacoit yesterday? Why did you not admit to it as your own?'

She came close to Archie, so close that he could see her fine, pale skin had an irreverent dusting of freckles across the bridge of the nose.

'My father's self-esteem is of the utmost importance.'

Archie said, blushing a little, 'Heaven knows, Miss Beresford, I'm no student of human nature, I've no business to point out anyone's mistakes but – but might your father not see such an action as condescension? Might – I mean suppose he saw it as more a blow to his self-esteem than, well, than a boost?'

'Oh, no,' she said with certainty, 'he would never do that.'

'You are a cracking good shot, Miss Beresford, in any case. And I haven't seen many women who sit a horse as well as you do. It's a pity you haven't been to England. I think hunting would suit you.'

Her eyes clouded for a moment and then she moved away from him and said in her old hard way, as if the spell were broken, as if the mood of Maymyo were slipping from her, 'No doubt I should, Mr Tennant. I am accustomed to excel.'

Archie began to laugh. She watched him for a moment and he thought she was about to be very angry, he could see her knuckles white around her riding crop. But then her face relaxed abruptly and she gave him another of those rare and brilliant smiles. She shook her crop at him.

'One day I shall prove it to you, Mr Tennant, and then it will be my turn to laugh. Now I must go and rouse Papa. We should be getting back to the bungalow.'

If Hubert had not been present, Archie reflected, conversation during that day and the following one as they descended the hills to Mandalay once more might have been as easy and surprising as that short half hour in the sunshine at Maymyo. But Hubert seemed content – or even, Archie began to suspect, determined – to be silent, so none of them spoke much and when Archie tried, as he frequently did, to catch Maria's eye, she seemed always to be looking ahead or at her father. What was more disconcerting was that, as they approached Mandalay, her old habit of imperiousness seemed to settle back upon her, like a miasma rising from the city itself and enveloping her as she came closer. Archie began to think he had imagined the brief softness and breadth of mind that had mellowed her during their conversation and when at last the rose-red city walls came into view once more and he said to her, daringly, 'The end of an adventure, Miss Beresford?' and received in reply only a look of the most chilling reproof, he hardly felt surprised.

As their roads parted by the city walls, she held out a hand to him.

'Mr Tennant, goodbye. And I trust that your first season in the forests will not be too unpleasant.'

He held her hand firmly.

'Then I shall not see you until the spring?'

'My duties at court resume the moment the royal child is born. You must realize that my time is fully taken up.'

He smiled at her, hoping to elicit even a flicker of what she had responded with at Maymyo, but she regarded him stonily. He released her hand.

'Goodbye, Miss Beresford. Goodbye, Sir.'

Neither Maria nor Hubert looked back as they rode away. In fact, they did not even mention Archie beyond Maria's saying, in a tone that had an edge of supplication to it, 'Well, Papa? And what did you make of our escort?'

Hubert did not smile. He simply gave a small sigh, as if the matter were utterly without interest and said, 'A most undistinguished companion, my dear.'

Maria looked at him quickly, her mouth open to reply, but something in his face daunted her and she merely urged her pony homeward in silence.

13

Grace lay in her dim and shuttered bedroom and felt the fever ebb and flow from her like a scorching tide. It seemed so silly to be ill; she was sure it had no connection with her fright three days before. In fact she could remember, in odd lucid moments, that the headache which had now clamped itself upon her skull relentlessly had begun even as they left Mandalay, long before she was attacked. Lots of people had a fever in Mandalay; Europeans were always taking to their beds; it seemed almost a matter of course, but she had never been really ill, not all those five years in Burma. There had been times in Rangoon when she suffered from the results of the rather haphazard kitchen arrangements at the convent – the nuns, being so little interested in food, were quite content to leave it to zealous but unfastidious Burmese converts – but that sort of affliction was part of life in the East, everyone knew that no-one was immune.

But this, Grace thought, pushing vainly against the thudding waves of fever, this is quite different. I can't seem to control my thoughts and my arms and legs go wandering off and I wish everything didn't throb and pound so. How can I think when I am all scattered and pulsing like this? The nights are horrible. I know when it is night because my brain goes screaming off into nightmares and of course I believe them when I am in them, I believe that they are real. Where is Archie, she thought, struggling to raise her head and look for him, he should be here, he should be, I have asked and asked—

Tom sat with her during the nights, administering himself the quinine Frederick Winser had sent to the mission. A terse note had come with the medicine to the effect that these jungle fevers came and went, but reliably went with rest and regular dosing. Tom, who had never known a day's illness himself – chiefly, other people had always supposed, because he forgot for nine-tenths of his live that he was possessed of a body – felt curiously adrift sitting by Grace's bed watching her mutter and toss, her smooth hair plastered damply to her cheeks and forehead and her skin alternatively burning or clammy. It wasn't that the ability to pray had deserted him but the form of prayer he needed now was foreign to him. He had always begged for direction and inspiration, never for any worldly thing; the blessing of a good wife and child had been, he considered, a sign of divine bounty; he had never consciously asked for any benefit for himself. He had asked, day in, day out, over nearly fifty years for the chance to serve, that the way of best service be made plain to him, that such talents as he had be used only and fully in the life he had chosen. And now he needed a favour. Now he wanted a direct gift from God, a selfish gift to himself alone – and he did not know how to ask for it. It seemed to him that some bargain should perhaps be made, but felt that there was nothing he possessed of any value that he had not surrendered long ago as a curate of twenty-two. So he prayed shyly and with difficulty, like a novice uncertain of being heard.

Denzil brought Maria the news of Grace's illness. She was surprised to find how much it disquieted her so in order to disguise this from him she said brutally, 'Hardly a surprise, I think. One would expect her to succumb to the slightest thing.'

He said, 'I think it is serious.'

A pair of slippers being embroidered for Hubert had lain unfinished by her chair for weeks. Maria now snatched them up as if their completion was a matter of the utmost urgency. She bent her head and sent her needle stabbing in and out of the velvet almost viciously, hardly looking to judge the accuracy of her stitches. Supayalat had been delivered of a daughter that morning and no one in the palace had been in a high good humour except for Thibaw, who, for all his indolence and sulky weakness, was truly attached to his children. Also, there was still no news from Pierre, not so much as a letter to say he had reached Paris. Now Grace. Maria was not in the least superstitious – at least she told herself so – but she could not help observing that Grace's illness made the third preoccupying fact in her life, all three of them facts that hardly made for reassurance or stability. There was still no direct heir to the Burmese throne; there was no certainty that the future would bring the position and security of the last five years; and Grace, insignificant, unremarkable as she might be, represented some kind of order and continuity in this strange life in Mandalay. Maria shook herself resolutely and pricked her finger deeply in the process.

Denzil held out his handkerchief. 'You will put blood on the slipper.'

She took his handkerchief in silence and pressed it to her forefinger.

'How is the mood in the palace?'

'The King is pleased,' she said, 'but he was drunk this morning. Those *pwes* – those *pwes*—' she put her hand briefly to her forehead, remembering a ceaseless banging of gongs that had beaten, like a headache, all morning. 'Denzil, they go on almost day and night now. The palace theatre is never quiet, there are musicians and dancers everywhere. The King shouts for more, louder and louder, if they so much as stop for a moment.'

'It's to distract his mind. Just as the champagne is. He is no more fit to govern than the sacred white elephant and his conscience smites him at all the deeds of cruelty done in his name. You look tired.'

'I am perfectly well.'

'Something is the matter.'

'No,' she said, 'nothing.'

He got up and began to walk about the room. He said, with a certain hardness, 'It is difficult for all of us, this waiting. I know no more of Pierre than you do. I am just as helpless. But you and your father – Maria, it is of no assistance to our cause, our standing in Mandalay, our morale, if you and Hubert quarrel—'

'We have never quarrelled in our lives,' she said sharply, looking down at her lap.

'You are beginning to behave very stupidly,' Denzil said. 'I begin to think you are losing your head. Or if not, it has been so turned for you it is abandoning all commonsense. True, we could not do without you and your influence with the Queen, but by the same token, you would not be laden with those jewels if it were not for the rest of us and our various talents. May I remind you that it was I who secured that very first audience your father had with Thibaw. Without me the entire scheme would not exist; without Pierre we should not know how to go about the technicalities; without Hubert we might not so easily be able to raise the money. Don't forget that, Maria, not for a moment.'

She said nothing, but went on sewing, jabbing at the velvet with her needle. He came close to her chair and stood looking down at her bent head.

'Sulk if you will, my dear. But don't imagine yourself indispensable. And don't be fool enough to think that any of us, *any* of us, your father included, would have the smallest scruple in doing without you should we need to, should you become impossible to deal with. It is utter folly to alienate yourself from your father—'

She glanced up, her eyes hard with fury, and said, 'Please go.'

'In a moment. When you have heard me out I shall leave you to reflect upon what I have said. Listen, Maria—' He stooped close to her. 'Do not, for your own sake entertain the smallest delusion of grandeur. I don't know what you have done to offend your father – I don't wish to know – but I know you have done something from his own changed behaviour and I must deduce that you are acting towards him as you are now to all of us. If you wish to stay here my dear, if you wish to keep the position you so enjoy, you must give as much as you take. I don't care one iota if your heart is in it or not, I only care for appearances.'

'Oh, yes,' she said savagely, jerking her thread, breaking it, 'that is perfectly evident. You have no more heart than a stone.'

Denzil said, laughing, 'And you do, my dear, you do?'

She thrust the needle into the slipper and pushed it off her lap to fall onto the floor. 'You should go.'

He bowed. 'If I may be assured that you have both heard and comprehended what I came to say.'

She rose and stood regarding him. 'I understand you perfectly. My opinion of what you say will remain my own affair—'

'Naturally.'

'—but you must know that I am extremely resentful that you should suppose me in any way careless of the future.'

He moved towards the open double doors. 'Maria my dear, how could you be careless? Hardly, I feel, with this – this new-found heart of yours.'

When his step had gone lightly down the verandah, Maria found that she wanted very much to sit in one of her rose-pink chairs and cry her eyes out. Instead, she kicked the slipper spinning across the polished floor and then rang violently for a servant to retrieve it.

'Are you there?' Grace said, 'Did you come?'

Archie tried to loosen the burning fingers a little from his own.

'Yes,' he said. 'Two hours ago.'

Her eyes opened briefly, regarding him in puzzlement, and closed again.

'I asked for you. I asked and asked. I wanted you to save me from the dreams.' Her head rolled fretfully on the pillow, damp strands of hair peeling from her cheeks as she moved. 'I'm so hot. My head is terrible, you can't think how much it hurts. I don't want to be brave, I don't want to be ill—'

With his free hand Archie took up a sponge that floated in a basin of water beside him and squeezed it to dampness. He began clumsily – for it was his right hand she clung to so desperately – to wipe her forehead and cheeks, but she rolled her head faster and faster as if trying to escape his ministrations, and trickles of water ran down into her ears and the dark moistness of her hair.

She said, 'I didn't want Maria to come, I didn't ask her. Why did she come?'

'She isn't here. You are thinking of the expedition. That is all past, forgotten. You must not think of it, you must only think of getting well.'

'I can't be well,' she said peevishly, opening her eyes to show him that they were filled with tears, 'I am only ill, I hate being ill, it tires me, it tires me right out. Send Maria away. Say I don't want anyone, just you, just you and Papa. Don't go!' she cried suddenly, although he had never moved. 'You mustn't leave me! You mustn't go!'

He checked a small sigh. 'I am not going. I am staying by you. As long as you want me.'

The room itself made him uncomfortable. It was not simply the overpowering heat or the sickroom smell or the pathetic and defenceless sight of Grace, shrunk with fever, but the warring components of the room itself. A crucifix hung above the bed, symbolically enshrined in clouds of folded mosquito net, a small porcelain virgin and child stood tranquilly on the bedside table among the bottles and glasses and the walls were hung with slightly sentimental pictures of Christ surrounded by improbably plump Jewish children and St Francis liberally loaded with wild birds. But besides these things were a looking glass, several hats on pegs, bunches of ribbons hung on nails – one even on the corner of St Francis – stools and chairs laden with piles of crumpled gauzy stuffs no-one had seen fit to put away, scattered slippers, brushes, combs, a fat pink satin pillow bristling with what Archie took for hairpins. The sheer economy of Hnin Si struck him again – guiltily in such a situation – the spare neatness of her gestures, the small tidy pile of her discarded clothes, the single prong with which she skewered her glossy hair. Except for her physical self, she often left no other trace at all of her presence in a room. But this clutter, this disorder, this conflict of piety and self-indulgence—

Grace gave a little cry from the pillow. Her closed lids were pulsing with the misery of some inward image and her mouth was puckering childishly as if she would cry.

'Don't,' Archie said, 'dear Grace, don't—'

Tears slid from beneath her closed lids.

'I can't bear to watch you,' Archie said, 'you poor little thing, poor little Grace—'

From the doorway, Tom said, 'How good you are to stay, I know how distressing it is. But school is finished now and I can relieve you.'

'It's all right sir. I'll stay. I – I think she wants me to. She keeps waking just for a moment and I wouldn't like her to think I had deserted her.'

Heavily, Tom took the chair on the opposite side of the bed. He reached to take Grace's free hand, but she tore it from him, flailing about wildly with it.

'Archie! Archie! Oh, why don't you come?'

Archie took the roaming hand and held both hers between his own. Her skin was as dry and hot as burning paper. She opened her eyes briefly and then closed them and sighed and muttered a little.

'Of course—' Tom said, 'and this is something I should not have known how to say to you had she not been ill – of course, you know how devoted she is to you. I shouldn't want you to feel her affection a burden on you, you know, but if – if it were to make a difference to her – her recovery, you know, if you were to – if you could, in some way, reciprocate just – just a little, enough to give her hope, enough to give her something to recover for—'

He stopped. Archie, overcome with the most horrible confusion, looked down at his hands holding Grace's. Very carefully he laid Grace's hands on the sheet.

'Don't misunderstand me,' Tom said hurriedly. 'I can't expect any promises. I don't look for any commitment. I don't know what else to do, I don't know who else to turn to. I just thought perhaps as you were, are, a little fond of her—'

'Oh yes,' Archie said, 'yes, I am. Fond—'

Grace opened her eyes, looked at him with great clarity and firmly retrieved his right hand with her own. 'Of course – of course, I want her to recover. More than anything. You must know that. And – and I'd do anything I could to help. But – but not that sort of promise. It would not be true, not fair—'

'No promises! I don't ask for promises! Just a word of encouragement, of affection, just a word, you know.'

'Even that would be unfair. I couldn't do it.'

Tom shut his eyes and gave a sound like a stifled cry. He said, 'No. No, of course not,' and then he opened his eyes and smiled and said, 'I shall fetch you something to eat. You must be very hungry.'

Archie said too heartily, 'I am afraid so, sir. I always am you know.'

'Stay,' Grace said to him sternly from her pillow. 'Don't leave me. Stay.'

Tom stood up and remained for a while looking down at her. 'Only jungle fever,' he said after a moment, 'that's all.'

'You should see Winser,' Archie said, 'straining at the leash to be off in the forests and he was like this only a few days ago.'

'Yes,' Tom said, 'yes.'

When he had gone, Archie looked down to find Grace staring at him intently. He smiled.

She said earnestly, 'You must send Maria away. You will, won't you?'

Grace died before dawn the following day. She died in her father's arms quite silently while Archie slept on a cotton quilt on the floor of the living room. The fever had climbed steadily all the previous evening and her room had become an inferno of darkness, and pain and wild cries. Several times Archie felt ready to promise anything if only the delirium would calm, but he doubted, even in the most frenzied moments, that he possessed any magic potion in any case. Tom knelt and gazed at Grace and shot Archie glances of terrifying beseechingness. After midnight the fever suddenly seemed to subside and Tom sent Archie for a few hours' rest, promising he would call if he needed help. When Archie had gone, he put his arms about Grace and she lay so tranquilly in them, so limp and quiet and still, that she must have been dead some time before he observed it. Even then he could not release her at once but continued to cradle her and gaze down at her, devastated by such a sense of absolute desolation and abandonment that he wondered if he himself were still alive.

He could not speak to Archie, he could only touch and point. He let himself be led to a chair and be fed sips of sweetened tea as if he were an invalid. He heard Archie's voice in other parts of the mission, and then cries and wailings and after a long time in which his thoughts stumbled helplessly about in no direction at all, Archie saying, 'I'm awfully sorry, sir, but I don't think all the servants will stay. I've tried to persuade them but they say there will be ghosts now. It isn't more than three or four but they are packing now—'

'Christians,' Tom said softly. 'I taught them to love Christ.'

'Can I get you anything? They are preparing breakfast.'

'No. Nothing. Absolutely nothing. Nothing, nothing at all—'

'Could you sleep? You should you know, you have been up for nights.'

'I want to sleep,' Tom said a little petulantly, 'I want to—'

Archie put pillows behind his head. 'Don't worry about anything. I will arrange it. I will see to things.'

'But you are going! To the forests. You must, you said so.'

'A day or so will make no difference. Please lie still.'

Tom caught Archie's hand. 'She knew how to love, Archie. She knew about people. I wonder – I begin to wonder – if I know nothing, if my idea of love bears no relation to humankind at all—'

Gently, Archie freed his hand. 'Don't think about it. Not now, just sleep.'

Tom watched him leave the room, his clothes like rags after the ordeal of being slept in. He wanted to call him back, to see that tired, kind young face turned towards him again, to ask if he, Archie, thought that perhaps this was not the end but the beginning after all, that the lessons of this world were the only ones that really schooled you for divine service, that heaven was in fact bought on earth. He said, very faintly, 'Archie,' but he said it to empty air.

He woke to find oblongs of midday sunlight on the floorboards at his feet since the double doors had not been shuttered while he slept. He turned his head a little in the first bewilderment of waking, then remembered Grace in an onrush of wretchedness and saw that Maria Beresford was sitting near him, watching him with an expression of uncharacteristic uncertainty.

'Mr Prior, I hope I did not wake you.'

He struggled free of his pillows. 'No, not at all. I have slept for several hours.'

'I have watched you the last one,' she said surprisingly. 'The news was brought to me at breakfast. I postponed my visit to the palace.'

He inclined his head in silence.

'You are very good to come so soon,' he said after a while.

She spread her hands.

'I can think of nothing else I can do. If I could, I would do it. Sitting here is of no use to you, I know, but I do not know how else to show you what I feel.'

He smiled at her. 'It does me a great deal of good to see you here, to hear you speak so.'

Maria said, 'I was not always – gracious to your daughter. We did not have sympathetic temperaments I think, but that is no excuse. I know – I know—' she stopped, and then said in a great rush. 'I know what you have lost.'

Tom leaned forward. 'I think I hardly know myself yet. But I value your sympathy and your courage immeasurably.'

She snorted. 'Courage! Courage is of no value. It only means you have not the imagination to fear the right things.'

Tom rubbed his hands over his forehead tiredly. 'No, my dear, no. Courage is most assuredly not that. Courage is seeing what there is to fear and going on bravely all the same.'

'That is real courage. Your kind of courage.' He heard her catch her breath a little. She said, 'Mr Tennant!' and Archie came into the room with a tray of toast and fruit which he put beside Tom.

'The servants would have brought it—'

'They are busy,' Archie said awkwardly, averting his thoughts as best he could from the deft activity in Grace's bedroom.

'Then I am not the first caller,' Maria said.

'Yes, you are, Miss Beresford. I was here all night.' He indicated his clothes. 'As is all too evident.'

'Did you send the message to me this morning, Mr Tennant?'

'Yes,' he said.

She looked at him for a long moment with her

300

wonderful directness and then she said, 'Thank you.'

'Eat,' Archie urged Tom, 'just a little.'

Maria rose. 'I believe you go into the forests any day, Mr Tennant?'

'Yes,' he said, 'as soon as—'

'You should go,' she said. 'Life must go on. If there is any help of any kind that Mr Prior needs, I shall be happy to give it. More than that, it would be a kind – a kind of relief. That is, if you will let me help.'

Tom rose also and held out his hands to her. 'Whenever you wish, my dear Miss Beresford. Any hour, any time.'

Maria held out her hand to Archie. 'And we shall look forward to seeing you back in Mandalay in the spring, Mr Tennant.'

He wanted to hold her hand a moment longer but she disengaged herself firmly. Then, without looking back, she went, head high, down the verandah steps to the bullock cart waiting in the lane.

PART THREE

14

Isolation, Archie discovered, had little to do with merely being on one's own. Before two months in the forest were out, he could feel a sense of the most piercing – and exhilarating – isolation in the midst of a clearing full of trampling elephants and shouting *mahouts*, a knowledge as sharp as a physical sensation of his aloneness, his alienation from the dank forest trails and the huge beasts and brown men who worked them. It was a knowledge he relished, just as much as he relished being beholden to no-one, expected to conform to no social rules, and it had come upon him almost the day Frederick Winser had left him to his own devices.

'Pretty uncomplicated, your duties,' Frederick had said their first night in the chill darkness of the forests. 'The elephant men will show you how to work the timber. We work from them, they work from their forefathers. Your main responsibility will be the transport and safeguarding of all those damned silver rupees. You give each forester an advance and pay him off finally at the end of the season. The negotiation of the advance is up to you and, I'll tell you, bad debts are not

The main street of Maymyo was quite unlike Mandalay, being lined in part with timber buildings, but also with houses and shops of carved grey stone on which clumps of bright green ferns had settled here and there in cracks between the blocks. It was only a small place as yet, and an exclusively Burmese one at that, but there was an air of solidity and dignity about it that Mandalay, for all its splendour, conspicuously lacked. The air was glorious, warm in the sunlight but with a sharp clarity to it that was a wonderful relief after the humid heat of the plain, and even the light seemed sharper and clearer, all objects more brilliantly defined.

Hills rose all around, spreading away to north and east and south and falling to Mandalay in the west, blue still but now clearly seen to be thickly wooded. Maymyo itself was wooded, not in the dense, heavy jungle manner of Mandalay, but with tall and graceful trees around whose slender trunks poinsettias grew in green and scarlet profusion. It was easy to see where houses might be built on the level ground around the village, houses which would have wonderful views to the west while the Shan hills would rise up on all other sides to shelter them.

'Look,' Archie said, as much to break the silence between them all as anything, 'that would do wonderfully as a cricket pitch.' He pointed with his whip to a smooth oval clearing among looked kindly upon by the company. In the morning I'll show you which trees to select for girdling.'

Waking to his first forest morning had been unforgettable. The mutterings of darkness had given way to a rowdy bright green world full of movement and chatter, and in the bamboo clump only feet from his tent door a group of pigeons with backs the colour of jade sat droning companionably. They breakfasted under a handy acacia tree, Frederick more absorbed in maps than food, and then set off down a series of, to Archie, eerie and indistinguishable trails towards the faint cries and shouts that led them to the elephant men.

That day he watched trees being selected and girdled. And the next and the next. Day after day, acre after acre, until teak trunks danced in his sleep like a vision of eternity, he watched the long saw cut being made deep into the heartwood of the tree, girdling it entirely, to stop the circulation of the sap.

'Dries it out,' Frederick said, 'In a couple of years. Not only makes it lighter for the elephants but a dead tree will float. Living ones sink.'

After two weeks he was marking trees of his own accord; after three, standing on the river bank, he could see that measuring by eye was going to be a rapidly acquired accomplishment. After four, Frederick left him, to chart new land to the east.

With Frederick went all chance to speak

English except for the limited amount possible with Ah Chun. To Hnin Si, who had made herself an inconspicuous part of his baggage without any direct request on his part that she should do so, he spoke French; to the *mahouts* he attempted stumbling sentences in Burmese. He had a group of thirty-nine in his charge, thirty-nine working elephants, thirty-nine men and seven elephant calves. The advances he had to pay them had been settled by Frederick before he left, and the store of silver coins necessary for the final payment at the end of the dry season was the only thing that weighed at all heavily upon his mind. He was reduced to carrying a good deal of it about with him on the elephant that became as familiar a mount to him as horses had once been.

Time took on a different, more elastic dimension. Days were spent in swaying elephant rides to reach particular clearings and, if night overtook him, he slept tentless on a groundsheet under a dense rug to protect him from the dew that fell as thick as snow in the cold forest nights. If he was in camp, Ah Chun cooked for him with pointless punctuality; if he were not, he hardly seemed to notice hunger for the first time in his life. His day was measured by the chattering brilliance of early morning, the thick and stifling heat of midday, where mud and dust vied with each other for supremacy, and the cold sudden nightfalls lit by the flames of his camp fire.

Ah Chun roused him at daybreak to shout

hoarsely for the *mahouts*. Invariably one or two were missing – the excuses Archie neither understood, nor cared much about. In his green and strange kingdom his concern, apart from a perpetual and fascinated examination of his own state of mind, was to get a sufficient number of good trees girdled and the required number of logs, carefully selected and measured, dragged to the river banks and lowered into the water on the first stage of the journey to Rangoon.

'Forest officers,' Frederick had said in parting. 'Loneliest fellows in Asia.'

If he was lonely, he hardly felt it as such. Monotony had not eaten into him; he only felt the days to have a seductive and languorous rhythm. The evenings were long it was true, with little to fill them but the solitary gulping of Ah Chun's curry and then reading or mapwork by the dim yellow glow of the oil lamp, but sleep came swiftly and heavily to him, speeded on by Hnin Si's fingers soothing his neck and shoulders into perfect relaxation. She was there each night he was in camp, kneeling waiting for him in the darkness, small and strong and amenable. Every so often he gave her money which she took with perfect composure.

One night about the turn of the year, he said to her, 'And what will you do in the spring? Will you go back to the cigar factory?'

'No,' she said, 'I stay with you, *thakin*.'

'Suppose – suppose we tire of each other—'

She glanced at him calmly. She was kneeling

beside him, smooth and pale brown, no bigger than a tall child.

'Then I stay with Ah Chun,' she said, 'for you are, as he told me, a good master,' and Archie saw, as he supposed he had always suspected, that she was Ah Chun's mistress too, perhaps even, in the Burmese sense, his wife. He put his hand on her shoulder.

'Ah Chun by day, me by night.'

'You always, if you order it.'

He laughed. He was astounded to find how little he was outraged. He said aloud, thoughtfully, 'Do you suppose I have no pride?'

She did not understand him.

He turned to look at her. 'I should beat you for sleeping with another man.'

'If you please. But that I only do when you are not in need of me. If you need me I am ready. Ah Chun also.'

A sudden unattractive and grimy image of rooms in the Jericho slums of Oxford rose before him. He rolled away from Hnin Si and lay staring at the rough walls of his hut.

'You are angry, *thakin*?'

'No,' he said, suddenly tired.

'You are weary of always the elephants.'

'No,' he said, again, 'not that, something I can't explain to you.'

'I go?'

He did not want her to go to Ah Chun. He said, 'Stay until I sleep,' and before he slept, while her fingers moved round and round the muscles at the base of his neck, he saw Maria in his mind's eye, as clearly as if she were before him, saying, 'I do not seem to feel sure of anything up here, I seem to feel almost another person,' and he thought that's how I am too, really, here in the forest. I wonder where I have got to? Then he plunged into sleep and in his dreams Hnin Si followed him among the teak trees, flitting persistently behind him, from one to another, beseeching, 'I don't please you, *thakin*? I don't please you?' and because it was a dream, he didn't care about it at all one way or the other.

After that, things changed a little, not so much in themselves but more in the emphasis he put upon them. The long repetitive days in the forests became each a separate and comparable challenge – a certain number and standard of trees to be marked and dragged, a tightening of discipline among the *mahouts* – and the dream world of the nights, the fantasies he wove in the darkness, became a luxury he treasured and longed for. The half-dream, half-reality of Hnin Si – half-dream to Archie because nothing in his upbringing had led him to suppose one could possess a girl for one's pleasure so simply – lost the astounding enchantment of the early weeks. She became for him one of the few comforts of his life in the forest, but without the romance she had first filled him with. He pondered for a long time on his feelings for her after her revelation of her relationship to Ah Chun and was forced to admit that he could not, deep down, resent Ah Chun being either Burmese or a servant but merely another man. A small, smooth-skinned, almost, to Western eyes, girlish-looking man, but a man none the less. Archie saw that he had seen in Hnin Si an image of submissive devotion that was entirely of his own romantic making; the master–slave relationship had seduced him as much as the girl herself. She, on the other hand, had been entirely practical throughout and he must now imitate her.

So his dreams took over. He worked harder, physically, than he had ever worked in his life, often, if away from camp, spending thirty-six hours in the same sweat-soaked collarless shirt. He had always, because they were so universally the fashion, spurned either moustache or beard, but now he let both grow luxuriantly. If Ah Chun had not fallen upon his hair and nails with such vigour, he would, by January, have been a veritable old man of the woods. He wished he had brought more books with him – the Gibbon he had instructed Ah Chun to pack in a sort of romantic ambitiousness had already been re-duced to pulp by the forest damps – for there was a limit to the amount of re-reading he could do. Dreaming, on the other hand, he could always repeat, even embellish, and the long monotonous miles on elephant back, or evenings when the tedium of a day prevented him from sleeping with his customary suddenness, he beguiled with fantasies. Fantasies of Mandalay and the gilded palace and the hidden royal couple, no bigger than his own servants but dressed and jewelled like idols exuding their irresistible power, their barbaric and beastly charm; fantasies of his imagined influence with them, his exposure of that tawdry collection of gambling Europeans who clawed at the coat tails of the palace; fantasies of his achieving a second Tennant Phillipson, a teak company to rival the Bombay-Burmah, born out of his unique relationship with Thibaw and Supayalat, the French wiped out of Burma, as well as the Greeks and the Italians and the Germans, Burma British throughout perhaps, with Thibaw a puppet king . . . Sometimes the fantasies even involved Maria, though hardly in a clearly defined role. Her ability to be both admirable and despicable, alluring and repellent, provided splendid fuel for his imagination. He scarcely knew her, yet he told himself he knew a great deal about her. Her image remained more clearly upon his mind's eye than any other and the fleeting look of beseeching that he had caught on her face once in Maymyo, once in the mission, remained powerfully with him and worked upon his romantic self just as Hnin Si had done, quite unconsciously, when she first led him to bed in Mandalay.

A month before the rains began, an elephant went berserk. It was a cow elephant in the early stages of pregnancy whose previous calf had been born dead, Archie was told, and she suddenly

cast aside the log she was carrying – the twentieth
such log she had moved impeccably that day –
crushing the near forefoot of the elephant working beside her, scraped her *mahout* off savagely
against a tree and turned, bellowing and trampling, upon the team behind her.

Archie was perhaps two hundred yards away.
It sounded to him as if the world were being
torn apart. Men came tearing through the undergrowth towards him, screaming in panic,
clutching at his arms and hands, and then he saw
the beast, among the trees, flailing and trumpet-
ing like some monstrous machine of destruction.
His rifle was strapped to his own elephant who,
though normally as docile as a lamb, was displaying distinct and understandable signs of unease,
shifting and grunting, swinging its great head. He
shouted to the *mahout* to make it kneel.

Behind him the din was fearful. The maddened
elephant was going round and round in circles
while before her trees crashed and splintered and
the terrified *mahouts* tried to urge their own
beasts out of her path.

'Boy's adventure book,' Archie said in English
to the *mahout*. 'Schoolboy hero stuff.'

The *mahout* said the *thakin* did not make himself plain.

'I am not trying to. I am keeping my own
courage up.' He said in Burmese, 'Will the
elephant go close?'

'No,' the *mahout* said, 'no!'

The rifle was slippery in his sweating hands

and he was glad there were no witnesses of his shaky loading of it.

'Send my belongings to my mother,' he said to the *mahout*, smiling. 'In England it is customary.'

The *mahout* said that if the *thakin* wished to give orders he must do so not in English.

'No orders,' Archie said. 'But I shall tell you, in English, how terrified I am because you won't understand me but it will relieve my own feelings.'

He grasped the rifle and began to walk away. The *mahout* shouted. Ahead of him, he could make out very little. Which elephant was which? It was madness to be on foot, he was bound to be crushed, but at this moment he could see no other form of mobility that was any use—

The frantic elephant whirled into view. He raised his rifle, took clumsy aim, fired and missed her. The scream that rose from the clearing was deafening. He pinned himself against a tree and swore. Twenty yards away a huddled body lay in the undergrowth and an elephant calf with a raw wound in one leg in which splinters of bone gleamed like teeth was circling wretchedly round and round, howling, on three legs. All round the clearing, shouts and bellowings echoed from among the denser clumps of trees, and occasionally a high wild scream charted the progress of the demented elephant.

He dared not move. He waited perhaps ten minutes before she appeared again and this time managed to graze her in the shoulder, enough to halt her in her charge. She swung round towards him, blood streaming from her where she had dashed herself into trees and he raised his rifle, shaking so hard he could hear the rhythm of his teeth chattering and echoing in his skull, and fired, blind and wild, hitting her in the base of her throat. She sank, huge and flailing, to her knees and then, like a ship tilting into the sea, heaved over onto her vast grey side. In the ecstasy of mingled relief and misery at not having acted sooner, Archie fired twice into her skull.

She had maimed seven elephants and two men lay dead, one her own *mahout*. Nobody would work further that day. Back in camp that night, Archie met Ah Chun in a highly excited state for dacoits had, for the first time that winter, set upon the camp and, though they had stolen nothing, the boy whom Ah Chun had used as his own servant in the kitchen had been taken with them and all Archie's possessions had been thrown about in search of valuables. Hnin Si had been washing her hair in a nearby stream or she would undoubtedly have been raped.

Archie slept badly, for the first time in the forest. What recompense – if any – the corporation made to the elephant men customarily he did not know, but if he was to return next winter, he felt some kind of payment must be made before he struggled back to Mandalay. One thing was certain and that was that in the weeks to come neither rupees nor rifle should leave his side for a moment. When Ah Chun came to him

315

at dawn as was his custom, he brought the news that another of the elephants, one not involved in yesterday's catastrophe, had anthrax.

'I suppose,' Archie said, 'that this is really what I came for.'

Ah Chun performed the sketchy shiko from which he always contrived to eliminate all respect.

'*Thakin*,' he said, 'that is so.'

15

No-one told Maria of Bonvilain's return. She had taken to spending far more time in the palace than before, though the din of the ceaseless *pwes*, the gongs and the singing and the drums, made it a far from peaceful place to be. Noisy though it was, far changed though it was from the first day when Maria had seen the gardens full of water-falls and birds and children and the pretty little maids of honour in their rainbow silks, something held Maria to it, something quite as powerful as Supayalat herself. Fear had always been part of life in Mandalay, inseparable from the unpredict-ability of any way of life that hung upon savage royal whim, but that fear now seemed to stalk visibly in the palace itself, seemed to pursue even the King and Queen, so that Maria, to whom fear was largely a hysterical ailment only indulged in by those with nothing better to do, even she felt that the sands were stirring uncomfortably be-neath her feet and she was reluctant to be away too long, afraid only of missing something vital.

People were dying in the palace, and being violently dismissed. Favourites, like vulgar little Hosannah Manook summoned back from

Rangoon to teach the court photography, was thrown out summarily with screams.

'A traitor!' Supayalat howled. 'A traitor! A *kalā* who cares nothing for us! If I think you have betrayed me I shall get permission from Calcutta, from the Governor General, to kill you, kill you!'

Thibaw's old mother died from blood poisoning in a welter of extravagant accusations. She had taken a lover, Supayalat insisted, a young lover from among her own attendants, she should die alone, like a dog; no-one should wait upon her.

'And you!' the Queen cried to Maria. 'You! Do you have a lover?'

Maria drew herself up, her court manners swamped by outrage.

'Naturally not.'

The Queen laughed and clapped her hands.

'You!' she said. 'You! If all the English were like you, perhaps we could not drive them out so easily.'

'*Ashin-nammadaw-paya*,' Maria said, using the formal court manner of addressing the Queen. '*Have* you driven all the English out?'

Supayalat leaned forward, her small face as flickering as a snake's. 'Not all, but soon will be all. Soon. If a bird has a wing long enough ready to fly, cut the wing. Cut it! There shall be no power here but our power. The English shall fear us.'

'And after the English? What then?'

'Ah!' Supayalat smiled. 'Ah! After them a great

Burmese nation where the only *kalās* will work for us, bow to us, bring tribute to us.' Her brow darkened suddenly and, snatching off her slipper, she hurled it across the room to catch the cheek of one of the young Shan maids in the King's service. It was a commonplace. Thibaw's glance had only to rest upon a pretty face for more than a moment for the Queen to take revenge. She stood up.

'Traitors!' she shrieked, 'All traitors! All traitors will die—'

Thibaw, from his couch, gestured feebly. Supayalat ran towards him, seating herself beside him, taking his hand and stroking and crooning over it.

'You make all people fear you,' she insisted to him. 'All those who would betray you are in fear of their lives, their lives—'

For such scenes, Maria stayed. In any case, nothing held her now at home. Hubert had withdrawn from her to such an extent that she felt her presence at meals was only to satisfy her own sense of propriety, not for his pleasure at all. The dull and leaden ache of misery with which his behaviour left her she dealt with by hardening herself to it, surmounting it, subduing it with the imperiousness with which all her life she had crushed all things she did not understand or like. He smiled at her absently at meals sometimes and she returned his smiles, but her own were more the carefully contrived ones she had once given to Horace Browne, to Murray Shaw, not

319

the spontaneous expressions of love. Once, and only once, she had caught Hubert's sleeve as he left her drawing room and had said in a voice of pleading which sounded as strange to her as if it had belonged to someone else, 'Papa – dearest Papa – why have I displeased you so?'

And he, gazing down at her with the mild, indolent, withdrawn look that was now habitual with him, took his sleeve away gently and replied, 'I do not understand you, my dear. I do not understand you at all. When has such a word as displeasure had any significance between us?'

And for a moment her heart had leaped up and she lifted her face smiling for him to kiss, but he had stared blankly down at her as if that proffered cheek were nothing to him at all, nothing, and then he had bowed a little and smiled and had left the room.

After that, she had taken her cue from him. She knew that his days were spent chiefly among the halls of audience in the palace and that his nights – unnaturally long nights which engulfed most evenings as well – were passed behind the closed door of his bedroom. Their conversation was mostly palace gossip of an entirely trivial kind, since Maria did not feel she could convey the unease that filled her days with Supayalat to a father whose responses to her had dwindled to those of a courteous stranger. So when Bonvilain came back, although Andreino, because he knew most things, knew of his arrival, and so did Denzil Blount and Hubert and the rival engineers who had squatted on the palace floors all the months of the Frenchman's absence, hoping to advance themselves behind his back, Maria knew nothing. She went into the palace as she had always done, to assist at the ritual dressing of the morning, and left it, as she had become accustomed to do, after the ritual dressing of the evening, before the King and the Queen processed in their diamonds and gold-shot silks to the ceaseless din of the royal theatre. Then Maria returned, dressed for dinner, ate it more or less in silence across the table from Hubert, and withdrew to the lamplit solitude of her drawing room while he, after a short ceremony with a cigar, went to his room.

Without Mattie Calogreedy, her ignorance might have been extended from days into weeks. Mattie had lived all the period of Bonvilain's absence in the security of her own conviction that he would return, rich enough on account of the concession to work Mogok to defy his parents and marry her. He had told her, she confided to an uncaring Maria as they jolted into the palace, that in his country, in France, a man might not marry without parental consent before he was twenty-five. Well, she had pouted, soon he would be rich enough to cock a snook at parents and in any case, he and she were married already. This notion, this peasant belief that cohabitation made a marriage, seemed to Maria no less than one would expect of the Burmese. She drew her skirts away from Mattie Calogreedy in distaste. What the Queen saw in her could not be imagined but there she was, European maid of honour, though she was getting so plump, so coarse, that she lolled about in Burmese dress mostly now, presumably to avoid the discomfort and discipline of corsets. Bonvilain had sent Mattie a dress from Paris and Mattie had offered to show it to Maria who, burning to see it, had laughed and said she thought it would hardly be to her taste.

Mattie, who had shown surprising resilience to Maria's disagreeableness throughout the five years of their acquaintance, had suddenly looked crestfallen, more than that, almost wounded at Maria's scorn of her Paris dress. She had not the capacity to see that to have a bourgeois Frenchman as a lover was, in Maria's eyes, beneath contempt, and so she was dismayed and disconcerted at Maria's refusal and put the dress away in the room she used in the palace and said no more about it. It was such a forgotten subject that when she came stumbling into Maria's house late one afternoon, dressed in a profoundly unbecoming European dress which strained hideously over her plumpness and was unforgivably blotched with sweat, Maria did not at first recognize her.

'He is married!' she wailed, her hat awry over one eye. 'Married! He has brought back a French wife to whom he has given a ring! He never gave me a ring – She is a pale little thing, I saw her, but he was so stern with me, he said I should never have expected marriage—'

She fell into one of Maria's French chairs and burst into noisy tears.

Maria said, standing quite still in the doorway onto the verandah, 'Then Monsieur Bonvilain is back in Mandalay?'

Mattie screamed, 'Married! Married! He is married!' and rocked herself about.

'I know,' Maria said.

'He promised.' Mattie sobbed, not listening. 'He promised me! I was his wife, he my husband, he cannot leave me, he cannot! He must be making a joke—'

'No,' Maria said, 'no. European men marry their own kind. You must know that.'

'I am half-Greek,' Mattie said, rolling her handkerchief into a damp ball. 'Half-Greek. And my mother has light skin, very light. Oh, speak to him for me, Miss Beresford, speak to him, I implore you, I beg you, speak to him!'

Maria said nothing but looked out into the heavy gold and green of the garden, gold and green soon to be deluged with the rains, those awful ceaseless rains.

Behind her Mattie said, in tears again, 'I believed him, Miss Beresford, I believed him. I believed his promises. What shall I do without him, oh, whatever, *ever* shall I do?'

Maria did not mean to be touched. Mattie was so absurd, ugly even, with her grief-mottled face and her hair coming down, her body straining away at the dress like too much sausage inside a too tight skin, and her dreadful peasant credulity and vulnerability. Almost against her will, Maria moved to sit opposite her, to hold out a clean, dry handkerchief, to say, 'There is nothing I can do. If speaking to him would help you, I would do it. But it will not. You must make your life in the palace now. You must not have dreams of Europe, you must turn your back on them.'

Mattie looked back at her for a moment, submissive and subdued. Then her face contorted and she screamed, 'He will pay for it! He will, he will! And so shall you all, all you *kalās*, all you people who take what you want, using us as your slaves, your toys!' She got up hastily, gathering up her bag, her gloves, her parasol, jumbled in her arms like a carelessly held baby. 'He had his pleasure with me, he thought he could take, take, take and not give. I will show him! I will teach him! I am not a mistress. I am a wife! His wife! He will live to regret treating me as a woman of the street. You'll see, you'll see!'

At dinner that night Maria attempted to be particularly charming and animated so that she might have a hope of a full response to her question when the moment came to put it.

'And Papa! Guess what happened today! I heard – quite by chance – that Pierre Bonvilain has returned!'

Hubert said easily, 'Oh yes. Yes, I do believe that he has.'

'I heard it from Mattie Calogreedy. She was dreadfully distressed because she believed he meant to marry her and then, of course, to go down to the bund and meet him off the steamer today and find that he had brought a wife, well, that, even for her—'

'Oh, not today,' Hubert said calmly, laying down his fruit knife. 'His steamer did not come today. He arrived a week ago, a week ago precisely. With the mails.'

Maria held the edge of the table. 'A week ago? A *week*? And you knew and said nothing of it to me?'

Hubert rose. 'No, my dear,' he said and smiled down at her, 'No. Nothing at all. After all of what possible interest to you could Monsieur Bonvilain's return be?'

He turned and was about to leave the room, but she rose rapidly and hurried after him, reaching his side just as the doors began to open for him.

'Papa! Papa, what can you mean? Of no interest to me? Who told the Queen of Mogok, who showed her all the plans, who gained the chance of the concession almost alone? Do you know what you are saying?'

'Perfectly,' Hubert said, still smiling. 'And we are very grateful to you for the charming manner in which you have interested the Queen in our project but, my dear, things must now – as I am sure you see yourself – go beyond that. It is the affairs of men, my dear Maria. You need trouble yourself about it no more, it is no concern of yours at all,' and then, with a steady determination she could only have broken by casting herself physically in his path, he moved out of the room and, within seconds, she heard the quiet click of his own door closing behind him.

In the morning, before her departure for the palace, Maria wrote a letter to Denzil Blount. She would be glad, she wrote, to see him at teatime, that day, after her return from the palace. It was, she added, quite like old times to have Pierre Bonvilain back in Mandalay and perhaps Denzil would bring him so that she might have the chance of asking what day would be suitable for her to call upon Madame Bonvilain and welcome her to Mandalay.

At the palace, Maria knelt and touched her forehead to the floor. '*Ashin-nammadaw-paya*, the Frenchman has returned.'

'Oh, yes,' Supayalat said, leaning forward for one of her little maids to light her cheroot. 'He brought me carpets, and a looking glass framed in gold lilies, and a camera. A good camera with a tripod. Perhaps you will learn to use it better than that fool Manook.'

Maria took a deep breath. 'And Your Majesty, did you give him what he asked for?'

In the doorway, one of the ministers hovered, the old *Taingda Mingyi*, with his carved merciless face. Supayalat waved her maids away.

'Go, go! Go, all of you. And you!' She gestured at Maria, her free hand held out to the old man. 'Go too! Your Frenchman has his rubies, you have what you wanted. Go!'

In the antechamber the little maids were crouched, whispering. They looked over their shoulders at Maria but did not beckon her to join them. She stood by one of the long openings that served both for window and door and looked out at the empty palace platform, the deserted gardens, the shining tin roofs between their wings of red and gold, and heard the wailing throbbing of the music of the *pwes* pulsing from the theatre. Her sleeve was plucked. The girl at whom Supayalat had thrown her slipper stood looking up at her.

'We wish to know, because you are so much in the confidence of the *Ashin-nammadaw-paya*, if the *Taingda Mingyi* has often had audience just recently?'

'Yes,' Maria said, thinking of nothing much but her own bewildering position. 'Yes. Every day that Her Majesty has been in the pavilion by the waterfall. He comes to her there.'

'And you hear them?' the maid said, scarcely audibly while the others crept closer. 'You hear what they say?'

'Naturally I wait outside the pavilion. Her Majesty has assured me that their conversations concern solely the best interests of the King.'

Supayalat was closeted with the *Taingda Mingyi* for above an hour and afterwards was remote and thoughtful, smoking furiously and spinning the diamond bracelets on her wrist in a glittering circle of white fire. She spoke to no-one, not even to Maria, and the King kept to his own rooms and came nowhere near her. Her dinner was brought in in the customary jewelled lacquer urns, and she pushed the curry and rice about her plate for a while but ate nothing, merely smoked and drank water, glass after glass, her eyes fixed upon the view outside but not seeing it, seeing nothing.

Maria was afraid to leave her, but afraid, too, of not being at home. She ordered the bullock driver to go quickly and arrived at home shaken almost to pieces and smothered in dust. Within twenty minutes, changed and outwardly composed, she was waiting in the drawing room with tea, as was her custom, at her elbow. For two hours she waited, while the light thickened and the coppersmith bird beat out his relentless knocking and then a message was brought from Denzil saying how much he regretted being unable to come. Another day perhaps, when Madame Bonvilain was over the fatigues of the journey . . .

Hubert did not appear at dinner. Long after midnight, wakeful and restless, she heard his steps pass her door without pausing and go on down the verandah to his own room. I will go to Tom Prior, she thought, I will go and ask him what I have done, what is happening. I will tell him what I have seen in the palace. And then she thought, I cannot, I cannot tell him, I cannot tell anyone that I am afraid of failing. And he would not know what is going on, he would not care about the palace. The only thing he would understand about is my – my losing Papa and that I do not want to admit to anyone, anyone at all.

When Denzil finally came, he found Maria unprepared for him and he brought Bonvilain and his wife. Marie-Thérèse Bonvilain was slight and blonde, dressed in dove-grey silk. She had perfect poise and eyes for no-one in the room but her husband.

Maria said to Bonvilain, dispensing tea as she spoke, 'And France? Did you amuse yourself well in France?'

'Admirably,' he said, smiling at her and then with an intimacy which exasperated her, at his wife.

'And profitably too, I trust,' she said directly to him, her eyes fixed upon him.

He grimaced faintly at his wife. 'We have promised not to speak of that, heh? A weekend of wickedness at Deauville, Mademoiselle, among bachelor friends was not, as my wife will tell you, profitable in any way. *Les diamants, chérie*,' he said to his wife. 'Show Miss Beresford your ring.'

Marie-Thérèse held out an impeccably kept pale hand and displayed a marquise of diamonds of an impressive size.

Maria said coldly, 'Charming.' She looked across at Denzil. 'And you seem to have been much occupied of late, Mr Blount,' she said. 'I have not seen you in weeks.'

'Times change, my dear Maria. And so do habits. I cannot always do what once I did. But I know you are well. I have seen your equipage going in and out of the palace with a punctuality that would do credit to a railway timetable.'

Maria said as lightly as she could, 'You have seen me but have not seen fit to speak.'

He laughed and shrugged. 'My dear, you know how it is in such communities as ours. So little happens there is so little to say. We amuse each other far better if we see as little of each other as we can. Think how much you saw of Grace Prior when she was alive!'

Maria fought back sudden hot tears that sprang to her eyes. Head high, she said with an attempt at playfulness, 'Since, by your own account, this is the last I shall see of you for some while, I must make the most of it. Tell me how plans for Mogok are going.'

Bonvilain stretched out his long legs and took his wife's right hand. 'Well enough, I think, to promise *ma chère femme* – and you also, Miss Beresford – a companion ring for this charming but unadorned hand.' He kissed it and smiled, replacing it in her lap. 'Do you know, Miss Beresford, that this bad little girl of mine says she does not care for rubies?'

There were, as was her habit, rubies in Maria's ears and round her neck and wrists. She said to Denzil, ignoring Bonvilain, 'I don't wish to speak of jewels. I wish to speak of the concession, the concession to work Mogok. Do we have it? There are rumours in the palace, but I wish to know what the facts are—'

'Madame,' Denzil said to Marie-Thérèse across Maria, 'Madame, Englishwomen are intrepid beyond belief. I should not be at all surprised to see Miss Beresford mine a ruby for herself. Indeed, I almost had to prevent her forcibly, once, from plunging into the earth's depths to see for herself. I am sure you have heard what a favourite she is in the palace, and to spend much time around the Queen requires one to be very intrepid indeed.'

Madame Bonvilain smiled, showing perfect teeth, and resumed her contemplation of her husband. He said, 'What news from the palace, Miss Beresford? There are rumours that all those political prisoners they have confined down there, beneath the palace, are plotting against the King. But you, naturally, would know more of this than anyone else in Mandalay.'

'And equally naturally,' she said to him in revenge, 'I should tell you nothing I see or hear in confidence. Any information I may have I regard as my own.'

Denzil said quietly, 'In that case, my dear Maria, we understand each other perfectly.' He rose. 'We should detain Miss Beresford no longer—'

A step sounded on the verandah. Hubert came in, perfectly composed, kissed Madame Bonvilain's hand, with the appearance of having done so already several times, nodded cordially to the two men and brushed Maria's cheek lightly with his own.

He said to Marie-Thérèse, 'How good of you to call so soon upon my daughter. I know she wished to call upon you first, but pressing engagements at the palace take up so much of her time. There is a terrible noise up at the palace tonight; the *pwes* have become quite deafening.'

'We were just leaving,' Denzil said, his eyes upon Maria. She turned her head away and looked out into the garden.

'Let me come with you,' Hubert said. 'Let me take you down to the lane at least.' He offered his arm to Marie-Thérèse. 'How charming you look. My daughter's hair was as blonde as yours, you know, when she was a child—'

In the doorway Pierre and Denzil turned to bow farewell.

'It was delightful to see you,' Pierre said, smiling. 'I should have been disappointed to find you any less stern or beautiful. It would quite have changed Mandalay for me.'

She bowed. 'My congratulations on your marriage, Monsieur.'

Denzil said, 'Goodbye, my dear.' He paused a little and then said, 'When next you construct yourself a bed, my dear Maria, you must use your considerable intelligence to reflect upon the fact that one day you must lie upon it.'

She did not even incline her head to acknowledge that she had heard him.

That night in the palace a massacre took place, a far more savage massacre than that of five years before. On the orders of the *Taingda Mingyi*, himself acting upon instructions from the Queen, the prisoners in their unspeakable pits below the palace had been told that they had a chance to escape, that their irons would be struck off. Disguises were left for them in their cells, words of encouragement that the plan came directly from the exiled princes who were poised to overthrow the King and his all-powerful Queen were passed to them from their gaolers, posing as allies. And then, as they struggled, dazed with weakness and hope, into the clothes provided for them, the prisons were set on fire and became at once an inferno of panic. Those who were not trapped to die in the flames fought their way out of the blazing holes to be hacked to death as they took their first breaths of free air.

The King, cringing in a corner of the palace, his head buried against his Queen in an agony of terror and horror, begged that no enemy should be left alive, that the insurrection in the prisons should be quelled, that all those who opposed him and had striven to rise up against him beneath his own palace should be killed, every one. In silence Maria and Hubert stood on their verandah while flames and screams tore across the hot black sky and the throbbing of the *pwes* from the royal theatre went on and on, on and on.

In the morning, Maria set out as usual for the palace and, as usual, made her way towards the western gate, the only gateway to the city permitted to foreigners, because of its ill-omened associations with death. On that brilliant morning, she found the ground beyond the moat by the western gate was choked with bodies, pile upon pile of hideously mutilated corpses, between two and three hundred of them, men, women and children, naked and pitiful in the merciless light. The stench that rose from these butchered bodies was beyond description.

'Let them lie,' Thibaw had cried, his eyes hidden against his Queen. 'Let them lie unburied! Let all men see what a thing it is to offend the King.'

Convulsed with nausea, shaking and retching, Maria ordered the bullock cart turned about and made her way blindly home.

16

'And now,' Andreino said, 'now that you are rested, there is much to tell you. Much.'

'I might have been on the moon,' Archie said musingly, his legs stretched out before him in clean drill trousers whose ironed creases were a source of wonder and delight to him after months of Ah Chun's jungle laundry methods. He pulled his tunic up and slid his hands inside his waistband. 'Look at that. Just take a look, will you? I am inches thinner, *inches*—'

Andreino said, 'It won't last my boy, not if you eat as you have just done.'

Archie closed his eyes. 'It was wonderful. Wonderful. The mutton—'

'Listen to me.'

'I am.'

'Open your eyes. Otherwise you will be dreaming of food. Open them. Ever since you came to Mandalay I am warning you, warning and warning. Now we must do more than keep our eyes open, we must be prepared to take action. People are fleeing over the border into British Burma, hundreds of them, every day. For why? Because the royal purse is empty, the soldiers of the King are not paid so they have taken to the jungle and its laws. They terrorize the villages, they make the roads impassable, they massacre whom they please in the name of Thibaw. And in the royal city things are little better. That villainess of a Queen! She may be clever but she is not clever enough to see that you do not eradicate opposition by massacre. She reigns by terror and that is no secure basis for the future. And now she needs money. Where do you think she will turn?'

'To us?' Archie said. 'To the corporation?'

Andreino flung out his hands. 'To the English, my friend? The *English?* To the nation who shelter the exiled princes of Burma in India, the nation who already possess the lower half of her country? Never! Not in a thousand years, a million. I told you we should watch the French, I told everyone. For years and years I am telling people that they must never take their eyes off the French, never. But the British government and the government of India, they will not look at Burma, they will not regard it as important. What has happened now? Khartoum has fallen, the British are defeated again, your great General Gordon is dead and when I write to the Chief Commissioner in Rangoon and tell him of what the French do here, he says only Khartoum to me, Khartoum, Khartoum—'

Archie said, 'What about the French then?'

Andreino leaned forward, his black eyes fixed on Archie's face. 'I will tell you, my friend. I will tell you. Monsieur Bonvilain – that is a good

336

name, ha? – has returned from Paris where he clung to the Burmese delegation like a shadow, with the concession to work the ruby mines at Mogok. It is a remarkable achievement for an adventurer like Bonvilain. But then, of course, we know who helped him to it.'

'Yes,' Archie said, unwillingly.

'Our handsome Miss Beresford begged for the Queen's favour and got it. And her father will assist in raising the three lakhs of rupees to pay the Burmese government, and Mr Blount will see that the scheme spreads to no-one further.'

Archie said, 'I don't believe Miss Beresford would do such a thing to help the French.'

Andreino smiled. 'Your months of solitude have made you gallant. But you are right also. She interceded with the Queen on behalf of herself and her father for their part in the scheme, just as she once did for the mines at Minhla. I think she did not believe – for she must have known – that Bonvilain might enlist the help of the French Foreign Minister. I tell you, Archie, that Jules Ferry has extracted from the Burmese delegation the right to take over almost everything in Mandalay but the throne. The French are to build a railway, found a bank, take charge of the army. And the others, the other *kalās*? My own country is a cauldron of political troubles and cannot spare a moment from Abyssinia for the outside world, and Germany's parliament has declared it no longer supports Bismarck's colonial policy, and the British – the British I told

337

you of. So there is no-one to oppose the French, no-one. They will run arms through Burma to Tonkin, they will pillage the country of her natural resources, they will take the teak and the jewels from beneath our noses. I am afraid my friend, afraid that the Bombay-Burmah are in grave danger of being driven out of the forests. We have only to displease the palace in the smallest degree and pouf! our concession goes. So you see, you have not come back to much of a place. Mandalay is falling apart before our eyes. Sensible people are going to Rangoon. Even, I tell you, even Tom Prior is going down to Rangoon, even he.'

Archie got up and began to pace about the room. 'How is he?'

'He? Tom? Not so good. Something in him has broken, he does not burn with zeal now. He will be better in Rangoon back in the capable hands of Doctor Marks, shown where to go once more.'

Archie said, his back to Andreino. 'I want to see Miss Beresford. I don't understand all this, her connection with Bonvilain. It isn't like her, she is no traitor—'

'No,' Andreino said softly, 'she is an unhappy woman.'

'Her father?'

'Precisely so. Bonvilain is using the father. You will see. When the father has raised the money to pay for the first year's contract, the father will go. He does not know it, but he will. Miss Beresford is not needed already, matters are beyond pleading with the Queen, they involve the French Foreign Minister and the Burmese government these days. Her usefulness has gone. So, I think, has her father's love for her. He only resents her now.'

'What fools,' Archie said, furiously. 'What blind, duped fools.'

'So you agree with me? We must not let the French get away with it?'

'Absolutely not.'

'Then you will help me?'

'Of course. Only tell me how.'

Andreino came to stand close to Archie. 'I need proof, my friend, written proof. I need evidence of French undermining of British influence here, copies of contracts, letters, any reference we can find to the Bombay-Burmah in correspondence between Ferry and Mandalay. You can work upon Hubert Beresford, you can also work upon little Mattie Calogreedy, who has access to all sorts of things in the palace and who is burning for revenge upon Bonvilain.'

'Why are you doing all this? Who for? After all you are an Italian—'

Andreino shrugged. 'The British pay me.'

'And if someone else offered you more?'

Another shrug. 'Perhaps. Perhaps. Who knows? But only I think if that someone else had a chance of final victory. And I don't believe the French have that. They will give us all a bad fright, but I shall do everything in my power to see that that is all they do.'

In the comfortable bungalow that had been secured in the expectation of a French consul arriving shortly in Mandalay, Pierre Bonvilain lounged as Archie had been doing a mile away, his long legs stretched before him and his hands beneath his chin, pressed finger tip to finger tip. Beside him, on a low rattan table, lay a pile of papers weighted with a glimmering lump of ore such as Maria had filled the Chinese bowls in her drawing room with, and his gaze returned with satisfaction time and again to the topmost paper of the pile.

It was a letter, dated a month ago, and the address heavily embossed in the top right-hand corner was the Quai d'Orsay. It was, next to the written concession given to him by the Burmese delegation in Paris to work the Mogok mines – a copy of which, incidentally, he must retrieve from Hubert and that quickly, before Denzil discovered that vainglory had led him to do anything so unwise as to show it off – the most satisfactory and flattering letter of his life. It was, Jules Ferry wrote to him – to him, personally, Pierre Bonvilain by name – of great satisfaction to the French government to hear of his achievements in Burma and in particular his securing of sole rights to mine for rubies in Mogok. It had initially been thought that the money for the venture must be put up by Bonvilain himself on account of the adventurous nature of the scheme, but another complexion had been put upon the matter by the success in securing influential treaties with the Burmese that made France in Burmese eyes, the 'most favoured nation'. In view of this turn of events, Ferry was pleased to tell Monsieur Bonvilain that the necessary three lakhs of rupees would now be guaranteed by the French government and that Monsieur Bonvilain need look to no-one else for assistance.

Pierre smiled beneath the moustache that his Marie-Thérèse was not the first to admire so profoundly. His schemes were turning out far better than he had ever, arriving in Mandalay five years before as a penniless engineer, dreamed of. The Beresfords had been of inestimable use to him and, now that they were becoming a hindrance, he must extricate himself from all connection with them. This was facilitated by the disintegration of their own relationship, and Bonvilain had no doubt that he could in some way insinuate to Hubert that his no longer being necessary as a fund raiser was in some measure due to the impossibility of his daughter's temper nowadays which, coupled with her greed, made her an unpredictable and dangerous partner.

Denzil Blount was rather another matter because there was something in him of which Bonvilain, even in his most self-satisfied and cavalier moments, was a little afraid. Without Denzil, he might still be a penniless engineer and also have been unable to disentangle himself from the Beresfords as painlessly as he seemed to be doing. He resented the prospect of sharing the profits from Mogok with Denzil but, on the other hand, could think of no alternative that did not fill him with distinct alarm. Denzil, caring for nothing but himself, was without a single scruple and Pierre, the new darling of the Quai d'Orsay, found that for the first time in his life he had something to lose that he cared very much about. Things would, there was no doubt, have to remain as they were for the time being. If he antagonized Denzil there was a strong chance that Denzil, in revenge, would reveal to the Bombay-Burmah Trading Corporation the French plans to usurp the concessions to the teak forests, plans that Ferry had entrusted to Bonvilain and which Bonvilain's boastfulness had allowed to escape, just as it had permitted Hubert to see the copy of the concession to work Mogok. If Denzil ever went down in life, he would make sure he brought down as many with him as he could—

'Pierre,' Denzil said from the verandah, 'I received your note. I am delighted the mails brought you good news—'

Bonvilain laughed. A renewed sense of his own invincible success flooded through him and dispelled any doubts. He stood up and put his hands on Denzil's shoulders.

'My good friend, how glad I am to see you. Yes, indeed, I do have good news. Excellent news. Excellent, that is, for you and for myself, but bad I fear, very bad, for Monsieur Beresford.'

Denzil moved away as if he disliked to be touched. 'Am I to understand that your government will finance us?'

'Precisely so.'

'Guaranteed?'

Pierre drew the letter from beneath the lump of ore and handed it to Denzil. 'See for yourself.'

Denzil read it rapidly with intense concentration.

'Well?' Bonvilain said.

'You have done excellently.'

Bonvilain grinned. 'Rare praise—'

'Rarely deserved. But deserved this time.'

'You will inform Hubert?'

Denzil stared. 'I do it? Oh, no, my dear Pierre, not me. As a last task before they withdraw to lick their wounds in Rangoon – and withdraw they must now there is nothing to keep them in Mandalay – I shall ask Miss Beresford to tell her father for me. It will, as I am sure you will agree, be so very much better coming from her.'

Bonvilain began to laugh. 'Villain! My friend, you are a villain!'

'Yes,' Denzil said evenly, 'And don't you ever forget it.'

343

17

Tom Prior left Mandalay with only Maria Beresford to wave him away. He stood on the bund for a long time before boarding, his battered possessions in an untidy heap at his feet, a heap which seemed to have a life of its own, sliding and shifting and changing contour as if it were trying to adjust its contents more comfortably. Tom had breadcrumbs in his beard, two buttons missing on his coat and, Maria could not help but notice as he stooped absently to caress the dusty head of a nearby child, odd socks. He looked about him at intervals as if he expected someone, as if a ghostly horde of past familiars of Mandalay might come drifting through the trees along the top of the bund – Colonel Browne, Grace, old Manook rubbing his hands – and restore to him the spiritual vigour of his past.

'Andreino—' he said suddenly, 'Signor Andreino—'

Maria looked about her. There was no European in sight, nothing but a chattering and distasteful mass of Burmese. Tom looked at Maria.

'Archie,' he said in deep reproach.

'Perhaps he does not know you are leaving. At least, he does not know it is today.'

Tom lifted his face, screwing his eyes up against the sun. 'You should be coming with me, my dear. You should not be staying. What am I thinking of, going down to safety and allowing you, a woman, to remain here? Go and pack your things at once, at once, don't delay a moment, come with me, come down to Rangoon!'

He clutched her arm and she saw that his eyes were quite glazed with fatigue. 'Maria, come with me, I beg you, come with me, don't stay, don't let me—'

His fingernails digging into the stuff of her sleeve were far from clean and, close to, he emitted a frowsty smell of unwashed clothes. With an effort, she put her own hand on his.

'It would not help you if I came. In your heart you know that. At best I can only be a brief distraction. And I do not want to come. It sometimes seems to me that I have spent five years insisting to one man or another that I am not afraid to stay, that I want to stay.' She paused and took her hand away. 'In any case, I have nowhere else to go.'

'You are wrong, my dear, so wrong. We all, always, have a place to go. We are never alone in this world, never, when we have a Father who loves us in whom we trust—' he shut his eyes again, 'in whom we trust and trust—'

She eyed him sceptically. 'Do we?'

From the river the steamer hooted mournfully.

345

'You must go aboard, Mr Prior. Where are the mission coolies?'

Tom said, 'I sent them back. I can manage quite well, I have so little, nothing that matters—'

Maria made a sound of impatience. 'Of course you cannot carry your own baggage. It would be unthinkable. I begin to think I should come with you in order to ensure at the very least that you do not disgrace the name of England.' She turned and called sharply. Her own servants, lolling against the wheels of the bullock cart, grinning and spitting red jets of betel juice into the dust, came scampering up the bund. Maria indicated the collapsing canvas mound of Tom's possessions and ordered it aboard.

'I will see you again?' Tom said, his eyes upon her face.

'Of course,' she said briskly.

He looked over his shoulder at the dusty road that led back to Mandalay, back among the dispirited wooden houses of the *kalā* town to the dangerous glitter of the royal palace.

'The City of Gems.'

Maria touched her ears. 'So it seems.'

'Goodbye, my dear.'

Their hands touched. His eyes were full of tears. He said, 'God keep you.'

'Goodbye, Mr Prior.'

She watched him stumble down the steps towards the landing stage. One of her servants fielded him as he lost his footing among the

346

broken stones and, with another, guided him along the gangplank, crabwise as they were too many to walk abreast. Once on the deck, Tom turned as if he were about to wave, but seemed to forget what he had turned for and went shuffling along holding the taffrail until the upper decks of the steamer hid him from her view.

Back in her drawing room, Archie was waiting. He had leapt up, hearing the rushing sweep of her dress along the verandah, and with this sudden movement had precipitated an avalanche of small silk cushions to the floor. She regarded him for a moment as he frantically chased the sliding cushions across the slippery surface of the polished boards.

'Mr Tennant.'

'Do forgive me, Miss Beresford. I am so sorry – I don't think anything is damaged—'

She stepped past him and rang the bell. 'Of course it isn't. Please leave them. The servants will pick them up. It is of no consequence at all.'

He straightened up in relief. 'I am so very glad to see you, Miss Beresford.'

'Are you?' she said, without coquettishness. 'And will you sit down? Somewhere less hazardous—'

A servant slipped in and retrieved the cushions deftly. Maria said, looking at Archie with her usual directness, 'You look extremely well, Mr Tennant. A beard becomes you.' It was the most intimate remark she had ever made to him.

Blushing helplessly, he said, 'If – if I had thought a beard might please you, I should have grown one earlier. Shaving arrangements in the forests were – a little rudimentary.'

'And you are in Mandalay now for the wet season?'

'Yes,' he said, glancing out into the garden, 'any day now.'

She said, 'I dread it.'

He turned to look at her. She had grown much thinner, thin to the point of gauntness around her face and neck, so that her eyes seemed much larger and her hair more luxuriant, heavier.

'I have to chastise you, Mr Tennant.'

'Oh,' he said, immediately repentant.

'Tom Prior left Mandalay this morning for Rangoon. He would most evidently have liked to see you before he left.'

Archie's face was flooded with contrition. 'Oh, my God – forgive me, Miss Beresford, but I would not have missed his going for worlds. But I knew nothing of it, I mean, I knew he was going, but not when, not that it was today—'

'He will be better in Rangoon. He is not really fit to look after himself.'

'Then he did not recover? He did not recover from – from Grace's death?'

'No,' she said, 'he did not.'

'Is – is this place a destroyer, Miss Beresford?'

She turned her head away from him. 'Only, I think, Mr Tennant, if you permit yourself to be a victim.'

He said, 'I was under the impression that your days were spent in the palace.'

He caught in her eyes a fleeting glance of unease.

'I regarded Mr Prior's departure as a priority.'

'How are things in the palace?'

In a low voice, her head bent towards her lap, she said, 'Unstable. Dangerous, perhaps.'

'That is what I heard myself. Acute shortage of money, savage repression of opposition, weakness and vacillation on the part of the King—'

'All those things.'

'Is it really safe for you to go there still?'

She looked at him. 'Safer than anywhere else.'

'Should you not have gone to Rangoon with Mr Prior?'

'No.'

'Because of other matters which keep you in Mandalay? Business matters?'

She got up abruptly. 'It is impertinent to crossquestion me, Mr Tennant. What I do is no affair of yours. My decisions are entirely of my own making.'

Archie rose too so that they faced each other across the beautiful faded Chinese rug. 'What you do may at the moment be no affair of mine, but I have to tell you, Miss Beresford, that I wish it were. I have thought about you so much in the forests, so much that in the last weeks thoughts of you have almost obsessed me. You may have done your utmost to discourage me in the past, as you seem to have done with all other human contact, but the effect of your behaviour upon me has merely been to arouse first my interest and secondly my admiration – and – and fascination, Miss Beresford. I don't really seem to care about your interest in me, indeed I should think it is minimal since you have not asked me one single question about my time in the forest, but that aspect is beside the point. The point is that I find I am in love, quite violently in love with you, and the only way I can appease my feelings is to ask you, however hopeless my chances, if you will consider marrying me.'

Maria's face betrayed nothing. 'I am sure you will quite appreciate that I must refuse you, Mr Tennant.'

'Must?' he shouted. 'Must? Why must?'

She folded her hands calmly before her. 'I am a woman of independence, Mr Tennant. I am not a woman who needs looking after, I am not a woman who needs a man—'

'I don't want to look after you necessarily – at least, I do, but not if you don't wish it. I want to have you, I need you even if you don't need me.'

'What you need, Mr Tennant,' she said, her lip curling, 'is any woman. It is common knowledge that you went into the forests with more than simply your manservant. How you can outrage me by such a proposal when your behaviour is so utterly – disgusting, *depraved*, is beyond my comprehension.'

Archie spread his hands. 'Oh Miss Beresford,

don't demean yourself by speaking so. What does a mistress mean in a place like this—'

'Get out,' she said, her hands over her ears.

He stepped forward and took her hands away, holding them hard in his own. 'I will go when I have been properly answered. Do you refuse me because you have no feeling for me at all, because you intend never to marry anyone, or because I have kept a Burmese mistress for a few months?'

She struggled a little in his grasp but found it was fruitless, so let her hands lie in his and said impatiently, 'All those things, Mr Tennant.'

He let her go. 'So it does not matter a whit to you whether or not I try again?'

'Not a whit.'

'And your father? Does he wish to see you die an old maid?'

An expression very like pain crossed her face. 'My father's views coincide entirely with my own.'

'I don't believe you, Miss Beresford.'

She gave a small, immediately suppressed gasp. 'Please – please go, Mr Tennant.'

He held out his hand to her. 'If you will shake my hand.'

She put hers into his. Hers was trembling very slightly.

Archie said, 'We are more alike than you will admit, Miss Beresford. We have so few human intimates. I suppose my closest relationship is with an old man in England who has no reason except for his loneliness and goodness of heart to love me, but love me he seems to.'

'Then you are most fortunate, Mr Tennant.'

'Yes,' he said, 'yes, I am. And you might have made me as fortunate as I ever hoped to be.'

She took her hand away abruptly. 'No,' she said, 'I could not. I could not do that for anybody.'

'May I ask you one small last favour?'

'You may *ask*—'

'I don't need to tell you how much we all live on the edge of a precipice here, nor how the danger level rises every day, nor how growing French influence here makes our own position more uncertain at every moment. All I do wish to tell you is that, given all these imponderables, I want you always to remember that I am there in time of need. After what I have said to you this morning, you will understand that I am not just prepared to help you if ever you are in difficulties, but hoping against hope that such an occasion might arise.'

She bowed her head very slightly but said nothing.

'Goodbye,' he said, 'Maria.'

She still did not speak and her face was turned away from him again so he sighed, involuntarily but loudly enough for her to be in no doubt as to his feelings, and clumped disconsolately down the verandah to his waiting cart in the lane.

*   *   *

It required for some reason all the self-discipline Maria possessed to dress herself for the palace later that day and to order herself driven there. Supayalat and Thibaw would have eaten in the fountain room as usual, Thibaw drinking steadily, Supayalat watching him with her intent, unblinking stare, and they would now have retired to their own apartments and be sleeping in the heavy afternoon heat, heavier now with the approaching rains than ever. Maria planned to be waiting for the Queen when she awoke. The afternoon would be like all other afternoons, spent in a pavilion in the gardens, lighting one after another of the Queen's cheroots, listening to story after story told by nervous maids of honour – nervous because of the increasing unpredictability of Supayalat's temper – watching scornfully while Mattie Calogreedy sought to oust her, Maria, from royal favour in revenge for her lack of sympathy over Pierre Bonvilain and his insipid little wife . . .

At the palace walls, just as she was about to cross the white bridge over the mirror-still moat, her cart was stopped.

'Miss Beresford,' Andreino said from the road-way.

She looked down at him with distaste. He wore a dreadful coat of figured velveteen and smelt strongly and sweetly, like some essence of over-blown roses.

'Forgive me for halting you. I shall only take a moment of your time.'

The sun blazed down even through Maria's parasol, she could feel it like a brand on the base of her neck.

'I have some hard things to say to you, Miss Beresford, and I only say them out of respect for your intelligence. It is imperative that you leave at once for Rangoon. Even to travel the streets here as you now do will soon become impossible. The position of the English here becomes more perilous every hour—'

Maria glanced up at the shining roofs that flew above her. 'Not mine, Signor Andreino.'

He grasped the side of the cart. 'Even yours, Miss Beresford. That is precisely why I wish to speak to you. You have too good an intelligence as I said to be misled any longer by your father, by Monsieur Bonvilain or Mr Blount. The truth is, signorina, that your father has, for whatever reason, long decided that you shall have no further part in the concessions to any mines in Upper Burma. What is more, Bonvilain, as you know, has secured all he went to Paris to secure and he and Blount are in the process of divorcing your father from all their plans also. Your father was in touch with Bonvilain all the time he was away, but did not tell you, and furthermore – these are cruel things to say to any woman, signorina, but for your own safety they must be said – he agreed with the other two that your part in their business affairs must cease. He now finds himself in the same position – or at least, he will do very shortly. If you wish to warn him, that is a matter for your own discretion. But I cannot urge you too strongly to leave. Bonvilain is the favourite, a French consul is coming, the future for the English is very black. Mr Blount only stays because he has some hold on Bonvilain, but you will see, he too will go if the fire gets hotter.'

Maria looked steadily ahead all the time he was speaking, her back straight, her chin raised. 'Why should I believe you, Signor Andreino?'

'You will be gravely mistaken not to.'

'Please take your hands from the cart sides.'

He stepped back. 'Despite your ungraciousness, Miss Beresford, I will offer you any help I can. You must not hesitate to ask me. The next steamer leaves on Thursday and it is imperative that you are on it. If times get much worse, there may *be* no steamers.'

The bullock cart ground forward, missing his glossy boot toes by inches. He gazed after it for a while with a mixture of admiration and indignation and then, tucking his cane beneath his arm, set off briskly in the direction of Archie's bungalow.

Maria, creaking forward towards the palace, would not even allow herself to think. She rode as she had always done, bolt upright and looking resolutely before her, as if the butterfly crowd of little Burmese who thronged the royal city simply did not exist. At the outer postern, she climbed out of the cart, furled her parasol and stepped inside. The *Hlutdaw* soared before her as it had done hundreds of times before, scarlet and gold and massive, its great steps empty of any sign of life but the odd bird investigating corners for insects. At the postern to the palace platform she was stopped.

'Nonsense,' she said, 'I am Miss Beresford. I am never stopped.'

The guard was joined by another. 'Orders of the Queen.'

Maria looked at them in incredulity. Her first instinct was to ignore them and march forward as if they simply were not there. But some slight movement caught her eye and she stayed where she was, gazing across the green lawns and waterfalls where she had spent afternoons without number. Moving across the gardens, in the distance but unmistakable to Maria's clear vision, was Queen Supayalat, attended by her fluttering band of maids of honour and in their midst, her blond hair clearly visible beneath a charming hat of pale straw, walked Marie-Thérèse Bonvilain.

'I am so sorry,' Andreino said, 'I feel for you so. A father—'

'No,' Archie said, 'not my father. But like one. Better in some ways, I think.'

The letter lay between them where Andreino had laid it on a stool.

'But you are rich now, my friend. A great house, servants, money – There is no need for you to go back to the forests.'

Archie put his hands over his eyes.

'But I want to go back. He would want me to.

If it wasn't for him I should be idling about as some penniless and inky clerk in Chancery Lane. It's the least I can do—'

'My dear fellow. Believe me. I do feel for you.'

'Would you think me churlish if I asked you to go? I'm sorry but I – I can't seem to manage anything else today—'

Andreino stood up. 'Forgive me. I shall leave at once. I should just tell you that I saw Miss Beresford today and told her of her position here. I think you should consider yours, communicate with the manager in Rangoon—'

'Get out!' Archie shouted.

'Forgive me,' Andreino said again, 'forgive me.'

'Go. *Go.*'

When he had bowed himself out, Archie stumbled to his bedroom. It was as orderly as usual, evening clothes laid out, polished boots, mosquito net in symmetrical folds, water jug and upturned glass on a tray by the bed. With flailing arms, Archie crashed around the room, sweeping his clothes to the floor, kicking his boots wildly about, sending jug and glass flying in a hail of glittering splinters. Then he cast himself down across the bed and burst into noisy uncontrollable tears.

Two days later, the rains began, sweeping, blinding deluges of water surging in from the Bay of Bengal. Frederick Winser came back from the forests too in a strange and intractable frame of mind, curiously uncommunicative about his

357

months of solitude. Archie could not even wring from him the smallest details of what he had achieved in his winter of map-making and after an awkward week in which Frederick answered Archie only in grunts he announced that he was taking the next steamer to Rangoon.

'Rangoon!'

'Yes. Coming?'

'But – but why?'

Frederick waved a letter with a nonchalance Archie did not trust. 'Company business. They want to see me.'

'Not – not trouble?'

'Oh, no!' Frederick said, avoiding Archie's eye and plunging with elaborate vigour into the dissection of a mango. 'Not that. Do assure you. Want to come?'

'No thanks. I want to see the action here.'

'Might be nasty. I've warned you.'

'Yes,' Archie said, 'everybody does. That's what I am staying to see.'

When Frederick had gone, lethargy stole upon Archie like a constant drowsiness. He began to eat too much and tried to rouse himself from a luxurious anticipation of the next meal by giving himself a strict timetable – beginning with being shaved once more each morning – and from which he lapsed inevitably at some point in each day. He ordered a pony brought round before the afternoon deluge drowned Mandalay with its appalling regularity but some days could not rouse himself to mount it. Ah Chun cleaned his gun faithfully each evening, whether it needed it or not, with a kind of steady reproachfulness. Andreino, calling at intervals in his busy round of inquiry and intrigue among the half-worlds of Mandalay, was the only European he now saw.

Until Hubert came. Archie had told himself that to sleep after luncheon was not only destructive to his willpower but also wasted one of the few dry moments of the day, but each afternoon was a battle against slumber that required superhuman efforts on his part. He came stumbling out of the dining room, Ah Chun padding in his wake with the cheroots he had taken to in the jungle, and found Hubert waiting for him, immaculate as ever in white linen, his handsome face now so expressionless that it was difficult to tell if he was aware of any other human being on earth but himself.

'Mr Beresford!'

'Mr Tennant.'

Archie fumbled hurriedly with the buttons of his tunic. From behind Ah Chun tugged and tweaked him surreptitiously into place.

'This is not a convenient time? You were lunching?'

'A little late—' Archie said shamefacedly.

'You could spare me a few moments?'

'Of course, of course—'

From the only comfortable chair, Ah Chun removed an untidy heap of *Rangoon Gazettes* and dusted the cushions obsequiously with the flat of his hand. Hubert handed him his hat and cane with no indication that he saw in him any more presence than that of a piece of furniture.

'We are quite alone, Mr Tennant?'

'Entirely, Mr Beresford.'

Archie turned and gave orders to Ah Chun who went out closing the door elaborately.

'I have no reason to doubt your manservant's discretion, but I cannot, in the present instance, be too careful. You would oblige me, Mr Tennant, by drawing your chair as close to mine as possible so that I may speak low.'

Intrigued entirely out of his drowsiness, Archie leaned forward, his elbows on his knees. 'How can I help you?'

Hubert put his hand over the right hand breast of his jacket.

'I have something here that I am anxious to entrust to you. I think you will by now be aware of the position which I have held in Mandalay since my arrival here in seventy-nine and I also assume that you will know that I and my partners gained the concession from the palace to work the ruby mines in Minhla soon after our arrival. Is all this known to you?'

Archie nodded.

'I am aware that as a forest officer you have been out of touch with affairs in Mandalay this last cold season, but I am certain that Signor Andreino has been most assiduous in putting you in possession of all details. You will therefore have heard rumours that the French wish to supersede British influence here in Upper Burma and that they are prepared to replenish the empty royal coffers in return for concessions in mining, banking, railways and so forth. Indeed, a French consul, a Monsieur Haas, disembarked from a steamer here only yesterday.'

'Yes,' Archie said, 'yes, I heard.'

Hubert drew a deep breath and leaned forward so that his fine, blank eyes were no more than a foot from Archie's.

'It was my understanding, Mr Tennant, that I was indispensable to the partners of whom I spoke to you earlier. I have, of course, on account of my background, no difficulty at all in raising for our partnership the vast sums of rupees necessary to pay the leases on the concessions. It seems, however, from an interview I had only yesterday with Mr Blount and Monsieur Bonvilain that they have no further desire to take advantage of the talents I can offer them.' He stopped and drew back and Archie saw that expression had crept into his glance for the first time, an expression of anger and – and of something else, something more dangerous. 'I do not care for speaking frankly, Mr Tennant, but in this instance I feel I must tell you that I am in no way prepared to bow to such treatment. Mr Blount and Monsieur Bonvilain entirely forget with whom they are dealing. More to the point, perhaps, Mr Blount does not know, and Monsieur Bonvilain has temporarily overlooked the fact, that in a moment of bravado inspired by the success of his time in Paris, Monsieur

Bonvilain lent me copies of the signed treaties between the French and Burmese governments.' He put his hand to his jacket again. 'He will live to regret both his boastfulness and his lack of discretion.'

Archie said, pointing, quite forgetting his manners in his eagerness, 'Do you mean, Mr Beresford, that you have proof, written proof that the French are in league with the Burmese and that the palace is being encouraged to oust the British?'

'I do,' Hubert said calmly. 'I have a copy of the signed concession for the French to manage and finance banks and a letter from the French foreign minister, Jules Ferry, to the *Kinwoon Mingyi* saying that the French will arrange for the Burmese to import arms through Tonkin. I have been able to use some influence at court and persuaded Miss Calogreedy to obtain copies of the Burmese reply to that letter and to others which are evidence of Burmese favour towards the French. Miss Calogreedy had an admirer in a clerk in the *Kinwoon Mingyi*'s office and the matter was easily arranged. I also possess the copy of a letter which will interest you in particular, Mr Tennant. It is from the new consul, Monsieur Haas, and it assures the palace that if an excuse can be found to cancel the Bombay-Burmah Trading Corporation's leases upon the teak forests, France will be more than ready to take them up.'

Archie was too excited to sit still. He got up

and began to pace about the room, his hands in his trouser pockets. Hubert watched him calmly. After a while, shaking his head, as if too bewildered to think coherently, Archie came back to his seat and said, 'But the French don't want war, do they? I mean, they are hardly powerful enough in this part of the world to defeat us—'

'Precisely. That is one reason why Haas has come. His mission is to persuade the Burmese government to make treaties with Germany and Italy by which they will join with France and declare Upper Burma neutral. England could not defy three such powerful nations as that. But the time is not yet ripe. France does not want to provoke England yet because, as things now stand, England is strong enough to drive out the French.'

'And you—' Archie said, almost in a whisper, 'you wish to precipitate things. You want those letters made public to London and Calcutta. You want an English army to march into Mandalay. You want revenge—'

'You take my point precisely, Mr Tennant.'

Hubert put his hand inside his jacket this time and drew out a flat packet of papers. He held them out to Archie. 'You will oblige me, Mr Tennant, by taking these papers to Signor Andreino. He is in private correspondence with Calcutta and, as you well know, with the Bombay-Burmah Corporation in Rangoon. I would be grateful if you would act with the utmost dispatch.'

'But why me, Mr Beresford? Why not take them to Andreino yourself? Of course, I will do it for you, for – for the corporation, for England, of course I will, but why choose me?'

Hubert stood up. 'No suspicion or intrigue attaches to you, Mr Tennant. Signor Andreino is surrounded by it and as I believe I am closely watched these days, I do not choose to run the risk of being seen in his company. The connections could be made so obviously. In your case, as a forest officer only out of the jungle a few weeks and also as one of the few Englishmen left in Mandalay, my calling upon you will seem a commonplace courtesy.'

Archie looked down at the packet in his hands. 'I can't believe it – I can't believe that you – Mr Beresford, what will you do now?'

'I leave for Rangoon this afternoon. The steamer is due to depart at four o'clock. At that hour precisely, when you hear the departing signal from the river, I would be obliged if you would deliver this packet to Signor Andreino.'

'And – your daughter? Miss Beresford?'

Hubert's face betrayed nothing. 'I believe she chooses to remain. I do not burden her with my plans.'

'And this?' Archie waved the papers. 'She knows nothing of this?'

'Naturally not.'

Archie shouted, 'So you intend to escape retribution by running away to Rangoon, but you don't mind leaving her to face it?'

'She has nothing to face. She is not in the least involved.'

'But what will she live upon? How will she live? What will she do?'

'Money is not a problem, Mr Tennant.'

'I wish,' Archie said furiously, 'I wish I could feel anything but contempt for you. I wish I could see anything remotely patriotic in your gesture, anything but a desire for personal revenge on Blount and Bonvilain. I wish I saw something in your behaviour to your daughter that savoured of anything but the most inhuman callousness.' He brandished the papers, 'I will run your errand, Mr Beresford, because greater things are at stake than your petty vengeance, but don't for one moment suppose that I am doing it for you.'

Hubert said blandly, 'Your motives do not concern me in the very least, Mr Tennant. I am only concerned that these papers reach Signor Andreino and in that matter, since as you say, great issues are at stake, I know you will not fail me.'

He moved towards the door. 'You would be so good as to ask for my hat and cane, Mr Tennant?'

'If you cannot look after your daughter, I can!'

Hubert turned at the doorway with the faintest of smiles. 'I am not a believer in advice, Mr Tennant. It is invariably inappropriate. But I feel it only fair to warn you that the outcome of any

such chivalrous intent will only lead to the loss of
your own self-esteem. You may assume, if you
wish, that I speak from my own experience.' He
paused and then said lightly, 'My own bitter
experience.'

PART FOUR

18

On 2 November 1885 in Madras, the Burma Field Force loaded its stores and weapons onto steamers of the British India Company in deluging rain. The night was spent in the greatest possible misery under canvas at Fort St George and the tent which Murray Shaw shared with another adjutant was flooded to a depth of six inches and had to be abandoned. If he spent the night wretched and sodden, with his high spirits at the prospect of the Burma campaign as dampened as his clothes, so too did the ten thousand other men of the force, gathered from the armies of Bengal and Madras on the instructions of the Secretary of State for Foreign Affairs in London and Lord Dufferin, Viceroy of India.

To men jaded with hanging about the garrison towns of India, the instructions to embark for Burma had come as a welcome relief. Murray Shaw himself saw it partly as a chance for promotion to major and partly as an opportunity to see if the 2nd battalion of the Hampshire Regiment could actually put all the theories he felt he had enriched them with in his small way into practice. He had, like most officers in India, felt very little interest in Burma during his seven or eight years in the East but the behaviour of that preposterous little savage of a king in Mandalay in recent months had aroused both his fascination and his fury.

His colonel, George White – a man he admired chiefly for the Victoria Cross he had won on the North-West Frontier – had been extremely helpful in explaining what seemed to Murray Shaw a pretty complex and tricky situation. Of course, old White had been military secretary to the previous Viceroy of India for a while and therefore you would expect him to have a better grasp of the things political johnnies got up to than many, but all the same, he did put the situation remarkably plainly, so plainly in fact that Murray felt himself able to repeat what he had heard to fellow junior officers without, for once, feeling he might have got hold of the wrong end of the stick.

'It's pretty simple, really. Somehow the news of what the French were up to leaked out to Calcutta and then to London and then, to cap that, this Thibaw fellow tried to throw out the Bombay-Burmah chaps by claiming that they had defaulted on payments for their leases. Apparently they are supposed to pay a royalty on each log they export, and Thibaw said they had smuggled some out without paying. White told me that the Burmese parliament – some rum name I can't remember – said the Bombay-Burmah had defrauded the King out of over seventy-three thousand pounds and the forest

370

workers of thirty-three thousand. Can you believe it?'

'Just as well we are going,' someone said, beside him. 'Teach them a thing or two—'

'But you haven't heard the whole. Apparently the Burmese said that they would fine the Bombay-Burmah twice the amount owed and, if they refused to pay, they'd have all their timber seized. So, of course, we sent the Burmese an ultimatum.'

'Of course—'

'We said that the Burmese must allow the fine to go to proper arbitration, and then we said that they must receive and treat a British Resident properly – after all, they have some Frenchman up there having the time of his life – and that they should not enter into any foreign relations without consulting us. Apparently the Queen, who really rules the roost up there, wouldn't hear of it. They said they didn't mind having another British Resident and they would listen to the Bombay-Burmah's case, but they wouldn't on any account have their foreign affairs interfered with. So there you are. Old Thibaw wants a fight!'

'And that,' someone else said, 'makes two of us.'

Murray was to wonder later if his colonel had actually overheard his enlightening lecture on the background to the need to march on Mandalay. When 3 November dawned, thankfully bright and cloudless after the drenching night, and

371

Murray found himself on the quayside next to his commanding officer while the sepoys were embarked in the steamers, White said, 'Of course, we mustn't underestimate the Burmese. I don't want you or any other junior officer of mine to do that. We have made a lot of mistakes recently in this respect and suffered terribly. Between you and me, Shaw, I hope that Thibaw's answer will be defiant, so that we have a soldier's duty to perform, not a policeman's.'

The crossing to Rangoon took only three days, across sea like a millpond, but most of the sepoys were sick nevertheless. Rangoon, Murray considered, looked a low dull place, but the Burmese girls, clustered along the river banks with chattering immodesty, looked both pretty and approachable. Not for the first time, Murray was glad that the sudden excess of romanticism that had seized him at a regimental ball in Madras the previous winter had not led him, as for a moment or two he had feared it might, to propose to a very pretty Miss Purvis who had laughed so obligingly at everything he said. He knew the sudden headiness that seized him as they sat out in a shadowed corner between pillars had been partly champagne, partly sheer frustration and partly because Miss Purvis, being tall and fair, had summoned up the memory of a magnificent girl he had known briefly in Bombay in '79. Maria Beresford had remained in his memory long after she had followed her father on some extraordinary expedition to Burma, whence she was by now bound to have travelled on and was doubtless now queening it as the wife of some distinguished fellow in Government House in Calcutta. He had wondered once or twice if the powerful imprint of her personality had prevented him from finding any subsequent girl desirable enough to marry, but such speculation was usually quickly quenched by a hearty recognition of the advantages of bachelorhood. Murray was under no illusions about the catch he represented being heir to a baronetcy and now in possession, six years past his twenty-fifth birthday, of a handsome income. He could afford better polo ponies than anyone else in the regiment, old White included, higher gambling stakes and a vastly superior cellar. There were many moments – and this, steaming gently into Rangoon with the prospect of a fight and all those pretty little things lined up before him, was one – when he felt he had got life entirely measured up, tailor-made to fit him.

There was, he soon discovered, to be no hanging about in Rangoon. Within five days, the Field Force had moved north by rail from the capital to an undistinguished little hole called Thayetmyo on the Upper Burma border, where a vast convoy of steamers and flats from the Irrawaddy Flotilla Company lay on the great shining breadth of the Irrawaddy. The steamers, which for years had carried chiefly Burmese and their bundles and the mails and occasionally Europeans with their accompanying mountains of luggage, had been fitted out hastily with arms racks, water tanks and latrines and the flats they were to tow had been adapted to carry artillery. The convoy was to be escorted by steam launches equipped with machine guns to sweep the river banks as they moved northwards.

In common with all the other officers, Murray was issued with a ration list for his men which specified, among other things, an ounce of lime juice for each man per week, and in addition to that, a list which Murray himself found quite baffling. Not liking to ask any fellow officer for enlightenment, he sought out a journalist chap called Moylan, employed by *The Times* as Rangoon correspondent, who was accompanying the Field Force to Mandalay.

'That,' Moylan said, giving Murray one of his keen, sharp glances, 'that is a list of the most celebrated antiquities in Upper Burma, books and scripts and Buddha images, that sort of thing. So if you come to sack a monastery, Captain Shaw, you would be obliging the world infinitely if you safeguarded any library or shrine you find rather than permitting your sepoys to rampage through it.'

'And if the enemy rally in monasteries?'

'You must refer to your colonel. But in such a case, I should suppose unhappily that the soldier must precede the preserver of antiquities.'

'Rum language—' Murray said, gazing at the sheet in his hand.

'Now that,' Moylan said, following his glance

and pointing to a name on the list, 'that one you will be quite safe with. The Tripitaka commentaries. That is the world's greatest book on Buddhism, it says everything there is to say. But I am delighted to tell you that the pages are of marble, set into marble plinths. Not easy to damage, Captain Shaw.'

After a day at Thayetmyo, Murray was dispatched with a small force back to the railway terminus at Toungoo to assist in the safe embarkation of many employees of the Bombay-Burmah Trading Corporation who had come south when Thibaw had refused Lord Dufferin's ultimatum and were headed for Rangoon and temporary safety. Murray's brother Digby, when they had seen each other briefly before the Hampshires embarked for Rangoon, had said in his careless way that he had met a Bombay-Burmah fellow the year before in Bombay, destined for the forests of Upper Burma.

'Pleasantish chap,' Digby said. 'Big. Seemed not to know whether it was Christmas or Tuesday. Expect he's lost in some jungle now. Somebody Tennant – Archie, I think it was. Keen on polo.'

Having dispatched all the corporation's employees south and elicited all their names, Murray found no-one called Archie Tennant among them. As Digby had said, he was no doubt lost in some jungle which was, if Murray's martial ambitions were to be realized, the safest place for him.

He returned to Thayetmyo to find great excitement. It appeared that a steamer had arrived from Mandalay two days earlier with the news that the city was in a ferment and that some Italian fellow, a Signor Andreino, whose connection with the Bombay-Burmah Corporation Murray could not for the life of him make out, had gathered all the foreigners he could find into a single house and barricaded them in. The streets were no longer safe as roaming bands of dacoits prowled day and night and it was not possible even to move guarded about the *kalā* town, let alone attempt to enter the royal palace. The din of music and gongs and the Burmese notion of singing still reverberated from the royal theatre and it was reported that Thibaw, grasping his Queen's hand for reassurance and licking his lips nervously as he spoke, had told his ministers, 'It is only by war that I can save the honour of my kingdom. The trade and business of every subject of mine has suffered because of the English who have made improper demonstrations of war—'

And his Queen, pregnant again the report said, had risen and shrieked, 'Improper! Improper! What the English do is unlawful! Do you hear us? Unlawful!'

These stories had stirred up Murray's blood wonderfully but Moylan, always visible somewhere among the troops with his notebook, had been sceptical. 'There won't be a fight, Captain Shaw. I am sorry to disappoint you, but there'll only be a lot of noise. Shall I tell you something that came up to me by telegraph from Rangoon today and which you may disseminate among your fellow officers? The French are getting out as quickly as they can. They don't want to fight the English. The consul, Monsieur Haas, is being recalled at once and will be reprimanded for, as they say, acting without authority. End of his career, I shouldn't wonder. There's another Frenchman up in Mandalay, an engineer and his wife, but Andreino has them safe. Also, I am told, a bevy of intrepid American lady missionaries, one of the Bombay-Burmah's forest officers who was disinclined to miss the fun and an Englishwoman. What she is doing there, I could not say, but she appears to be quite without family. A Miss Beresford.'

'Maria Beresford?'

'I have no idea.'

'Must be,' Murray said, while quite a new anticipation took its place beside his eagerness to fight. 'There can't be two Miss Beresfords. Not in a place like Mandalay.'

Sixty miles above Thayetmyo lay the only place where the Field Force anticipated any difficulty. It bore the name of Minhla and was distinguished by being reasonably well fortified and also by possessing considerable ruby mines to the west of the river. On the way north towards Minhla, two Italian army engineers in the pay of King Thibaw were captured during their failure to blockade the river and the diary of one revealed the interesting information that they two alone had been entrusted by the royal palace in Mandalay with the task of closing the frontier.

'You see?' Moylan said to Murray Shaw. 'You won't get a battle. As the Burmese would say, it's a fish to fight a dog.'

'There's Minhla,' Murray said doggedly. 'They say there are eight thousand Burmese troops waiting for us across the river from Minhla.'

There were, but Captain Murray Shaw was fated hardly to see them. His brigade, led by White – now a general for the duration of the campaign – was ordered to follow as a reserve upon the brigade commanded to attack the great brick fort at Minhla, the strongest, Moylan said, in Burma. They disembarked from the steamers at dawn, watched with considerable envy the Royal Welch Fusiliers and two companies of Madras Infantry march off and then listened impatiently to the gunfire that resounded some hours later. By early afternoon when they reached the fort themselves, they found it in British hands, every Burman fled. There was nothing to do but march disconsolately back to the river and listen, with ill-concealed resentment, to tales of the lively fighting that had taken place all day in the thick jungle on the opposite bank of the river. The commander-in-chief, General Prendergast, was heard to say that not only had Jack Burman put up a lively fight but that he considered the infantry skirmishing over the hills at Minhla one of the prettiest sights he had ever seen.

After such bitter disappointment it was not even balm to Murray Shaw's feelings to see the wooden houses of Minhla ablaze that night, nor to watch Burmese soldiers driven from their hiding places to drown in the Irrawaddy. As the night wore on, thickening cloud began to obscure the brilliant stars and before dawn it began to rain, to the misery of the troops and the astonishment of any who knew Burma and declared it to be far too late in the year for such a downpour. When day broke, grey and chill and impossibly wet, news was brought to Murray that one of his sepoys had cholera. It was, as he said to a fellow officer from whom he borrowed a rubber cape, all he needed to hear.

19

'They are through Pagan,' Andreino said. 'They scuttled the royal steamers—'

It seemed almost impossible to imagine, the huge efficient steamers of the Irrawaddy Flotilla Company bristling with khaki coats and Manchester-made guns opposing the gilded steamers of Thibaw with their cargoes of soldiers in scarlet and white and purple-red, the officers in state beneath golden umbrellas, every head crowned with velvet and the curious tin helmets with upturned wings.

'Listen,' Maria said suddenly, commandingly.

A faint booming came on the hot wind from the south, a rumble like thunder.

Archie said, 'Guns—'

'Guns, English guns. They must have reached Myingyan, perhaps more. Maybe they are only forty miles away.'

Marie-Thérèse Bonvilain began to cry again. It not only irritated Maria that she should cry at all, but that she could manage to do so becomingly without so much as a hint of swollen eyes or a reddened nose. But she sobbed inevitably as she wept and the sound, shut up together as they were in the house that had belonged to the British political agent in Mandalay twenty years before, was sufficiently exasperating in itself.

Andreino had not ceased to marvel at the apparent docility with which Maria had finally agreed to leave her own house. All summer, after all, he had begged and cajoled her to leave Mandalay, to go down to Rangoon, to Madras, to Calcutta, anywhere, anything but remain. She had refused adamantly upon every occasion. What she did all day he could not imagine, living there in virtual seclusion, seeing almost no-one, no longer welcome at the palace. His quick ear caught the news that she was selling things, pieces of French furniture, Japanese lacquer, Chinese porcelain, but she appeared to him, on each occasion he called, as impeccably dressed as ever and her drawing room as charming as it had ever been. Rubies still clustered at her ears and round her neck and wrists, but she was absolutely, maddeningly uncommunicative about any single thing except her determination not to leave Mandalay.

In the last week of October he had almost despaired. It had become entirely apparent to him that there was no-one but himself to whom the foreigners left in the neighbourhood of Mandalay could look. On instructions from the corporation, Archie had not gone back to the forests for his second winter but had chosen – in defiance this time of the manager in Rangoon – to remain in Mandalay, and for that Andreino

could only be thankful. Between them, they
selected the most impregnable of the houses
in the *kalā* town that had once had European
occupation, and into this they induced any
foreigner remaining in Mandalay and those who
arrived daily from outlying missions, drawn by
rumour, to take refuge. Miss Beresford remained
adamant and, for some strange reason, Archie
seemed reluctant to visit her. Only at what
Andreino considered to be the last moment,
when news came that the Burma Field Force had
arrived in Rangoon, did Archie at last agree to
go.

'I don't say I shall have any more luck than
you. If I don't we shall have to go together and
carry her away by force.'

Maria received him with perfect composure.
She looked a little pale, her pallor thrown into
relief by a dress of the same colour as her jewels,
but he could at first detect no outward sign that
her strange isolated summer since her father's
departure had had any ill effect upon her.

'Please sit down, Mr Tennant.'

He lowered himself gingerly into one of the
rose-pink French chairs.

'If you have come, Mr Tennant, to tell me all
the things I am weary of hearing from Signor
Andreino, I must tell you that you are wasting
your time.'

'Then I will start with some other matters to
divert you, Miss Beresford. The first is that
Monsieur Haas has left Mandalay, recalled to

Paris in public disgrace. He will be, it seems, the scapegoat to save French face. The second is that I was witness three days ago to an interview between Signor Andreino and Denzil Blount, the upshot of which was Mr Blount's refusal to come under any kind of protection and his subsequent vanishing. Both Ah Chun and Andreino's servants have done a considerable amount of searching and inquiring and it seems Mr Blount has entirely disappeared. The third is that Monsieur and Madame Bonvilain have cast themselves upon our mercy since the contracts with which he hoped to make himself a fortune are now, of course, not worth the paper they are written on. I quite see that they are hardly an inducement for you to join us, but join us, Miss Beresford, you must.'

She did not speak, but looked out past his shoulder to the heavy green garden where the coppersmith bird still beat out his aggravating rhythms, and the pulsing gongs of the royal *pwes* throbbed in the sunlit air. After a while, in which he watched her intently and observed that there were dark circles under her eyes and that her hands shook however hard she clenched them together in her ruby silk lap, he said with all the gentleness he could summon. 'Won't you tell me why? Won't you trust me? Me, Maria, of all people?'

He was not at all sure what made him choose those words. He had scarcely seen her all summer and had determined not to examine his feelings at her rejection of his proposal, but rather to plunge with Andreino into the complexities and intrigues that followed the dispatch of those fateful papers to Rangoon. But she looked so vulnerable to him at this moment, a vulnerability made all the more poignant by her endeavours to overcome it.

'Maria,' he said again, coaxingly.

She said, without looking at him, 'I am so bitterly ashamed. I cannot hold my head up in any company.'

'But why? What have you done?'

'The world knows what my father did. And I did. The world knows we tried to line our pockets at the expense of British interests and that my father, for revenge, betrayed the people who were his partners. I saw the contracts in his bedroom – I was looking for evidence of quite another kind – and two days later they were not there.'

'No,' Archie said, 'the world does not know.'

'It must. It must—'

'I will tell you something. If your father chooses to say anything in Rangoon, it is only his own reputation he will destroy. Nobody but you and I know how I came by those papers. You know because you saw the papers in his bedroom. I know because your father came to me. And Mattie Calogreedy knows because she obtained copies of the Burmese replies ostensibly for your father but in truth for her own revenge. But she will say nothing. She is quite stricken enough by the consequences of her actions already and won't risk anything else. When I took the papers to Andreino, I did not tell him where I had obtained them and he, though he must have a shrewd idea, did not ask me. I suggested he send them to the Chief Commissioner in Rangoon as if he had come by them himself, which he was extremely pleased to do because his position is very precarious and he needs the good opinion of both the British government and the Bombay-Burmah. He is delighted to take all the credit. So you see, no one knows. They know your father left for Rangoon but it is generally supposed that – that relations between you both had become too strained to bear. Opinion condemns him as a bad father, but not as a traitor to boot.'

Maria was breathing very fast, her eyes fixed upon Archie's face. 'You have told no-one? No-one at all beside myself?'

'No-one.'

She gave a little gasp and stretched out her hand. He took it and found it unaccountably cold.

'Perhaps you think me mad, Mr Tennant. Perhaps I am a little. But all the time that I have suffered for feeling I have not been a good Englishwoman, I have suffered far more violently for feeling that my father had in some way betrayed Queen Supayalat, that he had delivered her, as indeed she will be delivered, into the rough hands of British soldiery. You may despise me for any allegiance that I have for her because I know she is violent and barbarous, but for me, Mr Tennant, she represented the first place I could belong to in my adult life, the first great lode star, the first chance to fulfil any ambition, the first society which I could feel, if I am to be honest, to be worthy of me. She is in a sense more than a queen to me, Mr Tennant, she is a country, a belief, a mother. She gave me chances I could never have hoped for elsewhere and even when she denied me audiences these last months, she has not forgotten me. Gifts come from the palace. I am allowed to remain here in the house she built for me when all other foreigners are driven from Mandalay. So when I realized my father had betrayed her, you may perhaps conceive of the agony and bitterness I suffered. I will not leave Mandalay because I must be near her even if I can give her no help. I cherish the hope that maybe at the end I can mediate with the English commanding officers for her – oh, anything, even light her cigar. It utterly broke my heart that the world should know what my father had done to her and I could not show my face. But you tell me, Mr Tennant, you tell me—'

'That nobody knows but we two. It will seem perfectly natural that Andreino should have sent the papers to Rangoon since the Bombay-Burmah was so closely involved and he is, after all, their agent. The secret is utterly safe.'

She said in a steadier voice, 'Thanks to you.'

He ducked his head.

'I owe you a great deal, Mr Tennant. I cannot repay you in any way except by the courtesy of more frankness than I feel comfortable in indulging in. I imagine you have had great satisfaction in being so entirely right about my father—'

'No!' he said, shocked, 'Not satisfaction, how could I—'

'You told me during that memorable conversation at Maymyo a year ago that I was destroying my father's image of himself. I disbelieved you entirely and have lived to regret my disbelief bitterly. I am mortified at my own cruelty, aiding and abetting my father into greater depths of folly and vanity until his eyes were suddenly opened and he saw himself as the puppet I had made of him. And I had gone on in my own way so long it hardly seemed that I knew how to change. He withdrew himself from me completely, first emotionally and then, finally, physically. I have heard nothing from him since he left, only a note from Hosannah Manook to whom he confided, during a chance meeting in the street in Rangoon, that he intended to return to India. He did not, apparently, in the few minutes they spoke together, mention me at all. I should not, of course, expect it.'

'Oh, Maria,' Archie said, 'Maria—'

She said, 'I am not afraid for myself, but what will they do to the Queen? Oh, Archie, what will they do to her?'

'Nothing violent. That I promise you. And try to remember that if your father betrayed the

Queen, she, in her turn, attempted to betray us, we English! The army is coming up the Irrawaddy with almost no opposition; in fact Andreino says they are losing more men through cholera than bloodshed. The aim of the British government is to annex Upper Burma, to run it like Lower Burma, not to conquer it like some invading medieval horde—'

'But it will all be gone, won't it? The City of Gems will be just another British-run Eastern place, like Bombay, like Rangoon. I know the cruelty is a bad thing and the savagery, but, oh, the pride of it all, the lovely arrogance, the way that the King and Queen are life and belief to their people, the beauty of everything here, the wonderful unconsciousness of anything else—'

She fumbled with uncharacteristic clumsiness for a handkerchief.

Archie rose and came and knelt by her chair, taking her free hand in his. 'Maria, you must come away with me, away to relative safety. If you stay here, in this house, there is an increasing chance that you will be harmed. Not by official Burmese soldiers, but by one of these marauding bands that are hardly particular about their victims. The army will be here in about a fortnight, we estimate, and if you wish to cling to any chance at all, however slender, of serving the Queen, you must make sure you are alive to do it. Everything you have said is safe with me. You know you can trust me. That – that I want you to. And you must trust me now to know what is best for you and to come with me.'

She blew her nose and said with something of her old briskness, 'What may I bring?'

'As little as possible. What we can carry in a bullock cart.'

'Can you wait one half hour?'

'If you can be quicker, I should be grateful.'

She was twenty minutes. A small trunk was carried down to the lane, a hatbox and another box tied with cord. She came back into her drawing room dressed for travelling, holding only a parasol and a reticule Archie supposed held her jewels and, after a businesslike look around the room that had been her heart's delight, she reached up and unhooked two water colours that hung on the gleaming teak walls. She handed them to Archie.

'These have been on the walls of every drawing room I have ever known, so I must keep them to grace the next one.'

When they were seated in the cart and it had jerked forward among the ruts on its journey towards the agent's old house, she said with a kind of diffidence, 'Would it be foolhardy to have one more glimpse of the palace walls? Could you ask the driver to go round that way?'

It was foolhardy and they went. For several minutes they sat alone and conspicuous, two Europeans in a bullock cart among the jostling Burmese, gazing at the glittering palace, silver and gold and scarlet roofs swooping like wings above its walls of rose-red brick, the barbaric splendour of it softened by the gauzy green of the tamarind trees and acacias, by the soft blue backdrop of the Shan hills, grave and lovely behind so much overwhelming gorgeousness. They sat spellbound, Archie as he had always done, Maria as she had never done before, and then a harsh cry rose from a group of men near them and a hail of stones spattered the cart, and the driver stood up and lashed the bullocks into a stumbling sickening canter among the ruts. Andreino, seeing Archie come in some ten minutes later with his prize upon his arm, felt that nothing now was too improbable to happen.

The mood of wonder could not last. Some seventeen adults shut up with each other in a stifling wooden house in uncertain circumstances was no breeding ground for a sense of the miraculous. Pierre Bonvilain was foolish enough to test the remnants of his charm upon Maria and found himself publicly humiliated; the lady missionaries – whose clothes and manners aroused in both Maria and Marie-Thérèse Bonvilain the only fellow-feeling they shared on any subject – sang rousing evangelical choruses at headache-inducing volume and smiled cheerfully with exasperating monotony; Andreino and Archie came and went with an unannounced suddenness that was wearing to everybody's nerves; and Maria, having made the supreme sacrifice of leaving her own house, was prepared to make absolutely no more. Marie-Thérèse's perpetual elegant tearfulness was a weak-willed luxury that Maria felt she should be prepared to forgo.

'I can only warn you, Madame, that the English private soldier has a very low opinion of poor-spirited women.'

At night the throbbing of the *pwes* that had disturbed the sleep of every inhabitant of Mandalay for almost six years was supplemented by bursts of gunfire. The black sky glowed scarlet at intervals and sometimes, lying in bed in a room she was forced to share with two young American missionaries who, shrouded in thick cream flannel, prayed loudly and relentlessly each night for twenty minutes before climbing into bed, Maria could detect the wild cries of human beings on the rampage. She kept her revolver under her pillow at night and in her pocket by day and her rubies with it. Both the weapon and the jewels represented far more to her than their intrinsic value.

Food was scarce and dull, the servants mostly terrified Indians from the Methodist missions, except for Ah Chun and two Burmese loyal to Andreino. Hnin Si was also inconspicuously about the place but her offer of acting as maid to Maria – upon Archie's suggestion – had been so violently rejected that she preferred to remain in the background. Maria dressed herself and her own hair, rousing everyone's reluctant admiration but endearing herself to no-one but Archie. He rejoiced to see her every day, lamenting to himself that it was always so publicly, but he watched her as much as was possible, so that when her glance did stray towards him and rested there, even for only a second, he might not miss the chance.

Even Andreino's habitual jauntiness could not disguise the perilousness they were all in. He might be a little irritated by Marie-Thérèse Bonvilain's tearfulness but he could well understand her fears. They were all, as he explained to Archie and Maria, in a blind alley.

'You will understand now why I wanted you to leave, Signorina, why I begged you to go down to Rangoon. We are now dwellers in a city where there is no law but that of the jungle; there is no-one to be in authority here any more. The King's power dies every day, the British are not yet here. And if the King's rule dies quite – before the British come—'

Maria looked at him steadily. 'Should we be the first victims?'

'Of the people of Mandalay? Most certainly. Many hate the King and Queen for their oppression with as much vigour as they love them for their royal omnipotence, but quite as many hate us *kalās*, whom they think have exploited them, grown fat on them—'

'We have,' Maria said.

Archie turned to look at her.

'If the money from all the ruby mines had gone to the people of Upper Burma, to feed and clothe them, they would be a very different race. Of course, that is a foolish dream since, even if we did not take the money, the palace would. The people never benefit.'

Archie began to laugh. 'Maria! Maria, what humanitarian feelings for such an iron-clad heart as yours—'

'I have had time to think recently. Months. And one cannot drive about Mandalay for six years and not see how people live. The squalor may disgust me, but I also find myself comparing it with the way of life of the palace.'

'Signorina—'

She turned to Andreino.

'Signorina, is it possible that you do not know fear?'

'I know it intimately, but it is not of the kind you suppose. I am not physically afraid.'

'Do you know what you may have to face? If, in the next few days, law and order break down utterly here and the crowd goes wild, like a horde of maddened beasts?'

'Of course I don't know. But I can well imagine.'

Andreino stood up. 'I admire you, but almost I find Madame Bonvilain a more natural woman.'

'Go then,' Maria said, 'and pay compliments to her.'

'You astound me,' Archie said when he had gone. 'How can you be so calm, when any day, any hour even, a band of drunken brutes may slash their way in here? How can you not be afraid?'

'I keep telling you. I am not afraid of that.'

'What then, what—'

She said softly, 'You know quite well, Archie. Of an obscure and empty life.'

However calm she might be, the tension in the house was a palpable thing. The three men, and the four manservants who could be trusted not to be reduced to gibbering incompetence by panic, took turns to patrol the house, moving from window to window, armed with rifles. At night they took it in turns to do sentry duty, Archie proving much the steadiest at this, claiming that forest life had made him sharp-eared and eyed in the dense nights. Even with his comforting presence moving softly across the wooden floors, sleep could only be fitful and unrefreshing, broken constantly by screams from neighbouring houses and lanes, and gunshots which echoed whining among the trees of the compound. Bullets were found once or twice, lodged in the balustrade of the verandah, or in the door frames, and one morning, before any of the men had observed and removed it, a body was found slumped upon the verandah steps, the body of a young Burman, his throat most thoroughly slit. Even the missionaries could not sing that day, but stayed near Madame Bonvilain, huddled all together in the centre of the house, as far from windows and doors as was possible.

Minutes passed like hours. Fear robbed most of them of appetite so there was not even the welcome diversion of mealtimes to break the monotony and the anxiety. They were afraid to talk too much for fear of attracting anyone's attention – and anyone might so easily be crouching among the mango trees which, with a flimsy wall of matting, was all that protected them from invasion – and in any case, no subject could hold any interest for them except their plight and that, somehow, seemed worse if discussed. So the endless daylight hours were passed mostly in silence, straining to hear any sounds closer than the distant jangle of Mandalay being taken over by the mob . . .

On 24 November, Mandalay erupted with delight at the news that the best of Thibaw's generals had defeated the British at Myingyan. There was singing and dancing in the streets and a procession went past the besieged house on its way to the river, bearing golden bowls and cups and medals for distribution among the victorious troops.

'It was nonsense,' Andreino said next morning. 'All the Burmese did was withdraw. They never so much as raised their rifles. The British artillery silenced the Burmese batteries before a Burmese soldier had fired so much as a shot—'

Later that day Archie, whom Andreino had warned against going about too freely in daylight, returned with his tunic slashed after a scuffle down by the river, but also with some dramatic news.

'The royal barge of state has just gone down the river. Forty golden oars – it was flying a white flag and there were two envoys, under hat umbrellas in the bows. It seems they are taking a letter from the *Hlutdaw* asking for an armistice, saying that the British government had not understood that Thibaw needed time to do all the things he promised.'

'And if Prendergast refuses?' Maria said, her face white. 'If he refuses an armistice? What will become of the palace?'

Archie said soothingly, 'He won't, you'll see. You'll see by tomorrow.'

On 26 November, General Prendergast replied to the envoys in the golden barge by saying that he could not grant an armistice.

'The Queen!' Maria said to Archie in a whisper of anguish. 'What will happen to the Queen?'

He touched her hand briefly. 'Prendergast has asked the King to surrender himself, his army and Mandalay. He says if he gets to Mandalay, finds that all these requests have been granted and that none of us have been harmed, he will spare Thibaw's life and that of his family.'

'Then don't endanger yourself,' Maria said. 'Don't keep going out and exposing yourself to harm. If anything happened to you, revenge would be taken upon the Queen.'

'And do you,' Archie said in half-mocking despair, 'not care what happens to me?'

She looked at him directly and then she said, in exactly the tone she used to admonish Madame

Bonvilain for weeping, 'Oh yes, Mr Tennant. I care.'

Two days later, Andreino roused the household at dawn. No-one had slept because the anti-*kalā* feelings in Mandalay, which rose as the British army came nearer, had culminated in a night of stone-throwing and hostile yelling outside the house which had reduced almost all the inmates, tense with long strain, to hysteria. An hour before dawn, the bands of Burmese had straggled off, spent by their own lawlessness, and the inhabitants had fallen into an exhausted slumber, only to be aroused almost at once by Andreino.

'You must rise all of you! The British army is come, the whole flotilla will be here by mid-morning. It takes up five miles of the river! We must be down on the bund to greet them, to show that we are safe!'

The lady missionaries declined to come, saying they would not add to the crowd, and as Andreino and Archie, Maria and the Bonvilains made their way towards the river, they could be heard on the first of their jolly morning choruses, praising the Lord for the day He had made. The Irrawaddy was choked all across its breadth with steamers and flats, both they and the bund seeming to swarm with red coats. General Prendergast, upon being presented to Maria and finding himself asked at once what he intended to do with the Queen, whom his troops referred to as Soup-plate, was quite taken aback and for a moment felt himself not to be in charge of the situation at all.

'Miss – er, Miss Beresford. I – I have received no reply to my request for the King's surrender. It is my intention that we march to the palace and gain an answer directly.'

Maria's chin went up and she gave her parasol a little shake. 'General, I should be obliged if you would permit me to accompany you. For five years I was accustomed to have daily audience with Her Majesty and I am familiar with the ways of the palace and with court language. I believe I should be of assistance to you.'

From the deck of a steamer some distance away, Murray Shaw had his field glasses trained upon that elegant figure in blue. He saw her presented to General Prendergast and then he saw them exchange a few words and then, to his astonishment, he saw her accept the arm the general offered. As they moved away among the trees at the top of the bund, Moylan said at his elbow, 'Your Miss Beresford?'

'By jove, it is,' Murray said. 'My Miss Beresford!'

20

From the Lion Throne Room could be heard
the regular approaching tramp of marching men.
Supayalat, attended by a weeping Mattie
Calogreedy, had mounted one of the wooden
watchtowers that stood at the palace walls and
together they had watched the first columns
come into view up the four white roads that led
to the City of Gems. For some minutes they
had stood there together, the vibrant, pregnant
little Queen and the plump, coarsened maid of
honour, watching those steady ranks of red-faced
Englishmen and brown-faced Indians and then,
abruptly, Supayalat had rushed screaming down
the spiral stair of the watchtower and cast herself
howling to grovel in the white dust of the courtyard, tearing her hair down from its knot,
scattering the diamonds that had decorated it like
raindrops. The violence of her grief – maybe even
her remorse – had only lasted moments. Under
Mattie's bewildered, sorrowful gaze, she had
picked herself up, twisted her hair back onto her
head and, dusty but still magnificent, had gone
to the Lion Throne Room where Thibaw sat
motionless except for the restless shifting of his

eyes. Silently, Supayalat slipped onto the *salun-daw* beside him and took his damp and trembling hand in hers.

'*Poon-dawgi-paya*,' she said. 'My Lord. The Lord of all the Universe.'

'They are coming,' Thibaw said. 'They are coming to execute us.'

She said, soothingly, 'No. No. Not that. Never that. Lord of the White Elephants, Lord of the Lion Throne—'

She left him briefly for the last ritual bathing and dressing of her time in Mandalay. Mattie stayed by her, but many of the little butterfly maids had gone, driven by a terror of the English soldiers back to their relations. They hardly spoke, she and Mattie, but simply went through the familiar motions of the bathing with scented water, the oiling of that smooth brown skin still as unlined as a girl's after half a dozen pregnancies, the brushing and arranging of her gleaming black hair, the richest tamein, the finest muslin jacket, the most impressive diamonds in her hair, at her neck and ears, weighting her thin supple brown wrists and fingers . . .

Back on the Lion Throne, Thibaw waited for her. Side by side they sat in their brilliant silks and diamonds, even their majesty dwarfed by the huge gilded and fretted screens of the throne that soared behind them, edged with flames of gold carved out of teak. Before them, descending some fifteen feet to the floor, fell steps to a red and golden balustrade that kept everyone at a distance. The room, lined now with ministers and court officials, was quite still except for that advancing, shuffling stamp, the army of the great white queen from the West, coming nearer and nearer at every moment through the white dust of Mandalay.

It seemed that despite the approaching tramp of marching men the British officers were in the Throne Room with startling suddenness, big and red-faced, their huge feet heavy-booted on the floor where only velvet slippers had been before, velvet slippers and submissive bare feet. Supayalat stretched out her hand to her husband and peered at the Englishmen. One she knew, a Colonel Sladen, chief political officer, a friend of Burma in the old days. But the others, all strangers, all of them. Thibaw's fingers tightened on hers. Her eye caught a flash of blue among the drill coats of the officers and as she watched it a voice she knew well from days and days of idleness among the fountains and lawns of the palace gardens said, 'Is it really necessary, General, to wear swords in the presence of Their Majesties?'

She gave Thibaw's hand a little jerk. 'Miss Beresford—'

He was not listening. He was very afraid, she could tell. Sweat had broken out gleaming upon his upper lip, his forehead.

'Great Lord of my life,' she said, 'Lord of the House of Alompra, the Kingdom of Ava. Eye of the Universe, Jewel among jewels of the City of Gems—'

Colonel Sladen and General Prendergast stood below them, armed and shod.

'Are you my executioner?' Thibaw asked.

Edward Sladen, who had known Burma for twenty years, shook his head in reassurance. He indicated Prendergast.

'This is the English general, Your Majesty. He has come to request you to keep your promise of yesterday and to surrender yourself to his charge.'

Supayalat could feel the bones of the King's fingers pressing painfully on hers. He cleared his throat and said in a voice that was much steadier, 'And will the general spare my life and the lives of my family?'

'Certainly, Your Majesty.'

Thibaw's fingers slackened their grip. He gave her hand a little squeeze and withdrew his own to his lap.

'Your Majesty,' Sladen said gently, 'the general will treat you with great respect and consideration and will allow you to take anyone with you that you please, together with your personal property.'

Thibaw licked his lips. 'And – and will the English soldiers protect me from my own people?'

Prendergast said something in English, his eyes fixed all the time upon the King.

'Your Majesty, the general wishes me to tell you that he will see that you are surrounded by soldiers on your way to the ships.'

Ships! Supayalat gave a startled, almost fearful, glance at her husband. Where were they going? Where were they to be taken? Where was there in all the world, but Mandalay?

Sladen said, as if reading her thoughts, 'We will escort you to India, Your Majesty. A house – a fitting house – has been prepared for you at Ratnagiri on the Kolkan, the southern coast of India, not far from Madras. The government of India will supply you with a pension, a generous pension.'

'But I am to be an exile?'

'Yes, Your Majesty. You must be an exile.'

Thibaw's gaze went slowly about the Lion Throne Room, travelling over the scarlet and gold lacquer, the mirrored pillars, the gleaming floorboards of polished teak where the sunlight fell as thick as syrup from the open doors onto the palace platform. He took a deep breath and spoke with a dignity that brought a glow to his wife's face.

'When I go into captivity, those who love me may follow me, but those who like themselves best will stay and look after their own property.' He paused and glanced briefly at the Queen. She was gazing at him, intent upon his every breath. 'I shall leave my palace now. I shall go into a summerhouse in the gardens and there, tomorrow, my formal surrender to the general may take place—'

Supayalat leaned towards him, whispering.

'You will grant my request that the Queen's

ladies may be permitted to use the western gate freely tonight.'

The Englishmen exchanged glances. They moved together and conferred in that strange, muted tongue of the English and only Maria, standing behind them, her eyes fixed upon the jewelled dolls on the Lion Throne heard Sladen say, 'Damn it! You can't refuse such a thing to the ladies! One night—'

Prendergast hesitated. 'Very well. I'll put White and the Hampshires on the western gate. Even if the King did attempt to escape, dressed as a woman, which is my fear, I don't think he would get past White—'

'There would be no question of such a thing,' Miss Beresford said sharply from behind them, 'no question at all. The King will remain entirely faithful to his Queen and she, as I am sure you will observe, is in no condition to ride anywhere upon an elephant.'

'Miss Beresford is very familiar with both King and Queen,' Sladen said. He turned to the King. 'The ladies of the court may go freely in and out, Your Majesty. You will understand the need for a guard for your own safety, but you have no need to be in any way alarmed by their presence.'

From her golden height, Supayalat leaned down a little. 'Miss Beresford, you will attend me this night.'

And Maria, in the presence of the English officers, knelt on the floor of the Throne Room amid the billowings of her skirts and touched her forehead on the ground in humble thankfulness.

'*Ashin-nammadaw-paya*. It will only be an honour.'

It was a strange and horrible night. Neither Supayalat nor Thibaw slept but sat upright and watchful, hand in hand upon the *salun-daw* in the little pavilion that had seen so many games and intrigues in the past, and listened to the howls and cries as Mandalay was looted. Thibaw's people, the citizens of Ava who had struggled for so long under the burden of corrupt and savage rule, had erupted into a screaming horde. Maria, stiff and cold, knelt by her Queen, the only servant remaining beyond the two old ministers who had helped to drive the monarchy into British arms, and the handful of court ladies left from the three hundred who had once surrounded the royal pair. In the shadows of the gardens, by the streams and waterfalls, at every flight of steps, in every doorway, at each corner of the palace platform, English sentries stood, uniformed, thick-booted men of the guard of the 67th Hampshires. No-one spoke, not one word in all those long and bitter hours, and the only movement in the sorrowful and dignified little group in the pavilion was Supayalat, leaning forward at intervals from the couch, for Maria to light a fresh cheroot for her.

21

'You must be the fellow my brother met. In Bombay,' Murray Shaw said.

'Oh?' Archie said idly, not really listening, his eyes fixed upon the little procession of women that had been trotting past them, either in or out of the palace, since dusk fell.

Murray shifted his feet. The recent unseasonal rain had made a marsh of the outer palace compound and it was a pretty damned uncomfortable place to be. Still, it was his men who were on guard duty, even if standing ankle deep in Burmese mud watching a crowd of rough-looking peasant women was hardly a substitute for the action they had all been hoping for – and endure it they must.

'He said he met you at dinner somewhere. Said you played polo—'

'I tried to. I say, I know I am not a soldier, and therefore you probably won't listen to me, but you know all these women are looters, don't you?'

Murray gave him the pitying glance soldiers reserve for unprofessional civilian misconceptions. 'No, they are not, old fellow. They are the

Queen's ladies-in-waiting. Old Soup-plate's little lot, as my sergeant says. We gave them free access as a favour to the Queen.'

Archie said mildly, 'Take a look at them.'

By the light of the flares that had been lit on the massive white walls of the western gate and which threw jagged flames and shadows over the soldiers stationed either side of it, Murray peered at the women scuttling through.

'Not what I had expected, I grant you. Always thought the Burmese women would be finer looking—'

'They are,' Archie said. 'These are the wives of fishermen from the bund, from the river, whores from the town, peasants from the fields round Mandalay. And beneath your military noses, they are carrying away everything of small size and great value from the palace. If you don't inform your commanding officer, there won't be a diamond left to take home to Queen Victoria.'

Murray said, nettled, 'What do you know about it in any case?'

'Enough,' Archie said. 'Are you going?'

'Why did you come up here, Tennant? What are you doing in the palace in any case? Why aren't you with the other civilians and that Italian fellow? May I remind you that it is the Burma Field Force that have taken Mandalay—'

'Ah,' Archie said, 'so it was. Walked in and took it. I came up to the palace because there is someone here I want to be sure is safe. An English person. A lady.'

Murray said, with the air of someone whose job it is to know everything, 'I imagine you mean Miss Beresford. She is in the garden pavilion with the King and Queen.'

'I know.'

'Of course,' Murray said, 'I knew her years ago. In Bombay.'

'Busy place, Bombay.'

'I dined with them several times. I was a guest at her twenty-first birthday party in fact. She must have been the handsomest girl in Western India. And the most spirited. Knew her pretty well, to tell the truth.'

A soldier came up, stamped to attention in the mud, and presented Murray with a folded paper.

'Sorry, old chap,' Murray said to Archie with a grin. 'General's orders. All civilians to leave the palace. All, that is, except the ladies-in-waiting.'

Archie said, 'Will you inform him that these are no more court ladies than angels?'

'Theory of yours, old fellow. Nothing to do with me. Wilkes here will escort you out. Night, Tennant.'

When Archie had gone, Murray took out his notebook and after a considerable amount of thought and a false start or two, succeeded in scribbling a message. He summoned the returning Wilkes.

'Take this to the guard at the pavilion, would you? Where the King and Queen are. And see it is given to Miss Beresford there. Miss Maria Beresford.'

*   *   *

Dawn came at last, rising rosy over the long blue lines of the Shan hills and behind the tall cone of Mandalay Hill where the giant golden Buddha, placed there by King Mindoon, stood and pointed down to the city of the kings of Ava. Soft plumes of mist rose from the wet gardens around the summer pavilion, swathing the harsh and brilliant outlines of the palace, the implacable forms of the English soldiers, the menace of the day ahead. A small procession of ladies-in-waiting, dressed in their customary brilliant silks as if this day were no more irregular than any other day, came across the misty spaces bearing the lacquerwork urns that contained the royal breakfast. It was spread before the King and Queen, golden dishes of curry and rice, rice-flour pancakes smeared with a paste of sesame seed, mangoes sliced to translucent thinness and laid on leaves, dried prawns arranged in a wheel on a silver plate, a gilded basket of pineapples, a jewelled goblet for Thibaw, French crystal for his Queen, for his second Queen, for the Queen Mother. Maria rose to attend them.

Supayalat said, 'Take it. Take it all away.'

'*Ashin-nammadaw-paya*—'

The Queen clapped her hands together and raised her voice. 'At once! Take it away! Everything!'

Thibaw said nothing. His pale plump face was slack in the dawn, his eyes dull and tired. His second Queen, Supayalat's plain and older sister, made some small move towards the dish nearest to her, caught her sister's commanding eye, and withdrew her hand. She had put on the apricot robes of a nun and sat behind her sister, apprehensive and suppressed, Thibaw's wife only in name. Supayalat leaned towards the King, her hard little brown fingers laid upon his plump soft hand.

'You must dress, my lord. You must dress for the English general.'

Thibaw looked down at his clothes in some surprise, at the gorgeous ripple-woven silk of his paso, silk woven on a loom of two hundred shuttles, the pattern done by eye. He had worn it since yesterday, since the afternoon of yesterday, he, who was accustomed to wear nothing for more than a few hours together. He glanced at his Queen and nodded faintly.

'For the English general of the great white Queen—'

For the last time, Supayalat's litter was carried across the gardens to her, the litter that had carried her about the palace for six pregnancies in as many years. It was a little pagoda-shaped cage, scarlet and gold, with gilded gauze windows, set in a golden boat and slung on poles covered in velvet. Maria rose to attend her as she had done for the unwanted breakfast and Supayalat said, 'You. Just you,' and bowed her sleek black head to step behind the doors of golden gauze.

Maria dressed her in silence. All around them, in other rooms of the great rambling palace, voices shouted and laughed and feet went stampeding by, the feet of the women of the town, their brawny arms straining round velvets and silks, cushions and stools, golden cups and looking glasses framed in gems, ivory combs, boxes of lacquer and scented woods, fans and bottles and gilded umbrellas. Maria looked about the little room where she knelt by the Queen, the room which had witnessed a hundred ritual dressings and which held only four great teak wardrobes inlaid with silver and mirrors and a huge looking glass swinging on a golden stand.

'There is nothing here to take,' Supayalat said.

She was wound into a tamein of cream, thickly embroidered in gold, and wore over it a jacket of a pattern only permitted to royalty, the hem wired up into stiff little points like wings, each wing edged with golden teardrops. Round her neck Maria clasped a diamond necklace of dazzling splendour – paid for, Archie might have told her, by the Bombay-Burmah Trading Corporation who had purchased it three years before, on royal orders – and then she knelt to slip onto those smooth brown feet golden slippers lined in red velvet, the edge of the sole studded with rubies.

'Nothing to take,' Supayalat repeated bitterly, 'only myself.'

'Your Majesty, I do assure you that you will be treated with the utmost deference.'

Supayalat spat. 'Exiles!'

Maria waited, watching the vehement little

figure struggle with itself before the looking glass.

'The letter!' Supayalat said suddenly, 'You received a letter! In the night!'

'It was from a gentleman I once met in India. Many years ago, Your Majesty. He is come up with the army. He simply wishes to be remembered to me.'

Supayalat's eyes gleamed. 'You must not waste your chances! You are a girl no more, you are old to be married. Of course—' She stopped and in the looking glass her brilliant dark eyes met Maria's blue ones, 'You might come with me to India.'

'*Ashin-nammadaw-paya*, Your Majesty, the honour you do me—'

'I shall not rest. Not in India. There are many scores to be paid. The English will feel me still, here in Mandalay, they will not be free of me.' She stopped and laid her hands either side of her swollen belly. 'Call the litter. The *Poon-dawgi-paya* needs me. Call it.'

'Your Majesty, are you asking me to come to India with you?'

'I would order,' Supayalat said, 'but now I ask.'

'And would you permit me a little time to reflect upon your request?'

'Yes,' Supayalat said, 'yes.' She went past Maria, smiling, tapping the pocket where she had thrust Murray Shaw's note. 'There are things to be seen to, heh? Gentlemen from Bombay—'

Maria drew herself up. 'Such consideration

would not influence my decision in the least, Your Majesty.'

Supayalat's smile faded. She looked at Maria with her hard searching gaze.

'They should, Miss Beresford,' she said, her tone sharp with reprimand, 'they should.'

On the open verandah of the pavilion, Thibaw waited, simply dressed in white, his head swathed in a turban of white and pink. Behind him, his second Queen still knelt, and beside him the old Queen Mother, mother to both Queens, crouched in meditation, her lips moving silently, her little old brown claws held out in supplication to some unseen source of strength. Thibaw sat cross-legged upon a carpet, quite without occupation apart from a betel box, shaped like a golden bird with emerald eyes, which had been his father's, which rested upon the floor within reach. The boards of the verandah were already splashed with blotches of betel juice, scarlet stains like blood. Supayalat was handed from her litter and went swiftly to seat herself by her husband, coiling herself beside him, supple and watchful, the teardrops on her winged jacket winking in the strengthening sun. Stiff and aching, sour-mouthed and sore-eyed from a sleepness night in the open air and the discomfort of the clothes of the previous day, Maria sank upon the verandah steps and waited with them, her thoughts a confused and exhausted jumble of a future in Ratnagiri and a past in Bombay.

At noon, General Prendergast came, complete with pith helmet and riding boots polished to a dazzling brilliance. Maria moved away from the verandah steps as the soldiers approached, but Thibaw made no attempt to rise, only glanced about him apprehensively and then, as the English general bowed and shook him firmly by the hand, looked much astonished. He remained for some time afterwards gazing down at his hand as if having such a liberty taken with it must surely have changed it out of all recognition.

'Your Majesty, you are asked to come to the ship with us now, at once.'

'Tomorrow,' Thibaw said, his eyes sliding past the soldiers, 'only tomorrow—'

'Today, Your Majesty. There can be no more delaying.'

'Two hours, one – one hour—'

'Ten minutes,' the general said inexorably.

Maria's vision was blurring. The Queen's voice, only a whisper, was repeating steadily, 'Lord of my life, Lord of the White Elephants, Lord of the Lion Throne, King of Ava, of the House of Alompra—'

The general said, 'I must order you, Your Majesty. It pains me but I must.'

'A little while,' Thibaw's gaze went swinging wildly round the gardens and grottoes, the fountains and groves of so many days of idle pleasure, 'a little while, a little—'

He stopped, his eyes sinking to the ground. 'We have two children alive. Three are buried in the northern garden here. Let—' He paused again and then said with gathering resolution, 'Let Sladen govern the country for five years and when he has everything in good order then I will come back and be guided by him.' He lifted his eyes and looked at Prendergast with diffidence. 'You English think I killed all my relations, but it is not so. I was under guard myself and they were murdered. I only ordered that they should be imprisoned to avoid a disturbance in the country. Some – some people have tried to murder me—' He caught his breath and licked his lips. 'I wish – I wish the English people to know I am not a drunkard. I am a religious Buddhist. I have given up the crown jewels – Let me stay an hour more, an hour more, an hour only, an hour—'

'No,' Prendergast said, 'no more time. We have drawn up one of your coaches. Will you and your Queens mount so that you may ride in fitting style to the river?'

Maria fought back her tears. If she wept, she would not be able to see and she must see, she must—

Thibaw rose to his feet, a strange, small, plump figure, dignified and absurd.

'I scorn to ride,' he said, 'I scorn it. My Queens and I will walk.'

He stooped and with a sudden and heartbreaking tenderness offered a hand to either Queen. Prendergast stepped back and all the soldiers with him, back until they formed a wide aisle across the green gardens to where the great royal red gate stood flung open, the gate used only by the King, the gate scarcely opened for Thibaw in all the seven years of his reign. Slowly and with irreproachable dignity, the King and his Queens walked across the gardens hand in hand, the sunlight glancing irreverently off their jewels and gold ornaments so that they moved in a halo of dancing lights. Maria longed to follow and would not, would not for these final and fleeting moments take from them their last glory in even the smallest measure. She put her hand to her face and found it slippery with tears.

'Miss Beresford,' Colonel Sladen said and pressed into her hand an immaculately laundered handkerchief.

On the bund, Archie waited behind a double file of men from the Liverpool Regiment. He had waited there through the heat of the afternoon while the royal procession, after the interminable formalities of leaving the palace, made its snail-paced progress through the crowds that thronged the *kalā* town. The SS *Thoreah* lay at the landing stage and round it, on the broad waters of the Irrawaddy dyed apricot by the rapidly setting sun, bobbed the inquisitive boats of the fisher-men of Mandalay. The crowd pressed at his back, the dusty-footed, garlic-scented Burmese crowd in its rags and tatters of turbans and pasos, chattering comfortably as if it were about to see a pageant rather than the dethronement of a king. Here and there lanterns began to be lit, glowing

416

yellow in the thickening dusk and then a whisper began, growing to a mutter and a cry, 'The King is coming! The King! The King!'

Two small bullock carts came into view, with eight white umbrellas held over the first.

'Nine,' Archie said to himself, 'there should be nine. As King he is entitled to nine—'

In the second cart Maria sat upright with Mattie Calogreedy beside her, sobbing and dusty, dressed in a peculiarly unbecoming European dress several sizes too small for her. In the dusk, Maria's face was no more than a pale triangle beneath a hat of blue velvet flowers, but Archie felt he could deduce her expression from her attitude and that even, from fifteen feet away, he could sense the distaste she felt for Mattie's lack of self-control and her absurd and inappropriate dress. So strange, he thought, so strange and wonderful – Are the great events of the world always so amazing in their littleness at close quarters? A king is dethroned and a little plump fellow in a pink checked turban is bundled away in a bullock cart in the dusk, without ceremony, without pomp and splendour and hardly any sense at all that an age has passed, that a chapter is closing, that whatever the future brings, it can't bring back kings to Mandalay. I am looking at history, Archie told himself, peering to see clearly, I am looking at the end of an age, at the machinery of the British Empire in visible motion, and what do I see but two little brown Eastern people helping each other to descend from a cart like any fond peasant couple at a market, watched by a few soldiers, a crowd of Burmese and me. The Kingdom of Ava is dying. Even as they step onto the gangplank, with the Queen holding out her hand as if to a child, persuading, urging, cajoling and motherlike, with each step the kingdom breathes slower, more shallowly, and when they are gone we shall be left here with a sense of mission accomplished and an awful emptiness, a hollow aching void because an era is over; every minute carries us farther from it, from any sympathy we felt for it. The spell is breaking, the spell of Mandalay, and those little creatures are taking it with them—

A sudden movement caught his eye. Maria had descended from the second cart and had hurried forward towards the gangplank of the *Thoreah*, followed by the still-weeping Mattie stumbling behind and blotting her eyes on the backs of her grey kid gloves. For a moment Archie thought Maria meant to run up the gangplank behind the Queen and he began to shout, wildly and urgently, pushing his bulk roughly through the crowd that held him from the shore, and then he saw that Maria had halted suddenly and was simply standing there, between two soldiers, gazing up at the side of the steamer where Supayalat was coaxing Thibaw to take his final steps onto the deck. Archie reached her side a moment later, breathless and tumbled.

'Don't go, Maria, I beg you, don't go, reflect a little—'

She shook his restraining hand off impatiently but said nothing, only continued to look almost imploringly upwards at the tiny figure climbing towards the deck.

Mattie said, sobbing, 'I never meant this; I never wanted this to happen, it wasn't the Queen I hated, it wasn't her. Oh, tell her I always loved her, tell her it was Pierre I wanted to hurt, I didn't think, I didn't think—'

Maria said in disgust, without turning, 'Control yourself.'

Archie put an arm about Mattie's shoulders, feeling her warm puttylike flesh squeezing against the fabric of her dress.

'Oh, Mr Tennant, I am so unhappy, I am so confused. And now there is no-one left in Mandalay for me. I am quite alone. What will become of me, what will happen?'

A gleam of grinning teeth among the nearest soldiers indicated to Archie that the darkness did not cover his embrace of Mattie. He took his arm away from her shoulders but found she still leaned against him, sodden and heavy with misery like a damp flour sack.

'You should go to the convent of St Joseph.'

'Oh,' she said, beginning to cry again, 'nuns—'

'They are going,' Maria said suddenly. 'Look, oh, look—'

The *Thoreah* hooted mournfully and the throb of the engines began to pulse in the dark waters of the Irrawaddy. Mattie peeled herself from Archie's side and rushed forwards to the river, screaming for the Queen, her voice quite drowned by the rising note of the engines and the splash of water. Side by side behind her, Archie and Maria stood and watched the *Thoreah* pull away to midstream, bearing with her the doll-like royal couple, upright and motionless upon the deck, their backs turned resolutely upon Mandalay. Archie wanted violently to put not one but both arms about Maria, but her rigidity and concentration deterred him. He stood beside her, peering passionately at her in the fitful light of surrounding lamps, his fists clenched at his sides and at last burst out, 'Shall you go? Shall you go with her?'

Maria said, as if from far away, 'She never turned. She never turned to bid me farewell.' She paused, and then said in a more normal tone, 'Naturally I shall follow her. I have one more thing to do in Mandalay – and if nothing comes of that, then I shall go to India. What else is there for me to do?'

'You know what you might do,' he said urgently. 'You might marry me.'

'Archie, we have already had this conversation—'

'But things are different now. You are different, so am I. You can't follow her, you can't. India won't be like Mandalay, it can't be. Ratnagiri will be some fly-blown bungalow where life will be nothing but staggeringly boring and full of petty intrigue. There will be nothing left of life here, nothing. The Queen will grow ever more whimsical and tyrannical—'

He stopped. Silent tears were sliding down her face and hanging ignominiously on her cheeks and chin. Mattie, stumbling up from the river, looked astonished out of her own wretchedness.

He said, 'I'm so sorry. Forgive me,' and put a crumpled handkerchief of doubtful purity into her hand.

She said furiously, 'I never weep. Never. And this is the second time today.'

'You are tired. And too much has happened.'

'Tired,' she said, 'yes, tired.' She gave herself a resolute shake and straightened her shoulders. 'Would you find me a bullock cart? I think I should like to go to bed.'

'Come to the convent,' Mattie begged. 'Come to the convent with me.'

'No thank you,' Maria said. 'I have had quite enough of pious women but at least I will remain with those who are familiar, however irritating—'

'You are a cold, hard woman!' Mattie screamed, 'You have no thoughts for anyone else, you have no feelings, you are stone!'

'And you,' Maria said savagely, 'are soft and weak and – and *treacherous*.'

Archie caught Mattie as she lunged across him at Maria. They struggled clumsily together for a while but Mattie's instincts would not allow her to interpret a man's touch save in one direction for long. She gave up abruptly and began to wail into Archie's shirt front, clutching at him with her frantic little fat hands. Over her head he looked in despair at Maria.

'Hysterical,' Maria said shortly and then, raising her voice, she almost shouted at Mattie, 'To make a spectacle of yourself is one thing, but to make one of Mr Tennant is quite another! Let go of him this instant!'

Moments later, with Maria upon one arm, touching him so lightly he could hardly feel her, and Mattie dragging upon the other, Archie descended the landward slope of the bund towards Mandalay. Behind them the *Thoreah*, invisible now in the sudden blackness except for the lights strung along her decks like a necklace, swung her bulk slowly around in the river and began the slow journey south to Rangoon and exile.

22

'I want no-one to leave this compound,' Andreino said, 'without my express permission and the escort of either myself, Mr Tennant or Monsieur Bonvilain.'

The lady missionaries, huddled together in a grey-brown serge flock, listened obediently. Some wore the bright smiles that were as habitual with them as breathing, but others, who had found that their spontaneous ability to burst into rousing evangelical song had unaccountably deserted them in the last few days, looked grave and biddable.

'Now that the King and Queen are gone,' Andreino said, 'I am afraid that lawlessness will again take over Mandalay. I have no doubt but that General Prendergast will institute order as soon as he can, but even he cannot prevent the hordes who will pour into the city from the jungle and the villages from being, initially, a great threat. And the Queen has left many spies and supporters behind and you must not forget that for Supayalat, England is first among her enemies and therefore any English civilian will be a prime target for her revenge—'

'I come,' one of the lady missionaries said loudly, 'from Allentown, Pennsylvania!'

Andreino glanced at Archie, smiling. 'My dear signorina, I fear you cannot expect a Burmese dacoit to make the distinction between an American and an English citizen.'

'More's the pity for that, poor heathen soul,' the lady from Allentown declared roundly.

One of the others stood up, a small fresh-faced young woman with more of an air of having spent the last years on a farm than in a steaming Burmese jungle. 'I have a request, Mr Andreino.'

'Certainly, Miss Newman.'

'Three years ago, when I first came to Burma, I spent nine months at the mission school here in Mandalay with Mr Prior. It would ease my mind very much if I might go back to the school and bring out any Christian souls who remain there and are in peril—'

'Miss Newman, if any Europeans had remained at the mission, I should naturally have rescued them myself the moment the British arrived in Rangoon.'

Miss Newman regarded him reprovingly. 'God makes no distinction as to colour, Mr Andreino. I feel you may have overlooked some *Burmese* Christians.'

From his watchful position at the window, Archie said, 'I will go for you, Miss Newman.'

'I should be glad of your company, Mr Tennant, but I should prefer to go myself.'

'I cannot allow it,' Andreino said, 'unless there is excellent reason—'

'I insist upon going,' Miss Newman said levelly. 'There are various mementoes in the school that I should like to take to Mr Prior in Rangoon before they are in danger of being destroyed. You cannot know what to choose.'

'Miss Newman—'

'I am not afraid of danger, Mr Andreino. And I am fully determined to do what I see to be my duty.'

Andreino looked across at Maria, sitting a little removed as she always did, and shrugged. 'You ladies of determination—'

'We become much worse,' Maria said, with a ghost of a smile, 'if thwarted.'

Miss Newman clearly did not relish the thought of being linked with the worldly and aloof Miss Beresford in anyone's mind. 'I am not being perverse, Mr Andreino, merely asking for your help.'

'I'll come with you,' Archie said. 'I said I would. I should be pleased to.'

'It must be daylight, signorina—'

'Naturally.'

Andreino sighed. He showed no outward marks upon his face of the strain of the past week, but his elaborate linen was now grimy to a point that made Maria reluctant to go near him.

'Will you listen to me one more moment? I must outline plans for your leaving Mandalay—'

Marie-Thérèse began to weep again. Her

425

husband, most solicitous to her in public, despite having been heard, by the shocked missionaries, to speak quite sharply when he did not think himself overheard, tried a smile of male complicity with Archie which evoked no response and put an arm, with elaborate resignation, around his wife's trembling shoulders. Between sobs she was heard to say that she should never live to see Paris again, nor her beloved parents, nor the little spaniel which had been her childhood companion, nor her old nurse, nor the room which had been hers since babyhood, indeed right up to the very night of her marriage, the marriage that had led to so much danger—

'I would beg you, Madame,' Andreino said, 'to weep as softly as it is in your power to do.'

She took her face from her husband's shoulder to glare at him.

'The scheme I have devised,' Andreino said, 'depends upon the patience of you all. The Irrawaddy Flotilla Company, having suspended its steamer service for the past few weeks, now intends to resume it. If an opportunity arises for me to – to borrow, shall we say, a military escort from the British force, I will make sure that you are all upon the first steamer bound for Rangoon. If it is thought that your departure in smaller groups would attract less attention from the bandits, who will, I fear, harass all shipping south as far as the border with Lower Burma, you must be patient and wait your turn. Mr Tennant—' He paused and looked at Archie, 'Mr Tennant is remaining in Upper Burma and will assist me. May I say to you all that I regard you all as my responsibility and I will do everything in my power to ensure your safety.'

A burst of hoarse shouting arose from the lane some twenty yards away and a hail of stones, flung from behind the matting fence which still remained miraculously intact, pattered noisily onto the tin roof above their heads.

'We should hurry—' Archie said.

'As soon as possible!'

'When is the first steamer?'

'Not before I have been to the mission!'

'Will the British give us no protection?'

'If only we were all armed—'

Archie, stooping over Maria, said, 'On my way back to the mission, I will look at your house.'

She glanced up at him. 'If you would. I long to return there—'

'There can be no question of that.'

'I must. I cannot think here. I cannot put my thoughts into any kind of order.'

'But it is the only place where you have any chance of safety.'

'Oh!' she said impatiently, tapping her foot. 'Safety—'

'Maria—'

'Yes.'

'Have you made up your mind? About – about anything?'

'I told you,' she said, 'I have already said so. I

can think of nothing here. All these women, the lack of privacy, the chattering – it is impossible.'

'You are so difficult to persuade to anything,' he said in despair.

She looked up at him again, on the verge of a smile.

'I should have thought, in a situation like this, that it was a relief to have at least one person who knew their own mind.'

Miss Newman was well equipped for her journey to the mission. She appeared before Archie in the serge dress he had begun to think grew upon her like a skin, stout boots and a solar topee, one hand clasping a green cloth umbrella, the other a capacious bag made apparently of carpet. It was but ten minutes' walk to the mission and Archie had chosen the early afternoon as the most suitable moment since a large number of the inhabitants slept then, slumped beneath trees or carts, even at such an excitable time as this. He carried his own double-barrelled revolver in one pocket and Maria's – astonishingly handed to him in silence as he left – in the other. He had offered one of these to Miss Newman, who had said that as a servant of the Lord, she never touched firearms.

'Not even to defend another?'
'The occasion has never arisen, Mr Tennant.'
He held out Maria's revolver. 'It might today.'
'I prefer not to take it, Mr Tennant.'
He shrugged. 'A little illogical, if you will

forgive me for saying so. A dead servant of the Lord is not so much use to Him as a living one.'

Miss Newman gave him a quelling look.

The lane outside the compound was still and empty in the heat. It was lined with compounds and bungalows such as the one in which they had taken refuge, but in a haphazard way, with rough spaces here and there in which Burmese had set up their matting hovels. Goats roamed unsteadily in these dusty clearings, but they were almost the only sign of life beyond a still body or two, humped in the shade, its turban wound about its face.

'I think,' Archie said in a low voice, 'that conversation would be a mistake. The dust is thick enough to muffle much of our tread. Would you be so good as to walk slightly ahead of me?'

Miss Newman struck out purposefully, her umbrella held over her head and casting a round black block of shadow on her serge-clad shoulders, swinging her carpet bag with almost military precision. Archie trod behind her, his eyes moving from side to side, slipping watchfully over matting walls and mango trees, their heavy leaves drooping and motionless in the heat. It was a long ten minutes, following Miss Newman's resolute back and expecting all the time that someone might leap from the foliage – foliage which somehow managed to give an impression of concealing something watchful. Two turnings were safely negotiated and Maria's house came into view. The doors onto the verandah stood open but within Archie could glimpse the gleam of the gilding on those familiar rose-pink chairs. Guiding Miss Newman out of her determined course, he steered her onto the verandah and looked within. The Chinese bowls had been broken, littering the floor with blue and white fragments, but the furniture stood where she had left it around rugs rumpled by hurried feet – but still there. In silence, regarded disapprovingly by Miss Newman, Archie pushed the broken china pieces into a corner with his foot, straightened the rugs and then closed the shutters upon the room. Then, still without speaking, he shepherded Miss Newman back down the lane.

The mission house itself looked almost untouched. Together they climbed the worn steps to the verandah and pushed open the shutters warily to let sunlight into the room where Grace had dispensed tea and the seed cake learned from faraway cookery lessons in her Brighton school. Apart from the dust and a strange greenish-grey mould that had settled like a veil over the cushions and upholstery, the room was just as Archie remembered it; the highly coloured saints still frozen in acts of heroism and martyrdom on the walls, Grace's tea table, the sagging chair in which Tom had crashed to sleep the night of her death, the hooked wool rug the mission school children had made in a thoroughly Burmese mixture of turquoise and apple green and yellow. 'There!' Miss Newman said in triumph. 'Quite untouched! Poor heathens they may be, but not in their souls. They know better than to touch what is the Lord's.'

Archie said, running his finger along the edge of the table and revealing, under the dust, the rings where cups and saucers had stood, 'I fear it's not so much that as fear of ghosts. The Burmese believed ghosts took over when Grace died. Ghosts would keep even the most hardened marauder away.'

'What a sad cynic you are to be sure, Mr Tennant.'

'Perhaps,' he said, 'perhaps.'

'You will remain here,' Miss Newman said firmly, 'while I see if there are any little remembrances in Miss Prior's room that her father might wish to have.'

Archie put a hand on her arm. 'Look by all means. But don't bring anything. It would only hurt him to see—'

'The Lord gives us succour in our grief. He will not suffer us to be long troubled.'

'It has often seemed to me,' Archie said with some energy, 'that Buddhists, for all they are heathen, have an excellent human sympathy.'

'I do not understand you, Mr Tennant.'

'Miss Newman, I dared not hope that you might.'

She returned ten minutes later to the sitting room bearing the picture of St Francis upon which Grace had hung her ribbons and the small china virgin and child which Archie had last seen lost in a forest of physic bottles.

'Of course, there was a lot of girlish foolishness in there,' Miss Newman said, 'which naturally, I left.'

'Naturally.'

'And now, Mr Tennant, the school. The school and the chapel.'

It was evident at once that the ghosts of the house had not been deemed powerful enough to afflict the school and chapel also. Complete devastation reigned, the schoolroom a debris of smashed furniture and broken pictures, the chapel a melancholy scene of heaped destruction surmounted by a crucifix which had been thrust in, like a sword, as a final gesture. Out of the mound of splintered wood in which winked fragments of coloured glass from the broken windows, Christ protruded on His Cross, His face disfigured and His bronze legs obscenely twisted below the knee. Not a thing remained whole, not even the altar, a solid teak structure, which had been hacked at viciously, and stood on its side, as undistinguished as a tea chest, naked of the cloths that forty years of embroidery by lady missionaries had adorned it with – now probably in use as items of apparel somewhere in the Mandalay bazaar. The banners of the Sunday School and the Bible society had gone, the pages of hymn books lay scattered like white leaves over the chaos and above it all, as a sickening last insult, hung the stench of human filth.

Miss Newman gripped her umbrella more tightly. 'Barbarians!'

'Only poor heathens – I thought.'

She moved forward a step. 'I must at least take the crucifix.'

'And show to Tom Prior evidence of the fate that has overtaken the place he loved so much, where he had such high hopes?'

She turned to him. 'Mr Tennant, are you an unbeliever?'

'Not at all.'

A slight sound came from beyond the shattered window frames. Archie looked round at once but the compound between the chapel and the school house was empty of everything but a solitary hen.

'Will you now pray with me in this desecrated place of the Lord?'

'I think we shouldn't linger, Miss Newman. I think we should go now. You see there is no human life here—'

Miss Newman dropped to her knees, laying down her bag and umbrella that she might clasp her hands before her. Then, with closed eyes, she began to pray, calling upon the Lord in strident and demanding tones.

'Please—' Archie said.

Unaccountably, the hair on the back of his neck was prickling, his hearing seemed suddenly intensified, acute. He stooped and seized her arm. 'Miss Newman, *please*—'

'Amen,' she said loudly, glaring at him and getting to her feet. 'My bag, if you please, Mr Tennant, my umbrella—'

Outside in the still afternoon heat, a small

433

band of men was waiting. There were four of them, with broad mahogany faces and sullen mouths, naked except for loincloths and, in one case, a ragged shirt of checked cotton. Their feet were bare and white with dust and in each of their right hands a *dah* swung, catching the sunlight on the blades.

Archie put his hand to his pocket. 'Please take the pistol—'

'Certainly not,' Miss Newman said.

One of the men came forward and two began to move sideways so that they were treading in a horseshoe shape of which Archie and Miss Newman were the centre.

'Then get behind me—' Archie shouted, plunging a hand into either pocket.

There was a swish in the air like a sudden gust of wind and the centre *dah* blade went up at the sight of the revolvers. There followed a moment of extreme confusion, Archie much impeded by Miss Newman's frantic grasp at his waist and by his having nothing with which to cock the pistols except his teeth. The men were all coming forward, moving faster now, their weapons gleaming in the cloud of dust they were trailing and then Archie fired, right- and left-handed simultaneously, and saw one man fall. Miss Newman was screaming now, dragging him backwards as she hung upon his waist, but he leaned against her weight with his own and fired again, wildly. One of the men began to shout. Sweat was running down Archie's forehead into eyes already filmed with dust. He had to drop Maria's revolver to reload his own and the *dahs* would be upon him before he could do that, any second now—

'They have stopped,' Miss Newman said from under his right arm.

Stock still, ten strides away, the men stood, weapons hanging. Archie raised his empty pistol. They ducked in unison, flinging their arms up across their faces.

'Get out,' Archie said, using the dialect with which he had learned to swear at the *mahouts* in the forest. 'Move. Quickly. Or I will kill you all.'

They stepped backwards a pace or two.

'Move! At once!'

In a moment the compound was empty except for the fallen man in the centre. It had been over in not much more than a minute.

'Is he wounded?'

'Don't touch him!' Archie said. 'Stand there, holding Miss Beresford's pistol as if you would shoot with it – do not argue, Miss Newman – while I load this one—'

Warily, crabwise, they left the compound, retreating backwards up the steps to the mission house and the safety of the ghosts.

'I have to thank you, Mr Tennant,' Miss Newman said with the air of one doing her duty.

'Please do not.'

'It would, of course, have been a martyrdom—'

'It most certainly would not. A tawdry picture

of St Francis is not worth being hacked to pieces for.'

'I was at *prayer*, I would remind you, Mr Tennant.'

They crossed the dusty floorboards to the verandah which fronted the lane. The lane itself was empty still but Mandalay was waking up in the distance and the sounds of gongs and shouting echoed in the hot air.

'Are you ready to attempt our return?'

'Certainly, Mr Tennant.'

She tried to return Maria's pistol, but he shook his head, pushing her before him.

'My umbrella, my bag—'

'A small price to pay for whole skins, Miss Newman.'

She set out, her head high, holding the pistol stiffly in front of her. Only once did she turn her head, when they passed Maria's house once more.

'Mr Tennant.'

'Miss Newman.'

'I am aware that you saved my life this afternoon. I am also aware that there are other lives which you would have preferred to save.'

Over her shoulder, Archie could see that only a hundred yards now separated them from safety. A quick glance behind him showed him that the lane was empty and before them only a group of children was visible, straggling along in the scanty shade dragging a bullock calf on a rope. He prodded Miss Newman to make her go faster.

'Only one,' he said, 'only one.'

23

'So the Lion Throne Room is to be a church,' Maria said, her voice taut with scorn.

Murray Shaw, uncomfortable in a miserable little upright chair and wondering why on earth he had come, nodded.

'And the passage behind it the vestry? And the Lily Throne Room a club? A *club*. I suppose the sacred Red Gate is open always now. And Lord and Lady Dufferin are coming from Calcutta, I gather, to confer a blessing on the noble work of the Burma Field Force—'

He muttered, 'We expected a fight, Miss Beresford. We thought the King would resist. Indeed we did.'

Maria snorted and looked past him out of the doors. They were seated in a room she insisted upon calling her drawing room which contained nothing whatsoever except the two chairs on which they sat and drifts of dust on the polished floor. She had described in tediously intimate detail all the furnishings the room had once possessed, many of which lay smashed and ripped out in the heavy green tangle of the garden, and there had been an awkward moment when she surveyed the gilt legs and wads of torn stuffing that lay littered about and her chin had distinctly trembled. Murray couldn't take women crying. Never had been able to. He sighed and drew his boot toe through the dust at his feet.

'It was unrealistic of you to expect to find me unchanged, Captain Shaw,' Maria said.

He blushed hotly.

'Miss Beresford, I never – I mean, I hardly, indeed you are scarcely—'

'I am quite changed. So I may say are you. The diffidence of the young man I knew in Bombay is quite gone.' She looked down fleetingly at her dress and remembered with what extraordinary care she had dressed for this interview, what trouble she had taken with her hair and the choice of a hat which would shadow the lines that years of taxing climates had drawn on her brow and round her eyes. 'I believe you have carried about a quite false impression of me all these years and I am sorry for it.'

He did not know how to handle her at all. He did not want to look at her because doing so destroyed the image of the delightful girl in blue that had saved him from various entanglements over the years, and he found himself very much afraid of what she might say next. It seemed to him that she was just as much in charge as she had been at twenty-one but with less charm and lightness, more eccentricity. He said nervously, 'No – oh, no—'

'I am sorry for you, but I am much sorrier for

myself, Captain Shaw. I have learned so much about myself just recently that not only am I quite sick of the subject but also very much afraid that I have nothing left of what I thought I was. When you requested an interview I believed I should recapture some of the buoyancy of my time in Bombay, that you would bring back to me that other Maria with all her optimism and confidence. But how could you? I don't even look the same. And my sharp tongue alarms you. I shall try not to let it alarm you further, although it is difficult for me to express approval of what the British have done to Upper Burma. Perhaps in time I shall get to think such interference a good thing. At the moment the desecration of the palace by your army only disgusts me. A club! No doubt the green edges to the moat will provide a splendid track upon which to run the first Mandalay Gymkhana.'

'It has been mentioned—'

'And so I believe has the erection of a brewery and a distillery since, I am told, you cannot keep an army here without beer and gin—'

Murray stood up. 'It was better for the Burmese to be conquered, Miss Beresford,' he said stoutly.

'Conquered! Better! Yes, better in the sense that the natives will be fed and policed and doctored and governed, but that is only half the story. I will not bore you with the other half because you would not understand me.'

'I must go, Miss Beresford.'

439

'Yes,' she said, 'yes, you must.'

He shifted his feet and looked about him. 'This is really your house?'

'Certainly. It was built for me by the Queen. I have no servants just at present but that is a small matter.'

He held out his hand, forcing himself to look at her and finding, to his resentment, that her face, close to, was quite as captivating as it had been in Bombay six years before, lines and gauntness and all.

'Goodbye, Miss Beresford.'

Her hand in his felt as fragile as a bird. She smiled at him but her eyes were cold and blue. 'Perhaps you would find your own way out, Captain Shaw.'

'Yes,' he said, 'certainly.'

'And I am sorry for your disappointment.'

He flushed with indignation. 'It was not a disappointment, Miss Beresford.'

Seconds later, negotiating fragments of porcelain which littered the verandah, he reflected that although the interview had indeed been a disappointment, that was not what he had minded so badly. What he minded was her continuing upper hand, a supremacy which the young Murray Shaw had found exciting, but which the older one found only intolerable. He had come away, he told himself crossly, shaking like a disgruntled dog, thoroughly worsted; even if he didn't want her any longer, he had not been prepared to be so absolutely unwanted himself.

What the dickens she had sent for him for, he could not imagine.

In the lane a second bullock cart was pulled up behind his own. It contained a handful of Burmese and the fellow from the Bombay-Burmah Corporation who was chatting away to the natives with what seemed a pretty astonishing degree of familiarity. Murray said, 'Afternoon, Tennant.'

Archie demanded, without preamble, 'What are you doing here?'

Murray shrugged. 'Renewing old acquaintance. Talking over old times.'

Archie grunted.

'I was just leaving,' Murray said. 'You'll have to announce yourself. She hasn't any servants.'

'I know. I've brought her some.'

'Funny place, Mandalay. Seems to affect people a bit. Know what I mean?'

'No,' Archie said. 'But then, I am affected too.'

'Going out into the forests again?'

'In due course.'

'Best of luck, then.' Murray moved away and then retraced his steps. 'Do you know something, Tennant? Six years ago, Maria Beresford was the best-looking girl in Bombay. And the most spirited.'

'Yes, I know,' Archie said. 'You told me.'

Maria was standing with her eyes closed in the middle of her empty drawing room. The hem of her skirts had gathered up fragments of fluff and

441

horsehair, but apart from that, she looked dressed for a reception. And she was wearing all her rubies.

'I've brought you Ah Chun for a few days,' Archie said from the doorway. 'And two boys he recommends. And he will find you a maid tomorrow. I wish you wouldn't sleep here.'

'I want to.'

'Just because the British are here doesn't mean Mandalay is safe. There are hordes of bandits loyal to Supayalat and hordes more loyal to no-one. Ah Chun says he will sleep across your door tonight but I can't feel that's enough.'

'I couldn't bear another night with the hymn singers. I simply could not. This is my house, in any case. I belong here.'

'Until you go to India.'

Maria began to walk slowly up and down the gritty floor, little plumes of dust rising with her sweeping skirts.

'Until I go to India.'

'Then – then you really are going? Whatever it was you had to do, nothing came of it then?'

'Nothing.'

Archie crossed to the doorway and stood gazing out, his shoulder propped against the frame.

'Maria. Maria – is it a personal objection to me that makes you refuse me still?'

'No,' she said.

Knowing her by now, he did not turn, but waited, his back to the room and to her.

442

'I have money now,' he said after a while. 'I had much rather have had the old man still but that's something I can do nothing about. I shall stay in the East for a while because he would have wanted that, but I shall go home in the end. Home to a square brick house with its own frontage on the Thames. Even if you don't want me, wouldn't you rather that than a dusty bungalow in India with Thibaw drinking and Supayalat scolding?'

'You forget,' she said, 'I don't know England.'

'I don't forget. I suggest that I am the very person to introduce you to each other. I don't forget anything. I don't forget Maymyo. We might have a house up there where you could spend the forest seasons. Or you could come into the forests with me.' He spun round and said with a piteousness he did not intend and much regretted, 'Maria, do you care nothing for making me happy?'

She put her hands to her temples.

'Did you think yourself in love with that military oaf out there? Did you dream that you were the same as six years ago in Bombay? I wish – I wish that at the very least you would tell me what you think of me!'

Maria took her hands away from her head. 'Archie, you have the most attractive and admirable character I have ever met. You have a natural candour and sweetness that makes me trust you, confide in you. But I don't know that I want a good man like you. I don't know that I shouldn't prefer a fascinating but reprehensible creature like the Queen. To be truthful, I am horribly confused. Perhaps it is recent events, perhaps it is just too long in Mandalay. Mandalay, oh, Mandalay—'

He shouted, 'You are infernally obstinate!'

She smiled at him. He crossed the dusty space between them with huge strides and clamped his arms about her. She remained still in his embrace, but she did not resist him, even when he lowered his head and kissed her with more vigour than subtlety.

'Please,' he said, 'please marry me. I'll do everything to make you happy, I swear it. Think of life with me, think how much lies ahead—'

She detached herself gently, but she did not move away. A faint colour lay along her cheek-bones.

'I can't seem to believe in anything,' she said, 'so much has vanished here, died – Grace, my father, Tom Prior, Denzil Blount, ambition, pride, glory—'

'Then don't insist upon making it worse!' he cried in despair, seizing her again, 'Don't throw yourself away to live with a myth, the ashes of a legend. Her reign is over. Yours might just be beginning. New Burma! New beginnings!'

She said, 'The old one meant so much to me.'

'That man out there—'

'Oh,' she said tiredly, her head drooping so that it almost touched his shoulder, 'a great mistake, Archie. A very foolish thing to do.'

'He boasted—'

'Yes,' she said, 'yes. I am sure he did. He told me how they are turning the palace into a merry military compound complete with club room and chapel. I can hardly bear to think of it.'

'That is how Ratnagiri will seem to you,' he said stooping so that her hair might brush his cheek. 'A sham. A tawdry imitation of things vanished.'

'I promised that I would go.'

'Promised?'

'Myself.'

'And me?'

'Oh!' she said angrily, tearing herself free. 'I don't know, I don't *know*—'

He stood back and regarded her. Her face was pinched with fatigue and she was clasping and unclasping her fingers nervously.

He said, 'If I leave you alone tonight to think everything over, will you give me an answer tomorrow?'

She said nothing, only stared down at her twisting fingers.

'I have to go back into the forests quite soon. I don't suppose it will be much fun, I should think the jungle even more lawless than Mandalay now, but I am contracted to go when I can. I had much rather go, knowing.'

She straightened up suddenly, lifting her chin, folding her hands, giving him the old, imperious blue look.

'Certainly you may have an answer in the morning.'

'Whether it be Supayalat or me?'

'Whether it be Supayalat or you or neither of you.'

'I shan't sleep,' he said. 'I dread tonight.'

'I shan't sleep either.'

'I suppose I should derive some consolation from knowing that periodically I shall be in your thoughts.'

'If you wish,' she said.

He came close to her and stooped to put his mouth gently on hers without touching her with his hands.

'Until tomorrow,' he said.

'Yes,' she said, 'until tomorrow.'

On the verandah steps Hnin Si was crouched combing her hair with a wooden comb. She had had no instructions to come with Ah Chun but these days she ignored instructions anyway. As Archie passed, she stopped the sweeping movement of her arm, put down the comb and shikoed to him. He paused and looked at her for a moment sadly, at her curious high-coloured Shan face, her flexible wrists and hands, her slanting brown eyes as blank as almonds. He could not now remember at all what it was like to desire her.

'*Thakin* wants me?' she said.

Archie sighed. 'No,' he said, 'no, I don't.'

She leaned forward and in an echo of a year before said, 'I don't please you, *thakin*?'

A great melancholy was settling on Archie like a fog. Through it he peered down at Hnin Si.

'Not in that way,' he said, 'not any more,' and then he stooped and laid two silver rupees on the step beside her before he went on down to the lane.

THE END